CW01636170

Born ... g at the age of fi ... iversity of Leice ... olitics. He work ... modern-day equivalent of the Whigs. He now lives in Bristol.

Praise for Jonathan Lunn's Killigrew series:

'A hero to rival any Horatio Hornblower. Swashbuckling? You bet.' *Belfast Telegraph*

'A cracking adventure crafted by a writer who has clearly inherited the talent to tell a jolly good yarn' *Newton & Golborne Guardian*

'If you revel in the Hornblower and the Sharpe books, grab a copy of Jonathan Lunn's action-packed saga' *Bolton Evening News*

'A rollicking tale with plenty of punches' *Lancashire Evening Post*

'Full-blooded, action-packed with a wealth of historical background and naval and warfare detail, a spread of characters and a racy narrative make this a rollicking good read' *Huddersfield Daily Examiner*

*Also by Jonathan Lunn*

Killigrew and the Incorrigibles
Killigrew and the North-West Passage
Killigrew's Run

# Killigrew R.N.

and

# Killigrew and the Golden Dragon

Jonathan Lunn

headline

Copyright © 2000, 2001

The right of Daniel Hall to be identified as the Author of the Work has been asserted by him in accordance with the Copyright, Designs and Patents Act 1988.

KILLIGREW R.N. first published in Great Britain in 2000 by HEADLINE BOOK PUBLISHING

KILLIGREW AND THE GOLDEN DRAGON first published in Great Britain in 2001 by HEADLINE BOOK PUBLISHING

First published in this omnibus edition in 2005 by HEADLINE BOOK PUBLISHING

A HEADLINE paperback

10 9 8 7 6 5 4 3 2 1

Apart from any use permitted under UK copyright law, this publication may only be reproduced, stored, or transmitted, in any form, or by any means, with prior permission in writing of the publishers or, in the case of reprographic production, in accordance with the terms of licences issued by the Copyright Licensing Agency.

All characters in this publication are fictitious and any resemblance to real persons, living or dead, is purely coincidental.

ISBN 0 7553 2661 X

Typeset in Times

Printed and bound in Great Britain by Mackays of Chatham plc, Chatham, Kent

Headline's policy is to use papers that are natural, renewable and recyclable products and made from wood grown in sustainable forests. The logging and manufacturing processes are expected to conform to the environmental regulations of the country of origin.

HEADLINE BOOK PUBLISHING
A division of Hodder Headline
338 Euston Road
London NW1 3BH

www.headline.co.uk
www.hodderheadline.com

# Killigrew R.N.

For Macer

# I:

## The Prize

You could always tell a slave ship from any other vessel.

The sharks knew that.

Any ship that crossed the Atlantic could expect at least a couple of sharks to follow in her wake in the hope of catching some scraps tossed overboard by the cook. But a slave ship would have a couple of dozen fins slicing through her wake. Sharks were not the most clever of the ocean's denizens but they were patient and they knew from experience that sooner or later there would be deaths on board a slave ship and when that happened there was nothing for it but to throw the body over the side. Often a member of the crew would die, usually from yellow fever, but twice as often it would be one of the slaves. The sharks did not discriminate between black and white. To them it was all food.

The sharks could tell it was a slaver from the stench.

Mate Killigrew could smell it now as he was rowed across from Her Majesty's paddle-sloop *Tisiphone* to the *Maria Magdalena:* a compound of stale sweat, urine, excrement and vomit. Even on Her Majesty's yacht *Victoria and Albert* the sanitary arrangements for the crew were primitive at best, and on most ships the stench of the effluent which gathered in the bilges could be overpowering to a landsman during high summer. On a slaver, the sanitary arrangements for the slaves were non-existent.

'Sweet Jesus!' one of the rowers gasped as they approached the slave ship. 'What a stench! She stinks like the nethermost pit of Hell!'

'Keep silence in the boat, there,' ordered Killigrew. He sat in the long boat's stern, his saturnine face turned towards the *Maria Magdalena*. His mind was already on the deck of the slaver, planning what tasks the prize crew would have to perform once on board, and putting them in order of priority.

There were fourteen men crammed in the *Maria Magdalena*'s long boat. The three officers – Mate Killigrew, Assistant Surgeon Strachan and Midshipman Parsons – all wore navy-blue pea jackets, white kerseymere pantaloons, and peaked caps. Killigrew was also entitled to wear the China War Medal but he preferred not to. He was not proud of having taken part in that small but dirty conflict, which some called the Opium War, even though he had been promoted to mate – a halfway house between midshipman and lieutenant – as a reward for his part in the taking of Chingkiang-fu in 1842. That was five years ago now, but still the nightmare of that butchery sometimes haunted his dreams.

The remaining eleven men were all ratings and wore no uniform as such, except that they all drew their clothes from the purser's slops and there was inevitably a uniformity to their white trousers, blue jackets and broad-brimmed straw hats.

Killigrew glanced across to where Strachan sat with his handkerchief held delicately over his nose and mouth. The assistant surgeon was in his early twenties, the same age as Killigrew, with blue eyes behind wire-framed spectacles and a tangle of light brown hair. A graduate of the University of Edinburgh, where he had qualified as a Licentiate of the Society of Apothecaries, Strachan was a relative newcomer in the navy. Killigrew suspected the assistant surgeon could not have graduated very high in his class at medical school, otherwise he could have worked in a country practice: far more pleasant than a paddle-sloop in the Tropics, and far more remunerative than the nine pounds and sixteen shillings a month he earned as an assistant surgeon.

It was six bells in the afternoon watch, or three o'clock, as the landsmen would have it. The *Tisiphone* – 160 feet long from stem to stern, with a single funnel between the two masts – and the *Maria Magdalena* were hove-to alongside one another about fifty yards apart. The sun beat down mercilessly on the shimmering blue sea. Back in Britain it was winter but the Tropics knew nothing of winter and summer, only the dry season and the wet season. It was the dry season now and hardly a breath of air disturbed the sails of either vessel.

During the first part of the chase a fresh off-shore breeze had propelled the swift Baltimore-built barque along at a good twelve knots which the paddle-sloop, with her sails and her engines, had barely been able to match. But the *Tisiphone* had persisted, her crew knowing that as long as they could keep the slaver in sight then time and the doldrums were on their side. Eventually, as the morning gave way to afternoon, the breeze had slackened and died, leaving the *Maria Magdalena* helpless. A blast of chain shot from the *Tisiphone*'s sixty-eight pounder had brought down the slaver's upper spars and she had run down the American colours she had been flying, colours which Killigrew did not doubt were false.

The Stars and Stripes was a good flag of convenience for slavers. Both the British and the Americans maintained an anti-slavery squadron off the coast of West Africa, but the British one was by far the larger and more active of the two. The United States did not have a treaty with Great Britain to allow British ships to stop and search US vessels: the memory of the War of 1812 and its primary cause – the Royal Navy's unjustifiable habit of stopping American merchant ships and pressing their crewmen into service on board British men-o'-war – still rankled with American politicians and naval officers who were old enough to remember those days. Thus no vessel of the Royal Navy could stop an American ship, and no vessel of the United States Navy could stop a British one. All the slavers had to do was hoist the Old Glory when chased by a British vessel, or hoist the Union Jack if chased by the Americans. Any Royal Naval officer stopping a ship flying the US flag had to be damned sure of his ground if he did not want to spark off a diplomatic incident.

The starboard side of the barque loomed over them and Killigrew glimpsed the surly faces of some of the crewmen left on board. As soon as the *Maria Magdalena* had surrendered, the *Tisiphone*'s captain, Commander Standish, had ordered her master to cross over to the paddle-sloop with a dozen of his crewmen. Those men were now captives under the muskets of the *Tisiphone*'s marines, while the rest of the slavers waited on board the barque for Killigrew and his men to board and take command of the vessel.

'Way enough,' said Olaf Ågård. One of the *Tisiphone*'s two quartermasters, the Swede was the senior petty officer in the long boat. He had served on British ships – first Hull whalers, then Royal Navy vessels – for so long that scarcely a trace of any Swedish accent remained in his voice. 'Toss and boat oars.'

The rowers shipped their oars and allowed the long boat to cover the last few yards under her own momentum until the bow bumped gently against the clipper's side where a rope ladder hung down from the gunwale.

Killigrew went up first. At the top he hooked both hands over the gunwale, heaved himself up and swung his feet on to the deck. There were a dozen sailors gathered there, some looking fearful, others glaring at Killigrew with venom in their eyes. The moment he stood on the deck he unhooked his 'pepperbox' – a multi-shot pistol with six revolving barrels – from his belt and levelled it at the sailors. It was not unknown for the crew of a captured slaver to murder the prize crews put aboard her, although they usually waited until the vessel which had caught them had sailed away. But Killigrew was damned if he would take any chances with this villainous-looking bunch.

'Which one of you is in charge?' he demanded.

The sailors exchanged glances. None of them spoke.

Killigrew repeated his question in Portuguese and gestured with his pepperbox. 'Come on, speak up. I haven't got all day.'

'I am,' said one, a heavily built man with greasy black hair and a cast in one eye.

'What's your name?'

'Ramón Barroso.'

'Are you the first mate?'

'Yes.'

The rest of the prize crew gathered on board the *Maria Magdalena*'s deck, armed with pistols and cutlasses, and some of them at once covered the slavers. 'Keep those men under guard until we can get irons on them,' ordered Killigrew. 'I'm sure there'll be no shortage of those on board. Boulton, Evans, Ivey and McFee: you four search the ship for other crewmen and weapons. Mr Parsons, be so good as to hoist our colours. Mr Fentiman, make an inventory of what spars we'll need to jury-rig her until we make it to Freetown. You help him, Sails. See what you can find in the ship's stores; what's missing we'll have to bring across from the *Tisiphone*.'

Fentiman and 'Sails' – the chief carpenter's mate and the sailmaker respectively – nodded and went about their work.

'I'll check the slave deck,' said Strachan, heading below.

Killigrew gestured at Barroso with the pepperbox. 'Show me the ship's papers.'

'The *senhor capitão* has the papers. He took them across to your vessel to show to your *capitão*—'

'I mean the *other* ship's papers,' said Killigrew. 'I never stopped a slaver yet which didn't have more than one set of papers.' He followed Barroso into the captain's day room where the Portuguese indicated a padlocked strongbox.

'I don't have the key.'

'I do.' Killigrew shot the padlock off with his pepperbox.

Barroso moved to open the strongbox, blocking it from Killigrew's sight with his body. ''Vast there!' Killigrew snapped before he could raise the lid. 'Move over there. Turn your face to the wall, spread your legs and put your hands against the bulkhead. Good boy. Now don't you bat an eyelid.'

He lifted the lid of the strongbox. A pistol lay on top of the papers inside, an old-fashioned single-shot flintlock. Killigrew picked it up and showed it to Barroso. 'Is this what you were looking for?'

Barroso did not reply. Killigrew tucked the pistol behind his belt and turned his attention to the rest of the strongbox's contents. There were no ship's papers, no log, no cargo manifest, no owner's instructions, just a slight haze and a smell of burning in the day room.

There was a knock on the door. 'Who's there?' Killigrew demanded without taking his eyes off Barroso.

'Me, sir. Parsons.'

'Come in, Mr Parsons. What can I do for you?'

'It's the quack, sir. He wants you to join him on the slave deck.'

'All right.' Killigrew seized Barroso by the scruff of his neck, rammed the muzzles of his pepperbox into the small of his back, and marched him out on deck. 'You can go back with your shipmates for now.' He pushed Barroso roughly across to where the barque's other crewmen waited, and then descended through a hatch and down a companion ladder to the slave deck.

Below decks the stench of sweat, urine, excrement and vomit was even worse and Killigrew found himself gagging. Strachan waited outside the door. The sounds of moaning and weeping came from the other side.

'I thought you'd want to see this for yourself, sir,' said Strachan, grim-faced.

Killigrew glanced at him. Strachan had already been aboard several other slavers in his short time with the West Africa Squadron; if he thought this one was worthy of particular attention, then it had to be especially bad. The forewarning braced Killigrew, as much as anything could have braced him for the stench and sight which greeted him when Strachan opened the door.

A wall of hot, stinking air hit him at once, and he had to choke back the bile which rose to his gorge. The one mercy was that the dim lighting prevented him from seeing too much.

If Killigrew lived to be a hundred years of age – which with his career and personal habits was unlikely, he reflected – he would never understand the mentality of slavers. Even if the very concept of slavery had not been entirely contrary to all laws of natural justice, surely it would have made sound economic sense to look after the slaves. True, they would have transported fewer slaves per voyage, but then they would have lost a smaller number on the way and sold a higher proportion of those they had paid for on the African coast.

But instead they packed the slaves on deck as closely as it was physically possible, and on average roughly a third of them died during the middle passage to the New World. 'O brave new world, that has such people in it!' he thought ironically. And it was not even a reflection of the complete indifference to the lives of their slaves, which his various encounters with slavers had taught him was a given. To the slavers, their cargo was not even human, merely a superior form of ape. But the diseases which spread like wildfire through the slave decks of these death hulks – dysentery, smallpox, ophthalmia – could transfer just as easily to their crews, and it was not unusual for a sixth of the crewmen to die as well.

The deck had been split into two levels, with less than three feet of headroom between the two. Like most people Killigrew had seen the graphic plans of slave decks published by the abolitionists, and had read the statistics about how little space each slave had. But those were only pictures and statistics, and could never capture the full horror. There were over four and a half hundred slaves crammed into that cramped, fetid hold, all of them naked and in irons, their ankles raw and blistered where the fetters chafed their flesh. A shallow wave of piss and puke swept across the deck each time the barque rolled. As soon as the door opened, the moans and cries intensified as they jabbered at him in their incomprehensible tongue.

And the worst of it was that the vast majority of them were children.

When the slave trade had been legal, slaves of all ages had been transported to the Americas. But now that fewer ships dared to make the crossing and the supply was strangled, it made more economic sense to import younger slaves from whom the owners would get more years of work. And since children were smaller, the slavers could pack more of them on board.

'Jesus Christ,' breathed Killigrew. 'All right, does anyone here speak English? Speakee Krio? *Est-ce qu'il y a quelqu'un qui parle français? ¿Habla español? Fala português . . .?'* A firm believer in self-improvement, Killigrew had found that there were usually one or two foreign ratings on board most British ships, and one way to pass the time on long voyages was to employ them in teaching him their tongue; in this manner he had picked up the languages of the most common seafaring nations, including Spanish and Portuguese in addition to the French most naval officers learned as a matter of course.

'I speak Portuguese,' said one of the older ones, a woman of about twenty.

'What's your name?'

'Koumba, *senhor*.'

'My name's Kit. Now listen, Koumba, I want you to translate what I'm going to say for everyone else here. Can you do that?'

She nodded.

'Good girl. Tell them everything's going to be all right, do you understand? I'm an officer of the Royal Navy, we've come to save you from the slavers. We're going to get you out of here and take you all up topsides as soon as possible, and the doctor here will care for your sick. Then we'll take you back to Africa, all right? But you have to be patient.'

She nodded again.

'Good girl. Be strong. The ordeal's nearly over.'

He went back on deck and gestured for Barroso to approach. 'The keys for the irons. Where are they?'

Barroso grinned. 'The *capitão* has them. He keeps all the *chaves* on him all the time . . .'

Killigrew shook his head. 'What about the spare set?'

'Spare set, *senhor*? What spare set?'

Killigrew punched him in the stomach. As Barroso doubled up, Killigrew drove his knee into his face. Barroso's head was snapped back and he sprawled on the deck.

The British seamen on deck stared at this display of gratuitous violence, half shocked, half admiring. None of them cared for slavers, of course, but Mr Killigrew hated them with a passion. He knew what they would be thinking: *A rum cove, that Mr Killigrew, most of the time as staid and sober as any English gentleman, yet every now and then prey to the most violent passions. But then he did have a foreigner for a mother, it was said, so what could you expect?*

Ignoring their stares, Killigrew kicked Barroso viciously in the side, grabbed him by the scruff of the neck and hauled him to his feet. Then he smashed his face against the mainmast.

Barroso sank to his knees with blood streaming from his nostrils and a livid bruise weeping blood on his temple. He spat a mouthful of blood on the deck and several teeth with it. Killigrew felt nothing. He had no doubt this was not the first time blood had been spilled on that deck.

'The spare set.'

'Hanging on a . . . *o que é . . . o prego*?'

'A nail?'

'*Sîm*, a nail. Hanging on a nail behind the door to the *capitão's* day room.'

'It's amazing how co-operative these people can be when you ask them nicely,' remarked Killigrew. 'Go and fetch them, Mr Parsons.'

As the midshipman scurried off to fetch the keys, Boulton, Evans, Ivey and McFee returned from below decks. 'There's no one else hiding on board, sir,' reported Boulton.

'You're sure? I don't want anyone you overlooked sneaking out once we've parted from the *Tisiphone* freeing their shipmates here so they can slit our throats. Remember the *Felicidade*.'

'Yes, sir.'

The *Felicidade* had been another slave ship captured by the Royal Navy off the coast of Africa two years earlier: the slavers had overpowered the prize crew and thrown the survivors overboard. Worst of all the slavers had later been captured and despite their guilt having been established, a judicial appeal had ruled that a British court had no jurisdiction over a vessel owned by a Brazilian who had murdered a British prize crew. The slavers had been sent back to Brazil at British expense.

Killigrew turned to the chief carpenter's mate from the *Tisiphone*, who was waiting to report. 'Well, Mr Fentiman?'

'It ain't good, sir. They must've chucked most of their stores overboard when we was chasing 'em. And most of the timbers and rigging that's still home is as rotten as a politician's conscience. There ain't enough rope and timbers on board the *Tisiphone* to replace 'em all. Christ – pardon me language, sir – but we'd need to build a whole new ship to replace this floating coffin. We'll be lucky to get halfway back to Africa.'

'Well, there isn't enough room on board the *Tisiphone* for all the slaves, so we'll just have to make do. Galton, I want you and Evans to row Fentiman and Sails back to the *Tisiphone* to arrange the transfer of stores.'

'Aye, aye, sir.'

Parsons returned carrying a bunch of keys. 'Good lad,' said Killigrew, taking them from him.

'Sir, there's something I think you should see in the captain's cabin.'

'All right.' Killigrew turned to Boulton and handed him the keys. 'I want you and the others to start bringing up the slaves from below. And bring up some irons for these fellows,' he added, indicating the slavers. 'Once we've got all the slaves on deck we can put these swines in their place, let them see how they like it down there. It's a pity there aren't more of them, so they can get a flavour of how cramped it is.'

Killigrew followed Parsons aft to the master's day room. 'What is it, Mr Parsons?'

'It's . . . um . . . it's difficult to explain, sir. I think you'd better see for yourself.' Parsons echoed the phrase Strachan had used not five minutes earlier before showing him the slave deck. Killigrew wondered what new atrocity awaited him.

Parsons opened the door to the cabin. A handsome black woman in her early twenties stood at the window, gazing out across the sea. Like the slaves in the hold she was completely naked, but better kempt, and Killigrew would have been less than human not to admire her long, lithe limbs and supple curves.

'Ah-ha!' said Killigrew. 'No need for alarm, Parsons. That is what is known as a "woman". A remarkably fine specimen, at that.'

Parsons flushed. 'I know that, sir . . .'

Hearing voices, the woman turned and crossed quickly to where Killigrew stood on the threshold. She dropped to her knees at his feet and entwined her fingers in the material of his coat, her eyes pleading. 'Doan' hurt me, mas'er. Please doan' hurt me . . .'

Killigrew grimaced and gestured helplessly, unsure of what to do with his hands. In the end he settled for patting her on the head and motioning for her to rise. 'It's all right, it's over. No one's going to hurt you. We're officers of the Royal Navy. We're going to take you back to Africa.'

'Oh, t'ank you! T'ank you!' Sobbing with relief, she buried her face in his crotch.

He gently took her under the arms, prised her away, and helped her to the bunk. 'What's your name?'

'Missy, mas'er.'

He shook his head. 'Not the name the slavers gave you. Your *real* name.'

'Onyema.'

'Well, you sit there, Onyema, and I'll send someone to make sure you're not hurt as soon as I've got a moment.' He headed for the door and gestured for Parsons to follow him.

'Do you suppose they . . . you know . . .?' asked Parsons as soon as the door was closed.

'I don't doubt it,' Killigrew said tightly. 'You'll often find the master of a slaver picks out the handsomest of the women for his own personal pleasure during the voyage to the Americas. Sometimes he'll let the whole crew do likewise.'

'My God!' stammered Parsons. 'Savages! So this is how the white man brings civilisation to the dark continent.'

'At least she didn't seem too badly knocked about. It doesn't make up for the violation, of course, but in some ways she'll have been better off in the master's cabin than she would have been down in that slave deck with the others.'

The others were being brought up on deck now. Some of the little ones were so sick after only a few hours on board they could no longer walk and had to be carried up. Even before they had been brought on board the *Maria Magdalena*, they might have spent weeks in equally vile imprisonment in a barracoon on the African coast. As each one emerged, Strachan directed one of the seamen from the *Tisiphone* to play water from the ship's pump over their besmirched bodies. Some of the children howled when the salt water entered their sores, but brine was better than excrement.

At length all the slaves were brought up – including half a dozen dead – until the decks were crowded with their bodies: not only the barque's waist, but the forecastle, quarter-deck and poop deck, so that it was hardly possible to move without stepping on one. They lay about listlessly, a few of the children still crying, some of the older ones addressing the navy seamen in their strange tongue – Koumba told Killigrew they were offering their thanks – but most still too drained by the suffocating heat of the hold to do more than lie there. Strachan moved amongst them, checking for any signs of infectious disease and doing what he could for them, while Killigrew directed two of the seamen to rig up a sail as an awning over the waist to provide some shade from the glaring heat of the sun for the sickest of the freed slaves. The slavers, meanwhile, were put in irons and carried down to the filth of the slave deck, enabling the marines to stand down at last.

'There's no sign of any disease,' Strachan reported at last. 'I think it's safe to put some of the stronger ones aboard the *Tisiphone.*'

'Good. I'll see to it. There's a woman in the captain's cabin. I don't think she's hurt as such, but I'd be grateful if you could . . . you know . . . make sure she's all right.'

Strachan nodded. 'Very well, as soon as I've collected some things from the sick berth.'

By now the *Tisiphone* had manoeuvred alongside the *Maria Magdalena*, and as timber, ropes and sails were transferred across one way, about eighty of the slaves were carried across the other. Killigrew and Strachan went back aboard the *Tisiphone*, the latter collecting medical supplies from the sick berth while the former presented himself to Commander Standish.

Standish was in his forties, long overlooked for promotion to post-captain, and Killigrew knew that it rankled. There were men younger than Standish who were commodores by now. It was not because Standish was the kind of pompous, unimaginative officer who did everything by the book to conceal his own incompetence – although he was – but because he lacked the 'interest' of a senior officer: that magical quality which meant all the difference between the advancement and stagnation of a naval career. Without it, it did not matter how bold or efficient an officer was.

Standish stood by the window in his day room, staring out, and he did not turn to face Killigrew as the younger man entered his office. There was no love lost between the two of them. Another reason for Standish's slow career progression was the fact that he was a graduate of the Royal Naval College at Portsmouth. Most senior officers sneered at college graduates, deriding them as 'X-chasers', and preferring the majority of officers who had learned their trade at sea, the way they themselves had done, the way the navy had trained all its officers since time immemorial. That had been how Killigrew had learned, and Killigrew had the 'interest' which Standish lacked. If Killigrew played his cards right he would be a post-captain long before he was Standish's age.

'Fentiman tells me she's in an appalling state, Mr Killigrew.'

'By navy standards, sir, yes.' By any standards, for that matter, but there was not enough room on the *Tisiphone* for all the slaves; the only way to get them back to Africa was to try to sail the *Maria Magdalena* to Sierra Leone, so Killigrew knew there was no point in complaining.

'Think you can make it?' Standish did not sound as if he cared either way, but was obliged to ask out of good manners.

Killigrew did not imagine it would be easy, but he was confident in his own ability and that of the men who had been appointed to the prize crew. 'It shouldn't be too much trouble, sir.' It went without saying that Killigrew's definition of 'too much trouble' meant much more trouble than most other people's definition.

Standish grunted. 'It's now' – he checked his fob watch – 'just coming up to four o'clock. We should reach Freetown some time after noon the day after tomorrow. We'll wait for you there until the morning tide on Monday; in any event, if we have to leave before you get back, I'll leave orders at the prize court.'

Finally some supplies, especially water and fresh fruit, were transhipped aboard the *Maria Magdalena* in an effort to improve the stock of rice and yams which the slavers had taken on board for the slaves. Then Killigrew and Strachan went back aboard the barque and the two ships parted company, the *Tisiphone* tacking eastwards back towards the African coast.

Killigrew felt a pang of loneliness as the paddle-sloop sailed away, but it was only momentary. It was always a thrill for a young man to find himself in command of his own vessel, even if it was only the temporary command of a captured prize. He was never happier than when there was a seaman's work to be done – except when he was in amenable female company with a plentiful supply of good whisky and cheroots, of course – and there was no shortage of work to be done aboard the *Maria Magdalena.*

The first task was to repair the spars and rigging damaged by the *Tisiphone*'s chain shot during the chase, so they could get the barque under way at the earliest opportunity. The simple fact that the slaver was now in the hands of the Royal Navy would not prevent more deaths from occurring amongst the recaptives – as the technically freed slaves were known – and the longer it took them to reach Sierra Leone, the more recaptives would die. The transfer of eighty Africans to the *Tisiphone* had left more space on deck, and the seamen chivvied the ones left behind to leave gaps between them through which they could cross the deck while they worked.

It did not take long to hoist those sails that had not been damaged, and Killigrew at once directed Ågård to take the helm and put her about. The wind had freshened a little now – no more than five knots, force two on Admiral Beaufort's scale – but it was off-shore, against the *Tisiphone*. No sailing ship could head directly into wind, but by bracing up the yards they could travel on a starboard tack, at an angle to the direction they wanted to go, before changing to a port tack. In this way they could follow a zigzag course which would eventually take them to Freetown, but it would be a slow and laborious process – for every ten miles of ocean covered they would actually have to cross thirty – especially with the winds so light. At least they would pick up speed as soon as they had replaced the upper sails.

Killigrew heard a woman's scream from below decks. He vaulted over the poop-deck rail and landed nimbly on the quarter-deck, narrowly missing one of the Africans who lay there. He kicked open the door, passed through the master's day room into the cabin and quickly surveyed the scene. Onyema sat on the bunk, her thighs pressed against her chest with her arms wrapped around her knees. To Killigrew's right, Strachan pressed himself into the corner of the cabin furthest from the bunk. He was dabbing at a split lip with his handkerchief.

'What the devil's going on in here?' demanded Killigrew. Both Onyema and Strachan began to speak at once. Killigrew waved for silence. 'One at a time. Ladies first.'

'She's no lady,' muttered Strachan.

Onyema indicated Strachan. 'Him me touch—'

'I was examining her, damn it!' snapped Strachan.

'Him touch Onyema paps. Him try touch Onyema cunny.'

'That's a damn lie!' spluttered Strachan. His native Scots burr, usually hardly discernible, became more pronounced when he was upset. 'I had nae even got as far as taking her pulse when the black bitch went crazy on me. She hit me, damn it!'

Killigrew studied Strachan's red face, trying to judge whether he was telling the truth or if it was just bluster. It was unthinkable that a naval officer could act in such an ungentlemanly fashion, but Strachan had not been in the navy for very long and Killigrew did not know him well enough to be sure either way. He could not blame a man for being tempted – Onyema was a fine-looking woman – but a gentleman resisted temptation if his advances were unwelcome. To take advantage of a woman who had just been through the kind of ordeal Onyema had been subjected to was the behaviour of the vilest scum.

'Get out,' he told Strachan.

'You're going to take her word for it over mine?'

'Why should she lie?'

'How should I know? She's crazy. She just went for me all of a sudden.'

'A man's innocent until proven guilty,' Killigrew said tightly. 'I'll allow you that much. Now get out of my sight.'

'For God's sake! You don't seriously think I'd try to take advantage of her? After what she's been through?'

'Get out!'

Strachan stared at Killigrew and apparently decided it would be safest to do as he was told. As soon as he was gone, Killigrew turned to Onyema. 'I must apologise for allowing this to happen. It won't happen again, I assure you.'

'Thank you, mas'er.'

He grimaced. 'It's Mr Killigrew, not "mas'er",' he told her, and then softened. 'Or "Kit" to my friends.'

'Mas'er Killigrew Onyema friend?'

He smiled. 'I hope so.'

'Onyema like Mas'er Killigrew. Mas'er Killigrew, him have kind face. Face woman trust, can.'

Killigrew laughed. 'Well, that's the first time anyone's ever accused me of that.' He opened the closet, hoping to find a shirt he could give her to put on – the sight of her smooth ebony skin was starting to distract him to the point where he could almost sympathise with Strachan – but instead found a woman's muslin shift. He handed it to her. 'Here, put this on.'

She pulled the shift on over her head. It fitted perfectly. 'Ship go Africa long time?'

'Three, maybe four days.'

'What happen, ship go Africa?'

'We'll take you to Sierra Leone. That's a British colony. There's no slavery there.' Which was not entirely true: ironically, since Sierra Leone had been set up as a colony for freed slaves, it was one of the few places in the British Empire where slavery was still allowed, but only for domestic slaves. But he saw no need to confuse her. 'The British government will maintain you – pay for food and shelter, I mean – for a year. After that, it's up to you. You can stay in Sierra Leone and try to get work, although I don't recommend it. You may decide you're better off going to the British West Indies under a scheme of apprenticed labour. But all this will be explained to you when we reach Freetown.'

'Onyema work Mas'er Killigrew? Onyema servant Mas'er Killigrew?'

He chuckled, but without much humour. 'I'm afraid I can't afford to keep any servants.' His closest living relative, Admiral Killigrew, was wealthy, but he refused to go cap in hand to his grandfather, and lived as best he could on his navy pay and any prize money he earned.

'Now you must excuse me,' he told Onyema. 'I've got important work to do.'

He made his way into the day cabin, took out the charts and navigational instruments he had brought on board with him and plotted a course to Freetown. When he had finished he stood up, crossed to the window and opened it to let in some fresh air. He wedged himself in the frame, with one foot on the sill, his knee against his chest, and lit a cheroot while watching the sun set the sky aflame as it sank towards the horizon. Beneath the ship's stern the sharks' fins still swam in the wake. When he had finished his cheroot he flicked the butt out and watched the glowing tip arc down through the gloom to the waves.

'That's all you're getting out of me, you bastards,' he murmured softly to himself.

'Mas'er Killigrew?'

He turned his head. Onyema stood framed in the door to the cabin, the light from a hurricane lantern shining through the diaphanous material of her shift to silhouette her nubile figure. She toyed with the stays at the neck of the shift, pulling them down between her breasts – whether by artifice or not Killigrew did not know – to emphasise her cleavage.

'Nothing. I was just thinking out loud.'

'Onyema make Mas'er Killigrew happy?'

'Mas'er Killigrew already happy.'

'Mas'er Killigrew, him have wife?'

'No.'

When a knock sounded on the door before he could say anything more, his reaction was one of relief. He waved her back into the cabin and she closed the door behind her. 'Come in.'

Fentiman thrust his head around the door. 'Begging your pardon, sir, but there's five foot o'water in the well.'

'Five feet!' With that much water in the bilges the orlop deck must have been completely awash. 'My God, it's a miracle we've not foundered already. Set two of the hands to work the bilge pump immediately.'

'Begging your pardon, sir, but I've already done that. It's just that I checked the water in the well when we first come aboard, and there was less than six inches then.'

Killigrew stared at him in incomprehension for a moment, and then took out his fob watch and flicked open the cover. It was nearly five o'clock. 'You mean to tell me we've shipped four and a half feet of water in less than two hours? We must have a bad leak.'

'Yes, sir. I've set Ivey and Lidstone to look for it and I'll be going to help them in a moment, but with that much water coming in we're going to need to man the pump all the way from here to Freetown, and even then I wouldn't care to lay odds on our staying afloat till we arrive.'

'You'd better get on with looking for that leak then, hadn't you?'

'Aye, aye, sir.'

Killigrew followed him out and ascended to the poop deck where Parsons stood yawning besides Ågård at the helm. He glanced up at the tops of the masts. Fentiman and the sailmaker had done a fair job of jury-rigging the damaged upper spars, sails and rigging, but if they had five feet of water in the well then the benefit of the upper sails would be counteracted by the drag of the hull. Boulton and Evans had stripped off their shirts and were working steadily at the bilge pump. The recaptives lay quietly on the deck while Strachan moved amongst them, treating their sores. *Trying to atone for earlier misdeeds*, mused Killigrew.

The sand in the half-hour glass by the ship's bell ran out and one of the seamen turned it over before ringing the bell four times to signify the beginning of the second dog watch. With the help of two seamen Killigrew measured the barque's speed with the log-ship and -line. Then he crossed to the log-board and wrote '2' under the column marked 'K'. 'How's her head?' he asked. There was no reply. 'Mr Parsons?'

The midshipman blinked. 'Wha—?'

'How's her head, Mr Parsons?' persisted Killigrew.

Parsons glanced at the compass in the binnacle. 'East by north, sir.'

Killigrew made the appropriate entry on the log-board, followed by a note of the wind direction, and then turned to Parsons. 'You're asleep on your feet, lad.'

'Yes, sir. Sorry, sir. It won't happen again.'

'It will if you don't get some rest. You've been on duty non-stop since the start of the forenoon watch. Go down to the day room and get your head down.'

'Thank you, sir.' Parsons went below.

Just under two knots, mused Killigrew. The loss of speed would be partly due to the fact the wind had dropped off again, but also because they were wallowing with five feet of water in the bilges. He glanced to where the two men still worked at the bilge pump. At this rate it would take them more than a week to get back to Sierra Leone; and if things were as bad as Fentiman had implied, they would be lucky to stay afloat that long. If Killigrew had known about the leak before they had parted from the *Tisiphone*, he would have asked Standish to tow them into Freetown.

'Something wrong, sir?' asked Dando.

Killigrew forced himself to smile and took out another cheroot. 'I was just wondering . . . I don't suppose you noticed if there were any women amongst the crewmen from this ship who went on board the *Tisiphone*?'

'Women? No, sir. Leastways, if there was, they were the ugliest women I ever clapped eyes on. Why d'you ask?'

'Just wondering.' He glanced at his fob watch. 'Time to change tack,' he decided.

Ågård nodded. 'Stand by to go about!' he boomed, prompting some of the recaptives on deck to raise their heads. 'Haul of all!'

The seamen scurried about the decks, cursing the recaptives who got in their way.

'Hard a-lee,' ordered Killigrew.

Ågård span the helm to starboard. 'Helm's a-lee.'

As the barque's bow came around into the wind the sails sagged back against the masts. The barque began to lose way and the bow swung to starboard. The hands hauled on ropes to adjust the sails, bringing them around to catch the wind from the other side. The mainsail filled with wind once more as the head continued to come around to starboard.

'Ease the helm,' Killigrew told Ågård, who span the wheel to bring the rudder amidships.

At last the barque came around far enough for the wind to fill the sails from the port tack, and they gathered way once more. The hands adjusted the trim of the sails accordingly.

Ågård was not used to handling the barque and the bows came around too far. 'Meet her,' said Killigrew. Ågård span the wheel to compensate. 'Handsomely does it . . . helm amidships. Luff and touch her.'

'Aye, aye, sir.' Ågård steered the barque as close to the wind as he could without letting it spill from the sails.

'How's her head?'

'East by south, sir.'

'Keep her so,' Killigrew told Ågård, and turned to Dando. 'Be a good chap and run along to the galley to see if you can find some tea, would you? Make some for everyone who wants it.'

'Aye, aye, sir.' Dando turned away and was about to go below when a thought occurred to him and he turned back. 'Does that include the darkies, sir?'

'Negroes, Mr Dando, and if you can find enough tea for all of them don't let me stop you. Actually, it's about time they had a bite to eat and something to drink, and it seems to me you just volunteered. No more than half a pint of water each. We've only got enough to last us a week.'

'Aye, aye, sir.'

Killigrew entered the master's day room and lit an oil lamp to update the log: even a prize ship had to keep a log. When he had finished he glanced around the cabin. There was not much to reveal the personality of the previous occupant. The only personal touches seemed to be a couple of rather bad watercolours depicting maritime scenes. He found himself wondering if the master had bought them under the mistaken impression they had any artistic merit whatsoever or if he had painted them himself. There was no evidence of any artist's materials in the day room so he had to assume that the former was the case.

There was a knock on the door. 'Come in.'

The door opened and Dando entered bearing two mugs.

'Your tea, sir. I brought some for Mr Parsons too, in case he wanted a cup. Is he in the cabin?'

Killigrew frowned. 'That's a good question.' He had told Parsons to sleep in the day room, but there was no sign of him. Of course, if Parsons had changed his mind and decided to chat to Onyema, there was no harm in that, but then why was there no sound of voices coming from the cabin? It occurred to him that Parsons and Onyema might have found another way to pass the time, and the thought did not shock him too much: after all, the lad had to learn sooner or later, and somehow Killigrew suspected that Onyema would be as good a teacher as any. But the deathly hush from the cabin did not suggest the sport of Venus was in play.

He stood up, crossed to the door, and tapped on it gently. 'Parsons?' When a few seconds had passed without any reply, he tapped again. 'Onyema?'

Still no reply. Killigrew exchanged glances with Dando and opened the door.

The light of an oil lamp illuminated the scene with its guttering yellow flame. Parson's coat was tossed carelessly on the floor while Parsons himself lay on the bed, staring up at the deck head. His pantaloons were around his ankles. There were no marks on him, nothing to suggest a struggle, just the gaping wound in his throat and the blood-soaked bedclothes.

'Sweet Jesus!' gasped Dando.

Killigrew backed out of the cabin and turned and ran out on deck, Dando hard on his heels. 'Turn out the hands,' he snapped, reloading the empty barrel of his pepperbox with a fresh cartridge and ball. 'We've got a murderess on board.'

# II:

## Floating Coffin

'Evans! McFee!' Killigrew waved across two of the sailors who had pistols thrust in their belts. 'Look lively, you two. Go down to the slave deck and stand guard over the prisoners. No one goes near them, do you understand? Shoot if you have to.'

'Aye, aye, sir!' The two sailors drew their pistols and cutlasses and dashed below.

'What's going on?' asked Strachan.

'It seems I owe you an apology, Mr Strachan.'

'About the captain's belly-warmer? I told you she was mad.'

'Not mad, Mr Strachan. Just very, very cunning. She's one of them.'

'What?'

'One of the slavers, damn it! I was a fool not to see it. She cooked up that yarn about you trying to molest her to sow dissension amongst us. She's been biding her time, waiting for us to drop our guard so she could free her friends.'

Killigrew wondered how he could have been so stupid: the only black on board who spoke English; the absence of any signs of cruelty on her body; the shift in the master's closet that fitted her so perfectly . . .

He cast his eyes over the deck, mentally mustering the men

under his command: Dando and the sailmaker standing by for orders, Quartermaster Ågård at the helm, Boulton and Galton at the bilge pump, O'Connor moving amongst the slaves with a cask of water, and the other two men working at the bilge pump.

''Vast pumping, there,' he told them. 'Check your pistols. Where are Fentiman, Ivey and Lidstone?' Then he remembered: they had gone below to look for the leak. 'We'll have to search the ship, deck by deck. Boulton and Galton, you two stay on deck with Mr Ågård. Sails, you take Dando and O'Connor and start at the bows. Strachan and I will start from the stern and we'll work our way for'ard until—'

He broke off as a scuffle sounded below. They heard a thump, and then the report of a pistol followed by a man's scream, cut off short.

The sailmaker crossed to the main hatch. 'Dick? Johnny?' he called down. 'Are you boys all right down there?' When there was no reply, his expression became grim. 'Looks like they've got themselves a couple of pistols now, sir.'

'Everyone up on the poop deck, chop-chop!' ordered Killigrew.

'What about the recaptives?' asked Stachan, gesturing at the bodies strewn across the deck.

'We'll just have to leave them, that's all . . .'

Two shots rang out. Killigrew felt something scorch his cheek. A moment later Galton was on his knees clutching his stomach. Killigrew whirled in the direction from which the shots had come from in time to see the slavers rush out of the accommodation hatch behind the mainmast, only a few yards away. He fired his pepperbox twice. Boulton, Dando and O'Connor also fired their single-shot pistols. Three of the slavers went down, falling amongst the recaptives on deck who scrambled to get out of the way, crying out in panic and confusion.

Killigrew fired again, and then the surviving slavers were retreating back down the hatch. He shot one more in the back before they were all out of sight, then grabbed Galton by one arm, hoisted him to his feet and helped him up the companion ladder to the poop deck after the others.

Boulton, Dando and O'Connor quickly reloaded their pistols and crouched at the rail at the leading edge of the poop, from where they could cover the rest of the barque's decks and hatches. Killigrew reloaded his pepperbox while Strachan crouched over Galton. A dark, thick stain was already spreading over the front of the seaman's shirt. Strachan tore the cloth apart to reveal the wound in his stomach.

'He's been gut-shot,' he said, while Galton groaned in agony.

Killigrew nodded, understanding that the seaman's chances of survival were slim. 'Do what you can.'

'What do we do now, sir?' asked the sailmaker. 'We can't stay up here for ever . . .' Apart from the fact that the recaptives needed to be looked after, the seamen could not trim the sails from the poop deck. Nor was there any food or water up there.

'It's worse than that,' said Killigrew. 'The ship's sinking.'

Strachan looked up sharply. 'What?' he spluttered in panic.

'Slowly,' Killigrew hastened to reassure him. 'But sinking nonetheless. That's why Fentiman went below with Ivey and Lidstone: they were searching for the leak.'

'I suppose the slavers got them, then, sir,' said Boulton.

'Maybe. I didn't hear anything.'

'Surely the slavers are in the same boat as we are,' said Strachan. 'No pun intended. We may be trapped up here, but they daren't show their faces on deck. If the ship's sinking, they'll drown first.'

'If the water in the hold gets that deep, then we'll be foundering and we'll soon drown with them.'

'Can't we talk to them?'

Killigrew grinned and jerked a thumb towards the hatches. 'You can try it if you like . . .'

'There's someone moving down there!' hissed Boulton.

'Hold your fire,' ordered Killigrew, and glanced over the rail. 'It's one of the recaptives. Let him up.'

'Him' was a 'her'. Koumba crept up the companion ladder and found herself face to face with the multiple muzzles of Killigrew's pepperbox. Her eyes widened, showing white against the blackness of her face in the twilight. He grabbed her by the arm and dragged her on to the poop deck. She gasped but did not cry out. 'What is happening?' she asked him in Portuguese. 'The slavers – you let them escape.'

Killigrew grimaced. 'Not on purpose, I assure you.'

She jerked her head to where four of the slavers shot earlier lay on deck. 'Two of them are not dead.'

Strachan had finished tending to Galton's wound as best he could. 'I should go to them—'

'You stay where you are, mister,' snapped Killigrew. 'It's them or us now. I can't have you getting shot trying to give them medical attention.'

Strachan looked relieved and did not try to argue.

'We have to do something, sir,' said Ågård.

Killigrew nodded. 'Someone has to go down there and deal with the slavers.'

'Are you mad?' asked Strachan. 'They've had plenty of time to reload their pistols. Whoever goes down will be shot the moment he appears at the top of the ladder.'

'That's why I'm not going down the ladder.' Killigrew crossed to the taffrail at the stern of the poop deck and glanced down.

Strachan stared at him. 'You're going to go down there alone?'

'I'd like one volunteer to come with me.'

Everyone spoke at once. Killigrew waved them to silence.

'Just one of you. Mr Dando, I think.' He turned to the sailmaker and handed him a boat hook. 'Get ready to pass this down to me.' He took off his coat and hung it from a belaying pin.

'For God's sake, man!' protested Strachan. 'There's at least eight of them. Not to mention the bitch that slit poor Parsons's throat. Just two of you, against eight of them?'

The sailmaker laid a hand on Strachan's arm. 'Mr Killigrew knows what he's doing.'

'So do I. He's committing suicide.'

'We're wasting time,' said Killigrew. He took a coil of rope from a belaying pin and handed it to Dando. 'The longer we leave it, the more time we give them to cook up a plan.' He crossed to the skylight in the middle of the poop deck and raised it. 'We'll go in through one of the stern ports,' he explained. 'The password is "whisky". Anyone comes up through those hatches without calling that out first, you can blow his head off. Just make sure you don't hit any of those poor negroes. If we're not back in half an hour, you'll know we're dead.'

'Then what do we do?' asked Strachan.

Killigrew clapped him on the shoulder. 'You'll be in command then, so that's your problem.' He jumped down into the master's day cabin before Strachan could protest and landed lightly on the balls of his feet. Dando followed him.

'Belay one end of that rope to that beam,' ordered Killigrew, as he crossed to the window and opened it. Dando made the rope fast and Killigrew dropped the other end out of the window and into the barque's wake.

'Want me to go first, sir?' offered Dando.

'Toss you for it,' said Killigrew. 'Heads I go first, tails you do.' He tossed. 'Heads it is.' Killigrew slipped his double-headed coin back into his pocket. Taking a knife from a sheath strapped to his ankle he clenched it between his teeth and climbed out through the window, feeling like one of his piratical forebears.

He glanced up and saw the sailmaker at the taffrail above him. The sailmaker lowered one end of the boat hook towards him, but Killigrew shook his head and shinned down the rope. There was a stern port on either side of the rudder. The barque was so low in the water there was barely a foot of freeboard between the water and the sills of the ports. Within an hour water would be pouring through those ports if they did not get pumping again.

The port on the starboard side of the rudder was open, blackness behind it, and—

There was a blinding white flash from the port and a loud report filled Killigrew's ears. Something burned his shoulder and he almost lost his grip in shock. He slipped down the rope until his feet splashed into the water. Gripping the rope in one hand, he took the dirk from between his teeth and flung it through the open hatch. The action made him spin on the rope. As he swung back to face the port, he saw one of the slavers topple out to splash into the barque's wake.

The sharks at once closed in. Killigrew quickly shinned up the rope until he was out of the water. A feeding frenzy erupted below him as the sharks tore at the slaver's body, quickly falling astern.

No more shots came from the stern port, but it was only a matter of time before more of the slavers came to investigate. Killigrew had to move quickly if he did not want to be dangling helplessly when they arrived; next time he might not be so lucky. The overhang from the stern prevented him from reaching the port. He glanced up to where the sailmaker stood at the taffrail with concern on his face.

'Drop it!' hissed Killigrew.

The sailmaker looked puzzled. Killigrew held up one hand, and gestured. Sails remembered the boat hook he was holding.

He held it out over the taffrail vertical, and allowed it to fall, straight down, just to one side of Killigrew. The mate snatched it out of the air, near the blunt end. The hook twisted down towards the water and a shark's head emerged, snapping at it. Killigrew jerked it clear, swung it at the stern port and hooked it over the sill. He pulled himself in towards the port and scrambled through.

He was in the after hold on the orlop deck, standing in several inches of water. Footsteps sounded outside and the door began to open. 'Eduardo?' called a voice, and the door opened as one of the slavers entered. He paused on the threshold and squinted into the gloom. 'Are you all right? What happened? What were you shooting at?'

'Me,' said Killigrew, and hit him on the head with the blunt end of the boat hook. The slaver slumped to the deck.

Killigrew was still tying the man's hands behind his back with his belt as Dando climbed in through the stern port after him. 'You all right, sir?' he whispered, glancing at the unconscious man.

'Better than he is.' Killigrew took out his handkerchief and used it to gag the slaver, propping him up in a seated position with his back to a bulkhead so that he would not drown in the water which sloshed about on the deck.

Then he stood up and pressed himself against the bulkhead to one side of the door, listening. The only sounds he could hear were the creaking of the ship's timbers and the sloshing of water.

He drew his cutlass in his right hand and his pepperbox in his left, and the two of them slipped out through the door into the dark bowels of the ship. Down here the slavers had the advantage over them, because they would be familiar with the barque's layout below decks. But so far, he hoped, the element of surprise was on his side.

Killigrew and Dando crept along the deserted orlop deck

until they stumbled across something in the dark. Killigrew fell over and sprawled on something soft and sticky. Realising he was lying across the bodies of Fentiman, Ivey and Lidstone, he scrambled back in horror.

All three had had their throats slit from ear to ear. There were no other wounds on them to suggest they had died fighting: the slavers had murdered them in cold blood.

'Bastards,' whispered Dando. 'Begging your pardon, sir.'

'That's all right, Dando. You took the word right out of my mouth.'

They continued along the orlop deck until they reached a companion ladder leading up to the main deck, and paused. They could hear voices speaking Portuguese above.

'What's taking Ferrando so long?' asked one. 'I told him to come straight back here.'

'Maybe something happened to Eduardo. I'm going to check.'

'Do you want me to come with you?'

*Please say no,* thought Killigrew.

'Yes.'

Footsteps came down the companion ladder. Killigrew and Dando ducked behind the mainmast where it descended between decks to the mast step at the keel. He slipped his pepperbox into its holster and listened to the footsteps splashing through the water. Eerie shadows danced on the bulkheads: one of them carried a lantern. Killigrew and Dando exchanged glances as the two slavers walked past their place of concealment, heading for the after hold.

Killigrew and Dando stepped out behind them. Killigrew hit one with the hilt of his cutlass and Dando laid out the other with a belaying pin. They dragged the two men to the empty slave deck, gagged them and fettered them. Nonetheless they would have to work quickly now, as these two men could quickly raise the alarm by rattling their fetters when they came to.

The two British seamen returned to the foot of the companion ladder. They heard footsteps above and froze.

'Where are Carlos and José?' Killigrew heard Barroso ask. 'Curse them, I told them not to move!'

A face appeared at the top of the steps and Killigrew and Dando quickly ducked back out of sight. 'Carlos? José? Where are you?'

*Why don't you come down and find out?*

'I don't like it, Ramon . . .'

'Me neither. There's something strange going on . . . damn it, some of those English pigs must've gotten below somehow! I'll wager that devil Killigrew is with them. Tomas, Rodrigo, I want you two to go down there and flush the bastards out. Simão and I will stay at the main hatch.'

Tomas and Rodrigo descended the ladder with a lantern. As they headed into the darkness, Dando regarded Killigrew quizzically in the gloom. Killigrew nodded, and as Dando headed aft to take care of the two men, Killigrew went up the companion ladder and made his way to the main hatch. One man crouched beneath the grating, the barrel of his pistol pointed aft towards the poop deck.

Killigrew readied his cutlass. He felt guilty about creeping up on the man and striking him down from behind, but he reminded himself that this man would almost certainly murder him if the opportunity arose. Besides which, with the odds stacked against him, this was no time to fight fair: he would only be giving the advantage to his enemies.

Something clanked behind him and he half turned before a loop of chain was dropped tight around his neck and pulled hard against his throat, choking him. His cutlass clattered to the deck.

'Simão! I have him!'

The man with the pistol turned and levelled it at Killigrew's head. Killigrew kicked at his hand and sent the pistol flying.

There was a bright flash as it discharged itself harmlessly into a bulkhead.

Killigrew scrabbled at the chain which bit into his throat but the man who held him was too strong. He tried to draw his pepperbox but the man took both ends of the chain in one hand and clamped the other over Killigrew's wrist.

Simão snatched up the cutlass and came at Killigrew, slashing. Killigrew launched himself backwards and slammed the man behind him against a bulkhead. He gasped and took his hand from Killigrew's wrist. Killigrew drew his pepperbox and shot Simão between the eyes. Then he felt for the other man's side and rammed the muzzles against it, pulling the trigger. The man groaned and the chain became slack enough for Killigrew to break free.

The man with the chain was Barroso. A dark stain spread around the wound in his side, but he was still on his feet and Killigrew guessed he had not hit any vital organs. He swung the chain at Killigrew's hand, knocking the pepperbox away into the darkness.

A lithe, dark shape leaped out of the shadows from one side and crashed into Killigrew's side. Onyema sank her teeth into his wrist. The pain was excruciating. Barroso dropped the chain, snatched up the cutlass and charged forwards.

Killigrew and Onyema rolled over and over on the deck, her teeth still deep in his wrist, her fingernails raking his face, searching for his eyes. As Barroso brought his cutlass down, Killigrew allowed Onyema to roll on top. The cutlass buried itself deep in her shoulder. She gasped in shock. Barroso stared down in horror at what he had done, and then pulled the cutlass free. Onyema screamed and her blood splashed down on to Killigrew.

Killigrew still had the single-shot pistol in his waistband and he levelled it at Barroso. 'Drop the cutlass.'

'I'd do as he says, friend,' growled Dando, appearing

behind Barroso. The slaver snarled and tossed the blade to the deck.

Killigrew crawled out from underneath Onyema and unbuttoned his waistcoat. Shrugging it off, he folded it and held it over the awful wound in her shoulder. 'Hold this in place,' he told her. 'I'll send the surgeon down to look at that wound.'

She spat in his face.

'What about my wound?' demanded Barroso.

'I hope you bleed to death,' Killigrew told him, collecting up all the weapons he could find. He turned to Dando. 'The other two?'

'Out like lights and trussed like turkeys, sir.'

'Good work, Mr Dando.' Killigrew made his way to the main hatch. No sooner had he raised his head above the level of the coaming than a report sounded and a bullet bit into the deck inches from his hand. 'Whisky!' he bawled. 'Whisky!'

The men on the poop deck rose to their feet. 'By God, Mr Killigrew!' exclaimed Strachan. 'Is that really you?'

'What's left of me.' Killigrew climbed up on deck. He suddenly felt utterly drained.

'What about Mr Dando?'

'In fine fettle. There are wounded down here for you to take care of, Mr Strachan.'

'Of course, of course.' Strachan hurried down the companion ladder and crossed the deck to the hatch.

'You'd better go with him, Boulton, in case they try anything,' said Killigrew. 'Help Mr Dando put the slavers back in the slave deck. And watch the woman, too. She's a real hellspite. Sails, you'd better find that leak chop-chop. O'Connor, go with him and help him.'

'Aye, aye, sir.'

Almost fainting with fatigue, Killigrew staggered into the

master's day room. Koumba followed him inside. 'Are you all right?'

He lit a candle and grinned. 'I was wondering when someone was going to ask me that.' He stripped off his shirt and examined his shoulder. The bullet which had creased him as he hung from the stern had not gone deep, but he was also bleeding where Onyema had bitten him.

Koumba saw the teeth-marks and her eyes widened. 'What made that mark?'

Killigrew shrugged. 'Onyema – the slave master's woman – bit me.'

'She bit you?' Her eyes widened, and then her face hardened. 'You must kill her, Senhor Killigrew.'

'What?'

'She's a leopard woman.'

Killigrew was too tired to listen to what sounded to him like it was going to turn out to be nonsense. He wondered if his comprehension of Portuguese was not as good as he had supposed. 'A what?'

'A leopard woman. Have you not heard of the leopard people? They have the form of men and women, but in truth they are evil magicians. They have the power to transform themselves into leopards, in which shape they roam abroad at night committing the most terrible atrocities.'

'Superstitious nonsense. You can't go round killing people just because they bite you. I used to know a girl called Eulalia Pengelly, she bit me once when we were children. You're not suggesting *she's* a leopard woman, are you?'

Koumba ignored the interruption. 'The leopard people murder men and use parts of their bodies to create *borfima.*'

'*"Borfima"?*'

She nodded. 'Powerful medicines which give them great wealth. I tell you this: the leopard woman must be killed, before she brings more death and destruction.'

'Nonsense. If she lives she'll get a fair trial in Freetown. As captain of this vessel I have wide-ranging powers, but I'm damned if I'll use them to take the law into my own hands.' A bottle of *aguardiente* stood on the table and he pulled out the cork with his teeth, taking a long pull at the fiery liquor. Then he swabbed away the blood from the wound in his shoulder, poured a little of the *aguardiente* into it, and set it alight with the candle.

Koumba winced as the smell of burning flesh filled the room. 'Is that the white man's magic?' she asked.

'Got to cauterise the wound, keep out infection,' he grunted. The blue flames disappeared and he poured more *aguardiente* over the blackened skin before he repeated the procedure with the teeth-marks in his wrist. She helped him dress both wounds.

'What is the "Royal Navy"?' she asked him.

'The ships of her Britannic Majesty Queen Victoria. And the men aboard them, of course.'

'And is this what you do? Rescue black people from slavery?'

'That's part of it.' Killigrew gently lifted Parsons' body from the bunk and carried it through to the day room where he laid it on the deck.

'Because your Queen Victoria orders you to do this?'

'Yes. And for tonnage bounty. And because it's the right thing to do.' He re-entered the cabin and removed the blood-soaked sheets from the bunk. The blood had soaked through to the mattress below, but Killigrew was too exhausted to care.

'The ways of the white man are strange indeed.'

Killigrew thought about that. 'Yes, I suppose they are.'

The sun was streaming through the skylight by the time Dando roused Killigrew with a mug of tea. Killigrew sat up sharply. 'What time is it?'

'Nearly eight bells in the morning watch, sir.'

'Why the devil didn't anyone wake me?'

'The quack said you needed rest, and Sails agreed with him.'

Killigrew climbed off the bunk and pulled his shirt on. 'The ship? Is she still sinking?'

Dando looked dubious. 'We managed to find the leak and patch it as best we can, though there's still some water coming in. We had to use the fore t'gallant to fother her. There was no spare canvas, 'cept the sail we used for an awning. Sails wanted to use that, of course, but the quack overruled him.'

Killigrew thought about it. Taking down the fore topgallant sail would knock a fraction of a knot off their speed and delay their arrival in Freetown by an hour or two, all told. Some of the recaptives might die in that hour, but more would die if they were left on deck without shelter or shade from the tropical sun.

Killigrew took the mug of tea from Dando and followed him out on deck. The recaptives were starting to look a lot more lively than they had done the previous day and Sails was teaching some of the fitter young men the rudiments of seamanship so that they could help to run the *Maria Magdalena* back to port. They spoke no English and he spoke no . . . whatever language it was they spoke . . . but he seemed to be managing by pointing to various parts of the ship, saying their names over and over until the recaptives repeated them parrot fashion, and by demonstrating himself he taught them some of the simpler chores required in trimming sails. Killigrew nodded thoughtfully. With only eight men left in the prize crew, including the two officers, they would need all the help they could get.

Two more of the recaptives were busy working the bilge pump, and even as Killigrew watched them another recaptive emerged from one of the hatches carrying a bucket of water which he carried to the side and tipped over. No sooner had he carried the empty bucket back down below than a second recaptive emerged with a bucket and did exactly the same thing.

'The only way we can keep pace with the leak, I'm afraid, sir,' explained Dando.

'At least we've got plenty of hands to keep it up,' Killigrew remarked wryly.

To one side several bloodstained sacks about six feet long lay in rows on the deck. Ordinarily Sails would have sewn them up in canvas, but canvas was too precious on board the *Maria Magdalena* to be squandered in the burial of the dead.

'Why haven't those been dumped overboard yet?' demanded Killigrew.

'Mr Ågård said we should wait for you to read the burial service, so we can do it proper, like,' said Dando.

Killigrew counted the sacks. There were a dozen. Had so many really died in the fighting last night? Remembering now, it all seemed like no more than a nightmare. He did some quick mental arithmetic. 'Who are the other four?' he asked Dando.

'I'm afraid Mr Galton didn't last long, sir. And three more of the slaves died as well. Fever. They must've picked it up on the coast.'

Killigrew nodded. 'Are many more of them sick?'

'The quack counted about two dozen. He's put them in the sick bay.'

'Where's Mr Strachan?'

'Up on the poop, sir.'

Still holding the mug of tea, Killigrew climbed the companion ladder to the poop deck where he found Boulton spelling Ågård at the helm. Strachan sat sleeping on the deck with his back propped up against the bulwark, while two sleeping recaptive children nestled on either side of him.

Koumba sat opposite him, watching the sleeping doctor with an amused smile on her face. In the light of day he could see that she really was quite presentable now that she had had a chance to clean up, and her broad smile lit up her whole face. As Killigrew stepped on deck she glanced at him and her smile did not falter.

'Good morning, Menina Koumba,' he said in Portuguese, saluting her.

'Good morning, Senhor Killigrew. I trust you slept well?'

'My God, what was I thinking? I slept on that nice comfortable bunk and left a lady to sleep on deck . . .'

'A lot of ladies slept on deck last night,' she reminded him, nodding to where the other recaptive women sat in the ship's waist. They were chatting amongst themselves, and some of them were even laughing. This morning there was hope in their eyes where yesterday Killigrew had seen only despair, and in that moment he was reminded that everything he had gone through last night had been worth it.

'We couldn't all have fitted on that bunk,' said Koumba. 'Please do not feel guilty about it, Senhor Killigrew. If anyone earned a good night's rest last night, it was you.'

Killigrew grunted non-committally. Thanks to his carelessness in trusting Onyema, seven members of his prize crew were dead. 'We'd better get the burial of the dead over and done with,' he said.

They rigged up planks from which the bodies could be tipped overboard while Killigrew rooted around inside his sea-chest and came up with his King James's Bible and his Book of Common Prayer. His grandfather had given them to him on the day he had first joined the Royal Navy as a first-class volunteer, aged twelve. 'These were your father's. I know he would have wanted you to have them.'

Inside the cover of the Bible the following had been written in his father's hand, bold and flourishing, yet meticulously precise:

*A gentleman is made, not born. He is defined by his actions, not his wealth.*
*A gentleman protects those who cannot protect themselves.*
*A gentleman respects the feelings and beliefs of others.*
*A gentleman is guided by his own sense of justice and fair play.*
*A gentleman treats others according to their merit rather than their station.*
*A gentleman is not boastful, but lets his actions speak for themselves.*
*A gentleman is as careless of the debts he is owed as he is careful of those he owes to others.*
*A gentleman does not stand idly by in the face of injustice.*
*A gentleman asks no man to do what he is not prepared to attempt himself.*
*A gentleman takes responsibility for his own actions.*

Killigrew knew those lines by heart. He had no way of knowing if his father had merely written them in an idle moment or if he had deliberately put them down so that his son might be guided by them. But like many children deprived of a fatherly role model at an early age, he seized upon any clue towards his father's character and clung to it. Those lines were the strongest clue he had, and all his adult life he had struggled to abide by those rules.

The prayer book was less well thumbed. This was the first time Killigrew had opened it since he had said, 'Thank you, sir, I'll treasure it always.' And he had kept it, if only to prove to himself that he had meant those words. It was not that Killigrew was an impious man as such, it was just that there always seemed to be more important things to do than pray and go to church.

By the time he emerged on deck once more the others were ready. He opened the prayer book at the contents page and was relieved to discover there was a section 'For the Burial of the Dead at Sea.' Killigrew had seen plenty of burials at sea, but this was the first time he had ever been called upon to conduct one himself.

He riffled through the pages until he found the right one. 'Shall we begin?'

The seamen doffed their hats.

Killigrew cleared his throat. '"Forasmuch as it hath pleased Almighty God of his great mercy to take unto himself the soul of our dear brothers here departed, we therefore commit their bodies to the deep, to be turned into corruption, looking for the resurrection of the body, (when the Sea shall give up her dead), and the life of the world to come, through our Lord Jesus Christ; who at his coming shall change our vile body, that it may be like his glorious body, according to the mighty working, whereby he is able to subdue all things to himself."'

He nodded to Ågård, and one by one the bodies were tipped overboard. They hit the water with a splash and went straight under, pulled to the bottom by the iron shot Sails had sewn inside the sacks.

Killigrew passed the prayer book to Strachan and pointed to the next line. 'Perhaps you'd care to read this part?'

Strachan looked a little shocked at being called on to help, but he took the book from Killigrew. '"I heard a voice from heaven, saying unto me, Write, From henceforth blessèd are the dead which die in the Lord: even so saith the spirit; for they rest from their labours."'

He passed the book back to Killigrew. 'Our Father, which art in heaven . . .'

They all joined him in reciting the Lord's Prayer, and when they had finished he read the collect. Then he concluded:

'"The grace of our Lord Jesus Christ, and the love of God, and the fellowship of the Holy Ghost, be with us all evermore."'

He closed the prayer book and stood with his hands clasped before him as they stood in respectful silence for a moment with their heads bowed. Then Dando raised a hand to his breast and sang 'How Sweet the Name of Jesus Sounds' in a surprisingly competent tenor.

Afterwards Killigrew sent O'Connor to fetch him breakfast before retiring to the master's day room, checking the log-board on the way so he could update the log. Then, while he was waiting, he took out the chart and calculated their progress so far. It was slow; damned slow.

There was a knock on the door. 'Come in, O'Connor.'

'Not O'Connor,' said Strachan. 'Me.'

'Well, come in anyway. I owe you an apology, Mr Strachan.'

'You mean about the black woman?' Strachan gestured dismissively. 'You apologised last night.'

'All the same . . .'

'I can't blame you for thinking what you did,' said Strachan, and grinned sheepishly. 'After all, coming in and seeing what you saw . . . What must I have looked like?'

Killigrew was grateful for Strachan's magnanimity, but he could not bring himself to smile. 'If I'd listened to you last night, perhaps none of those people need have died.'

'And what *would* you have done, if you'd believed me last night? Put her in irons, just for being over-sensitive? It's always easy to be wiser after the event. You can't blame yourself for what happened. It wasn't your fault Parsons and the rest of our men died, and as for the slavers you and Dando killed . . . well, I don't imagine anyone will mourn their passing.'

'Even blackbirders have mothers, wives . . .'

'Mothers and wives who'll have given up their sons and husbands as worse than dead the moment they learned what line of shipping they were in, if they had any milk of human kindness in their breasts. Look at it this way: how many would have died if those men had shipped with a legitimate merchant ship, instead of taking to blackbirding? They knew the risks they were taking. You know, I'm starting to think that for some of those swines cocking a snook at the Royal Navy is part of the thrill of it. Well, they've cocked their last snook at us now, and the world's a better place for their passing. So instead of worrying about their eternal souls, why not give a thought to the three hundred and sixty odd slaves up on deck whom you've saved from a lifetime of servitude and misery?'

O'Connor arrived with breakfast, two bowls of lobscouse: a seaman's stew of *bouilli* beef, ship's biscuits, potatoes, onions and spices. Most landsmen would have turned their noses up at it, but to a mariner it was considered a delicacy. Thinking of the slaves on deck subsisting on a diet of rice and yams, in all conscience Killigrew could not bring himself to eat it. 'Thank you, Mr O'Connor, but I'll just have whatever the slaves are having.'

'That *is* what the slaves are having, sir.'

'You made enough lobscouse for three hundred and sixty-six slaves?'

O'Connor shifted from one foot to the other. 'Well now, sir, I had to take some liberties with the traditional recipe . . .'

Killigrew picked up a spoon and tasted it tentatively while O'Connor eagerly awaited his approval. He smacked his lips. 'Very good, O'Connor,' he said dubiously. 'It *is* a little different, I'll admit. Rice?'

'Yes, sir.'

'And something else I can't quite put my finger on . . .'

Strachan tasted a mouthful. 'Yams.'

O'Connor beamed.

'Very good, O'Connor.'

The sailor went out and Strachan spat his mouthful of lobscouse back into the bowl. 'My God, it's disgusting. Even by navy standards.'

'I should eat up, if I were you. It's the only kind of food we're likely to get from here to Freetown.'

'And how long will that be?'

'I've just finished charting our progress. If my calculations are right we're still ninety-two miles from the African coast.'

'Nautical miles, I take it?'

'Of course.'

'I've never understood: what's the difference between a nautical mile and a normal one?'

'About eight hundred feet.'

'More or less?'

'More.'

'Capital,' Strachan said wryly. 'How long's that going to take us?'

'Well, taking into account the fact that we're low in the water and short of a fore t'gallant, and having to tack because the wind's against us, and what wind we can take advantage of is no more than a force two . . .'

'Don't beat about the bush, Mr Killigrew. Give it to me straight.'

'About five days.'

'Five days! How long do you think we can keep this floating coffin afloat?'

'Oh, about five days, I should say. Of course, we may get there sooner if the wind picks up between now and then.'

'How likely is that, in these latitudes at this time of year?'

'Are you a gaming man, Mr Strachan?'

'Sometimes. Why? What kind of odds would you give us?'

'Very good ones. If you're the kind of man who likes to wager on a long shot.'

* * *

'Fire! Fire!'

Killigrew was woken by the sound of shouting and the clump of feet on the deck above his head. He rolled off the bunk, his hand snaking under the pillow to draw out the pepperbox he had concealed there, and took in his surroundings. He was in the master's cabin on board the *Maria Magdalena*. Little light came through the tiny porthole, which suggested it was still night.

He had fallen asleep fully clothed but for his waistcoat and tail-coat, so he went straight out on deck. In the early morning light he could see recaptives streaming out of the forward hatch while the seamen on board charged through the recaptives on deck and fought to descend through the crowded hatch, cursing and swearing at those that got in their way.

Smoke billowed out of the hatch.

Panic stirred in the pit of Killigrew's stomach. Of all the dangers a man faced at sea, fire was one of the most terrible.

He descended below decks via the empty main hatch and made his way forward. The smoke became thicker the closer he got to the bows, until it was acrid and choking. The stench was horrible. It smelled like charred pork.

A few recaptives blundered into him in the dark as they fled from the fire. The companion ladder leading up to the forward hatch was still crowded. A few crushed bodies lay at the foot of the ladder, trampled in the rush to get out. Some recaptives were still crawling out through the door of the sick bay, from where the smoke seemed to issue.

Ågård was trying to descend against the tide, a bucket of water held high. He reached the sick bay only a moment ahead of Killigrew, who followed him inside. The smoke stung his eyes and clawed at his throat. Through the thick black cloud he could just make out the fire: one of the cots was ablaze, the flames tinged with blue. There was another odour in the smoke, something Killigrew could not place at first until the smell of burning flesh and those blue-tinged flames reminded him of how he had cauterised his wounds just before going to bed the previous night: *aguardiente*.

He saw with horror that there was a body on the cot being consumed by the flames.

Ågård hesitated only for a moment, and then stepped forward and tipped the contents of the bucket on the cot. The flames were extinguished at once with a hiss, and steam filled the room.

Killigrew stumbled to the ports and opened them to let in some fresh air. Then he and Ågård started to pick up the bodies of the fever victims who had passed out in the smoke. Strachan himself was there, unconscious, slumped in a chair. Killigrew lifted him over his shoulder and carried him up on deck while other seamen descended to carry out the other victims of the fire.

Two of the recaptives still worked at the bilge pump and Killigrew filled a bucket from the pump before tossing it over the assistant surgeon. Strachan spluttered into life, choking and retching. Killigrew took a ladleful of water from the scuttled butt and poured some of it between Strachan's lips. Strachan coughed and spewed up. He writhed on the deck for a moment and then rose on his hands and knees. 'Wha . . . what happened?'

'There was a fire in the sick berth. Don't you remember anything?'

'Fire? No. I was sitting in the chair reading a book . . . that's all I remember. I must've dozed off.' He broke off, coughing again, and wiped his sleeve across his eyes. 'A fire? How could there have been a fire? Did one of the lamps fall?'

'Perhaps, but I don't think so.' Killigrew turned to where Ågård was trying to give a small child the kiss of life. But the child was dead. Ågård rose with tears in his eyes, which might have been caused by the smoke, but somehow Killigrew did not think it was just that. For all his rough manners and boisterous behaviour, Jack Tar was a sentimentalist at heart.

'There's three others suffocated from the smoke and two more trampled to death at the foot of the companion ladder,' said Dando, as more bodies were brought out through the hatch. 'There's some more that's badly injured or sickly from the smoke. I think this one's got a broken leg,' he added, indicating a young boy.

Strachan pushed himself to his feet. Killigrew put a hand on his arm. 'Are you going to be all right?'

'I'll have to be, won't I?' Strachan shrugged his arm off and went to tend the injured.

'What happened?' Killigrew asked Dando.

The seaman shook his head. 'I don't suppose I know much more'n you, sir. I were on the poop with Mr Ågård there when we hears screaming from the fo'c'sle. We looks up and sees smoke a-coming from the hatch. Mr Ågård tells Boulton to take the helm and rushes for'ard with me. By the time we gets here the darkies are running out of the hatch. You was already there by the time I got down the hatch after Mr Ågård. Do you think the fire was started deliberate, like?'

'I don't know. Better go and check on the prisoners, Dando.'

'Aye, aye, sir.' Dando descended the main hatch and returned a couple of minutes later to report that Barroso and the other slavers were still securely in their irons and thoroughly frightened by all the clamour.

'Did you put their minds at rest?' asked Killigrew.

'No, sir. Begging your pardon, sir, but I'm afraid I couldn't resist the temptation to tell 'em the ship was afire and we was abandoning 'em to their fate.'

Killigrew listened for a moment. He could just hear Barroso

and the others screaming in terror for someone to come and let them out. 'Good work, Dando.'

'Why, thank'ee, sir.'

Killigrew descended to the sick bay once more. Some residual smoke still lingered in the air and the stench was appalling, but the air blowing through the open ports made it possible to breathe in there. The only sign of fire apart from the smoke-blackening on the bulkheads and deck head was the charred corpse on the burned cot, completely unrecognisable except that it might have been a woman.

Killigrew heard a sound behind him and whirled, but it was only Strachan. 'I've tended the wounded as best I can,' he reported. 'We'll need a new sick berth. We can't leave the poor devils out on deck.'

Killigrew nodded. 'Use the master's day room.'

Strachan took in the scene. 'This fire was started deliberately, wasn't it?'

'Yes. My guess is someone poured *aguardiente* all over this poor devil and set her alight. I don't suppose you can recall who—'

'Onyema. But it wasn't the fire that killed her.' Pinching his handkerchief over his nose and mouth, Strachan indicated the crushed head of the charred corpse. 'Her skull was smashed first.'

# III:

## Reeled In

'You mean someone stove her head in and then set fire to her to make sure?' said Killigrew.

'I'm saying that's what it looks like,' replied Strachan. 'Poor bitch. She probably wouldn't have lived much longer anyway with that shoulder wound.'

'But why?'

'How should I know? Damned savages.' Strachan started to pack his small supply of medicines, surgical instruments and dressings into his bag.

'Even savages don't do something without a good reason. At least, a reason that seems good to them.' Killigrew frowned. 'They used to burn witches, didn't they?'

'Who did?'

'In the Middle Ages, I mean.'

'Oh. Yes. So?'

'Just thinking out loud. I don't suppose you saw anyone nosing around the sick berth earlier, did you?'

'No one who shouldn't have been there; but I told you, I fell asleep.'

'At what time?'

'How should I know? I remember the ship's bell ringing twice . . . that would have been at one o'clock, wouldn't it?'

Killigrew nodded and reached for his watch, only to

remember it had been in the fob-pocket of his waistcoat, which he had given to Onyema to help her staunch the flow of blood from her wound. 'My waistcoat . . .'

'Hm? Oh, here it is.'

The blood-soaked waistcoat had been tossed on the floor. It was ruined, but the watch was still ticking. Killigrew snapped it open. 'Five past four. So our murderous arsonist had about three hours to go about his – or her – work.'

He left Strachan to arrange the transfer of the sick and injured to the master's day cabin and made his way up to the poop deck. Koumba was still there, sitting with her back to the gunwale. 'What happened?' she asked.

Killigrew did not reply, but indicated her to Boulton. 'How long has she been there?'

Boulton glanced at her. 'She's been there since Ågård woke me a few moments ago.'

'When the fire broke out?'

Boulton nodded.

'What's going on?' asked Koumba. 'I don't understand.'

'You stay there,' Killigrew snapped at her, making his way down to where Ågård was helping Strachan and Dando carry the sick to the master's day room. 'How long was Koumba on the poop deck?'

'You mean the negress that speaks Portugee, sir?' said Ågård. 'I don't think she left the poop deck all night. Oh, except once, to perform the necessary.'

'Did she use the heads?'

Ågård shook his head. 'No, she just went down to the waist and pissed into a scupper, sir. Why? You don't think she was the one who started the fire, do you?'

'Could she have been?'

'No, sir. That was the only time she left the poop, and I could see her the whole time.'

'Did she speak to anyone while she was down there?'

'She might've done, sir, I don't know. It's not like I was watching her or anything. Even a negress is entitled to her privacy. It was only because I was at the helm looking for'ard that I noticed. But she couldn't have started the fire, I'd stake my life on it.'

'Did you see if any of the other recaptives went below?'

'Plenty, sir, but don't ask me to tell you which ones. They all look the same to me. Especially in the dark.'

Killigrew sighed. 'All right. Thank you, Mr Ågård.' He made his way back up to the poop deck, caught Koumba by the arm and hoisted her to her feet.

'What is it?' she asked.

'I want a word with you,' he told her. 'In private.'

'By all means,' she said.

He took a hurricane lantern and dragged her below decks to one of the store rooms where they could talk undisturbed. She regarded him nervously and ran her tongue over her sensuous lips. 'Senhor Killigrew, I do not think you are the kind of man who would take advantage of—'

'Onyema was murdered tonight,' he told her, hanging the lantern from a nail in an overhead beam. When she said nothing, he ploughed on. 'Her skull was smashed in and her body was burned.'

'I cannot pretend I am sorry. She was *evil*.'

Killigrew grabbed her by the shoulders and slammed her back against the bulkhead. 'I know you didn't do it, but I think you know more about it than you're letting on. I think you know who did. In fact, I think you put the murderers up to it.'

'I don't know what you are talking about.'

'Someone poured *aguardiente* all over her body and set fire to it. The way you saw me pour *aguardiente* over my wounds earlier and set fire to that. Why burn her after she'd already had her skull smashed in? To destroy her evil spirit? Is that it?'

'Perhaps I mentioned to some of the other Africans on board that Onyema bit you. Perhaps they surmised, as I did, that she must have been a leopard woman. What does it matter? Whether or not you believe in the leopard people, you cannot deny she was evil. She tried to kill you, tried to kill us all . . .' She smiled, and pushed her breasts out towards him. 'But that is not the real reason you brought me here alone, is it?' she asked, licking her lips.

He turned away quickly. 'You're no better than she was. You do realise that six others were killed as a result of that fire?'

'God decides who lives and who dies. If Onyema died it was because God wanted to punish her for being a leopard woman. Perhaps God also wanted to punish the six who died for crimes of which we know nothing. Vengeance is mine, saith the Lord.'

Killigrew stared at her. 'You're a Christian?'

She nodded. 'A Catholic.'

'Of course. That's where you learned Portuguese, isn't it? Jesuit missionaries.' He ran his fingers wearily through his hair. 'Get out. Go on. Get out of my sight. And there'll be no more burnings of witches or leopard people or any other superstitious nonsense like that, d'you hear?'

Her head held high, she crossed to the door. On the threshold she paused and turned back to stare at him gravely. 'The leopard people are real, Senhor Killigrew. You *will* believe.'

Killigrew felt a shudder run down his spine, then shook his head dismissively. 'Superstitious nonsense,' he muttered to himself.

The sea was glassy. The sails hung limply from the yards,

without a breath of wind to stir them. The heat of the sun was oppressive. The recaptives lay listlessly on the deck; the sailors were not much better off. Killigrew had gambled on rationing the food and water for five days, knowing that they could not stay afloat much longer than that anyway, but even so they were weakened by thirst and hunger.

The only sounds were the creak of the timbers and the squeaking of the pump which two Africans continued to work, knowing that their lives depended upon it now. Killigrew stood at the taffrail where he had rigged up a fishing line. Their only hope now lay in putting the long boat into the water and towing the *Maria Magdalena* to the shore; but he was not convinced his men had the strength for the feat. Still, short of a miracle – the freshening of the wind – it was their only chance. He took out his fob watch and glanced at it. Five minutes to noon. *If the wind doesn't pick up by noon,* he told himself, *we'll have to try it.*

Strachan climbed on to the poop deck, dabbing sweat from the underside of his jaw with a wadded handkerchief. He joined Killigrew at the taffrail. 'We're going to die here, aren't we?'

'Never say die, Mr Strachan,' Killigrew told him with a breeziness he did not feel. 'We're not dead yet.'

'We might as well be, if the wind doesn't pick up soon.' He took Killigrew's telescope and turned it to the east. 'Wait a minute! I can see land!'

Killigrew shook his head. 'Smokes.'

'What?'

'Those are smokes. Low-lying fog banks, Mr Strachan. They're quite common in these waters at this time of year. They can look like land, from a distance.'

'To a landlubber, you mean.'

'I didn't say that. Mind you, if the smokes weren't there – and if my calculations are correct – you would be able to see the coast of Africa.'

'Jings! Are we that close?'

'It's still about seven miles. It might as well be seven hundred miles without any wind.'

Strachan had been keeping his voice low, but now he lowered it even more and moved closer to Killigrew. 'But if we're *that* close, couldn't we get in the long boat and row?'

'All three hundred and fifty-seven of us, Mr Strachan?' Sickness had continued to take its toll of the Africans despite Strachan's best efforts; Killigrew had to be content with the small consolation that an average of three deaths a day was not bad for a slaver, even one which a Royal Navy prize crew was trying to get back to a harbour.

'It's pointless us all dying,' murmured Strachan. 'There must be room for twenty in that boat . . .'

'Twenty-four, actually. Probably more, if you took some of the children instead of the adults. But how do you choose which ones?'

'Well, we Britons should go, naturally . . .'

'Why "naturally"?'

Strachan thought about it. 'Well, because we've got the guns and I'm a selfish swine.'

'Your honesty does you more credit than your generosity of spirit, Mr Strachan.'

Killigrew's fishing line twitched in the water. 'You've got a bite,' Strachan told him.

Killigrew glanced down. 'It's just a sprat. Not even worth the effort of reeling it in.'

Strachan shrugged. 'I'm not saying we should leave *all* the negroes,' he continued. 'There's seven of us, that leaves room in the boat for seventeen of them. More if we took the children: they've got longer lives ahead of them anyway.'

'Is it your medical training which allows you to think such things through so coldly and calculatingly?'

'Just common sense, I'd have thought. Listen Killigrew, if

you want to be a hero and go down with your ship that's fine by me. I just don't see why you should want to take the rest of us down with you.'

'I don't intend that anyone should go down with this ship, Mr Strachan,' Killigrew said coldly. 'I've already lost thirty-five people since I took command of this vessel. I've no wish to make it three hundred and fifty-two—'

Killigrew's fishing reel span with a screech. Something big had taken the hook and was moving away fast. 'That's a sprat?' Strachan asked incredulously as everyone gathered around the two of them.

'Something that ate the sprat, Mr Strachan.' Killigrew took the fishing rod from its line and braced himself to fight the fish.

Everyone else was suddenly an expert on deep-water fishing. 'Let it run, sir! Let it run!' urged O'Connor.

'No, fight him!' said Boulton. 'Wear him down.'

'It's a marlin! It's got to be a marlin.'

'No, it's a shark!' Strachan pointed to where a fin cleaved through the water about a hundred yards or so off the stern.

'Good,' said Killigrew. 'Have you ever eaten shark steak, Mr Strachan? It can be surprisingly tasty. In China, the fin is considered a delicacy.'

'Hit him, sir! Hit him now!'

The line went slack and Killigrew at once began to reel it in.

'All right, now reel it in,' Boulton said unhelpfully.

'Why don't you tie the line to the bows, maybe we can persuade it to tow us ashore,' sneered Strachan.

'You've lost him, sir,' said Boulton. 'The line's snapped.'

'No, he's hooked,' said O'Connor. 'He's hooked good and proper.'

'He's gone, I tell you,' insisted Boulton.

The reel screeched as the shark ran again.

'He's running, sir!' said Boulton.

'Let him go . . . that's it . . . Right, now hit him! Hard!'

'Sail ho!' cried one of the recaptives Sails had trained to be a lookout.

Killigrew twisted and glanced up to where the African sat on the foretop. 'Where away?'

The African just pointed off the port side of the *Maria Magdalena*. 'Sail ho!' were probably the only two words of English he knew, Killigrew reflected.

He handed the fishing rod to Strachan. 'Here, take this.'

'Wha—? No! No, I don't know anything about this . . .'

'Boulton and O'Connor will teach you soon enough,' said Killigrew, picking up his telescope. 'They both seem to be experts.'

As the two seamen at once began to bombard Strachan with contradictory advice, Killigrew moved to the bulwark and pointed his telescope to the north, in the direction which the lookout had indicated. He couldn't see any . . . no, wait, there it was: the upper sails of a ship, the hull down below the horizon. Killigrew descended to the quarter-deck and jumped lightly on to the gunwale before ascending the ratlines to the mainmast top. He paused on the platform about a third of the way up the mast and raised the telescope to his eye once more.

Yes, he could see her all right. A clipper, her sails hanging just as limply as the *Maria Magdalena*'s. Killigrew could just make out three boats in the water before the clipper's prow. They had to be towing the ship.

And she was headed towards the *Maria Magdalena*.

Killigrew slammed the telescope shut and shinned nimbly down the ropes to the deck. ''Vast angling, there!' he roared as he ascended to the poop deck.

Boulton was helping Strachan to reel in the shark while O'Connor readied a boat hook as a makeshift gaff. 'Hold on,

Killigrew!' called Strachan. 'We've almost got the blighter! By jings, he's a leviathan!'

'Belay that! All hands to quarters!'

Boulton and O'Connor at once left Strachan to it, leaving him with a forlorn expression on his face. A moment later the rod was torn from his grip, leaving him with the skin flayed from his palms.

'O'Connor, I'll wager there's a Brazilian ensign in the flag locker,' said Killigrew. 'Fly her upside down from the mainmast. Mr Ågård, see if you can get this pivot gun ready for action. Round shot, if you please. I noticed some in the shot locker the other day.'

'Aye, aye, sir!'

As O'Connor and Ågård hurried off to do Killigrew's bidding, Strachan came across wiping his bloody palms on his handkerchief. 'We almost had him there,' he said petulantly.

'Sorry to spoil your sport, Mr Strachan, but this is more important.'

'What's going on? You look as if you're preparing for a fight.'

'That I am. The ship has the look of a slaver to me.'

'She's not a steamer, is she? I don't see any steam. How is it they're moving while we're becalmed?'

'They're using their boats to tow her.'

'You can do that? Why didn't we think of that?'

'I did. But it's seven miles to the shore and our men are weak with hunger and exhaustion. Pulling a ship of three hundred and fifty tons burthen seven miles to shore is no laughing matter, especially when she's low in the water. That's what they call a counsel of desperation.'

'I'd say we were in pretty desperate straits.'

'I was hoping something would turn up. And it has.' He gestured off the port beam. 'She's headed south along the coast. If she's a slaver that means her slave deck's empty; otherwise she'd be sailing out to sea.'

'And you think they'll give us passage to Freetown?'

'It may take a little persuasion.' Killigrew patted the muzzle of the thirty-two-pound pivot gun on the poop deck.

'Do you think we can beat them in a fair fight?'

'Good God, no. That's why we're using guile.' Killigrew nodded to where O'Connor was hoisting a Brazilian ensign to the top of the mainmast.

'That's not a British flag.'

'No.'

'Isn't it upside down?'

'Unofficial sign of distress. With any luck the slaver should come to investigate, which I very much doubt she'd trouble to do if we flew the Union Jack. Take your coat off. You look too much like a naval officer.'

'I'll tell Commander Standish you said that. He's usually weighing off at me for not looking *enough* like a naval officer.'

Killigrew made his way to where Koumba stood in the waist. She had avoided the poop deck ever since Killigrew had confronted her about Onyema's death. 'There's a ship coming,' he told her curtly. 'It's our only chance to get everyone off this floating coffin alive, but if we're going to take her we need her to get close. The only way we can do that is if they think we're just another slaver. That means that all these people have to get out of sight.' He gestured at the recaptives on deck.

'Go back down on the slave deck, you mean.'

'I'm afraid so. We'll put the irons on them but not lock them. Can you explain to them? Make them understand it's for their own protection?'

She nodded. 'I'll try.'

'The slaving fraternity is a close-knit one, sir,' Ågård warned Killigrew. 'If you're going to try to pretend to be the master of this vessel there's a good chance the captain of that clipper will know you're not who you claim to be. He probably knows the real master of the *Maria Magdalena.*'

'I know, but that's a chance we've got to take. Anyway, I'm not going to pretend to be the master of this vessel; you are.'

'Hunh?'

'I'm the only white man on board who speaks more than a few words of Portuguese. If only one of us does any talking it's going to look damned suspicious. So you're going to pretend to be American. You'll never pass for Brazilian anyway, with that blond hair and those blue eyes. Think you can manage a Yankee accent?'

Ågård grinned. 'Waal, Ah guess Ah sure kin try.'

'That's good, but don't overdo it.'

'An American master of a Brazilian vessel?' said Strachan. 'Isn't that going to seem even more suspicious?'

'Brazilian slavers often carry American captains, Mr Strachan,' said Killigrew. 'To go with their false American colours and forged papers.'

Koumba persuaded the recaptives to descend below decks, leaving only two of them on duty at the bilge pump. Dando went below with Koumba to make sure the recaptives put the irons on their ankles so that it would seem to the casual observer that they were secure. They took the slavers, gagged them, and escorted them to one of the store rooms where they shackled them and locked them in.

Killigrew made his way to the cabin to fetch his pepperbox. He passed the sailmaker on the way. 'Sails, can you check the level of water in the well for me?'

The sailmaker nodded and made his way to the well. Killigrew entered the cabin and made sure all the barrels of his pepperbox were primed and loaded. He thrust it into his holster and then took the single-shot flintlock, loading and priming that as well. He unfastened his sword belt, loath to part with his cutlass but aware that as navy-issue equipment it would give the whole game away. On his way out he took the keys from the nail on the bulkhead and slipped them into his pocket.

On deck, he met the sailmaker returning from the well. 'How much longer do you think?' Killigrew asked him.

'Half an hour, an hour maybe? Then the water reaches the lower ports. I've battened the ports down, of course, but that'll only buy us a few minutes.'

'How long until the other ship reaches us?' asked Strachan.

Killigrew took another look through his telescope. 'No more than half an hour.'

'That's cutting it damned fine.'

'Assuming, of course, that they trouble to come and investigate.'

'What if they don't?'

'Then I hope we can all swim.'

The clipper troubled to come and investigate.

The men in the small boats towed the clipper to within a cable's length of the *Maria Magdalena* and the master of the clipper – the name painted on the stern was the *São João* – hailed them in Portuguese with his speaking trumpet.

'You are in need of assistance? You seem very low in the water.'

'I'd better pretend to be the ship's interpreter,' Killigrew said to Strachan, and raised his own speaking trumpet to reply. 'We're sinking. We were chased for over a hundred miles by a damned British steamer. We managed to give her the slip in the end, but not before she damaged us below the waterline.'

'You have slaves on board?'

Killigrew was about to reply when Ågård laid a hand on

his arm. 'If this turns out to be a US Navy ship posing as a slaver . . .'

'Don't even think such thoughts,' said Killigrew. 'Don't worry, the Yankees don't have that much imagination.' He raised the speaking trumpet to his mouth. 'Yes. Three hundred and forty-one of them. You can have fifty per cent commission on them, if you'll just get us out of this mess.'

'Seventy per cent!'

'Nothing doing!'

'Killigrew!' hissed Strachan. 'What the hell do you think you're playing at?'

'I've got to haggle, or they'll know there's something rum going on.'

'Seventy, or we leave you all to drown!' called the master of the clipper.

'Fifty-five. My owner will kill me anyway when he hears about this.'

The master of the *São João* laughed. 'Sixty-five.'

'Sixty. Any more than that and I'm bankrupted.'

'Sixty-five. That's our last offer, take it or leave it.'

'You drive a hard bargain, my friend.' Killigrew hesitated, as if indecisive. 'Very well, sixty-five it is.'

'Come on over. We'll talk.'

'All right, but don't let's talk too long. This ship is going down fast, and if we don't get the slaves on board your ship your commission will be sixty-five per cent of nothing.'

Boulton, Dando, Sails and O'Connor swung the *Maria Magdalena*'s jolly boat out on its davits and lowered it into the water. Killigrew produced the flintlock and thrust it into Strachan's hand. 'Here. Stick this in your belt.'

Strachan accepted the weapon dubiously. 'Won't they see it?'

'That's the general idea. They'll think it odd to see a slaver who isn't armed.'

'Will I have to use it?'

'When the time comes you may have to wave it around threateningly. If we can do this without unnecessary bloodshed I'll feel much happier. If you must shoot it, here's how you aim it.' Killigrew clamped his hand over Strachan's and held the muzzle close against his own side. 'Like that. That's the only sure way of hitting your target with one of those things. And remember it's a single-shot weapon, so once you've pulled the trigger you're defenceless. Unless you want to use it as a club, of course.'

Strachan grimaced and thrust the pistol behind his belt. 'Let's hope it doesn't come to that.'

Killigrew turned to Boulton and the sailmaker. 'Stay away from the pivot guns – they'll be watching you. But if you hear shooting or it looks like we're in any kind of trouble, try to sink the small boats. The important thing is to keep the *São João* here until we're all aboard her – including the recaptives. Without the small boats they're as helpless as we are, until the wind picks up.'

'Good luck, sir.'

'Thank you. And you.'

Killigrew and Ågård shinned down a rope into the jolly boat. Strachan followed them gingerly, lost his grip when he was only a few feet from the boat and sprawled on the bottom boards. Killigrew helped him up, and then Dando and O'Connor began to row them across to the *São João*. Most of the *São João*'s crew were in the small boats riding off the clipper's bows. Strachan wondered when they would return to the ship so that they could start transhipping the slaves; it could not be long before the *Maria Magdalena* foundered. Still, the more slavers there were in the small boats the fewer there would be on the *São João*'s deck for them to deal with.

The jolly boat bumped gently against the clipper's side and a rope ladder was tossed down for them to climb up. Two of the slavers climbed down first to hold the rope ladder for the others as they climbed up. They stayed in the jolly boat after Strachan had climbed up on deck after Killigrew, Ågård, Dando and O'Connor and began to row it back to the *Maria Magdalena.*

Someone on deck said something in Portuguese to Ågård. Killigrew turned and saw a middle-aged man with silver hair and a tanned face wearing tolerably good clothes. He guessed this would be the master of the *São João.*

'Hey, Barroso!' Ågård called to Killigrew in an execrable attempt at an American accent. 'Come over heah and translate whut the hell this dude's saying. Whut else do I pay you fuh, Gawdamnit!'

Killigrew turned smoothly away from the gunwale to obey, but the silver-haired man held up a hand. 'You only speak English, Captain?' he asked Ågård.

'The only language Ah know is American, suh.'

'Ah, an American. I was wondering what that accent was supposed to be. Of course – an American captain would help to convince any ships of the Royal Navy that tried to stop you that you are an American ship. Very clever. Allow me to introduce myself: I am Raimundo da Silva, master of the *São João*, out of Pernambuco.' He held out his hand delicately.

Ågård shook it a lot less delicately. 'Abram Tyler, at your service. And this heah's mah first mate and translator, Senhor Ramón Barroso, and mah ship's doctor, Tex Polk.'

'Er . . . howdy,' said Strachan.

'Well, gentlemen, shall we retire out of this fatiguing sun into my day room and seal our bargain with a drink while my men tranship your slaves – or perhaps I should say *our* slaves – to my ship?' He gestured to where the slaves were being brought up on to the deck of the *Maria Magdalena.* Killigrew noticed that the use of whips was much in evidence and he stifled a wince. 'I have an excellent bottle of sherry—'

'Let's stay out here, shall we?' suggested Killigrew.

'You do not trust me?' Da Silva smiled. 'That is very wise. I respect a cautious man . . .'

A commotion broke out on board the *Maria Magdalena.* Some of the slaves, outraged at having their hopes of freedom dashed by their apparent transfer to another slaver, started to struggle. A couple of shots rang out, and two young recaptives fell to the deck.

'Have your men take care, Senhor da Silva,' warned Killigrew. 'That's valuable merchandise.'

'So you do not have your cargo broken to the lash yet, eh? Personally, I always find a couple of dead niggers a most excellent investment. It encourages the remainder to be still for the rest of the passage. But tell me, Senhor Barroso, I always thought my old friend Capitão Videira was master of the *Maria Magdalena.*'

'Capitão Videira fell ill,' Killigrew explained smoothly. 'The owners employed me to stand in for him on this voyage.'

Da Silva turned to his first mate, a burly man with black curly hair and a greasy, matted beard. 'You see, Figueroa? Did I not tell you it could not be Videira you saw led in chains from the deck of that British paddle-sloop we saw in Freetown two days ago?'

Killigrew realised the game was up.

# IV:

## Land Sharks

Killigrew drew his pepperbox from its holster and touched da Silva beneath the jaw with the muzzles. In the same instant he felt the cold touch of a pistol muzzle behind his ear.

'I believe this is what is known as an *impasse*,' da Silva said coolly. 'You shoot me, and Figueroa shoots you.'

'I think not,' Strachan said somewhere behind Figueroa, and Killigrew felt the gun taken away from his ear. Ågård, Dando and O'Connor also drew their pistols and covered the slavers close by.

Da Silva's face turned grey. 'Royal Navy?' he spat.

'In the best traditions of the service,' agreed Killigrew.

With da Silva and his first mate at pistol point, they waited until all the recaptives and the rest of the prize crew had been transhipped from the *Maria Magdalena* to the *São João*, only moments before the former floundered and keeled over, turning turtle.

As the slavers were herded down to the slave deck, Killigrew marched da Silva back into the day room. The ship's papers were made out in French, Spanish, Portuguese, Danish and English – both British and United States. Killigrew did not doubt there was a different flag in the bow locker for each of the different nationalities represented amongst the forged papers. There was also a cargo manifest: even now the slavers still carried out their trade by the book, as if it were all still perfectly legal and above board.

He cast his eyes over the manifest. The cargo consisted of *aguardiente*, copper wire, cotton goods, gunpowder, iron pots, looking glasses, muskets, rum and tobacco; all of them typical goods of exchange for the slave trade. According to the owner's instructions they were supposed to take them to the Owodunni Barracoon to exchange them for a cargo of slaves to be transported to Bahia.

'Where's the Owodunni Barracoon?' Killigrew asked da Silva.

'I have never heard of it.'

'Really? You were supposed to be sailing there.'

Da Silva took out a cigar and struck a match to light it. Before he could apply the flame to the cigar's end, Killigrew had snatched the cigar from his mouth, crushed it in his hand and tossed it out through the window.

'You shouldn't have done that,' da Silva said with an infuriating mildness. 'That really was a waste of a fine Havana cigar. I suppose you think you are very clever, eh, young man?'

'Clever enough to defeat you, if that counts for anything,' retorted Killigrew.

Da Silva chuckled. 'Defeat me?' He shook his head. 'Oh, no, my friend. Perhaps you have won this battle, but you can never win the war. You know as well as I do that once we get to Freetown you will have to let us go. You have no power over foreign nationals. Why you persist in stopping our ships is a mystery to me.'

'Because it's our duty?' suggested Killigrew. 'Both as officers of the Royal Navy and as decent human beings.'

'Humanity is a relative concept, my young friend.' Da Silva crossed to the open door and gestured at the recaptives being brought back on board the *São João*'s deck from the boats. 'To you these cattle are human beings. To me they are no more than apes. Apes that can be trained to take their rightful place in the service of a higher form of life.'

'That counts you out, then. Compared to you, even a slug is a higher form of life.'

Da Silva was unperturbed. 'You English make me laugh. Always so arrogant, so convinced that you are in the right. What gives you the prerogative to interfere in the trade of other nations, to act as the self-appointed watchmen of the seas?'

'What gives you the right to trade in human flesh?'

Da Silva sighed mockingly. 'Such passion and idealism in one so young. One day, when you are my age perhaps, you will come to understand that nothing in life is as clear cut as you seem to think it is . . .'

'Oh, I think that when it comes to issues you'll find the inhumanity of the slave trade is as clear cut as they come.'

'Perhaps. Perhaps you are right. But being right makes no difference. You know what is important?' He reached into his pocket.

Killigrew put a hand on the grip of his pepperbox. Da Silva smiled, and slowly drew out a fistful of gold coins. 'This. This is what is truly important. This is why you will never end the slave trade. Because men will always love this more than they love justice. You could take this – share it with your men, if it makes you feel better – and let us go.'

Killigrew stared at the coins as they glittered in the sunlight. With the money that da Silva had in the palm of his hand, Killigrew could buy himself out of the navy and set himself up for life in a comfortable town house in London. He licked his lips, and then took the money from the slaver's hand.

The smile that started to spread across da Silva's face froze as Killigrew tossed the money out of the window. 'You shouldn't judge other people by your own standards, da Silva.'

'You're a fool. You should have taken the money. I will

still be free within days of our landing at Freetown.'

Da Silva's self-assured smugness was so irritating that Killigrew struggled to suppress the urge to smash his face in. 'We'll see,' he said tightly.

'It is the ruling of this court that since the *Maria Magdalena* and the *São João* were separate ships with separate owners, the two cases must be dealt with separately.' Of the three admirals who sat on the panel of the court of mixed commissions, it was the Dutch one – the neutral one, the others being British and Portuguese – who read out the summation and verdict. He at least had the decency to look regretful at the verdict that he and his colleagues had reached.

The courthouse in Freetown was a dry, dusty place with pretensions to civilisation. It was a long way from civilisation, but it was even further from the blood-soaked deck of a slaver.

'Firstly, the *Maria Magdalena*. The captain of the arresting vessel, Commander Standish of Her Majesty's paddle-sloop *Tisiphone*, has presented no conclusive evidence that the crew of the *Maria Magdalena* were at any time engaged in the trading of slaves . . .'

Killigrew kept his face impassive, merely closing his eyes for a moment. He refused to give da Silva and Videira the satisfaction of seeing that to him the verdict was like a dagger being twisted in his guts. But the *Tisiphone*'s other mate, Eustace Tremaine, leaped to his feet. 'No evidence!' he protested. 'What about the slaves, damn it?'

'Sit down, young man, or I'll have you in contempt of court,' snarled the British admiral, a fat, red-faced, gouty old man.

'I *am* in contempt of a court which takes the word of a gang of murderous slavers over and above that of four officers of the Royal Navy!'

The British admiral banged his gavel. 'Sit down! I *shall*

have order in this court! You will conduct yourself with the decorum becoming an officer of the Royal Navy.'

Killigrew reached up and took his friend by the arm, gently pulling him back into his seat.

The Dutch admiral continued. 'Since there is no concrete evidence to convict the crew of the *Maria Magdalena*, it is the verdict of this court that Captain Videira and his men are to be released at once. As to Captain da Silva and his crew, we likewise find that since the only evidence that he and his men were engaged in the slave trade other than the slaves which Mate Killigrew himself shipped aboard from the *Maria Magdalena*—'

Tremaine banged a fist against the table. 'But this is farcical! You can't deny the existence of those slaves in one case, and then use them as evidence in another! If you'd only get some of them in here to testify—'

The British admiral banged his gavel again. 'Silence! If you had been here earlier, young man, you would understand that the testimony of natives is inadmissible evidence. As indeed were the papers which Mate Killigrew claims to have found on board the *São João*, papers which Captain da Silva claims were planted in his cabin by the aforementioned Mate Killigrew. The court therefore finds the captain and crew of the *São João* innocent. They are to be released at once, and the Portuguese vessel *São João* to be surrendered back to them by the Royal Navy at the earliest convenience.'

Videira and da Silva shook one another's hands, and then the hands of their plump and over-paid lawyers. Videira's lawyer rose to his feet. 'Your lordships, I would like the record to state that not only will my client be suing Mate Killigrew for the loss of the *Maria Magdalena*, but he will also be pressing the families of the honest mariners so callously slain by Mr Killigrew to sue him for excessive brutality in the execution of his duties.'

At the back of the court, the seamen of the *Tisiphone* present groaned.

'That is a private matter between yourself, the families of the dead seamen, and Mate Killigrew,' the Dutch admiral remarked drily. 'It is no concern of this court. We will now adjourn.'

Killigrew went outside and leaned back against the wall of the courthouse. He looked at his hand and saw that it was shaking. He clenched it into a fist, and then lit a cheroot to calm his nerves.

Tremaine followed him out. The same age as one another, Killigrew and Tremaine were good friends. They both resided in the gun room, but since they were in opposite watches they rarely saw one another, like the eponymous heroes of Mr Morton's new farce, *Box and Cox.* They had grown up together in Falmouth and shared the same dream of becoming captains in the Royal Navy like their fathers. But when they had reached the age of twelve their ways had parted, Tremaine attending the Royal Naval College at Portsmouth while Killigrew had gone straight to sea as a first class volunteer.

There was a self-mocking rivalry between the two of them – college graduates were often derided for their more theoretical approach to seamanship – and they played up to it, but each was secretly jealous of the other. Tremaine envied the kudos Killigrew enjoyed amongst his superiors for being an officer raised in the old tradition of hands-on experience; while Killigrew knew that times were changing and that one day the college graduates would run the navy. Already the navy was becoming more and more scientific. Steamships might lack the romance of sail, but there could be no doubt that one day they would supplant them altogether.

'Damn it, what a travesty!' huffed Tremaine, outwardly more upset by the verdict than his friend. 'That wasn't justice, that was a farce!'

Killigrew shook his head. 'It's not a question of justice, it's a question of law. The two are rarely the same thing. Forget it, 'Stace. It's not important. What's important is that most of the negroes we found on board the *Maria Magdalena* are saved from a life of slavery. That's what counts.'

'Yes, but you'd think you'd get some gratitude out of it, instead of being treated as though *you're* the criminal.'

Strachan came out next. 'Damnably sorry, Killigrew. Outrageous verdict. Listen, about that private action Videira's lawyer was talking about. My Uncle Andrew is a QC, I'm sure I could persuade him to accept your case.'

'Thank you, Mr Strachan. I may just take you up on that offer—'

Standish steamed out of the court, red in the face. Seeing Killigrew, he rounded on him angrily. 'Well, I hope you're satisfied, young man. One midshipman and six of my best hands killed; a slaver I went to a considerable amount of trouble to catch only for you to sink it, cheating me and the rest of the crew of our share of prize money; and for what? So I could stand up in that court and be made a fool of, a laughing stock! All I can say is, I hope Videira's land-shark *does* bring that personal action against you. I won't defend you, for one. Perhaps it will teach you not to be so damned zealous in future.' As Standish had repeatedly informed Killigrew, if there was one thing he could not abide it was a *zealous* officer. 'I mean, what in the name of all that's holy did you think you were playing at?'

'My duty, sir?'

'None of your jaw now, laddie! I shan't have it, d'ye hear? I shan't! You're a disgrace, Killigrew! A damned disgrace! Carrying on like some kind of latter-day buccaneer. Well, let me tell you there's no place for buccaneers like you in today's Royal Navy. If you'd followed proper naval procedure and brought the *Maria Magdalena* straight back here, instead of rushing off trying to catch another slaver, then Parsons and the others might still be alive . . .'

As much as Killigrew wanted to smash Standish's face in, there was part of him which could not help wondering if the commander was right about him being responsible for the death of the seven men who had been under his command as part of the *Maria Magdalena*'s prize crew.

The two slaver captains emerged from the court with their lawyers, laughing and joking. Seeing the four naval officers, they smirked. 'See you in the civil courts, Mr Killigrew,' called Videira.

'How are those high-minded ideals of yours now, Mr Killigrew?' asked da Silva. 'A little dented, perhaps?'

Killigrew's temper finally snapped. He lunged for da Silva's throat, but Strachan and Tremaine both caught him and hauled him back before he reached the slaver. 'Easy, Killigrew, easy,' said Strachan.

'I'm not finished with you,' Killigrew snarled at them. 'I'm coming after you, and all your kind.'

'I hope that's not a threat, Mr Killigrew,' said da Silva's lawyer. 'The courts here take a very dim view of threatening language.'

'There'll be a reckoning yet.'

Da Silva smiled. 'I shall await that day with interest.'

Killigrew watched the two lawyers hurry their clients on into the hustle and bustle of the streets of Freetown, and sighed. He wished he could learn to control his temper, widely supposed to be a legacy from his Greek mother. She had been a fighter in the Greek War of Independence, and quite a firebrand by all accounts. That had been where she had met his father, of course. Captain John Killigrew had served as an officer in the Royal Navy during the war against Napoleon and afterwards became a sailor of fortune, serving with his old patron Admiral Lord Cochrane in the Chilean,

Brazilian and Greek navies in turn.

'Are you all right, Killigrew?' asked Tremaine.

Killigrew nodded, and banged a fist against the side of the courthouse. 'Damn those scum! Da Silva was right, damn his eyes. He's going to go straight back on board the *São João* and pick up a cargo of slaves further down the coast, and it's as if there's nothing we can do to stop him!' He sighed. 'Oh, well. Standing here grumbling isn't going to help matters.'

Strachan nodded. 'Gentlemen, as a fully qualified apothecary, it is my recommendation that we repair at once to the nearest hostelry, partake of intoxicating liquors, and indulge in the company of the lowest sort of females that Freetown can boast of.'

'Capital notion,' said Killigrew. 'Let's go.'

When Killigrew had finished dressing he left a guinea on the bedside table and glanced back to where the prostitute, a freed slave, sat at her dresser, touching up her hair in preparation for her next client. Most of his sexual liaisons were with prostitutes – striking up a relationship with any other kind of woman in a port could only end in heartbreak for one or both parties, and possible ruin for the lady if it resulted in pregnancy – but that night he went downstairs feeling uncharacteristically ashamed. *Aguardiente*, copper wire, cotton goods, gunpowder, iron pots, looking glasses, muskets, rum, tobacco: it was all the same. The rape of a continent.

A brawl between the Tisiphones – it was traditional for sailors from a ship to be known by its name – and the crew of an American frigate had been in full swing in the saloon below when Killigrew had headed upstairs, but it was over by the time he returned. Here and there a few unconscious bodies snored amidst the wreckage of tables and chairs, while a slave swept up the broken glass. 'Goodnight, Mas'er Killigrew.'

'G'night, George.'

*Just another night at Maggie's Place*, he thought to himself.

George suddenly remembered something. 'Oh, Mas'er Killigrew? Wait there a minute, mas'er. I have something for you.' He scurried into the back room. Killigrew was curious enough to wait until he returned; it did not take long. George re-emerged carrying a tall black beaver hat. 'Mas'er Standish, him done left this in Missy Molly's room last night.'

'Did he, by God? Don't worry, I'll see that he gets it back. Thank you, George.' Killigrew tipped him a shilling and went outside.

He paused on the veranda and leaned on the rail, watching the people coming and going for a while until he had finished his cheroot: Krumen as naked as the day they were born, Muslim traders in elegant long blue robes of fine country cloth, and Creoles dressed in European clothes wholly unsuited to the tropical climate. It was barely eight o'clock, but already things were winding down in the town. Freetown was so shameless it practised its debauchery during daylight hours; it had to get up to go to chapel early the next morning.

Freetown was a city of contradictions: a young settlement with an air of tumble-down decrepitude about it. None of the whites who came to this fever-stricken coast expected to live more than a few years, so no one bothered to invest much time or money in building to last or even repairing that which collapsed. To landward, green-carpeted mountains, slashed here and there with scars of red earth, and dotted with the homes of the colony's wealthier whites, provided a backdrop to the port, rising up until they disappeared into the low-lying clouds which wreathed them. Houses of wood or stone, washed white or yellow, with green-painted jalousies beneath their verandas and wide-caved shingle roofs, crowded towards the sea. The dusty streets, which turned into rivers of mud during the wet season, were broad, and prolific gardens provided microcosmic reflections of the jungles which crowded around the edges of the settlement. St George's Cathedral dominated the town – not that the town needed much to dominate it – with turkey-buzzards perched on the roof during daylight hours, and chapels of every conceivable Protestant sect jostled for space with countless rum-houses.

Freetown had been set up on the coast of Sierra Leone as a colony for freed slaves nearly sixty years ago. In those days its population had consisted of four hundred negroes and sixty prostitutes, and while its population had expanded considerably since then – particularly with the arrival of black settlers from Nova Scotia, of all places, in 1797, and of Cimaroons from Jamaica in 1800 – the general tenor of the place had changed little. Most of the town's permanent inhabitants were, as its name suggested, freed slaves. They were maintained at the British government's expense for a year and then left to fend for themselves. Some opted to go to the West Indies as apprenticed labourers or to serve in a black regiment; for those who stayed behind in Sierra Leone there was little choice but to become a labourer, and despite Freetown's steady growth there were always more labourers than there was labour for them to perform.

The white population of the town was no more than five hundred, although that number was bolstered by a constantly fluctuating tide of seamen: sailors from the vessels of the various navies which patrolled the coast for slavers, and to make sure the flags of their countries were known throughout the world; and the crews of captured slavers. The combination of men from rival navies, freed slaves and disgruntled slavers made for a volatile mix, and it was not unknown for African tribesmen to raid across the river and kidnap freed slaves to sell them on to the white man once more.

Yes, Killigrew was going to miss Freetown when he got back to England in a few weeks' time. But there was something else that saddened him about his imminent departure from the West Africa Squadron: the feeling that he was only just beginning to find his feet and the sense that the squadron's work in suppressing the slave trade, far from being over, was only just begun.

He took a final drag on his cheroot and headed back for the wharf. He had not gone a hundred yards when he heard someone groaning down an alleyway between two shacks. He went to investigate. 'Hullo? Are you all right? Who's there?'

A man was sprawled amongst the fetid rubbish, pawing feebly at the ground.

'What's up? One too many to drink? I know the feeling. Come on, let's have you . . .'

As he tried to turn the man over he saw the glint of moonlight on a blade and jumped back, but slowly, too slowly, his reactions dulled by alcohol. He felt no pain, but when he glanced down at himself he saw that the fabric of his shirt was sliced through and blood was seeping from a long, thin line scored across his chest.

The man came at him again. Killigrew knew no better cure for drunkenness than danger. He dodged back from the man's next lunge and caught him by the wrist. Spinning the man away from him, he slammed him against the side of a shack and twisted his arm up into the small of his back until he dropped the knife. He punched him in the kidneys to make sure, and the man sank into the rubbish with a groan.

He turned to the mouth of the alley and saw three shadowy figures blocking his path.

'You know something, my friends?' asked Barroso. 'If I could have just one wish fulfilled, it would be to catch Senhor Killigrew alone down a darkened alley. And it looks as if it has just come true.'

# V:

## Pursuit

Killigrew reached for his pepperbox only to remember that he had left it on board the *Tisiphone*. He glanced back down the alley for an escape route at the other end, but there were three more burly figures blocking off his only escape route. He cursed himself for his carelessness in leaving ship unarmed; and for walking right into Barroso's trap.

'Get him!' snapped Barroso.

The six men charged down the alley from either end. Killigrew weighed up the odds and charged to meet Barroso and his friends. As Barroso pulled out in front, he swung some kind of club at Killigrew's head. Killigrew ducked beneath it and drove a fist into Barroso's side. The slaver doubled up. Killigrew span him around and used his back as a stepping stone to launch himself up towards the roof of one of the houses adjoining the alley. He caught hold of the eaves and swung himself up just as the other slavers converged beneath him, grasping for his ankles and bumping into one another. Killigrew's feet scrabbled against the wall for a moment and he trod on a head to push himself up. He ran up one side of the shingles and then down the other, leaping across the narrow alley on the far side of the building.

He landed easily on the next roof. Behind him, Barroso and his friends were coming round the first house, shouting to one another. Killigrew surmounted the next apex and began to run down the slope on the other side. The next alley was a good ten feet wide. He measured the steps of his pell-mell descent, putting his right foot on the edge of the roof and launching himself into space, his hands clawing at the air as he sailed through the darkness. He was aware of the alley yawning beneath him, and then the other roof rose up to meet him.

*Made it.*

His feet landed squarely on the shingles, and then they collapsed under the impact. He fell through with a splintering crash, landed on a counter and fell forward. He hit the floor, rolled over and rose quickly but unsteadily to his feet, bruised, scratched and dazed.

He could hear the shouts of the slavers outside growing louder, their footsteps soft on the compacted earth of the street. He looked around for something he could use as a weapon.

He was in a millinery shop.

He unbolted the back door and rushed out. A moment later something slammed across his stomach and knocked the breath out of him. He doubled up and fell down in winded agony, and his assailant brought the plank of wood down on him again. He rolled on to his hands and knees so that it hit him across the back, knocking him flat on his stomach, and then a foot connected with his ribs.

'I've got him! He came out the back!'

Killigrew rolled on his back and kicked the man in the crotch. The man gave a high-pitched scream and dropped the plank. Killigrew scrambled to his feet and ran down an alley just in time to meet Barroso and three more men coming to meet him. He knocked down one with a right cross, and then they were on him, raining blow after blow. His felt his legs crumple and slid to the ground. The slavers gathered in a circle, kicking at him savagely. He heard more footsteps running up

– how many of them were there? – and a cry of 'Remember the Alamo!'

*Remember the Alamo?*

A shot rang out. Killigrew felt something smash into his head and then . . .

Someone was slapping him gently on the cheek. After the beating he had been taking only seconds earlier it was a distinct improvement. Was he still alive, then?

'It's a Limey navy officer, Loot!' exclaimed an American accent.

'I think you must be mistaken, Charlie,' said another voice, the rich and melodious tones of the Deep South with a hint of Creole thrown in to spice it up. 'British naval officers are always far too dignified to be found brawling in back alleys,' it continued mockingly. 'No, this must be some fellow who stole the uniform of a British navy officer. Maybe we should hand him over to the authorities. What do you say, Charlie?'

Killigrew reached up and grabbed the first thing that came to hand: Charlie's throat. 'Hey, take it easy, *amigo*!' gasped Charlie.

'Who are you and what do you want?' rasped Killigrew, still woozy from his beating.

'Lieutenant Jean-Pierre Lanier, of the United States' frigate *Narwhal* at your service, sir,' said 'Loot'. 'My companions and I are merely acting in our capacity of good Samaritans, so if you would be so kind as to release my bosun's throat I should be much obliged to you.'

Killigrew let go of Charlie's throat and the American sailors helped him up. 'My apologies. I wasn't sure whose side you were on. Mate Christopher Killigrew, of Her Majesty's paddle-sloop *Tisiphone*. Sorry about half strangling you there,' he added to Charlie.

'That's oh-kay, *amigo*. It'd take more than one Limey to half strangle me.' Charlie shook him by the hand, and from the strength of his grip Killigrew knew he spoke the truth.

'I'm sure you could easily have sent off those bully-boys without our assistance, but I know how you Lime-Juicers think we Americans are always holding back when it comes to suppressing the slave trade,' Lanier said with a hint of amusement in his voice.

'You came along in the nick of time, and there's no denying it,' Killigrew told him. 'I'm indebted to you.'

'Not at all, sir, not at all. It was our pleasure.'

Killigrew tried to take a step but his knees gave way and he would have fallen to the floor if Charlie had not caught him. 'Hey, take it easy, *amigo*. You sure you're oh-kay?'

'I'll be all right in a minute,' said Killigrew. 'I just need to . . .'

'Nonsense, nonsense,' said Lanier. 'You need to sit down and get a good stiff drink inside you. Mr Killigrew, I should be honoured if you would be a guest in the wardroom of the *Narwhal* tonight. In fact, I must insist upon it.'

'In which case, it would be churlish of me to refuse,' Killigrew said cheerfully, although he was still a little suspicious. There was no love lost between British and American seamen – assuming these *were* American seamen, for it was so dark Killigrew could not make out what Lanier was wearing. Crimping was still a common practice in some of the world's less salubrious seaports, and it would be too embarrassing if he woke up the next morning and found himself pressed into service as a common seaman on an American vessel. But there were four of them, and he was in no condition to resist.

It was only a few hundred yards to the wharf overlooking St George's Bay where the USS *Narwhal* rode at anchor. Further out, Killigrew could see the *Tisiphone*. Two American seamen waited by the *Narwhal*'s launch, tied up at the wharf's single wooden jetty. As soon as he saw them he felt reassured:

he had seen the American frigate enter the bay earlier that day, and knew then that these men were genuinely US Navy, and unlikely to provoke a diplomatic incident by kidnapping an officer of the Royal Navy.

Once on board the frigate Lanier took Killigrew to the wardroom where he struck a match and applied it to an oil lamp which he hung from an overhead beam. He was in his mid-twenties, tall and rake-thin, with a lean jaw and high cheekbones which gave his face an angular, wedge-shaped look. The wardroom was not unlike that of the *Tisiphone*, except that there was slightly less head-room, and a daguerreotype of President Tyler hung on the bulkhead in place of a portrait of Queen Victoria. Killigrew was helped into a chair and a black servant took his hat while the ratings made their way back to their own quarters.

'Two whiskeys, Skip,' said Lanier. 'Then be so good as to rouse Mr DeForest from his bunk and have him attend to Mr Killigrew here.'

'Yes, sir.' The black poured out two glasses of rye whiskey and put them on the table before silently slipping out of the wardroom.

'Mr DeForest?' asked Killigrew.

'Our ship's surgeon,' said Lanier, and raised his glass. 'To Her Britannic Majesty Queen Victoria.'

Killigrew raised his own glass. 'To President Tyler.'

'I'll overlook the fact that you did not rise to salute our president, sir, and ascribe it to your current condition,' Lanier said coldly.

'My apologies,' Killigrew said quickly. 'In the Royal Navy it's the custom to give the loyal toast seated. Ever since the last King rose too quickly to accept it on board ship once, and banged his head on a beam.' Lanier smiled, and Killigrew rose to his feet. 'To President Tyler and the United States of America. Your health.'

'And yours.'

They downed their drinks. Killigrew gasped as the liquor churned a fiery wake down his throat. 'Good God, what is that?'

Lanier grinned. 'Kentucky rye whiskey, Mr Killigrew. It's an acquired taste.'

'Pass me that bottle. I think I may just have acquired it.'

The black returned with a middle-aged man dressed in a nightshirt and nightcap. 'Well! If someone had told me there was a celebration in progress, I might not have cursed poor Skip here quite so heartily for rousing me from my beauty sleep which, the good Lord knows, I'm in need of.'

'Mr Killigrew, may I introduce you to our surgeon, Mr DeForest? 'Bones, this is Mate Christopher Killigrew, of the *Tisiphone*.'

'Pleased to make your acquaintance, sir,' said DeForest. 'Sweet Jesus! You look like you've gone twenty rounds with Ben Caunt.'

Killigrew smiled at the reference to the boxing champion, and then winced as his split lip split again. 'Twenty-one, actually.'

'What you need is a good stiff drink,' said DeForest, and the black refilled Killigrew's and Lanier's glasses while pouring out a fresh one for the surgeon. 'What are we celebrating, anyway?'

Lanier glanced at Killigrew, and then raised his glass in a fresh toast. 'The end of the slave trade.'

'I'll drink to that,' said DeForest.

Killigrew glanced at the black servant and left his glass on the table.

Lanier grinned. 'Yes, Mr Killigrew, Scipio's a slave. I said death to the slave trade, not slavery.' He turned to the servant. 'Hey, Skip. You realise, of course, that Sierra Leone is a British colony and there's no slavery here? All you have to do is step off this ship, and you'll be a free man. I won't stop you.'

Scipio beamed. 'Why, thank you, sir. But I've already been ashore today and I didn't think much of what I saw. No, sir, I'm quite happy where I am, thank you all the same.'

'Then again, Scipio's a domestic slave,' said Lanier. 'And since Sierra Leone's one of the few colonies where the British allow people to keep domestic slaves he wouldn't be free anyway, as I understand it.'

'If it were up to me it would be a very different story, I can assure you,' said Killigrew.

Lanier shook his head. 'It's the cruelty I despise, Mr Killigrew, not the principle of slavery. There are no whips on my father's plantation, I can assure you. We feed our slaves well, give them clean and adequate accommodation, and they're grateful for it. They work all the harder knowing they're well looked after.'

'I don't doubt it, but I'll wager it's a different story on some of your neighbours' plantations.'

'True, but then I'll wager they're no worse off than the negroes you British transport to the West Indies under your system of apprenticed labour. You ask Scipio here: slavery doesn't have to be unpleasant.'

'For myself, it's the principle as well as the cruelty.'

Lanier shook his head again. 'We're all slaves to something, Mr Killigrew.'

'And what is it that you are a slave to, Mr Lanier?'

Lanier's face cracked into a grin. 'Why, to duty, of course.'

'I'll bet being a slave to duty is a damned sight more comfortable than being a slave to a plantation owner with only a loose understanding of your noble but discriminating bill of rights.'

Lanier shrugged uncomfortably. 'How about you, Mr Killigrew? What are you a slave to?'

'I don't know. I'll have a think about that one.'

'Say, I thought this was a celebration,' protested DeForest. 'Seems I was mistaken. Sounds more like I've walked into a debate on slavery. If I'd wanted that I could've gone to a meeting of the Society of Friends.'

'Agreed,' said Lanier. 'But not at two bells in the first watch. Let's at least put our differences behind us and drink to what we have in common: our contempt for the slavers.'

The three of them raised their glasses.

'That's what we need to do,' said DeForest. 'It's high time our navies learned to put their differences behind them. The War of 1812 was a long time ago. We'll never beat the blackbirders until we learn to work together.'

'It's a nice idea, but it's been tried before,' said Killigrew.

'It has?'

Lanier nodded. 'A few years ago the captain of the USS *Grampus* tried working with the captain of HMS *Wolverine*. The idea was that since only US Navy ships can stop American vessels, and only the Royal Navy's ships can stop British vessels, they'd sail together. If a slaver hoisted a US ensign then the *Grampus* would stop her; and if they hoisted the Union Jack, then the Royal Navy did the honours.'

'What went wrong?'

'Oh, it worked just fine,' said Lanier. 'Until our government heard about the arrangement and declared it *ultra vires*. Those damned fools in Washington think that asserting the freedom of the seas for American vessels is more important than stopping the slavers. Personally, I don't see what the problem is. I'd be happy for Royal Navy ships to stop and search American merchantmen when and where they pleased. If the merchantmen are engaged in an honest trade, then they've nothing to fear.'

'It's not only your politicians who are at fault,' said Killigrew. 'If statesmen like Lord Palmerston didn't take such a high-handed attitude with the diplomats of other nations, then perhaps those other nations might be a little bit more co-operative.'

The Americans could not disagree with that. DeForest swabbed Killigrew's cuts and bruises, cleaned and bandaged the cut across his chest – it was too shallow to justify stitches – and they drank several more toasts together before having the crew of the *Narwhal*'s jolly boat row Killigrew back to the *Tisiphone*, where the men of the anchor-watch carried him to his berth.

Killigrew was awoken at dawn by a squad of marines shuffling into the *Tisiphone*'s gun room and singing a rousing chorus of 'Early in the Morning'. He fell out of his hammock and crouched on the floor, holding his head which throbbed agonisingly despite his not having banged it on the way down.

He glared up at them. 'And to what do I owe this dubious pleasure, Corporal?'

'Begging your pardon, sir, Commander Standish's orders. He said it would teach you not to rouse him at little one bell by coming on board singing "The Star-Spangled Banner".'

'Did I do that?' It was all coming back to him: not slowly, but memory after drunken memory crashing helter-skelter into a skull too numbed to cope with them all. 'Did I remember to salute the quarter-deck as I came on board?'

'Yes, sir. And you doffed your hats.'

'Hat*s*?'

The corporal pointed to where Standish's beaver hat, now thoroughly battered, sat on Killigrew's sea-chest. 'You were wearing your cocked hat and had that in your hands, sir.'

Killigrew massaged his temples. 'I must say, this is a revelation. I never knew Commander Standish had a sense of humour.'

'I believe it was Mr Tremaine's suggestion, sir.'

Killigrew glanced across to where Tremaine's hammock

was stowed. 'Was it, by God? I shall bear that in mind.'

The corporal coughed into his fist. 'Begging your pardon, sir, but Commander Standish presents his compliments and requests you present yourself in his day room at six bells.'

'I don't suppose he told you what it was about, did he?'

'No, sir.'

'What time is it now?'

'Four bells, sir. In the morning watch.'

'Thank you, Corporal. Dismissed. Oh, send the ship's barber in here, would you?' Killigrew's hands were shaking too much for him to want to risk shaving himself. 'And tell him he'd better have a mug of tea in his hand when he gets here. Two, if he wants one himself.'

'Aye, aye, sir. Shall I have some food brought down to you?'

'No thank you, Corporal. Just some tea.'

Shaved, dressed, and with some tea inside him, Killigrew began to feel human again. He made his way to the captain's day room where another marine stood on guard. The marine knocked on the door.

'Who is it?' called Standish.

'Mr Killigrew here to see you, sir.'

There was a pause, the sound of feet on the deck – Standish striking up a pose in front of the window, guessed Killigrew – and then: 'Enter.'

The marine opened the door and ushered Killigrew inside. Predictably, Standish stood at the window gazing out. 'I've had a complaint from one of Freetown's saloon-keepers, Mr Killigrew. A demand for payment for damages, in fact. Something to do with a brawl?'

'Yes, sir. There were some American sailors in there and when the Tisiphones met them I understand things got a little out of hand. They were just blowing off steam.'

'To the tune of fifty pounds, Mr Killigrew. I thought I

banned all shore leave for the ratings? Aside from the risk of contracting yellow fever, I will not have my men brawling . . .' Standish turned away from the window and his face became grim when he saw the bruises on Killigrew's face.

'I ran into some of the men from the *São João* on my way back to the ship last night, sir.'

'I suppose you were at Maggie's Place too, were you? What were you doing there?'

'That's not the sort of question a gentleman answers, sir.'

'That's not the sort of hostelry a gentleman frequents, Mr Killigrew. I don't suppose you ordered any of the Tisiphones you saw at Maggie's Place to return directly to the ship, did you?' Standish frowned and tried to peer past Killigrew to see what he held behind his back in his left hand.

'I felt it would have been hypocritical of me to tell them to leave when it must have been obvious I was there to have a good time myself.'

'Damned right. You shouldn't have been there at all. You're a disgrace, man. Exceeding orders, brawling with common seamen, coming back on board roaring drunk in the small hours of the morning. You needn't think that I shall be asking you to join me on my next command when we get back to England, Killigrew . . . Damn it, man, stand up straight! What the devil are you holding in your hand?'

Killigrew held out his empty palm. 'Nothing, sir.'

'Your *other* hand, damn it!'

'Oh! I'd almost forgotten. Your hat, sir.' Killigrew dusted the beaver hat off with his sleeve and proffered it to Standish.

'My beaver! I've been looking all over for that. I thought perhaps that damned fool Gibbons had put it away somewhere. Where on earth did you find it?'

'Maggie's Place, sir.'

Standish turned puce. 'Get out, Killigrew.'

'Yes, sir.'

* * *

'Sail ho!'

'Where away?'

'Two points on the port bow.'

Killigrew skipped up on to the *Tisiphone*'s port-side paddle-box, extended the telescope and raised it to his right eye, looking in the direction the lookout at the masthead had indicated. 'Can you make her out at all?' called Standish.

'Two-masted, rakish, square-rigged . . . could be a Baltimore brig, sir.' When a good breeze was blowing Baltimore brigs were amongst the fastest ships on the sea, including steamers, and as such were beloved of slavers.

'Can you see an ensign?'

'None flying, sir. I don't believe she's seen us. No, wait a moment: she's altering course slightly; turning to loo'ard.' Killigrew lowered the telescope and snapped it shut before descending to the deck once more.

'Damned suspicious,' said Standish. 'She must be a slaver.'

'*Too* suspicious, if you ask me,' said Killigrew. 'Sir.'

'And what the devil is that supposed to mean?'

'It's as if she's trying to provoke our interest by acting suspiciously, sir. She could be trying to draw us away from the African coast to give other vessels – the real slavers – a chance to slip past us. When I was on board the *Dido*—'

'When you were on board the *Dido*, when you were on board the *Dido*,' Standish echoed pettishly. 'I was serving on this station years before you were on board the *Dido*, Killigrew. Believe you me, merchant ships have better things to do than lead Her Majesty's vessels on wild-goose chases, be they slavers or otherwise. Give chase, Mr Darrow. Make all plain sail.'

'Aye, aye, sir.' The boatswain relayed the orders, and the topmen in the rigging unfurled those sails which had previously been furled.

'She looks like a trim vessel to me, sir,' said Killigrew. 'Hadn't we better wet the sails?'

'Damn you, Killigrew. How many times must I tell you not to instruct me in my duties?'

'My apologies, sir.'

Standish turned back to the boatswain. 'Dampen the sails, Mr Darrow.'

'Aye, aye, sir.'

The *Tisiphone* was back in her old cruising grounds off the Guinea Coast, a few miles to the south of the Sierra Leone peninsula. Killigrew could see the low outline of the coast off to windward; a landsman might have mistaken it for a bank of low-lying cloud on the eastern horizon. Beneath an azure sky the sun glistened on the waves and shone dazzlingly on the paddle-sloop's pale deck. There was a slight haze in the air, caused by the red dust blown out to sea by the Harmattan winds. The north-east trade wind blew a moderate breeze from the land, filling the *Tisiphone*'s sails from the port quarter.

Beneath their sponsons the paddle-wheels hung lifeless in the water, and no smoke issued from the funnel. Standish rarely used the engine, partly because it made sense to conserve coal for when it was really needed, but mostly because he had learned his trade on sailing ships and was not used to having the benefits of a steam engine at his command. In fact, he disdained to use the engines unless he really had to, and even then did so grudgingly. Besides, all that soot made a dreadful mess of his beautiful sails.

Killigrew continued to watch the suspect vessel through the telescope. When he had gauged the relative speeds of the two vessels, he would be able to calculate how long it would be before the other vessel came within range of the *Tisiphone*'s bow-chaser; assuming the paddle-sloop could out-run her prey, which was by no means a given. The *Tisiphone* had perhaps half a knot on her quarry, if they maintained their current course and the wind did not change; it would be about twelve hours before they came within range. A stern chase could be a long and tedious business, and by now even the most inexperienced midshipman on the paddle-sloop knew better than to rush down to the gun room to sharpen his dirk.

In the meantime the day-to-day running of the ship continued as normal. The crew still had to be mustered, the deck holystoned, the rigging maintained, the crew's clothes washed, the log-board filled in, dinner eaten, marines paraded, seamen exercised with cutlasses and small arms, noon sights taken. All the while they drew closer and closer to their prey, and more and more men began to glance towards it more frequently. By the end of the forenoon watch it could be seen clearly from the deck with the naked eye.

The hands tried to give out an air of calm indifference but they fooled no one, not even themselves. The air of tension on board the *Tisiphone* was tangible; muted, at first, but increasing as the wearing of the hours brought the brig cable by cable closer to the paddle-sloop's guns. There was fear there, for it was not unknown for a slaver to put up enough of a fight to kill or maim navy seamen, although on the West Africa Squadron there was a greater risk of death from yellow fever than there was from action. But mostly there was excitement: a long, drawn-out stern chase was a chase nonetheless, a break from the monotonous routine of cruising, the chance to do some fighting and break some slavers' heads, and the possibility of prize money.

At midday Killigrew went below to dine in the gun room with Tremaine, Strachan, the captain's clerk and the *Tisiphone*'s two surviving midshipmen. Even though all of them were thinking of the ship they were chasing – with the possible exception of the clerk – there was a tacit agreement between them not to speak of it. Since there was little else to discuss, conversation was stilted.

After dinner Tremaine and Midshipman Radmall went up on deck and Strachan went to the sick bay, refilled with a fresh batch of cases of yellow fever after their last run ashore. The clerk had paperwork to attend to in the captain's day room, leaving Killigrew, off duty until the first dog watch, in the gun room with Midshipman Cavan. He knew he would not be able to sleep so he turned to his sea-chest for something to read. His bookmark was stuck between the pages of Gordon's *The Economy of the Marine Steam Engine*, but he knew that in his present state of mind he would not be able to concentrate on the technical information. Virgil's *Aeneid* seemed a better proposition, even on a second reading.

Cavan drew his dirk from his scabbard and began to sharpen it. The grating of the whetstone against the edge of the blade soon became irritating. 'For heaven's sake belay that scraping, Mr Cavan.'

'Sorry, sir. I just wanted to be ready for when we board her.'

'It'll be a couple of hours before she's in range, even. And I don't see Standish choosing someone as young as you for the boarding party.'

'But how am I ever to become experienced enough if I never get the opportunity because of my lack of experience? Can't you speak to the captain for me?'

'By God, Cavan, you're a bloodthirsty young shaver, aren't you? Are you really so keen to feel the edge of your sword biting through flesh, spilling blood and snapping bone?'

Cavan pulled a face. 'I hadn't thought about it like that, sir.'

'Well, I suggest you do. Better to come to terms with it now rather than when you're face to face with some slaver in the thick of a mêlée. Because if the idea of killing a man gives you pause for thought, then just remember that pause may be all the time your opponent needs to slice your head off.'

'Oh! I wouldn't have any qualms about killing a slaver.'

'Well you should. They've got rights, the same as any other man.'

'Even criminals?'

'They're not criminals until they've been proved criminals in a properly constituted court of law. Our job is to bring them before that court, not to inflict our own justice. D'you understand me?' As he spoke the words he had believed in for so long, he found they had a hollow ring to them now.

Cavan hung his head. 'Yes, sir.' Then he perked up. 'But it's all right to kill them in self-defence, isn't it?'

Killigrew smiled. 'That it is, Mr Cavan.'

'*Please* won't you speak to Commander Standish, sir? I have to get some experience of fighting sooner or later.'

'Later rather than sooner, believe me. Anyway, even if I did think you were ready, my talking to Standish wouldn't do you any good. You know how he hates having to go along with anything I suggest.'

'How old were you the first time *you* killed someone?'

'Sixteen, as I recall. Two years older than you are now, so don't worry, you've got plenty of time.'

'How many men have you killed?'

'Does it matter?'

'You were in Syria, weren't you, sir? And at the storming of Chingkiang-fu during the China War?'

Killigrew grunted but refused to be drawn. He was not ashamed of the battles he had fought against pirates and slavers, but the China campaign was not one he was proud of. At least in Syria the cause had been just, fighting alongside the Ottoman Turks against the rebel Viceroy of Egypt, Ibrahim Pasha. He remembered storming the Boharsef Heights with the combined force of the British Naval Brigade and the

Turkish soldiers. He remembered marines and Turks falling dead on all sides around him as they dashed across the open ground to engage the Egyptian Musselmen. And then, with the smell of blood in his nostrils and the memory of the atrocities the Egyptians had inflicted on the Lebanese fresh in his mind, he had been amongst the enemy, his cutlass whirling as he avenged the murder and rapine. Sometimes the nightmare still came back to haunt him, and in his dream he was watching himself from a distance. For it had not been Midshipman Killigrew who had taken part in the assault – as an officer of the Royal Navy he had been far too civilised to engage in that kind of savage bloodletting – but someone else, caught in the grip of an uncontrollable rage. And of all the horrors that had terrified him in that campaign, the one fear that still came back to haunt him was the fear that that Killigrew might not be dead but still locked deep within him, ready to emerge given sufficient provocation and to inflict atrocities as grim as any he sought to avenge. It was sobering to think that for all he was a product of the most civilised nation on earth he was just as capable of savagery as the most primitive Patagonian cannibal or Borneo head-hunter.

'What's wrong?' asked Cavan, snapping him out of his reverie.

Killigrew forced himself to smile. 'Nothing. I was just thinking, that's all.'

'About what?'

'Merely reflecting on human nature.'

'Oh.' Cavan shrugged.

The afternoon watch wore on. The ship's bell tolled the half hours, marking the slow dragging of time, with a lifetime between each bell. Killigrew could see the tension etched in every line of Cavan's young face, and at last he tapped him on the shoulder.

'Relax. Put the slaver from your mind. A watched kettle

never boils, and a watched slaver is never overhauled.'

'That's easy for you to say, sir. Dash it, how can you be so cool-headed at a time like this?'

'A naval officer is cool-headed at all times, Mr Cavan. It's a question of self-control. There's an old Chinese proverb: Any man who would conquer the world must first conquer himself.'

The hands were clearing the deck for action by the time Killigrew emerged on to the quarter-deck just before four o'clock. The bedding stowed on deck was now draped over the rails to provide some protection against flying splinters in case the enemy opened fire on them.

The brig was less than a mile off the port bow and the *Tisiphone* continued to overhaul her. 'Still no sign of any colours, sir,' said Killigrew, eyeing the brig through the telescope.

'All right,' said Standish. 'Let's see if we can wake them up, eh? Fire a blank shot, Mr Jeal.'

'Aye, aye, sir.' The gunner made his way to the bow-chaser on the forecastle.

One of the disadvantages of paddle-steamers was that the paddle-boxes on the sides took up so much space it was impossible to fit them with a broadside. To counteract this, the navy equipped them with bigger guns. The *Tisiphone* had three guns in all, two thirty-two-pounders and the bow-chaser in the forecastle: a sixty-eight-pound pivot gun.

A silence fell over the decks of the *Tisiphone*, just as if they were about to engage in a gunnery exercise. The gunner and his crew loaded the sixty-eight-pounder with a blank cartridge and primed it with a friction tube. They then raised it to its maximum elevation. The gunner's mate took the lanyard in his hands while the gunner glanced back to where Standish stood on the quarter-deck.

Standish nodded.

'Fire!' ordered the gunner. His mate jerked back the lanyard and the sixty-eight-pounder boomed, belching a great mushroom of pale-grey smoke from its muzzle.

The brig ran an ensign up her jackstaff. 'She's showing her colours, sir,' called the lookout.

'Can you make them out?'

Killigrew already had the telescope raised to his eye. 'Claiming to be a Yankee, sir.'

'Don't they all?' sighed Standish.

The brig showed no signs of stopping. Within half an hour they were within six cables – two-thirds of a mile, just within the extreme range of the sixty-eight-pounder – of their quarry. 'Ask Mr Jeal to give them a warning shot,' Standish ordered Cavan.

'Yes, sir. I mean, aye, aye, sir.' The midshipman saluted and scurried the length of the deck to the forecastle.

The gunner and his crew sponged out the gun, loaded her with a cartridge and a sixty-eight-pound round shot, over eight inches in diameter. The gunner's mate inserted a fresh priming, the crew aimed it at a spot in the water alongside the brig: they were too far away and at the wrong angle to fire the traditional shot across the bows. 'Ready.'

'Fire!'

The pivot gun boomed and the shot screeched through the air towards the brig. It ploughed into the water on the starboard side of the vessel. The message to the crew of the brig was clear: *You are within range of our guns*.

'Is she heaving to?' called Standish.

The lookout was silent for a moment as he peered through his telescope, waiting for some indication of the brig's next move. 'No, sir. She's bearing away.'

The brig's bows went about; she turned four points to starboard so that she ran south-west with the wind right astern.

'Stay with her,' ordered Standish.

'Aye, aye, sir.' The quartermaster span the helm, mimicking the brig's turn. But now the brig had the wind full abaft and the paddle-sloop began to fall astern.

'That's odd,' remarked Killigrew.

Standish said nothing, refusing to give Killigrew the satisfaction of asking him what was odd and waiting for him to elaborate; but Killigrew knew how to play that game too, and it was Standish who broke first. 'What is it?' the commander asked with a sigh.

'She must've known she could outpace us with the wind full abaft. Why not bear away the moment we gave chase?'

'I really couldn't say. Why don't you ask her master when we catch her?'

'Perhaps I shall.' Killigrew snapped the telescope shut.

The gunner and his crew quickly reloaded the pivot gun and were ready to fire before the brig slipped out of range again. But there was no point in firing a warning shot – the brig already knew they were there – and a shot aimed at the vessel could only hit the hull at that range and risk killing any slaves on board.

'We're going to lose her, sir,' prompted Killigrew, seeing Standish's indecision.

'I can see that! Tell Mr Muir to start up his engines. She can beat us with sails alone, but not with sails and steam.'

Killigrew crossed to the engine-room telegraph and signalled full speed ahead. If Standish had expected smoke to billow from the funnels and the paddle-wheels to start churning the water immediately, he was disappointed. After perhaps a minute, one of the greasy, grubby denizens of the engine room emerged on deck and tugged at his forelock. 'Begging your pardon, sir, but we'll have steam up just as soon as we can,' he announced in a thick Geordie accent.

'What the devil's the delay? Start the engines at once!'

'Can't start the engines with cold boilers,' said the engineer.

'We've got to light the fires in the furnaces and boil the water until we've got enough steam pressure, like.'

'How long will that take?'

'Two hours maximum.'

'Damned steam engines. More trouble than they're worth. Just . . . just do your best, Mr Muir.'

They should have lost the brig then. But as soon as the vessel was two miles away, she changed back to a southerly course and the *Tisiphone* began to overhaul her once more. As soon as the paddle-sloop came within range, the brig ran before the wind and slipped away again. They went through this pantomime several times as the sun sank towards the horizon.

'She's leading us a merry dance,' the *Tisiphone*'s second lieutenant remarked to Killigrew on one side of the quarter-deck, out of earshot of Commander Standish, in his aristocratic drawl. Lieutenant the Honourable Endymion Hartcliffe was the younger son of the Duke of Hartcliffe. A stout moon-faced man in his late twenties, he had a vague manner which belied the decisiveness and tenacity he could show when necessity demanded. 'I'm inclined to think you were right, Killigrew: she *is* only a decoy.'

Killigrew nodded. 'While the real slaver is getting further and further away, sir.'

'We'd better catch them soon. It will be dark within an hour or two and they'll easily give us the slip.'

# VI:

## Breaking the Circle

The sun had just kissed the horizon when suddenly the engines' valves hissed and the machinery clanked into life. The deck shuddered and vibrated beneath their feet and the paddle-wheels turned in the water, slowly at first but then with increasing speed, twenty revolutions a minute. The water beneath the paddle-boxes churned and the *Tisiphone* surged forwards.

From that moment it was all over. The brig turned to the south-west, but even with the wind full abaft and her sails drawing well, the moderate breeze meant she could manage no more than four knots to the *Tisiphone*'s eight. Within minutes the paddle-sloop was close enough to fire chain shot at the brig's masts, and even as the gunner's crew prepared to fire, the brig ran down her colours and hove to, backing her fore topsail while leaving her fore-and-aft sails set. The *Tisiphone* ranged alongside, stopped her engines and boxed her sails.

Standish called across to the brig – the name *Leopardo* was painted on the stern – and ordered the master to lower his sails and come on board at once.

'*No intende inglese.*'

'*Parlez-vous français?*'

'*No intende.*'

'No intende, no intende,' Standish muttered irritably.

'Would you like me to try, sir?' offered Killigrew.

'Don't bother, Mr Killigrew. I'll address them in the common tongue of the seas. Sergeant Rennie! Have your men fire at his jib halyard block.'

'Aye, aye, sir.' The sergeant of marines saluted Standish and then turned to where his corporal and ten privates were arrayed on deck, resplendent in their scarlet coats and white crossbelts, their muskets already primed and loaded. 'You heard the captain, lads. Present arms! Ready . . . take aim . . .'

'Begging your pardon, Sarge,' said the corporal. 'But what's . . .'

'The block on the rope supporting the triangular sail at the front,' hissed Standish.

'I've got it,' said the corporal, and he and his men levelled their muskets with more confidence.

Standish rolled his eyes. 'I must have the only marines in the whole blasted regiment who don't know a halyard from a hole in the ground,' he sighed.

'Fire!' roared the sergeant. The eleven muskets boomed as one.

The rope above the halyard block parted and the jib collapsed and folded itself over the brig's forecastle.

There was a polite round of applause from the seamen who stood idle on the *Tisiphone*'s deck. 'Belay that!' snapped the boatswain.

'Oh-kay, oh-kay!' the man on the brig called peevishly. 'We give in!'

Standish raised his speaking trumpet to his lips once more. 'May I congratulate you at the rapidity with which you have acquired a grasp of the English language?'

'Go to Hell!'

Standish turned to the other officers on the quarter-deck. 'Fluent, isn't he?'

A boat was lowered from the clipper and a dozen of the sailors rowed across. Even as they were taken aboard and covered by the muskets of half a dozen marines, the *Tisiphone* lowered one of her cutters and Lieutenant Hartcliffe, Mate Tremaine, a dozen seamen and the rest of the marines rowed across to the *Leopardo*.

The leader of the men from the *Leopardo* brushed aside the muskets and marched straight on to the quarter-deck, heading for Standish. Killigrew quickly levelled his pepperbox at him.

The man stopped short and glared at Killigrew. He was only a couple of years older than the mate, a tall, heavily built man with dark hair and a Quaker's beard, his upper lip clean-shaven. He wore a black frock coat and a low, round hat, his clothes dark and drab. Nearly everything about him screamed 'Quaker'; the Society of Friends had been foremost amongst the slave trade in the first part of the previous century, until they had seen the light and become foremost in the fight for its abolition. But there was nothing Quaker-like about the eyes he now narrowed at Killigrew: they glittered menacingly in the twilight, as black and soulless as a shark's, warning Killigrew not to underestimate him.

The man put one hand on the grip of his own pistol without drawing it from its holster. 'Where I come from, mister, it's not good manners to point a gun at a man unless you aim to use it.' He spoke with the nasal twang of a New Englander.

'I aim to use it all right, if you give me cause. Put your hands in the air.'

The man studied Killigrew, as if trying to gauge whether he really would use his gun. Something in Killigrew's mien assured him that the mate was in earnest, for he raised his hands.

'All right, Killigrew, that's enough of that,' snapped Standish.

The man turned to him. 'You the captain?'

'Yes. You're the master of that brig?'

'No. The captain's resting in his cabin,' the New Englander said with studied insolence. 'I'm the chief mate.'

'What's your name?'

'Coffin. Eli Coffin.'

'You're from Nantucket?' asked Killigrew.

'What makes you say that?'

Killigrew shrugged. 'Coffin's a common name there. That's not the sort of name one forgets in a hurry.'

'It had better not be,' growled Coffin. 'What did this man say your name was? Killigrew? Well, I don't aim to forget that name in a hurry, either.' He turned back to Standish. 'Now, mister, perhaps you'd care to tell me what you think you're doing?'

'I'd've thought that was pretty obvious. Stopping and searching you.'

'It may have escaped your attention, friend, but that's an American flag flying at our masthead. And these are American papers,' he added, thrusting a sheaf at Standish.

The commandeer did not even glance at them. 'Forged, I don't doubt.'

Coffin grinned triumphantly. 'Maybe a stiff letter from our State Department to your Foreign Office will convince you.'

'I'll believe it when I see it.'

'Oh, you'd better. Because when my government hears that a British warship stopped a United States vessel engaged in its lawful business, then there's going to be trouble. Your government's going to be looking for a scapegoat to save them from an embarrassing diplomatic faux pas, and guess what, my friend? You just put your head in the noose.'

Hartcliffe and his men soon returned. 'Not a trace of any slaves on board, sir.'

'What?'

'We searched the whole blessèd ship, sir. No slaves, no shackles, no evidence at all, rot it.'

'What did I tell you?' demanded Coffin, grinning from ear to ear.

'Then why did you run the moment you saw us? Why didn't you heave to the moment we hailed you with a blank shot?'

'We figured maybe you were pirates.'

'Damn you, man! You could see our British ensign clear enough, couldn't you?'

'They could've been false colours.' Still smirking, Coffin tucked his ship's papers back inside his coat. 'I hear that's a common trick in these waters.'

'There are no pirates in these waters, Mr Coffin. The Royal Navy sees to that.'

'Is that so? And what do you call stopping and boarding a ship illegally using the threat of arms, if not piracy?'

'If you return to your ship you'll find nothing's been removed or damaged, apart from the jib halyard,' Standish said stiffly. 'And we've wasted no more of your time than you have of ours.'

'Good day to you, gentlemen. Your Admiralty will be hearing from our government in due course.' Coffin nodded to his men, signalling for them to follow him back down to the *Leopardo*'s boat.

'She's a slaver, all right,' said Standish, watching the boat row back to the brig. 'And as for that insolent swine, he deserves a good flogging.'

'It'd take a brave man to administer it,' said Killigrew. 'I've met some dangerous men in my time, but that one . . .' He broke off as a shudder ran down his spine.

'Stuff and nonsense. You can't tell if someone's dangerous or not just by talking to them for five minutes. Well, I suppose you're gloating now, Mr Killigrew? Go on, then. Tell me you told me so.'

'Gloating isn't really my style, sir, but if you're ordering me to . . .'

Standish turned his back on Killigrew. 'You have the watch, Lord Hartcliffe.'

'Yes, sir.' Hartcliffe was a good naval officer, and yet somehow he could never bring himself to say 'aye, aye, sir'. Standish, who always became fawning and obsequious in the presence of nobility, even when they were his subordinates, was not going to argue.

'I take my hat off to you, Mr Killigrew,' said Hartcliffe when Standish had gone below. 'You *knew* it was a decoy, didn't you? And now the real slaver is far beyond our reach,' he sighed.

Killigrew rubbed his jaw and cast his eyes to leeward. 'Not necessarily, sir.'

'Face facts, Mr Killigrew. She has several hours' start on us already . . .'

'We have steam up. The wind's been blowing a steady nor'-easter at about thirteen knots all day. The other ship can't have gone more than forty-five miles, even if she was faster than the *Leopardo*. And she'll have run south-west before the wind, to get clear of our patrols as quickly as possible. I'll bet she's no more than fifty miles west-nor'-west of us.'

'That's still a deuced big lead.'

'My guess is that she'll stay on that course for another two days. If we headed west-sou'-west at full steam I'll wager we'd cross her path within seventeen hours.'

'Assuming she set out from the same point we did, more or less.'

'Why else would the *Leopardo* have gone to so much trouble to lead us on a wild-goose chase?' asked Killigrew. He nodded to where the brig's crew were taking their boat aboard and making sail once more. 'The other ship must've been out of sight of us, but within sight of the *Leopardo*. That would put her right on the Guinea coast. The *Leopardo* must've signalled to her somehow, telling her to stay in port until she could draw us away.'

'I don't know, Killigrew. It's a big ocean out there. It'd be like looking for a needle in a blessèd haystack.'

'We can narrow down our search. After all, we know roughly where she started out from, roughly where she was headed and roughly how fast she travelled.'

'That's an awful lot of "roughlys", and there's no place for "roughly" in navigation.'

'All right, I'll admit that the chances of us finding her are slim. But what have we got to lose? Time? We're as well cruising for slavers out here as we are a couple of miles off the coast.'

'I suppose you're right. But Standish will never go for it. Not if it's your idea. Not even if I tell him it was mine.'

'So don't tell him. You know as well as I do he won't be up again before the forenoon watch. He said you had the watch. He didn't say where you should take it.'

Hartcliffe stared at him. 'Rot it, Killigrew, you're going to cost me my commission!' he said with a grin. 'Make all plain sail, bosun! Steer a course west-sou'-west, Mr Ågård. Order the engine room to give me full steam ahead.'

Killigrew smiled and went below with the sailing master to the chart room to plot a course for their quarry and a course to intercept. As twilight turned into dusk, the *Tisiphone* steamed off after the sun below the horizon.

The sun had gone all the way around the globe and risen abaft of the *Tisiphone* by the time Standish emerged on deck the following morning at the start of the forenoon watch. He gazed about, searching for the land, and doubtless noticed that the paddle-sloop was sailing westwards, further into the Atlantic. Hartcliffe and Killigrew had been searching the horizon in vain for a glimpse of their quarry ever since first light. Now they were ready to give up the chase and head back to the coast.

'Where the devil are we?' Standish demanded of Hartcliffe.

'Er . . . fourteen degrees and ten minutes west, six degrees and twenty-nine minutes north, sir,' Hartcliffe replied.

'Where the devil's that?'

'About a hundred and ten miles off the Guinea coast, I think sir.'

'A hundred and ten . . . We're in the middle of the Atlantic Ocean, damn your eyes! Are we lost?'

'No, sir. We . . . I thought that since the *Leopardo* was obviously a decoy, we could perhaps try to calculate the course of the ship she was attempting to decoy us from and intercept her . . .'

'Don't lie to me, Hartcliffe. This hare-brained scheme smacks of Killigrew to me. Well, Killigrew? This is your doing, sir.'

'Yes, sir. Your night orders weren't specific, so I thought—'

'You *thought*, did you? You do a damned sight too much thinking for my liking, Mr Killigrew. Perhaps you should have *thought* about the possibility that there was no other ship, and that even if there had been, the chances of us being able to find her in the middle of the Atlantic Ocean were so astronomical—'

'Sail ho!'

'Where away?' Hartcliffe called up to the lookout.

'Two points on the starboard quarter.'

'Behind us?' exclaimed Killigrew, climbing on to the starboard paddle-box. 'She's making poorer time than I anticipated.'

'It's probably not the same ship,' muttered Standish. 'The devil take it! That ship probably never even existed in the first place.'

'Perhaps not, sir,' admitted Killigrew, his telescope raised to his eye. 'But this one has the look of a slaver all the same.'

'Well, since she's abaft of us . . . and since we have to go back that way anyway . . . I suppose there's no harm in our going to investigate her, whatever ship she may be,' Standish admitted grudgingly. 'Put her about, Mr Watmough,' he told the quartermaster, and turned to Midshipman Radmall. 'Have the engineer start up the engines.' With both the *Tisiphone* and the other ship sailing with the wind directly abaft, putting about meant turning head on into the wind.

The engine still had steam up, and within moments the paddle-wheels plashed into life. The *Tisiphone* turned in a tight circle, her bows coming around to meet the vessel coming up behind them.

A moment later the other ship likewise turned her head into the wind, and Killigrew got a good look at her sideways-on. He lowered his telescope and snapped it shut. 'It's the *São João*.'

'Don't be ridiculous, man. You can't possibly tell at this distance.'

'It's the *São João*,' insisted Killigrew, jumping back down to the deck.

The clipper turned her nose as close to the wind as she dared, trying to get away, but it was hopeless. Sailing on a port tack, with the wind coming in off the port bow, her speed was greatly reduced. The steam-powered *Tisiphone* was little troubled by such considerations and quickly gained on the other vessel.

The clipper continued to turn in a broad circle, trying to get the wind behind her once more so she could slip past the *Tisiphone* beyond the range of her guns. At Standish's command the quartermaster at the helm adjusted the course and moved to intercept her. Within minutes they had closed to within three miles. The clipper completed its turn, running free before the wind, but even with its sails drawing well it could not outpace the steam-powered sloop.

'We've got the blackguards!' exclaimed Hartcliffe, forgetting himself in his excitement.

Standish scowled and nodded. 'Clear the decks for action. Man the foremost quarters on the main deck.'

The hands scurried across the deck, bracing the sails, draping hammocks over the rails, and loaded the guns. It was another bright, cloudless day, the sun glittering on the sea. The wind had picked up during the morning, blowing a fresh force five, and the clipper had a bone in her teeth and cut a feather, as seamen referred to the foam at the stem and the wake respectively of a fast-moving ship.

Killigrew took up position in the bar, the wind whipping at his clothes. Spume bounced off the paddle-sloop's stem. The glittering waves raced past, and he could see flying fish skipping over the surface, racing the *Tisiphone*, while porpoises swam before the bows, launching themselves exuberantly out of the water as if leading the paddle-sloop. Standing in the forecastle, Killigrew felt himself share in their exultation. The *Tisiphone* had a knot and a half, maybe two knots on the *São João*; with less than three miles between them and the *Tisiphone* closing fast from astern, the slaver would be in range of the bow-chaser within an hour and a half. He hoped da Silva was on board, and wished he could have seen his face when his lookout had sighted the *Tisiphone* lying ahead of him when he must have supposed her to be far behind.

He raised his telescope again. In grim contrast to the porpoises racing the *Tisiphone*, a dozen sharks' fins cut through the clipper's wake. She had slaves on board, of that there was no doubt.

The time passed quickly as the two ships raced across the ocean, but it could not pass quickly enough for Killigrew.

Excitement coursed through every vein in his body. Da Silva and his crew had already escaped him once; this time they would not be so lucky. Taken with slaves on board, they could not escape being condemned by the prize court.

The gunner fired a blank shot. The clipper hoisted the Stars and Stripes but showed no sign of stopping. Raising his telescope once more, Killigrew could make out the crew throwing casks, spars, timber and coils of rope overboard. They were trying to lighten the load in the hope that they might still outrun the *Tisiphone*.

The gunner's crew reloaded the pivot gun, and waited for the *São João* to come within range. The *Tisiphone*'s bell marked off the half-hours. Killigrew made sure his pepperbox was fully loaded.

'Tell the captain we're in range now,' the gunner ordered one of his men, just when Killigrew felt he could bear the tension no longer. 'We can't elevate high enough to hit their spars, but I reckon we can put a shot close enough to them to give the men on the poop a shower bath. Maybe that'll persuade them to give up.'

The order came back within moments. 'Commander Standish says to fire when ready.'

The gunner checked the aim and elevation of the bow-chaser one last time and then hauled on the lanyard. The gun boomed and a few seconds later the shot plunged into the water abaft of the *São João*'s stern, sending up a great plume of water which drenched the men on the poop. A great cheer went up from the men of the *Tisiphone*, and the gunner's crew reloaded.

The clipper showed no signs of heaving to. The crew must have guessed the *Tisiphone* would not fire to hit at that range – a shot penetrating the hull would most likely kill many of the slaves tightly packed below decks, which rather defeated the object of the exercise – so they pressed on, still hoping the paddle-sloop would abandon the chase.

But the *Tisiphone* had the smell of blood in her nostrils and was not going to give up now. Within a quarter of an hour the paddle-sloop was close enough for the pivot gun to fire chain shot at the clipper's masts. The gunner's crew fired shot after shot, working with monotonous regularity. As the chain shot screeched through the air towards the clipper, the other crew retaliated with a pivot gun of their own, a twenty-four-pounder located on their poop deck. But their firing was as erratic as it was sporadic. Every now and then a plume of water would rise up in the *Tisiphone*'s vicinity; sometimes close enough to splash the deck, sometimes as much as a cable's length away. They did not hit the *Tisiphone* until she had almost ranged alongside her, and then a round shot smashed through the *Tisiphone*'s wooden hull close to the bows.

Killigrew felt the deck shudder beneath his feet and a moment later word came up from below: the shot had smashed through the sick berth and killed three cases of yellow fever, as well as cutting off the attendant's leg. A growl of anger ran through the *Tisiphone*'s crew. 'Why don't they give it up? They can see we've got the rate on them.'

The wind was freshening, increasing the *São João*'s pace. The two vessels were neck and neck for speed. 'Cram on all sail!' ordered Standish. From the tautness in the commander's voice Killigrew could tell that even he was caught up in the excitement of the chase, and determined to avenge the deaths of the three men in the sick berth.

Then the crew of the clipper began to throw their cargo overboard.

Killigrew did not believe his eyes as the first pair of fettered Africans were thrown over the side, their screams echoing faintly back to the *Tisiphone* above the sound of her paddles in the water. He raised the telescope, pressing his eye hard against the eyepiece. He could see the men on the clipper's deck clearly enough, marching the slaves up through the main hatch two at a time with whips and guns. As the slaves realised what their fate was to be they tried to put up a struggle, but they were either shot or clubbed to the deck. Dead or alive, their bodies were heaved unceremoniously over the side as the crew tried to lighten their load and dispose of the evidence at the same time.

The heavy iron fetters on the Africans' ankles pulled them straight under the surface as soon as they hit the water. Killigrew could imagine them screaming as they were dragged down to the ocean floor, their lungs filling with water, struggling, drowning helplessly. He felt sickened. He knew there were few forms of life lower than a slaver, but they were human beings after all, and it astonished him that any man should be so bereft of humanity that he could so callously slay his fellow men – in such large numbers – to save his own hide for what would probably amount to no more than a loss of employment for a few weeks.

Not all the slaves thrown overboard drowned. The sharks quickly caught on to what was happening and they too raced forwards, snatching at the sinking bodies, ripping them to shreds in a feeding frenzy which left a scarlet slick in the *São João*'s wake. As one pair of Africans was thrown overboard, an especially large shark lunged out of the water to snap at them before they even hit the surface. On the clipper's deck, the slavers saw this and laughed. They even tried to aim the next pair of slaves so that they fell into the gaping maw of the next shark which tried that trick. Ranks of vicious teeth snapped on limbs, tearing flesh and snapping bone. The screams of the slaves became more frenzied; even those still in the hold were screaming in terror now.

'Jesus!' said a seaman standing close to Killigrew, and the mate made no attempt to berate him for his blasphemy.

'Bastards!' agreed another.

Still the slaves were brought up, kicking, struggling, only to be beaten down and tossed overboard. Ten, twenty, thirty, forty . . . more and more, until it seemed the whole sea was red with blood. More sharks came from miles around, drawn by the smell. Killigrew clenched his trembling fists until his fingernails drew blood from his palms. Until the *São João* hove to there was nothing he could do but look on impotently. It was not even worth lowering any boats in an effort to pull the Africans from the water: they would either sink or be torn to shreds long before the boats could get to them; besides which, it would have necessitated stopping the paddle-sloop, allowing the clipper to get further away and giving the crew time to drop even more slaves over the side.

Finally a shot from the *Tisiphone* brought the *São João*'s mainmast crashing down in a tangle of sails, spars and rigging. Immediately the clipper lost way and the paddle-sloop overhauled it and hove to alongside less than a cable away. The slavers realised they were beaten and quickly hauled down their false colours.

There was so much confusion on the slaver's deck there seemed little point in calling across with the speaking trumpet and ordering them to send a boat over. One of the *Tisiphone*'s cutters was lowered into the shark-infested waters. This time it was the turn of Lieutenant Jardine and Midshipman Radmall to go aboard the captured vessel with a crew of seamen and marines. Killigrew slipped into the boat behind Strachan without waiting to be invited.

As the cutter pushed off from the *Tisiphone*'s side, Standish appeared at the rail above them. 'Killigrew? What the devil are you doing down there? I didn't tell you to go aboard with the prize crew. Come back here at once!'

Killigrew sat in the stern sheets with his back to the *Tisiphone*. The rowers had already propelled the cutter halfway across the distance between the two ships. He pretended not to hear.

'Do you want us to bring him back, sir?' called Lieutenant Jardine.

'No. But he comes back with the cutter, you understand me? I don't want any more farces such as happened aboard the *Maria Magdalena.* Is that perfectly clear? I'm going to get my share of tonnage bounty out of this.'

The sharks paid no attention to the boat. There was already enough fresh meat in the water to satisfy every shark off the Guinea Coast. Moments later the cutter bumped against the side of the clipper and a rope ladder was thrown down to them.

Killigrew went up first. Whoever had dropped the ladder had returned to help the other crew try to cut free the men who were trapped beneath the tangle of spars and rigging on the deck. One of the slavers had his legs crushed underneath a spar, and a tide of blood spread around him on the pale deck. Killigrew looked at him and felt no pity whatsoever.

Jardine took control of the situation while Radmall went to hoist the colours and Strachan went below to the slave deck.

'Hey, Killigrew! You gonna stand there looking like a dumb sonuvabitch or you gonna help me?'

It was Barroso, trapped beneath some rigging but otherwise unharmed. Killigrew crossed to where he lay and drew his cutlass, raising it above his head. Barroso flinched, but Killigrew only hacked through the rigging.

The slaver grinned as Killigrew sheathed his cutlass and helped him to his feet. 'You can't hurt me, right? You've arrested me, now you gotta deliver me to the prize court in Freetown, right?'

'Wrong.' Killigrew rammed his fist into Barroso's stomach.

The slaver doubled up and sank to his knees with a gasp of agony.

'Aw, come on! You're not still angry about the other night in Freetown, are you?'

'No, I've forgotten all about that. Now I've got a whole new list of scores to settle with you.'

Killigrew hauled Barroso to his feet and ran him across to the side. Caught off balance, the slaver realised Killigrew's intention too late to do anything about it. He hit the rail and toppled over. He screamed, convinced he was going to fall into the shark-infested waters, but then he bumped against the side and found himself hanging upside down, a rope fast around his ankle. He gazed down into the bloody water only a couple of feet below his head, and craned his neck to where Killigrew stood at the rail above him.

'*Jésus*, Senhor Killigrew! You *loco* sonuvabitch!'

'What's the matter, Barroso? Lost your sense of humour? You seemed to find plenty to laugh about when you threw those slaves to the sharks earlier.'

'What slaves? Ain't no slaves on this ship. We're engaged in honest trade.'

'It's true.' Killigrew turned to see Strachan emerging from the hold, his face ashen. 'There are no slaves on board. The swines must've thrown them all overboard. No slaves, no shackles, nothing. Not even enough extra water butts to convict them of slaving.'

'You mean, they're going to get away with it *again*?' asked Radmall.

'All right, that's enough,' said Jardine. 'Let him up, Mr Killigrew. You've had your fun. Killigrew? Where are you going? Come back here. Come back here at once! You get back on that cutter *now*, mister . . .'

Killigrew ignored him and marched into the roundhouse. He found da Silva seated behind the desk in his day cabin, looking as calm and self-assured as ever. 'Ah, Senhor Killigrew. Is it not the custom to knock before entering a room in England?'

'You son of a bitch.'

Da Silva smiled. 'So how are those high-minded ideals of yours, Mr Killigrew? Have they been dented at all yet?'

Killigrew kept his clenched fist at his side. 'Get up. Stand up, you filthy son of a bitch.'

'Are you threatening me, Senhor Killigrew? I think you are in enough trouble already. You're wasting your time, you know. I have papers which prove I'm engaged in legitimate commerce – see for yourself . . .' Da Silva opened the drawer at his right-hand side.

Killigrew's pepperbox appeared in his hand. 'Stop that. Move away from the desk.'

'For God's sake! You know as well as I do that you are not going to shoot me.'

Killigrew levelled his pepperbox at da Silva's forehead. 'Do it! Get back – right back. Against the window.'

Da Silva sighed ostentatiously and did as he was bidden. Killigrew stepped up to the desk and glanced into the drawer. There *were* papers in there, weighed down by a pistol.

'You think I was going for my gun? Ah, now you are just being foolish, Senhor Killigrew. I don't need a gun to protect me from *you*.' He smiled broadly. 'I have the law to do that for me. You know as well as I do what happens now. You take this ship into Freetown as a prize. But there is no physical evidence that we were ever engaged in the slave trade, so the court lets us go. I keep telling you that you are wasting both your time and mine.'

Killigrew knew da Silva was speaking the truth, and the truth hurt so much he wanted to smash the slaver's smug face into pulp.

'And in a few weeks' time I am back at sea aboard this

very ship, and you are cruising for slavers in your ship. What will you do if our paths cross once more, I wonder? Force us to go through this whole charade again? There must be some way we can break this ridiculous vicious circle we find ourselves in.'

'Oh, I can think of a way,' said Killigrew.

'And what is that, pray tell?'

The sound of the shot was deafeningly loud in the close confines of the cabin. The window behind da Silva shattered, leaving a large, jagged hole in one of the panes, with the slaver's blood and brains spattered around it.

# VII:

## Beached

Three chandeliers hung from the ceiling of the ballroom: a main one in the centre flanked by two slightly smaller ones. The thousands of beautifully crafted pieces of crystal caught the light of the candles and cast it into a thousand coruscating rainbows. Huge gilt-framed oil paintings adorned the walls, depicting scenes of naval battles, and rich drapes of red velvet hung across the windows. All of this magnificent opulence paled into insignificance, however, once contrasted with the gathering.

There were perhaps two hundred people in the ballroom, with a fairly even split between men and women and a broad range of ages from sixteen to eighty, with débutantes, midshipmen and sons of financiers at one end of the scale to dowagers, financiers' fathers and admirals at the other. Ornately uniformed footmen stood at the doorways while waiters moved amongst the guests with trays of drinks. The women wore magnificent full-skirted dresses of silk and velvet and fluttered fans, while the men were clad in full-dress naval uniform or civilian evening wear: black trousers or pantaloons, white waistcoats and cravats, and tail-coats. In the middle of the floor dancers moved about with slow and sedate steps, going through the intricate patterns of a quadrille to the strains of a full orchestra. A heady odour pervaded the room, a cocktail of scent, pomade and sweat.

The hostess, Lady Grafton, stood close to the door where she could greet her guests. A nod of acknowledgement was neither more nor less than etiquette demanded for Killigrew, but after excusing herself from the guests she was talking to she came across to greet him in person. She was in her late twenties, a handsome, Junoesque woman. 'I don't believe I've had the pleasure, sir . . .'

'Killigrew, your ladyship. Christopher Killigrew, lately of Her Majesty's paddle-sloop *Tisiphone*.'

'Ah, yes. Admiral Killigrew's grandson. I'm pleased to make your acquaintance.'

She offered him a gloved hand and Killigrew took the tips of her fingers lightly in his, bowing low with practised elegance. She received his bow with a curtsey. 'The honour is all mine, ma'am.'

'I understand you are recently returned from the Tropics, sir?'

'Yes, ma'am. The West Africa Squadron.'

'And you are in good health?'

'Never felt better, ma'am.'

'I'm so pleased to hear it. You must excuse me, I have other guests to greet. I do hope we shall have a chance to get to know one another better.'

'Indeed, ma'am.' As he watched her move on, he decided that a worse fate could befall a man than to find himself in her bed. Nor would it do his career any harm, provided the lady's husband did not actually catch him there.

He helped himself to a champagne flute from a passing footman and surveyed the gathering, looking for someone he recognised. He was used to such gatherings, having attended balls and levees at various governors' mansions and suchlike in the far-flung outposts of the Empire, and he usually felt at ease. But now he was strangely uncomfortable. He had only been back in England for a few days and he was still adjusting to shore life, where the threat of an encounter with slavers at any moment did not provide that added *frisson* of constant excitement. *This isn't real*, he found himself thinking, and then caught himself. *It* is *real – it's just a very different reality from the one off the Guinea Coast.*

It was not a question of which he preferred – he was equally at home in both – but after two years at sea he was due for a rest. He told himself to relax and enjoy the evening. But not too much: there was work to be done. The *Tisiphone* had gone to Woolwich to have her boilers replaced, and the crew had been paid off. Killigrew was on half-pay until he could find himself a berth on a new ship, and for that he needed the interest of an influential patron. He was in no hurry to do so, but he did not want to spend the rest of his life ashore.

'Hullo, Killigrew. Out of rig?'

Killigrew was not dressed in uniform. He had been in uniform for two years now and, keen to wear something different for a change, had used some of the money from being paid off to purchase himself some new evening clothes: black trousers, white waistcoat and a mulberry tail-coat, the muslin cravat at his throat knotted with careless elegance.

He turned and saw Tremaine standing there, now dressed in the uniform of a lieutenant. Both he and Killigrew had undergone the examination shortly after they had arrived back in England. Tremaine had stayed on board the *Tisiphone* as far as Woolwich, where he had been examined by Standish, newly promoted to post-captain (by God, there was no justice) and two other captains on board a ship of the line. Bearing in mind his own strained relations with Standish, Killigrew had thought it prudent to leave the *Tisiphone* at Portsmouth, and had undergone his own examination on a ship anchored in Spithead.

'How did your examination go?' Tremaine asked him

coyly, obviously wondering if the fact that he was in civilian clothes meant he had failed.

'Not bad,' said Killigrew. 'You'll never guess who was on my panel.'

'Who?'

'Captain Crichton.'

'Good God! Not "Nose-Biter" Crichton?'

Killigrew was of above average height, but Crichton had towered above him when he had leaned over him to address his questions during the examination. Killigrew's examination for midshipman had been a simple enough affair: he had been made to write out the Lord's Prayer from memory before the doctor had told him to take off his clothes and jump over a chair, after the completion of which task he had been given a glass of sherry to congratulate him on being in the navy. But the examination for lieutenant was a much more serious business.

'You are the officer of the watch, sir,' Crichton had said. 'It is blowing fresh, and you are under double-reefed topsails and t'gallants. Mark that! The captain comes on deck and asks how the wind is. You make the proper response. He then puts his hand into his pocket and produces a small leather case. Mark that! He opens it and presents you with a cigar. Now, sir – quick – which end would you put into your mouth? Quick! Which end?'

'The twisted end of an Havana, sir, and either end if a cheroot,' Killigrew had replied without hesitation.

'Right, by gad, sir! You have presence of mind. I have no further questions to ask.'

'Did you pass?' Tremaine asked him now.

'With flying colours, apparently.'

'Why, that's capital!' Tremaine pumped him vigorously by the hand. 'Not that I ever doubted you would, of course.' He lowered his voice and raised his glass to his lips: 'So come on, Killigrew. See anything you fancy?' he asked before sipping.

Killigrew smiled. 'I've not yet looked.'

Tremaine grinned. 'Miss Spencer's here tonight.'

'Oh, Lor'!' groaned Killigrew. He had already encountered Miss Spencer at a dinner-dance a couple of nights earlier, and found her to be a tedious, simpering ninny, an increasingly common breed these days.

'Don't you like her? She's very pretty. And her father owns half the cotton mills in Lancashire.'

'What would I want with cotton mills?'

'It's not the mills, it's the income that comes with them.'

'If I wanted a good income I'd've gone into trade myself, as you well know. God knows, Uncle William is always pressing me to swallow the anchor and become managing director of his company. Anyway, I'm not here to find a prospective wife. It's a posting I'm interested in. There are a lot of influential people here tonight, 'Stace, so make sure you're on your best behaviour if you don't want to swallow the anchor prematurely.'

Tremaine adopted a tone of injured innocence. 'Don't I always? I've got my eye on Mrs Fairbody.'

Killigrew arched an eyebrow. 'A married woman?'

'A widow. Still young, mark you, and deuced pretty. Her husband died of the Bengal flux a year ago. She's only just out of mourning. But her father's as rich as Croesus, so the suitors are going to be queuing up. Fortunately I've already arranged to have the fifth waltz with her.'

'How very enterprising of you. And does she fit her name?'

'See for yourself.' Tremaine nodded to where a blonde woman wearing a pink silk ball gown was surrounded by admiring beaux, like a first-rate ship of the line at anchor with tenders, gigs and bumboats swarming round her. 'A lovely creature. I must congratulate you: your taste is impeccable. Good luck to you.'

'Would you like me to introduce you?' Tremaine said, clearly out of politeness and terrified that Killigrew would say yes.

'No, thanks. I wouldn't want to cramp your style. You know what they say: two's company, three's a crowd.' *And seventeen is a positive mob*. 'Have you seen Old Charlie?'

'Rear-Admiral Napier? I think he's by the fireplace in the library saloon with all the other old bores.'

'Old fogies they may be, 'Stace, but they're also very influential.'

Killigrew took his leave of Tremaine and made his way to the library saloon. There were no ladies present, just the older men – senior naval officers, financiers and politicians – seated in armchairs around the fireplace smoking fat cigars and drinking brandy or whisky while pontificating.

Sir Joshua Pengelly – a short, stocky, bow-legged man and the owner of a successful shipping company – was holding forth. 'Palm oil!' he declared. 'That's the thing. It's one of the biggest crops on the African coast. If we can persuade the tribes to stop warring with each other and selling their captives as slaves, and instead to devote their energies to the production of palm oil, why, then we'll have the whole problem of slavery licked. And it's a sound investment, too. These days everything's steam powered, and engines need lubrication. You mark my words, if you've got some spare money and any sense at all, you'll put it all into palm oil.'

'It's a nice idea,' said the host of the evening as he stood with his back to the fire, his hands clasped behind his broad backside, inadvertently lifting the tails of his coat into a tuft like the plumage of some strange but dowdy bird. 'But you're ignoring the basic laws of economics. Demand creates supply. If you want to end the slave trade, you have to cut off the demand, and that means abolishing slavery in Brazil, Cuba and the United States. A task which is quite beyond the powers of our government.'

As a young man, Sir George Grafton had made his fortune in the China Trade, shipping opium from the Honourable East India Company's estates into the Celestial Kingdom in exchange for tea. It had not been easy. The Chinese, ignorant heathens that they were, seemed to object to having opium smuggled into their country, and the British government in London was slow to understand what was obvious to every trader in Canton: the Chinese needed a sound drubbing to show them who was in charge. So Grafton had left the China side of his business in the competent hands of his junior partner and retired to Britain, where he had bought himself a safe seat in Scotland in a by-election. He had never visited the constituency – it was a dismal, dreary place, by all accounts – but that had not mattered, since all the landowners wealthy enough to possess a vote there lived in London, so it was in that great city he had had his campaigning done for him.

Once safely ensconced on the government backbenches, he had been perfectly placed to lobby for what Britain's trade needed: war with China. The Celestials were a backward people, having spent the last two hundred years living in peace and creating great works of art: they were no match for the steamers and shell-guns of the British Expeditionary Force. After much slaughter, the Chinese had been forced to sign the Treaty of Nanking, opening five ports to Western trade and ceding Hong Kong to the British.

After that Mr George Grafton esquire had become Sir George by dint of his generous contributions to the coffers of the Whig party, and the mercantile shipping company Grafton, Bannatyne & Co. had gone from strength to strength, winning lucrative government contracts to run prison hulks and convict ships to transport thieves, Irish rebels, Chartists, trade unionists and other such undesirables to the penal colonies in Australia.

Sir George Grafton was one of the Whigs' 'nautical' members of parliament, although his only qualification to speak on naval matters was the fact that he had most of his money invested in merchant shipping. But with the Whigs in power it was necessary for Killigrew to cultivate the patronage of men like Grafton, no matter how offensive he found their politics.

'Only because Palmerston takes such a high-handed attitude,' said Sir Joshua. 'It's all very well being *right* all the time, but sometimes it helps not to be so self-righteous about it. It doesn't win friends. It's not that there aren't plenty of people in those countries who are as opposed to slavery as Wilberforce ever was. But every time they try to speak out, the vested interests just wrap themselves up in their flags and say that the anti-slavers are grovelling to us British.'

'Quite right too,' said Grafton. 'So they should. Damned foreigners.'

'Yes, but perhaps they don't quite see it that way.' Pengelly glanced up, saw Killigrew, and at once rose to his feet. 'Why, it's young Christopher, isn't it? Oh ho, but not quite so young any more, eh? Glad you could make it, Kit. Forgive me if I don't get up, my damned gout's giving me blue murder these days. Sir George, may I present Mr Christopher Killigrew?'

'Sir George.' Killigrew acknowledged the MP with a cautious nod.

Grafton nodded absently without even glancing at him.

'Pull up a chair,' said Pengelly. 'Get yourself a drink.' He waved across a footman, and indicated Killigrew.

'Whisky, please,' said Killigrew. The footman nodded and hurried off.

'You know Sir Charles, of course,' continued Pengelly.

'Bless my soul, of course I know Kit Killigrew,' said Rear-Admiral Sir Charles Napier, KCB, GCTS, KMT, KSG, KRE, MP. He was sixtyish, a portly man with a double chin and scraggly grey bushy sideburns. He was in full dress uniform, decorated with the Order of the Bath, the Grand Cross of St George of Russia, and the insignia of the Second Class of the Order of the Red Eagle of Prussia. This brave display was in sharp contrast to the thick dusting of snuff on his tail-coat.

He looked like a genial, harmless old buffer, which was exactly what he was: a genial, harmless old buffer who had once taken on three French ships of the line in nothing more than a gun-brig, delaying them long enough for the rest of the English fleet to catch them; a genial, harmless old buffer who had fought as a sailor of fortune in the service of Queen Maria of Portugal against the usurper Dom Miguel, defeating his navy at sea and then – fancying himself an amateur general – giving his army a sound drubbing by land; and a genial, harmless old buffer who less than seven years earlier had exceeded his orders in dictating his own terms to the Viceroy of Egypt.

'Killigrew was one of the snotties on board the *Dreadful* during the Syria campaign; and a damned useful aide-de-camp ashore. Blew up the magazine at Acre, so he did; and when I landed with my men the next day, we found Killigrew here sitting amidst the smoking ruins with the *Dreadful*'s schoolmaster and a couple of others, taking tea as coolly as if they were on the lawn at the Naval Academy! Good to see you, Killigrew. Still only a mate?'

'Recently promoted to lieutenant, sir.'

'Why, congratulations! Splendid stuff! Not before time either, I might add.' As the footman returned with Killigrew's whisky, Napier ordered another round of drinks to celebrate. 'Got yourself a posting yet?' he asked at last.

'Not yet, sir.'

'Well, we'll have to see what we can do,' Napier said with a wink which was meant to be encouraging.

Killigrew smiled, although he did not welcome the thought

of Napier's patronage as much as he felt he ought to. Despite his respect and admiration for the rear-admiral, Killigrew knew that Napier was not popular at the Admiralty, partly because of his eccentric ideas on abolishing the flogging of seamen and encouraging the building of steam vessels, but mostly because of his tendency to air them at every available opportunity.

'Kit's just back from the West Africa Squadron,' said Napier. 'He can tell us all about how to suppress the slave trade from the sharp end. Can't you eh?'

Killigrew smiled tightly and glanced down into his glass. 'One tries to do one's duty.'

'If you want my opinion, the West Africa Squadron is no more than a waste of men and money,' said Grafton. 'I intend to bring a private members' bill to the House of Commons to have the squadron disbanded.'

'Abolish the West Africa Squadron?' spluttered Napier. 'My dear sir, if you abolish the West Africa Squadron, who will suppress the slave trade? Surely you do not suggest that we leave it to the French or the Americans?'

'No man opposes the evils of slavery more vigorously than I,' said Grafton. 'But one must face facts. It is forty years since we declared the slave trade illegal and our navy set about suppressing it. Have they succeeded? Not at all. If anything, the West Africa Squadron's attempts to suppress it only make it worse for the slaves. Did you know, when slave ships find themselves pursued by a navy vessel and have no hope of escape, they throw their slaves overboard to drown, in order to dispose of the evidence?'

'And you would let such men carry on their trade unhindered, sir?' Killigrew was careful to keep his expression mild, although inside he seethed with rage at the very suggestion. 'Believe me, sir, if you saw such a thing happen you would feel very differently about it.'

'Ah, but you've been too close to the issue to consider it objectively,' Grafton said with a dismissive wave of his hand. 'Such decisions are best left to wiser heads here in England—'

Napier slammed down his glass. 'Stuff and nonsense.'

Grafton blinked. 'I beg your pardon?'

'You heard me, Sir George. Stuff and nonsense is what I said, and stuff and nonsense is what I meant. By God, if there's one thing I've grown heartily sick of during my time as a member of parliament, it's pompous asses blethering on about subjects of which they are clearly in utter ignorance. Nothing but fools and idiots, sir!'

'Sir Charles! I must protest.'

'You must protest? *You* must protest? After I spent five years listening to damned fools taking up issues not because they believed in them, but because they knew that by backing them they could promote their own careers? Pursuing half-baked policies drawn up in complete ignorance of the maladies which they sought to remedy—'

'I can see you are a passionate man, Sir Charles. But you must understand that there is no place for passion in the art of government. These things must be considered logically, in the cold light of reason. If there were no West Africa Squadron, the slavers would have no reason to throw the slaves overboard.'

'Yes,' said Killigrew, rising to his feet. 'Then they could go on to sell their cargoes into a lifetime of slavery in the Americas and reap rich rewards from the vast profits. Is that your solution, Sir George?' he demanded heatedly.

Pengelly quickly stood up and took Killigrew by the arm. 'This is all very interesting, gentlemen, but if you'll excuse Mr Killigrew and myself, there is someone present I'm keen to introduce him to. I'm sure we can resume this debate at a later date. At the Gresham, perhaps.'

Grafton nodded grudgingly, clearly annoyed at being prevented from having the last word, and at having to concede it to a young whippersnapper like Killigrew at that.

Killigrew turned to where Napier sat. 'Sir Charles.'

'We must have dinner sometime,' said Napier.

'Thank you, sir.' Killigrew left Grafton out of his leave-taking, in a calculated snub which he knew he would later regret, although for now he was too angry to care.

Hobbling on his gouty foot Pengelly steered him out of the library saloon and back into the ballroom. 'Sorry to drag you away, Killigrew,' he said. 'Between you and me I was really rather enjoying that. I think you and Sir Charles had Sir George squarely on the ropes. But I couldn't afford to let you ruin your career for the sake of my own entertainment, now could I?'

'No, sir. I'm obliged to you for your timely intervention. I must apologise to Sir George for my outburst . . .'

'Good Lord, I hope not. Grovel to that pompous ass? You'll do no such thing. Let the matter rest. He'll have forgotten all about you come tomorrow morning; and there are plenty of other people who can help you in your career. Now, I wasn't lying when I said there was someone I wanted you to meet. You remember my daughter Eulalia?'

'Eulalia? How could I forget?' *I still have her teeth marks in my arm.*

'Well, she's here tonight, and I just know she's eager to renew your acquaintance . . .' Pengelly gazed around the throng and then shook his head. 'Damn it, where's the girl got to? You wait here and I'll see if I can find her.' Pengelly plunged into the crowd and left Killigrew to sip his whisky in peace.

But peace was never something Killigrew seemed to be able to enjoy for long. He looked up and saw Tremaine heading towards him from one direction and Mr Spencer heading towards him from another, with his simpering ninny of a daughter in tow.

'Killigrew, have you seen Mrs Fairbody?'

'Good evening, Mr Killigrew,' said Mr Spencer. 'My daughter was wondering if she might have the pleasure of the next dance?'

Miss Spencer giggled and fluttered her eyelashes over her fan at Killigrew.

'Of course she may,' he said, taking her by the hand. Then he put her hand in Tremaine's and gently pushed them both towards the centre of the floor. Mr Spencer gaped and turned puce, at a loss for words. The orchestra struck up a lively polka, and Miss Spencer shrugged and gripped Tremaine tightly, sweeping him around the floor. Tremaine mouthed curses at Killigrew over her shoulder. Grinning, Killigrew shook his head and slipped through another door before Mr Spencer could find his tongue; or before Tremaine could pester him about Mrs Blasted Fairbody, for that matter.

The French windows were open so he went outside and stood on the terrace, leaning against the stone balustrade which faced across the ornamental gardens. The cool night air was fresh after the tobacco fug of the library saloon and the sweaty atmosphere of the ballroom, so he stood there a while, sipping his whisky and smoking a cheroot, reflecting.

It went against the grain for Killigrew to toady to anyone, but he had chosen the navy as his career and that was an end to the matter. He had every intention of retiring on an admiral's pension, and he knew that in order to achieve his aim he would need patronage. If that meant toad-eating the likes of Sir George Grafton, then it was just too bad. He had made his bed; now he had to lie on it. When he had achieved flag-rank, he could starting working to make sure that men were promoted because of merit rather than patronage.

He thought about the West Africa Squadron. Glad as he

was to be given a break in England, part of him still wished he was back there chasing slavers. He did not like leaving a job unfinished, and even after two years he felt he had hardly made any impact at all on the slave trade. Perhaps Grafton was right; perhaps the West Africa Squadron was a waste of time . . .

'Excuse me, you haven't seen Christopher Killigrew, have you?' he heard Mr Spencer's voice ask someone in the room behind him.

Killigrew hurriedly drained the last of his whisky and vaulted over the balustrade, landing lightly in the flower-bed below. He slipped behind a yew hedge and made his way through the shadows to the gazebo. He was about to sit down on the bench when he perceived someone already sitting there in the darkness. 'My apologies. I was unaware that this gazebo was already occupied . . .'

'Sit down,' said a woman's voice. 'There's plenty of room for two.'

'May I ask what you're doing out here all alone?'

'The same as you,' she responded. 'Hiding.'

He smiled, and sat down on the bench opposite her. As his eyes adjusted to the gloom he was less than devastated to recognise his co-fugitive as Mrs Fairbody. He raised his cheroot to his lips and was about to puff on it when he hesitated. 'I . . . er . . . hope you do not object to the smell of tobacco.'

'Not at all. As long as it's reasonably good quality.'

'Oh, the best,' he assured her. He tucked the cheroot in the corner of his mouth and stood up to bow. 'Christopher Killigrew at your service, ma'am.'

She stiffened. 'Not . . . *Kit* Killigrew?'

He frowned. He did not know many women in England, and if he had inadvertently slighted her in some far-flung port he was sure he would have remembered. 'I'm sorry, ma'am, I don't believe I have the pleasure of your acquaintance.'

'Perhaps not; I was wondering if you still had my teeth marks in your arm.'

He stared; he may even have gaped. '*Eulalia*?'

They both stood up and hugged each other. 'Kit! After all these years. How long has it been?'

'Eleven years?'

'Eleven years.' They parted and she put her hands on his arm, holding him at arm's length so she could look him up and down. 'And look at you now. Quite the young gentleman.'

'And look at *you*. A friend of mine pointed you out to me earlier as Mrs Fairbody. I never guessed for a moment that it was you.'

'Tush! And after you told me that you'd love me for ever.'

He held up a hand. 'I refuse to be held accountable for anything I said below the age of twelve. I was still a minor, don't forget. Anyway, you were the one who got married.'

'Only after you ran away to sea.'

After the deaths of his parents, Killigrew had been raised in the austere environment of Killigrew House under the stern eye of his grandfather. Rear-Admiral Killigrew had never approved of his son marrying a foreigner, and to him Kit was the product of that unnatural union. If he could have left the care of his grandson to the Naval Benevolent Society he would have done, but there was no question that the society could be lumbered with one more orphan when the child had a well-off grandparent still living.

Kit had hated Killigrew House. His grandfather was as much of a martinet in his own home as he was reputed to have been on board his ships, and Killigrew had often been beaten for playing with the children of the local fishermen. Then, shortly before Kit's fifth birthday, the Comte Duchargny – an impoverished nobleman who had been forced to flee his native land during the terror of the French Revolution – had turned up on the doorstep of Killigrew House offering his services as a private tutor. The Rear-Admiral had accepted, reasoning that an aristocratic tutor was just what was needed to instil discipline in the unruly child, and Kit's education in all the gentlemanly studies – Greek, Latin, French, fencing and dancing – had commenced.

The *comte*'s methods had been unconventional to say the least. Even though he was in his sixties, he remained nimble and spry, and in the midst of a bout with *epées* he would shoot questions at his young pupil. If Kit answered incorrectly, then the *comte*'s blade would slip under his guard and give him a stinging blow. Nowadays Kit often joked that he had had a simple choice between becoming fluent in the Classics or becoming an adept swordsman, and he still could not hear Latin verbs conjugated without instinctively reaching for a sword.

But he had liked the old *comte*. What his grandfather had never known, because he had never taken the trouble to find out, was that the *comte* was an old friend of Kit's father. As a young man, the *comte* had been one of those liberal nobles who had renounced their aristocratic privileges one fateful night in 1789, little imagining what it would lead to. Four years later his parents had been beheaded in the Place de la Guillotine and the young *comte* had barely escaped the same fate. He had served with the French Royalist forces against Napoleon, but when the French monarchy had been restored in 1814 it had been too much of a return to the bad old days of the *Ancien Regime* for his liberal tastes. He had become a soldier of fortune and it had been while fighting for Chilean Independence he had met Captain Jack Killigrew.

The *comte* told Kit stories about his adventures with his father in Chile, Brazil and Greece, and in an effort to explain the principles they had been fighting for he had introduced him to works by Rousseau, Wollstonecraft, and Burke. Then, when Kit was twelve, his grandfather had found a copy of Thomas Paine's *The Rights of Man* in his room. After a brief enquiry, the *comte* – seventy now – had been sent packing.

Kit had always been terrified of his grandfather, but his rage at his tutor's dismissal finally gave him the courage to stand up to his grandfather and the two of them had had a blazing row, the ancient naval officer versus the precocious twelve-year-old. The only thing they were both able to agree on was that they could no longer live together under the same roof, no matter how wide that roof might be, and that since Kit was now old enough to join the navy as a first-class volunteer, it was high time he did so. Killigrew had been relieved just to get out of the oppressive atmosphere of his grandfather's house. Certainly it had never been a home to Kit, and since that day he had had no communication whatsoever with his grandfather. Nor had he ever looked back.

'Still in the navy?' asked Eulalia.

He nodded. 'I've just been promoted to lieutenant.'

'Congratulations. You know, even after all these years, I still find myself sneaking a peek at Papa's copy of the *Naval Gazette* to see if you've been mentioned.'

'And have I?'

'Not since that business in China. I was so proud! When I went back to school the next term I took the cutting to show all my friends. They refused to believe that I'd known Midshipman Killigrew, the hero of Chingkiang-fu. And then, after that, nothing. Where've you *been* all these years, Kit?'

'After China I was posted to the West Africa Squadron for two years. I've only just returned. What about you? Who was this Mr Fairbody? Or would you rather not talk about it?'

'Oh, I don't mind. It's over a year since he passed on. This is only the second time I've been in Society since I came out of mourning; it's funny, rather like having to go back to square one in snakes and ladders. I think Papa wants me to get married as soon as possible. I can't think why, Mr Fairbody left me . . . comfortable, so it's not as if I'm an imposition on him.'

'You're still young. You should get remarried.'

'Oh, I dare say I shall, some day. But not the moment I come out of mourning. It's all right for you men. You're not expected to get married until you're thirty or so. It's different for us women, Kit. For us it's straight out of school and into marriage.'

'You didn't care for Mr Fairbody?'

'Heavens, did I make it sound like that? Peter was a good husband. He was Father's choice rather than my own, but I didn't protest.'

'Handsome?'

She grinned mischievously, her teeth shining white in the gloom. 'Devilishly. But . . . oh I do envy you, Kit. You've been off to see the world, gone to places I can only dream of or read about.'

'You could too, you know. If Mr Fairbody left you a moderate legacy, what's to stop you from travelling?'

'I expect I shall. I just need to pluck up the courage, that's all. That's why I don't want Papa to rush me into getting remarried. You know, I get the feeling he's already got someone in mind for me.'

'Yes,' said Killigrew. 'And I think I know who.'

'You do?'

He nodded. 'I was talking to him earlier. He said there was someone he wanted me to meet and asked me if I remembered you.'

She laughed. 'That's so like Papa. Childhood sweethearts reunited.'

'Would that be so terrible?'

'Oh, Kit! Don't take this the wrong way, but . . . I'm just not ready to dedicate the rest of my life to a man. Don't tell me you came here looking for a wife?'

He shook his head. 'As you said yourself, I'm a little too young to be worrying about marriage. It's a ship I'm after.'

'Ah. I've heard it said that naval men were married to their ships. That's why I'm not sure I want to marry a naval officer. No offence intended. But if and when I do get remarried, I don't intend to share my husband with three thousand tons of wood and a thousand horny-handed seamen.'

'Perhaps you should think about marrying the captain of a gun-brig. That way you'd only have to share him with a few hundred tons of wood and ten dozen horny-handed seamen.'

She laughed. 'You would not by any chance be in line for a posting to command of a gun-brig now, would you, Kit?'

He grimaced wryly. 'Right now I'm not even in line for the command of a dinghy. Still, perhaps we could go riding together next week? Catch up on old times?'

'I didn't know you were a horseman.'

'Oh, I'm never happier than when I'm in the saddle. Shall we say Friday morning?'

'Hyde Park?'

'Where else?'

'It's a little public, isn't it? Some people might get the idea that you're courting me.'

'Would that be so bad? If you're serious about not wanting to get married, it might help discourage some of your more ardent beaux if they think they're out of the running.'

'You *are* keen to get the bit between your teeth, aren't you?'

'I just thought that since *you're* not in any hurry to get married, and *I'm* not in any hurry to get married, we could not be in a hurry to get married together.'

She smiled. 'All right. Friday it is. Nine o'clock?'

'Better make it half past ten. I have an appointment at nine.'

'Not with some other woman who's not in any hurry to get married, I trust?'

He shook his head. 'Not unless she's a fellow of the Ethnological Society.'

'Did you say "Leopard People"?' Professor Llewelyn glanced up from behind the desk and pushed his spectacles back on to the bridge of his nose with a forefinger.

'I know it must sound crazy . . .' Killigrew told him apologetically.

'Believe me, young man, when you've studied ethnology as long as I have, then *nothing* sounds crazy.' Llewelyn picked up the fat, dusty tomes which lay under his desk and carried them across to an empty bookshelf. They had titles like *Seven Months with the Temne, Mating Rituals of the Kissi* and *Up the Niger by Canoe*. When he had placed them all on the shelf, he stood and stared at the spines, tapping a pen against the side of his nose.

'Let me see, I think I recall reading something somewhere about leopard people. Professor Phillpotts would have been the chap to ask. He was the real expert on West African cultures. Especially the Mende. In fact, now that I think about it, I seem to recall he said something about investigating the local myths and superstitions last time he left for the Guinea Coast. Unfortunately he never came back.'

'You mean he . . .'

'Died? Good Lord, no. Nothing like that. No, while he was on the steam packet he met some gypsy girl who was travelling to Spain with a circus and fell in love with her. Extraordinary behaviour. His wife was most upset. No, the last I heard of him, he was taming lions somewhere in central Europe.'

'The leopard people, Professor,' prompted Killigrew.

'Hm? Oh, yes. Let me see now, the Mende. Here we are: Gimson's *Encyclopaedia of the Peoples of Africa*, Volume Two. When in doubt, turn to Gimson, that's what I always say.' He riffled through the pages until he came to the entry he sought. 'Here we are: "the Mende is a large tribe which lives in the interior of Africa near the Guinea Coast. They are a handsome, negroid people" – have you ever noticed how these books never described a people as being ugly? – "who exist in a quasi-feudal society at a primitive stage of development. One interesting feature of their culture is the prevalence of secret societies . . ."'

Killigrew had never heard of a culture which did not have some kind of secret society. In China they had the Triads, in India they had the Cult of Thuggee, and in Europe and America there was Freemasonry. 'What sort of "secret societies"?' he asked.

'It doesn't say. Presumably because they're secret, hm? Ah, here we are: "Another interesting facet of Mende culture is the belief that certain people have the power to transform themselves into leopards through witchcraft. These leopard people are said to use parts of their victims to make *borfima*, magic potions which render the users rich and powerful. There exist in Mende societies witch doctors known as Tongo Players. These men claim the power to identify leopard people in their human form, using primitive and ornate rituals. It is believed that deaths caused by real leopards are ascribed to the handiwork of the leopard people and that the Tongo Players take advantage of this superstition to dispose of unpopular members of the community. When an individual is identified as a human leopard, he is beaten severely and then burned to death." That's all it says, I'm afraid.'

'Sounds like the witchfinder general of Jacobean times,' said Killigrew.

'Yes, they're a primitive people, aren't they?'

'Civilisation is relative in my experience, Professor. What must they think of the white men who come in ships to kidnap their people and carry them away by force across the great ocean to a life of eternal slavery?'

'Yes, but *they're* just ignorant. Where did you hear of the leopard people?'

'From one of the recaptives on a slaver I was bringing in as a prize. The master's mistress bit me in a fight, and when one of the slaves heard about it she starting talking about leopard people, and how the woman must be destroyed. The next thing I knew, the woman who bit me hard had had her skull smashed in and her bed set on fire.'

'Good heavens. She wasn't a negro, this captain's mistress, was she?'

'Yes, as it happens she was.'

'How extraordinary.'

'Not really. It was a pretty savage fight. Life and death, that kind of thing.'

'No, I mean the master of this slave vessel taking a negress as his mistress.'

'African women are no different from European women, in my experience, barring the colour of their skin.'

'Oh, I wouldn't go that far. You're aware, of course, that in the bush these people often go around . . .' Llewelyn looked about surreptitiously, as if worried that someone might overhear him, although as far as Killigrew could tell they were the only two people in the room. '. . . completely unclothed. Including the women. The negro may be similar to the Caucasian anatomically, Mr Killigrew, but up here?' He tapped his forehead. 'They must exist in a state of permanent – if you'll forgive the expression – *physiological arousal*.'

'You've never been to Africa, have you, Professor?'

'No. But I've read all about it. In books.'

'If you had, you might find it so humid that you'd feel more comfortable wearing fewer clothes than we are accustomed to wearing in our more temperate climes. It's the Garden of Eden, Professor, where man lived in healthy innocence, taking no shame in the human form until he partook of the fruit of knowledge.'

'I'm afraid that's one fruit I've eaten too much of ever to get back to Eden, Mr Killigrew,' Llewelyn said wistfully.

'I fear you may be right, Professor. Thank you for your assistance. It's certainly been an . . . educating experience.'

'Not at all. Glad to be of service. You're not going back there, are you?'

'To Africa? Well, I don't have any plans as such yet . . .'

'If you did learn anything more about these beliefs, I should be grateful if you could let us know about them if you return.'

'*If* I return?'

'Well, you might decide you're so happy living in primitive bliss in the Garden of Eden that you never want to leave,' said Llewelyn. 'On the other hand, you might die of yellow fever. They don't call Africa the white man's grave for nothing, you know.'

# VIII:

## A Game at Billiards

Killigrew quit the offices of the Ethnological Society and returned to where he had left his hired horse in the care of the crossing-sweeper at the junction of Queen Anne Street and Harley Street, tipping the sweeper every bit as generously as he had promised. When he was going to be sued by Videira's lawyers for every penny he had, a few extra crowns here and there did not seem to matter: better to give it to an honest crossing-sweeper than a slave captain and his pettifoggers.

It was a bright, crisp day in mid April and he enjoyed the ride through Mayfair's elegant streets to Hyde Park Corner. He reached the statue of Achilles on the dot of half past ten. There was no sign of Eulalia, but it would have been unladylike for her to arrive on time; that would have smacked of over-eagerness. She kept him waiting no more than ten minutes, arriving in the company of a groom acting as chaperone, both of them mounted. She looked even more lovely by day than she had done the other evening, the sunlight picking out the golden tresses pinned beneath a high-crowned riding hat perched at a rakish angle. Seeing him, she smiled.

'Good morning, Mr Killigrew. Your appointment at the Ethnological Society went well, I trust?'

He touched the brim of his top hat with his riding crop. 'Not as well as I'd hoped, ma'am,' he said, a little disappointed by her reversion to a more formal form of address than that which they had enjoyed the other night. He supposed it was due to the presence of the groom.

They at once set off at a slow, steady pace along Rotten Row, mingling with the other genteel riders, while the groom followed behind them at a discreet distance. The London Season was getting into its stride and the sandy track was busy with aristocratic young swells trying to catch the eyes of genteel ladies, and officers of the Household Cavalry showing off their latest mistresses.

'You were not able to learn anything more about those primitive native superstitions, then?' asked Eulalia.

'Nothing I didn't already know. Would you believe that their foremost expert on Africa had never ever been there?'

'Forget about Africa, Kit. It's behind you now.'

'I know. But it is still there.'

'Is it a beautiful country?'

'The parts of it I saw were – once you get out of Freetown, of course. But those were only on the coast. It's such a vast continent. I've not even scratched the surface . . .' He frowned. It was not the continent whose surface he wished to scratch, it was the slave trade. And he would do a damned sight more than just scratch it, if only he had the chance.

'You seem troubled.'

'I was just thinking.'

'About what?'

'The slave trade.'

'Fie on you, Christopher Killigrew. You come out riding with me, and all you can think of is the slave trade?'

'If you had seen some of the atrocities I have . . .' He shook his head. She did not want to hear of such things.

'It's not your problem any longer, Kit. Forget about it. Let someone else worry about it. Or do you think you're the only man in the whole world who can do that?'

'There are very few men who even seem to have the inclination.'

'You need something to take your mind off it,' she told him. 'Some vigorous exercise will do the trick, I think.'

'Oh?' he said, arching an eyebrow, but before he could come up with any suggestions she had turned her horse off the path and goaded it into a gallop, dashing off across the grass. He cursed under his breath and urged his own horse after her. The strollers of the lower orders cheered to see a fine woman galloping along so bravely, and laughed at the young gentleman who was hard pushed to keep up with her, using one hand to hold his top hat in place. If he was able to keep level with her it was only because she rode side-saddle. The groom was left far behind.

They passed along the bank of the Serpentine and crossed over the bridge, where pedestrians forced her to slow down, enabling him to catch up with her at last. She turned to smile at him, her cheeks flushed with exhilaration.

'So you *can* ride,' she acknowledged, and laughed merrily. 'You know, Kit, you haven't changed one bit. You always did have to excel at everything you attempted.'

He frowned. 'Do you think so? I've never thought of myself as competitive.'

'But that's what's so infuriating about you. It isn't a question of being better than anyone else. It's as if you already know that you're the best at everything you do, accept it without arrogance, and compete against yourself because there's no other competition.'

He shrugged. 'I've always felt that if a job's worth doing, it's worth doing well, if that's what you mean. If it makes you feel any better, there are plenty of things I'm hopeless at.'

'Such as?'

He thought for a moment. 'Gardening.'

She laughed.

'No, truly. Every kind of vegetation I touch withers and dies.'

'I don't believe you've ever tried your hand at horticulture in your life. If you did, I'm sure you would have a garden which would make the gardens at Kew look like a costermonger's vegetable patch.'

Red-faced and dripping with sweat, the groom caught up with them, which stifled the conversation from then on, but it was pleasant enough to amble through the park on horseback beside Eulalia. It seemed that scarcely a few minutes had passed before the bells of St Paul's in Kensington were tolling half-past eleven and Killigrew took out his watch.

'Am I boring you?' asked Eulalia.

'Not at all. I wish I could stay longer,' he said, with genuine regret. He could not remember the last time he had enjoyed a young woman's company so much. 'But I have an appointment at twelve. Perhaps I may be allowed to enjoy the pleasure of your company again some time?'

'When did you have in mind?'

'How about this afternoon?' he found himself saying.

She laughed. 'All right. Your appointment is for dinner, I take it? Shall we say two o'clock at Gunter's Tea Shop?'

'Better make it three,' he told her. 'I'm dining with Rear-Admiral Napier.'

He left Hyde Park at the same place he had entered, by the statue of Achilles, and rode up Piccadilly to St James's Street, where he had an arrangement with the landlord of the White Horse Cellar Coaching Inn for the stabling of his hired horse. It was only a temporary arrangement, for he had no idea how much longer he would be staying in London. He had only been in the city for a few days but already he was growing bored, and if it had not been for the possibility of a closer acquaintance with Eulalia Fairbody then he might have had a hankering to get back to sea.

There was not time for him to return to his own club to get changed, so he made his way directly to the United Service Club on Pall Mall. He was about to present himself to the porter in the hallway when he saw Napier coming down the stairs from above, deep in conversation with another gentleman who was smoking a cigar. The rear-admiral walked with his feet turned out, limping from one old war wound, and stoop-necked from another. He was too involved in his conversation with his companion to notice Killigrew.

'Can I be of assistance, sir?' asked the porter.

'It's all right, I'm here to see Sir Charles,' Killigrew told him, nodding up the stairs.

'And you are . . .?

'Christopher Killigrew.'

'Very good, sir. Sir Charles is expecting you.'

At the foot of the stairs Napier and his companion took their leave of one another, shaking hands warmly, and then Napier hailed Killigrew. 'Hullo, Killigrew. Come on up.'

Killigrew followed Napier up the stairs. 'That was Mr Brunel, the celebrated engineer,' Napier told him. 'Do you know him? Very clever chap, young Brunel. He's helping me with the designs for a new steamship I'm working on.' More than a quarter of a century ago, when steamships had seemed nothing more than a novelty, Napier had designed and built a small fleet of steamers for the River Seine at his own expense to prove how practical they could be; and only the previous year another vessel of his design, the first-class steam frigate HMS *Sidon*, had been launched and completed.

'Another steam frigate, sir?' asked Killigrew.

'No, no. She's not so big as the *Sidon*. A sloop. Well, a surveying ship.'

'Steam powered?' Killigrew asked in some surprise.

Napier nodded. 'Most of the navy's exploring ships are still sail-powered only; and all our charts are drawn up with sailing ships in mind. Steam vessels have completely different requirements, as I'm sure you'll appreciate. When steam supplants sailing ships altogether, as I have no doubt it will, then all the old Admiralty charts will be out of date. My new ship will be just the thing to update them; and being steam-powered, she'll have no difficulty navigating narrow creeks and inlets.'

They entered the reading room and sat down at a table, Napier ordering drinks for them both from a waiter. 'Yes, I've got big plans for my little surveying ship. I'm trying to design her to be something of a jack of all trades, you see. The danger is that if you try to compromise too much you end up serving no useful purpose at all. I don't want her to be a jack of all trades and master of none. And I'll need a crew of energetic officers to run her,' he added with a wink. 'Mind you, I can't see her being ready for at least another three years, so you've got time to get another posting under your belt before then. Who knows? By then you may have been promoted to post-rank.'

Killigrew smiled. 'That would be too much to dream of.'

'Why not? You're a capable and energetic young man. You'll be how old three years from now? Twenty-six, twenty-seven? Worse men than you have been promoted to post-captain at a younger age.'

Killigrew was pleased to think that Napier thought him worthy of the command of a vessel which was obviously a pet project of his. But just because Napier had designed another ship, there was no guarantee that the Admiralty would approve its construction, or that if they did they would approve Killigrew's appointment to the crew when it was ready. Besides which, all of that seemed a long time in the future and Killigrew knew he had no chance whatsoever of obtaining post-rank within three years if he spent them all ashore.

They dined heartily – Killigrew had a young man's appetite,

and that Napier was a good trencherman was testified to by his stout girth – and talked of the navy, the problems with manning and the slowness of promotion, and of steam engines and the relative merits of paddle-wheels and propeller screws. While all these subjects were close to the hearts of the two naval officers, Killigrew sensed that none of this was why Napier had asked him to dinner; a hunch which was confirmed when Napier told the waiter they would take coffee in the billiards room.

'D'you play billiards? Splendid game. Very scientific, d'ye see? It's all about *angles*.'

'I'm afraid I never was much good at trigonometry, although I have played billiards on occasion,' admitted Killigrew.

'Splendid! We shall play a game or two, and talk while we do so.'

The billiards room was empty at that time of day. Killigrew took two cues from the rack and offered Napier his choice. Then the two of them stood side by side at the baulk and each strung a ball up the table, bouncing them off the top cushion so that they rolled back towards the lower cushion.

'Ha! I win,' said Napier, when his ball came to rest nearest the bottom cushion. 'Although I suspect you let me, out of deference to seniority. Well, no matter. I shall break the balls, and you'll soon see I've no need of a handicap. I must warn you, Killigrew, I've been playing this game a good deal of late, and though I say so myself I've become rather a dab hand at it. First to score one hundred? I'll take spot white,' he added, placing that ball in the baulk and lining up a shot. He at once knocked Killigrew's ball into one of the pockets. 'First hazard to me, I think,' he said smugly, lining up his next shot. 'By the way, you do realise that Captain Standish thinks you murdered Captain da Silva in cold blood?'

'Oh?' Killigrew said cautiously. When Lieutenant Jardine

had entered the day room on board the *São João* to see da Silva's corpse stretched out on the deck and Killigrew with a smoking pepperbox in his hand, Killigrew had merely indicated the pistol in the open drawer of the desk and allowed Jardine to draw his own conclusions. 'Has he said anything?'

'Good heavens, no! Not as such. Standish is no fool; at least, not that much of a fool. He knows perfectly well that it could never be proved that you murdered da Silva – which you didn't, of course – and that if he said so publicly you'd be well within your rights to call him out. And we both know how *that* would turn out. No, he's just made some . . . shall we say *insinuations*. Oh, damn and blast!' he added as he missed a shot.

Killigrew stepped up to the table and took a shot.

'Oh, well played! Now, if it was up to me, I'd shoot every last slaver and be done with it. But you know what these damned Whigs are like: can't kill a man without a fair trial, and all that. As if there were such thing as a fair trial! Which reminds me, I read your report to the Slave Trade Department at the Foreign Office. Interesting reading. You're not the first naval officer on the West Africa Squadron to hear of this Owodunni Barracoon, either; although the information you found on the *São João* has helped to narrow down its location to within two hundred miles.'

'With all the creeks and inlets on that stretch of coastline, it should only take the entire squadron a couple of years to find it – if they dedicated all their energies to surveying that stretch of the coast, that is.'

'Which they won't, of course. The only thing we know about the Owodunni Barracoon is that it lies somewhere between Sierra Leone and Monrovia, it's run by a man called Francisco Salazar – Portuguese or Brazilian, no one knows for sure – and it seems to have picked up most of the slave trade which was lost when Denman and his colleagues destroyed the barracoons on the Gallinas, Sherbar, and Pongas rivers. In fact the department estimates that over twenty thousand slaves are shipped from this one barracoon to the Americas every year. Can you imagine that? Twenty thousand men, women and children, every year? Why, at an estimate of one-third dying *en route*, that's nearly seven thousand killed on the middle passage alone; and the rest condemned to a life of misery and degradation. Oh, capital shot, Mr Killigrew! I gather from the support you gave me in our rather heated debate with that pompous ass Sir George the other night that you feel rather passionately about the slave trade?'

'I'd give anything to see it stopped,' said Killigrew, concentrating on his next shot.

'Anything?' Napier chuckled. 'I wonder . . .'

'If you'd seen some of the atrocities I witnessed last month alone, you'd understand why I feel so strongly about it.'

'I dare say. But there are plenty of other men in the squadron who've seen sights every bit as atrocious as the ones you've witnessed, yet precious few of them seem to have your zeal for crushing the slavers. Well played! You're better at this game than you let on, Mr Killigrew. It is as well you're not a member of this club; I do believe you are what they call a "shark". Tell me, if you had the power, how would you go about stopping the slave trade?'

'There are a number of ways . . .' said Killigrew, taking another shot and potting Napier's ball once again. 'And I'd use all of them.'

'Go on.'

'Well, the most important thing is to abolish slavery in the Americas.'

'True. But given that this is beyond our powers?'

'Discourage the African princes from selling the slaves to Europeans; make other forms of trade more profitable. Like that palm oil Sir Joshua is so keen on. I'd use carrot and stick techniques. The carrot is the vast profits they could realise from palm oil; the stick is stepping up the activities of the West Africa Squadron. We should smash the barracoons as they did a few years ago, before Captain Denman was taken to court. Damn the law! If a merchant has goods at a barracoon, then he's aiding and abetting the blackbirders at the very least. His goods should be forfeit. I say we smash their barracoons and smash their goods and smash their ships until we've forced them out of business.' He struck the cue ball savagely and managed to sink all three balls.

'An eight stroke, by God! But will putting the barracoons out of business be enough, do you think?'

Killigrew stared at the green baize while he considered the question. 'No,' he decided. 'To tell the truth, the trade is just too damned profitable. It's the men who make the real money out of it we have to hit. The investors.'

'Very good!' Napier beamed like a teacher listening to a favourite pupil.

'But they're all foreigners so they're beyond the reach of the British law.'

'Supposing I were to tell you that one of the biggest investors in the slave trade today was an Englishman; and not only an Englishman at that, but a leading member of the Establishment?'

Killigrew almost dropped his cue. 'Who?'

Napier chuckled. 'My dear boy, if we knew his name you could rest assured the whole world would know about it by now. No, all we know are a few hints we've picked up here and there from reports such as yours handed in to the Slave Trade Department. But a definite picture is beginning to emerge. We even have a scrap of a letter of instructions to a slaver captain written on the House of Commons own headed notepaper!'

'A member of parliament?'

'Makes one think, does it not?'

'You don't suppose it could be . . .?'

'I know what you're going to say; don't say it. We need proof before we go making any accusations, otherwise we'll just ruin both our careers. And that's where you come in, Mr Killigrew.'

'I?'

'I want you to become a blackbirder.'

Killigrew miscued. Unmindful of the balls clinking on the baize, he looked up at the rear-admiral in astonishment.

'Yes, you heard me correctly,' Napier told him. 'The tighter we clamp down on the slavers, the more organised they become. The only way we're going to get the proof we need is to infiltrate their ranks.'

'You mean join the crew of a slaver under an assumed name?' Killigrew shook his head. 'It's a nice idea, but it will never work. The blackbirders are as thick as thieves, and I've crossed swords with so many there's too great a risk that one of them will recognise me as a naval officer.'

Napier nodded. 'I suspect that's the mistake I made with the last naval officer I sent on this mission.'

'You mean . . . you've tried this before?'

'Yes. You remember Lieutenant Comber, don't you?'

'Comber? Yes, he's a good man.'

'Ah . . . *was* a good man.'

'Please tell me he's working as a lion-tamer somewhere in central Europe.'

'Eh? No, no. I fear it more likely that Lieutenant Comber is currently somewhere at the bottom of the Atlantic Ocean. But I won't make the same mistake with you as I made with him.'

'No?'

'No. I intend for you to join a slaver under your *real* name.'

'I know you well enough by now to know there's method

in your madness, sir, but I fear you'll have to explain it to me.'

'We'll make it look as if you've been dismissed from the service in disgrace; guilty of something so vile that you'll never be able to get honest work on any ship again, navy or merchant. What more natural than for you, embittered and twisted, to seek revenge by signing on with the kind of crew which the navy works so hard to foil?'

'What more natural than the aforementioned crew should take the opportunity to thrash the living daylights out of me as soon as we're at sea, just for devilment?'

'Not if we pick the right captain, Mr Killigrew. One clever enough to realise the distinct advantages he'll enjoy from employing an ex-naval officer – one with a grudge towards the navy – on board his vessel. A man who is completely familiar with all the tactics the navy employs.'

'It might work,' Killigrew allowed. 'You have such a captain in mind?'

'There's an American, a man named Caleb Madison. He's the master of the *Madge Howlett*, a Baltimore-built brig out of New York. She lands at Liverpool two or three times a year and loads with manufactured goods ostensibly destined for Havana. Cotton textiles, gunpowder and muskets, looking glasses, copper wire, kitchen utensils . . .'

'All the usual goods in the slave trade.'

'Precisely so. A brig plying between Liverpool and Havana could make the crossing more than four or five times a year. Furthermore, our consul in Havana keeps a close watch on shipping which might be involved in the slave trade and sends regular reports to the Slave Trade Department. He's never seen any ship named the *Madge Howlett* land there.'

'So she's changing her name between Liverpool and Havana.'

'Or sailing directly to the Guinea Coast. But the *Madge*

*Howlett* belongs to the Bay Cay Trading Company, the same company which owned several other ships which have been condemned as slavers; one of which contained the fragment of the letter with the House of Commons heading. There's a mass of paperwork and red tape between the Bay Cay Trading Company and its real owners, but I'm willing to stake my life that if you berth on board the *Madge Howlett* for a voyage, you'll learn something which will lead us to our high-placed slaving investor.'

'That's easy for you to say, sir,' said Killigrew, lining up his next shot. 'It's not your life that will be at stake.'

'I know I'm asking you to undertake a perilous enterprise, Mr Killigrew, and believe you me, I'll not think any the less of you if you decline my offer.'

'And if – *when* – the voyage is ended and I return to England? I'll have my naval rank reinstated and my honour restored?'

'A hundred fold. You're going for a ten stroke? You'll never make that shot, Mr Killigrew. A guinea on it.'

'What odds will you give me?'

'A hundred to one.'

'And what odds would you give on my even *surviving* a voyage on a slaver, never mind finding out the information you require?'

'I'll not beat about the bush, Killigrew. About the same.'

Killigrew took his shot, striking first the red ball and then the spot white, pocketing both before his own ball slipped slyly down the top pocket.

''Pon my soul! Done it, by Jove!' exclaimed Napier. 'Which takes your score up to . . .'

'A hundred and one. My game, I believe.'

They replaced their cues in the rack and went downstairs and outside, waiting on the steps while the porter stepped out into the street to flag down a passing hansom for the rear-admiral.

A young girl – no more than eleven or twelve, gauged Killigrew – approached them with a bundle of heather. Her face was scrubbed, but there was grime around her neck and behind her ears, and her out-sized clothes were grubby and patched. 'Buy some lucky heather, kind sirs?' she asked.

'Oi! I've told you before!' growled the porter. 'We don't want your sort round here. Hop it!'

Killigrew waved him away. 'I think I'm going to need all the good luck I can get if I'm going to undertake this enterprise.'

Napier was delighted. 'You accept, then?'

'Did you ever doubt I would?'

'Capital fellow!' Napier clapped him on the back. 'I know you won't let me down.'

Killigrew handed the girl a sovereign in return for a sprig of heather.

'I can't change this, mister!' she protested.

'That's all right,' said Killigrew, smiling benignly. 'Keep the change.'

'Coo! For this much change I'll suck your sugar stick,' she offered.

Killigrew's smile grew thin. 'That won't be necessary. Why don't you buy some food for your family?' She nodded and ran off up the street.

'You realise, of course, she'll probably spend it on gin?' said Napier.

'If I had to live by selling heather and performing lewd acts on strangers, I'd probably spend all my money on gin, too,' said Killigrew.

'To return to your enterprise,' said Napier. 'If, as I suspect, the man we're after is high up in London Society, then there's a good chance he may have spies in all manner of unexpected places; such men usually do. For your own safety, I suggest that the fewer people know of this, the better.'

'How many people did you have in mind?'

'Ideally, just the two of us—'

He broke off at the sound of horse's hoofs clopping on the cobbles and they both turned to see a gig come racing down Pall Mall, a young swell standing with the reins in one hand while he lashed the horse's flanks with a whip held in the other. As the gig careered down the thoroughfare the man swayed on his feet, and it was only a drunkard's luck which kept him from being pitched into the road. The porter, standing halfway into the road to flag down a hackney, had to leap aside to avoid being knocked down.

Further up the road, the flower-girl was not so lucky. She heard the horse's hoofs and the rattle of the wheels on the cobbles, turned to see the gig bearing down on her, and froze. Killigrew launched himself towards her, but it was a purely instinctive reaction and he was too far away to do anything.

The driver of the gig did not even see the girl. She squeaked briefly before falling under the horse's hoofs, and then one of the gig's wheels bounced over her chest. The man in the gig fell back into the seat, giggling drunkenly, unaware that anything untoward had occurred, and the gig veered off Pall Mall on to Cockspur Street.

Killigrew reached the girl's body. Plenty of other people walked past, but none troubled to stop. She was barely conscious, and the blood which bubbled past her lips indicated that at least one broken rib had pierced a lung. Killigrew cradled her head in his lap and looked up at the passersby. 'Someone fetch a doctor, for God's sake!'

A fit of coughing racked the girl's body, and she lay still. Napier stood over Killigrew and put a hand on his shoulder. 'It's too late, Killigrew,' he said softly. 'There's nothing anyone can do.'

Feeling shaken, Killigrew pushed himself to his feet. He was not unaccustomed to the sight of violent death, but it was not something he associated with the genteel streets of St James's. 'We'd better fetch a constable,' he told Napier. 'Someone has to give that fellow's description, though I doubt they'll catch him.'

Napier nodded. 'No need for us both to wait. You must have things to do.'

'So must you, surely? And more important than what I'd had planned for this afternoon.' Killigrew glanced at his watch: it was nearly three o'clock.

Napier smiled. 'You had plans? Concerning a young lady, perhaps? No need to keep her waiting. You run along.'

'All right. When the police get here, give them my name. If they do catch that swine, I'll be happy to stand against him in the witness box. I'm staying at the Army and Navy.'

Napier nodded, and after one last regretful glance at the dead girl, Killigrew headed up Regent's Street. As he made his way towards Piccadilly Circus, he thought about her. There were those who would have said the death of one reduced to such circumstances was probably for the best, but Killigrew would have dismissed them as self-righteous asses. He felt sick. He had been so close to the incident, perhaps if he had been a little more vigilant he could somehow have prevented it. But there had been nothing he could do – how he hated to be an impotent bystander! – and it was done now anyway.

As he turned off Piccadilly and headed up Berkeley Street, he forced himself to put the girl's death from his mind and tried to think about the mission he had agreed to undertake for Napier. He wondered how he could inveigle Captain Madison into taking him on board the *Madge Howlett*. Killigrew had little taste for the duplicity which would be required of him to maintain his imposture, although he had confidence in his ability to carry it off, and it would be well worth it if it would enable him to bring some of the men foremost in the slave trade to justice. And it would be exciting; more exciting than cruising off the Guinea Coast on the *Tisiphone*, and certainly more exciting than mooching around in London. Yes, the more he thought about it, the more he realised he was looking forward to the adventure.

He reached Berkeley Square with a couple of minutes to spare, although Eulalia was already there, seated in a calash parked with the top folded down a short distance from Gunter's Tea Shop. There were several other carriages parked nearby, and waiters moved back and forth between the tea shop and the carriages delivering ice creams and sorbets. There was no sign of the calash's driver; Killigrew guessed that Eulalia had sent him off on some errand. Gunter's was popular with the younger members of Society, and the only place Killigrew knew of where a gentleman could talk to an unescorted lady without giving rise to scandal.

'Are you all right, Kit?' she asked as he approached. 'You look pale.'

'I saw a nasty accident just now,' he explained. 'A young girl knocked down by a gig.'

'Good heavens, how awful! Was she all right?'

'No. She died.'

Eulalia looked shocked. 'It's more genteel to say she "passed on", Mr Killigrew.'

'And not referring to her death directly makes it all right, does it?' he asked heatedly, removing his top hat to run his fingers through his hair in agitation.

'I'm sorry. You are right, of course. It will not bring her back. I forgot I was dealing with a plain-speaking navy man.'

'No, I'm the one who should apologise. It was not my intention to address you so intemperately, ma'am. I was angered by what I saw, and improperly expressed my anger towards you.'

'It is not improper to be angry, if the anger is justified,' she allowed, and smiled. 'But we are becoming formal once more, are we not? I think two people who played together as children might be permitted to address one another by their Christian names.'

He smiled and waved across a waiter, ordering them both a sorbet. 'So, are you going to tell me what all these mysterious appointments you keep having to leave for are?' she asked, when they had finished eating and the waiter had taken away the bowls once more.

'Oh, I'm just doing some work with the Slave Trade Department at the Foreign Office,' he told her absently, mindful of Napier's injunction not to discuss their plan.

'Still trying to suppress the slavers, Kit?'

'I have to. I'm sorry if I seem obsessive about them, but if you'd seen what I saw . . .' Even there, in the leafy surroundings of Berkeley Square, the mental image of the slaves being thrown off the *São João* had lost none of its impact.

'You had a bad time with the West Africa Squadron, didn't you?'

'I? No. I can think of no place better for a young naval officer wishing to see some adventure, both for its own sake and with an eye to getting noticed by his superiors. Nor can I think of any cause more just to fight for.'

'Does it come to fighting?'

'Indeed, yes. They're a rough crowd, the slavers: murderous scum who'll stop at nothing.' *And the only way to beat them is to play by their rules*, he found himself thinking.

He felt a raindrop on the back of his hand, then another on his cheek. 'It's starting to rain,' said Eulalia.

'Let's get the top up,' he suggested, unclipping the folded-down hood.

'Let me do it,' she insisted. 'I'm afraid there's a knack,

and if you're not careful you'll tear . . . oh!' she finished, as he raised the hood effortlessly and clipped it into place. She laughed. 'Oh, Kit! You really are the most infuriating man I've ever met!'

'What do you mean?'

'Because you're too good to be true. Are you going to stand there all day and get soaked?' she added, opening the door for him.

'I'm not sure it would be seemly of me . . .'

'Don't be silly. Look, here comes Giles,' she added, nodding to where her coachman emerged from the tea shop. 'He can chaperone us.'

Killigrew climbed in beside her while the coachman took his place on the driving board and got soaked. 'Where to, ma'am?'

'Better take me back to my club,' said Killigrew. While he would have been happy to spend all day in Eulalia's calash, he was concerned for her reputation despite the presence of her coachman, although inside he despised the new-found prudery of Society and longed for the days of the old King's reign, when a gentleman might do as he pleased and Society be damned. 'The Army and Navy, in St James's Square.'

The coachman glanced at Eulalia, who nodded, and he flicked the tip of his whip at the backs of the horses. They clipped through the rain-soaked streets at a comfortable pace.

Killigrew found himself staring at Eulalia until she blushed, but he could not take his eyes from her face. 'What are you staring at?' she asked at last.

'A Kit may look at a queen.'

She smiled; he knew it was a bad joke and worthy of no more, and appreciated the fact that she did not go out of her way to laugh at the jest. She was a rare woman, of that there was no doubt. When so many of Society's young ladies were brought up to be brainless girls interested only in home-making, it was a delight to meet someone like Eulalia who had a brain to match her looks and was not afraid to let it show. He suddenly realised that if he and Napier went ahead with the rear-admiral's plan to get Killigrew shunned by Society, then he *would* feel unhappy about it. Like her, he did not much care what Society thought of him, but the notion of being in her ill-graces was more than he could bear.

Could it be that he was in love with her?

Of course he was. Hopelessly, stupidly, pointlessly. Had she not said she was in no hurry to get married? But then neither was he. Was there any chance she would wait for him?

Of course not, if Napier's plan worked.

'Eulalia?

'Mm?'

'If something happened . . . if I were accused of some terrible crime, and found guilty and shunned by Society, would you think any the less of me?'

'What a strange question! Well, I suppose it would depend on the crime . . . and whether or not you had committed it.'

It was an intelligent response, as he would have expected of her. 'But would you believe in my innocence when everyone else was convinced of my guilt?'

'Of course.'

'You say that, but is it just because you think that is what I want to hear?'

She laughed. 'When have you ever known me to say something just because I thought it might please *you* to hear me say it?'

'True,' he admitted with a rueful grin.

'Why, have you done something . . . or rather, been accused of something?'

'Not yet.'

'Not yet?' she echoed, and then dug an elbow into his ribs. 'Oh, you're just teasing me!'

The calash pulled up in St James's Square. 'Here I must take my leave of you,' said Killigrew, climbing out into the rain. 'Perhaps I can see you again some time?'

'I've taken a box at Her Majesty's for the Season. My father and I are going with some friends to see Jenny Lind in *Roberto il Diavolo* next month.' Already celebrated on the continent, the silvery voice of the Swedish Nightingale had London Society in a froth of anticipation. 'I'm sure I can squeeze you into my box,' she added.

'I can think of no way I'd rather spend an evening.'

'I'll have an invitation sent round,' she told him, and ordered the coachman to drive on. Killigrew stood there on the pavement outside the Army and Navy Club and grinned like an idiot as the rain dripped from the brim of his hat until the calash had disappeared from view. Only then did he realise he was getting soaked through by the rain, and he hurried up the steps and into the club.

The porter looked up from where he sat in his lodge, and the expression on his face when he recognised Killigrew told the young lieutenant that something was wrong. 'There's a couple of gentlemen here to see you, sir,' explained the porter, the tone of his voice implying that he considered the visitors to be anything but gentlemen. 'I told them you were out and asked them to leave their cards, but I'm afraid they insisted on waiting.' He jerked his head to where two men sat on chairs in the lobby.

Both wore greatcoats and hats; one was a stout man of middle height, aged about sixty, with sharp eyes set in a round face, and half-whiskers; the other a red-headed, bony man with a turned-up nose. 'That's quite all right, Josephs,' Killigrew said, as the two men rose to their feet. He went to greet them.

'Mr Killigrew?' asked the sharp-eyed man. 'I'm Inspector Blathers, and this here's Sergeant Duff. We're from the

Detective Department at Scotland Yard. We're given to understand that you may be able to assist us in our inquiries into the death of a young flower-girl who was knocked down on Pall Mall earlier today.'

'Oh, that business. Yes, I shall be delighted to give you whatever help I may.'

'Would you mind accompanying us to Bow Street Police Court?'

'Is that really necessary? I'm soaked to the skin and I wouldn't mind changing out of these wet things. Couldn't I drop by later to give you a description of the man responsible?'

Blathers and Duff exchanged glances. 'Oh, we already have a full description of the man. And his name.'

'His name? Why, that's splendid! Fast work, I must say. Who is he?'

'The name we've been given is Mr Christopher Killigrew.'

# IX:

## The Pall Mall Child-Killer

'This is ridiculous!' Killigrew protested as he was pushed forcibly into the cell at Bow Street Police Court. 'I was there, yes, but it wasn't I who drove the gig. Ask Rear-Admiral Sir Charles Napier. He was there; he saw the whole thing. He'll vouch for me.'

'We already have,' said Blathers. 'As a matter of fact, he was the one who gave us your name.' He slammed the cell door, turned the key in the lock, and walked away.

'Gave you my . . .' stammered Killigrew, and then felt relief flood through him. At last what had seemed like a terrible misunderstanding had been explained. The rear-admiral was certainly a fast worker; but then, the timing of the girl's death had been too good to ignore. It was notoriously difficult to find witnesses in such cases; the only man who could deny that Killigrew was responsible was the driver of the gig, and he was unlikely to come forward.

It was perfect. If a gentleman like Killigrew pleaded guilty to manslaughter then he had every chance of being let off with a hefty fine – which suddenly struck him as unfair, although now was hardly the time to complain – but the repercussions would be more far-reaching. The navy would dismiss him for conduct unbecoming the character of an officer and a gentleman, and Society would shun him as a child-killer.

As would Eulalia.

He felt a momentary pang. But she would believe in his innocence – wouldn't she?

And then he could inveigle his way aboard the *Madge Howlett*; and with any luck return to England a few months later, honour redeemed, to have his rank restored and, he hoped, able to point the finger at whoever was behind the slavers.

Assuming, of course, he was let off with a fine. Assuming he was successful in joining the crew of the slavers. Assuming the slavers did not see through the imposture and slit his throat and throw his body overboard as soon as the *Madge Howlett* was out at sea.

Killigrew realised he was not alone in the cell. He turned in time to see three heavily built men rise from the bench. They were not smiling. 'So, you're the bastard who killed that little girl on Pall Mall today?' snarled one.

Killigrew guessed that now was probably not the time to plead guilty. Such men rarely found themselves in a position where they could beat up a member of the gentry – assuming they were not rampsmen who did so for a living, which was not entirely improbable from the look of them – and any man would naturally want to inflict some kind of punishment on someone guilty of such a crime. 'Accused,' he said. 'There is a golden thread running through British justice which says a man is innocent until proven guilty—'

Two of the men quickly moved forwards, grabbed Killigrew by the arms and slammed him back against a wall while the third rammed his fists repeatedly into his stomach. Fire exploded in Killigrew's midriff. A fist smashed into his face and threw his head back against the wall, cracking his skull. His eyes rolled up in his head and the two men released him, allowing him to slump to the floor, then the third kicked him in the mouth.

'That'll teach you not to go around killing little girls,' he snarled.

Killigrew tried to get up but a boot slammed into his side and he collapsed to the floor again.

'Break 'is bleedin' neck, 'Arry.'

As the man came at him again, Killigrew barely managed to roll away from the blow. He spat out a mouthful of blood and crawled into the far corner.

'Still got some fight left in you, eh?' snarled Harry.

Killigrew pushed himself unsteadily to his feet and turned in time to see Harry swinging a fist at his head. Then the rampsman's eyes widened in shock as Killigrew's hand came up as fast as a striking cobra and stopped the fist in its tracks. Killigrew closed his fingers over the fist, squeezing tightly until Harry gasped, and then began to twist. Harry turned away from him in an effort to relieve the pressure on his shoulder, and Killigrew punched him in the kidneys.

Harry fell to the floor with a grunt. One of the other men came at Killigrew. The naval officer punched him in the stomach once and the man doubled up in winded agony. Killigrew hit him on the back of the neck and lifted his knees into his face. The man lay still.

Killigrew glanced at the third man, who backed into the furthermost corner and raised both hands placatingly. Killigrew knew he need expect no more trouble from that quarter. He glanced down at his trousers. There was blood where he had kneed the second man in the face, and the fabric had ripped. 'Damn it!'

'My missus'll mend it,' offered the third man. 'Be good as new, it will. I'll give you her address.'

'Mr Killigrew?' called the gaoler. 'You made bail.'

Killigrew looked up in surprise from where he sat on the bench in the cell. 'No I didn't!' he protested. He had been in the police cell for nearly a week now and his clothes were ragged and filthy. Bail had been posted at a hundred guineas, the same amount that Napier owed him after their wager, but as an impecunious naval officer Killigrew preferred a couple of weeks' board and lodging at Her Majesty's expense and some cash in hand at the end of it.

The gaoler was not having any of it, however. 'Come along, Mr Killigrew. There's a gentleman waiting to see you.'

The gentleman was the lawyer who had posted his bail, a burly, prematurely-balding man with deep-set eyes beneath bushy eyebrows. He gave Killigrew his card. 'May I ask the name of my benefactor?' asked Killigrew.

'You may ask,' said the lawyer. 'But I can only reply that I am not at liberty to divulge my client's name.'

'My grandfather,' guessed Killigrew. 'Probably worried that I'll bring the family name into disrepute.'

'I could not possibly comment on that,' said the lawyer, gnawing the side of a forefinger. 'However, I have been instructed to engage Sir Abraham Haphazard, QC, MP, to speak at your trial.'

'But you cannot instruct a barrister to act as my counsel without my consent.'

'True.'

'Then you may kindly inform your client that it is my intention to conduct my own defence.' Even if the danger of being acquitted had not been entirely at odds with Napier's plans, Killigrew would not have accepted help from his grandfather even if his life had depended on it.

'That is entirely your prerogative,' admitted the lawyer. 'Although if I were your lawyer then I should advise you against it. Still, you seem to be a young man who knows his own mind. If that is your last word on the subject, it remains only for me to inform my client that I have done everything within my power to carry out his instructions. Good day to you, Mr Killigrew.'

'Mr Killigrew, you are hereby charged with manslaughter; to whit, that on Friday the fourteenth of April in the year of our Lord eighteen hundred and forty-seven, while incapacitated through over-indulgence in alcohol, you did drive down Pall Mall in a gig with wilful negligence, and that furthermore by doing so your actions resulted in the death of Elizabeth Williams, a minor. How do you plead?'

Killigrew rose to his feet. 'I wish to lodge a plea of guilty to both charges, m'lud, but would also like to plead mitigating circumstances.' He glanced up towards the gallery. Eulalia was there with her father and Eustace Tremaine, although as soon as Killigrew announced his guilty plea the three of them rose to their feet with expressions of disgust on their faces. Killigrew knew he could not blame them for their reaction, but it was still a knife in his heart that Eulalia could really think him guilty of such a crime.

'Very well,' said the judge. 'Does the counsel for the prosecution still wish to call its witnesses?'

The counsel for the prosecution stood up and bowed. 'If it pleases m'lud, counsel for the prosecution would like to demonstrate that there are no acceptable mitigating circumstances for a crime so heinous as that of which Mr Killigrew now stands accused.'

'Very well. Pray continue.'

Killigrew stood in the dock feeling dazed. He knew that in effect the whole trial was no more than a sham, although the fact that he was the only one who knew so was not very reassuring. His only consolation was the sealed letter from Napier brought to him by the solicitor appointed on his behalf. The letter had briefly confirmed that this was all part of the plan, and that while no one except himself and Napier knew the truth of the matter, Chief Justice Denman – the father of the author of the *Instructions for the Guidance of Her Majesty's Naval Officers Employed in the Suppression of the Slave Trade* – had assured Napier that if Killigrew pleaded guilty then he was unlikely to receive any sentence tougher than a fine of a few guineas, which Napier had agreed to pay – admittedly out of the money he owed following Killigrew's final shot in their game of billiards.

'Call the first witness.'

'Will Mr Simon Gubbins please take the stand?'

An elderly and filthy-looking man entered, evidently unnerved by his surroundings, and swore to tell the truth, the whole truth and nothing but the truth. Killigrew was glad that as the accused he had not been sworn in; he was not much of a church-going man, but even so he would have been uncomfortable about perjuring himself on the Bible, albeit in a noble cause and at no one's expense but his own.

'You are Mr Simon Gubbins, of Blue Gate Fields, London?' asked the counsel for the prosecution.

'Yes, sir.'

'And can you tell us where you were at ten minutes to three last Wednesday?'

'Yes, sir. I was on Pall Mall. Looking for pure.'

'And did you see the incident—'

The judge held up a hand, interrupting the counsel for the prosecution, and leaned forward to address the witness. 'I'm sorry, could you repeat that? What were you looking for?'

'Pure, your honour. Dog-muck. That's what I do. I'm a pure-finder.'

The counsel for the prosecution closed his eyes as if in pain. Normally he would ask his witnesses what they did for a living if the respectability of their profession would lend credence to their testimony. Mr Gubbins being a pure-finder, the prosecution had felt that his profession was best left unmentioned, unless the defence were so crass as to raise the issue.

'Let me make sure I understand you correctly,' said the judge. 'You were looking for excrement?'

'That's right, sir.'

'And what did you intend to do once you had found it?'

'Why, put it in me bucket, your honour. That's what I always do. Then, when I've got a full bucket, I takes it down to one of the tanneries in Southwark. They'll give you a good price if it's the right kind of pure. They like the white, limey kind best of all; they use it in puring the leather, I'm told, though I ain't never seen it done myself. That's why we calls it "pure".'

'And this is how you make your living?'

'Yes, your honour. It may not be much of a living, but it keeps the wolf from the door.'

'That's as maybe, but I don't think I shall ever feel comfortable in the saddle ever again,' said the judge, and a polite titter ran around the court. 'Pray continue with the cross-examination of your witness,' he told the counsel for the prosecution.

'Thank you, m'lud. Mr Gubbins, did you see Elizabeth Williams knocked down?'

'Yes, sir.'

'And did you get a good look at the man driving the gig which knocked her down and ran over her?'

'Why, yes, sir. I told you before, didn't I?'

'For the court, please.'

'I saw him, all right. A moment later he almost ran me over, too, so I got a good look at his face.'

'And can you see him in this courtroom today?'

Mr Gubbins had a good look around. 'No, sir.'

'Try again, Mr Gubbins. And I suggest you pay particular attention to the gentleman standing in the dock.'

Gubbins peered at Killigrew. 'No, sir. 'Tweren't him. Definitely not.' The counsel for the prosecution looked stunned; if he was not careful, thought Killigrew, he was going to lose this case. 'He was there, all right, but he weren't driving the gig. He—'

'Just answer the question: yes or no,' snapped the counsel for the prosecution.

'No.'

'I have no further questions for this witness, m'lud. May I respectfully request an adjournment?'

'You may,' said the judge. 'And I shall respectfully decline it. Since the accused has already pleaded guilty, I really don't see why this case should take more than a few minutes and I have a luncheon appointment at one. Does the defendant wish to cross-examine the witness?'

'Yes, m'lud,' said Killigrew, reflecting that when the accused had to help the prosecution prove their case it only went to show just how complete an ass the Law could be. 'Mr Gubbins, have you ever drunk alcohol?'

'I am an occasional imbiber, sir, but then who isn't? I only ever drink when it's cold, to keep the chill out.'

'There are a great many pure-finders on the streets of London, are there not?'

'Oh, yes, sir!'

'And not many dogs.'

'Sadly, no, sir.'

'So there must be a great deal of competition to find pure.'

'Oh, yes, sir. It can be quite a dog-eat-dog business.'

'Which means you must have to get up very early in the mornings.'

'Yes, sir. When it's still dark.'

'And still very cold at this time of year. So it would be natural for you to fortify yourself with a nip of something alcoholic before going out in the morning?'

'Objection, m'lud!' protested the counsel for the prosecution. 'The defendant is putting words in the witness's mouth.'

'Since the defendant seems to be doing a better job of prosecuting your case than you are, I hope you won't think me too harsh for overruling your objection,' the judge said drily. 'Continue, Mr Killigrew.'

'Mr Gubbins, had any alcohol passed your lips on the morning of the fourteenth? And may I remind you that you are under oath.'

'Well . . . maybe just a drop or two . . .'

'Yes or no, Mr Gubbins?'

'Yes.'

'Thank you. No further questions, m'lud.' Killigrew resumed his seat.

'Does the counsel for the prosecution have any further evidence it would like to present?'

The prosecutor looked flustered. 'No, m'lud.'

'Very well. Mr Killigrew, is there anything you would care to say by way of a plea for mitigation?'

Killigrew rose to his feet once more and read out his prepared statement.

'I only wish to say that no matter how great a punishment you seek to impose on me, it will pall into insignificance beside the burden of guilt which now tortures my conscience; and that as a God-fearing Christian, I know I will receive my due punishment in the next life as well as in the present. Furthermore, I wish it to be known that I have now sworn off alcohol for the remainder of my days.' He crossed his fingers behind his back before he said the last part.

'Very well. The jury may now retire if it wishes to consider its verdict. In summation I can only draw attention to the fact that, despite the hesitancy of the prosecution's sole witness, the accused has pleaded guilty, and I therefore direct you to find Mr Killigrew guilty as charged.'

The jurymen briefly exchanged a few whispered words, and the foreman rose to his feet. 'We have considered our verdict, m'lud.'

'And how do you find the accused, guilty or not guilty?'

'Guilty, m'lud.'

'Christopher Iguatios Killigrew, this court finds you guilty as charged. In view of your hitherto blameless reputation, and the sterling work done by you in the service of Her Majesty's Royal Navy, this court does not consider that a custodial sentence will be appropriate in this instance. Fined fifty guineas.' The judge banged his gavel like a salesman at an auction.

As he walked out of the court, Killigrew felt almost as guilty as if he really had been responsible for the girl's death. And meanwhile the man who had killed her was walking free, without any danger of ever being brought to justice. Of course, if Napier had not decided to take this opportunity, then it was unlikely that the man would have been in court; but all the same, Killigrew had been guilty of perverting the course of justice.

*Justice*? After that farce, he was no longer sure what justice was. *Fifty guineas*, he thought bitterly. If he had been a member of the labouring classes he might have been given ten years' hard labour, or transportation to New South Wales. So much for justice.

He was just about to leave the courthouse when a young midshipman stopped him. 'Lieutenant Killigrew, sir?'

'Yes?'

Red-faced, the midshipman said nothing more but merely handed him a letter. Killigrew noticed the Admiralty stationery at once. He ripped it open. The letter was polite but none the less curt: would Lieutenant Killigrew consider himself under open arrest until he presented himself to a court-martial to be held on board HMS *Icarus* at Deptford at ten hours *ante meridian* on Friday the seventh of May, yours faithfully, Vice-Admiral Lord Richardson, etc., etc. It was dated that very day; the letter must have been written the day before, and the midshipman given instructions to hand it to Killigrew as soon as a verdict of guilty was returned. 'You may tell his lordship I'll be there,' he told the midshipman, who saluted and turned on his heel.

Killigrew took a hansom to St James's Square and bounded up the steps to his club. He went straight past the porter in his lodge who called after him. 'Excuse me, sir? Letter for you.'

Killigrew returned to the lodge to take the letter from him. He was about to tuck it inside his coat when the porter called after him once more. 'I think you'd better read it now, sir.'

The letter was from the secretary of the Army and Navy Club and written in the same polite, formal but curt tone as the letter from the Admiralty. Following an extraordinary meeting of the club's executive committee it had been unanimously decided that Lieutenant Killigrew was no longer a fit and proper person to be a member of the club.

'Your dunnage has already been packed, sir. I'll fetch it for you now, shall I?'

Dazed, Killigrew nodded. He had expected it, of course, but it still hit home. He had joined the Army and Navy as soon as he had been promoted to midshipman, but this was his first stay there and he had only been in residence a few days. Nonetheless, it was his only home and now that too had been taken away from him.

He took his sea-chest and made his way to the White Horse Cellar Coaching Inn. From the looks he got there from the innkeeper and his wife, it was clear that news of his arrest and trial had spread with astonishing swiftness, and while the innkeeper was not too proud to have a disgraced naval officer living under his roof, he did not treat Killigrew with the same deference as he had done previously. Not that Killigrew cared for the deference; it was the civility he missed.

To his complete lack of surprise he heard nothing from Eulalia over the next few days. He called on her at her father's house in Knightsbridge on more than one occasion, but she was never in; or if she was, she was not receiving. Knowing that there would no longer be a place for him in her box at Her Majesty's Theatre, he managed to get a dress circle ticket through the good grace of an opera dancer of his acquaintance in the hope that he would at least get a chance to speak to Eulalia. He was not sure what he was going to say to her. He did not want to tell her all the details of Napier's plan, more because he did not want her to worry about him than because Napier had told him to tell no one. The force of the pang he had felt seeing her walk out of the courtroom had told him that he loved her; if he could not trust the woman he loved, whom could he trust?

There were several people of his acquaintance in the gas-lit finery of the theatre foyer when Killigrew arrived on the night; all of them studiously avoided meeting his gaze. Indeed, whichever way Killigrew turned, an avenue seemed to part through the crush for him. He tried to find the situation amusing, but could not.

He was unable to find Eulalia and her party before the last bell rang, and went in to watch the opera. Jenny Lind's singing was unquestionably delightful – for once *Punch* had got it right when they said that to call her the Swedish Nightingale was a compliment to the bird – but even her dulcet tones were not enough to distract Killigrew from his troubles. He was more concerned to speak to Eulalia, whom he could see seated in one of the boxes with her father, Tremaine, and several others Killigrew knew only vaguely. He studied her through his opera glasses – God, she looked lovelier than ever – but could not catch her eye as she concentrated on the stage.

At last the first interval came and he made his way through the crush to the saloon. Many of the people in the boxes would remain there and have their drinks brought to them, but Killigrew guessed that Mr Pengelly and his daughter would prefer to stretch their legs and socialise with the other opera-goers in the saloon.

He guessed correctly: he was standing by the bar when Eulalia entered with her friends. They were chatting gaily, Eulalia laughing at something Tremaine had said. Then they saw Killigrew and froze for a moment, before Eulalia abruptly led them off in another direction.

Killigrew headed off through the crowd after them. 'Eulalia! I need to talk to you, to explain! For God's sake! Just a minute, that's all I ask . . .'

She did not even turn her head. Tremaine broke off from the group to block Killigrew's path. 'Damn it, Killigrew, I'd've thought that you of all people would have had the taste and decency to know better than to remind Society of Mrs Fairbody's former connection with you.'

'I just want to explain . . .' Killigrew said desperately. 'Can you at least give her a message from me?'

'Oh, really! Stay away, damn you, or I'll be forced to call you out.'

'Then call me out!' snarled Killigrew, knowing that he could beat Tremaine any time he pleased, with sabre or pistol.

Tremaine knew it too. He blanched and backed away. Some instinct stopped Killigrew from following. Tremaine was right, of course, as far as he understood the situation, and Killigrew could hardly blame him for that. To have pressed the matter any further would have embroiled Eulalia in an ugly scandal, and that was the last thing he wanted.

He returned to the bar, and when the third bell summoned the audience back to the auditorium he ordered another whisky. He was in no mood to sit through any more of *Roberto il Diavolo*. He was the only one left in the saloon when the second act began; a moment later Sir Joshua Pengelly entered surreptitiously, with an embarrassed look on his face. 'Mr Killigrew?'

'Sir?'

'Look, I'm sorry I had to cut you dead earlier, but you understand . . .?'

Killigrew nodded.

'I'm dreadfully sorry about what happened. For you, I mean. You're a good man, I know. You made a mistake, that's all. I . . . I understand you've forsworn alcohol? I'm sorry there's not much I can do for you now, but perhaps in a year's time or so, when the scandal has died down, I can have you appointed as an officer on board one of my steamers . . .?'

'That's very kind of you, sir, and I'd be honoured. But a year is a long time, and anything can happen in—'

'Your whisky, sir,' said the barman, placing a glass at Killigrew's elbow.

Killigrew shrugged sheepishly. 'Force of habit,' he said. 'I meant to order soda water . . .'

Pengelly just shook his head grimly, turned away with an expression of disgust and hurried back towards the auditorium.

Killigrew finished his drink and went outside, dining alone in a chop-house – none of London's more fashionable restaurants could find a table for him any more, even if he booked in advance. Even in the chop-house, he was aware of people nodding towards him and muttering to one another under their breath. He could imagine what they were saying: 'That's Lieutenant Killigrew, that is, the Pall Mall child-killer. You can tell he's a villain just by looking at him – that swarthy complexion, a touch of the tar-brush in him, they say. Not really an *English* gentleman at all.' Thanks to his mixed heritage he had had to put up with that kind of remark during his early days in the navy, and although he had not been troubled by such taunts in recent years he had no doubt they would all be dredged up and used to account for his sudden disgrace.

He knew the opera was due to finish around half past ten and after he had paid his bill at the chop-house he found himself ambling back towards the theatre, he was not sure why. The Haymarket was crowded with prostitutes, lining up on the pavements like cabbies queuing for fares. Several of them called out to him – they at least were not too proud to accept the custom of the Pall Mall child-killer, he mused wryly – but he merely shook his head.

'Killigrew?'

He turned. It was Strachan. 'Hullo, Mr Strachan. What are you doing here?'

Strachan blushed. 'Oh, just . . . er . . . taking the night air.'

'Are you sure you want to be seen talking to the Pall Mall child-killer? Everyone else in Society is snubbing me these days, you know.'

'Well, I'm not sure that I qualify as a member of Society yet. What happened, Killigrew? The papers said you pleaded guilty to manslaughter.'

Killigrew nodded. 'It's true.'

'That you killed that girl? Or that you pleaded guilty?' Strachan asked shrewdly. 'I know you, Killigrew. That's just not the kind of thing you'd do . . .'

'Perhaps you don't know me as well as you thought you did.'

Strachan shook his head. 'No. I may not be the brightest fellow on God's earth, but I've always been a good judge of character. And I think there's something deuced rum going on here. What happened? Were you framed?'

Killigrew just shrugged. He was pleased that at least someone did not believe the pretence, even though he himself had confessed to the crime; he just wished it could have been Eulalia instead of Strachan.

'Look, Killigrew, it's obvious that whatever's going on you don't want to talk about it – or you can't. That's up to you. I just want you to know that anything I can do to help, just let me know. Money, a letter of recommendation, anything within my power. Here's my card. Don't hesitate to get in touch, all right?' Strachan moved on, embarrassed by his own effusion, but Killigrew called after him.

'Mr Strachan?'

'Aye?'

'Thank you.'

Strachan shrugged. 'You know what they say. A friend in need . . .' He turned and disappeared into the crowd.

*A friend indeed*, thought Killigrew, and then had to move quickly to avoid being engulfed as the patrons emerged from the theatre. He quickly took one of the hansoms waiting for trade before they were all snapped up. 'Where to, guv?'

'Do you mind if we just wait here a moment?'

'I'll have to charge you waiting time.'

'Fine.' Killigrew was more intent on the crowd than on what the cabbie was saying.

A slatternly-dressed woman stood on the running board so she could thrust her bosom at him. 'Looking for company, handsome?'

'Yes, but not yours, I'm afraid.'

'Impudence!' The woman stepped back on to the pavement and turned to her friends. 'Bleedin' window-shopper.'

Killigrew saw Eulalia emerge from the theatre with her friends. They said their goodbyes amongst the crowd, and then she got into a carriage with her father and Tremaine. 'Follow that carriage,' Killigrew ordered the cabbie. 'But discreetly, if you please.'

'All right, guv.' The cabbie flicked the tip of his whip across his horse's back and the hansom rattled off across the cobbles after the carriage as it headed up the

Haymarket towards Piccadilly Circus.

'Is that young lady your missus, then?' the cabbie asked as they headed west along Piccadilly towards Hyde Park Corner. He evidently thought that Killigrew was a cuckold tracking his wife in the hope of catching her in *flagrante delicto* with her young escort.

'Mind your own damned business,' said Killigrew, seeing no reason to disabuse him of that notion.

At last the carriage turned off Knightsbridge into the grounds of the Pengelly mansion. 'Pull up just down the road,' Killigrew told the cabbie, taking out his pocket telescope and squinting down the drive to where Eulalia and her father were climbing out of the carriage underneath the mansion's portico. Killigrew was terrified that Tremaine would also get out and go inside with them, even though the rational part of his mind knew that that would be unthinkable. But the rational part of his mind was in abeyance that night, as his act in trailing Eulalia back to her home – and what he planned to do next – demonstrated.

Tremaine did not get out of the carriage, which pulled back down the drive and out of the gate once more, heading back towards Mayfair. Killigrew waited until it was out of sight and then climbed out of the hansom, paid the cabbie his fare and tipped him generously. As the carriage rattled off into the night, Killigrew walked along the pavement until he came to the next turning and cut down a side street which looped around the back of the mansion. The street was unlit and deserted at that late hour, but Killigrew nonetheless looked about to make sure he was unobserved before he jumped up and grabbed hold of the top of the eight-foot-high brick wall which surrounded the grounds. His feet scrabbled against the brickwork, until at last he was able to haul himself over and drop down amongst the bushes on the other side.

There were lights on at the back of the house, in the kitchen downstairs and on the landing above. Enough light filtered out to enable Killigrew to navigate his way across the lawn to the rear of the house. There were bars on the ground-floor windows and the only door led into the kitchen where Killigrew could see the cook making cocoa, but a stout iron drainpipe leading up to the guttering at the eaves provided easy access to a landing window on the first floor; easy, at least, for a vigorous young man who had spent a goodly part of his teenage years skylarking about the rigging of a man-o'-war. He stood on the stone window ledge and held on to the drainpipe with one hand to steady himself while with his other he took a clasp knife from his pocket and opened the blade. He eased it into the gap between the sash windows and slid the catch open. Then he pushed the sash up, slipped through and stepped lightly on to the landing.

The first floor was silent, the only sounds from below the gentle murmur of voices: Eulalia and her father, although what they were saying was none of his business even if he could have made out the words, which he was too much of a gentleman to try to do. *A peculiar sort of gentleman*, he reflected, *who breaks into a lady's bedchamber at night*. The gas lights were low, but bright enough for him to find his way.

Six doors led off the landing. The first he tried was a bedroom, well furnished but obviously unoccupied. The next room was distinctly feminine without being girlishly so; since Eulalia lived alone with her father, it had to be her room.

He took off his hat as he entered. There were no pictures of the late lamented Mr Fairbody, which did not surprise Killigrew: whatever her feelings had been towards him, she was not the type who would spend the rest of her days pining for a departed husband. In fact there were no pictures at all, only a sampler above the bed: 'The wrath of man worketh not the righteousness of God – James i,20'. The needlework looked recent, but somehow Killigrew did not think that Eulalia had stitched it: she was not the kind of woman who could find pleasure in menial, repetitive tasks.

He put down his hat on the dresser, lit the oil lamp on the bedside table and sat down. He did not have long to wait. There were footsteps on the stairs, and then: 'Goodnight, Papa.'

'Goodnight, my dear.' A door opened and closed across the corridor while Killigrew watched the doorknob turn. He rose to his feet as the door opened and Eulalia came in. She had closed the door behind her and was halfway across the room before she saw him standing there. She froze in shock.

'Get out of here before I scream,' she said at last.

'If you were going to scream, you would already have done so.'

She snatched one of the pillows off the bed and threw it at his head. 'God damn you, Kit Killigrew. Infuriatingly right as ever.'

He pulled the pillow down from his face. 'Sorry. And sorry for breaking in here, but I had to talk to you and there was no other way.'

She put her hands on her hips. 'Did you kill that child?'

'No.'

'Then why did you plead guilty?'

'It's a long story.'

She indicated a carriage clock on the mantelpiece. 'You have one minute to convince me.'

'I'm going to join the crew of a slaving vessel so I can find out who's financing their voyages and where the slaves are coming from. I'm too well known amongst the slavers as an officer of the Royal Navy, so the only way to do it is to pretend that I've been disgraced and am after a petty revenge by working for those men I previously tried to catch. When Rear-Admiral Napier and I saw a child knocked down outside the

United Service Club, it seemed like a perfect opportunity, so I confessed to the accident.'

'And you really expect me to believe that?'

'Frankly, no. But it *is* the truth. How am I doing for time?'

'You've still got about half a minute. And a long way to go before you convince me.'

'Remember a couple of weeks ago, when you gave me a ride back to the Army and Navy, and I asked you if you'd think any the less of me if I were accused of some terrible crime, and found guilty and shunned by Society? If you would believe in my innocence when everyone else was convinced of my guilt?'

'So this is what all that was about?' He nodded. 'Look me in the eye and tell me you were in no way responsible for the death of that child.'

'I was in no way responsible for the death of that child.'

She took two quick steps to where he stood and embraced him, burying her face in his shoulder. 'Oh, Kit! I knew you could never have done such a thing. But when you pleaded guilty I thought . . . to tell the truth I didn't know what to think.'

He held her close. 'It's all right. I understand. I'm sorry I couldn't warn you before, but Sir Charles told me I was not to tell anyone. He thinks that the financier may be a member of the British Establishment.'

She stiffened, and then broke away to stare at him. 'Someone we know, perhaps?'

'Perhaps. But we need proof before we can make any accusations.'

'Won't it be dangerous?'

'Only a little bit.'

She turned away. 'You're trying to stop me from worrying about you. Of course it will be dangerous. For the love of God, Kit! If the slavers find out you're a spy, they'll kill you!'

'They can try.'

'It's too dangerous, Kit. What if something happens to you? I couldn't bear to think that I might never see you again.'

'I thought you weren't in a hurry to get remarried? There are plenty of other men out there. Eustace Tremaine, perhaps?'

She turned back to him and seized him by the lapels. 'I don't want Eustace Tremaine,' she said fiercely. 'I want—'

She broke off, and he tried to save her the embarrassment of having to finish the sentence by kissing her. It was a wasted effort, however, for the way she kissed him back finished the sentence more eloquently than words might have done. The next thing he knew she was trying to pull off his coat without breaking off the kiss while he fumbled with the fastenings at the back of her gown. So great was his passion that it required reserves of willpower he had not previously known he possessed to break off and back away. 'Slow down!' he protested.

'What's wrong?'

'Are you sure you want to do this?'

'No. My head says no, but the rest of me says yes, *yes*.' She blushed at her own passion, and lowered her eyes demurely. 'Do not misunderstand me, Kit. I loved my husband as a dutiful wife ought to. The feelings I have for you are stronger, but I'm not sure they're feelings of love. I . . . I think I'm . . . I'm weak, Kit. You'll have to help me be strong.'

He shook his head. 'You don't need me for that. You're the strongest woman I've ever known, Eulalia, and you're intelligent enough to realise that if there's something you want to do which will be to no one else's detriment, there's no reason on earth why you shouldn't.'

She considered his argument for a moment, and then turned away from him. For a moment he feared she was going to tell him to leave at once and never return.

'Help me take off this gown, Kit.'

* * *

She bit him in the shoulder at the end. If she had been trying to stop herself from crying out it did not entirely have the desired effect, for he yelped in surprise and pain; she bit deep. She always had. But he did not mind. *Nothing can ever be this perfect again*, he told himself. *I wish I could die right now*.

The two of them subsided on the mattress and lay entangled in one another's limbs, gasping for breath like two shipwrecked sailors washed up on a sun-kissed beach.

After a few moments Killigrew became aware of a knocking sound on the door. 'Eulalia?' called Sir Joshua. 'Are you all right?'

Flustered, she raised a hand to her chest, visibly trying to catch her breath. 'What? Yes, I'm fine, Papa. I was . . . I must have been having a bad dream.'

'I told you not to have the Stilton so late at night.' His shuffling footsteps sounded on the landing and a moment later his bedroom door closed.

Killigrew and Eulalia stifled giggles, and then she looked up at him with wonderment in her eyes. 'That was . . . strange. I felt so scared and yet . . . I never wanted it to stop. Oh, Kit! Why did it have to stop?'

'Sorry. I'm only human.'

Smiling, she reached up and touched him on the cheek. 'You're a god, Kit. A perfect Greek god. An Adonis.'

'That'll be my mother's nose.'

'Is . . . is it always like that, between men and women?'

'I've never known it *quite* like that,' he admitted, and frowned.

'What's wrong?'

'I don't believe that matches are made in heaven, that two people are meant for each other. Life doesn't work like that. People just drift through life . . . sometimes they connect, more often they don't . . .'

'I think we connected just now.'

'That's what I'm thinking. I know you're not in any hurry to get married . . .

'Yes. On the other hand, it's a woman's prerogative to change her mind.'

'I can't afford to marry you yet. But when I'm a post-captain . . .'

'How long will that take?'

'It depends. If I can pull off this mission to expose the slavers . . .'

Her face fell. 'I love you, Kit. The truth is I loved you before tonight. In fact I think I've loved you since we were children. I don't want to lose you.'

'Promise you'll wait for me, and I'll promise to come back alive.' He took off the small medal he wore around his neck and put it around hers.

'What's this?'

'A St Christopher.'

'I thought only Catholics wore saints' medallions.'

'And Greek Orthodox Christians.'

'You're not Greek Orthodox, are you?'

'No, but my mother was. She gave it to my father, and he left it to me. St Christopher is one of the patron saints of sailors.'

'Hadn't you better keep it? You're the one who's going to sea.'

He shook his head. 'I want you to have it, as a symbol of our engagement. May I consider us engaged, or would that be presumptuous of me?'

'You'd better,' she said gruffly, and then kissed him and grinned impishly. 'Must you go? I'll be so afraid for you. Haven't you already done more than your fair share towards suppressing the slave trade?'

'How much is a fair share?' He shrugged. 'Believe me, I'd much rather stay here in London with you. But I have no choice. My pleading guilty to the killing of that poor child may have been a ruse, but the trial was real enough.'

'You can pay the fine, can't you? I shall gladly lend you the money if you cannot.'

'There's more to it than that. I have to restore my reputation in the eyes of Society. My honour.'

'Pooh to Society. Your honour's intact in my eyes. Isn't that all that matters?'

He shook his head. 'If we're to be married I'll need a good steady income, and for that I'll need the good opinion of the navy.'

'Haven't you already got that?'

He grimaced. 'Not for much longer.'

HMS *Icarus* was a small frigate anchored in Greenwich Reach; these days larger ships could only navigate so far up the Thames with difficulty, if at all. Deptford had only been chosen as a venue because it was traditional to hold courts-martial on board ship and the town was convenient for London; Killigrew had no doubt it was the admirals' convenience that they had in mind rather than his own.

On the appointed day he presented himself in full dress uniform at the wharf where a jolly boat waited to row him out to the ship. The seamen on deck stared at him impassively as he made his obeisance to the quarter-deck. He recognised the faces of a few hands from the *Tisiphone*, men who would usually have grinned and knuckled their heads to him; these men now just stared as impassively as their new shipmates. Killigrew had told himself that he did not care what other men would think of him when he was disgraced, so long as he knew in his own heart that he was blameless; but seeing the condemnation in that lack of expression on their faces, he realised he had been wrong.

The court-martial was held in the *Icarus*'s great cabin before a panel of no less than nine admirals, including a straight-faced Napier. Killigrew presented himself before them, tucked his cocked hat under one arm and bowed first to the president of the court, Vice-Admiral Richardson – a smooth, white-haired, sharp-faced man – and then to the rest of the panel. The judge advocate recited the court's authority to assemble and then explained the circumstances which had led to its being convened. The rest of the trial was mercifully brief. Even if Killigrew had been of a mind to contest the accusation, the facts of the matter were clear: he was charged with conduct unbecoming the character of a commissioned officer of Her Majesty's Navy; he had been found guilty by a civilian court of manslaughter through drunkenness and wilful negligence.

'Lieutenant Killigrew, have you anything to say in your defence?' asked Richardson.

Killigrew hesitated. Even though this was all part of the plan he had hatched with Napier, the court was real enough and its decision would be binding. He could not merely declare his innocence at a later date, even with Napier to back him up; in the eyes of the Admiralty, he would have to do something pretty extraordinary to redeem himself. It would not be enough just to spend a voyage on board a slaver: he would have to come up with some hard evidence to prove that the enterprise had been worth while. But he hesitated only briefly, for he had thought this through countless times in the preceding days, and he grinned inwardly, knowing that the need to pull off a spectacular success would only be an added encouragement to him, as if he needed any in his fight against the slave trade. He stood up, his back as straight as a propeller-shaft, and looked Vice-Admiral Richardson in the eye.

'No, sir.'

'Very well. In which case I see no need for this court to adjourn to consider its verdict; the facts speak for themselves.' He glanced at the other members of the panel to make sure that they were in agreement, and saw only nodding heads. 'Lieutenant Christopher Iguatios Killigrew, it is the solemn duty of this court to find you guilty of a most gross breach of conduct. Your behaviour proves you to be wholly unfit to hold either your current rank or any other rank within Her Majesty's Navy. Therefore you are hereby stripped of your rank and commission and dismissed the Service . . .'

Even though it was all part of the plan and entirely expected, it was like being kicked in the chest by a mule. He had lost his home, his friends and now his career. The only thing left for him to lose was his life. Indeed, the navy was more than a career to him, it *was* his life. If he failed in his mission now, then he might as well end it all.

He was stripped of his lieutenant's epaulette and rowed back to the wharf. He went back to the White Horse Cellar Coaching Inn and took off the uniform he was no longer entitled to wear. He folded it carefully and put it in his chest, wondering when he would be allowed to wear it again. If ever.

# X:

## The *Madge Howlett*

He stood in the shadows beneath the eaves of a tavern near Liverpool docks and waited. The sound of raucous singing accompanied by an accordion came from another tavern further along the waterfront. He could not make out the words, but he knew the tune and did not doubt that they were singing one of the lewder versions of that classic sea shanty, ''Twas on the Good Ship *Venus*'. The sound of an accordion seemed strangely archaic: for some reason it always made him think of how the navy must have been in the days of his father's youth, when Napoleon's fleets threatened the shores of Britain.

It contrasted with the sound of an hydraulic crane lifting bales of cotton fabric on to a clipper in the harsh glare of limelight, for time was money and the sooner the cotton cloth produced in the mills of Lancashire could be returned across the Atlantic to the country from which the raw cotton had come, the sooner the credit could be transferred to the British banks, and whichever company delivered its goods first could corner the market while it waited for the others to catch up.

American cotton, produced by slave labour. Perhaps da Silva had been right: it was easy for the British to be holier than thou about the slave trade, but they still profited from it indirectly. And at least one Englishman – one very important and well-respected man – still profited from it directly. And that man was as responsible for the slaves thrown over the side of the *São João* as da Silva himself had been.

*I don't know who you are*, Killigrew thought to himself, *but I'm going to find out. And when I do, there's going to be a reckoning.*

The door to one of the taverns opened, spilling firelight across the cobbles with a hubbub of voices, and a man stood framed in the doorway, so tall he had to stoop to accommodate the tall, rather old-fashioned stovepipe hat he wore. Killigrew could only see the man's silhouette, but he had spent so much time studying him through a telescope over the past two days it was enough to recognise him by.

As the man walked away from the tavern, two heavily-built shadows detached themselves from a pile of bales of cotton stacked on the quayside and quickly moved to block his path. 'Can I help you gentlemen?' asked the man in an American accent.

'We were wondering if you could spare us the price of a drink,' one of the shadows asked gruffly.

'Sorry. The First Epistle of Paul and Apostle to Timothy: "For love of money is the root of all evil: which while some coveted after, they have erred from the faith, and pierced themselves through with many sorrows."'

'We asked for money, not a sermon. Give us some or we'll break your head open.'

The American took a step forward, when anyone else would have backed away in fear. As he did so a light from a window fell across him, revealing a face which, though weather-beaten, was otherwise wholly unremarkable, except that he was smiling in a situation which offered him nothing to smile about. The smile crinkled the crow's feet at the corners of his eyes, but there was no humour in those eyes: they were like hard chips of flint and managed to make even his smile seem menacing.

He chuckled ruefully. 'Well, I guess that puts a whole different complexion on the matter, doesn't it?' he said, reaching into a pocket. 'How much did you want?'

'All of it.'

'All of it? What are you planning to drink, champagne?' He took out a fistful of sovereigns and threw them on the cobbles at the feet of the two men.

*Clever*, thought Killigrew. *One of them bends down to pick up the coins, and the American kicks him in the head, leaving him with one opponent instead of two.*

But the menacing men were wise to that trick and both ignored the coins. They attacked fast, one of them trying to grab the American. Instead of turning to flee, he suddenly moved in to meet them. He swung his fists and managed to land a couple of blows which would have decked an ordinary man.

But neither of these men were ordinary. They received his blows with little more than grunts, and then one of them pinioned the American in a full-nelson, holding him fast while the other twisted in front of him to pummel him. The American kicked savagely at his kneecaps, but the attacker was expecting it. He side-stepped easily and rammed a fist into the American's stomach.

Killigrew decided it was time to intervene. He left the shadows and moved silently across the cobbles, stepping up behind the man who drove his fists repeatedly into the American's stomach. He got one hand on the man's shoulder and span him away from his victim, paying him in his own coin by driving a fist into his gut. The man gasped and swung at Killigrew's head, but Killigrew ducked beneath the blow and hit him in the stomach again, before clipping him on the jaw with a fast uppercut. The man's head snapped back and he went down.

The other man threw the American against a stack of barrels and charged towards Killigrew. The young man awaited his attack, adopting the classic pugilistic pose with both fists raised ready to strike. When the man reached him, Killigrew stepped aside at the last moment and tripped him up with an extended leg which sent him sprawling on the cobbles.

Something – probably the first man – slammed into Killigrew from behind and threw him against the wall of the tavern. Killigrew rammed his elbow into the man's midriff and broke free. They faced one another, circling warily, and then Killigrew stepped in close and tapped the man twice on the chin with his left. The man was evidently something of an expert pugilist, for he glanced to his left, expecting Killigrew to follow up with a right, which was when Killigrew decked him with a left cross.

He turned to see the second man advancing on him again, when suddenly the American loomed out of the darkness, holding a cask above his head which he brought down sharply against the second man's head.

'Are you oh-kay?' asked the American, once it was clear that neither of his attackers was in any hurry to get up and resume the combat.

Killigrew nodded, resting with his hands on his knees, breathing hard. 'Thank you.'

'No, thank *you*. I'm not entirely sure I could've handled them both if you hadn't stepped in. Tough little sons of bitches, weren't they?'

Killigrew crouched down to gather up the coins, and held them out to the American, who gestured dismissively. 'Keep 'em.'

'What I did I did out of Christian charity, not out of hope of a reward.'

'I know. That's why I'm giving you one.'

'I thank you for your kindness, but I'm not in need of charity.'

The American looked him up and down, taking in his unshaven face and the threadbare clothes he had purchased from a second-hand shop in Monmouth Street. 'Well, at least let me buy you a drink,' he said, taking back his money and gesturing towards the tavern.

Killigrew licked his lips as if torn between pride and thirst. 'All right,' he said.

They went inside and crossed to the counter. 'Back so soon, Cap'n?' asked the tavern-keeper.

The American grinned. 'You know me, Jake. I just can't stay away.'

'What can I get you?'

'The usual, please, and whatever my friend here is having.' He indicated Killigrew, whom the tavern-keeper looked up and down suspiciously.

'Well? What's it to be, young feller?'

'I . . . I wonder if I could have a cup of tea?' stammered Killigrew.

The American and the tavern-keeper laughed. 'Where did you find him, Cap'n? At a temperance meeting?'

Killigrew shook his head. 'No. I . . .I had an accident recently. I'd been drinking and . . . well, I'd rather not talk about it, if it's all the same with you.'

'I'm sorry, I didn't mean to pry. If it's tea you want then it's tea you shall have. I'm sure Susie must have some tea in the kitchen?' he asked the tavern-keeper, who nodded and poured out a glass of whisky for the American before disappearing into the back. 'My name's Madison, by the way. Caleb Madison.' The American offered his hand. He had a surprisingly powerful grip.

'Kit Killigrew.'

'Killigrew, Killigrew,' mused Madison. 'I'm sure I've heard

that name somewhere recently.'

Killigrew hung his head as if embarrassed. 'It's a common enough name in Cornwall.'

Madison's smile did not falter, but there was suspicion in his eyes. 'But we're not in Cornwall. And you don't have a Cornish accent.'

'No, well, I came from a good family. The tavern-keeper called you "captain". Am I to assume then that you are a fellow mariner, sir?'

'United States merchant marine. I'm the master of the *Madge Howlett*.'

'That fine Baltimore brig tied up in front of the Goree warehouses?'

Madison nodded. 'You know your ships. You're a sailor too? Which vessel are you with?'

'I'm between ships at the moment,' Killigrew responded with poorly-concealed circumspection. 'I, er . . . I don't suppose . . .?'

Madison shook his head. 'I'm sorry, I've got a full complement right now.'

Killigrew nodded hurriedly, as if embarrassed that he had enquired.

'You said "came",' said Madison.

'What?'

'You said you "came" from a good family. Most people would've said: "I *come* from a good family", but you said you "*came* from a good family". What happened? Did you disown them? Or did they disown you?' Madison was grinning, as if to make light of the matter, but his eyes watched Killigrew's face carefully, missing nothing.

Killigrew grimaced. 'They disowned me. I don't mean to be rude, but I'd really rather not discuss it.'

Madison held up his hands. 'I'm sorry. You helped me out

just now, and all I can do is ask impertinent questions. Please forgive me.'

The tavern-keeper returned with a mug of tea which he plonked on the counter before Killigrew. 'Thanks, Jake. Put it on my slate.'

'Right you are, Cap'n.'

Madison turned to stand with his back to the counter and cast his eyes across the gloomy tavern as he sipped his whisky. An expression of pain crossed his face. 'Goddamn it!'

'What's wrong?' asked Killigrew.

'There's one of my crew over there. He's supposed to be on watch tonight. I'm sorry, will you excuse me for a moment?'

'By all means.' Killigrew turned back to the counter and sipped his tea while watching Madison in the etched-glass mirror behind the shelves there. Madison crossed to where a man sat at one of the tables, wedged between two buxom serving girls. The man – dark-haired, olive-complexioned – was if anything perhaps below average height, but everything about him suggested bulk. He had the kind of physique which gave the impression of being as wide as it was tall – an impression which in this instance was not too far from the truth – and as far as Killigrew could see very little of it was flab.

The man looked up and grinned as Madison approached. Killigrew could not hear what they said above the hubbub of voices in the tavern, but whatever Madison said prompted the man to glance to where Killigrew stood at the bar. Killigrew saw the words 'Don't look now, you fool' form on Madison's lips, and the man quickly turned his head back to face his captain. He pursed his lips, and then rubbed his jaw as if trying to think. Then he nodded confidently, and spoke at length, prompting Madison to glance surreptitiously at Killigrew.

*Got you hooked, you bastard,* thought Killigrew. *Now to reel you in.*

'Get out of here, you idle dog!' Madison said, unnecessarily loudly. 'I don't pay you to sit idling in a tavern, consorting with loose women! Get back to work!'

'Sorry, Cap'n.' The massively built man squeezed out from between the wenches, the very image of contrition. He took his leave of them and hurried out.

Madison returned to where Killigrew stood. 'As a seaman yourself, you'll understand the importance of keeping good discipline amongst the crew.'

Killigrew nodded. 'Absolutely. In the navy we used to—' he said, and then broke off sharply as if he had said too much.

'You're in the Royal Navy?'

'Used to be. The bastards chucked me out,' he added savagely, and then looked embarrassed, as if he had revealed too much.

'Yes, your "accident".' Madison drained his glass, set it on the counter and turned to Killigrew. 'Well, my thanks to you once again, Mr Killigrew. That was a right Christian thing you did, and I'm much obliged to you. You have a place to stay tonight?'

Killigrew nodded. 'The Spotted Dog, up along the way.'

'I'm sorry I couldn't give you a berth on my ship, but as I say—'

'Think nothing of it. There's a steamer leaving for the Orient tomorrow, I understand they're looking for hands.'

'The SS *Ophelia*? I wouldn't recommend a voyage on her.'

'Why not?'

'Captain Jacobs has one of the worst reputations for cruelty on the seas.'

'I fear I'm not in a position where I can afford to be choosy about whom I work for.'

'Wait a couple of days. Something better is bound to come

along. Besides, a man with your experience could do better than a berth as an ordinary seaman on a steamer. With your background and training, I'd've thought that ship's captains would be queuing up to have you in their crews.'

Killigrew grimaced. 'Unfortunately I have what you might call a . . . a reputation.'

'Your accident?'

Killigrew nodded.

'It wasn't at sea by any chance, was it?'

'No. It had nothing to do with the sea. But as soon as I'd got a criminal conviction for what was only an accident those hypocritical swine at the Admiralty decided it was the perfect opportunity to get rid of me. I never was one of them, not really. My mother was Greek; the bastards never tired of reminding me of the fact.'

'Maybe you should think about getting a berth on a foreign vessel. Countries like Brazil and Cuba are always happy to have European officers on board. It lends them . . . shall we say, an air of respectability?'

'Slavers sailing under false colours, you mean.'

'Ah. You disapprove of slaving, I take it?'

Killigrew pursed his lips. 'It's against the law in this country. Not that I have a high opinion of the English law. I never really thought about it. I spent two years sailing with the West Africa Squadron, but I can't say I cared for the work. Sometimes I think we did more harm than good.'

Madison regarded Killigrew with a mixture of astonishment and amusement. 'Are there many more in the navy like you?'

'Unfortunately not. Pah, I'm better off out of it.'

'You'll certainly get better pay in the merchant service, once you find yourself a berth. And you strike me as a singularly intelligent young man. I'm sure you'll be oh-kay.'

'You're probably right. Well, thanks for the drink. Perhaps I'll see you around?'

'Perhaps. I was supposed to sail three days ago, but the damned harbourmaster's saying there's some irregularity concerning my ship's papers – which is a damned lie – and I can't leave until I've been cleared. Each day my ship rots in this port is costing me a fortune, and not doing me any favours with my owners, either.'

'Have you tried bribing him?'

Madison shook his head. 'He's one of those self-righteous ones, the kind who'd take great pleasure in throwing the money back in my face.'

Killigrew shook his head. 'Try sending him a crate of fine wine. Just as a gift. Let the *quid pro quo* remain unspoken.'

'You think that would work?'

Killigrew shrugged. 'Compare the cost of each day you're stuck in this harbour with the cost of a crate of fine wine. It's got to be worth trying, hasn't it? Who's the harbourmaster here, Jack Tolliver? I think I knew him vaguely in the navy. I seem to recall he's rather partial to a glass of Madeira.'

'You know, I think I'll give that a try. Thanks for the advice, Mr Killigrew. Once again, I'm in your debt.'

Killigrew watched him leave and sipped his tea to hide his smile.

He finished his mug of tea and left about five minutes later. As he made his way along the waterfront he heard his footsteps echo where there should have been no echo. He stopped abruptly and pretended to read a poster advertising a dinner-dance at the local assembly rooms. Out of the corner of his eye he caught a glimpse of a shadow ducking out of sight behind him. He smiled to himself and went on his way until he reached the Spotted Dog, a tavern which was on the right side of respectable, but only just.

'Evening, Mr Killigrew,' said the pot-boy who, in his capacity as night-porter, let him in.

'Evening.' Killigrew touched the brim of his hat and went

upstairs to his room. It was small but comfortably furnished. He lit the oil lamp and took off his hat, drew the curtains, and sat down at the table to write a letter and smoke a cheroot. When he had finished he dried the ink with blotting paper – afterwards burning the blotting paper over the ashtray so the ink could not be deciphered by means of holding it up to a mirror – folded the letter and put it inside his coat. He stubbed out the cheroot in an ashtray, put out the light and slipped out of the room.

He made his way to the water closet at the end of the dingy corridor. It was unoccupied, so he closed the door behind him without locking it and stood on the seat of the commode to open the window. There was no light in the water closet so he had no difficulty observing the alley below. It was deserted. He opened the window all the way and climbed out on to the ledge. Then he jumped into the night.

It was only one flight down. He hit the ground, rolled over and rose quickly to his feet. A couple of cats scavenging amongst the rubbish ran off with a hiss, startling him, but they were the only creatures to have observed his unusual mode of departure. He dusted himself off and went on his way, sticking to the shadows.

The Fouled Anchor was on the wrong side of respectable, but dressed in his second-hand clothes and grubby after rolling in the alley at the back of the Spotted Dog, Killigrew's arrival excited no interest whatsoever. He made his way upstairs and tapped gently on one of the doors.

'Who's there?' asked a voice.

'Tom Bowling,' said Killigrew.

The door opened and one of the men who had attacked Madison earlier stood there. The other sat before a mirror, wrapping a bandage about his own head. Killigrew slipped inside without waiting for an invitation. Corporal Summerbee of the Royal Marines quickly closed the door behind him.

'Are you fellows all right?' Killigrew asked them.

'Nothing that won't soon heal up,' said Summerbee. 'How did it go?'

'Splendidly. You did very well. I was utterly convinced.'

'So was I, sir. You didn't tell us he was such a tough customer.'

'I didn't know it myself. Hope I didn't hit you too hard there, Private Whitehead.'

Whitehead grinned. 'Hardly felt a thing, sir. Unlike when that Yankee bastard brained me with a keg. Begging your pardon, sir.'

'That's all right.' Killigrew took out the letter and handed it to Summerbee. 'I want this delivered to Rear-Admiral Napier. There's no reply necessary. I've got one more task for you. There's a house of ill-repute in Leopold Lane, at number sixty-nine. There should be a package for you to pick up there.'

'What sort of package, sir?'

'The kind that has two arms and two legs. Don't worry, he'll have been drugged to the gunnels, so you won't have any difficulty handling him. Take a wheelbarrow and a blanket to throw over him. Then take him to where the SS *Ophelia* is docked and deliver him to one of the boatswain's mates. He'll pay you a shilling. You might as well keep it between you. That should be all. Once again, thank you for all your help. When this is over I shall be writing a letter of commendation to your commanding officer.'

'I just hope that when this is all over, a letter of commendation from you is worth having, sir. For your sake, as well as for our own.'

'So do I, Summerbee. So do I.'

'Sir? Rear-Admiral Napier didn't tell us what any of this is about – although I think I can guess – but whatever it is, good luck with it anyway.'

'Thank you, Summerbee. That's much appreciated.'

Killigrew opened the door and was halfway across the threshold when he heard the corporal mutter under his breath, 'God knows, you're going to need it,' and Whitehead sniggered.

Killigrew's steps faltered only momentarily before he set his jaw and continued on his way.

The following day Killigrew sat down to luncheon and awaited his visitor. He dined alone, an impressive spread of roast mutton, potatoes and sprouts with lashings of gravy on the broad plate before him, a pot of tea steaming at his elbow.

*Cheer up, Kit,* he told himself. *If you don't succeed in pulling this off, you can always change your name and start a new career on the boards.* But it was difficult to imagine Eulalia being happy married to anything so disreputable as an actor.

Even though he expected company, there was no sign of it at the table, which was set for one. He was just tucking in when the door opened and Madison entered with an agitated look on his face. He gazed about the room, saw Killigrew, and at once came across to speak to him, holding his hat before him.

'Good day to you, Mr Killigrew. And how is my good Samaritan?'

'Very well, thank you. And you?'

'The same. May I join you?'

Killigrew gestured to the chair opposite him. 'Pull up a berth. Tea?'

'Thank you kindly.'

Killigrew twisted in his seat to address the landlady, who waited attentively by the dresser. She had not heard of the disgraced Christopher Killigrew, but despite his clothes she could tell that her guest was a gentleman. 'Could you fetch another cup for my friend, Mrs Hines?'

'Of course, sir.' She took down a cup and saucer and laid them on the table before Madison. 'Milk and sugar?'

'Thank you.' As soon as she had retreated to her earlier position, Madison turned back to Killigrew. 'You seem to be dining well.'

'Mm. As it happens, I've had a bit of good joss. A friend of mine is an acquaintance of Mr Brunel, the eminent engineer. It seems Mr Brunel will be looking for a new second officer for the *Great Britain* as soon as he can get her floated again.' Brunel's revolutionary transatlantic steamer the SS *Great Britain* had run aground in Dundrum Bay the previous year.

'Assuming they can get her off,' Madison pointed out. 'They've been trying for months.'

'This *is* Mr Brunel we're talking about,' said Killigrew.

'That's a good point.'

'The pay is excellent, and . . . well, if one must serve in the merchant navy, then there can be few finer or more prestigious vessels to serve on than the *Great Britain.*'

Madison's face fell.

'Is something wrong?' asked Killigrew.

Madison cleared his throat. 'First of all I want to thank you again, Mr Killigrew. I took your advice and had a case of Madeira sent to the harbourmaster's office first thing this morning. Now maybe it's just coincidence, but come noon I get a message from one of his boys telling me that I'm cleared to leave harbour whenever I please.'

Killigrew smiled. 'The British way of doing things, Captain Madison. It's a very genteel form of corruption. So, when do you sail?'

Madison grimaced. 'Well, that's just the problem. You remember last night I told you I had a full complement?' Killigrew nodded. 'Well, this morning my second mate had disappeared.'

'Does he drink? Take it from me, Captain, intoxicating liquor does terrible things to a man. Perhaps you should try having your men search all the waterfront taverns and gin palaces.'

'I already tried that. I understand the crimps were busy last night shanghaiing hands for the *Ophelia*, and I fear Mr Cutler may have been caught in their net.' Madison ran a finger through his thinning hair. 'If it was just one of my hands it wouldn't matter. But my second mate . . .? Men like that are difficult to replace.'

'Oh, I say! What rotten bad timing. If you'd come to me a few hours earlier I could have volunteered my own services – if you'd've accepted them.'

'Of course I would! That's why I came here this afternoon. I'm in a pickle, Mr Killigrew. I've already been stuck in this port for four days; I can't wait any longer.' He leaned across the table and lowered his voice. 'I'll pay you twelve dollars a day.'

'US dollars?' asked Killigrew, and Madison nodded. Killigrew carefully put down his knife and fork and dabbed at his lips with his napkin. 'Mrs Hines, it seems to me I'm being remiss. Unlike myself, Captain Madison here enjoys a glass of wine, in moderation. I wonder if you could fetch us a bottle? No, better still make it champagne, since I'm celebrating my new good fortune.'

'I don't think we have any champagne, Mr Killigrew.'

'Couldn't you send your son out to fetch some?'

'I could if he were here, Mr Killigrew, but I'm afraid he's run off for the day.'

'Oh that *is* a shame . . .'

'I could run out myself and get some, if you wouldn't mind keeping an eye on the place while I'm gone. The wine merchant is just down the road, I wouldn't be gone more than ten minutes.'

'Not at all, Mrs Hines. That would be awfully decent of you.'

She hurried out. Killigrew leaned back in his chair and looked Madison straight in the eye. 'Where are you bound?'

'Cuba, by way of Africa.'

'The Guinea Coast?' Madison nodded. 'You're a blackbirder, aren't you?'

'I kind of gathered last night that you had no principled objections to the trade.'

'In principle no. But in practice . . .? I've been humiliated by the Royal Navy enough as it is, Captain Madison. What if I should be on board your ship when it was stopped by a Royal Navy vessel? As a British citizen they could take me and put me on trial. We have the death penalty for slaving in this country now, you know.'

'But it's never been enforced. Besides, my ship's clerk is a very skilled individual, Mr Killigrew. He can . . . shall we say "arrange" some US papers for you. Not that you'll need them. The *Madge Howlett* is the fastest ship in the Atlantic. There's not a vessel in the Royal Navy that can catch her, not even a steamer. And I'll wager twelve dollars a day is a good deal more than you're being offered for this job on the *Great Britain*.'

'I couldn't tell you until I'd checked the current exchange rate. But there's also the prestige of working for such a well-respected company.'

Madison nodded sadly and for a moment Killigrew feared he might have overplayed it, but then the American looked up with determination in his eye.

'Prestige? Tcha! I know your sort, Mr Killigrew. You're a sailor. One of a long line of sailors, I'll be bound. Which would you prefer? The stuffy, formal atmosphere of a transatlantic steamer with its starched collars, grubby engines, tedious, middle-class passengers with their foolish questions, and a life that's regulated by a strict timetable, repeated again and again, voyage after voyage? Or the life of a fast merchant brig, with a free and easy attitude, no dress code, and the possibility of some excitement?'

'It's a tempting offer, Captain Madison. I can't deny I've a hankering to put the stuffy world of civilised society behind me. But what about you? Are you sure you want an ex-naval officer on board? One who spent two years serving on the West Africa Squadron?'

'That's why I'm so keen to have you in my crew, Mr Killigrew. We've been blackbirding for many years now and we know most of the tricks. But you understand the naval mind. You know the navy's tactics and her ships. You know who the captains are of each ship, and which ones will pursue a slaver to the ends of the earth and which ones will give up after the first couple of hours. And from talking to you last night I got the impression that you'd jump at the chance to use that kind of knowledge against them.

'I'll lay it on the square and on the level for you, Mr Killigrew, because I like to think of myself as a straight-dealing man and if we're going to be working together – which I hope we are – I wouldn't want us to get off on the wrong foot. I've been checking up on you. You had a promising career in the navy until you made one little, tragic mistake, and then they took it all away from you. Well, here's your chance to pay them back. By proving that no matter how many steamers they put in their West Africa Squadron, they'll never end the slave trade. What do you say?'

Killigrew sat back and lit a cheroot, shaking out his match and tossing it into the fireplace. He blew out a long stream of blue-tinged smoke and watched it curl lazily towards the oak beams overhead as if deep in contemplation. 'Twelve dollars a day?'

Madison nodded. 'Half in advance, the rest when we reach

Havana. And if it works out oh-kay then you can stay in my crew for as long as I'm captain of the *Madge Howlett*.'

'Are you sure you trust me that much?'

'I'll be honest with you, Mr Killigrew: no, I'm not. This is only the second time I've spoken to you; and while my instincts tell me I can trust you, I know a man's a fool if he relies on his instincts alone. So I'll tell you straight: you cross me once, boy, and I'll kill you. It's as simple as that.' Madison's eyes glittered as he leaned across the table once more. 'You breathe so much as a single word of our activities to the authorities, then no matter where you run, where you hide, I'll find you. No matter what it takes, I'll track you down and kill you, and as God is my witness you'll be a long time a-dying.'

Killigrew was in no doubt that Madison meant every word of it and was perfectly capable of carrying out his threat, but he managed a smile nonetheless. 'Well! You're certainly candid, I'll say that much for you.'

Madison smiled. 'I don't mean to scare you . . . aw, heck, yes, I *do* mean to scare you. Because if I'm wrong about you, then that's the only guarantee I've got that you'll keep your mouth shut. But something tells me I can trust you.'

'Well then, I hope I can prove myself worthy of your trust,' said Killigrew as the front door opened and the landlady returned with the champagne. 'And here's Mrs Hines, right on cue. Let's drink to our first voyage together, if you don't mind raising your glass with a man drinking coffee.'

Madison only stayed for one small glass of champagne – Killigrew guessed the American was not much of a champagne drinker, but ordering the bottle had been a suitable ruse to get Mrs Hines out of the house so they could talk in private – before he left, promising to send one of his men to help Killigrew with his things. As soon as he had gone, Killigrew settled his account with Mrs Hines and went upstairs to pack his sea-chest. It was a small chest for an officer, being only large enough to contain his sextant, writing equipment, clothes, washing things, and a couple of novels by Dumas, and Virgil's *Aeneid*.

Oh, yes. And his pepperbox, of course.

Finally he sat down, wrote a brief note, and laid it carefully on top of everything else in the chest. It was addressed 'To whom it may concern', inviting the finder to feel free to rifle the chest's contents while assuring him he would not find anything of interest unless he was a fan of Mr Dumas. Then he locked it with the key he wore on a chain around his neck, although he did not doubt there would be someone on board skilled enough to pick the lock so they could examine its contents at the earliest opportunity. He did not expect the presence of the pepperbox to raise too many eyebrows amongst such men.

He was carrying the heavy chest downstairs in both hands when Mrs Hines appeared at the foot of the steps. 'That gentleman's come to help you with your things, Mr Killigrew.'

'That gentleman' was the same squat, muscular man Killigrew had seen Madison talk to in the waterfront tavern the previous night. 'Meester Killigrew?' he rumbled.

'Yes.' Killigrew held out his hand and almost had his fingers crushed to a pulp when the man shook it.

'I am Manoel Duarte, the bosun of the *Madge Howlett*.' He spoke with a thick accent that Killigrew guessed was Portuguese. 'Capitão Madison send me to take you to the ship. You have you things?'

Killigrew indicated the chest he had put down to greet him. Duarte bent over, grasped one of the handles, and hefted it on to his shoulder as effortlessly as if it had been empty and made of paper. 'We go.'

Killigrew tipped his hat to Mrs Hines. 'Thank you for a thoroughly pleasant stay, Mrs Hines. I shall be sure to stay here next time I'm in Liverpool.'

She blushed and curtseyed. 'If you don't like us, tell us. If you do, tell your friends. That's our motto, Mr Killigrew.'

'And a fine one it is too. I shall be sure to recommend you.'

'We go,' insisted Duarte.

'Uh . . . we go,' Killigrew echoed to Mrs Hines, who giggled.

The waterfront was crowded at that time of day, but Killigrew had no difficulty following Duarte through the crush; he carved a path through the sea of bobbing heads like Moses parting the Red Sea.

Killigrew had not recognised the *Madge Howlett* when he had first laid eyes on her a couple of days earlier, which was unfortunate because that was the kind of mistake which might have cost him his life. But although he had a good eye for ships, one Baltimore brig looked pretty much the same as another built to the same specifications, while a simple readjustment of the sails and rigging could change the appearance of a ship entirely, unless one was looking for one ship in particular. Killigrew had been looking for the *Madge Howlett*, so when he had seen that name painted on the stern he'd assumed that was what he had found.

The *Madge Howlett* was a two-masted brig, about a hundred feet from stern to stern, the deck looking uncluttered without as many men or guns as a man-o'-war would have had. Killigrew had already studied her through his telescope, although this was the first time he had seen her close to and he noted with approval that she was in good condition, the brass fittings well polished, the decks holystoned until they shone palest yellow in the spring sunshine, the sails furled neatly under the yards, and the rigging neat and well maintained without any 'dead men' – untidy rope's ends – dangling loose over the sides. It was clear that Madison ran a tight ship; not as tight as a navy vessel, perhaps, but tight nonetheless.

There were perhaps a dozen men at work on deck, preparing to set sail. All had dark, Latinate looks and Killigrew guessed that if there were any genuine ship's papers on board they would prove that the *Madge Howlett* – if that were her real name, which he very much doubted – was in actuality a Cuban or Brazilian vessel.

Madison emerged on to the deck. 'Ah, there you are, Mr Killigrew. Welcome aboard. Now that we have permission to sail we'll be leaving just as soon as the chief mate returns.'

'He's not on board?'

Madison shook his head. 'I sent him down to London on an errand for me. He was due to catch the three o'clock train back, so he should be here within the hour. As soon as we're safely under way I'll have him fill you in on the details of your duties, but basically I'll expect you to take charge of navigation. The rules on board are fairly simple. There's a strict hierarchy on board. It runs from God to me to the chief mate to you to Senhor Duarte here. I expect orders to be carried out promptly and efficiently, and so should you. Do you speak Portuguese?'

'A little.'

'Good. Most of the men speak some English, but they can be a little slow to understand in that language. They're a good bunch on the whole. As far as punishment goes, I don't want to have to undermine you by overruling any of your orders, so if you're not sure of anything I suggest you clear it with me first. If that isn't convenient, you could do a lot worse than allow yourself to be guided by Duarte here. We've been sailing together for over ten years and he has my complete confidence; I suggest you give him yours. You'll get the hang of how I like things run soon enough.' He turned to the boatswain. 'Manoel, perhaps you'd like to show Mr Killigrew to his cabin and then give him a quick guided tour of the ship before we set sail?'

'*Sîm, senhor capitão*,' growled Duarte.

'Thanks.' Madison clapped Duarte on the shoulder and turned back to Killigrew. 'Manoel here may not have much in the way of social graces, but I assure you he's loyal and reliable, and that's all I ask of my men. Supper will be in my stateroom at eight; I'll introduce you to the other ship's officers then. Dress is informal at all times, although I expect certain standards of hygiene from my men which I doubt you'll have difficulty abiding by. Cleanliness is next to Godliness. As for the rest of the men, I dare say you'll get to know them soon enough. Manoel, when you've shown Mr Killigrew around the ship take him to the chart room so he can familiarise himself with the course I've plotted.'

'*Sîm, senhor capitão*.'

Killigrew followed Duarte below deck to his cabin. It was the first time he had ever had a cabin on board ship. He indicated the second cot. 'I'm to share this cabin with the chief mate?' he guessed.

'*Sîm, senhor.*'

'All right. Just put my dunnage down over there, I'll unpack later. Shall we take a look-see at the rest of the ship?'

Killigrew followed Duarte out of the boatswain. 'I might as well leave my hat in the cabin,' he said. 'Wait here, I shan't be a moment.'

Killigrew went back inside the cabin, took off his top hat and placed it on top of his chest. Then he plucked a single hair from his head and stuck it over the catch of the chest so that any attempt to open it would dislodge the hair. Then he went outside and followed Duarte on a guided tour of the ship.

The *Madge Howlett* was little different from any slaver Killigrew had been aboard in terms of layout – officers' quarters below the quarter-deck, stores in the bows, and a large hold running the whole length of the ship – but a good deal cleaner and less noisome. Killigrew doubted its current state would last long once they had slaves on board. The hold was piled high with bales of cotton cloth, rolls of copper wire, the long low shapes of crates of rifles, barrels with the word 'GUNPOWDER' stencilled on their sides, and various other boxes and crates. Killigrew wondered which boxes contained the shackles, handcuffs and padlocks. He also noted about three hundred empty barrels, enough to carry water for all the slaves for the duration of the middle passage, as well as a large stack of timber which could easily be used to make a slave deck.

There was an open hatch with a grating in the deck head, and Killigrew glanced up as a shadow from a man fell through.

'Everything stowed securely?' the man asked, another American. 'Good. That you, Manoel? The cap'n tells me you've got our new second mate with you. Well, stand forward out of the shadows, mister. Let's have a look at you.'

Killigrew took a pace forward and gazed up through the grating at the chief mate. Their eyes locked, and the man's eyes widened as he recognised Killigrew.

'You!' exclaimed Eli Coffin.

# XI:

## Blackbirders

'Hold him fast!' snapped Coffin. 'I'm a-coming down.' He disappeared from sight, and Killigrew at once felt Duarte's massive hands grip him by the arms. He made no attempt to resist; it would have been useless anyway.

It was not until Killigrew had seen Eli Coffin that he realised he had seen the *Madge Howlett* before, albeit with a different name and a different figurehead on her prow. Once he had been given the Coffin connection, he realised at once that she was merely the *Leopardo* under another name.

Coffin's feet clumped down the companion ladder from the forward hatch and a moment later he appeared in the hold. He was not smiling.

'You know this man, Senhor Coffin?' Duarte asked ponderously.

Coffin hawked and spat on the deck. 'Yeah, I know him. He's a goddamned British Officer.'

'An *ex* British Officer,' corrected Madison, entering behind Coffin. 'I take it you two are already acquainted, then?'

'This bastard was on board that navy steamer we led on a wild-goose chase a couple of months ago,' snarled Coffin, glaring at Killigrew with hate-filled eyes. 'What was she called?'

'The *Tisiphone*,' Killigrew offered helpfully.

'It's all right, Manoel,' said Madison. 'You can release Mr Killigrew.'

'You *knew*?' Coffin asked Madison in disbelief.

Madison smiled. 'Mr Killigrew is no longer in Her Majesty's service, Eli. It seems he's been . . . how can I put this? . . . guilty of an indiscretion.'

'The hell he has. You're not serious about having this whoreson on board, are you? He'll betray us to his friends at the first opportunity! He's probably here to spy for his navy!'

Madison shook his head. 'Calm down, Eli. Mr Killigrew here's seen the light. Acts, chapter nine, verse eighteen: "And immediately there fell from his eyes as it had been scales: and he received sight forthwith". It's oh-kay, I've made some enquiries and his story's on the level. I had a difficult enough job persuading him to join us. Don't mind Eli, Mr Killigrew. He hates the English, so don't take it personal. Once you two have had a chance to get to know one another you'll get along fine.'

'I'm sure,' Killigrew said drily.

'Don't count on it,' snarled Coffin.

'You'll get along with him, Eli, or I'll know the reason why. You've known me long enough to know that when I've made up my mind, it stays that way. Killigrew replaces that good-for-nothing Cutler until I say otherwise, you hear me?'

'Aye, aye, sir,' Coffin said surlily.

'Oh-kay, let's get to work. There's plenty to be done before we set sail. You've seen the ship, Mr Killigrew? Good. Take him to the chart room, Manoel. Eli, you come with me.' Madison headed out of the hold and Coffin made as if to follow him, but turned back to address Killigrew in a low, menacing voice.

'Now you listen to me, you Limey sonuvabitch. I don't know what your game is, but if you're on the level then I'm a Dutchman's uncle.' He touched Killigrew under the jaw with the coils of his whip. The bull-hide felt cold, coarse and dry, like the scales of a snake. 'Sooner or later you're going to slip up, and when you do I'll be waiting.' He turned away and went out of the hold, chuckling to himself in anticipation.

Duarte took Killigrew to the chart room. It was well ordered, and the relevant charts for their forthcoming voyage were easy enough to find. The route was straightforward: out into the Irish Sea, through St George's Channel, around Land's End, across the mouth of the Bay of Biscay, past the coasts of Spain and Portugal and south-sou'-west to the coast of Africa. The course veered well away from the Guinea Coast, presumably to evade the Royal Navy vessels which patrolled off-shore, and terminated vaguely somewhere near Sierra Leone, as if Madison had not been bothered to think that far ahead; evidently he did not trust Killigrew enough to reveal the precise location of their destination before they had even left port.

He made his way up on deck to where Madison and Coffin stood on the quarter-deck close by the helm. 'Ah, Mr Killigrew,' said Madison. 'You approve of the course I've plotted?' he asked with a smile.

'Yes, sir,' said Killigrew. 'Although it seems to be incomplete . . . ?'

Madison's smile did not alter. 'Our destination is a month's sailing away. We'll concern ourselves with that nearer the time. All ready, Mr Duarte?'

'Aye, aye, *senhor capitão*.'

'Then we'll waste no more time. Perhaps you'd care to take her out, Mr Killigrew?'

'Very well, sir.' Killigrew guessed that Madison was testing him: not to see if he was up to the task, if he had doubted that for a moment then he would never have taken him on as his second mate; more to assess his style of ship-handling – and crew-handling. 'Let go the bow-fast!' When the crew did not obey at once, he repeated his order in Portuguese, but still they exchanged glances of mocking bewilderment as if Killigrew's command of the language was wanting, which he knew it was not. It was not just the master of the *Madge Howlett* who was testing the new second mate.

'You are responsible for discipline on board this vessel, are you not, Bosun?' Killigrew asked Duarte.

'Yes.'

'Then see to it that my orders are obeyed promptly,' Killigrew said mildly.

Duarte glanced at Madison, who nodded almost imperceptibly. 'You heard Senhor Killigrew!' Duarte roared at the hands. 'Let slip the bow-fast!'

'Hoist the jib and let fall the foresail,' ordered Killigrew, glancing sidelong at Madison. The master was smiling faintly, indicating approval of Killigrew's handling of the reluctant seamen. The brig's bows turned away from the pier. 'Now let go the stern-fast. Fore braces, tacks and sheets. Meet her,' he added to the helmsman, who nodded and span the helm to stop her head from coming around any further.

The mooring lines cast off, the *Madge Howlett* slowly gathered way, moving out from the dock into the Mersey. The tide was approaching the high-water mark so there was no appreciable current, and the wind coming in from the brig's port quarter made her easy to handle.

'Port the helm . . . Ease her . . . Helm amidships . . . Steady as she goes.'

'Steady it is, sir.'

The actual task of conning the brig into the channel was child's play for Killigrew, and with a fresh breeze blowing they had soon passed New Brighton, the North Fort and the South Fort, crossed the bar, and emerged into Liverpool Bay. They hoisted all canvas, sailing close-hauled towards the setting sun. At seven bells Madison ordered Coffin to take the watch and, after reminding Killigrew supper was at eight, went below.

Killigrew returned to his cabin for a quick shave, a change of shirt and a brush-up before dinner. The hair he had left on his sea-chest had been dislodged, but it had been unnecessary: the searcher, prevented from concealing his search by an impulsive rage, had screwed Killigrew's mocking note into a tight ball. Somehow he knew it was Coffin who had done the searching. There was a feeling of violence about the chief mate, and not very deep below the surface, either. Of all the men on the *Madge Howlett* – including the chunky Duarte – Killigrew feared Coffin most of all.

Making his way to Madison's cabin he encountered a small man, dressed as smartly as his obviously cheap clothes would allow, with a sallow complexion and a bulging, watery-looking pair of eyes. 'You must be Senhor Killigrew,' said the man. He had a nervousness about him, and a voice like egg-white poured over sandpaper.

'If you insist,' Killigrew responded lightly. 'I fear you have the advantage over me, Mr . . . ?'

'Pereira. Cirurgião Antônio Pereira, at your service.' He extended his hand, and Killigrew shook it. It was like touching the petals of an orchid, the feel of clammy, dead flesh. If Pereira was the ship's surgeon, Killigrew was determined not to fall ill on this voyage.

He gestured at the door to Madison's cabin. 'Shall we go in?'

'To be sure, to be sure.' Pereira raised a hand, hesitated, swallowed hard, and tapped gently.

'Come in, Pereira,' Madison called from inside. 'I'd recognise your weak-livered scratching at my door any day. And Mr Killigrew,' he added, seeing Killigrew enter behind the surgeon. 'Come in, gentlemen. Take a seat.'

Coffin was already there, seated at the table. There were

only four of them to dine that night, which was just as well for the table only seated four; there was not room for a bigger one in the cramped cabin. One wall was dominated by the window which gazed out from the stern, while the remaining three were decorated with samplers: 'They that go down to the sea in ships, that do business in great waters; These see the work of the LORD, and his wonders in the deep – Psalm 107, 23-24'; 'It is good for a man that he bear the yoke in his youth – Lamentations iii, 27'; 'Judge not, that ye be not judged – Matthew vii, 1'.

Killigrew took them in as he seated himself opposite Pereira. The samplers reminded him of the sampler on the wall of Eulalia's bedroom, which reminded him of Eulalia, and he felt a fleeting pang as he thought of how much he would have preferred to be with her than in the company of these murderous rogues. He forced himself to put all thoughts of Eulalia from his mind: he would need his wits about him if he was going to stay alive for the next few months.

A black steward – Killigrew wondered if he were a slave or a freeman – stood by with a bottle in one hand, and as soon as everyone was seated he began to pour out the wine: first Madison, then Pereira, then Coffin. When it came to Killigrew's turn, he almost forgot to put his hand over his glass. He suddenly realised he had not had anything alcoholic for several hours, and regretted not being able to drink now. He wondered how long it would be before he could have another drink, and the thought made his mouth water.

'What's the matter, Killigrew?' sneered Coffin. 'Not drinking? You're missing out. It's a good year. What are you afraid of? There are no little girls for you to run down out here in the Irish Sea.'

'All right, Eli,' growled Madison, although secretly Killigrew welcomed Coffin's taunting: it would make it easier for him to abstain, if by doing so he would be disappointing a heartfelt wish in Coffin that he should fall off the wagon.

But the chief mate would not be silenced so easily. 'Or maybe he's afraid that he'll get drunk and let something slip. Like what he's *really* doing on board this ship.'

'I said *that will do*,' Madison said firmly, and Coffin lapsed into a sullen silence. 'Mr Killigrew will have a cup of coffee,' Madison told the steward, who nodded and went out. When he returned with a pot and a china cup and placed them in front of Killigrew, the latter hesitated before drinking. If they wanted to poison him, he had given them a perfect opportunity: it could be doctored without the others having to drink it; and the bitter taste would mask any poison. But then, if they wanted him dead he had given them all the opportunity they would ever need simply by coming aboard.

Madison turned to Killigrew with an apologetic smile. 'I noticed you admiring my wife's handiwork when you came in, Mr Killigrew.'

'The samplers?'

Madison nodded. 'A woman's touch. Are you a married man yourself?'

'I do not have that pleasure,' said Killigrew.

'That's a great pity,' said Madison. 'A man should be married. Proverbs, chapter five, verse eighteen: "Let thy fountain be blessed: and rejoice with the wife of thy youth."'

'Since we're playing at Bible quotes, Cap'n, I have one for you,' said Coffin. 'From the Book of Jeremiah, I think: "Can the Ethiopian change his skin, or the leopard his spots?"'

That pointed barb effectively stifled any further attempts at polite small talk at the supper table, but service as an officer in the Royal Navy prepared a man for many things, and stilted table talk in an uncomfortable atmosphere was one of them. The steward served them a simple but hearty meal of beef, carrots and potatoes and Killigrew tucked in with vigour, apparently oblivious to Coffin's hostility and the discomfort of Madison and Pereira, enthusiastically asking the steward to pass on his compliments to the cook. Finally Coffin muttered that he had had enough and went below.

'You'll have to forgive Mr Coffin, Mr Killigrew,' said Madison. 'As I said, he hates the English.'

'Any particular reason?'

'Just family tradition. His grandfather was killed at the battle of Trafalgar.'

'On which side?'

'The British side. Against his will.' In those days it had been the habit of the Royal Navy, forgetful of the United States' new-found independence, to stop American merchant ships and press their seamen into service aboard British men-o'-war; this had been the main cause of the War of 1812. 'But he's a good man.'

'A good man? Or a good seaman? The two are not necessarily one and the same, in my experience.'

'Aye, true enough. I'd say he's both, when he doesn't let his prejudice get the better of him. You'd be wise to try to win him over, Mr Killigrew. He's not a good man to have for an enemy.'

'You speak from personal experience?'

Madison chuckled. 'There's not a man who's experienced Eli's enmity who's lived to tell the tale,' he said. Killigrew, sensing the captain spoke the plain truth, felt a shudder run down his spine. 'Fortunately for me, Eli and I have always been friends.'

'Until now?'

'Oh, we don't always see eye to eye, but we can usually agree to differ.' Madison snipped the ends off a couple of Havana cigars and handed one to Killigrew. 'I don't know. Maybe he *is* right about you. What do you say?'

'I say you should trust your own judgement first.'

'Aye, well, I've not yet made up my mind on that score.

You've still got to prove yourself to me, Mr Killigrew. But help us pick up our cargo from the Guinea Coast and get it across the Atlantic to the slave markets of Havana, and perhaps then you'll have my trust.'

'I hope I can win it. I'm not so sure about Mr Coffin's. I never was one for visiting the sins of the fathers upon the sons myself. My own father was killed in a fight with the Ottoman fleet, but that didn't stop me from fighting with the Turks in Syria.'

'I understand you distinguished yourself considerably in that campaign?'

'I only did my duty.'

'In support of a crumbling Empire which your father once fought against?'

'You should judge each nation by the cause it is fighting for at any one moment in history, Captain Madison. My father fought for Greek independence. I fought for the freedom of the Lebanon from the Egyptians. The Lebanese may have had no great love for their Ottoman overlords but, believe me, they preferred being ruled from Constantinople to the rule of the viceroy in Alexandria.'

'Your father fought as a mercenary?'

'As a sailor of fortune. He served Admiral Cochrane against Napoleon's navies, and when Napoleon was beaten they went wherever there was a just cause to be fought for: Chilean and Brazilian independence, then for the Greeks.'

'And you wanted to follow in his footsteps? Is that why you went to sea?'

'Yes. What about you? What made you go to sea?'

'The same thing as you, the same thing as Mr Coffin. We followed in our father's footsteps. Mr Coffin and I served together aboard a whaler until we realised the advantages of blackbirding.'

'And they are?'

'Money, Mr Killigrew,' said Madison. 'I know the Good Lord taught us that love of money is the root of all evil, but a man must make a living. Besides, it's charitable work, too. As you said yourself, we're rescuing the niggers from a life of ignorance and Godlessness and taking them to a new life in the New World.'

Killigrew forced a smile on to his lips to conceal his revulsion. 'Of course,' he said. Madison could be dangerously likeable at times, and Killigrew was glad when he expressed such opinions. It would make it easier for him when the time came for him to bring Madison down.

'I say, Sir George!'

Emerging from the portals of the Reform Club with one of his parliamentary colleagues, Sir George Grafton heard his name called out and glanced down Pall Mall to see Rear-Admiral Sir Charles Napier limping towards him. 'Oh, Christ,' he muttered. 'Look out, William, it's that lunatic Napier. I thought we'd seen the last of him.'

Unsmiling as ever, his companion merely inclined his head with a dour expression.

Sir George pasted a broad smile on to his face. 'Why, Sir Charles! Good morning to you, sir. May I be one of the first to congratulate you on your recent appointment to the command of the Channel Fleet?' *God knows, I worked hard enough to get you sent back to sea so you'd keep your interfering nose out of parliamentary business.*

'Why, thank you, Sir George, thank you. Although I must say, it did come rather unexpectedly. And just when I was starting to find my feet in the House of Commons, too.' He chuckled. 'You know, if I didn't know better, I'd say one of my political enemies was trying to get me out of the way.'

'Nonsense, Sir Charles. There are no enemies in the House of Commons. Only adversaries.'

'I fear my command of the finer intricacies of Shakespeare's tongue is not up to the task of discerning the difference. But then as you know, I'm just a simple, bluff old sailor at heart.'

*In a pig's ear*, thought Sir George, and indicated his companion. 'You've met Mr Gladstone, I take it?'

'I know of his father,' said Napier. Mr Gladstone senior owned a plantation in the West Indies and profited from the trade in apprenticed labour, shipping coolies from India in conditions little better than slave ships.

'Mr Gladstone is one of the rising stars of our party,' said Grafton.

'Our paths have crossed,' said Napier. 'Although not yet our swords.'

'And nor will they ever,' sniffed Mr Gladstone junior. 'I have always felt that duelling is the kind of childish behaviour that gentlemen should avoid. And, I might furthermore add, it is contrary to the laws of our nation.'

'I was merely speaking metaphorically, Mr Gladstone. Of our parliamentary swords.'

'Oh,' sniffed Gladstone.

Napier turned back to Grafton. 'Sir George, I wonder if I might have a word with you *in camera*.'

'By all means, but I pray you be brief. I have important business to conduct . . .'

'As have I. Channel fleets don't run themselves, you know.'

'You must excuse me, Mr Gladstone. I'll speak further on this matter with you at a later date.'

'I shall look forward to it,' said Gladstone. 'Good day to you, Sir George, Sir Charles.' He doffed his top hat to them, and wandered off in the direction of the Haymarket.

'Now then, Sir Charles. How may I be of assistance to you?'

'Shall we walk a little way?' suggested Napier. 'It's a

splendid morning, and the exercise will do us good.'

'As you will.'

The two of them set off down Pall Mall towards Trafalgar Square, Napier limping. 'I'm just trying to tie up my parliamentary affairs before I hoist my flag on HMS *St Vincent*,' he explained. 'As grateful as I am finally to be given an important command, I am a little concerned that I shall be absent from the House of Commons at a not-entirely opportune moment. Now, while I realise that we have not always seen eye to eye over the past few years, I know I can rely on your honesty and decency as a gentleman to fight my corner for me in my absence.'

'Why, Sir Charles, I should be delighted to. And may I add that I am honoured that you should choose me for such a task?'

'Well, I have so many affairs that need to be looked after in my absence, I'm trying to spread them as thinly as possible. Most of my trusted friends have been given my more important matters to deal with, but there are still one or two insignificant ones that nonetheless would benefit from having a fatherly eye kept on them.'

'Indeed?' Sir George said drily.

'I dare say you recall Lieutenant Christopher Killigrew?'

'Ah, yes. That unfortunate young naval officer who disgraced himself so . . . er . . . disgracefully. Drinking, I believe, and being responsible for the death of a little girl.'

'That's the way it looked,' agreed Napier. 'Sir George, before we proceed any further in this matter, I must ask you to keep what I am about to tell you in the uttermost and strictest confidence. You must swear not to reveal this to another living soul until the time is right, on your word of honour as a gentleman.'

Grafton was intrigued. 'You have it, by God.'

'Mr Killigrew did not kill that child.'

'But . . . did he not confess to it?'

'A ruse the lieutenant and I cooked up between us,' Napier explained smugly. 'We wanted to disgrace him.'

'I'm not sure I understand. This fellow Killigrew and yourself cooked up a calumny to blacken his name, with his consent? But to what object?'

'Through my work with the Slave Trade Department at the Foreign Office I have lately become aware that there is someone in this country who is living off the profits of that most evil trade. And, I fear, a senior member of the British Establishment. Perhaps even a member of the House of Commons.'

'That is the most outrageous suggestion I have ever heard!' blustered Sir George. 'Do you have any evidence whatsoever to back up this assertion?'

'No. But I am relying on Mr Killigrew to provide me with it. That is why we had him disgraced, you see. As a private individual he was able to do what he could not as an officer of the Royal Navy: take ship aboard a slave vessel.'

'No slave vessel would ever take an ex-naval officer on as a member of its crew.'

'One already has. Even as we speak, Mr Killigrew is bound for the Guinea Coast on board the *Madge Howlett*, a suspected slave vessel. I have every confidence in that brave young man's ability to expose the name of the man who is financing the voyage.'

'The *Madge Howlett*? I cannot say I am familiar with the vessel. How many other people know about this scheme of yours?'

'No one. Except yourself, now, and once again I must entreat you to keep this matter in the strictest confidence. If word should get to the slavers that Mr Killigrew is acting as a spy aboard their vessel then his life would be imperilled.'

'To be sure, to be sure.'

Napier sighed. 'And that is why I need your help, Sir George. Both Mr Killigrew's trial and court-martial were real enough, I fear, though based only on his confession. I have promised that when he returns he will be exonerated and both his rank and good name restored. But if I'm with the Channel Fleet there will be no one in Britain who can speak up for him.'

'Say no more. You may rest assured that if . . . I do beg your pardon, *when* . . . Mr Killigrew returns, he shall have the full influence of my position to support him.'

'Thank you so much, Sir George.' Napier pumped Grafton's hand vigorously. 'I knew I could rely on you.'

'And now if you'll excuse me I have urgent business to attend to. Good day to you, Sir Charles.'

'What are you reading?' growled Madison, turning away from the helmsman.

'The Good Book,' said Killigrew, lifting up his Bible so that Madison could see the title on the spine.

'I never figured *you* for a religious man, Mr Killigrew. Not that I disapprove, of course. Quite the opposite.'

Killigrew smiled beatifically. '"Happy is the man that findeth wisdom, and the man that getteth understanding . . ."'

'". . . For the merchandise of it is better than the merchandise of silver, and the gain thereof than fine gold",' continued Madison. '"She is more precious than rubies: and all the things thou canst desire are not to be compared unto her." Proverbs, chapter three, verses thirteen to fifteen.'

'He's just trying to curry favour,' sneered Coffin. 'Any fool can read the Bible.'

'Maybe you should try it, Mr Coffin,' Madison said drily.

Coffin shrugged. He and Madison had sailed together for many years and if they disagreed over the issue of Killigrew's trustworthiness, then in most other respects they were of one mind, as Killigrew had not been surprised to discover over the past few weeks.

As soon as the *Madge Howlett* had been well out into the Atlantic they had radically changed the brig's whole appearance by the simple expedient of rearranging the spars and rigging; changing the figurehead and painting out the name '*Madge Howlett*' and replacing it with '*Leopardo*' was merely the icing on the cake. After that the voyage had been as dull and uneventful as only a sea voyage could be. Killigrew's duties kept him busy. He was in charge of the boatswain's locker and it was his job to issue spun-yarn, marline, marline-spikes and serving boards to the hands. Although he was next in seniority after Coffin, there was a wide gulf between the chief mate and the second mate. Killigrew was expected to go aloft with the rest of the crew to reef and furl the topsails, and yet in spite of this he was expected to maintain his dignity before them in the interests of discipline. But in this respect his years of service in the Royal Navy put him in good stead: as a midshipman he had been expected to go aloft with the hands, and the skills of reefing and handling the sails soon came back to him. It had always been a tricky balance, maintaining one's superior dignity while working alongside men, but a good officer knew how to turn it to his advantage by showing he was not ashamed to get his hands dirty without making any pretence at being just one of the lads. Once again he found he was neither one thing nor the other, but it was a position he was growing accustomed to.

Even though he shared a cabin with Coffin he was spared the chief mate's hostility, for on the whole the two of them lived a box-and-cox existence, one working while the other slept. When they did encounter one another, at first Coffin would growl some barbed comment, trying to provoke Killigrew into a fight. But Killigrew did not rise to the bait; in truth he welcomed Coffin's hatred, for it meant that Madison did not suspect him; if he had, then he would have taken the chief mate aside and ordered him to mask his hostility. After a while Coffin grew bored of needling Killigrew, or at least ran out of barbed comments to make, and settled for a growled acknowledgement. But his hatred remained unabated, as the occasional venomous glance he shot at Killigrew bore witness. Still, at least they made no attempt to poison him or slit his throat while he slept, and after a while Killigrew knew he could allow his vigilance to drop a little.

The days slipped by one after another as the waves were broken beneath the *Leopardo*'s prow and left churned by her wake; the future turned into the past, and the days became weeks, the weeks marked off by Madison conducting a prayer meeting on deck for the crew every Sunday morning. Attendance was compulsory. Nearly three weeks after they had sailed from Liverpool they entered the Tropics, and a few days later they made landfall at São Tiago in the Cape Verde Islands to take on board fresh water and fruit and vegetables. The *Leopardo* and her crew seemed well known there, and although it must have been obvious that she was a slaver no one made any attempt to stop her. Without the transatlantic trade the Cape Verde Islands would die, and for the moment the greater part of the transatlantic trade meant the slave trade. Killigrew realised all over again that the slave trade would never be crushed as long as men could make money out of it.

Perhaps the answer was to make it too expensive a trade to carry on.

From São Tiago they steered south-east, angling in towards the Guinea Coast, and that afternoon Killigrew was making his way to the boatswain's locker when he glanced in the galley as he passed. He was surprised to see the cook reading.

Like any cook on any ship Killigrew had ever been on, the cook was known only as 'Doc'. A short, wiry but broad-shouldered slave somewhere in his mid-twenties, with skin the colour of mahogany, Doc seemed to accept his status cheerfully. He played the guitar during his off-watches, sometimes a seaman-like shanty for the benefit of his shipmates, sometimes a haunting Spanish air which added a kind of beauty to the long watches of the night. He was always free for a chat whenever Killigrew popped into the galley for a light in the middle of the night watch, although so far he had failed to impress Killigrew with anything approaching mental acuity. Killigrew had met educated free slaves on the London lecture circuit, uneducated slaves on the Guinea Coast, African slaves and black seamen, and his experience was broad enough to suggest that those ethnologists who claimed that black people were mentally inferior to whites was so much gammon. But just as there were intelligent whites and foolish whites, there were intelligent blacks and foolish blacks. In Doc's case, there seemed to be no getting away from it: he was just plain thick.

So when Killigrew saw Doc reading, he was surprised to discover that the cook knew how. As he approached the galley, Doc quickly put the volume aside and placed a pan over it to hide it.

'Good afternoon, Doc,' Killigrew said cheerfully.

Doc grinned broadly and rolled his eyes like any Ethiopian minstrel. 'Why, good afternoon, mas'er.'

'What were you reading?'

'Reading, mas'er?'

Killigrew tried to reach past and lift the pan off the book, but Doc moved to one side to block his path. Killigrew tried to reach past him on the other side, but again Doc moved to block his path, still grinning inanely. The two of them continued this comic ballet in the cramped confines of the galley for a few seconds more, until Killigrew feinted to the left and then lunged past the cook on the right. He lifted the pan and seized up the book: Shelley's *Prometheus Unbound.*

Doc actually looked ashamed.

'Heady stuff,' said Killigrew.

'Why, I can't make head nor tail of it myself, mas'er. Mr Tristão, he been learning me to read and all, but I ain't a good learner, nossir.'

Killigrew flicked through the pages until a couplet leaped out at him, and he read it out loud: '"Kingly conclaves stern and cold/Where blood with guilt is bought and sold."'

'I don't know what it means, mas'er, but that sho'nuff pretty,' said Doc.

Killigrew gave him back the book. 'Are you happy on board this ship, Doc?'

'Happy, mas'er? Why shouldn't I be happy? Mas'er Madison, he hardly ever beats me, and the others treat me good. 'Cepting that Mas'er Coffin . . .'

There was a commotion outside the galley and Killigrew left Doc to his cooking, emerging to see Duarte dragging one of the hands up the companionway to the forward hatch. Killigrew followed them up on deck.

The man staggered, partly because of Duarte's rough handling but also because he seemed to have limited control of his own legs. The man giggled at Duarte's curses, and the more Duarte cursed him the more the man giggled. At last, when the boatswain had dragged him the length of the deck, he threw him down at Madison's feet.

'Drunk, *senhor capitão*,' said Duarte.

Seeing Madison standing grim-faced over him, the man stopped giggling and the light of fear shone in his eyes as he realised how perilous his situation was. His name was Nicolau Tristão and he had a wife and baby son waiting for him in Maranhão. Killigrew had not wanted to get to know the hands other than their names: the names of men he would be sending to prison if all went well, or to their graves if anything went wrong. He did not want to know about Susana and little Rico waiting at home for a husband and father who might never return. But you could not spend weeks on board ship with men without getting to know something about them. About how they had gone to sea, driven by starvation or shanghaied by crimps, or even willingly in the hope of adventure and riches.

'I don't abhor alcohol on this vessel, Mr Killigrew,' said Madison. 'Unlike your navy, I believe in treating men like equals. If I am allowed to drink, there is no reason why they should not enjoy the same pleasure. But I do abhor drunkenness.'

'Isn't that asking for trouble?' asked Killigrew. 'The one generally leads to the other.'

'I treat my men like adults, Mr Killigrew, and expect them to exert their own judgement from time to time. But tell me, what would you do with this man if you were in your navy?'

'It's not my navy any more,' Killigrew reminded him, and then continued cautiously, 'but that would depend upon the captain. There are some men who would have him flogged to within an inch of his life. And a few who would flog him beyond.'

'And you?'

'On my ship I wouldn't allow men to drink any more than their daily ration of rum. If they exceeded it – and sailors always seem to be able to exceed it – then I would hang them upside down over the side and dunk them into the sea a few times to sober them up. A flogged man cannot work.'

'And a man who cannot trust himself to stay sober cannot be trusted at all. Mr Coffin, show Mr Killigrew why there are so few cases of drunkenness on board the *Leopardo*.'

Coffin grinned. 'With pleasure,' he said, taking a crowbar from where it was clipped alongside a boat hook.

Duarte hoisted Tristão to his feet and left him standing

there. The sailor had sobered up with remarkable rapidity and he turned to Madison with tears in his eyes. '*Por favor, senhor capitão* . . . I will never be drunk on duty again, I swear it . . .'

'Damn right you won't,' snarled Coffin, circling Tristão while gently tapping the crowbar against the palm of his left hand. The sailor tried to turn to face him, but Coffin put a hand on his shoulder and span him back to face away. Then he smashed the crowbar across the sailor's kidneys.

Tristão cried out and sank to his knees, but the punishment had only just begun. A blow to the head or neck from that iron bar might have killed him at once, but Coffin was careful not to deliver such a blow: he wanted to make this last.

The bar swung down again and Killigrew winced as he heard the distinct sound of a rib cracking. Under different circumstances he would not have hesitated to intervene, but it suddenly occurred to him that Madison and Coffin had been waiting for an opportunity like this ever since they had set out from Liverpool. They were testing him once again, wondering if he had the callousness in his heart to stand by and watch a man being beaten to death. Seeing the other men on board going about their duties as if this was a not-infrequent occurrence, Killigrew tried to display the same nonchalance.

Coffin continued to swing the bar expertly, breaking Tristão's arms and legs. Duarte might have been a more suitable man to inflict the punishment, but Coffin was too obviously enjoying it.

'Proverbs, chapter thirteen, verse twenty-four,' said Madison. '"He that spareth his rod hateth his son: but he that loveth him chasteneth him betimes."'

Splintered bones burst out through the skin and blood ran across the pale deck. Killigrew felt sick and wondered when Coffin would stop. For a while it seemed as if the chief mate would not cease until he had beaten Tristão to death, but then he stopped abruptly: he had other plans for this man. He ordered Duarte to have a rope looped about Tristão's ankles, and then the sailor was hoisted from one of the yards on the foremast and swung out over the ship's side. He screamed in agony and terror. They dangled the man less than a foot above the waves, his blood dripping into the blue sea.

Those crew who were not engaged in other duties crowded the rail to watch. They were laughing and joking, betting with each other as to how long it would take, but Killigrew could see that the laughter was forced. They knew that a similar fate awaited them if they made a mistake.

As it waited for Killigrew.

The sharks did not take long to arrive. They had no difficulty keeping up with the ship, their dark blue-grey fins cleaving effortlessly through the water. One burst out of the water, jaws snapping, and narrowly missed Tristão before crashing back down into the waves.

Tristão screamed. He was blubbering in terror now, pleading for Madison to forgive him. But Madison was not even paying any attention to him, instead discussing something with the helmsman. Killigrew wondered which was the more repulsive, Madison's indifference or Coffin's enjoyment.

By glancing at Madison, Killigrew was mercifully spared from witnessing the end. There was a splash and a cheer, and when he glanced back Tristão's head had been bitten clean off at the neck. Blood gushed from the torso. Killigrew choked back the bile that rose to his gorge.

The corpse was brought in to the ship's side and cut loose. The sharks closed in and tore the body to pieces. Coffin indicated the pool of blood on the deck. 'Have that mess cleaned up,' he ordered Duarte.

'You see, few of my men try to thwart my will,' Madison told Killigrew. 'And no one does it more than once.'

'You should be careful,' Killigrew told him with a beguiling smile. 'There's a first time for everything.'

Madison's own smile did not falter, although he knitted his eyebrows. 'Not on this ship, Mr Killigrew.'

Killigrew knew he could not afford to look too shocked by what had happened so he remained on deck for a while, fighting the urge to go below and wash the taste of bile from his mouth. After about half an hour had passed, he went down to his cabin, stopping off at the ship's barometer to check the atmospheric pressure. It had dropped alarmingly in a short space of time.

'Looks like we're in for a storm,' he remarked to no one in particular.

# XII:

## Force Twelve

If Killigrew had had a farthing for every old sea dog who had told him that the sea was like a woman and needed to be respected by those that would earn their living from her, he would have had enough money to buy himself several pounds of sea salt. He could only presume that they had known some pretty frightening women. He had known plenty of women – and men, for that matter – whose wrath could be unnerving, but he had yet to meet the human being whose ire could even begin to match that of an angry sea. If Congrieve had been right when he had claimed that Hell had no fury like a woman scorned, then Hell was an afternoon boating on the Thames on a sunny summer's day compared to a storm at sea.

He had endured cyclones in the Indian Ocean and typhoons in the China Seas, and the one thing his experience had taught him was that the sea did not care if you respected it: when it made up its mind to destroy you, you were going to go down whether you liked it or not.

But there were certain precautions one could take to stave off the worst, and as the sky became overcast and the wind backed from south-east to north the crew of the *Leopardo* battened down the hatches, cleared the decks, made fast everything that could be made fast, and took in all canvas except the foresail and the main topsail, both of which were close-reefed.

The wind hovered around ten knots – force three on the Beaufort scale, barely a moderate breeze – with a gentle swell running under the *Leopardo*, but it was the calm before the storm and Killigrew knew it could not last. 'What do you think?' Madison asked him and Coffin.

Killigrew knew that a seasoned mariner like Madison would already have made his mind up about what to do next, but was looking for confirmation. 'It looks like she's coming up out of the south-east,' he said. 'If we're not careful we'll get caught in the dangerous quadrant.' A tropical revolving storm in the northern hemisphere revolved anti-clockwise, and a ship caught in the dangerous quadrant was in danger of being blown into its path.

Coffin nodded without reluctance, his hatred and mistrust of Killigrew and everything to do with him held in abeyance in the face of the coming danger. 'There's a slim chance we might make it back to São Tiago, but I wouldn't risk it. Best we run with the weather and try to get on her good side. If she catches us all we can do is turn into the seas and hope for the best.'

Madison nodded. 'Steer south-west,' he told the helmsman. 'Better break out the oilskins,' he added to Duarte. 'When this bitch hits she's going to hit fast and heavy.'

Even though Killigrew was on the lookout for clues to the coming storm's ferocity, he was caught out by the abruptness with which the sky turned dark. All of a sudden leaden clouds boiled up out of the south-east, and the first spots of rain fell on the sea, fat drops which pattered heavily on the oilskins they all wore. The sky was so dark it might have been twilight, although it was barely five o'clock and at that time of year in those latitudes it should still have been bright. Then the wind hit them, snapping at the sails and driving the rain hard against their backs. The creaking of the timbers grew ever louder as the masts and spars laboured under the incessant pressure, and the wind screamed through the thrumming rigging.

'Reduce sail,' ordered Coffin. 'Reefed foresail and reefed mainstay sail only.'

The wind increased steadily over the next two hours while the sky grew blacker. The gravid clouds were so low it seemed as if one only had to shin to the very top of the mainmast and reach up to touch them. The *Leopardo* scudded along with the wind full behind her. At first the gentle swell seemed unaffected and the brig rode the waves easily, but by seven o'clock the seas increased in size and she started to pitch. Killigrew watched the compass and the dog-vane: when the wind started to come from due north he would know they were clear of the dangerous quadrant.

The wind whipped Killigrew's oilskins against his limbs and forced him to lean back into it to maintain his balance. Its noise rose to an ear-splitting shriek for a while and then all at once fell to a low, eerie moaning, although its speed continued to rise: sixty knots gusting to ninety, force twelve – a hurricane.

'Furl those staysails!' Madison had to shout through his speaking trumpet to make himself heard above the wind. Killigrew was not the most imaginative of men, but even he could not help thinking it sounded like the souls of mariners drowned at sea singing a dirge for those soon to join them. As the hands struggled to furl the staysails, one of them was ripped from its fastenings and whipped out to sea. A stay slashed across the face of one of the topmen and he fell to the deck with a scream which was sharply cut short.

'Cut it loose!' Coffin roared to the men trying to furl the other staysail. They would lose that one too, but better that than lose the whole mast. The topmen gladly complied and climbed down from the rigging.

The man who had fallen to the deck was not dead. Duarte ordered two of the men to take him down below to Pereira in the sick bay, although what that gentleman was supposed to do for the seaman – whose back was clearly broken – was beyond Killigrew.

The seas rose to forty feet and started to break over the *Leopardo*'s stern. Killigrew braced himself as the water on the deck surged between his legs. It ran out through the scuppers, but not quickly enough for his liking. 'All hands to the bilge pump!' he ordered.

As the seas increased in height they came closer together, thus steepening between crest and trough. As each wave broke over the brig's stern she laboured to rise over the crest. As the waves passed under her she slipped easily down the back of the wave, her stern pounding the trough with a shudder which ran the whole length of the ship; then the next sea would break over her and they would go through it again, each time worse than the last. There was nothing they could do now but keep pumping out the bilges, hang on for dear life, and pray.

Forked lightning shattered the sky, like bright limelight behind cracked, black-painted glass, but the rumble of thunder was masked by the wind's ululating threnody. The gale blew the rain at such an angle it was impossible to tell where the rain ended and the spume began. Water foamed and boiled across the deck. After a while it did not even break, remaining grey as it slid waist-deep the length of the ship. Killigrew could only marvel that such a delicate vessel still floated under the onslaught, although he knew it was only a matter of time.

He began to consider the possibility of his imminent death. He found he could face it with an equanimity which surprised him. He felt a pang at the thought of never seeing Eulalia again in this world, but apart from that he had little to lose. He thought of the Chinese he had met, with their philosophy of 'joss': either he would survive the storm, or he wouldn't –

it was as simple as that. There was little he could do about it and no point whatsoever in worrying: now his fate was in the hands of the gods.

The *Leopardo* was lifted on another crest and exposed to the full fury of the wind. It was like a living thing, full of rage and hatred and determined to sink this ship which defied its capricious will. It slammed into Killigrew's body and would have knocked him off his feet if he had not been gripping the rail tightly. He heard a shout behind him and turned his head, tears coming at once to his eyes as the wind stung them.

Coffin had raised his face to the black, lightning-slashed sky and shook his fist at it. As the brig slipped down into the next trough, sheltering them from the worst of the wind, Killigrew could just catch his words: 'Come on, you bastard! Do your worst! I'm ready for ye!'

'Don't you think that's rather asking for trouble?' Killigrew asked with a wan smile. But Coffin could not hear him above the noise.

Incredibly, conditions worsened. More incredibly, the *Leopardo* stayed afloat. But she could not take much more of this pounding. Killigrew remembered an old rhyme he had heard as a child from the fishermen of Falmouth: 'Long foretold, long last; short notice, soon past.' Experience had taught him there was truth in those words whether one encountered a storm off Lizard Point or a typhoon in the South China Sea. This tornado had risen quickly, yet after four hours it still showed no sign of abating.

His exposed skin was numb from exposure to the wind and spume and every limb in his body ached with the effort of simply remaining upright. Another wave lifted the *Leopardo* dizzyingly high – he would have said the waves were seventy feet from trough to crest if he had not known better – and then a sudden gust of wind slammed into her like a giant fist. There came an horrendous crack like the firing of a sixty-eight pounder. At first he thought it must have been the thunder, but then he realised that thunder would not have made the deck shiver so.

He looked at the foremast and saw it topple. It was broken clean through close to the deck, the snapped windward rigging flapping in the gale. It pitched forward as the next wave lifted the brig's stern, and would have toppled had not the rigging held it upright. When they reached the crest, the full weight of the wind hit the mast once again, and the stays attaching it to the mainmast made the latter bend perceptibly.

Killigrew pointed to the masts and had to cup his hands over Coffin's ear to make himself understood. 'If we don't cut it free we'll lose the mainmast as well!'

Coffin nodded and the two of them at once went forward to the mainmast. It was at moments like this that one could understand what the brotherhood of the sea was all about: Killigrew might secretly despise Coffin as a slaver, while Coffin openly detested him as an Englishman, but the two of them were instantly ready to put their differences aside and work together to save the ship; their lives depended upon it.

They hauled themselves hand over hand along the rail as the seas crashed over the deck. Killigrew indicated the stays which ran from the top of the mast down to the dead-eyes on the starboard gunwale, and made a slicing motion with the edge of his hand. If they cut the starboard forestays and timed it with the pitching of the deck then the mast would topple forward and sideways overboard. That was the theory, at any rate.

Coffin shook his head firmly and pointed up to the stays which ran between the foremast and the mainmast. The important thing was to cut those first; but it would be impossible to cut them without ascending the rigging.

Killigrew nodded, jerked a thumb at his chest, and then pointed up into the shrouds.

'You're crazy!' bellowed Coffin.

'Got any better suggestions?' Killigrew yelled back.

'You'll never make it! You'll be killed!'

'Then you'll be happy, at least.' Killigrew gazed up into the shrouds once more. Coffin was right: he *was* crazy. Still, it was a sensible exchange: one life for two dozen.

*One honest man for the life of two dozen slavers*, he reminded himself. *If you're going to die, wouldn't it be better to take the bastards with you?* Was it his place to judge these people? Surely that was the Lord's decision. But he had taken that decision into his own hands when he had executed da Silva. Perhaps this storm was God's way of punishing him. *One murderer and two dozen blackbirders*, Killigrew told himself. No wonder God wanted this ship sunk with all hands. *Watch it, Kit my bucko: you've been spending so much time with Madison you're starting to think like him. You've never been a Jonah before now, and this is hardly the time to start!* He found himself grinning as some of the defiance Coffin had expressed earlier infected him with its violent energy. 'Come on, then!' he roared at the heavens. 'Take me, if you want me!'

And with that he hauled himself up into the ratlines.

He ascended a step at a time. It seemed to take all of his strength just to cling to the sodden rigging, never mind to pull himself up at the same time. The rain hammered him and the wind sought to tear him away. He was glad it was so dark, for he could hardly see the mountainous seas around him and the deck pitching below; occasionally a flash of lightning would pick out the white caps of the wave crests, but Killigrew had enough to do without worrying about that.

The mainmast creaked threateningly. It was the only thing keeping the foremast up, and soon it too must snap. Killigrew forced himself to climb faster, throwing caution – literally – to the howling winds. The rain soaked clean through his oilskins and seemed to slice into the skin underneath.

Before he realised it, he had reached the doubling where the topmast reached the topgallant mast. Up here the wind was even stronger. He lost his footing and slipped, dangling from his arms. The strength of the wind seemed to make gravity irrelevant: everything span around him and he no longer knew which way was down. The wind blew him forward at an angle, and nothing he could do would get his feet back on to the ratlines. He thought about pulling himself across the shrouds hand-over-hand, but knew that as soon as he released the grip of one hand, the other would be broken by the strength of the wind.

Then the *Leopardo* sank into another trough and the mast swung backwards, swinging Killigrew with it until he could entangle his legs in the ratlines once more. *Just a few more inches*, he told himself. He climbed up: one step, two, and then he could see the stay less than a foot away through the stinging rain.

He wrapped both legs and arms around the shrouds, clinging on with all his might, then eased a hand into his pocket and took out his clasp knife. *Whatever you do, don't drop it*, he thought to himself with a grim smile. The rain was like a thousand white-hot needles against his flesh and his hands were so numb he could barely open the knife. But at last the blade snapped into view. He reached across with one hand and started to saw at the thick rope which ran from the mainmast to the foremast. The blade was razor sharp and quickly parted the strands. It was hard work nonetheless, and it seemed to take for ever before the weight of the foremast was enough to break the strands which remained. There was a snap like a pistol-shot and the rope snaked away into the night.

Killigrew closed the knife and began to descend, grateful for every step which took him a foot nearer to the safety of the deck. Only one other stay ran between the foremast and mainmast, where the topmast met the lower mast. He swung himself underneath the ratlines and lowered himself to the maintop. He missed his footing in the darkness and the wind, and his sea-boots slipped on the rain-washed planks. He scrabbled desperately at the boards, his numbed fingers searching for a grip. He felt his feet slip out over the leading edge, then his calves and his knees, and then he had hooked one arm around the mast itself. Half dangling over the edge, he braced himself where the mast itself afforded him some protection from the murderous wind.

He risked a glance down to the deck. He could just make out pale faces staring up at him, while the deck itself was awash with soaking waters which sloshed between the bulwarks. Each time a wave broke over the *Leopardo*'s stern the faces would be buried beneath a maelstrom of white water, but they were still there when the waters receded. Coffin was at the foot of the starboard forestays, already hacking through them with a hatchet.

Killigrew took out his clasp knife once more and reached down towards the stay with the blade. His arm was just an inch too short. He withdrew it and altered his grip on the haft of the knife so that he held it between his fingertips. That way he found he could reach the rope, but the amount of pressure he could apply was negligible. The strands parted, but slowly, far too slowly.

The rope snapped so suddenly that Killigrew lost his grip on his knife and it was whipped away; only the lanyard tying it to his belt saved him from losing it altogether. Coffin had hacked through the forestays and as the ship was lifted on another wave the foremast toppled forwards and then swung sideways as the port-side forestays took up the strain. There were still plenty of stays running from the foremast to the bowsprit, but Killigrew could not cut those in time and could only hope that they snapped. There was a chance the bowsprit itself would be ripped away, but better that than losing the mainmast.

The foremast crashed into the sea and was swallowed up by the blackness at once. Coffin lunged through the knee-deep water on deck to hack at the port-side forestays which still attached the mast to the ship's side. A moment later there was a great crack as the jib-boom snapped off the bowsprit, and then the last of the ropes snapped and the danger from that quarter was gone.

Killigrew descended to the deck feeling shaken and used-up. He crossed to where Coffin hacked through the last of the forestays, but the job was done by the time he got there. Coffin did not even acknowledge him.

As the brig descended stern-first into the next trough Killigrew turned aft and then froze in horror.

A rogue wave rose up behind them, towering, mountainous. An immense wall of water a hundred feet tall if it was an inch. Such a wave could not support its own weight and Killigrew saw foam at its peak as it began to topple forward on to the poop deck. Either it would snap the ship clean in two or else flip it stern over bows: either event signalled the death of the *Leopardo*.

'Hold on!' he yelled as the vast breaker tumbled down towards the brig's stern like the jaws of some vast leviathan of the deep closing on its prey. He felt the whole ship shudder and pitch crazily as hundreds of thousands of gallons of water slammed on to the poop. The deck fell away sickeningly from beneath him and he went over backwards, splashing into the knee-deep water. Still the breaker descended, a vast wall of cascading water eating its way up the length of the deck from stern to stem.

Towards Killigrew. Floundering, he rolled on to his front and half crawled, half doggy-paddled towards the stump of the foremast. He threw his arms around it, took a deep breath, and then the water crashed down on him. The weight of water drove the breath from his body and seemed intent on pushing him clean through the deck. It was strangely silent beneath the water after the howling of the wind and the crashing of the waves.

The pressure on his back slowly receded, and then the waters surged about him, transferring the weight to his arms and shoulders as the flood tried to drag him away from the mast-stump. Even if he had been at full strength he could not have hoped to resist that pressure; as it was, his trip into the rigging had left him hopelessly drained. His arms gave way and the water swirled him away: up, down, sideways, it was impossible to tell. Something heavy slammed against him, and then a fresh surge of water span him through its inky depths.

He thought about swimming towards the surface, but dismissed the idea as nonsensical: he did not even know which way the surface lay. There was nothing he could do but enjoy the strange feeling of peace which filled him as the water swept him where it would. Was he drowning? Probably. He had always supposed that one day it would come to this, but he had never thought it would happen this early in his career. There had been so much he wanted to do with his life, so many battles left unfought, it seemed a shame it should all come to an end now. Others would remain to fight those battles, of course, but he was not sure he could trust them to do the job properly. And then there was Eulalia waiting for him in London . . .

Something else slammed against him, and he clung to it instinctively, just as he clung on to his life by holding on to what little breath remained in his lungs. The water tried to pull him away again, but with less determination now. Then a roaring filled his ears. At first he thought it must be the blood roaring in his head as he died, but then he realised it was just the turbulence of the storm-tossed waves.

A moment later whatever he clung to broke the surface, and Killigrew surfaced with it. The wind, rain and spindrift stung his face and he gulped air into his lungs.

He was clinging to the rails of the head. By a miracle, he was still alive. By an even greater one, the *Leopardo* was still intact and afloat. Shaking his head to clear the rain and hair out of his eyes, he saw other members of the crew on deck looking about them with wonderment as if astonished to find that they still lived, and he shared in that wonderment.

'Man overboard!' boomed Duarte.

*No rest for the wicked.* Killigrew pushed himself to his feet and crossed to where the boatswain stood at the rail, pointing out into the inky blackness beyond. Killigrew could just make out a figure floating level with the storm-tossed ship, perhaps thirty yards from the side. At that distance his face was no more than a white blur, but Killigrew somehow sensed that it was Coffin. If he had thought about it he would have left the chief mate to drown. Not even Madison could have blamed him for doing nothing after all he had already been through, and trying to save the chief mate was suicide anyway. But there was no time to think. He quickly unwound a coil of rope which had been thaned up tightly round a belaying pin. He gave one end to Duarte and tied the other around his waist.

'Make that fast!' he snapped at Duarte, and then jumped overboard thinking: *There's trust for you.*

His narrow escape from the rogue wave had filled him with a sense of exhilaration, as if part of him had got the impression he was indestructible. He knew the idea was false, and yet somehow it inspired him with renewed strength. He started to swim out with a strong, easy crawl-stroke to where Coffin struggled in the water. But his strength had deceived him and quickly gave out. *Just a few more feet*, he thought, as his exhaustion caught up with him.

He reached Coffin as the chief mate was going down for the third time. Killigrew caught him underneath the chin and dragged him back to the surface. It was all he could do to float on his back supporting Coffin. Then the rope around his chest tugged against him and he realised that the muscular boatswain was hauling them both back to the ship.

'You'll die when I decide it, and not before,' he heard someone snarl at Coffin, and it was only by process of deduction he realised it must have been himself. If the half drowned chief mate heard him, he gave no indication of it.

Then they bumped against the *Leopardo*'s side and strong arms hauled them both over the bulwark. The storm seemed to have abated a little. Killigrew hoped it was over now, rather than a temporary lull. Coffin sprawled on the deck, vomited sea water, and lay still.

'Is he dead?' asked Madison.

Duarte put an ear to Coffin's chest, and then shook his head. 'He lives.' The brawny boatswain lifted Coffin in his arms and carried him almost tenderly below deck to the sick bay. Killigrew followed.

Pereira looked distinctly seasick in the dim glow of the oil lamp which swung wildly from an overhead beam. There was only one cot in the sick bay, and it was already occupied by the man who had fallen from the rigging earlier. But from the way Pereira had pulled the sheets up to hide the man's face he was no longer in need of a comfortable bed. Killigrew hoisted him out unceremoniously and Duarte lay Coffin in his place.

Before Pereira could do anything, a spasm shook Coffin's body and he leaned over the side of the cot to fetch up more sea water. Gasping for breath, he looked up at the boatswain. 'What happened?'

'You were washed overboard,' said Duarte. 'Senhor Killigrew saved you.'

Coffin glanced across at him. If Killigrew had expected gratitude he was disappointed, but even he was stunned by the look of sheer venom in Coffin's eyes, as if the chief mate would have preferred to have been left to drown. Then Coffin turned his eyes on Pereira. 'Brandy,' he gasped.

'I have none,' said Pereira.

'There's a bottle of *aguardiente* in Madison's cabin,' said Coffin.

'I'll fetch it,' offered Killigrew.

As he made his way aft below decks he thought about Coffin's reaction on hearing who had saved him, and began to understand it. How hateful it must have been to a confirmed anglophobe like Coffin to owe his life to an Englishman! The thought afforded Killigrew a small modicum of amusement, but it was short lived. He remembered how the Chinese believed that if one saved a man's life, one was responsible for that man for the rest of his existence; a very Chinese logic, but a kind of logic nonetheless. Any atrocity Coffin committed from now on would lie on Killigrew's head. It was a thought which filled him with a distinct feeling of unease.

He went into Madison's day cabin. Despite the tarpaulin which had been stretched over the skylight in the deck head, the glass had shattered under the pressure of the waves and now lay in shards all over the floor, while water dripped steadily from above. In spite of this, the shutters which protected the windows were still in place, and the oil still burned in the lantern which swung from an overhead beam, casting eerie, swaying shadows across the scene.

By some miracle the bottle of *aguardiente* in a drawer of Madison's desk had not been broken. Killigrew took it out and pulled out the stopper, pouring a generous and – in his opinion – well-earned measure down his throat. He gasped with pleasure as the fiery liquid burned its way down to his stomach.

So much had happened during the past few hours that he had forgotten he was on board the *Leopardo* for a specific purpose, and it was only in that instant he remembered it. This was the opportunity he had been looking for from the moment he had joined the crew. He went to the door and glanced out. Seeing no one, he closed the door and went to work.

He carefully searched the other desk drawers, taking care not to drip water on to the papers within, but found nothing to indicate who the financier behind this slaver was. Then he turned his attention to the safe. It was locked, of course, and the key was doubtless on Madison's person. Killigrew did not know anything about picking locks, but there was no harm in inserting the key to his own sea-chest to see if that fitted: it would only take a couple of seconds.

But a couple of seconds can mean the difference between life and death. Just as he was trying to withdraw the key, having failed in his attempt, the cabin door opened and Duarte's massive bulk filled the frame.

# XIII:

## Flotsam

'So!' snarled Duarte. 'Senhor Coffin was right about you! You *are* a spy!' He quickly pulled his pistol from its holster. 'No tricks. Keep your hands where I can see them.'

'Certainly.' Killigrew raised his hands.

Duarte crossed the cabin and came around the desk, keeping his pistol on Killigrew the whole time. He gestured for Killigrew to back away from the desk. 'There's a perfectly good explanation for all this,' said Killigrew. 'But I'm sure it will sound better coming from your lips, Captain Madison,' he added, with a nod of acknowledgement towards the door.

Duarte only half-turned before he realised he had been tricked, but it was all the time Killigrew needed. He snatched the bottle of *aguardiente* from the top of the safe and smashed it over Duarte's head.

The boatswain straightened and turned away from the desk, the liquor running down his face. He levelled the pistol between Killigrew's eyes and pulled the trigger.

Killigrew did not even flinch. 'I've yet to see the pistol that still worked after the kind of drenching we've both had.'

Duarte threw the pistol at his head. Killigrew ducked and then lunged at the boatswain's throat with the jagged remains of the bottle. Duarte knocked his arm aside with one hand and drove his other into Killigrew's stomach.

It was like being butted by a charging bull. Killigrew doubled up in agony. Then Duarte caught him by the arm and dashed his wrist against the side of the safe. Killigrew dropped the broken bottle. Duarte lifted his knee into his face, smashing his head back against the safe door.

Killigrew slumped to the deck. Duarte reached down and seized him by the lapels, lifting him to his feet once more. The boatswain was bigger and stronger than Killigrew and furthermore he had not spent the past hour climbing about the rigging in a force-twelve hurricane, or swimming in tempest-tossed seas. Killigrew knew that if he was going to survive this encounter then he was going to have to kill Duarte as quickly as possible, while his little remaining strength held out.

He drove one fist into the boatswain's stomach with all his might, and then the other. Duarte grunted, and then hoisted Killigrew's feet clean off the deck, swinging him around and slamming him against the far bulkhead. Killigrew punched him on the jaw, snapping his head around, but when it came back to face the young Cornishman it was still smiling. Duarte punched him in the stomach again, following it up with a hammer-like blow to the back of the neck as he doubled up.

Barely conscious, Killigrew fell face down on the deck and tried to crawl away. Duarte stood over him and rolled him on his back before wrapping his massive hands around Killigrew's throat, squeezing.

Killigrew felt himself choking. He flailed wildly at the boatswain's torso, but it was like trying to dig a tunnel through a mountainside with his fists. His vision swam and he felt himself suffocating as Duarte increased the pressure on his windpipe.

A red mist filled Killigrew's eyes. He fumbled blindly about him on the deck for something he could use as a weapon, anything. His searching fingers found the pistol. He gripped it by the butt and thumbed back the hammer.

Duarte laughed. 'That won't do you any good, *inglese.* Wet powder, remember?'

Killigrew brought the pistol up between Duarte's legs with his final reserves of strength until it slammed hard against the boatswain's crotch. Then he pulled the trigger. The hammer fell and Duarte screamed in agony. He released Killigrew and the Englishman broke away and pulled himself to his feet.

He snatched up a chair and brought it down against Duarte's head. It was the boatswain's neck rather than the sturdy chair which snapped, silencing his screams.

Killigrew quickly closed the door and prayed that the noise of the storm had muffled the sounds of the struggle from the rest of the ship. If it had not, he was a dead man. But if he did not move quickly he was a dead man anyway. He opened the windows at the rear of the cabin. In the flashes of lightning he could see that the seas were still mountainous; no sooner had he opened the shutters behind the window than a wave crashed against the stern, drenching him.

He picked up Duarte and dragged him across to the window. It was almost impossible to fit him through. 'Why the devil couldn't I have got into a fight with Pereira?' he wondered out loud. He gave a final push and the corpse popped out like a cork out of a champagne bottle to be swallowed up by the sea.

Killigrew closed the shutters and the windows behind them, turning to survey the cabin. It was a mess, but no more than could be accounted for by storm damage. Ditto his own face, which he supposed was no oil painting after the beating Duarte had given it. An inch of water sloshed about his feet; Killigrew could only pray it would be put down to the water dripping through the tarpaulin over the smashed skylight.

He adjusted his neckcloth and returned to the sick bay. 'What happened to you?' asked Pereira, wide-eyed.

'I slipped and fell in the dark as the ship lurched,' Killigrew explained glibly. 'Where's Mr Coffin?'

'He went back on duty. Said the ship needed him.'

'The same goes for me.'

Killigrew went back on deck and found Madison and Coffin standing on the quarter-deck. Lightning still flashed in the heavens, but further away now, and the wind had died down to a shriek. Killigrew checked the compass and the dog-vane to make sure they were not in the eye of the storm; if they were, then the worst was yet to come. To his relief he saw they still headed south-west while the wind came steadily off the starboard beam: they were out of danger and putting distance between them and the tornado with every passing minute.

'What happened to you?' grunted Coffin.

'Slipped and fell,' said Killigrew.

'Holding the bottle of *aguardiente*, I suppose, since you haven't brought it with you.'

Killigrew nodded. 'I'm afraid the cabin's rather a mess. That rogue wave must have smashed in the skylight. There's glass and water all over the place.'

'We can clean up in the morning,' said Madison. 'Where's Mr Duarte?'

'I don't know. I left him with Mr Coffin in the sick bay.'

Madison glanced at Coffin, who shook his head. 'He went out after Killigrew.'

'He's probably somewhere down below,' said Madison.

'I'm sure you're right,' agreed Killigrew.

'*Coisa* ho!' cried the lookout at the masthead.

'*Coisa, coisa* . . . what the devil is a "*coisa*"?' Madison demanded.

'It's Portuguese for "thing",' offered Killigrew.

'I'm aware of that, Mr Killigrew,' Madison said irritably.

'What I meant was, what kind of a "*coisa*" is he referring to?'

'Let's find out, shall we?' Killigrew tilted back his head to call up to the lookout. 'Where away?'

'Fine on the port bow!'

Madison, Coffin and Killigrew levelled their telescopes in that direction and searched the horizon for the unidentified floating object, but saw nothing. 'Has the fool been drinking?' wondered Madison.

It was the morning after the storm. The sky was clear and the air fresh, the waves choppy. The dawn had revealed the full damage to the *Leopardo*: both to the ship itself and to its crew. In addition to the man who had been killed in his plunge to the deck, three men were missing and presumed swept overboard, Duarte included. Now the crew were hard at work trying to jury-rig the spars and rigging to compensate for the loss of the foremast and the jib-boom. With her spread of canvas thus reduced, the *Leopardo* was making poor speed as she resumed her south-easterly run to the Guinea Coast. Now she responded sluggishly to her helm and was almost impossible to steer. Madison would have given anything to have lost the mainmast rather than the foremast, but it had been the storm's decision, not his, and there was nothing for it but to make the best of a bad job. In addition, the storm had sprung several timbers, and while the carpenter and sailmaker laboured to plug the gaps other crewmen worked at the bilge pump.

Killigrew realised he was making the mistake of looking for a ship, which in those conditions would have been visible the moment its sail rose above the horizon if the lookout were attentive. But the lookout had not cried 'sail ho!' but '*coisa* ho!' Killigrew lowered his telescope accordingly, looking for something smaller. He found it almost at once.

'It's a mast.'

'Ours?' asked Madison.

'If it is, it's acquired some extra appurtenances.' There were three figures clinging to the floating mast. Somehow Killigrew doubted they were the men missing from the *Leopardo*'s crew, unless Duarte had been blackballed from entry to Davy Jones's locker.

'Castaways,' said Madison. 'From some other ship that foundered in last night's storm, I suppose.'

'We should leave them,' said Coffin. 'The last thing we want is strangers sniffing around on board. We've already got one of those,' he added, 'and as far as I'm concerned that's one too many.'

Madison said nothing, chewing over Coffin's proposal as if giving it serious consideration. The suggestion was anathema to Killigrew. If the castaways were left to their fate their chances of survival would be non-existent that far out from the coast, and Killigrew had been brought up to believe it was the duty of every seaman to go to the help of those in peril on the sea regardless of all other considerations. But he was not sure a slave crew would operate under the same strictures.

'We can't leave them to die,' he said. 'It would be damned unchristian of us.'

Madison nodded reluctantly. 'Mr Killigrew's right, Eli. We can't be like the priest and the Levite and pass on by. Matthew, chapter seven, verse twelve: "Therefore all things whatsoever ye would that men should do to you, do ye even so to them: for this is the law and the prophets."'

'And what if they find out we're blackbirders?' demanded Coffin. 'As soon as we put them ashore we'll have every navy vessel on the coast searching for us.'

'Then we'll have to make sure they don't find out, won't we?' Madison said crisply, and turned to the crewman he had appointed boatswain in Duarte's place. 'Lower the jolly boat, Mr Covilhã. We'll have that mast, too, to replace the one we lost last night. We'll drop them off a few miles down the coast from Freetown, within easy walking distance of one of the settlements but not close enough to excite the attention of any navy vessels in the harbour there.'

As the jolly boat picked up the castaways, Killigrew was aware that for them it was a case of out of the frying pan and into the fire. He was beginning to understand Madison's warped idea of morality: while the slave captain would pick up castaways out of Christian charity, he would not hesitate to have them murdered later if that was the best way to protect his own interests. But with any luck it would not come to that.

As the *Leopardo* hove to alongside the floating mast, the jolly boat bumped against the brig's side. There was a stir on deck as the hands gathered around the rail to help the three castaways over the bulwark, in particular the one that was female and pretty. They gathered around her, grinning inanely and knuckling their foreheads. But Killigrew was more concerned about the man who was barely conscious and had to be lifted over the rail. He seemed to be delirious, babbling away in a daze, quite oblivious to what was going on around him.

As the man was laid on the deck, Killigrew crouched over him. The man was in his late twenties, fair-haired, his smooth, pink face sunburned and now salt-blistered. He wore a dog collar.

The woman pushed her way through the crowd of sailors around her and Killigrew was aware of the hem of her dress at the edge of his vision, but he was too busy trying to ascertain what was wrong with the man to look up at her. 'Oh, you will take care of my brother, won't you, sir?' she asked. Like her brother, she spoke with a distinct American accent. *More damned Yankees*, thought Killigrew.

'We'll do our best, ma'am,' he said. 'What happened to him?'

'He got hit on the back of the head by a . . . by one of those things as our ship went down.'

Killigrew was finally forced to glance up at her. That she was the delirious man's sister there could be no doubting, but the features looked better on her than they did on him, for all that her lips were blistered, her eyes gummed with sea salt, and her blonde hair straggled wetly across her shoulders.

She was pointing to a block and tackle in the ship's rigging. Killigrew nodded. 'That's a block, ma'am.'

'It's "miss", not "ma'am",' she told him.

'Pleased to meet you, miss, though I wish it could be under more fortuitous circumstances. My name's Killigrew, by the way. Kit Killigrew.'

'We're just glad that your ship came along when it did,' said the woman. 'This is my brother, the Reverend Chance.'

'Which would make you . . .'

She nodded with a grimace. 'Miss Chance. No jokes, please. Believe me, Captain Killigrew, I've heard them all.'

He found himself warming to her at once. 'Then I'll have to see if I can surprise you. And it's just "mister", I'm afraid, not "captain". Captain Madison over there is the master of this vessel,' he explained, pointing to where Madison stood on the quarter-deck with Coffin. Both of them were avoiding the castaways, perhaps fearing that their faces might be identified later.

He turned to the nearest sailor. 'Carry the reverend down to the sick bay. Miss Chance, you and your friend here . . .'

The third castaway tugged his forelock. 'Donohoe, sir, Able Seaman Clem Donohoe,' he announced in an Irish brogue.

'One-time navy?' Killigrew asked him.

'As is yourself, sir, unless I'm very much mistaken.'

The presence of an able seaman who had served on one of Her Majesty's ships was a reassurance to Killigrew, a potential ally if things turned nasty. 'Very well, Able Seaman Donohoe.

You go below with Miss Chance here so the quack can make sure you're both all right. I'll have some hot food brought to you.'

As the three castaways were taken below, Killigrew turned to Doc. 'Some hot broth, Mas'er Killigrew?' suggested the cook.

'Good idea, Doc.'

As the cook made his way to the galley, Killigrew crossed to where Madison and Coffin waited. 'Well?' demanded Madison.

'Well what?'

'What did you find out?'

'The clergyman and the woman are brother and sister . . .'

'We saw that much for ourselves,' sneered Coffin.

'The reverend received a blow to the head when their ship went down. He looks like he might be in a bad way. Their names are the Reverend and Miss Chance.'

'Miss Chance!' guffawed Coffin. 'It was sure as hell a mischance that brought them on board *this* vessel.'

Killigrew smiled thinly. 'Yes, well, if I were you I should avoid making that joke in her presence. I got the feeling she might not see the humorous side of it.'

'What about the other one?' Madison demanded impatiently.

'His name's Donohoe. An Irishman – from County Cork, unless I'm mistaken. He's served in the navy.'

'Another goddamn Limey tar,' muttered Coffin.

Madison half-turned towards his chief mate. 'Haven't you got duties to be seeing to, Mr Coffin? Like getting that mast lashed up in place of the one we lost?'

'Aye, aye, Cap'n.' Coffin headed forward with a crooked grin.

'You were saying about this Donohoe fellow?' Madison asked Killigrew.

Killigrew shrugged. 'I suppose he was a sailor on board their ship.'

'Which was?' asked Madison.

'I didn't enquire. They've all been through an unpleasant ordeal and I thought the first priority was to make them comfortable.'

'Quite right, of course, Mr Killigrew. All the same, I'd feel a good deal happier if I knew a little bit more about them before I put them ashore.'

'I'm sure they don't represent any kind of threat—'

'I'm sure they don't intend to,' Madison cut in firmly. 'But of all the captains in the slave trade today, no one's got a longer record of avoiding capture than me, and that's because I take precautions. Find out more, Mr Killigrew.'

'Aye, aye, sir.'

'You seem to have a talent for . . . shall we say social chit-chat? Putting on a polite face for the gentry?'

'My grandfather made sure I was brought up correctly, if that's what you mean.'

Madison gestured dismissively. 'Whatever you want to call it. It was your suggestion that we pick them up instead of leaving them to their fate. I'm making you responsible for them. I'll tell Mr Covilhã to have the men watch what they say when our "guests" are around. And I don't want them sniffing around the hold, understood? They go in the sick bay, the officers' accommodation or on deck, but nowhere else. If the reverend is indisposed he'd best stay in the sick bay, and I suppose Mr Donohoe had better sleep with the other lads. Miss Chance can have my cabin.'

'And where will you sleep, sir?'

'I'll have your bunk, Mr Killigrew. You can bunk up with Pereira.'

'What a delightful thought,' Killigrew said drily.

'And Killigrew?'

'Sir?'

'I guess Miss Chance might scrub-up real pretty. But I don't want you trying to take advantage of her, you understand? Treat her with respect.'

Killigrew bridled. 'You forget. I used to be an officer and a gentleman.'

'I forget nothing. "Used to be" is right.'

Killigrew made his way down below. Half a dozen sailors crowded around the entrance to the sick bay. It was the first time any of them had seen a woman since they had left Liverpool, Madison having made sure that few of them left the ship at São Tiago and none of them had left the dockside. 'Haven't you men got work to do?' snapped Killigrew. 'Mr Coffin could do with a hand lashing up the new mast.'

'*Sîm*, Senhor Killigrew.' The men scurried away and Killigrew slipped into the sick bay. Pereira was examining the back of Reverend Chance's head while Miss Chance sat on the chair, a rough blanket thrown around her shoulders. Donohoe sat near her on the floor. If the *Leopardo* was poorly equipped with medical facilities, it was infinitely better than other slavers Killigrew had encountered, most of which did not even carry a surgeon on their books in order to save on expense.

'How is he?' Killigrew asked Pereira in Portuguese.

'Not good. He has a bad concussion, and fever too perhaps. I have given him a little laudanum to help him rest.'

'Is he going to be all right?' Miss Chance asked in English.

'The surgeon's doing his best for him,' said Killigrew, and she nodded. 'How about you two?'

'I'm fine,' she said. 'Well, still a little shaky maybe. I was ready to commend our souls unto God just before this ship turned up.'

'Didn't I tell you we'd be fine?' said Donohoe.

'How about you, Mr Donohoe?' asked Killigrew.

'Oh, I'll be right as rain, Mr Killigrew sir. I've been shipwrecked before. It'll take more than a few big waves to be putting an end to Clem Donohoe.'

'Were there many others on board your ship?'

'Seventeen of us in the crew, all told.' Donohoe smiled wanly, although he was obviously upset at the thought he would never see his shipmates again. 'The reverend father and Miss Chance here were our only passengers. I think maybe some of the others managed to get into one of the boats, but when she foundered she went down so fast . . .' He let the sentence trail off and gestured helplessly, hopelessly.

'Which ship was it?'

'The *Belinda Lovelace*, out of New York. Bound for Sherbro Island with supplies and mail.'

'My brother and I were on our way to join the American Mission there,' explained Miss Chance.

Killigrew nodded. He knew Sherbro Island, or at least he had seen it a few times: a large island immediately off the Guinea Coast. It was there that the slaves who had revolted against their captors on board the *La Amistad* had settled after their trial in the United States had cleared them of the charges of mutiny and murder a few years earlier. Many of them had become Christians during their incarceration in the States, and they had helped the newly formed American Missionary Association set up the Mende Mission at Komende on the island.

'I'll see if I can persuade Captain Madison to drop you off there. It's on our way.' As a matter of fact the course Madison had plotted – which had yet to be completed – trailed off immediately to the west of Sherbro Island, and Killigrew knew that Madison would be far happier to drop off his passengers at a Christian mission than he would at a British Crown Colony and naval base.

Doc turned up with three bowls of steaming broth on a

tray and handed two to Donohoe and Miss Chance. 'What about him?' he asked, nodding at the recumbent reverend.

'He'll be asleep for a few hours,' said Pereira, taking the third bowl for himself. 'A pity to let it go to waste. You can make him another bowl when he awakes.'

'Doc, could you fetch our guests some dry clothes from the purser's slops?' suggested Killigrew, and the cook nodded and went out. 'If you two are both comfortable, I'll leave you to Senhor Pereira here.'

'About accommodation . . .' said Donohoe.

'That's been arranged,' said Killigrew, and filled them in on the arrangements.

'I'm sorry if we're an imposition,' said Miss Chance.

'Don't be ridiculous,' Killigrew told her with a smile.

He reported to Madison in his day cabin. The captain was already packing up his things to make room for Miss Chance. 'Well?' he grunted.

Killigrew related the gist of his conversation with Donohoe and Miss Chance, and Madison nodded. 'We'll make better time once Mr Coffin gets the new mast in place. We should be within sight of Sherbro Island in just over a week if all goes according to plan. You'd better get some rest now. I want you to take the middle watch tonight.'

'Jesus!' Killigrew gasped when he came up on deck to take over from Madison as officer of the watch.

Madison grinned, his face turned into a ghastly devil's mask by the phosphorescence of the sea which cast its hideous glow over the ship. 'You never seen this before, Mr Killigrew?'

'After two years on the West Africa Station? But it still gives me the creeps.'

Above, the sky was as black as the Earl of Hell's waistcoat, without a star to be seen in the heavens. A few lanterns swung above deck, but their illumination was hardly needed: the whole sea was aglow with phosphorescence, from horizon to horizon, a bright, eye-searing pale green. It looked as if they were sailing through a sea of fire.

'Revelation, chapter fifteen, verse two: "And I saw as it were a sea of glass mingled with fire".'

Killigrew nodded. 'No wonder the ancients believed that a belt of flame circumscribed their world.'

'I'll bid you goodnight, Mr Killigrew. See you in the forenoon.' Madison went below.

Killigrew was left alone on deck with the helmsman and the lookouts. Apart from the hideous glow of the sea, all was well: a strong breeze blew from the south-west, carrying the *Leopardo* towards her destination on a starboard tack. Despite the jury-rigged foremast, the vessel rode easily on the broad swell of the ocean.

Miss Chance emerged from the aft hatch. When she saw Killigrew she smiled at him, but knitted her brow at the peculiar quality of the light. As soon as she was fully out of the hatch she saw the sea and her expression changed to one of wonderment.

She crossed to where he stood, treading carefully on the deck as if she feared that the ship might vanish from beneath her and plunge her into the glowing sea. She was dressed in clothes from the purser's slops, outsized and baggy on her slight figure, making her look even smaller and more vulnerable. She had somehow managed to wash her hair, and while she had been unable to have it properly coiffed, it spilled across her shoulders in a way which was natural and attractive.

'Am I dreaming?' she asked him.

He shook his head. 'Phosphorescence, miss. It looks eerie, I'll grant you, but it's common enough and quite harmless.'

They leaned against the rail, side by side, and stared down to where the ship seemed to strike veins of glowing gold from the green-tinged light. 'What causes it?' she asked.

'I've no idea. To tell you the truth, I don't want to.'

'Because you might fear the explanation?'

Smiling, he shook his head. 'The only thing I fear about the explanation is that it will prove to be perfectly banal and ruin the magic of it. How is your brother?'

Her face fell. 'Feverish. I'm afraid the blow to the head he received may have permanently addled his brains. Is . . . what kind of surgeon is Mr Pereira? I mean, is he a good one?'

'He's no better nor worse than any surgeon you'll find on a ship like this,' said Killigrew, meaning he was neither better nor worse than having no surgeon at all.

'What kind of a ship is this, exactly?'

'A merchantman. Trading manufactured goods to the Guinea Coast in return for palm oil.' He felt more uncomfortable lying to her about the purpose of their voyage than he did lying to Madison about his motives, but it was for her own safety.

'An American master and chief mate, an English second mate, and the rest of the crew Spanish or Portuguese,' she mused. 'Are all merchantmen as cosmopolitan as this, Mr Killigrew?'

He shrugged. 'It's not uncommon amongst merchantmen, or even navy vessels. A ship may be registered in one country and owned by a merchant in another, but the men aboard her don't much trouble themselves what flag they serve under. If they loved their countries so much, they'd've stayed in them instead of running away to sea. Unless they've been shanghaied, of course, but all the hands aboard this vessel are willing enough.'

'Why did *you* run away to sea, Mr Killigrew?'

He chuckled. 'With my family background, running away would have meant staying on shore. The Killigrews have been making a living from the sea since the fifteenth century. What about you, miss? What brings you so far from home?'

'I just want to help our black brethren, that's all. William – my brother – was the first to get involved in the Missionary Association, but I've always supported him in everything he's done.'

'Wouldn't you rather have a life of your own? Or is that an impertinent question?'

She shook her head. 'This is the only way I can have a life of my own. If I stayed in America my folks would press me to marry, and then I'd have to subsume my life into that of my husband. At least this way I get some choice of my own. And the condition of the Africans is something I care about passionately.'

'Ah, yes. Converting our heathen brethren to the path of righteousness.'

'From your tone I take it you do not approve?'

'I've not had much experience of the effects of missionary activity in Africa. In Guinea there's so much tribal warfare it's impossible to tell how much is caused by missionaries and how much is caused by the economic demand for prisoners of war.'

'The economic demand for prisoners of war? Is there one?'

'Slaves, miss.'

'Oh, of course. You seem to think that all of Africa's problems are caused by whites.'

'I wouldn't go that far. But Africa has more problems caused by Europeans and Americans than Europe and America have problems caused by Africans.'

'But surely you can't approve of the Africans living in unenlightened ignorance?'

'What you call ignorance is subjective, miss. Take the Chinese, for example. We call them heathens, but to them we're the uncultured barbarians. Who's to say we're right and they're wrong?'

'Surely common sense dictates—'

'European common sense, miss. The Chinese were living in ignorance of the teachings of Christ for hundreds of years before missionaries arrived in China to convert them. Were all those who lived before now to be condemned to an eternity in Hell simply because God himself made them Chinese?'

'They are all God's children, Mr Killigrew.'

'True. But you cannot deny that God seems to have represented himself in different ways to the different races on his earth. Since they are God's ways, can they be wrong?'

'You'd have to ask my brother, Mr Killigrew. He's the theologian, not me.'

'I think of myself more as a philosopher than a theologian, miss.'

'But you can't deny that the heathens of this world live in a state of wretched poverty and constant warfare?'

'There's plenty of poverty in Europe and America. And as for war, is there really that much difference between the tribal wars in Africa and the wars between nations in Europe and the Americas? Except that more people are killed in our wars, because we are more civilised and therefore better organised and efficient at killing.'

'But at least we know that to kill is a sin.'

'And yet still we do it. Does that make us better or worse? When I was in the navy—' He broke off and smiled. 'But I'm lecturing you, miss, and that's deuced tedious of me.'

'Mr Donohoe said something about you having the carriage of a naval officer, Mr Killigrew. Why did you leave the navy for the merchant service?'

'It's a long story, and not one that I'd want to bore you with.'

'Aren't you going to tell her?'

Killigrew turned and saw Coffin standing there.

'Tell me what, Mr Coffin?' she asked.

'Why, tell you about why he was kicked out of the Royal

Navy, Miss Chance. About his drinking problem. About how he got drunk one day and decided to race his carriage down Pall Mall, and in so doing knocked down an innocent child and killed her.'

She stared at Killigrew with an expression of shock and horror.

Coffin grinned. 'Not so much the gentleman he seems now, is he?'

She gave the chief mate an icy look, and then turned back to Killigrew with what might have been a hint of sympathy in her eyes. 'That's a terrible thing to have on your conscience, Mr Killigrew. I'll pray for your eternal soul.'

'Pray for us all, Miss Chance,' Coffin called after her as she headed back below. 'Did Mr Killigrew here neglect to mention this is a ship of the damned?'

Killigrew was woken by the sound of someone hammering on the door of the cabin he shared with Pereira. He rolled out of his hammock, landing lightly on the balls of his naked feet, and jerked the door open. 'What?' he snapped.

Miss Chance stood there. 'Please come quickly, Mr Killigrew!' she said in a rush. 'It's Mr Coffin! He's beating one of the sailors and if someone doesn't stop him I fear he may . . . oh! Mr Killigrew! Oh!' She raised a hand before her eyes and averted her gaze, blushing crimson.

'Oh! Sorry.' Killigrew stepped behind the door to cover his nakedness, reflecting that Miss Chance was going to have to get used to the sight of the naked human form if she was going to do missionary work in Africa. 'Go on.'

'Mr Coffin is beating one of the sailors. I fear that if someone doesn't stop him he'll beat the poor man to death!'

'All right, I'll come right up.' Killigrew quickly pulled on his pantaloons and shirt. The ship's bell rang urgently as he laced his half-boots, summoning the hands to their quarters.

It was a week since they had rescued the three castaways from the sea. Dawn was lightening the sky, revealing the coast of Africa off to port. And there, off the port bow, a frigate less than three miles away was running to intercept them. Covilhã was ordering the men to cram on all canvas, even at the risk of breaking the jury-rigged foremast, while Madison ordered the helmsman to steer a course to the south-west to avoid the frigate. 'Stand by to tack ship!' called Covilhã.

The object of Coffin's wrath lay at the foot of the mainmast in a pool of his own blood. He lay so motionless it was impossible to say whether he lived or died, but Coffin continued to kick him in the head regardless. 'You want to sleep, you idle, good-for-nothing sonuvabitch? I'll put you to sleep! I'll send you to sleep with the fishes!' He reached down to grab the man by the collar and dragged him across to the rail.

'For the love of God, Mr Killigrew!' pleaded Miss Chance. She stood by while Donohoe struggled to go to the aid of the unconscious man, held fast in the grip of a burly sailor. 'Stop him! Don't you see this is your chance to redeem yourself in the eyes of the Lord?'

But Killigrew was powerless to intervene.

'Take our guests below, Mr Killigrew,' Madison ordered gruffly.

'Please,' said Killigrew. 'You'd better do as the captain says.'

'Aren't you going to stop him?'

'Please, miss. For your own good.'

Coffin reached the side of the ship and lifted the man above his head with all the strength his insane rage gave him. The man went over the side without a scream and hit the water with a splash. Killigrew could not see the sharks from where he stood in the middle of the deck, but he knew they would be there.

'Oh, God!' sobbed Miss Chance. 'Heaven help us! Did you see that? He murdered him! Mr Coffin murdered that poor sailor, for the love of God! Just because he fell asleep on watch!'

Donohoe stopped struggling. 'Of course. Because that allowed the frigate to get so close without anyone on board this ship knowing about it.'

'So? What does it matter?' asked Miss Chance. 'That's not a reason to kill a man.'

'It is if they're slavers,' spat Donohoe.

'Sl-slavers?' stammered Miss Chance, as if she had believed that the slave trade had ended forty years ago when Denmark, the United States and Great Britain had all declared the trade illegal.

'Quite right, Mr Donohoe,' said Madison. 'I'm afraid this is a slave vessel you find yourself on, my dear,' he explained to Miss Chance. 'Take them below, Mr Killigrew.'

'Please,' insisted Killigrew, gesturing to the hatch. 'For your own safety . . .'

'Blackbirders!' spat Donohoe. 'I'd expect nothing less of these foreigners, but I'm surprised at ye, Mr Killigrew. I took ye for a Christian gentleman.'

Killigrew smiled wanly. 'You wouldn't be the first to make that mistake, believe me.'

Donohoe rammed an elbow into his captor's chest and broke free. He snatched a belaying pin from the bulwark.

'No!' shouted Killigrew.

Coffin heard footsteps on the deck and turned in time to see Donohoe running towards him, brandishing the belaying pin above his head. The chief mate pulled his pistol from its holster and shot him in the chest. The Irishman fell back to the deck, dead.

Miss Chance groaned and her eyes rolled up in her head. Killigrew had to move fast to catch her before she fell. 'Goddamn it!' he muttered.

'Take her below and put her somewhere out of harm's way, Mr Killigrew,' ordered Madison. 'I strongly advise you put her in irons. Then come straight back on deck.'

Killigrew nodded and carried her below decks. As he carried her to the orlop deck her eyes opened. Seeing Killigrew carrying her she began to pound at his face with her fists. He put her down, but with her feet on the deck it was only easier for her to beat him. He grabbed her by the wrists and tried to still her, but her face was twisted with hatred and loathing.

'You rats! You evil, murdering rats.'

'Listen to me! Stop it!' he pleaded. 'Listen to me, as you value your life!' But she continued to struggle in his grip. Nothing he could say could get through to her, so he kissed her on the forehead.

She stopped struggling and stared at him in astonishment.

'Listen to me,' he said, more calmly. 'You have to trust me. I can't explain now, there isn't time, but you must trust me. Do you understand?'

She nodded, wide-eyed. 'You . . . you're going to have to kill me, aren't you?'

'Not if I can help it,' he told her. 'That's a promise.' He steered her down to the orlop deck and gestured to a set of irons. 'Sit down.'

'You're going to shackle me here?'

He nodded. 'Please believe me, I beg you. It's for your own safety.'

As he clipped the fetters over her ankles the reality of her predicament hit her with its full force. 'What if the ship sinks? I'll drown!'

'The ship won't sink. That frigate won't fire at the hull. They probably don't think we have slaves on board but they'll want to find proof that we're slavers before they condemn us. So they'll aim at the spars and rigging. Believe me, this is the safest place to be. If they catch us, Madison won't want a dead American citizen on board, so you'll be safe enough.'

'And if they don't catch us? What then?'

Killigrew had no idea. 'I'll protect you. I promise. You've got to trust me, that's all.' He headed back towards the companion ladder.

'Mr Killigrew?' she called after him. He turned back. 'I . . . I don't know why . . . I've no reason to . . . but . . . I *do* trust you.'

He grinned ruefully. 'Yes, well, don't tell any of those scum up there you said that, or we'll both be as good as dead.'

# XIV:

## Barracoon

Killigrew returned on deck and studied the frigate through Madison's telescope. 'Do you know her?' asked Madison.

Killigrew nodded. 'She's the USS *Narwhal*.' He did not add that less than four months ago he had been drinking on board her with Lieutenant Lanier and his friends.

'Can she catch us?'

'I don't know. Before we lost our foremast she wouldn't have stood a chance, but now with this jury-rigging . . .'

It was strange to find himself being on the other side in the war against the slavers, running with the hare after spending so many years riding with the hounds. It would be embarrassing for him if the frigate caught them. He was not confident he could convince Lanier that he was working as a secret agent for Rear-Admiral Napier; also if there was nothing in Madison's safe to identify the man behind the slavers then this whole enterprise would have been for nothing, and he would never be able to redeem himself and be reinstated as an officer of the Royal Navy. Worse than that, if the Americans saw fit to hand him over to the authorities in Freetown as a British citizen caught on board a slave vessel, there was a good chance he would be hanged for it. So from Killigrew's point of view there was nothing to be gained from trying to sabotage the *Leopardo*'s efforts to escape the *Narwhal.*

But now he had Miss Chance's safety to think of. Madison would not let her and her brother go now that they knew they were on board a slaver. Was there any way he could keep them alive and help them get to safety? It seemed impossible. But was his mission more important than their lives? If he succeeded he would be saving thousands of Africans from being condemned to a life of slavery; but only if he succeeded. How could he balance that against the life of one man and one woman? And was it the Africans he was concerned about, or his own skin?

He wondered if Miss Chance could swim, at least long enough to stay afloat until she could be picked up by the crew of the *Narwhal.* Perhaps he could put her and her brother into a boat while everyone else was busy? But they would see what he had done sooner or later, and know he was up to no good. Unless . . .

'Perhaps we can buy ourselves some time by putting the Reverend Chance and his sister in the jolly boat and leaving them for the *Narwhal* to pick up?' he suggested to Madison. 'That way we get them out of our hair and force our pursuers to slow down at the same time.'

'Aye, and hand over a woman who can easily identify every man-jack of us to the authorities, Mr Killigrew. You'll have to do better than that.'

A cannon boomed distantly and Killigrew saw a plume of pale grey smoke rise from the *Narwhal*'s side. There was no answering splash of shot landing in the water closer to the *Leopardo* – it had been a blank.

'They're asking us to show our colours,' grunted Coffin.

Madison nodded. 'Hoist the Union Jack, Mr Covilhã. If they get within hailing distance you can do the honours with the speaking trumpet, Mr Killigrew. Maybe that Limey accent of yours will throw them off the scent.'

Close-hauled, the two ships raced to windward. Each time the *Leopardo* changed tack the *Narwhal* mirrored the manoeuvre barely seconds later. There was no doubting the American sailors knew their business, but it was impossible to say which of the two vessels was the faster.

The *Narwhal* came within a mile of the *Leopardo* as the latter ship tried to slip past her and at once one of her pivot guns boomed and raised a huge plume of water from the waves barely a cable's length to port of the brig. The Americans had used round shot and for a moment Killigrew panicked, thinking the *Narwhal* meant to sink them after all. He thought of Miss Chance, whom he himself had chained on the orlop deck. Then he realised that the Americans would know the range of their guns to within a few yards, even taking the wind into account. It had just been a warning shot.

Then the two ships were level, only three-quarters of a mile of ocean separating them. The frigate veered towards the brig, but for every yard towards the slaver she gained sideways, she fell a yard astern. When she was almost directly abaft the brig her bow-chaser boomed, sending up a fountain of water which showered the men on the quarter-deck.

'We'll use the sweeps,' decided Madison.

There were six sweeps on board the *Leopardo*, three for a side. There were not enough men on board to have more than three men to each sweep. Even Killigrew had to help, leaving Coffin to take the helm while Madison had the con. The sailors stripped down to their waists and hauled away to the strokes called out by Covilhã like the galley slaves of old, praying that the sweeps would give them that extra burst of speed they needed to elude the *Narwhal*.

It was hot and sultry, and the sweat soon poured from the backs of Killigrew and the others as they rowed under the blazing tropical sun. Working with his back to the bows, Killigrew could just see the sails of the *Narwhal* beyond the *Leopardo*'s stern. If the frigate were falling behind, it was doing so so slowly it was impossible to discern. His back and arms soon ached from the exertion.

'We're losing her,' opined Madison, staring aft through his telescope.

Coffin glanced over his shoulder. 'Aye, but they ain't giving up yet. They know we can't keep this up for ever.'

'Pace the men, Mr Covilhã,' ordered Madison. 'We may have a way to go yet.'

The sun climbed towards its zenith until it beat down mercilessly on the men labouring on deck. Madison disappeared below. Killigrew wondered if he had given up hope of outrunning the frigate and was going to burn the papers in the safe; if he did, then the chances were that Killigrew's mission was doomed to failure and he would have to live the rest of his life in disgrace. He was toying with the idea of leaving his place at the sweeps and going below to stop Madison when the slave captain reappeared a few moments later carrying a pail in one hand and dragging Miss Chance by the arm with the other.

'Fill the pail at the water butt and give the men some water,' ordered Madison.

'Do it yourself,' she snapped back. 'You think I want to help scum like you escape from justice?'

He thrust the pail into her hands, making her stagger. 'You'll do it, missy, or I'll have you pulling on one of those sweeps yourself!'

She glared fiercely at him for a moment as if defying him to do it, and Killigrew suppressed a smile, torn between admiration for her spirit and a throat-burning thirst. Then she glanced at the men at the sweeps and saw Killigrew amongst them. Her shoulders slumped and she crossed to the water butt. He was glad she had sense enough not to make straight for him, instead serving the men on the port-side sweeps first.

'Is there anything I can do to help?' she murmured as she lifted the ladle to Killigrew's parched lips. He swallowed the water – it probably had not even been that fresh when they had taken it on board at São Tiago eight days earlier, but it was still the sweetest liquid he had ever tasted – and then just shook his head, conserving his breath.

Madison suddenly peered forward, and raised his telescope to his eye, staring ahead. Then a grin spread across his face, and he lowered the telescope. 'Three points to starboard, Mr Coffin, if you please. Keep pulling, boys! There's a smoke a couple of miles ahead. If we can make it there's a chance we'll be safe.'

The men at the sweeps pulled even harder, knowing that the end was in sight. It occurred to Killigrew that Madison might have lied to the men in order to get them to pull faster, but he could not twist his head around far enough to check. Covilhã and five others shipped their sweeps briefly to trim the sails to their new heading, and then resumed rowing.

They had put another half-mile between themselves and the *Narwhal*, but still the frigate did not give up. It was rare for a frigate to fall in with a slaver it had a chance of catching – such ships usually only ended up on the West Africa Station because their navies had no other use for them – and, having smelled blood, her crew was reluctant to give up the chase.

A few minutes later the brig slid into the fog bank and the men gasped with relief as the low cloud masked them from the worst of the sun's rays. Killigrew felt the moisture prickle his bare skin.

'Keep pulling!' ordered Madison. 'We're not out of it yet. Hard a-port, Mr Coffin. Port-side sweeps back water!'

The *Leopardo*'s head came about in the opaque mists, and with the oarsmen on the port side reversing, the ship almost turned on her axis. 'Now forward again! One . . . two . . . three . . . four . . . five . . . way enough! Toss and ship sweeps. Way aloft! Take in all canvas! We'll drift with the smoke. Silently, now, silently!'

After pulling at the sweeps for the best part of three hours, the hands climbed into the rigging like octogenarians, but the sails were soon furled. 'Pipe down! Not a sound out of any of you, d'ye hear? The next man to make a sound other than me or Mr Coffin goes the same way as Tristão did, follow me?'

Coffin took his whip from his belt and looped it around Miss Chance's neck. 'That goes for you too, missy. One peep and I'll snap that pretty little neck of yours like it was driftwood.'

The hands climbed silently down from the rigging and tip-toed across the deck. The frigate would not have chased them so far if it was going to be put off sailing into a little low cloud, but Killigrew guessed Madison was counting on their last manoeuvre inside the fog to throw the Americans off the scent.

They waited. Everything was silent but for the creaking of the timbers and the gentle slap of the waves against the brig's sides.

'Heave to!' a voice with an American accent boomed barely two cables away. Killigrew thought he recognised Boatswain Charlie's voice. 'Counterbrace them yards!'

Everyone turned to look in that direction, and they could see a pale shadow looming through the mist behind them. Then a boatswain's whistle sounded the order to pipe down. The Americans had guessed that the slaver was hidden in the fog bank, and they were listening for a clue which would give away its location. All that was needed was a sudden gust of wind to tear a rent in the fog and the *Leopardo* would be exposed to the view of the *Narwhal* within point-blank range of her port broadside.

There was silence for one minute, two, three. Harsh laughter, faint muffled, and Boatswain Charlie hissing for silence, threatening dire warnings against the next man to make a sound. Coffin pulled tight on the whip he still had coiled around Miss Chance's neck, as if sensing that she was tempted to call out to the men on the frigate. She glanced across to where Killigrew stood, looking at him from under her eyelashes. He gave his head an infinitesimal shake.

'Ah, to hell with it!' said someone on the frigate. 'They're probably miles away by now. Belay that last order, men. Brace in the sails!'

The shadow moved on through the fog, but Madison quickly raised a hand, signalling for his crew to remain silent. It might yet be a ruse by the captain of the frigate to trick them into betraying their position.

They waited. An hour passed, then another. No one went near the ship's bell. As the afternoon wore on the mist slowly evaporated, until all of a sudden it was gone. There was no sign of the *Narwhal*, but the African coast was visible directly ahead.

Madison took a sighting on the coast with his sextant. He returned on deck a moment later. 'Take the helm, Mr Covilhã. Lay in a course east by north. Take the girl below and put her in irons, Eli, then join me directly in my cabin. You too, Mr Killigrew.'

Madison went below followed by Coffin dragging Miss Chance by the arm. Killigrew shrugged his shirt back on and gazed towards the bows. They were heading in towards the African coast. By his own dead reckoning they had passed Sherbro Island during the chase and now lay somewhere off the Guinea Coast to the south. Did that mean they were close to their destination?

He buttoned his shirt and went below, tucking it into the waistband. Madison was already waiting for him in his day cabin, poring over a chart. He said nothing apart from to respond to Killigrew's knock on the door, and from the tone of the captain's voice Killigrew deemed it wisest to stand back and say nothing until Madison looked up and addressed him.

Presently they were joined by Coffin. 'Well?' Madison asked him.

'We've no choice, sir. She was dead the moment her ship went down. You know it and I know it. Only this dumb Limey thought he could prolong her life.'

Madison sighed. 'You're right, of course, Eli. All the same, she is a woman.'

'All the more reason to kill her, sir.' Coffin grinned. 'You can't trust a woman to keep her mouth shut. I'll do it, if you like. I'll see to it she don't suffer too much.'

Killigrew was a patient man, but he had been subjected to Coffin's needling for over four weeks now, and the callous way in which he spoke of murdering an innocent woman in cold blood was more than he could bear. 'You'll enjoy that, won't you?'

Coffin turned to him. 'Perhaps you'd rather do it yourself, mister, since it was your idea to bring her aboard in the first place?'

'All right, you two, that's enough,' snapped Madison. He massaged his temples and sighed again. 'There . . . there is another way,' he said hesitantly. 'I'm not sure that I care for it overmuch, but at least it doesn't mean killing her.'

'Cut her tongue out?' suggested Coffin. 'Too risky. She'd still be able to write down all she's learned.'

Madison scowled at him. 'I was thinking of giving her to Salazar.'

Coffin pursed his lips, and then nodded. 'That's not a bad idea. All them nigger whores he keeps in his harem, I reckon he must get a hankering for a bit of white meat every once in a while.'

'What do you say, Mr Killigrew?'

Killigrew shrugged. 'Who's Salazar?'

Coffin chortled. 'Why, ain't you never heard of Salazar? No wonder you navy boys are always a-running round in circles. You don't know anything about the slave trade if you don't know about Francisco Salazar.'

'And he is . . . ?'

'You'll find out soon enough,' said Madison. 'As we should make landfall at the Owodunni Barracoon by nightfall.'

The sun was sinking into the ocean by the time the *Leopardo* anchored half a mile from the coast, casting an orange light like fire across the sky and sending a flaming path across the waves to where the brig floated. Killigrew stood on deck and gazed towards the land. Even with the telescope he could see nothing, but that did not surprise him. For most of its length the Guinea Coast presented nothing to the seaward observer but an unbroken barrier of impenetrable green foliage, but Killigrew knew that the foliage hid deltas and mangrove swamps, a hundred thousand tiny creeks and inlets which made ideal hiding places for the slavers' barracoons.

'They're all asleep,' sneered Coffin.

'Then let's wake them up, Mr Coffin,' ordered Madison.

They fired a blank shot from the *Leopardo*'s bow-chaser, and ran up some signal flags. A few moments later a flag appeared on the shore, barely visible even through a telescope in that light. It seemed to flutter over the jungle in the evening breeze, and Killigrew could just make out the design: a yellow and black leopard on a white background.

Madison closed his telescope with a gesture of satisfaction.

'That's the signal. Lower the gig, Mr Covilhã. Fetch the girl, Mr Coffin.'

'Where are we?' she demanded as she was handed down into the gig. 'Where are you taking me?'

'Somewhere where you'll be made comfortable,' said Madison.

Killigrew suspected that was far from true and wished there was some way he could warn her, but thinking about it he decided it would be better if she was allowed to remain calm for now. There were eight of them in the gig altogether: Madison, Coffin, Killigrew, Miss Chance, and four oarsmen. Coffin was carrying a sample of the *Leopardo*'s cargo, one of the rifled muskets they hoped to exchange for slaves.

The gig shoved off from the brig's side and they rowed across the bar which prevented ships of any reasonable draught from getting any closer into shore. Once they were across the bar a creek suddenly appeared as if from nowhere amongst the trees which crowded the edge of the stretch of white sand on the beach. The jungle seemed impenetrable on either side of the creek, and the tangled roots of the mangrove trees which clawed at the mud looked eerie in the failing light. Strange tropical birds cried out in the darkness, and mosquitoes buzzed infuriatingly about the heads of the people in the boat. Submerged shapes glided silently through the water without even causing a ripple. Killigrew took them for logs, until he realised they moved against the current: crocodiles.

Then they turned a bend in the creek and a wooden jetty came into view. Three men stood on the jetty, two rough-looking mulattos wearing broad-brimmed straw hats and cradling rifles, and a European, tall, lean-built, dressed all in white and bare-headed.

'Salazar? Is that you, you old son of a gun?'

'Captain Madison.' There was a hint of a wan smile and no trace of any particular accent in the man's rich and sonorous voice. 'Welcome back to the Owodunni Barracoon.'

The gig bumped against the jetty and two of the oarsmen quickly went ashore to make the painter fast, while the guards helped Madison and the others on to the jetty. 'And Mr Coffin, of course. And who are these?' asked Salazar, indicating Killigrew and Miss Chance.

'This is Mr Killigrew, my new second mate, who's been good enough to fill in for Mr Cutler, who was careless enough to get himself shanghaied aboard the *Ophelia*. And the lady is Miss Suzannah Chance, of whom more later.'

Salazar smiled. 'A woman of mystery. How intriguing. And a beautiful one at that,' he added, kissing her hand to her evident distaste.

Salazar was a younger man than Killigrew had expected, in his late thirties or early forties. Flecks of grey showed prematurely at the temples of his leonine head, and high cheekbones and a thin jaw gave his face an angular look.

'So, have you anything in stock, Salazar, or are we going to have to look elsewhere?' asked Madison.

'My dear Captain Madison, when have you ever known me to have nothing in stock? The question is, what have *you* got for *me*?'

'The usual. Guns, powder, textiles.' He handed Salazar a sheet of paper which the barracoon owner tucked inside his shirt without bothering to read.

'Shall we get in out of this unhealthy night air?' he suggested, slapping at a mosquito on the back of his neck. 'Dinner is almost ready. I do hope you will join me. I have the finest chef on the Guinea Coast in my employ, Miss Chance, and an excellently stocked wine cellar.'

Madison ordered the oarsmen to stay by the boat and one of the guards stayed with them while the other led the way up a short dirt track to an arch in the hedge which bordered the creek. Killigrew stepped through it into another world.

There were dozens of buildings: long, low barracks; workshops; clusters of mud huts; bungalows built in the colonial style; a huge stockade off to the left; and at the centre of it all what looked like an Italianate *palazzo*. There were guards everywhere, and Killigrew suddenly noticed a wooden watchtower a hundred feet tall growing up out of the jungle on a neighbouring island, largely camouflaged by the creepers which had been trained to climb up it.

'I had no idea there was such a large settlement in these parts,' said Killigrew.

'That depends how you define a settlement, Mr Killigrew,' said Salazar. 'All this is my barracoon. All these islands belong to me. My own private kingdom, if you like, in which I am master of all I survey.'

Killigrew was stunned, partly by the size of the barracoon but mostly by the fact that Salazar was obviously some kind of megalomaniac. 'It must be the biggest barracoon on the Guinea Coast?'

'In the world, Mr Killigrew. I employ over three hundred people here: guards, servants, clerks, lawyers, administrators, workmen. I pay them well, and in return I get their total and unquestioning loyalty.'

'And if you don't?'

'Every kingdom must have its laws, Mr Killigrew, and those laws are useless if there is no penal code to back them up.'

'A place like this must be very expensive to maintain.'

'It's all relative. I am a businessman first and foremost. I do not run my little kingdom simply for my own aggrandisement.'

'You don't?'

'This barracoon has a turnover of three and a half millions a year, Mr Killigrew. That's pounds sterling. And most of that is clear profit.'

The barracoon was much bigger than the Slave Trade

Department had estimated. 'That's a lot of money,' said Killigrew.

'Mr Salazar does very well for himself,' observed Madison.

'Yes. But not nearly as well as your owners do. I fear that is where the real money lies: transporting the slaves across the Atlantic.'

'The profit lies with the risk, Mr Salazar.'

'Indeed it does. I tell you, Mr Killigrew, when Great Britain declared the slave trade illegal it was the best thing that ever happened to our trade. Mr Madison can purchase a slave here for twenty to thirty thousand *reis* depending on its quality and sell it in the Americas for . . . how much would you say?'

'We expect to make a nine hundred per cent profit,' said Madison. 'That's before you deduct the cost of the voyage, of course.'

'Of course. But even so we can still afford to have two out of every three ships caught by the Royal Navy and the whole operation will still be worth while. Since the proportion of vessels actually caught by the navy is pitifully small, you can imagine what kind of profits we are looking at.'

They approached the colonnaded portico of the *palazzo* at the centre of the settlement. 'Welcome to my humble abode,' said Salazar. 'It was built in Umbria in 1502 as a summer residence for Duke Valentinois. I had it dismantled brick by brick and shipped out here to be reassembled as you see it now.'

'Gives a whole new meaning to the term "conveyancing",' remarked Killigrew.

They ascended the steps to the portico and a black butler emerged to hold open the door for them. Inside it was no more opulent than some of the grander governors' residences Killigrew had visited in some of Britain's better-established and more profitable colonies. Thick velvet drapes hung over the windows and the floor was marble. On the walls, magnificent oil paintings depicting scenes from classical mythology vied for space with hunting trophies in the most ghastly lapse of taste – gazelles, leopards, even a huge rhinoceros's head stuffed and mounted over the Adam fireplace.

Salazar turned to the butler. 'Inform chef there will be six of us to supper. Shall we say half past eight? That will give my guests time to freshen up after what I'm sure was a long and tedious voyage.'

'It was long,' admitted Killigrew. 'I'm not so sure about "tedious". I had no idea supper was going to be so formal, otherwise I'd have brought some evening clothes . . .'

'You can borrow some of mine,' said Salazar. 'We look to be about the same build. And I don't think finding clothes for the lady is likely to present a problem. Henriques, show the gentlemen and the lady upstairs,' he added, snapping his fingers at a liveried black footman.

'I'd rather we kept an eye on the lady, Salazar,' said Madison. 'She's kind of by way of being a prisoner.'

'A prisoner!' exclaimed Salazar. 'Even more intriguing. I shall not press you on the matter, Captain Madison, since I know you well enough to know you will reveal all at the appropriate time. I shall make sure she is watched.'

'If you think I'm going to get changed with one of your guards watching me . . .' she protested.

'Oh, heaven forbid, Miss Chance! I think I can provide you with a suitable escort. Henriques, summon Assata directly to escort Miss Chance to her chamber.'

Killigrew studied the paintings while they waited.

'I see you are admiring my Titian, Mr Killigrew,' said Salazar.

'Wasn't that one stolen from the Louvre a couple of years ago?'

'It may have been,' Salazar admitted with a dismissive

gesture. 'I paid full price for it, however, I assure you. When one has earned one's first million it becomes very difficult to find new ways of spending one's money.'

Killigrew smiled thinly. 'How you must long for a life of simple poverty.'

Salazar shrugged. 'I happen to like the best of things in life. Am I to be blamed if God has smiled on my enterprises over the years?'

'What about the stuffed heads? Yours?'

'Yes indeed, Mr Killigrew. Are you a hunting man?'

'I'm inclined to agree with Shenstone.'

'Shenstone?' asked Salazar.

'A British poet. What was it he said? Ah, yes. "The world may be divided into people that read, people that write, people that think, and fox-hunters."'

Salazar gestured dismissively. 'Foxes are vermin, Mr Killigrew, and their extermination should be left to the lower orders. You cannot know the full thrill of hunting until you have hunted big game. Take this fellow, for example,' he said, indicating the rhinoceros head. 'Five years ago, it was. Can you have any conception of the thoughts that go through a man's mind as one of those beasts bears down on him? At one hundred yards I fired my rifle, but it misfired. He lumbered on. I pulled my pistol from my belt, aimed, and fired – got him right between the eyes. I'll swear he ran on another fifty feet before he realised he was dead.' Salazar's eyes glittered as he recollected the event. 'When his body finally crashed to the ground, he was as close to me as I am to you now. I tell you, Mr Killigrew, one cannot appreciate the true exhilaration of life until one has looked death between the eyes.'

In the *aide-memoire* of his mind, Killigrew scrawled the words: *Mad as a March hare*.

Henriques returned with a tall, muscular black woman wearing a blue-and-white striped tunic belted at the waist and a white cap with a leopard device on the front. A carbine was slung over one of her shoulders, and a large dagger hung at her side along with a brace of pistols. 'Ah, Assata,' said Salazar. 'One of my personal bodyguards, gentlemen, a gift from King Gezo of Dahomey.'

'And all I got for Christmas was a cravat,' sighed Killigrew.

'Assata, take Miss Chance here up to the Chinese room. See that she is given a chance to wash and change for dinner. There are plenty of clean clothes hanging in the closet, Miss Chance. You should be able to find something to fit you.'

Madison and Coffin watched open-mouthed as Assata escorted Miss Chance up the grandiose staircase. 'Tell me, Salazar,' Coffin asked with a leer, 'is guarding the only thing she does with your body?'

Salazar smiled thinly, unimpressed by Coffin's rough manners. 'Believe me, Mr Coffin, it would be a foolish man who tried anything untoward with Assata. When one has seen a woman crack a man's ribcage between her thighs, one becomes very reluctant to place oneself in that perilous position.'

Henriques escorted Madison, Coffin and Killigrew upstairs and showed them each into a room. The rooms were large and every bit as richly appointed as the rest of the house, with grand four-poster beds and marble washstands in a corner. Presently Henriques returned with hot water and towels. It was the first chance Killigrew had had to wash properly in weeks, and he made the most of it, washing the salt out of his hair and scrubbing himself from head to toe. There was a complete supply of toiletries on the shelf above the washstand: macassar oil, pomade, eau-de-cologne. By the time he had finished, Henriques returned with underclothes, a clean shirt and a pair of white pantaloons. Killigrew dressed and went outside where he encountered Miss Chance emerging from another room, followed by Assata.

'You look ravishing, Miss Chance, if I may be so bold,' said Killigrew. It was true enough. She wore a pale-blue evening gown of light silk which swished and rustled with each step she took.

'I only wish you were the only one in this place with the word "ravishing" on his mind, Mr Killigrew,' she responded. 'There are hundreds of dresses in that closet, some of them the very latest fashions from Paris. Why do I get the feeling I'm not the first woman to visit this place? It gives me a creepy feeling.'

'I think it's rather charming myself,' said Killigrew, admiring the interior decoration. 'I'll say one thing for Salazar, his taste is impeccable – barring the dead animal heads on the wall downstairs, of course.'

'I suppose *you'd* like to live like this.'

'Who wouldn't? Although I think I'd grow tired of it after a while. My own tastes have always run to colonial simplicity.'

'After a week on that hell-hole you call a ship, this is all too good to be true.'

'I wouldn't disagree with you there.' He wanted to say more, but suspecting that Assata knew more English than she let on he thought it wisest not to. 'Shall we go downstairs?'

Madison, Coffin and Salazar were already waiting for them with a fourth gentleman, a huge African dressed in a curious combination of clothing: a spotless red tunic with enough gold braid on it to suggest it had once been the property of a brigadier-general if it had not been so obviously first-hand, white breeches, and sandals, the whole topped off with a leopard skin, the head resting on top of the man's shaven scalp, giving an even greater impression of height to his six and three-quarter feet. He was perfectly proportioned too: broad-shouldered and muscular of build, like an ebony sculpture of a Greek athlete.

The African held the rifled musket Coffin had brought from the ship and was turning it over in his hands, gazing down the barrel and snapping the hammer expertly.

'That's the latest in European military armaments, your highness,' Madison was telling him. 'The rifling in the barrel makes the bullet spin in flight, increasing the range and improving accuracy remarkably. You see, I don't try to fob you off with out-dated, second-hand muskets. I've got five hundred more like that on board the *Leopardo*, every one of them fresh from the manufactory where they were made. I'll let you test it tomorrow before I ask you to commit yourself. I hear you're a pretty good shot with a musket? Well, I'm a lousy one. But you use a musket, I'll use that rifle, and I'll beat you ten times out of ten against any target you choose to pick. Even British line infantry don't have rifles as good as that. Those weapons will make your leopard warriors the envy of the finest armies in the world.'

Salazar glanced up and saw Killigrew and Miss Chance descending the staircase. 'Ah, Miss Chance. May I introduce you to Prince Khari? Your highness, this is Miss Chance.' The prince bowed stiffly and clicked his heels, like a Prussian drill instructor. 'And of course may I present Mr Killigrew, your highness? Mr Killigrew, this is Prince Khari.'

'Charmed, I'm sure,' said Killigrew. 'I take it the two of you have a business association?'

Salazar smiled. 'It is thanks to Prince Khari's constant warring with his neighbouring tribes that I am never short of merchandise.'

'They are not "neighbouring tribes", as you call them,' Khari reminded Salazar. He spoke good English with a rich and melodious timbre. 'They are tributary states of my father's empire.'

'Of course, of course.' Salazar seemed amused, as if he was used to pandering to the pride of native chieftains. 'Prince

Khari is the son of King Nldamak,' he added to Killigrew and Miss Chance.

'Ah,' said Killigrew. 'And there was I thinking he must be one of the Buckinghamshire Kharis.'

A footman emerged from a small doorway and held up a small bronze gong, which he struck. 'Supper is served.'

'Shall we be seated?' Salazar, as host, led the way into the dining room, followed by Khari, Miss Chance, Madison, Coffin and Killigrew. A long mahogany dining table large enough to seat two dozen people stretched the length of the room, while another gilt-framed old master hung above the cold hearth at the far end. The furniture, as far as Killigrew could tell, was Louis-Quinze. The whole scene was dimly yet warmly illuminated by the many candles burning in the three candelabra on the table; the candelabra might have been silver-plate, but given Salazar's attitude to spending money Killigrew was ready to bet they were solid silver.

Salazar sat at the head of the table while the others searched for their place cards. Killigrew found himself seated at Salazar's left while Miss Chance sat opposite him. Assata entered the room and stood just inside the doorway with her arms folded, unsmiling, watching Miss Chance.

'I'm sorry I'm not wearing a coat or cravat, Mr Salazar, but these were the only clothes your footman brought me,' Killigrew said apologetically. 'However, I see from your own apparel you prefer a more casual approach to dress?'

'Indeed I do, Mr Killigrew. I find the heavy clothes worn in Europe quite unsuited for these tropical climes. I trust you have no objection?'

'None at all. A very sensible policy, if I may say so.'

'You may, and I shall take it as a compliment that you do. I trust that the clothes are a suitable fit?'

'Well enough. They're a little tight around the chest and shoulders.'

Salazar shrugged. 'That is to be expected. I fear I do not get as much exercise as I used to when I was a sailor. I try though, exercising with the foil. Do you fence, Mr Killigrew?'

'A little,' Killigrew admitted cautiously. 'I'm more used to a cutlass.'

Salazar tutted. 'Such a clumsy weapon. Hardly suited for a gentleman, I would have thought.'

'But more practical than a foil when boarding a hostile ship.'

'Mr Killigrew used to be an officer in the Royal Navy,' explained Madison.

'Indeed.' Salazar seemed completely untroubled by this revelation. That worried Killigrew at first, until he realised that in the heart of his own private kingdom a man like Salazar had nothing to fear from a lone man, ex-navy or otherwise.

'You used to be a sailor, Mr Salazar?' asked Miss Chance.

He nodded. 'Oh, yes. Once I was the captain of a slaver, just like Mr Madison here. I soon made so much money I was able to start building this place. How long until you can retire, Mr Madison?'

Madison smiled. 'With any luck I'll be able to retire after this voyage. I've got my eye on some land on the western frontier of the United States. Good cattle-farming country, I'm told.'

'Exchanging one form of cattle for another?' Killigrew suggested drily.

Madison beamed. 'Exactly so, Mr Killigrew. But cattle are a lot easier to handle than niggers. No offence intended, your highness.'

Prince Khari inclined his head regally.

'Ah, the wine,' said Salazar, as another footman entered and started to pour white wine into the crystal goblets. 'Graves. The best dry white in my cellar. A good vintage, and an excellent complement to the *consommé d'été*. You will have a glass, won't you, Mr Killigrew?'

'Mr Killigrew doesn't drink,' said Madison.

Salazar smiled broadly. 'Oh, but I think he does, Captain Madison. Don't you, Mr Killigrew? Or should that still be *Lieutenant* Killigrew? I'm afraid my informant was rather vague on the matter of whether or not you retain your rank while you're working as a spy for the Slave Trade Department in Whitehall.'

# XV:

## Bad Medicine

'What?' Salazar said with amusement. 'No heated denials? No protestations of innocence?'

'You seem to be pretty sure of your information,' Killigrew said mildly, although his mind was reeling. 'May I enquire how you came by it?'

'So you can return to England and exact your revenge on the one who betrayed you? Put such thoughts from your mind, Mr Killigrew. You will not be seeing England again.'

'You mean to say he was a spy all along? Spying on me?'

'Spying on us, Captain Madison,' said Salazar. 'It's the name of your financial backers he's really interested in, although I'm sure his navy would be grateful for the name of your ship and the location of this barracoon.'

'Goddamn it, didn't I always say that sonuvabitch wasn't on the level?' exclaimed Coffin, banging his fist on the table.

'Is it true, then?' Madison asked Killigrew, more in sorrow than in anger. 'Have you been a viper in my bosom all this time? I am sorely disappointed in you, Mr Killigrew.'

'I think we should congratulate him for carrying out his imposture so successfully,' said Salazar. 'It was a courageous effort, although doomed to failure. I must say, Mr Killigrew, you seem to be taking your defeat with remarkable composure.'

'I've lost this trick, but not the hand.'

'I think you'll find that you've played your last card.'

'Oh, I may have a few more left up my sleeve . . .' Killigrew suddenly leaped up from his chair, knocking it over backwards, and whirled, snatching the carving knife from the sideboard behind him. He hauled Salazar out of his seat and held the knife's serrated edge to his throat.

Madison, Coffin and Khari all jumped to their feet, but they were too slow. Too slow, that is, compared to Assata. In the blink of an eye she had drawn both her pistols and now levelled them, unwavering, at Killigrew's head.

'No!' Salazar called to her in panic. 'Don't shoot.'

Killigrew grinned nervously. 'Don't worry, Mr Salazar. If Miss Assata knows how to use those things – and from the look of her, she does – then she knows she's got as much chance of hitting you as she has of killing me.'

'I doubt it,' Salazar returned mildly. 'Assata is an excellent shot and she would have no difficulty putting out both your eyes at that range. No, my concern was for the Tintoretto on the wall behind you. So please, Mr Killigrew, do both art and yourself a favour and resume your seat so we can finish dinner like civilised gentlemen.' He held out a hand, palm upwards, and Killigrew, seeing the futility of further resistance, hesitated only for a moment before he surrendered the carving knife. Everyone sat down once more, the footman hurrying forwards to right Killigrew's chair for him.

'Better we kill him now and be done with it,' snarled Coffin. 'I'll do it myself if you like.'

'Please, please!' said Salazar. 'Nothing so uncouth as bloodshed at the dinner table, I pray you. Besides, I think it would be better if Mr Killigrew here informed us exactly how much Rear-Admiral Napier knows of our activities before we see to it that he takes his final leave of this world.'

'Torture, I suppose,' Miss Chance said coldly. 'Have you people no consciences?'

'I used to have one,' said Salazar. 'But I outgrew it. The vast wealth I have earned as a consequence is more than adequate compensation.'

Coffin shook his head. 'He won't tell you a thing. I know his sort. He's dangerous. Better to kill him now and be done with it, as I said before.'

'Oh, I'm sure Mr Killigrew can be persuaded to tell us everything he knows. Have you ever studied the history of the Spanish Inquisition, Miss Chance? Some of the techniques they used were really quite sophisticated. But tell me, Captain Madison: you have still not yet revealed the reason for Miss Chance's presence.'

'It was sheer mischance which brought Miss Chance to us, if you'll pardon the pun,' said Madison, oblivious to the look she shot him which suggested that pardoning the pun was not on her personal agenda. 'Her ship went down in a storm about a week ago. We found her, her brother and a sailor floating in the water the next morning. Mr Coffin was for leaving them to their fate; foolishly, I chose to be guided by Mr Killigrew's advice. I should have guessed then, when I realised he was still a sentimentalist at heart, that he was up to no good. Mr Coffin was kind enough to dispose of the sailor as soon as they realised we were slavers. Miss Chance's brother, the Reverend Chance, is so sick he doesn't even know his own name, so he's no threat; in fact I've a feeling he won't last the night,' he added with a sly smile which made Killigrew fear for the missionary's life.

'But as for Miss Chance herself, well . . . you can see we have a problem. Call me old-fashioned, Mr Salazar, yet I still balk at the thought of killing a woman. But as you can understand, we can't very well let her go. Least of all now that she's been here and seen this place. Then I thought of you. Might there be a place in your harem for her?'

Miss Chance leaped to her feet and flushed bright crimson. 'What? How dare you!' Assata quickly stepped up behind her and forced her back down into her chair. Miss Chance struggled against her, but the Dahomey amazon was bigger and stronger than her, and twisted her arm up into the small of her back until she cried out in pain. 'Let go of me, you . . . evil woman!'

'Enough, Assata!' snapped Salazar, and the woman released Miss Chance with a contemptuous curl of her lip.

'Let the girl go on her word of honour that she'll breathe nothing of what she's seen to a living soul, and I'll tell you everything you want to know,' Killigrew said tightly.

'But you are going to do that anyway, whether you like it or not,' Salazar pointed out reasonably. 'You are in no position to bargain, Mr Killigrew.' He turned back to Madison and Coffin. 'It is a generous gift, my friends.'

'The least we can do, under the circumstances,' said Madison. 'If it hadn't been for your informant in England, my carelessness in having Killigrew in my crew could have ruined us all.'

'Then I shall accept your gift. She will be a fine addition to my little menagerie.'

'For the love of mercy, Mr Killigrew!' implored Miss Chance. 'Surely you cannot mean to sit there and say nothing while these evil swine treat me like . . . like some kind of chattel?'

'There is not a lot Mr Killigrew can do about it,' said Salazar. 'If I were you, Miss Chance, I should not look to him for help. He is as good as dead. Whether that death comes swiftly and painlessly, or is lingering and agonising, is entirely up to him. The sooner you accept that and resign yourself to your fate, the happier you will be, I assure you. I pride myself on how well I treat my concubines, and I hope I am not without my charms . . .'

'You have all the charm of a rattlesnake, Mr Salazar. I wouldn't willingly associate with you if you were the last man in the world.'

Killigrew chuckled.

'That amuses you, Mr Killigrew?' said Salazar, evidently hurt by her rebuff. 'Laugh while you can. You will have nothing to laugh about tomorrow, I assure you.'

'I believe it's customary to give the condemned man a last request?' asked Killigrew.

'Of course, within reason. Perhaps you would like the pick of my harem? I often treat honoured guests so, and your bravery deserves reward. But not Miss Chance, however. I prefer my meat fresh, and do not care to taste of another man's leavings.'

'What a charming way of looking at things you have, Mr Salazar. Actually, I was thinking more along the lines of something to drink, since I've been on the wagon for about a month now and there's no longer any need for me to maintain the pretence of being teetotal.'

Salazar laughed. 'Of course. Some wine for Mr Killigrew, Henriques?'

'Actually, I know it's a little early in the meal, but I wondered if I might trouble you for something a little stronger? To help calm my nerves, you understand.'

'Then I entreat you to try my cognac. It was left in the cellars of Bonaparte's home on the island of Saint-Helena. I purchased it at auction for no less than five thousand pounds per bottle. A fitting last request, would you not say?'

'Genuine Napoleon brandy,' Killigrew remarked with a smile, as Henriques leaned over him to place a balloon glass on the table.

'It was well worth every penny I paid for it,' said Salazar.

'It has a splendidly smoky flavour.'

As Henriques leaned over the table with the bottle of cognac, Killigrew shifted his chair slightly and a moment later the footman had dropped the bottle and was hopping about, clutching his foot.

'Oh, I'm sorry, did I hurt you?' Killigrew quickly righted the bottle and mopped up the puddle of spilt cognac from the surface of the table with his napkin. 'My apologies. How clumsy of me.' He made as if to wring out the napkin, twisting it between his hands, and then thrust it into the neck of the bottle and touched the cognac-soaked cloth to one of the candles in the nearest candelabra. The cognac flamed at once and then Killigrew hurled the bottle at Assata. She ducked and the bottle smashed against the wall, spraying the far end of the room with flaming cognac.

Killigrew rammed his elbow into Salazar's face, knocking him backwards over his chair, and then tipped the table over sideways against Coffin, pinning him in his seat. He grabbed Miss Chance by the wrist and dragged her through the door leading to the kitchen before any of the others could recover in time to react. They slammed the door behind them and a moment later two bullets smashed the panels in quick succession.

A tall wooden dresser piled with crockery stood beside the door, and Killigrew at once tried to pull it over in front of the door. Seeing his intention, Miss Chance helped him and a moment later it crashed into place, scattering shards of broken crockery across the floor. The door opened an inch a moment later, and was then brought up short as the dresser blocked it. On the other side, someone started to throw their shoulder against it.

Killigrew and Miss Chance turned away from the door to see a heavily built chef with a scar down one side of his face staring at them in astonishment. Recovering quickly, the chef snatched up a large triangular-bladed knife and lunged at them.

Killigrew dodged the thrust and backed away around the kitchen table. A cauldron of consommé was gently warming over the hearth; Killigrew grabbed a butcher's hook, using it to tip up the cauldron so that a tidal wave of soup splashed across the floor towards the chef. Even further enraged at seeing his creation treated in such a cavalier manner, he charged forwards. As he thrust at Killigrew's throat, Killigrew caught him by the wrist. The two of them struggled chest-to-chest with the knife between them. The chef was the stronger of the two, and he forced Killigrew back into the flames in the hearth at the same time that he turned the blade's point towards Killigrew's left eye.

Then there was a dull thump and the chef's head jerked. His eyes rolled up and he slid down to the floor to reveal Miss Chance standing behind him wielding a heavy wooden chopping board in both hands.

The men on the other side of the door had stopped trying to open it and were now trying to smash it, the panels splintering as they attacked them with some sharp, heavy object. Killigrew grabbed Miss Chance by the hand. 'Come on.'

There was another door on the far side of the kitchen. It was locked but the key was in the hole. Killigrew unlocked it, took out the key and hustled Miss Chance through, before following her out and locking the door behind them. He looked around to get his bearings, and then dragged her after him as he dashed across the lawn. There was a brick wall nearly eight feet high at the far end of the garden. He leaped up and got his hands over the top of it, his feet scrabbling against the bricks until he was able to pull himself up. Sitting astride the wall he glanced down to help Miss Chance up after him, but there was no sign of her.

'Miss Chance?' he hissed urgently into the darkness.

'Behind you.'

He twisted, and saw her seated on the wall beside him. 'How did you . . . ?'

'What?'

'Never mind.' His hand found hers in the darkness and the two of them jumped from the wall, rolling over on the compacted earth below.

A bell tolled sonorously in the darkness, some kind of alarm, and in the glow of torches off to their right they could see armed men emerging from the low barracks they had seen earlier. 'Maybe they don't want us to leave after all,' mused Killigrew, leading the way between two single-storey thatched buildings.

Behind them torches and lanterns were being lit throughout the barracoon. Killigrew was tempted to find the slave pens to release all the slaves, using the confusion he would thus cause to effect his own escape. But the slaves would be locked in, fettered and shackled and under heavy guard. Releasing them would have to wait for another day, when he came back with reinforcements to destroy the barracoon once and for all. The only way he could make sure of that was to get out alive.

They plunged into the bushes beneath some trees, blundering through the thick undergrowth until he was sure they had lost their pursuers. He became aware that Miss Chance was pulling back against him, trying to slow him. 'Stop!' she hissed. 'We can't go anywhere without my brother!'

'I don't intend to.' He stopped to get his bearings. All around them the jungle was alive with the croaking of frogs and the chirruping of insects, but the sounds of pursuit were distant. 'They can't search the whole jungle for us and they won't be able to follow our tracks until it gets light, so we've got a few hours at least. They'll expect us to make for the shore and follow the coast south to Monrovia.' He glanced around. There were no less than four watchtowers, one at each corner of the barracoon, and he could just make them out against the purple night sky. Using his trained seaman's eye, he took a bearing on each of them so he could find his way back to where he stood now.

She suddenly pecked him on the cheek. He regarded her with gentle amusement. 'What was that for?'

'Thank you. You were wonderful back there.'

'You were rather splendid yourself, if I may say so. Can't say I've known many young ladies who'd've handled themselves as well as you did tonight. But we're not out of it yet. Do you think you can climb up this tree?'

She looked up at the branches overhead. 'Certainly, but why?'

'You'll be safe up there. If anyone does come by, just stay very still and keep quiet. You'd be amazed by how few people ever bother to look upwards when they're searching for someone.'

'Where are you going?'

'To fetch your brother. And to make sure they don't use the *Leopardo* to ship any slaves out of here before I can come back to destroy this place.'

'Why can't I come with you?'

'Do you think you can swim half a mile?'

'No,' she admitted. 'Can you?'

'I'll have to. Sit tight. I'll be back, I promise,' he added, conscious that time was against them.

Fronds and creepers lashed at him as he stumbled through the darkness. He knew he might blunder into the trunk of a tree at any moment, but he was racing against time now, knowing he had to get well away from the barracoon with Miss Chance and her brother by sun-up. The unmistakable sound of the surf booming on the shore guided him. He crashed through the undergrowth, tripped over a root, and suddenly found himself rolling over and over on fine, dry sand.

He stopped himself and scrambled back into the trees in case anyone was watching the beach. A full tropical moon cast its pale yellow light over the scene, and he could see the *Leopardo* anchored about half a mile out to sea. He hoped that the Reverend Chance was sufficiently recovered from his blow on the head for Killigrew to get him off the ship.

He sat down and unlaced his half-boots. He was not worried about sharks, at least not much. He was more worried that Salazar's men might be expecting him and Miss Chance to make for the beach; perhaps they were already watching the sand from the trees further up the beach, with their rifles primed and loaded. Still, the longer Killigrew left it the greater the danger became. He knew his chances of salvaging any kind of victory against the slavers were now slim, but he had reached the stage where there was nothing he could do but plough on and hope for the best. It was his duty to get out of this alive, not only for his sake and that of the Chances, but also for the slaves in the pens, both present and future.

He dashed out of the trees and sprinted across the white sand, half expecting a fusillade of shots to blast out of the night behind him. But there were no shots, no shouts, nothing. When Salazar and his men came to the beach – as they must do, sooner or later – they would see his footsteps in the sand. What would they make of them? Would they guess what he was up to? Perhaps not: it was so bold, he could hardly believe he was attempting it himself.

He splashed through the surf, deeper and deeper, until he could dive into the water and pull himself through the breakers with a strong crawl stroke. There was a strong current running across the coast and he had to stop every few minutes, pacing himself and redirecting himself towards the ship again. When it was only a cable's length away he used a silent breast-stroke so as not to alert anyone on deck of his approach, but as the *Leopardo*'s hull loomed above him a better idea occurred to him.

He trod water alongside the hull and waved an arm above his head. 'Hey, Covilhã! Ahoy there! Anyone up there?'

A man's head appeared silhouetted above him. 'Who's there?'

'That you, Covilhã? Throw me a line, for God's sake. Then weigh anchor and make sail. We've got to get out of here.'

A rope was thrown down from the side and Killigrew pulled himself up it, his stockinged feet braced against the brig's side. He was surprised by how much effort it took him just to climb aboard: the swim had drained him more than he had realised. As he scrambled over the bulwark, he saw the other members of the crew gathered on deck. 'Don't just stand there, for Christ's sake! Man the capstan! We've got to get moving straight away.'

'I take my orders from the *capitão*, not you,' snarled Covilhã.

'Not any more. He's dead. So are Coffin and the others. Wake up and look lively there, man! It's an ambush – the British were waiting for us. They must've taken the barracoon before we got here. There's no sign of Salazar and the others. I was lucky to get away with my life.'

Killigrew managed to project the right amount of urgency and panic into his voice to convince the boatswain, who turned to his men: 'You heard Senhor Killigrew! Man the capstan!' he ordered. 'Away aloft! Which way do we sail?'

'I don't know,' snapped Killigrew. 'Away from the coast, out to sea, to start with. There's probably a British cruiser waiting up the coast to close the trap, a steamer like as not. I'll go down to the chart room and plot us a new course.'

Covilhã nodded and Killigrew left him and the crew busily preparing to set sail while he went below deck. He made his way forward to the sick bay where the Reverend Chance lay on the cot. Dr Pereira was dozing in his chair. Killigrew went to the cot and tried to shake Chance awake, but at once saw by the light of the oil lamp that nothing would ever wake the clergyman again. He was dead, as stiff as a board, his face twisted into a ghastly rictus. He had not died easily.

Pereira stirred and looked up at him. 'What . . . what's wrong?'

'What happened here?'

Pereira looked puzzled. 'He . . . he's dead, *senhor*.'

'I can see that,' snapped Killigrew. 'How?'

'I used the strychnine.' He gestured to where a brown bottle stood on a shelf. 'Isn't that what Capitão Madison wanted?'

Killigrew felt sickened. He regarded the surgeon in contempt. 'You murdered him? In cold blood?'

'I . . . I was only obeying orders, *senhor*!' protested Pereira.

'Well, I've got new orders for you.' Killigrew took the bottle from the shelf and removed the stopper. There was still plenty of poison left. He held it out to the surgeon. 'Drink.'

Sweat broke out on Pereira's brow. 'Please, *senhor* . . . no!'

'Drink it! All of it.'

'Please, *senhor*, I beg you . . .' Pereira tried to dodge past Killigrew in his panic but Killigrew tripped him up. Pereira sprawled on the deck and as he rolled over on his back Killigrew sat on his chest. As he tried to pour the poison between Pereira's lips, the surgeon clamped his mouth firmly shut. Killigrew punched him in the throat and when he opened his mouth to gasp Killigrew thrust the neck of the bottle between his teeth. He pinched the surgeon's nose, closing his nostrils and forcing him to swallow.

'Have a taste of your own medicine,' Killigrew suggested grimly.

Pereira thrashed about wildly, first in terror and then as

the spasms gripped his body. Fortunately the sound of the anchor chains rattling through the hawse-hole smothered the hammering of the surgeon's limbs against the deck. His teeth clamped down so hard on the neck of the bottle they smashed it, but by then he was already as good as dead. Killigrew snatched the pillow from under Chance's head and smothered it over Pereira's face to stifle his horrid gurgling and retching. After a few moments he lay still.

Killigrew stood up, as sickened by what he himself had just done as he had been by the reverend's murder. Was he any better than the slavers were, at heart . . . ?

'*Que* . . . ?'

He whirled to see Covilhã standing in the entrance to the sick bay, staring down at Pereira's body. Killigrew glanced around for something he could use as a weapon, but Covilhã quickly pulled his pistol from his belt and levelled it at him. 'I do not know what you are doing, *senhor*, but I think you were lying about the Royal Navy ambushing *Capitão* Madison and *Senhor* Coffin. I think it is you who is working for the Royal Navy . . .'

Killigrew raised his hands. 'You have to trust me. You don't understand. It was Pereira who was the spy, not me . . .'

'I have had enough of your lies, *senhor*.' Covilhã raised his arm and levelled the pistol between Killigrew's eyes.

Killigrew braced himself for the shock of the ball smashing into his skull and prayed that the pain would be short-lived.

There came the sound of a soft 'chunk' and Covilhã's grip on the pistol faltered as blood trickled down his face. Killigrew stared in astonishment and saw a butcher's cleaver embedded in his skull. The boatswain's knees gave way and he crumpled, revealing the broad-shouldered shape of the ship's cook standing behind him.

'Doc,' said Killigrew. 'I can explain everything . . .'

'Don't bother. I know exactly who you are and what you're

up to. You're working for Rear-Admiral Napier, aren't you?'

'No, that's a . . .' Killigrew frowned. 'How the devil do *you* know?'

Doc grinned. 'Because I'm working for him, too.' Doc's pidgin-patois was gone, replaced by what sounded suspiciously like a London accent. 'Able Seaman Wes Molineaux, at your service, sir. The rear-admiral asked me to keep an eye on you. Looks like it was a good thing he did, too.'

'He might've let me know.' Killigrew eyed Molineaux dubiously. God knows, he needed all the friends he could get right now, but he was not sure if the black could be trusted. Certainly Molineaux was not on the side of the slavers, for if he had been he had had nothing to gain and everything to lose by killing Covilhã; and it would not have been unlike Napier to have sent Killigrew such an unusual guardian angel. He decided he had no choice but to trust his new-found friend.

Molineaux eyed Chance's corpse on the cot and then lowered his gaze to where Pereira lay beneath Covilhã. 'Did you hush the quack?'

'Yes.'

'Plummy for you. Never did like him. What's the plan, boss? You *have* got a plan, haven't you?'

'Yes. And it's "lieutenant" or "sir" to you, Able Seaman. Not "boss".'

Molineaux grinned. 'I know all about you, Killigrew. You may not have killed that ankle-biter, but it was a real court-martial that cashiered you. So until the day you get your rank back – if it ever comes – I'll call you what I like. In fact, seeing as how I'm an able seaman and you're just a plain civilian, I reckon it should be *me* who's giving the orders.'

'We'll worry about that later. First of all we've got to destroy this ship. You go to the hold and set one of the powder kegs to explode in ten minutes' time; I'll see if I can break into Madison's safe and find anything interesting.'

'You know all about cracking peters, do you?'

'How difficult can it be?'

'Bearing in mind a safe is a box which has been specifically designed to stop people from breaking into them—'

'And you're an expert, I suppose?' Killigrew snapped impatiently.

'As it happens, yes. That's why the rear-admiral chose me for this job.'

Killigrew nodded. He had already guessed from Molineaux's use of thieves' cant that the seaman had not always worked on the right side of the law. 'I'm surprised he bothered to involve me in this at all. You seem to know all the wrinkles.'

'The rear-admiral figured a ship's officer would have a better chance of learning something from Madison than a black cook. Seems he was wrong, though.'

'Save the sauce for later. We've got work to do. I'll meet you in Madison's day room in five minutes.'

Molineaux had sense enough not to argue. As he headed aft, Killigrew took down the oil lamp and fetched a candle from the purser's store and a coil of rope from the boatswain's locker. He looped the coil over one shoulder and slipped into the hold. He could hear the sailors moving about on deck above, and the timbers began to creak as the masts took up the strain of the billowing sails.

Killigrew put the oil lamp down on one of the kegs of gunpowder stowed in the hold and took his clasp knife from his pocket. He broached the top of another keg, wincing at the sound of the wood splintering, and prayed that no one on deck had heard it. Then he stirred the powder in the keg with his hands, hoping it had not separated into its constituent parts during the voyage. He scooped it up to one side, so that the surface of the powder in the keg formed as steep a slope as possible.

Now for the delicate part.

He took the candle out of his pocket, and cut it all off but for one inch. Lifting the glass cover from the oil lamp, he lit the stub of the candle. Holding his breath, he planted it in the powder. As the candle burned down, the powder would slide down to fill in the void, until at last it came into contact with the flame.

Still holding his breath, he replaced the glass cover on the oil lamp and backed away from where the candle flickered over the charcoal-covered powder. As the deck rolled the candle listed slightly and Killigrew's heart leaped into his mouth. Then it seemed to settle down. He hurried out of the hold and headed aft to Madison's day room.

Crouched in front of the safe, Molineaux was inserting a couple of picklocks into the keyhole when Killigrew entered. The seaman glanced up in alarm, but then recognised him and relaxed. 'Get it open?' Killigrew asked him.

'Not yet. These things take time.'

'Time is the one thing we don't have. There's enough powder in the hold to blow up this ship and ten more like her.' Killigrew crossed to the window and opened it, before tying one end of the rope to an overhead beam.

'If we don't find something in here to tell us who's behind this Bay Cay Trading Company, you can kiss goodbye to your commission.'

'And if we don't get out of here now you can kiss goodbye to that part of your anatomy on which you sit. And every other part of your anatomy, for that matter.'

'Got it!' The tumblers of the lock clicked, and Molineaux swung open the door.

The safe was empty.

Salazar reined in his horse on the beach to the south of the barracoon, where Madison and Coffin headed southwards with a band of Salazar's men, holding burning torches aloft. 'Any sign of them?' asked Salazar.

'No,' snapped Coffin. 'We're wasting our time here. Killigrew won't come this way, because he knows it's the first place we'll look.'

'It is the only sensible way for him to come,' Salazar pointed out reasonably. 'The nearest settlement is Monrovia, fifty miles to the south. Either he comes this way or he makes for Freetown, which is nearer a hundred miles to the north.'

Coffin hawked and spat upon the sand. 'You seem pretty sure he'll stick to the coast.'

'Of course he will. What chance do a young European and an American lady have of getting anywhere in the interior? They would not last five minutes. It would be complete madness to try that way.'

'It was complete madness for him to try to pass himself off as a slaver,' said Coffin. 'But he tried it – and almost pulled it off.'

'Prince Khari will take his leopard warriors into the interior to search for him,' said Salazar. 'If Killigrew has headed inland, he will not get far.'

'I wouldn't trust that uppity nigger and his goddamned leopard warriors to catch a dose of the clap,' snorted Coffin. 'Face it, Salazar. You let the Limey bastard get away.'

Salazar shrugged. 'Perhaps. It does not matter.'

'Doesn't matter!' exclaimed Madison. 'And just how do you figure that, Mr Salazar, bearing in mind that once he gets back to civilisation he'll tell the authorities everything: about you and me, about my ship and your barracoon . . .'

'*If* he gets back, which I very much doubt. And if anyone will believe him, which I also very much doubt. You forget: in England he is disgraced as a drunk and a child-killer.'

'He won't be when Rear-Admiral Napier speaks up for him.'

'Which is why I suggest someone goes to England and makes sure that an accident befalls the rear-admiral. Something fatal. Who will pay any attention to Killigrew if he does not have Napier to back him up?'

A smile spread slowly across Coffin's face. 'Maybe you ain't such a dumb sonuvabitch after all, Salazar.'

'I hope not. It would be a poor world indeed where a "dumb sonuvabitch" could amass as vast a fortune as my own. Are you volunteering to go to England to arrange the admiral's tragic and premature demise?'

Coffin grinned. 'It'll be my pleasure.'

Salazar turned to Madison. 'You see, captain? Even if Killigrew does make it back to civilisation – which is extremely unlikely – his story will not be believed. So I think that I shall be able to continue my trade uninterrupted for a few years yet, and nothing will stop you from using the profits of this voyage to fund your retirement. I don't think Mr Killigrew will give us any more trouble . . .'

They heard a thump from out to sea, and turned their eyes in that direction in time to see the *Leopardo* disintegrate in a huge, blossoming ball of orange flame accompanied by a tremendous roar. A thousand planks of wood were hurled in all directions, most of them high into the sky, and as the ball of fire faded into a black cloud the planks rained down on the surface of the sea, some of them landing on the beach a short distance away. Of the *Leopardo* they could see nothing, just the expanding concentric circles in the water to show where she had recently floated.

For a few moments the men on the beach stared in stunned silence. It was Madison who spoke first. 'And just in case that Limey bastard *does* get back to England,' he told Coffin with a calmness surprising for one who had just had his livelihood blown out of the water, 'make sure he suffers an accident, too. A very painful one.'

Both Killigrew and Molineaux duck-tailed under the water as the ship exploded less than two hundred yards behind them. The surface of the water above them burned as bright as sunrise with orange flame, and a moment later the shock wave hit them, knocking the breath from their bodies. They surfaced, gasping, just as the debris rained down about them.

'Bang go your chances of finding out who was behind the Bay Cay Trading Company,' gasped Molineaux as they trod water beside one another.

'I'll just have to hope that being able to reveal the location of Salazar's barracoon is enough to redeem myself and win back my commission,' said Killigrew.

'And we'll just have to hope that we can live that long.' Molineaux nodded to the beach perhaps seven hundred yards away where they could see torches. 'Looks like we've got a reception committee waiting for us on shore.'

'They won't be able to see us out here. Those torches will ruin their night-vision. We'll be all right so long as we steer clear of the circle of light.'

They swam across the bar, the current carrying them away from where the men on the beach spread out to meet any survivors swimming from the *Leopardo*. At last they reached the shallows and crouched low in the surf, gasping for breath. They were perhaps two hundred yards away from the nearest man, with fifty yards of open beach between them and the cover of the trees. 'Together, or one at a time?' asked Molineaux.

Killigrew shook his head. 'One at a time. Crawling. Less chance of being seen that way. You go first.'

Molineaux nodded and slithered up through the surf and out of the water, gliding with cat-like stealth over the sand while Killigrew watched the men with the torches, waiting for one of them to cry out at any moment. But they moved further away now, heading back towards the barracoon, as if they had given up any hope of catching Killigrew returning ashore; perhaps they thought he had been blown up with the *Leopardo*.

When he glanced back at Molineaux he saw the seaman was already near the trees, and a few moments later the black was swallowed up by the darkness beneath the trees. Killigrew did not hesitate before following him. As he crawled along in Molineaux's tracks, he realised there was another advantage to crawling over running. Salazar's men were bound to find their tracks with the coming of sunrise and if they had found two sets of footsteps they would have realised that Killigrew had an ally now, for there would have been no chance of mistaking Molineaux's prints for Miss Chance's. But crawling just left one confused track which could as easily have been the work of one man as of two.

He reached the trees and stood up beneath their boughs, dusting off the worst of the sand which clung to his sodden clothes. 'Molineaux? You there?'

'Yeah, I'm here,' Molineaux's voice came back. Killigrew found the seaman's presence strangely reassuring. 'I mean, it's not as if there's anywhere else I could go, is there? What do we do now, head down the coast towards Monrovia?'

Killigrew shook his head. 'No. First we have to fetch Miss Chance.'

'You managed to keep her alive, then? That's good.' Molineaux grinned, his teeth showing white in the darkness. 'I was beginning to think we'd run out of Chances.'

'Very droll.' Killigrew led the way through the belt of trees which lay between the beach and the barracoon, heading parallel to the shore.

'Are you going to tell me what went wrong, then?'

'Salazar knew all about me. Someone in England talked to the wrong person.'

'Impossible. The only people who knew what you were doing were you, me, and the rear-admiral himself. And you're not suggesting *he* peached, are you?'

'No. But I'm still not sure about you.'

'Well, thank you very much! I saved your life back there, you know.'

'Anyway, several people knew about my mission,' said Killigrew. 'Corporal Summerbee and Private Whitehead, to name but two.' *And Eulalia Fairbody to name a third*, Killigrew could not help thinking as he found his half-boots and sat down to pull them on. It was inconceivable to think that she might have betrayed him, and yet . . .

'Who are Corporal Summerbee and Private Whitehead when they're at home?'

'A couple of jollies who helped me inveigle myself on board the *Madge Howlett*; or the *Leopardo*, whichever you prefer. You still haven't told me how *you* got on board her, by the way.'

'I joined her in Havana,' explained Molineaux. 'Madison went to a slave market looking for a good seaman who could cook. He chose me. At least, that's what he thinks. Actually he chose one of the other slaves and I was substituted later with the British consul's help.'

'And you mean to tell me Madison never noticed the switch?'

'Of course not. Us darkies all look the same to you people.'

'I'll thank you not to put me in the same category as Madison, Coffin and Salazar,' said Killigrew. 'So the British consul in Havana knew about our plan as well?'

Molineaux shook his head. 'He knew Napier wanted me aboard a certain slave vessel, but he didn't know why. And I didn't tell him.'

'It couldn't have been him anyway,' mused Killigrew. 'Salazar said his informant was in England . . . Wait a minute: if Napier had you join the crew of the *Leopardo* in Havana, he must've been setting this thing up for months. But he only told me about it two months ago.' Two months! It seemed more like two years since he had played billiards in the United Service Club in London.

'Months!' said Molineaux. 'Man, I've been on that ship for two *years*. Something went wrong, badly wrong. The cove I was supposed to protect was someone called Comber, but he never even turned up. I managed to get in touch with Napier the next time we landed at Liverpool and he told me to sit tight until he could get someone else. When you turned up I *knew* you were one of his men straight away.'

'You've been living a lie for two years on that hell ship? I take my hat off to you. Or at least, I would if I were wearing one.'

'Yes, and it hasn't been fun either, I can tell you. You saw for yourself how Madison used to treat me.'

'You must be dedicated to the cause of anti-slavery.'

'To tell the truth I didn't have much choice. But don't believe any of that gammon I told you about not caring about the Africans. They're human beings, at least, which is more than you can say for bastards like Madison and Coffin. I don't know what made you so down on slavery, sir, but while Madison never had me flogged – as long as I toadied to him and grovelled and bowed and scraped like a bug-eyed watermelon-guzzling sonuvabitch – he weren't kind to every slave that came his way, I can tell you. Some of the things I've seen . . .'

'I've seen similar,' Killigrew assured him.

'So are we going to get those bastards and put them out of business for ever?'

'Damned right we are.' The two of them shook on it. 'But

first we have to get to safety. Now, where did I leave Miss Chance?'

Killigrew paused to look around. He could tell from where he stood in relation to the watchtowers that he was not far from where he had left her, but in the darkness all the trees looked the same. They were too close to the barracoon for him to want to risk calling out to her.

'You mean you don't know where you left her?' Molineaux hissed incredulously.

'She's around here somewhere . . .'

A woman's scream, loud and shrill in the darkness, sounded somewhere off to their right.

'This way,' said Killigrew, heading off in the direction of the scream.

# XVI:

## The Law of the Jungle

*Well, Suzannah, you wanted adventure*, Miss Chance told herself ruefully as she made herself as comfortable as possible in the tree's lower boughs. *You can't say that isn't what you've got*. Shipwrecked, picked up by murderous cut-throats, chased by the US Navy, threatened with being consigned to a megalomaniac's harem and rescued by a dashing young British naval officer; if she ever got a chance to write back to her family in Poughkeepsie they were not going to believe a word of it. She was not sure that she believed it herself.

The problem was, she had had more adventures in one week than she had planned to have in the five years she intended to spend working at the Sherbro Island mission. *Serves you right. Missionary work is supposed to be a way of serving God, not of looking for adventure . . .*

The night sky was lit up by an explosion which hammered her ears with its roar. Mr Killigrew had said something about making sure the slavers did not use the *Leopardo* to ship out the slaves in the barracoon, but had he intended to blow the ship out of the water? It was quite likely, but until he returned she had no way of knowing whether or not he had managed to get off the ship with her brother before the explosion. She hoped so. For one thing, she had little confidence in her ability to get back to safety without his help; she had studied maps of the Guinea Coast, of course, and guessed the barracoon lay somewhere between Sierra Leone and Monrovia, but which was nearest she had no idea. And for another, she found Killigrew so infuriating she was starting to wonder if she had fallen in love with him. First of all he had charmed her, then he had let her think he was a drunkard and a child-killer, then he had let her think he was a slaver, and now he had been revealed as a brave man prepared to risk everything in the noble cause of the fight against the slave trade.

'Pssssssst!'

The sound snapped her out of her reverie. 'Mr Killigrew?' she called softly. 'Is that you?'

'Pssssst!'

The noise was close. Too close. As if it were in the tree with her . . .

She twisted on the bough she lay on and came face to face with a snake. She froze instantly, but her movement had already startled it and its head reared back, inches from her own, so close she could clearly see its black eyes glittering in the light and its forked tongue flickering out at her.

She caught her breath. She could feel her heart pounding. The snake only wanted to get out of the tree, she knew, but she was in its way. Why did it not have the sense to turn around and go back the way it had come?

She tried to edge back down the bough towards the trunk, but even that movement seemed to anger the snake and it reared back again. It might not be deadly poisonous, she realised, but she had no wish to find out the hard way.

She was aware of someone moving about on the ground below her, silently and stealthily. She could not look down to see who it was without taking her eyes off the snake, and that she could not bring herself to do. Its gaze was hypnotic and forced her to focus all her attention on it.

She heard a snap from below. At first she thought it was a

twig breaking underfoot, but a second, identical snap followed hard on the heels of the first. It was no natural sound, but the noise of a brace of pistols being cocked. Out of the corner of her eyes she could see Assata below her, aiming her pistols up at her. The amazon gestured for her to climb down out of the tree.

'I can't move!' she hissed. 'There's a snake!'

Assata gestured with the pistols again, impatiently now. Miss Chance tried to ease her way back down the bough, but again the snake reared threateningly. Get shot or get bitten by a poisonous snake; what kind of a choice was that?

Then the snake struck.

Young ladies of genteel upbringing rarely have the opportunity to test their reflexes, so it was not until that moment that Miss Chance had any idea how good her own were. The palm of her hand hit the side of the snake, just behind its head, and without thinking about it she closed her fingers around it. It opened its jaws wide, baring vicious fangs at her, but she gripped it tightly, knowing that to let it go would be one of the last things she ever did if its bite were deadly poisonous. It hissed at her, and she hoped it was not the kind of snake which could spit venom into its victim's eyes.

Then she realised she had lost her balance on the bough and was slipping over sideways. She could not use her right hand and flailed about wildly with her left, but it met only thin air. She reached the point of no return, teetered for a moment, and then fell.

The fall seemed to last for ever, and yet at the same time it was over before she knew it. What little of the world she could see in the darkness tumbled around her, and then she hit the ground below, using her left arm to break the fall and taking care to hold the snake well away from her body with her right.

Assata said nothing – she never did – but she snorted what might have been a contemptuous laugh, and gestured for Miss

Chance to get up. Miss Chance tried to comply, but she could not use her right arm and she sprawled awkwardly on her left side. Assata moved in close, apparently oblivious to the particular impediment under which Miss Chance laboured, and kicked her in the side. The amazon was only wearing sandals, but she did not hold back and the blow was both painful and humiliating.

'All right, all right, I'm trying!' Miss Chance snapped irritably. 'Stop kicking me! Can't you see I've got this—'

She broke off, and looked from the snake to the amazon. Then she pressed the snake's mouth to Assata's ankle.

Assata screamed and dropped the pistols as the snake's fangs went home. Then she turned and ran off through the trees, shrieking, doubtless hoping to find someone who would suck out the venom before it was too late.

Miss Chance snatched up the pistols and sprinted off in the other direction without really thinking about where she was going or what she was going to do when she got there. Her problem was solved for her a moment later when she bumped into a dark figure. She gasped and almost discharged both the pistols at him, when another voice called out to her. 'Miss Chance? It's all right, he's with me!'

'Mr Killigrew?' She threw herself at him and wrapped her arms around him, and he hugged her back.

'It's all right, you're safe now. We're back. We made it.'

'What about my brother? Where is he?'

'I'm sorry,' whispered Killigrew, hugging her tightly and rubbing her back. 'I'm so sorry.'

She let out a sob.

'If it's any consolation, miss, we managed to take care of the swine that murdered him,' the black man said in an English accent. She recognised him as the cook from the *Leopardo* now, although his accent had changed.

She pushed herself away from Killigrew and dried the tears

that prickled her eyes on one of her elbow-length gloves before turning to the black man. 'No, as it happens it is no consolation whatsoever,' she told him coldly. 'It won't bring my brother back, will it? He was the gentlest, kindest man that ever lived. The last memorial he would have cared for is cold-blooded revenge.'

'I'm sorry, miss, but it wasn't cold-blooded, believe me,' said Killigrew, looking guilty. 'And there are plenty of other gentle and kind people out there who'll suffer if we don't put a stop to Salazar and Madison and their activities.'

She handed the brace of pistols to Killigrew. 'Who is this?' she demanded, tossing her head in the black man's direction.

'Able Seaman Molineaux,' explained Killigrew. 'It's all right, he's on our side.'

The black grinned. 'My friends call me "Wes", miss.'

'Do they indeed, Mr Molineaux?'

'Who was that screaming?' asked Killigrew.

'Assata. I was in that tree and there was a snake and then she appeared below me and pointed her pistols at me and the snake was going to strike so I grabbed it behind the head but I fell out of the tree and then she was kicking me so I made the snake bite her, heaven help me, and she ran off. I think I may have murdered her!'

'Self-defence, miss,' Killigrew assured her. 'No one will blame you for it. She'd've done the same to you, and with less provocation. But we'd better get moving. Even if that snake was poisonous, I suspect Miss Assata will live long enough to point Salazar and his cut-throats in this direction.'

No one argued with that and they set off through the trees, Killigrew leading the way. He held out one of the pistols to Molineaux. 'You know how to use one of these?'

'Just give me half a chance!'

'Well, don't. Not unless you really have to. The sound of a gunshot will bring Salazar's men running, and right now we have more than enough problems as it is.'

The foliage grew thicker and a moment later they emerged from the trees to find themselves standing on the south bank of the creek. 'Can we swim across?' Miss Chance asked dubiously.

'Yes,' said Killigrew. 'Unfortunately, so can they.' He pointed across to where dozens of crocodiles silently patrolled the water in the moonlight.

'Then we have to go back and head south, to Monrovia,' said Molineaux. 'It's closer than Freetown, anyway.'

Killigrew shook his head. 'That's exactly what Salazar will expect us to do.'

'Well, what do you suggest we do? We can't stay here, and now you tell us we can't head north or south. That only leaves swimming the Atlantic!'

'We go inland.'

'Inland! Are you crazy? Into the interior? We'll never get out alive!'

'Trust me. I know what I'm doing.' Killigrew motioned for Molineaux and Miss Chance to halt, and then pointed up ahead, to where Madison's gig was tied up to a wooden jetty which projected out into the creek. 'We'll head upstream in that.'

'Don't you think those two plug uglies with muskets might have something to say about that?' asked Molineaux.

Killigrew hefted the pistol in his hand. 'You two wait here.' He disappeared into the bushes off to their right. For a couple of minutes everything was silent and Miss Chance and Molineaux were alone with the sounds of the jungle at night. Things were livelier in the direction of the barracoon, where someone was shouting orders, trying to draw order out of the confusion. On the far side of the creek she heard the mournful cry of a whippoorwill.

The two guards on the jetty stood in companionable silence,

their muskets slung over their shoulders, one of them smoking a clay pipe. A moment later the pipe fell to the jetty, the guards gaped, and they both raised their hands. Killigrew emerged from the shadows, covering them both with his pistol, and motioned for Molineaux and Miss Chance to come and help him. They relieved the guards of their muskets, tied them up with their own belts, and then removed the boots of one so they could gag them with his socks.

'We'd better get a move on,' said Miss Chance, and nodded to where she could see lights in the trees further down the creek, where they had just come from. 'It looks like they're closing in.'

'All right,' said Killigrew. 'Get in the gig, Miss Chance. Cast off the painter, Molineaux.' He finished gagging the two men and then jumped down into the gig, taking up one oar while the seaman took the other and pushed them out from the jetty.

'My hands are still killing me after pulling on those sweeps all afternoon,' grumbled Molineaux.

'Mine too,' Killigrew said tightly, and nodded to where the men with torches were emerging from the trees. 'But if we don't keep rowing I don't imagine those gentlemen will be in a mood to tend to our blisters.'

'Is there anything I can do to help?' asked Miss Chance, feeling like useless baggage and hating it.

'Can you shoot?' Killigrew asked hopefully.

'I'm willing to try, but I'm afraid I'd only be wasting bullets.'

'All right. You sit tight, and maybe say a prayer for us. We'll soon have you out of here.' Killigrew and Molineaux sat side by side on the bench and hauled mightily on the oars, swiftly propelling the gig up the sluggish waters of the creek.

The men on the bank reached the jetty, stopped and levelled their muskets. Powder flamed in the darkness and a flock of ibises rose honking into the night sky as the first shots echoed over the mangrove swamps. The musket balls buzzed through the darkness, occasionally plopping into the water close to the gig, but none came too close for comfort. Some of the men tried to pursue the gig on the bank, but the undergrowth was thick and they soon fell behind.

Killigrew and Molineaux were too busy rowing to return fire. The firing died down once Salazar's men had all discharged their muskets and there was a pause while they stopped to reload. Then there was more firing, sporadic now as each man fired as soon as he was ready, but they were even further behind now and the shooting was yet more erratic. A few moments later another bend in the creek had hidden the gig from their view. Killigrew and Molineaux kept rowing, desperate to put as much distance between them and the slavers as possible before sun-up, which was only a couple of hours away now.

'Can we stop now?' asked Molineaux. 'I reckon we've lost them—'

A couple of canoes shot out of a side-channel off to their right, each containing six men. All the men had muskets slung over their shoulders, but they did not aim them yet, hoping first to overhaul the gig.

Killigrew and Molineaux redoubled their efforts, but it was hopeless. The sleek canoes were built for speed, and they had more rowers. 'Take this,' said Killigrew, handing Molineaux his oar.

'What? You're going to leave me to do all the work?'

'Trust me.'

The first canoe drew level with the gig. The men in the canoe still did not bother to unsling their muskets: presumably Salazar had told them to bring Killigrew and the others back alive if they could.

Killigrew felt under the thwart in the stern sheets and found a wooden cask. Taking it in both hands, he stood up suddenly, balancing easily in the rocking boat, hefted the cask above his head and hurled it at one of the men in the canoe. The man dived out of the way, upsetting the next man, and then the cask smashed through the bottom of the canoe. It filled with water and foundered at once.

The crocodiles in the water changed direction and closed in on the men swimming in the water.

The gig left the sinking canoe behind, but now the second canoe was moving in for the kill. This time they did not come too close, but two of the men in the bows of the canoe levelled their muskets. Even with only four men paddling, it easily outpaced the gig.

The muskets boomed and Miss Chance gasped as a musket ball splintered the gig's gunwale close to her hand. Then Killigrew had picked up one of the muskets they had taken from the men on the jetty, brought it up to his shoulder, aimed and fired, all in one smooth motion. The first musketeer did not even cry out, just fell back silently against his mate, his arms flung wide, his musket falling into the water.

Miss Chance was shocked by Killigrew's coolness as he executed these men, even though she knew he had no choice, and yet she was also glad she had someone as proficient at killing as him to protect her. He might kill just as unhesitatingly as the men who sought to capture them – perhaps even more so – but what made him different from them was that he would never harm her, was even prepared to risk his own life in order to preserve hers.

He picked up the next musket, fired again, and the second musketeer fell over the side of the canoe.

One of the men from the first canoe suddenly got his hand on the side of the gig and tried to grab Miss Chance. She shrieked in alarm and kicked him in the head. Another man appeared on the other side of them, and Killigrew smashed the butt of the musket into his face. A third tried to swim after them, but a crocodile surfaced behind him, its jaws gaping, and a moment later the man was dragged under. Horrified, Miss Chance covered her eyes.

'It's all right,' said Killigrew. 'It's just the law of the jungle. Kill or be killed.'

'Cannibalism, if you ask me,' said Molineaux. 'I've never seen reptiles eating reptiles before.'

Another shot rang out from the second canoe, which was still overhauling them even with only three men paddling now. Killigrew braced his feet on the bottom boards and took careful aim with his pistol. Another man died, and Miss Chance quickly snatched the other pistol from Molineaux's belt and handed it up to Killigrew. He took careful aim again, but then hesitated.

'Shoot, for Christ's sake!' urged Molineaux, still heaving on the oars.

'It's our last shot,' said Killigrew. 'And there's three of them. Miss Chance, could you look in the bow locker and tell me what you find?'

She opened the locker. 'There's a bag of tools . . . something made out of canvas . . . some rope . . . and a bag filled with water.'

'That'll be the sea-anchor, miss.' He tucked his pistol in his belt and reached into his pocket. 'And it isn't water. Pass it here.'

He took the bag from her and held it out over the side of the gig, puncturing it near the top with his clasp knife. A little liquid dribbled down the side and dropped into the river. Killigrew took the pistol from his belt and held the flash pan against the hole in the bag. He pulled the trigger. The bullet went wide, but the flash ignited the liquid. It flamed quickly, and he tossed the bag at the canoe. The bag burst against the prow of the canoe and sprayed the three remaining men with burning oil. They screamed and beat at their burning clothes and hair, before jumping into the water. The crocodiles closed in, and the burning canoe drifted away with the sluggish current.

Killigrew's own hand was on fire. He doused it in the river, and then resumed his place on the bench beside Molineaux, taking up the other oar. A couple of minutes later they had left the scene of carnage behind them.

'Now all we have to do is find our way overland to Monrovia,' said Killigrew.

Molineaux rolled his eyes. 'He makes it sound so easy.'

Killigrew grinned. 'Trust me.'

They did not stay in the boat much longer. About half a mile further on, the channel widened where the river led out of the mangrove swamps and shortly afterwards they came to some rapids. In other circumstances Killigrew would have suggested they carry the gig between them to the head of the rapids; the fact was that his hands were in no condition to help carry a boat several hundred yards through thick jungle with the prospect of more rowing at the end of it, and he doubted Molineaux's hands were any better. The blisters they had developed pulling on the sweeps earlier had burst now, and their palms were raw and bloody. He wanted to get away from the water as quickly as possible anyway. In another hour it would be first light, and dawn was when the miasma overlying tropical rivers and swamps which caused malarial fevers were at their worst.

They rowed into the river bank, where thick foliage overhung the water. Killigrew tested the depth of the water with an oar and then jumped over the side, landing chest-deep in the water. 'Come on,' he told Molineaux.

The seaman was about to follow him when he hesitated. 'What about the crocs?'

'I think we left more than enough to keep them occupied down river.'

Molineaux cast his eyes over the water as if to make sure there were no crocodiles now rushing through the river towards Killigrew, and then realising he had no choice he swallowed hard and followed Killigrew over the side. Between them they pushed the foliage aside and pulled the gig hard against the bank, handing Miss Chance out and on to dry land. Molineaux followed her up, and Killigrew tried to angle the gig's bows up on to the bank. 'Molineaux, take the prow and pull, I'll get behind and push.'

'Wouldn't it be easier just to sink it?'

'Yes, but if this turns out to be an island we'll only have to refloat it. Once we get it on the other side of these bushes it'll be invisible from the river, even in daylight.'

Molineaux pulled, Killigrew pushed, and between them they managed to drag the gig up the bank and through the bushes. A short distance from the bank the undergrowth thinned out and disappeared altogether, but so few moonbeams could penetrate the canopy it was pitch black beneath.

Killigrew wanted to get as far away as quickly as possible, but their chances of navigating through the trees in the darkness were non-existent. 'It'll start getting light in an hour,' he said, gazing upwards towards the canopy. 'We'll be able to get going then. Until then, two of us can sleep. Who's going to keep watch?'

'I'll do it,' said Molineaux. 'You swam from the beach to the *Leopardo* and back again, I only swam back. Stands to reason you'll be more in need of a doss than me.'

'All right,' Killigrew said gratefully. 'We'll sleep in the gig,' he told Miss Chance. 'We'll be more comfortable there.' Which was not entirely true, but he did not want to worry her by telling her that in the boat they would be marginally safer from snakes and spiders and scorpions and whatever other nasty stinging things inhabited the jungle.

Killigrew had no recollection of actually getting into the boat; the next thing he knew, he was awoken by a piercing shriek. Lying next to him, Miss Chance awoke too and clung to him in alarm. 'What was that?'

Killigrew shook his head woozily. He had had so little sleep he felt as if he would have been better off not sleeping at all. 'I don't know . . .'

There was another ear-splitting shriek, and then the whole jungle seemed to come alive with howls and screams. Although it was still dark, there was enough light to see by now, and they could make out the trees stretching high overhead, like the pillars of some great Gothic cathedral, reaching up to the vaulted forest canopy perhaps a hundred and fifty feet above them.

Miss Chance seemed to realise that she was clinging to Killigrew more tightly than propriety would have approved of, and let go of him quickly with a sheepish grin. 'Where's Molineaux?' Killigrew asked her. She shrugged.

There was no sign of the seaman. Had he headed back to the barracoon to lead Salazar and the others to where they were hidden?

A moment later Molineaux appeared, running through the trees with a look of sheer panic on his face. 'What the hell's that sound?' he demanded of Killigrew.

'I don't know. Whatever it is, it isn't human.'

'Is that good or bad?'

'It's probably just monkeys or something. Where did you go?'

'I had to pump ship.'

'"Pump ship"?' asked Miss Chance.

'Answer the call of nature,' Killigrew explained delicately, feeling guilty for having suspected Molineaux of betraying them.

Molineaux was peering at him with a curious expression on his face. 'Sir?'

'What?'

Molineaux gestured towards Killigrew's neck. 'You've got some kind of slug sticking to you.'

*A leech*, Killigrew realised with revulsion, and reached up to pull it off before remembering that if you did that they were supposed to leave their heads inside you. He quickly rummaged about in the gig's emergency supplies until he came up with a box of brimstone matches, and handed it to Molineaux. 'It's a leech. Burn it off.'

'You sure about this?'

'Just get on with it.'

'Hold still.' Molineaux struck one of the matches and held it under Killigrew's jaw until the leech curled up and fell off.

'You'd better avert your gaze, miss,' said Killigrew, stripping off his clothes. 'There may be more of these things. They must have stuck to me when I went in the water last night. You too, Able Seaman. Strip. You check my back, I'll check yours.'

'You're clear,' Molineaux told him at last. 'How about me?' He glanced down at himself. He was covered in them. 'Oh, yeuch! Gerremoff me!'

Killigrew painstakingly worked his way around Molineaux's body. He noticed that there were scars on Molineaux's back. 'I thought you said Madison never flogged you?'

'He didn't. I got those courtesy of the Andrew Miller.'

'The Andrew Miller?' asked Miss Chance, sitting in the gig with her back to the two naked men.

'He means the navy, miss. What did you do to deserve those?' he added to Molineaux.

'Sassed the bosun on my first ship.'

'Why am I not surprised? Why did you join the navy in the first place?'

'Just between the three of us?'

'Just between the three of us.'

'I signed on one step ahead of the peelers. I used to be a cracksman. The rear-admiral found out, I don't know how, but that's how he picked me for this job. Careful with them lucifers,' he growled, as Killigrew removed the leeches from his inner thighs.

'All right, I'm done. You're clear.'

'Those things aren't poisonous, are they?' asked Molineaux, as they got dressed once more.

'They're not venomous, if that's what you mean. They're even used in medicine sometimes.'

'Plummy,' sneered Molineaux. 'Maybe we should have left them on, if they're good for us.'

'All right, miss, you can open your eyes again,' said Killigrew when they had finished dressing. He raided the gig's emergency supplies to see if he could find anything else of use. The only things which might conceivably be worth taking were some hard tack and salt junk, a lead-line, and some rope. 'Right, let's get going.'

'Which way?' asked Molineaux.

'We'll follow the river until the sun comes up. Then we'll head east for a day, towards the sunrise, and then turn south until we hit the coast again.'

They set off walking beneath the trees. Killigrew was in a hurry to make good time but he did not force a punishing pace, knowing that their European constitutions were not up to the task of over-exerting themselves in the tropical heat. The sun came up and the screeching of the monkeys died away to be replaced by a brooding and oppressive silence. The weather grew hotter and hotter, until the sweat dripped off them. A couple of hours after noon, they heard rushing water and followed the sound until they came to a pleasant glade where a cataract cascaded from a rocky precipice into a crystal-clear pool. Molineaux at once started to take off his coat as if to plunge into the refreshing water, but Killigrew laid a hand on his arm.

'What's the problem?' demanded Molineaux. 'No crocs, no leeches, no sharks, just lovely cool clear water . . .'

Killigrew pointed to where a leopard sat watching them from a rock overlooking the pool, its haunches tensed as if ready to spring. 'I suggest we keep very, *very* still.'

'I second the motion,' muttered Molineaux.

'Oh, don't be ridiculous!' said Miss Chance, pushing between the two of them. 'It's just a big pussy cat.'

'A big pussy cat that can rip a man's throat out in the blink of an eye,' Killigrew warned her.

She ignored him, gesticulating at the leopard. 'Shoo! Scram! Go away!'

The leopard snarled at her, a cross between a roar and a miaow, showing sharp fangs. She bent down, picked up a stone, and lobbed it at the leopard.

'No!' yelled Killigrew.

The stone bounced off the rock near the leopard and it sprang to its feet, backing away a little before it held its ground and snarled again. Miss Chance picked up another stone and this time hit the leopard on the nose. It turned and sprinted off into the undergrowth with an amazing turn of speed.

'Plummy,' said Molineaux. 'What if it comes back with its mates?'

'Leopards hunt alone, Mr Molineaux,' said Miss Chance, easing herself into the water, her gown billowing out around her. 'And they almost never attack humans.'

'You're an expert on leopards, I suppose?' asked Molineaux.

'I've read about them,' she returned, striking off across

the pool with a sedate breast-stroke. 'I may only be a woman, but I'm not addle-headed enough to decide to spend five years in Africa without reading a little about the country.'

'It'll be getting dark soon, and I don't expect to find a better place to camp for the night than this,' said Killigrew. 'I'll see if I can get us something to eat.' He put down the bag he was carrying and took out the lead-line and some ship's biscuits.

'You want me to keep an eye on the lady?' asked Molineaux.

'I think it would be better to ask her to keep an eye on you,' Killigrew returned with a smile.

'Hey, you were just as scared of that leopard as I was!' Molineaux called after him as he headed off into the trees.

Killigrew had learned how to snare birds from the natives in the jungles of Borneo. Although most of the forest's inhabitants had avoided the three intruders, he had glimpsed several birds during the day, either fluttering through the tree canopy or running along the ground. Finding a likely-looking spot, he broke up a ship's biscuit and scattered the crumbs on the forest floor. Next he made a noose from the lead-line and laid it on the ground, running the line up to the hiding place he had chosen behind a tree. Then he settled down to wait.

He did not have to wait for long. A plump-breasted bird with brightly coloured plumage and a glowering expression which reminded him of Standish strutted along the ground, bobbing its head like a pigeon. It saw the crumbs, studied them with its head cocked on one side, and then edged cautiously closer to investigate. It stepped on the noose, and Killigrew was tempted to pull on the snare there and then, but forced himself to be patient and waited until it took another step, putting a claw fully within the circle of twine.

He pulled. The bird squawked and fluttered into the air, but the noose was fast around its leg and Killigrew had a firm grip on the line. He pulled it in and wrung its neck.

'What've you got there?' Molineaux asked when he returned to the side of the pool.

'Supper,' said Killigrew. 'I'll pluck it. You see if you can find some firewood and get a fire going. Don't go too far, though: I reckon you could only be a hundred yards off through the trees and still get lost in this jungle.'

'I ain't going to get lost,' Molineaux muttered under his breath, heading off into the trees.

Killigrew sat down on the pebbly beach at the side of the pool and began to pluck the bird, uncertainly at first but with growing confidence as he discovered there was a technique to it. Miss Chance climbed out of the water and shook herself off. The wet cloth of her gown clung to her body, outlining her figure alarmingly. Killigrew looked away, but she lay down beside him. 'Do you want a hand with that?'

'Have you ever plucked a bird before?'

'Have you?'

'No, but I seem to be managing.'

'Good heavens, look at your hands! Did you do that rowing?' she asked. He nodded. 'Here. Let me bandage them for you.'

'Have you got any bandages?'

'I'll use my petticoats. Avert your eyes.' He glanced away and heard the sound of material tearing. 'All right, now give me your hands. Here, wash them in the water first.'

He was overwhelmingly aware of her proximity as she bathed his hands in the cool water. 'You should have said something earlier,' she said. 'How typical of a man to suffer in silence, to no good purpose other than the protection of his pride. I don't suppose poor Mr Molineaux's palms will be in any better case than this. Really, the two of you are as bad as each other! There,' she concluded, tying off the makeshift bandage. 'You'd better let me pluck that bird after all. I don't know where you men would be without a woman to look after you.'

'In the navy we usually make do with a jolly.'

'I beg your pardon?'

'A Royal Marine. Every vessel has a squad of marines on board, usually with nothing better to do than to stand around getting in the way. We keep the private soldiers employed by using them as servants for the ship's officers. Most of 'em retire and become gentlemen's gentlemen.'

'And that makes up for the lack of feminine company, does it?'

'Oh, there are plenty of opportunities for that, if you know where to look for it.'

'A wife in every port, is that it?'

He grinned. 'Well, I wouldn't say that. I've never been to New York.'

She slapped him playfully on the shoulder. 'Not when you're at sea, though.'

'You'd be surprised. I've known ships where the captain took his wife to sea. It's not allowed, of course, but they do it anyway and everyone turns a blind eye. Sometimes they take their whole families.'

'But you're not a captain.'

He smiled. 'Not yet. Give me a few years. I've only just made lieutenant.'

'So what do you do for feminine company?'

'Sometimes the captain's daughter can be a comely lass,' he told her, with wistful remembrance.

'And when the captain doesn't have a daughter?'

'A cold shower-bath every morning. Um . . . that bird's not getting plucked, you know.'

'Oh!' Miss Chance at once set to work, which was just as well because a couple of minutes later Molineaux returned, backing slowly out of the trees.

'Did you get some firewood?' Killigrew asked him.

'Uh-hunh.'

'"Un-hunh"? What does "uh-hunh" mean? Did you or didn't you, man?'

'I got some firewood, but I had to drop it when I put my fams up.'

Killigrew glanced up and saw that Molineaux had his hands raised over his head. The reason for this was the tall African, naked but for a breech-clout and a necklace of cowrie shells, who followed him into the clearing with a spear levelled unwaveringly at the seaman's chest.

Killigrew and Miss Chance leaped to their feet. Another spear buried its head in the ground at Killigrew's feet, and he twisted to see a dozen more native warriors standing on the rocks overlooking the pool.

# XVII:

## The Leopard People

Killigrew thought about plucking the spear from the ground but decided against it in case the natives interpreted that as a hostile act. Instead he raised his hands above his head.

'Speakee Krio?' he hazarded, without much hope, a lack of hope which proved to be justified when one of the warriors jumped down from the rocks and moved across to face him, brandishing his spear and shouting angrily in a language which Killigrew could not understand. All of the warriors looked extremely hostile.

'Say something to them, Molineaux,' he hissed. 'These are your people.'

'*My* people?' spluttered the seaman. 'My people were prigging culls in St Giles. I don't understand these people's mumbo-jumbo anymore'n they'd voker the flash patter.'

The warrior shouted at Killigrew again and waved his spear in his face. Killigrew found his eyes transfixed by the spear's point. 'I don't suppose you caught any of that?'

'I think it was an invitation to dinner,' said Molineaux. 'With us as the main course.'

One of the warriors tried to grab hold of Miss Chance. She pushed him away. Killigrew moved to defend her, but before he had taken a couple of steps she had started shouting back at the men – in the same language. Their expressions showed as much astonishment as Killigrew felt. One of them responded, glowering, but she kept up the tirade. At length the natives began to look sheepish and lowered their weapons.

'You can speak their language?' asked Killigrew.

Miss Chance nodded. 'Fortunately they're Mende. I learned some of their language from an ex-slave I met in New York who was born in these parts.'

'You seem to be rather fluent.'

'Well, I only learned the basics, but I seem to be making myself understood. They thought we were slavers; that's why they were so hostile at first.'

'You put them straight, I take it?' asked Killigrew, and she nodded.

The man who appeared to be in command of the natives spoke to her again, more politely now. 'I think he's saying we're free to go, but they'd be honoured if we'd be guests at their village for dinner tonight.'

'I knew it!' groaned Molineaux. 'No prizes for guessing who'll be on the menu.'

'Oh, don't be ridiculous,' said Killigrew. 'There aren't any cannibals on the Guinea Coast.'

More words were exchanged between Miss Chance and the leader, and suddenly all the warriors burst out laughing at something she said. 'What's so amusing?' asked Killigrew.

'I told them Mr Molineaux was afraid they wanted to eat him.'

Grinning, the leader said something. 'He says his village would soon starve if they had to live off something as scrawny as Mr Molineaux,' explained Miss Chance.

'Scrawny?' spluttered Molineaux. 'Who's he calling scrawny?'

Killigrew smiled. 'Tell them we accept their invitation.'

Miss Chance made the introductions, but the only name Killigrew caught was that of the leader, Ndawa. In turn, the two Englishmen were asked for their names. The Africans laughed heartily on hearing them.

'What do they find so amusing?' asked Killigrew, not a little put out, as they set off through the jungle once more.

'They say we have strange names.'

'Tell them theirs sound peculiar to our ears.'

'They want to know what our names mean. Especially Mr Molineaux's. They say an African should not have a white man's name.'

'You can tell them I'm proud of my name,' Molineaux protested indignantly. 'It was given to my father by my grandmother, who was a close personal friend of Tom Molineaux.'

'Not Tom Molineaux the celebrated pugilist?' exclaimed Killigrew.

Molineaux grinned. 'Well, I hear Mr Molineaux was what you might call something of a ladies' man, and my grandma wasn't exactly what you'd call a lady . . .'

'A pity you didn't inherit his physique as well as his name,' Killigrew remarked drily.

Miss Chance explained to the natives that Molineaux had been named after his grandfather, a great warrior, and Ndawa nodded approvingly. 'He says he shall call you "Sekou", which means "fighter".'

'"Sekou",' mused Molineaux, and nodded. 'I like that.'

Ndawa asked Miss Chance a question, and Killigrew recognised his own name. 'He wants to know what it means,' she said.

'It's the name of a place in Cornwall. I suppose one of my ancestors must've come from there.'

This provoked further howls of laughter from the natives. Another exchange passed between Ndawa and Miss Chance. 'He says that life must have been very confusing in your ancestor's village, if everyone was named after the place they lived in,' she explained.

The undergrowth became thicker, and a few moments later they emerged from the trees to find themselves at the edge of a broad savannah through which a wide stream meandered sluggishly. A village of clay huts with conical thatched roofs stood on the bank of the stream about half a mile away. There were fields around the village where men and women worked, and they all stood up as the party of hunters returned with two whites and a black man in white man's clothing.

By the time they entered the village itself there was quite a crowd of people gathered to stare at them. Like Ndawa, men and women alike were naked from the waist up but for bracelets, necklaces and head-dresses of cowrie shells. Chickens roamed freely within the confines of the village, marked out by a seven-foot high fence, and there were goats everywhere. The place was dusty, but a lot cleaner than most parts of London. And the air was a damned sight fresher, too, reflected Killigrew.

He felt something touch the back of his hand and glanced down to see a small boy, completely naked, rubbing his hand to see if the white would come off. Ndawa chased the boy away with a cuff around the back of the head, shouting at him angrily.

'Tell him I don't mind,' said Killigrew.

'Actually, from what Ndawa said, I think he was afraid that the boy might get the idea that white men weren't dangerous after all,' said Miss Chance.

Killigrew nodded. Ndawa did not want the boy to go near white men because in this part of the world most white men were slavers.

Killigrew, Molineaux and Miss Chance were ushered into the largest hut, towards the centre of the village. This, they learned through Miss Chance, was the home of Ndawa's father, Momolu, the head man of the village. Momolu himself was there, a tall, plump, grey-haired man with a cherubic face. He rose to his feet to greet the guests, speaking the language with a deep, rich and melodious bass.

'He says we are welcome under his roof, and we are to stay as long as we wish,' translated Miss Chance.

'Will he be offended if we say we only want to stay for one night, but must be on our way tomorrow? Every day we delay increases the chances of another ship reaching Salazar's barracoon to carry off the slaves there.'

'That depends how I put it, I suppose.'

'Tell him we're extremely grateful for his hospitality, but I'm worried that if we stay too long we'll be in danger of outstaying our welcome.' Killigrew shot a hard glance at Molineaux, who was exchanging smiles with one of Momolu's daughters, a pretty young girl somewhere in her late teens. She smiled back at him shyly.

'He says we can stay for as short or long a time as we desire, and if we let him know when we want to leave, he will send guides with us to help us get to where we want to go.'

'Ask him how far it is to Monrovia.'

Momolu did not understand the question at first, so Killigrew drew a sketch map of the Guinea Coast in the dust with a stars and stripes where Monrovia was. Momolu chuckled and nodded, marking the location of his own village on it, and said something to Miss Chance.

'He says it is three days' journey from here, and if we wish to leave tomorrow he will arrange for a guide to take us there. And he likes your drawing of a canoe-house. I think he means a ship.'

'That's not a ship, that's a whale,' protested Killigrew, who had gone to some trouble to make it quite clear where the land ended and the sea began on his map.

'Looks like a ship to me,' said Molineaux.

'It's a whale!'

'It does look like a ship,' admitted Miss Chance.

So there was something else Killigrew was no good at: drawing. Eulalia would be delighted when he told her.

Food was brought in wooden bowls, rice with a sauce of fish, cassava and sweet potatoes. It was pleasantly spicy and none of the Europeans would have had trouble finishing it, had not Miss Chance warned them to leave just a tiny morsel in their bowls. 'In many African cultures it's considered bad manners to eat all the food that's put before one. It suggests that one's host has not provided one with enough.'

The meal was washed down with some kind of palm wine served in wooden cups, and all that was lacking in Killigrew's opinion was a cheroot to round off the meal.

A thought occurred to him. 'Ask him what he knows about the leopard people.'

Miss Chance nodded, and at once passed on the question to Momolu. The chief's reaction was astonishing, both angry and fearful, and he raised his voice for the first time since Killigrew had met him. 'What's wrong?'

Miss Chance had knitted her brows as if struggling to follow what Momolu was saying. 'I'm not sure, but I think you've said something improper. Something that isn't supposed to be discussed in front of the women and children.'

Killigrew was not satisfied, but did not want to be a bad guest by pressing the issue. 'You'd better give him my apologies. Tell him I'm an ignorant white man, that I didn't know any better.'

Miss Chance managed to mollify Momolu somewhat, but the chief did not recover his earlier good grace and sat there glowering. After that the atmosphere in the hut was unbearable and Killigrew made his excuses – through Miss Chance, of course – and went outside. He sat on the low clay wall which surrounded the village well, sipping his palm wine and trying to ignore the women who peered at him out of the doors of their huts, giggling. It was a beautiful evening and he gazed across the savannah, enjoying the sunset. Knowing that for now there was nothing he could do to help the slaves in Salazar's barracoon, he tried to put them from his mind.

Certainly his surroundings were pleasant enough, and he would have enjoyed a slightly longer visit, although he knew he would soon grow bored in such a place. He had always preferred the hustle and bustle of cities to idyllic rural villages, and the noisier and more crowded, the more he preferred them.

After a while Miss Chance emerged and joined him at the well. 'Our sleeping accommodation has been arranged,' she explained. 'We'll each be sleeping in separate huts to avoid overcrowding; several people have offered us places, I've left it to Momolu to worry about who has the dubious honour of being our respective hosts. The chief seemed to think that I was your wife and suggested that if we wanted he could arrange for us to have a hut to ourselves, but I soon put him straight on that score.'

'Good,' said Killigrew, thinking: *pity*.

She fanned herself with her hand. 'I can't say I blame you for coming outside. It really was getting rather stuffy in there. I was beginning to feel quite faint.'

He smiled and said nothing. He was lost in his own thoughts, and while he was happy to listen to her prattling on, he did not feel inclined to say much himself. 'It's a beautiful night, isn't it?' she ventured.

'A beautiful night, a beautiful country,' he told her.

'And the people are so kind! I wonder how many Africans would get the same kind of welcome in our countries as we have in theirs?'

'You know how your country treats Africans,' said Killigrew.

She lowered her eyes. 'That's not fair. You know I don't approve of slavery any more than you do.'

'I'm sorry. I just can't help thinking that the only way we're going to stop the slave trade for good is to abolish slavery in the Americas.'

'You're right, of course. Perhaps instead of dedicating my life to converting these people to Christianity I should instead try to convert my own countrymen. These people seem less in need of moral guidance than we Americans do.'

Killigrew shrugged. 'You can't blame yourself for being American. People are people. Some are good, some are bad. It's got nothing to do with where they were born or what colour their skin is. The one thing I've noticed, from Falmouth to Nanking, is that nearly every culture seems to arrive independently at some system of morals which allows them to live in peace with one another. The real problems only start when those cultures clash head to head.'

'You're certainly right there. You know, I asked Chief Momolu what the names of the gods were in his religion. The books I've read about Africa always say that the natives are simply heathens, so I'd always assumed they were pantheists. It turns out the Mende have only one God, the same as Christians and Moslems.'

'There you are, then. God is God in any language.'

She pressed an arm to her forehead. 'Oh! This heat!'

Killigrew frowned. It did not seem that hot to him, and he wondered if he had a chill. He glanced across to where Molineaux was talking to Momolu's daughter. 'He's not going to get us in trouble, is he?' he asked Miss Chance.

'The chief seemed to be quite pleased at Mr Molineaux's evident interest in Abena.'

'In what?'

'Abena. That's her name. Seems he wants to marry her off.'

'To a British sailor? You must be joking!'

'The chief seems to think Mr Molineaux has come a long

way in the world. He thinks that Mr Molineaux has come to Africa to settle in the land of his ancestors.'

'I doubt it. I've known Englishmen – white Englishmen, I mean – who were less proud of their British heritage than Molineaux seems to be. I don't know him that well, but he doesn't seem to be the kind who'd want to give up all the luxuries of European life to live in Africa.'

'You might be wrong about him.'

'I might be, but I don't think so. I've known plenty of seamen his age, miss, and apart from the colour of his skin he's no different from the rest of them. At least, no different than they are from each other.'

'Supposing he did want to settle down in Africa? Would you stop him?'

'He's a rating of the Royal Navy. Settling down here would be desertion,' Killigrew said firmly, but then smiled. 'Of course, since I'm not currently a commissioned officer of the navy, I'm not under any obligation to try to stop him from deserting. Just so long as he doesn't stop me from getting to Monrovia.'

'And what then?'

'I'll get passage to Freetown, make a report to the senior naval officer present, and press for an expedition to the Owodunni Barracoon to see that vile place wiped off the face of the earth.'

'You make it sound so easy.' A look of panic suddenly appeared on her face and she bit her lip. 'You . . . you'll have to excuse me for a moment.' She hurried back towards the huts and accosted one of the women. The woman nodded and led her away, smiling. *Gone to pump ship*, thought Killigrew with a smile.

Killigrew spent the night on a rush mat in Momolu's hut. The hut was more than big enough for the chief, his wife and daughter, and their guest. Miss Chance was the guest of Ndawa and his wife, while Molineaux was put up in the hut of one of the other village headmen. The African night was cooler than the day – to the extent that the villagers put on long, lightweight gowns of fine country cloth – but it did not trouble Killigrew. In spite of all his worries, he had no difficulty getting to sleep.

He was awoken in the small hours of the morning and found Ndawa shaking him by the shoulders. The African said something in Mande, the language of the Mende, his face concerned but his words unintelligible to Killigrew.

'What is it? What's wrong? It's no good, I don't understand. You'll have to get Miss Chance. Me no hear, you fetchee Missy Chance for to jam heads talkee Mande,' he said at last, lapsing into the pidgin English of the coast in frustration.

But Ndawa no more understood that than Killigrew understood Mande. He spoke again, and this time Killigrew caught Miss Chance's name amongst all the unfamiliar words. A trickle of cold sweat ran down his spine. Perhaps the reason Ndawa had not brought Miss Chance was because he could not bring her. Perhaps the problem had something to do with her.

A small oil lamp, such as the Arabs used, provided light in Ndawa's hut, and by its warm glow Killigrew could see that Miss Chance looked ghastly. Her face was ashen and beaded with sweat, and while Ndawa's wife had covered her with blankets and the night was still warm, she was shivering uncontrollably and her teeth chattered. Ndawa's wife now knelt beside her, mopping her brow with a damp cloth.

Ndawa spoke some more. Killigrew did not understand the words, but the meaning was plain to see. Miss Chance was seriously ill.

He knelt down beside her. 'Miss Chance?'

'Mr Killigrew?' she reached feebly for his hand and he took it at once, squeezing it affectionately. 'I think it might have been something I ate.'

'It's just a fever,' he told her. 'It'll pass.'

She smiled, but he could see in her eyes that she knew he was lying.

'Ask them if they've got any cinchona bark,' he said.

'I don't know how to say that in Mande. Will it help?'

'I've heard it can often help in cases like this,' he said. 'Try Jesuit's powder.'

She spoke to Ndawa's wife, and Killigrew recognised the words 'cinchona' and 'Jesuits', but neither seemed to elicit any understanding from the woman. 'She says they've already sent for the witch doctor, but he lives in a village a day's journey from here so it will be two days before he gets here.'

Killigrew did not argue. It was an African sickness, so perhaps it needed an African cure. If she had been in Europe a doctor would probably have prescribed leeches, and nothing an African witch doctor could prescribe would be much worse than that, in Killigrew's opinion. 'Just hang on. You'll be all right.'

Ndawa's wife said something to her husband, and he gently took Killigrew by the arm, lifted him to his feet and dragged him away. Probably telling him that she needed rest, which Killigrew agreed with.

As he emerged from the hut Molineaux arrived with a small boy. 'What's wrong?'

Killigrew led him some distance away from the hut, so there was no danger of Miss Chance hearing them speak. 'It's Miss Chance. She's contracted yellow fever.'

'Oh, Jesus!' groaned Molineaux. 'She'll be all right, won't she? I mean, people get yellow fever and survive, don't they?'

'Sometimes. If they're strong.'

There was no question of Killigrew leaving the village while Miss Chance was too ill to be moved. He spent the rest of the day moping around, worrying. Without her to translate there was no one he could speak to but Molineaux, and he felt strangely excluded. The people of the village were clearly sympathetic, but the language barrier was all but insurmountable.

He felt so impotent. He wanted to do something for Miss Chance, but the only thing he could think of was going to Monrovia to see if any apothecaries there could sell him some cinchona bark. That was three days' journey away, and there was no guarantee that there would be any cinchona when he got there, or that she would still be alive when he got back six days later. But at least he would be doing something.

Her condition deteriorated during the course of the day, and that night Killigrew slept fitfully.

The witch doctor arrived late the next morning by dint of travelling all through the night. If Killigrew had expected some outlandishly dressed man with a demonic horned mask, he was disappointed : the doctor dressed little different from any of the other Mende, except for the bag of charms and talismans he carried.

Rather more remarkable was the witch doctor's travelling companion, an individual Killigrew immediately recognised as a member of the Kru race, a people renowned throughout the world as expert sailors and equally skilled linguists, these talents making their services as pilots, casual labourers, interpreters and boatmen much in demand from European vessels which operated along the Guinea Coast. If most of the Krumen Killigrew had met spoke pidgin rather than English proper, it was because they had been given the impression that pidgin was the only language British sailors spoke and understood.

The witch doctor's companion was recognisable as a Kruman from the tribal markings on his face, a line of blue cuts from his forehead to the tip of his nose and arrows on his temples, and the sharpened teeth he revealed whenever he grinned, which, like most Krumen, he seemed to do a great deal. He wore a white top hat, a size too large for him so that it rested on his ears rather than the top of his head, a white cravat, and a white-and-pink chequered loin cloth; he was otherwise quite naked but for an ivory bracelet and arm- and ankle-bands of leopards' teeth and cowrie shells threaded on string. He carried a notched fighting-stick over one shoulder as a young Englishman might carry a cricket bat as he sauntered to the crease.

'Speakee English?' this apparition enquired of Killigrew, who nodded. 'Me Tip-Top, me speakee man.' Killigrew guessed that like most Africans, Tip-Top had two names, a real name and the name given to him by white sailors who were too lazy to try to remember African names. The Kru in particular seemed to revel in the ridiculous names with which white sailors christened them, in a way which suggested to Killigrew that somehow they were having the last laugh on the white men who sought to mock them, as if it was hilarious that these ignorant foreigners could not cope with Kru names, but the least the Kru could do was to tolerate their stupidity. 'You speakee what bad for white puss, Tip-Top speakee medicine feller.'

Killigrew related Miss Chance's symptoms to Tip-Top, who relayed them to the witch doctor. 'Me thinkee yellow jack,' concluded Killigrew. 'Savvy yellow jack?'

Tip-Top nodded, his top hat jiggling on his head. 'Medicine feller hear, him savvy yellow jack good. White feller's sickness. White puss live, doan' live, who savvy, can?' He went into Ndawa's hut with the witch doctor, who did not look optimistic. Killigrew realised it was too much to hope that the doctor would know a cure. He stood outside the hut and waited, pouring himself his third cup of palm wine of the morning.

Molineaux approached. He had 'gone native' – sensibly, considering the heat of the day – and was wearing only his undershorts. Killigrew wiped sweat from his own brow and held out the gourd to him. 'Drink?'

'It's a little early in the day for me,' said Molineaux, eyeing the gourd dubiously. 'Sun not over the foreyard, and all that. Are you sure you haven't had enough?'

'Yes.' Killigrew drained his cup in one draught, and refilled it. 'This is my fault. I should have listened to you. This would never have happened if we'd stayed on the coast.'

'If we'd stayed on the coast we'd've been nabbed by Salazar's patrols. You can't blame yourself.'

'Then who else am I going to blame?' Killigrew demanded savagely.

They heard shouting from the far end of the village, and looked up in time to see a boy running between the huts, his feet muddy from the rice fields where he had been working. He was shouting something.

'What's the palaver, d'you think?' asked Molineaux.

'I don't know, but I've got a bad feeling,' said Killigrew, throwing away his cup and gourd.

The two of them ran towards the entrance of the village in time to see a large group of strangers approaching, some of them mounted on small but sturdy horses, the rest following on foot. Killigrew still had his pocket telescope on him and he took it out to study these new arrivals more closely.

They were warriors, bearing muskets and spears and wearing an odd mixture of African clothing and European uniforms, but all of them wore leopard skins in one form or another. Focusing on the lead horseman, Killigrew at once recognised Prince Khari.

'Slavers!' he roared to the villagers. 'Slavers!'

They did not need to be told. Some of them ran to fetch their spears and bows, others readied the farming implements they held to use them as weapons. Killigrew wished he had a pistol or a cutlass, anything he could use as a weapon. The villagers gathered at the entrance to the village and formed a defensive line. They at once began to loose their bows, sending their long arrows whipping through the air towards the leopard men.

The horsemen reined in and the men on foot spread out on either side of them, bringing their muskets up to their shoulders. Prince Khari bellowed an order and the muskets crackled, a cloud of pale grey smoke rolling across in front of each fusillade as the villagers fell dead and wounded on all sides. As unreliable a weapon as the musket was, it had nonetheless achieved and maintained its place in the soldier's armoury for hundreds of years thanks to its ability to wreak havoc amongst closely packed bodies of men.

Those villagers who survived the initial onslaught continued shooting their bows, but the effect was negligible. The horsemen goaded their horses on, hoofs pounding the earth, and levelled their spears while the musketeers dropped their weapons and charged forwards with swords and war-clubs. A moment later the two sides slammed into one another.

Killigrew had found himself caught in mêlées before, and he did not much care for them. There was too much going on: no opportunity for skill or intelligence to keep a man alive. All one could do was lash out at the bodies that pressed close around one, and hope that one only hit the enemy. A man could be killed as easily by a blow aimed at another as by a blow aimed at himself, a blow from a friend as from an enemy. A man who walked away after such skirmish might simply be lucky, rather than a good fighter.

And that was just a fight between Europeans, where the colour of a man's coat might at least give you some indication as to where you should direct your blows. Here the best Killigrew could do was to lash out at any leopard skins he saw. Mêlées were confused enough at the best of times, but at least in the battles he had known in Syria and China he had caught the occasional command shouted in English or French to guide him. Here, where all commands were given in unknown tongues, he was completely lost. The only thing he could judge was that whichever way he turned, the leopard men seemed to be gaining the upper hand.

A leopard man swung a club at him. Killigrew ducked beneath the blow and rammed a fist into the man's stomach. The two of them grappled, and the leopard man pushed Killigrew back against the wall of a hut and pressed his club against his throat. Then a horseman galloped past, inadvertently bumping into the leopard man and giving Killigrew a chance to snatch the club from his hands. He swung the club and struck the man to the ground.

He heard more hoof-beats and started to turn, but something heavy slammed into him from behind. He sprawled in the dust alongside the man he had just clubbed unconscious. He was aware of hoofbeats pounding the earth all around his head, and managed to crawl out of the way.

The leopard men had fought their way through the entrance to the village and now they rode amongst the huts, setting the thatched roofs ablaze with torches. Killigrew pushed himself to his feet and saw Ndawa fighting off two leopard men at once. He brought down the club on the head of one, allowing Ndawa to finish off the other with a spear-thrust. He thanked Killigrew with an upraised hand, and then ran off to help some of his fellow villagers.

Killigrew looked around for another enemy and saw no shortage of them. As the women and children of the village ran from the blazing huts, the leopard men herded them down the main thoroughfare, guiding them towards the entrance. One of the women – Ndawa's wife – fought back, trying to snatch a spear from a leopard man. Another leopard man rode up behind her and clubbed her down.

Something inside Killigrew snapped.

The man whose spear Ndawa's wife had tried to take grabbed her by the ankles and began to drag her through the dust towards the village entrance. Killigrew stepped into his path. The man did not see him until he bumped into him. He dropped her ankles and began to turn, only to receive the full force of the club in his face.

The horseman saw this and charged forwards. Killigrew waited for him, readying the club. The horse reared in front of Killigrew, hoofs flailing wildly. Killigrew side-stepped and dashed the club against the side of the horse's head. The horse went down on its forelegs and pitched its rider over its head. He tried to get up, but Killigrew did not give him a chance.

He glanced up and saw Miss Chance, asleep on her feet, being dragged out of Ndawa's hut between two leopard men, supervised by Prince Khari. Killigrew tried to run to her, but another leopard man blocked his path. Killigrew smashed his skull in.

As Killigrew charged forwards once more, Prince Khari glanced around and saw him. Recognising Killigrew, he grinned broadly and pulled a pistol from his belt. The pistol brought Killigrew up short, frozen in panic. Khari levelled the pistol and was about to fire when suddenly Tip-Top stepped out from behind a hut and gave the prince's horse a sharp thrust in the hindquarters with his fighting stick. The horse reared as Khari squeezed his trigger and the shot went wide. Khari landed on his back in the dirt and Tip-Top was about to strike him on the head when another leopard man brought him down with a blow from a war-club, crushing his top hat. Khari jumped athletically to his feet, and another horse was brought for him.

Killigrew gazed about through the drifting smoke and dashing bodies, but Miss Chance and her captors had disappeared. He jumped on to the wall around the well to get a better view. Wherever he looked the young men, women and children of the village were being ridden down and caught in nets strung between two horsemen. He glimpsed Miss Chance being slung across the rump of a horse. He was about to jump down and go to her when another leopard man ran at him. Killigrew kicked him in the face. He saw a horseman about to ride past, and grabbed the rope by which the well's pail was suspended from the primitive wooden derrick. He swung himself out from the well, caught the rider in the chest with both feet and knocked him clean out of the saddle. The rope swung back, and Killigrew dropped to the ground, kicking the dismounted rider in the side as he tried to get up.

By the time he got to the horse another leopard man was trying to climb into the saddle from the other side. Killigrew ducked underneath the horse and grabbed the man by the ankles, pulling his feet out from beneath him so that he cracked his head on the ground.

Killigrew got a foot in the stirrup and swung himself into the saddle. The whole village was ablaze now. The acrid smoke stung his eyes and clawed at his throat. Whichever way he turned the horse, he found his path blocked by the flames. The only way out – using the phrase 'way out' in its widest possible sense – was a fence, five feet high and burning fiercely. He tried to ride the horse at it, but it balked and almost threw him from the saddle. He backed it up as much as possible, until its rump was scorched by the hut burning behind it. It broke into a gallop without any goading. Within seconds it was upon the fence, but by now it was moving too fast to have any chance of stopping or swerving in time.

It leaped.

For a moment smoke and flames filled Killigrew's vision, and then he was treated to a grandstand view of the savannah stretching beyond the fence. A moment later the cassava field immediately below the fence hurtled up to meet them, and he was jerked viciously in the saddle as the horse's hoofs hit the soft earth. The horse stumbled, and Killigrew almost fell to the ground, righting himself in the saddle at the same time that the horse regained its footing.

He looked around. The leopard men had got what they had come for and were herding their captives back towards the trees while a few of their number fought a rearguard action against Ndawa and the other men who had managed to avoid being taken. Killigrew dug his heels into the horse's flanks and galloped towards them.

'Ndawa!' yelled Killigrew. The young man turned and saw him. 'Spear!' Killigrew made a throwing motion. Ndawa understood, and tossed a spear up to him as he rode past. Killigrew caught it by the shaft and urged the horse onwards, towards the rearguard. Seeing him bear down on them, they scattered. Beyond them he could see Prince Khari seated astride his horse, riding alongside the horse over which Miss Chance was slung.

'Khari!'

The prince twisted in his saddle, saw Killigrew, and turned his horse to meet his charge. Killigrew readied his spear to launch it at Khari's chest, and saw the prince pull a second pistol from his belt. The pistol came up unwaveringly. Killigrew knew he was too far away, but hurled the spear anyway, trying to give it some spin in flight the way he had seen the Africans do, so it would fly further and straighter, like a bullet from a rifle.

He missed Khari by about three inches, the spear sailing past his head to bury itself in the ground behind him. Khari did not even flinch. A moment later he pulled the trigger and disappeared in the puff of blue-tinged smoke which burst from the muzzle of his pistol. The next moment everything went crimson and Killigrew was blinded. He felt his horse stumble beneath him and then he was thrown forwards. The ground slammed into him and he rolled over and over. Wiping the horse's blood from his eyes with his sleeve, he tried to get up but his ankle gave way beneath him. He tried again, and stood up just in time to be slammed to the earth as Khari rode him down. He crawled a short distance, and felt rather than heard the hoofbeats pounding towards him as Khari rode him down again. Through the muzziness which clouded his vision, he just managed to glimpse the horse's fetlocks, and then something smashed into his skull.

# XVIII:

## Coffle

Half a mile into the jungle they came to where the leopard men had left their mules, and the captives were reorganised into a proper coffle. Men, women and children alike had their wrists tied behind their backs, and the men were yoked in pairs, one behind the other. A rope ran from the wrists of the rearmost man in each pair to the wrists of the next captive, a woman, who had her hands tied behind her; another rope, tied around her neck, ran back to the wrists of the next man behind her, the first in the next pair with his neck in turn in one end of a double-ended yoke. The children were mixed in with them.

The leopard men reloaded their muskets to keep the slaves covered, and exchanged war-clubs for cat-o'-nine-tails which they used unstintingly on any slave who even looked as if he or she might try to cause trouble, lashing them until the blood poured from their flayed skin.

Molineaux saw Miss Chance pulled from the rump of a horse and then placed in a litter made by stretching a pole between two mules and slinging a hammock from beneath it. She looked unharmed, but it was obvious she was in no condition to travel. He wanted to go to her to give her a few words of reassurance, but he was in the coffle at the front end of a yoke, his wrists tied before him and linked by a rope to a noose around the neck of Momolu's daughter Abena. As the coffle got under way he had no choice but to follow her or else risk choking her. He gagged as the man behind him was slow to keep up, pulling back on the yoke which cruelly chafed both their necks.

So far none of the leopard men seemed to have noticed that whereas all the other male captives wore breech-clouts, Molineaux was wearing a pair of white cotton undershorts purchased from Mrs Cropper's penny bazaar in Liverpool. He thought about pointing out that he was not an African and that the leopard men had no right to enslave him, a British citizen, but decided against it. They had no right to enslave any of these people, but that had not stopped them from doing so. Any demand to see the British consul in Monrovia would be received at best with jeers and at worst a swift death to stop him from causing trouble.

Not that he was in a position to cause much trouble. The unspoken language of . . . well, not love, perhaps, but a certain mutual attraction . . . which had served him so well with Abena the night before last, was useless in any attempt to plot an escape with the other slaves. They called out to each other in Mande, words of hope and encouragement to give one another strength, he supposed. Not understanding, he felt horribly isolated.

He wondered if Killigrew was all right. Probably. White men always managed to survive somehow, and compared to the rest of his pasty-faced brethren, Killigrew had struck him as being particularly adept at looking after himself. Would Killigrew try to rescue him? Certainly he would not allow Miss Chance to be carried off by the slavers; and, to be fair, he would probably try to free Molineaux and the other captives if he could. But could he? Molineaux doubted it. No, if he was going to get out of this, he would have to do it himself. Secured to Abena in front of him, and another man behind him, under the vigilant eyes and guns of the leopard men, there was nothing he could do but watch and wait and bide his time until a better opportunity presented itself.

Some of the leopard men shouted at the captives and lashed them angrily. For some reason Molineaux was spared; when the other captives fell silent, he realised that the leopard men were ordering them not to talk.

Two of the leopard men fell into step alongside Abena, joking in whatever language it was they spoke, and laughing. It was obvious they were referring to her, and one of them reached across to grab one of her breasts. She shrank away, and the man grabbed a fistful of her hair at the back, pulling her head back to tilt her pain-ridden face to the sky, snarling something at her.

Molineaux was perfectly positioned to kick him in the crotch from behind, and saw no reason to refrain.

The man clutched at himself and sank to his knees, sobbing in agony. His friend turned and smashed Molineaux in the face with the butt of his musket. The side of his face exploded in pain and he went over sideways, jerking the man behind him forwards and twisting his own neck in the yoke. He lay there, half-throttled, unable even to move, let alone defend himself. The man stood over him and lashed at him with a cat-o'-nine-tails, and Molineaux cried out as the knotted thongs lacerated his skin. 'Ow! Jesus Christ! All right, I'm sorry, I'm sorry!'

The man stopped and stared at him, before whirling to where Prince Khari rode at the head of the column. He shouted something, and Prince Khari wheeled his horse and rode back to where Molineaux lay. 'You speak English?' Khari asked, reining in.

Molineaux said nothing, and shrugged as if he did not understand.

'You shrug like a white man,' spat Khari. He made it sound like an insult.

'And you've got a face like a warthog's arse,' Molineaux could not resist replying, 'but you don't hear *me* complaining.'

Khari said something to the leopard man, who lashed at Molineaux again, once, twice, three times. Molineaux bit his lip in spite of the pain, determined not to give them the satisfaction of crying out a second time. 'What's the matter?' he taunted Khari, when the leopard man backed away to admire his bloody handiwork. 'Haven't you got the grit to get down off that prad and fight me yourself? And me yoked and bound and all.'

'Where did you learn to speak English?' demanded Khari.

Molineaux decided this would not be a good time to speak of his British parentage. 'From a missionary. Where did you learn yours? 'Cause I'd ask for my money back if I were you, you big ignorant hunk of shit.'

Khari repeated his order to the leopard man, who lashed at Molineaux again. 'Brave feller, eh? I'd like to see you try that if I wasn't bound,' Molineaux spat through the pain.

Khari leaned on the pommel of his saddle to address him. 'You were not born in Africa. Perhaps you are a runaway, who was shipped back to Sierra Leone or Monrovia? I cannot place your accent, but it does not matter. I ought to kill you for your impertinence towards a prince of royal blood, but a slave who already speaks English will fetch a good price at market in the United States.'

'Yeah? Well, when I've finished with you, the only market you'll fetch any kind of price in will be a meat market.'

Prince Khari chuckled, and ordered the leopard man to give Molineaux another half a dozen lashes before riding back to the head of the coffle and ordering them to move on.

* * *

Killigrew heard voices. They did not make any kind of sense. He wondered if it was because they were speaking in a foreign language, or because the blow to his head had deprived him of his senses.

His senses certainly felt addled, at least those of them he was using. Aside from his hearing, he could taste the dust in his mouth, could smell smoke and blood, and could feel the hard earth pressing against his body and the agonising throbbing in his skull. He could not see because his eyes were shut. He kept them shut because he was afraid that if he opened them he might find that he was blind.

He felt hands on his shoulders, turning him on his back. He rolled over and opened his eyes. If he was blind, then keeping his eyes shut for the rest of his life was not going to make a – he winced – blind bit of difference.

He could still see. All he could see was blinding white light, but it was better than nothing. Then Ndawa's head eclipsed the sun.

'*O-ke*?' asked Ndawa, his face full of concern.

'No,' said Killigrew. He raised a hand to his head and discovered with astonishment that his skull had not been caved in, although a huge lump had risen on one side of it. The horse's hoof must have struck him a glancing blow. 'Not "*o-ke*".'

Ndawa helped him up. Killigrew tried to stand on his own two feet, but his left ankle gave way the moment he put his weight on it. He would have fallen if Ndawa had not caught him. Ndawa put one of Killigrew's arms across his shoulders and helped the white man limp back towards the village.

A scene of carnage greeted them. There were corpses everywhere: several of them leopard men, but not nearly enough to put out the rage that smouldered within Killigrew. Like a moorland fire it had gone underground and seemed to be extinguished, but in time it would burst out afresh, more fierce and destructive than ever before. And when the reckoning came someone, Killigrew was determined, was going to get very, *very* badly burned indeed.

Most of the people left in the ruins of the burned-out village were the elderly ones, too weak and feeble to be worth taking away as slaves. The women moved amongst the bodies of their sons and grandsons, weeping, while the men went to work, trying to clear up the mess.

Killigrew had hoped that the witch doctor would be able to give him some kind of ointment to put on his twisted ankle to take away the pain – he had tried heathen remedies in the past and found them at least as effective as the latest European techniques – but the doctor was dead, run clean through the body with a spear which had grotesquely pinned him to the side of Ndawa's hut. At least Ndawa's wife was there, and not too badly hurt. Then Killigrew remembered Miss Chance and his heart filled with despair. They had taken her. She was not well enough to travel; she would be lucky if she survived the journey back to Salazar's barracoon; he had no doubt that was where Prince Khari would take her. And even if she did live that long, what kind of a fate awaited her when she arrived?

'Where's Molineaux?' he asked Ndawa. The young man shrugged, not understanding. 'Sekou,' said Killigrew. Again Ndawa shrugged. He did not know. He turned away and went to help tend the wounded. These people had enough concerns of their own, without worrying about a British seaman and an American missionary. Killigrew tried to go in search of a horse, but before he had taken two steps his ankle gave way beneath him and he collapsed against the wall of the hut, sliding to the ground with a sob of frustration.

'*Ce n'est pas bon*,' said a voice beside him, and he turned to see Tip-Top standing over him, knocking his battered top hat back into shape.

Killigrew looked up at him in surprise. 'You speak French?'

'A little,' admitted Tip-Top. 'As do you, evidently.'

'I wish you'd said something earlier. It's better than messing about with pidgin English.'

Then Killigrew saw Momolu. There was a bloody graze on his temple and his face was ashen, but his voice remained strong as he said something bitterly to Killigrew. 'What did he say?' Killigrew asked Tip-Top.

'He says: "Now you know what the leopard people are."'

That evening Momolu held a palaver which all the remaining villagers attended. Killigrew went along and watched from the sidelines. He could not understand a word that was being said, but it was clear that passions ran high. 'Can you tell me what they're saying?' he asked Tip-Top.

'They are discussing what is to be done. Italo – the young man who speaks now – is saying they must gather together their kinsmen from the neighbouring villages and pursue the leopard people to their lair and rescue the prisoners before they are spirited off to Hell.'

Killigrew smiled without much humour. 'I think it more likely they'll end up in the Americas – not that there's much difference between Hell and the Americas for those condemned to a lifetime of slavery.'

Italo sat down, and Momolu rose to his feet. 'He is saying that he would do anything for the return of the captives, but attempts have been made to track the leopard people to their lair before; those that set out to find it never returned,' translated Tip-Top.

'Tell them I know where the captives have been taken,' said Killigrew. 'Tell them I have been there myself and barely escaped with my life, but I am willing to return to help them free their kinsfolk, if they will help me.'

Tip-Top stepped forward and removed his hat, holding it

in front of him like a petitioner. They heard him out as he translated what Killigrew had said, but as soon as he had finished Italo leaped to his feet and spoke so angrily that spittle flew from his lips, gesturing at Killigrew the whole time.

'I don't like the sound of that,' said Killigrew.

'He says it is your fault that the leopard people came to the village today,' Tip-Top murmured out of the corner of his mouth. 'That they came here searching for you and your friends.'

'He's probably right,' said Killigrew. 'Tell him—' He broke off when he saw that Italo's tirade had finished and Momolu was gesturing for his son to speak.

'Now Ndawa is defending you. He says that although your skin is white your heart is pure, and the way you fought today proved that. You saved him from being killed and his wife from being taken by the leopard people, and for that he is always in your debt. You fought as a lion, and the lion always defeats the leopard. If they listen to you, there is perhaps a chance you can show them a way to defeat the leopard people.'

Killigrew flushed. He pushed himself to his feet and leaned against the side of the well for support. 'Now tell them this: the leopard people are working together with white men. White men who make me ashamed to be a white man. There are other white men, like me, who would like to destroy the white men who bring shame upon my race by helping the leopard people carry your kinsfolk into slavery; but we cannot do it without the help of the Mende, just as the Mende cannot defeat the leopard people and free their kinsfolk without the help of the white men. By working together, we can destroy the leopard people and the white men who would help them.'

When Tip-Top had finished translating all this into Mande, Killigrew was surprised by the lack of reaction on the part of the villagers. He had thought it a fairly capital speech, and was disappointed. He could only assume it had lost something in the translation.

Momolu rose to his feet and spoke very briefly indeed, although his dry tone was unmistakable. 'He wants to know if you've got a plan,' explained Tip-Top.

Killigrew grinned with relief. 'Now he's talking my language.'

As it happened he did have a plan, and he explained it at length through Tip-Top. There was approval on the whole, but Italo was not entirely satisfied. 'He wants to know how they can be sure you will meet them when and where you say you will, and whether you can guarantee to bring the help of the white men with the great canoe-houses.'

'Tell him I cannot guarantee the help of other white men, although I will do everything I can to bring it about. But whether I come with help or alone to the place we have arranged, I *shall* come, on my word of honour as an English gentleman.'

Italo had one more question. Instead of translating it to Killigrew, Tip-Top looked about until he saw a solid-looking rock on the ground nearby. He picked it up and showed it to Italo, answering his question. That seemed to satisfy Italo, who nodded and sat down once more.

'What was all that about?' asked Killigrew.

'He wanted to know what the word of a British gentleman was,' explained Tip-Top, and grinned. 'I showed him.'

They had given him five days. Killigrew knew it would take him three days to get to Monrovia, even with native bearers carrying him in a litter; with his ankle twisted, he would not make it otherwise. He knew that the remaining two days would not give him much time to fulfil his side of the bargain, but it would have to suffice; every day's delay before putting their plan into action increased the chances that more ships would come to the Owodunni Barracoon and carry off the slaves imprisoned there.

He set out with Tip-Top and Ndawa's cousin, Dguma, acting as bearers, as soon as they could rig up a litter; even before they left, runners were sent out to the neighbouring villages to call for the help of their warriors. Tip-Top and Dguma, used to the stifling tropical heat, carried Killigrew at a pace that would probably have killed all but the fittest Europeans. As they rested at villages along the way each night, Killigrew exercised his twisted ankle as much as he dared. He was determined to be in shape for the attack on the Owodunni Barracoon, but did not dare over-exert the joint for fear of making it worse rather than better.

Monrovia, the capital of Liberia, had been founded a quarter of a century earlier. Like Sierra Leone, Liberia had been set up as a homeland for Africans and their descendants who had been slaves but now, being free, wished to return to live in Africa. But while Sierra Leone was a British Crown Colony, Liberia had been founded by Americans. The United States constitution forbade – for obvious reasons – the ownership of colonies, so quite what the Liberian state was in legal terms was not fully defined; the US Government, however, embarrassed by this colony that was not a colony, had decided that it was time Liberia stood on her own two feet and declared her independence, whether she liked it or not. Killigrew had heard that a convention had been called in Monrovia for the following month so that the settlers of the non-colony could discuss their future. But when he arrived, borne between Tip-Top and Dguma, the place seemed as sleepy as ever.

Even though they had been founded for the same purpose, Freetown and Monrovia were the complete antithesis of one another: where Freetown was a riotous, ramshackle town where alcohol-consumption and prostitution were the order of the day, Monrovia was God-fearing, decent, orderly, alcohol-free and all in all the kind of place that only Yankee evangelists could create.

Killigrew hated it.

But he forgot all his loathing the moment he spied the frigate moored in the harbour. 'We're in luck, Tip-Top,' he exclaimed.

'A British ship?'

Killigrew nodded. 'HMS *Thor*. I know her captain.' Whether the captain would be prepared to listen to the disgraced Killigrew was another matter entirely.

Tip-Top and Dguma finally stopped on the waterfront and Killigrew climbed down from the litter, hobbling on his ankle but able to move around unsupported now. He pointed to the Kru bumboats tied up below the wooden jetty. 'See if you can persuade one of them to take us out to the frigate,' he told Tip-Top.

The Krumen manning the bumboats took little persuading. They had doubtless already visited HMS *Thor* many times since she had anchored in the harbour, but they were clearly glad of another excuse to visit the ship and ply the crew with their wares. Killigrew picked the likeliest, to the disappointment of the other boatmen, who nevertheless rowed out to the *Thor* with their rival, so that Killigrew arrived with a commercial flotilla of honour.

As they drew near, a lieutenant about the same age as Killigrew crossed to the rail to wave them away, and Killigrew guessed they had suffered from bumboat boys smuggling alcohol on board to the crew. Prohibition might be about to become inscribed in the constitution that was being drawn up for Liberia, but Killigrew expected that that was one law which might well prove to be unenforceable, even in the face of evangelical zeal.

'Clear off, you wretches! We've already got all the cassava, sweet potatoes, spices, rum, peppers, rice and mangoes we need. Go on, get away!'

'That's no way to greet an old friend, Matt,' chided Killigrew.

Lieutenant Matthew Masterson performed a double-take. 'Killigrew? What the deuce are you doing here?'

'It's a long story and I haven't much time. May I come aboard?'

Masterson frowned, torn between loyalty to an old shipmate and the knowledge that Killigrew was *persona non grata*. 'Look, Killigrew, I heard about what happened in London and I'm dreadfully sorry, but—'

'It's urgent, Matt. Many lives are at stake. You have to believe me, I didn't kill that girl. I've been spying for the Slave Trade Department. Rear-Admiral Napier will confirm my story.'

'Napier's here?'

'No, he's in London.'

'It will take weeks to get confirmation—'

Killigrew pounded a fist against the side of the hull. 'Damn it, there isn't time! You'll just have to trust me. Matt, I know where the Owodunni Barracoon is.'

Masterson stared. 'You've been there? I was starting to think it was a mythical place, like an El Dorado for slavers.' He hesitated only a moment longer. 'Throw down a ladder for him, Bosun.'

Killigrew heaved a sigh of relief. 'Is it all right if I bring my friends aboard?' he asked, indicating Tip-Top and Dguma.

'Of course! Come on up.'

'Is Nose-Biter still captain of this tub?'

Masterson nodded.

'You think he'll be willing to sail there and help me destroy the place?'

Masterson looked uncertain. 'This isn't the old days,

Killigrew. We can't just go charging into barracoons, freeing slaves and bombarding them the way we used to. After the legal wrangle Denman got himself into at the Gallinas River . . .'

'At least let me speak to him.'

Masterson took a deep breath. 'All right, Killigrew. But this issue isn't as straightforward as it seems . . .' He motioned aside the marine who stood on duty at the entrance to the roundhouse and ushered Killigrew inside. They made their way to the captain's day room and were saluted by the marine who was likewise on duty there. A low murmur of voices could be heard coming from the other side of the door.

'Sorry, sir, but Captain Crichton says he's not to be disturbed,' said the marine.

Masterson cleared his throat. 'My apologies to Captain Crichton, but I think he will want to hear what Mr Killigrew here has to tell him.'

The marine knocked on the door. 'Captain Crichton, sir? Lieutenant Masterson apologises for the interruption but says he thinks you'll want to hear what Mr Killigrew has to tell you.'

The door was jerked open and Captain Crichton stood there, glowering at the marine. He was in his late fifties but despite his age he was of tall, imposing build, with wild white hair and watery eyes which bulged from his fish-like face. 'Killigrew? Lieutenant Kit Killigrew? Or perhaps I should say ex-lieutenant?'

'It's a long story, sir.'

'Well, you'd better come in.' Crichton stood aside and allowed Masterson and Killigrew to enter the day room. As Masterson closed the door firmly behind them, Killigrew saw that Crichton's guest was a tall African with widely flared nostrils, low brows and a pair of eyes which glinted like polished Minié balls. He was dressed smartly in European clothes: black pantaloons and frock coat, white shirt, waistcoat and cravat. What brought Killigrew up short was the leopard skin draped over his shoulder. He rose to his feet and bowed without taking his eyes off Killigrew for a moment.

'Your Majesty, may I introduce Mr Christopher Killigrew?' said Masterson. 'Late of Her Majesty's Royal Navy and currently working for the Slave Trade Department of the British Foreign Office. Killigrew, this is His Majesty King Nldamak.'

Killigrew knew the name, although it took him a moment to recall where he had heard it before, and even then he only did so because of the leopard skin.

Nldamak was Prince Khari's father.

The slave coffle had reached the delta at the mouth of the Owodunni River two days earlier. They had only marched for a day, but it had been a gruelling march nonetheless and no less than seven of the captives had died: three dropped from exhaustion and were left for the vultures with their throats slit, the other four were murdered with shocking casualness for showing the least resistance. After seeing that, Molineaux had shown his captors considerably more respect than before, but had been even more determined than ever to see the slavers put out of business for ever.

They could not see the barracoon at first – unlike Killigrew, Molineaux had not got a clear look at the place when they had been there a few days earlier – for the place was screened by the thick bands of jungle which grew all around the channels and swamps of the delta. But Molineaux saw the four watchtowers silhouetted against the sky – in the direction of the sea, he supposed – and knew they had arrived.

They came to where one of the channels barred their way. A wooden landing stage reached out into the brackish waters. Crocodiles sunning themselves on a nearby mud-flat seemed to pay the slavers and their prisoners no attention. There was no boat tied up at the stage, just a tall wooden post set in the earth with an ivory horn hung from it. One of the leopard men took the horn and blew into it, a series of resounding notes which startled a flock of ibises to flight. Molineaux tried to imprint the sequence in his memory; it might come in useful later.

They waited. Some of the leopard men lit pipes. At length Molineaux heard a gentle plashing and gazed down the channel in time to see a large canoe appear around a bend, manned by four mulattos. They quickly reached the landing stage and tied up. One of them eyed the slaves. 'Not a bad looking lot, your highness. Not the best I've ever seen, but they'll do, I'm sure. Every slave has his price. Senhor Salazar is keen to know if you got Killigrew and the Chance girl.'

Khari gestured to where Miss Chance lay in the litter. 'I have the woman. Killigrew is dead, as Salazar requested. I rode him down myself and crushed him beneath the hoofs of my horse, as I crush all my enemies.'

The man nodded and turned away, but Khari seized him by the arm, making him wince. 'I expect to be paid well for this, Tobias. If not in guns, then in gold.'

'You'll have to discuss that with Senhor Salazar,' said Tobias. 'But I'll tell you one thing: word is there's another ship due in in a few days' time.'

'With rifles?'

'Rifles, gunpowder, rum, the lot. Don't you fret, your highness. You'll get paid.'

Khari folded his arms. 'I hope so. Senhor Salazar seems to think he can order me around as if I were another one of his lackeys. There are plenty of other barracoons where I can sell my captives.'

Tobias chuckled. 'Maybe so, your highness, but not this

side of Cape Palmas, there ain't. Come on, let's get the first batch in the canoe.'

The first batch comprised Miss Chance, Molineaux, Abena, and five other captives. Tobias got in the boat with Prince Khari and three of his leopard warriors. They cast off from the landing stage, paddled off down the channel and left the others to wait.

For the first time since their capture, Molineaux was close enough to Miss Chance to talk to her. 'Miss Chance? You all right, Miss Chance?'

She muttered something without looking at him. He caught Killigrew's name, but the rest of it made no sense. She was clearly delirious, and the pallor of her skin was ghastly.

Something smashed into Molineaux's back, and he sprawled at the bottom of the canoe. He rolled on to his back and found himself staring up at Prince Khari. 'You may have the gift of speaking English, but I did not say you could use it.'

With his hands now tied behind his back, and consequently twisted under him at an awkward angle, Molineaux winced. 'You didn't say I couldn't.' He was perfectly positioned to tip Khari over the side with a kick to his knees, in the hope of feeding him to the crocodiles, but with the leopard men covering him with their muskets he would gain little from that other than his own death in return for the possibility of Prince Khari's. He decided to wait for a better opportunity to kill him.

Khari gave him a half-hearted kick to ram home the point and turned away. Molineaux managed to sit up and tried to memorise the route they took through the channels, but the delta was like a watery maze, and one jungle-covered river bank looked much the same as another to him. Finding the way out of the delta the other night had been easy: it had simply been a case of heading upstream until they reached the main body of the river; but finding the way to the barracoon at the heart of the delta would be impossible for a stranger. Salazar had chosen the location of his lair well.

At last another landing stage came into sight, and Molineaux began to appreciate just how big the barracoon really was. Most of the island where they landed was covered by a huge stockade surrounded by a wooden palisade at least twelve feet high. From inside the stockade he could hear pitiful groans and the rattle of chains, like Scrooge's nightmare of Marley's ghost multiplied a thousand times. The mangrove swamps did not smell sweet at the best of times; here the stench was appalling.

The captives were dragged out of the boat. 'Not her,' Tobias ordered when one of the leopard men made to lift out Miss Chance. 'She goes to the big house.'

The leopard man glanced at Khari, who silently nodded his acceptance, before straightening and leaving Miss Chance where she lay. Molineaux could imagine what kind of fate awaited her at Salazar's hands in the big house; he wondered if the slaver was the kind of man who would take advantage of a desperately ill woman – a man who could sell human beings by the hundred like so many heads of cattle was capable of any atrocity. Molineaux was reluctant to let her out of his sight and he pushed back against the leopard men who herded him towards the entrance of the stockade, but he was powerless.

Molineaux, Abena and the other captives were pushed into the stockade. The walls loomed over them menacingly, and Molineaux saw more guards armed with muskets patrolling the catwalk that ran around the top of the palisade. In the centre of the stockade there were a dozen sheds formed from wooden pillars lashed together with bamboo. The walls were about six feet high, and between the top of the walls and the roof thatched with palm leaves there was a gap of another four feet. The groans and rattling chains seemed to come from all around; Molineaux wanted to put his hands over his ears and scream until he had blocked out the sound of human suffering.

The captives were marched between these sheds to one towards the back of the stockade and ushered inside. As yet it was empty. A central row of wooden pillars supported the roof, and a chain ran the length of the row, with a large neck-link every two feet. The captives were each padlocked into a collar. 'Shackle him between those two,' ordered Khari, indicating Molineaux.

'You think he's dangerous?' asked Tobias. 'He don't look much.'

'No. But he is clever. Those can be the most dangerous ones of them all.'

*You better believe it*, thought Molineaux, as one of his wrists was shackled to the man on his right and the other to Abena on his left.

'If he gives you any trouble, give him a good beating,' said Khari. 'But don't kill him. He speaks English – he should fetch a good price.'

Khari, Tobias and the guards went out to fetch the next batch, bolting the bamboo gate to the shed and padlocking that too.

Now that Killigrew was dead it was all up to Molineaux. All he had to do was get out of his shackles, kill the guards, free the others and then use the resulting confusion to rescue Miss Chance from Salazar's salacious clutches before they all made their escape through the maze of crocodile-infested waterways and into the jungle. *Easy as caz*, he thought wryly to himself. He glanced at the padlocks on his fetters and cursed himself for leaving his picklocks at the village, not that he had had much choice in the matter. He turned to Abena. 'I don't suppose you'd happen to have such a thing as a bent nail on you?'

She looked at him blankly.

He sighed. 'Didn't think so.' He lay back on the planking which formed the floor of the shed, trying to feign calmness in the face of adversity, but his own frustration got the better of him and he pounded the planks with his fist.

# XIX:

## A Lamb to the Slaughter

'I had a dream,' said King Nldamak, and then grimaced. 'Well, actually it was more of a nightmare.' He glanced at the three white men in the cabin bashfully, as if worried they might be laughing at him for being superstitious, but all three met his gaze gravely. He continued. 'I dreamed that one day the white man would rule all of Africa, from the Barbary Coast to the Cape of Good Hope.'

'Great Britain has no territorial ambitions in Africa,' Killigrew assured him, truthfully enough. 'Colonies are expensive to run and more trouble than they're worth.'

'Expensive to run, Mr Killigrew?' mocked Nldamak. 'Has not your country plundered India for its riches? Is it not Indian wealth which has made Britain great, while enslaving the Indians?'

Killigrew flushed. 'Britain only wants to trade. Fair trade is mutually beneficial to both parties. Sometimes it is necessary to protect trade with force of arms. Sometimes it is necessary to displace corrupt local rulers and set up an administration until such time as government can be handed back to the local people . . .'

'And how long until you hand back local government to the Indians, Mr Killigrew? Ten years? Fifty years? A hundred years?'

Killigrew held up a hand. 'I'm not saying that the East India Company hasn't made mistakes by allowing itself to be drawn into a greater and greater role in the government of India, your majesty. But we British have learned from that experience. We won't make the same mistake again.'

'Won't you? Perhaps you are wise enough to see that, but what about your government? Is that wise?'

Killigrew thought of men like Sir George Grafton, and decided it was probably best to say nothing.

'Africa is a rich land, Mr Killigrew. One day your people, and the people of the other nations of Europe, will realise that. Some already do. The only thing which prevents the white man from penetrating further into this continent is the white man's fever. But I hear now that Jesuit's bark is being proved to be a cure for the fever. The bad airs which now prove so fatal to the white man's constitution will not protect us for ever, and when the time comes the white man will come in force to plunder Africa's riches. Africa must defend herself, Mr Killigrew. Not just the Vai, the Mende and the Temne, but *all* the peoples of Africa. We must stop allowing the white man to carry off the best and strongest of our people to slavery in the Americas.'

'I couldn't agree with you more, your majesty. That is why I must fight against your son.'

Nldamak looked away. 'Khari and I went our separate ways many years ago, Mr Killigrew. He believes the only way the African can defeat the white man is to accept the white man's ways and learn to beat him at his own games. But the white man's ways are not the ways of Africa.'

'There was slavery in Africa long before the white man came, your majesty,' said Masterson.

Nldamak looked up at him sharply. 'If a wrong has been done for hundreds of years, Lieutenant, does that make it more or less of a wrong? Let Africa make her own mistakes. If she must suffer, let it be through her own fault rather than the fault of the white man. But my son – who is no longer my son – does not see these things the way I do. He has spent too much time in the company of white men, and it has corrupted him. Now his cause is the white man's cause, and he would betray his own people if it were to his own advantage. I do not mean to insult you gentlemen. I know that your hearts are good. I thank you for working to stop the slave trade; you have seen for yourselves the suffering it causes. But there are others in your country who do not understand and do not care. *They* are the ones I fear. They are the ones who will one day decide that Africa must be plundered for her wealth, as she has already been plundered for her people.

'And as for my son, who is no longer my son . . . he chose his path a long time ago. Let it lead him where it will. He must do what he must do, just as you must do what you must do. If you kill him, I shall grieve, as any father must. But I will not stand in your way. And now, gentlemen, you must excuse me.'

They ushered him out of the great cabin and stood and watched from the deck as Nldamak climbed down to the captain's gig and was rowed back to the waterfront, his shoulders slumped dejectedly. Killigrew saw a man who predicted only pain and suffering as the future for his people, and his heart went out to him.

'He speaks well enough, I'll grant you,' said Masterson. 'But can we be sure he won't send word to Khari and Salazar to warn them of our imminent attack?'

Captain Crichton nodded slowly. 'Oh, I think we can trust him, Lieutenant.'

Killigrew nodded. Nose-Biter Crichton might have a reputation for being as mad as a hatter, but Killigrew knew the captain was a good deal wiser than he let on. 'Besides, if we set sail at once we can attack the barracoon long before he can get word there,' he said. He was concerned that every moment they delayed increased the chances of more slavers coming to take away the captives in the barracoon's stockade.

'Weigh anchor and set sail, Masterson,' ordered Crichton. 'Set a course for the Owodunni Barracoon. Mr Killigrew here will give you directions.'

Within an hour they gathered together in the day cabin for a council of war: Killigrew, Crichton, Masterson, Tip-Top, Dguma and the captain of the *Thor*'s marines, Captain Reynolds. Killigrew showed them the sketch map he had just finished.

'This is the barracoon, or at least as much of it as I saw. Salazar gave me a pretty good guided tour. The sandbar here prevents any ships from approaching within half a mile of the coast. There are watchtowers here, here, here and here. The men in them have telescopes, so it's a fair bet they'll see you coming the moment you round the headland two miles to the south. Salazar's house is here, at the centre. Over here we have adminstration blocks, these are the barracks, and this is the harem.'

'Sounds to me like this fellow Salazar knows how to live,' remarked Masterson.

Killigrew nodded. 'Let's just hope he knows how to die. If he doesn't, I know how to teach him.' He was aware of Crichton and Masterson exchanging worried glances at his bloodthirsty talk, but pretended not to have seen and concentrated on the plan. 'Over here is the stockade where the slaves are kept, at the eastern end of the delta, away from the shore. The barracoon's well laid out and easily defensible – Salazar's no fool – but he's made one fatal flaw. Provided you don't elevate your long guns above five degrees, if you anchor just outside the bar you can bombard the whole barracoon and hit everything but the stockade itself.'

‘What about the harem?’ asked Crichton. ‘Wouldn’t want to bombard innocent women.’

‘And Miss Chance,’ added Masterson. ‘Odds are she’ll either be in the harem or in Salazar’s house.’

Killigrew nodded. ‘That’s where your marines come in, Captain Reynolds. I’ll go with you to guide you. Ndawa – Chief Momolu’s son – promised to meet me there with some of his men and enough canoes to get us through the creeks. We’ll hit the barracoon at midnight. We use stealth. With any luck we’ll be able to get the women out of there before Salazar even knows we’ve been and gone. The other slaves will be safe in the stockade. At two bells in the middle watch you can start the bombardment.’

‘Then you’d better make sure you’re out of there by then,’ said Crichton. ‘Because I’m going to throw every shell I’ve got on board at that barracoon, and when I’m done there won’t be so much as a termite left alive in that delta.’

Captain Reynolds nodded. ‘If there are any survivors amongst Salazar’s men, we’ll pick them up. I’ve done this kind of thing enough times before.’

Killigrew shook his head. ‘Make no mistake, gentlemen. This is far and away the biggest barracoon I’ve ever seen. Salazar himself told me he employs over three hundred men.’

‘That’s a lot of people,’ said Crichton. ‘What arrangements are we going to make for prisoners?’

Killigrew looked up at him, his dark eyes glittering coldly in the light of the oil lamp. ‘Who said anything about taking prisoners?’

HMS *Thor* hove to a few miles to the south of the Owodunni delta at sunset the following evening and the anchor was dropped into the sea with a splash. The crew prepared to lower the launch.

‘Remember, you’ve got to be out of there by two bells in

the middle watch,' Masterson told Killigrew. 'Do you have a watch?'

'Yes, but it's broken. I think some water must have spoiled the workings. Damn it, you'd think someone would come up with a way to make these things impervious to water.'

'You'd better take mine. Shall we synchronise watches, sir?'

Crichton checked his own watch. 'I make it six thirty-seven, on the dot.' Six hours and twenty-three minutes to one o'clock, or two bells in the middle watch.

'Same here,' said Masterson, and handed his watch to Killigrew, who tucked it into the fob pocket of the borrowed waistcoat he was wearing along with a borrowed dirk and a borrowed cutlass. 'You'd better take this as well,' he added, handing Killigrew some kind of pistol.

Killigrew studied the weapon curiously. It was like a pepperbox, but whereas the pepperbox had six distinct barrels for each shot, this weapon had only one barrel, with a cylinder in the middle containing several chambers, each of which was brought into line with the barrel as the cylinder turned.

'Colonel Colt's invention,' explained Masterson.

Killigrew cocked the hammer experimentally, saw that it worked, and then lowered the hammer back into place. 'Ingenious.'

'Each chamber's already primed and loaded. All you have to do is cock, aim and fire. Effective range is about fifty yards.'

'Thanks, but if I have to use it I'll have failed. Stealth is the order of the evening, gentlemen.'

'Take it anyway,' said Masterson. 'Just in case.' Killigrew nodded and buckled on the gun belt Masterson handed him before climbing into the launch. 'Good luck,' Masterson called down to them as the boat was lowered to the water.

'I'll see you in seven hours,' Killigrew told him.

Masterson grinned. 'I'll have a bottle of whisky standing by.'

'I'll probably need it by then.' In fact Killigrew would have liked to have a drink or two there and then, to stiffen resolve, but he knew he needed to keep a clear head.

It was a tight squeeze in the launch with Tip-Top, Dguma and Reynolds and his squad of twenty marines. The jollies looked smart in their red coats and white crossbelts. They rowed proficiently across the bar and through the breakers, jumping out to drag the boat a few feet up on to dry sand so that the officers would not have to get their feet wet. The squad moved quickly across the beach with Tip-Top and Dguma while Killigrew gave one last glance to where the *Thor* rode at anchor, silhouetted by the last rays of the sunset.

'No turning back now,' said Reynolds. 'We're going to have to move fast now to get to the barracoon in time. My men are in first-rate condition, Killigrew. You'd better not slow us down.'

'I'll certainly try to keep up,' Killigrew promised him gravely. 'Let's just hope this breeze keeps up, otherwise we'll be left without naval support at the eleventh hour.' Without the bombardment from the *Thor*, even if the marines did succeed in rescuing the slaves from the barracoon, there was nothing to stop Prince Khari's leopard men from pursuing them as they escaped.

'I just hope that these natives are there with the canoes,' grunted Reynolds.

Dguma and Tip-Top exchanged a few words. 'What did he say?' asked Killigrew.

Tip-Top grinned, his pointed teeth showing white in the bosky gloom. 'He says the word of a Mende is as good as the word of an Englishman. They'll be there.'

As the light faded they headed inland through the jungle. Dguma led the way, used to moving stealthily through the forest at night. It was a clear night and a half-moon rose shortly after sunset, but beneath the trees it was pitch black. The marines were well disciplined and they marched silently, without talking. However irritating the jollies might be on board ship, there were no soldiers in the world Killigrew would have preferred to have around him in a scrap.

Nevertheless it took them nearly five hours to cover the few miles to the edge of the delta. They paused by a thick band of undergrowth beyond which Killigrew could hear the gentle trickle of water.

'Well, we're here. Where are they?' His ankle was throbbing again after the trek and he unlaced his half-boot to massage it.

Reynolds looked at him. 'Are you sure you're up to this, Killigrew?'

'Never felt better.' Killigrew laced his boot up tightly.

Tip-Top translated his question into Mande for Dguma.

Before Dguma could reply, a voice hissed at them in some African tongue, suspicious and full of menace. The marines quickly unslung their muskets, but Dguma answered the voice, and a moment later a shadowy figure emerged from the darkness. 'One of their watchers,' explained Tip-Top, after a brief exchange with Dguma and the stranger. 'Ndawa and the others are about five hundred yards off that way.'

They followed the man through the trees. Killigrew kept one hand on the butt of the revolving pistol holstered at his side in case the stranger should turn out to be one of Salazar's men, but before long they were surrounded by about a dozen Mende armed with spears, bows and war-clubs. Ndawa clapped Killigrew on the shoulders, and even Italo seemed pleased to see him. One of the Mende cupped his hands to his mouth and made some kind of bird-call, doubtless the signal to summon back the other men who had been watching for Killigrew and his companions.

Tip-Top asked Ndawa a question, to which the Mende replied evenly.

'What did you ask him?'

'I wanted to know if this was all the men he had with him,' said Tip-Top. 'He says more wanted to come, but twenty was enough.'

'He's right,' said Killigrew. 'Salazar's men might have noticed a larger force of Mende approaching and hiding here in the woods. Tell him that the naval bombardment has been arranged.' He hoped it was true. His worst fear – that the breeze might die and leave the *Thor* becalmed – had come true. But he sensed that Crichton and Masterson would not let him down and would get the frigate into position, even if that meant putting all their boats into the water to tow it.

Led by Ndawa, the Mende picked up the five bark canoes they had brought with them and moved off through the trees until they came to a spot Ndawa had reconnoitred earlier, where the bushes at the side of the channel thinned out enough for them to reach the water's edge. With Tip-Top's help, Reynolds and Ndawa organised their men, dividing them between the canoes. One canoe would head downstream and the men inside would silence the guards in the two watchtowers to the west, which would be the first to spy the approach of the HMS *Thor* as it rounded the headland to the south; another would take care of the guards in the easternmost watchtowers, which dominated the harem and the stockade. The remaining three would attack the barracoon and rescue the women in the harem.

'Fix bayonets, men,' ordered Reynolds. 'No shooting unless you have to. We don't want to raise the alarm.'

The Mende got into the canoes first and held them steady for the marines, but the marines were used to working with small boats and climbed in without fuss, four marines and four Mende to each canoe. Killigrew climbed into the largest canoe with Tip-Top, Ndawa, Dguma, Italo and Reynolds with three marines.

The canoes slipped silently through the water, the paddles making barely a sound. The jungle on either side of them was alive with the croaking of frogs and the chirruping of insects, while the sound of distant laughter floated through the night from the direction of the barracks. One of the canoes headed off down one of the main channels towards the coast, bearing the men who would kill the guards in the westernmost watchtowers; the rest headed inland, towards the harem.

Ndawa held up a hand, and the lead canoe slowed to a halt, the others doing likewise. Then he signalled one of the canoes forward to where a watchtower loomed over them about a hundred yards away. It tied up directly beneath the tower, and two of the marines got out. Killigrew took out his pocket telescope and was able to follow their progress as they ascended the ladder stealthily, silhouetted against the purple night sky. They were at their most vulnerable now, and Killigrew expected someone to see them and raise the alarm at any moment. His heart pounded in his chest, but his earlier fear had melted away and now only excitement filled him. He had been waiting for this night for a long, long time.

This was the night of the reckoning.

The first marine reached the top of the ladder, bayonet in hand. If either of the two guards made any sound as they died, Killigrew did not hear them. Their silhouettes disappeared and were quickly replaced by the marines, who put on the guards' broad-brimmed straw hats and assumed their positions.

Ndawa signalled again and the remaining canoes glided forwards. One moved on to deal with the second watchtower, the other three passed the stockade. Killigrew could smell the stench of excrement and hear the groans of the slaves and the occasional clank of their chains. *Just a few more minutes*, he thought, *and then you'll be free. Just hang on until then.*

The three canoes tied up at the next island, at the far end from the long, low building which formed the harem. Two guards stood on duty with muskets over their shoulders at either end of the building, but they looked relaxed. Ndawa was about to ease himself out of the canoe when Killigrew put a hand on his arm to stop him.

'Tell him to kill the guards, but not to enter the building,' he asked Tip-Top in a low voice. 'The women may all be there against their will, but we don't know that for sure, and it will only take one of them to raise the alarm.'

Tip-Top passed this on, and Ndawa nodded before climbing out of the canoe with Dguma, Italo and another man. They split into two pairs, tackling each end of the building silently. The guards never knew what hit them, and Killigrew could barely hear the soft thud of the bodies as they hit the ground with arrows through their throats.

Killigrew, Tip-Top and the marines climbed out of the canoe and hurried through the moonlight to join the others outside the building. Killigrew tried the front door. It was unlocked. He eased it open a crack and peered through. A long corridor ran the length of the building, illuminated by an oil lamp hanging from the ceiling, and a guard dozed in a chair towards the middle with his straw hat tipped forward over his eyes, snoring loudly. A door led off the corridor every six feet on either side, and Killigrew could hear sobbing coming from more than one of them. He eased the door shut once more.

'Two minutes,' he whispered to Reynolds. Tip-Top passed the word on to Ndawa.

Killigrew made his way around the outside of the building. Each room had a small barred window set in it. Most of the rooms were dark, but even without light he could see that none of them contained Miss Chance: all the captives of the harem were black. A light showed in one window, and as Killigrew peered through he could see a fat white man he did not recognise – his bronzed face and hands in obscene contrast to the white rolls of flab of the rest of his body – holding down a slender young black woman, bending her over the grim cot which served as a bed as he thrust himself into her from behind.

Filled with revulsion, Killigrew felt himself trembling with rage, but held himself in check. Being raped was probably traumatic enough without having someone kick down the door to witness your humiliation before brutally and bloodily murdering the man who was raping you.

He finally returned to where Ndawa waited with the others. 'No sign of Miss Chance,' he whispered to Reynolds. 'Salazar must have her at the house.'

'And you're going after her, I suppose?'

Killigrew nodded. 'Besides, I've got a score to settle with Salazar.'

'Want me to send some men with you?'

'No, thank you. I'll manage. Give me ten minutes, and then start getting the women out of here.' No matter how stealthy they were, Killigrew could not imagine that releasing the women from the harem and getting them through the delta was a task which could be performed without the alarm being raised.

Ndawa nodded as Tip-Top explained, and then asked a question. 'He wants to know what he should do if you're not back by the time we're ready to get back in the canoes,' said the Kruman.

'You go without me,' Killigrew said simply. He checked his watch. It was a quarter past midnight. 'You've got three-quarters of an hour before the bombardment starts.' *If it starts*, he added to himself: there was no sign of the breeze picking up again, and the night was deadly still. 'Don't be here when it does.' He hurried off into the darkness before Reynolds, Ndawa or Tip-Top could protest.

A water channel separated the island with the harem from the main island at the centre of the barracoon where Salazar's house and the administrative blocks stood. A narrow wooden bridge arched over the water, and another guard stood on duty there with a musket over his shoulder, smoking a clay pipe. Killigrew decided to adopt the bold approach and strode up the bridge as if he had every right to be going where he was. The man looked up as his footsteps sounded on the planks of the bridge.

'*Boa noite*,' said Killigrew.

'*Boa noite, senhor.*'

Killigrew produced a cheroot Crichton had given him earlier. '*Tem lume, por favor?*'

'*Sîm, senhor.*' The guard produced a box of lucifers, struck one on the wooden handrail of the bridge and lit Killigrew's cheroot for him.

'*Obrigado.*' Killigrew surreptitiously took out his knife and held it behind his back.

'*De nada.*'

'*Onde está a casa de Senhor Salazar?*'

As the guard turned away to point out Salazar's house, Killigrew clamped a hand over his mouth and slit his throat. '*Obrigado*,' he murmured, propping the man's body against the handrail so it looked as though he was staring into the water below the bridge. He kicked the man's pipe, which had fallen to the planks of the bridge, into the water, and wiped the blade of his knife clean before replacing it in the sheath at his side.

He crossed to where the *palazzo* stood, keeping to the shadows. There were no guards here. All the downstairs rooms were dark, although lights showed in some of the upstairs windows. He crept around the back and tried the kitchen door.

Locked. Kicking it open would raise the alarm. He looked around for another way in, and saw a drainpipe leading up to the roof. He looked around again to make sure no one was watching, but a hush lay over the barracoon. Everything was preternaturally quiet. Killigrew prayed he was not about to walk into a trap.

Or rather, climb into a trap, to be precise. Ignoring his throbbing ankle, he shinned up the drainpipe to the ornate stone balustrade that ran around the top of the *palazzo* and scrambled over it. There were perhaps a dozen skylights set at various places across the roof, but they were all locked and barred. Making his way around the edge of the roof, he came to where a balcony jutted out in front of some French windows that were dark. He lowered himself over the balustrade and dropped. He landed lightly on the balls of his feet but pain shot through his ankle nonetheless. He crouched there for a moment and peered through the glass. The room beyond was unoccupied. He tried the handle. The door was unlocked but the catch was on. He slid his knife into the gap and jiggled it until he was able to raise the catch, slipping inside and closing the door behind him.

He crossed to the far door and pressed his ear to it. No sound came from the other side. He opened it a crack and peered out. A single oil lamp illuminated the landing. There was no one in sight. He slipped out of the room and crept cat-footed across the carpet to the door opposite. Light shone underneath the door. He crouched down to peer through the keyhole and saw Captain Madison sitting up in bed, reading the Bible. *I'll deal with you later*, Killigrew thought to himself.

Voices came from a door further down. He peered through that keyhole. The occupants of the room were out of sight this time, but he could hear them talking. He recognised Salazar's voice: 'You should be grateful to me, Miss Chance.

If it had not been for the Jesuit's powder I gave you, you would be dead by now.'

'If you think I'm going to surrender to your disgusting embraces just because you saved my life – after first endangering it, of course – you've got another think coming, Mr Salazar.'

So at least one of the captives had not been violated; that was some small relief at any rate.

'You should be good to me, Miss Chance . . . May I call you Suzannah?'

'You may not. Don't touch me! Get your filthy hands off me!'

Killigrew straightened and was about to burst through the door when he felt a hand on his shoulder. He straightened, turned and found himself staring at Prince Khari's chest.

'I never took you for a peeping Tom, Mr Killigrew.'

'I'm a man of many parts,' Killigrew told him with a shrug, and tried to stab him in the stomach with his knife.

But Khari's hand swept down as fast as a striking mamba and gripped him by the wrist, halting the knife's point an inch from his skin. He span Killigrew around, slammed him against the wall and twisted his arm up into the small of his back until Killigrew gasped and dropped the knife.

Two of the bedroom doors opened and Salazar and Madison emerged, the former in white pantaloons and shirt, the latter in a blue-and-white striped nightshirt and tasselled nightcap. 'What's going on?' demanded Salazar.

'I found an intruder,' said Khari.

'Good evening,' said Killigrew, speaking with difficulty because of the way Khari was pressing his cheek against the wall.

Recognising him, Salazar relaxed and smiled, leaning negligently against the wall. 'Mr Killigrew. I've been expecting you . . .'

Killigrew groaned. 'Somehow I had a feeling you were going to say that.'

'. . . in spite of what his highness here told me about having killed you.'

'You don't have to call him "your highness", you know,' said Killigrew. 'His father's disinherited him. He won't even inherit a cracked chamber-pot when King Nldamak dies, never mind a throne.'

Khari punched him in the back and Killigrew gasped as pain exploded through his kidneys. 'Do not worry, Salazar. I'll finish the job.'

'No. I'll deal with Killigrew. You go down to the pens and make sure the slaves are all safely locked up for the night. Even Killigrew here isn't foolish enough to come back alone.' Salazar relieved Killigrew of his cutlass and revolver, keeping him covered so that Khari could release him and disappear downstairs.

'I'll get dressed,' muttered Madison, going back inside his room.

Salazar motioned for Killigrew to enter Miss Chance's room. She was sitting up in bed, her face drawn and pale with heavy bags under her eyes, but it was clear she was on the mend following her illness. 'Kit!' she exclaimed, spreading her arms wide.

Killigrew saw no reason not to go to her and hug her reassuringly. 'It's all right. Everything's going to be just fine.'

Salazar tutted, seating himself in a chair by the door while keeping Killigrew covered with the revolving pistol. 'You should not lie to the lady, Mr Killigrew. Or could it be you know something which yet escapes me?'

Killigrew glanced at the carriage clock on the mantelpiece. It said twenty-two minutes to one.

Salazar examined the revolving pistol, and started to knock the bullets out of their chambers, one after another, as if daring

Killigrew to come around the bed at him; but the cutlass was propped against the wall close by Salazar's hand. 'I admire your spirit, Mr Killigrew. I would like to say you have been a worthy adversary, but I fear your puny efforts to put me out of business have hardly taxed me. I noticed you glanced at the clock just now. Am I keeping you from an urgent appointment?'

'You know how it is. Things to do, people to see.' Killigrew tried to sound nonchalant, but his bravado sounded hollow even to his own ears.

'I wonder. Could it be that you managed to arrange for a naval vessel to come and bombard my little business concern? The suggestion that any man, disgraced and stripped of his naval rank, could pull off such a feat would normally make me laugh. But then, you are not just any man, are you?'

Salazar gestured with the revolver. Killigrew had counted the number of bullets he had knocked out and knew there was still one in there. 'An ingenious little toy,' said Salazar, and span the cylinder, before aiming the pistol between Miss Chance's eyes. He pulled the trigger, and she flinched with a gasp as the pistol banged, flames shooting from the muzzle, but the hammer had fallen on a chamber without a bullet in it. 'So tell me, Mr Killigrew, did you arrange for a naval bombardment, or not?'

Miss Chance clung to him. 'Don't tell him anything, Kit.'

'Perhaps Miss Chance thinks I am in jest,' said Salazar, aiming and squeezing the trigger again. The pistol banged again, but again there was no bullet in the chamber. 'Let me assure you, I'm not.' He aimed again, and smiled. 'Miss Chance has four chances left. Should I make arrangements for the reception of unwelcome guests, or not?'

Killigrew knew when he was beaten. He only hoped that Reynolds's marines had been able to get the women out of the harem in time. 'Give it up, Salazar. A Royal Navy frigate should be anchoring off the shore in the next fifteen minutes: the bombardment commences at one o'clock. You can kill me if you like, but either way you're finished.'

Salazar glanced down the barrel of the pistol. 'A wise decision, Mr Killigrew. The next shot would have blown her pretty little brains out.' He picked up the cutlass in his left hand and gestured with the revolver. 'Now let us leave Miss Chance to get her rest, which she is much in need of following her recent illness.'

As they emerged from the bedchamber they found Madison waiting for them outside . 'Well?'

'There's a British frigate coming to bombard us in a quarter of an hour.'

Madison laughed. 'One frigate? Was that the best he could do?'

Killigrew frowned. For two men who were about to be subjected to a bombardment of shells, they were both in remarkably high spirits. 'It should be enough to turn this barracoon into so much ploughed earth,' he told them confidently.

Salazar smiled. 'I think not.'

They went downstairs and Salazar pulled on a bell rope. Henriques appeared a moment later. 'Mr Sampson and his crew are to report to their action stations at once, Henriques.'

The footman nodded and hurried outside. Salazar and Madison followed him, taking Killigrew with them. The three of them went out of the *palazzo* and approached another bridge which led on to the next island, the one which bordered the shore. 'Before I kill you, Mr Killigrew, I want you to see why your pathetic attempts to destroy me have failed, so that you may die knowing that at the end you have lost, and I have won,' said Salazar. 'When you first came here I gave you a little guided tour, and I dare say you made good use of the knowledge you thus gained instructing the gentlemen of the

Royal Navy in how to bombard this barracoon. But there is one small but important detail I was careful not to show you.'

Several dozen men emerged from the barracks at the trot, and Salazar motioned Killigrew to stand back and let them pass over the bridge first. When the last of the men had crossed over, Salazar, Killigrew and Madison followed.

They passed through an archway in a hedge and came to where an escarpment sloped up slightly. A creeper-covered wall ran along the top of the escarpment, and at each of the twelve embrasures in the wall a ninety-eight pounder pointed out to sea. Killigrew's heart sank. If the gunnery of Salazar's men was up to anything, then the shore battery would blast the unsuspecting HMS *Thor* out of the water.

Salazar saw the despondency on his face, and laughed. 'Surely you did not think I would invest so much of my hard-earned money in an operation of this scale without spending something on the means to protect it?'

Some of the men took down the creeper-covered boards which shielded the embrasures from the sea while others crossed to a bunker about fifty feet behind the battery. One of them unlocked the door and carried an oil lamp inside. The others followed him, and had soon formed a human chain, passing out round shot and cartridge bags. As one group of men piled the shot and cartridges outside the bunker, others from the gun crews came down and fetched the first load for their cannons. They worked with startling efficiency and were clearly well drilled.

'I told you before,' said Salazar. 'I like the best of everything in life. That extends to my gunners. Mr Sampson was trained in gunnery by the best teachers in the world, Mr Killigrew: your own Royal Navy. I don't think my men will have any difficulty reducing one frigate to so much matchwood,' he added with evident relish at the forthcoming slaughter.

Salazar stepped up to the wall and motioned for Killigrew and Madison to join him. Below the wall Killigrew could see the steep slope of the escarpment stretching down to the beach, thick with foliage. Out to sea, HMS *Thor* was getting into position, towed by the ship's boats in the absence of any wind.

'Perfect,' said Salazar. 'With so many men in their boats, it will take several minutes to get them back on board and ready to fire their long guns. She's a sitting duck. Fire your first broadside as soon as you're ready, Mr Sampson!'

'Aye, aye, Mr Salazar!'

Killigrew had only one last card to play. 'If you sink a British frigate, the Royal Navy is going to come looking for you. And we've already left word with the authorities in Monrovia as to exactly where they can find you.'

Salazar smiled. 'I dare say you have. But I'll be long gone by then. Sinking this ship will buy me all the time I need to clear out of here and set up my operations at a new location. It will cost me a great deal of money, but that will be a drop in the ocean compared to the profits I make from the trade. You see, Mr Killigrew, your schoolboy heroics will result in nothing more than the loss of one year's profit for me, and the deaths of the crew of a British frigate. Oh, and your own death, of course. Which, I might add, is long overdue. Perhaps you'd like to do the honours, Captain Madison?'

'With pleasure.' Madison levelled the pistol at Killigrew's forehead. 'No pithy last words, Mr Killigrew? You disappoint me. Then let the Good Book supply your epitaph. Isaiah, chapter fifty-three, verse seven: "He was oppressed, and he was afflicted, yet he opened not his mouth: he is brought as a lamb to the slaughter".'

'Amen,' said Salazar. 'Goodbye, Mr Killigrew.'

# XX:

## The Reckoning

'Pull!' hissed Molineaux. 'Pull, damn your eyes!' He knew the other slaves could not understand his words, but he hoped they would get the general idea.

The captives pulled on their fetters, seeking to break them away from the wooden pillars which supported the roof. If they succeeded the whole roof would probably come down on their heads, but it was only made of palm leaves and a few bamboo poles, and a few cuts and bruises were preferable to a life of perpetual slavery. But the wooden beams were fixed deep in the ground, and they could not be budged.

Molineaux heard voices outside. He quickly motioned for everyone to stop pulling and resume their earlier positions. A light showed through the gate of the shed, and he saw Prince Khari standing on the other side with Tobias, who held an oil lamp aloft. 'See, your highness? There's no one here but these slaves, and they ain't going anywhere.'

'I want to be sure. Open the gate.'

The two men entered the shed, and Tobias moved the light of the lamp over the slaves, moving along the row. Khari eyed them warily, looking for anything which suggested that all was not well.

Molineaux rose up on his knees as they approached him, his hands clasped together. 'Please doan' make me no slave, mas'er! I beg you! I ain't no African, I is a freeborn Englishman! Oh lawdy, please doan' send me to th' Americas, please!' He grabbed Tobias by the belt in supplication. The slaver slapped him across the face with his left hand, and Molineaux fell back to the floor.

'Shut your noise, you crazy nigger sonuvabitch!'

'Poor dumb white trash,' Molineaux muttered under his breath, as Tobias led Khari to the end of the row. Khari heard him and glanced over his shoulder with one eyebrow raised, but he did not see that Molineaux had expertly filched the ring of keys from Tobias's belt.

'All right,' said Khari. 'Salazar was wrong. He *did* come on his own.'

The two of them turned and strode back towards the gate. Molineaux did not bother to wonder who had come on his own. He had about fifteen seconds. He inserted the key into the padlock on his left manacle. The other slaves shifted where they lay, clinking their fetters so that Khari and Tobias would not hear the keys jingle in Molineaux's hands.

The first padlock snapped open and Molineaux's left hand was free. Two more to go, but Khari and Tobias were only a few feet from the gate now. The right manacle was trickier, because he had to use his left hand to unfasten it. His hands were trembling so much he could barely get the key in the hole. He dropped the keys, cursed himself silently, and tried again. The key turned at once.

Khari and Tobias had reached the gate.

Now the neck-collar. But the first key did not fit. Molineaux tried the next one, and again found it did not fit.

Khari and Tobias went outside and closed the gate behind them. Tobias snapped the padlock on the gate back into place and then reached for his keys to lock it.

Molineaux inserted a third key into the padlock on his collar.

'What's wrong?' Khari asked Tobias.

'My keys . . . damn it, I must have had them a moment ago, otherwise how did I let us into the shed . . . ?'

Khari looked up and Molineaux saw his eyes peering through the gate. Their eyes locked in the same instant that the padlock on Molineaux's collar came free. Khari patted Tobias on the shoulder and pointed through the gate at Molineaux.

'Kill him. I'll raise the alarm.'

'What the . . . Goddamn it!' Tobias jerked the padlock off the gate just as Molineaux tore the collar from his neck and handed the keys to the next slave in the row.

As Khari disappeared, Tobias charged towards Molineaux, reaching for the pistol holstered at his side. Molineaux ran to meet him. The two of them clashed just as the pistol came out of its holster, and they struggled for a moment with the gun between them. Molineaux managed to force the muzzle down towards the ground and it went off with a flash that was blinding in the darkness of the shed. He broke free of Tobias's grip and threw him towards the row of chained slaves. One of them stood up to receive him, looped his fetters over the slaver's head and drew the chain hard against his throat. Tobias gurgled horribly as the slave throttled him.

'I'm going after Khari . . .' Molineaux told the slaves, and then gestured dismissively and turned and ran for the gate. 'Ah, what the hell. You can't understand a word I say anyhow.'

He emerged from the shed in time to see Khari sprinting towards the entrance of the stockade. The guards silhouetted on the catwalk peered down into the darkness below, trying to work out what was going on. One of them called down in Portuguese.

'Sound the alarm!' shouted Khari. 'Slave rebellion!' He reached the gate of the stockade and hammered on it. The gate was opened, and Molineaux saw two guards standing there in the moonlight with muskets in their hands. Khari shouted something at them in Portuguese and dodged past.

The guards raised the stocks of their muskets to their shoulders and levelled them at Molineaux. His eyes widened, and he threw himself behind the shed just as the muskets flashed and two bullets thrummed in his direction.

He rolled over on the compacted earth, picked himself up and ran around the far side of the shed nearest the main gate. The guards there were still trying to reload their muskets. Molineaux charged towards them, his naked feet pounding the earth. One of them raised his musket and fired. Molineaux swerved and felt the bullet sing past the side of his head. The other was still ramming his next shot home with the ramrod when Molineaux reached him.

The seaman snatched the musket from his hands and smashed the butt against the side of the guard's head. The guard went down, and Molineaux turned the musket on his companion, shooting him through the chest with both ramrod and ball at point-blank range.

The guards on the catwalk were shooting down into the stockade now, but not at Molineaux. The slaves were pouring out of the first shed, one of them unlocking the gate to the next and disappearing inside with Tobias's keys. Molineaux snatched a Bowie knife from the belt of one of the guards and went after Khari. Emerging from the stockade he glanced around, wondering which way the so-called Prince of the Leopard Men had gone. The tolling of the alarm bell soon told him.

The bell hung from a wooden pin between two tall upright posts on the next island. Molineaux sprinted across the bridge. Already the guards were pouring out of the barracks to suppress the rebellion. He cursed himself for his stupidity. Armed with muskets, they would easily slaughter the slaves.

Molineaux's one consolation was that he would at least be able to kill Khari.

But as he drew near to Khari the leopard prince turned and saw him. Molineaux slashed at him with the knife, but Khari caught him by the wrist and twisted his arm up into the small of his back. Molineaux cried out and dropped the knife, and Khari threw him towards the reeds which lined the bank of the nearest waterway.

Molineaux rolled over, stood up quickly and turned to meet Khari's next attack. Khari had picked up the knife and now he advanced on Molineaux, taking his time. 'I knew you were trouble the moment I laid eyes on you,' he snarled as the two of them circled. He lunged, slashing at Molineaux's throat. The Englishman leaped back and landed amongst the reeds on a mud bank. Khari came at him unhesitatingly and thrust at his stomach. Molineaux tried to catch him by the wrist, but the thrust was only a feint and Khari at once followed it up by slashing Molineaux across the chest. He hardly felt a thing other than a slight burning sensation, but when he glanced down at himself he could see a thin cut across his chest weeping blood.

Khari moved in for the kill.

Madison would have been less than human not to have turned his head when the first shot sounded from the direction of the stockade. An opportunity like that came along once in what would be a very short lifetime if one was careless enough to let it slip past. Killigrew seized it in both hands, along with the pistol Madison held to his head. He pushed the muzzle aside and the two of them struggled chest-to-chest for a moment. Killigrew twisted Madison around until the gun pointed at the stack of powder cartridges outside the bunker. He pressed down on Madison's trigger finger and the revolver discharged its single remaining shot harmlessly into one of the cartridges.

Snarling with rage, Madison threw the gun away and seized Killigrew by the throat. As his hands crushed his windpipe, Killigrew saw the slaver's eyes flicker past his head, and glancing at the ground he saw Salazar's shadow in the moonlight, poised to swing the cutlass at his back.

Killigrew whirled Madison around as a human shield. The slave captain gasped as the heavy blade bit deep into his spine. Then his legs crumpled and he fell to his knees. Killigrew watched him without compassion. 'Ecclesiastes, chapter three, verses one to two,' he said coldly.

Madison puckered his brow. 'Ecclesiastes . . . ?'

'"To everything there is a season, and a time to every purpose under the heaven: A time to be born, and a time to die".'

Madison nodded, and died.

Salazar stared down at Madison's body, and then levelled the point of the cutlass at Killigrew's throat. 'You are going to spend a long, long time dying for that, Mr Killigrew.'

Killigrew tried not to stare as behind Salazar, one of Sampson's men picked up the powder cartridge that had been pierced by the bullet from the pistol. As the man carried the cartridge on his shoulder, he was oblivious to the gunpowder which spilled out of the bullet-hole and left a trail in his wake.
'Do I get a last request?' Killigrew asked Salazar.

'Such as?'

'A last cigar.'

Salazar shook his head. 'My cigars are back at the house, and I don't intend to give you a chance to think up some new trickery while I send someone to fetch one.'

The man carried the powder cartridge to the cannon closest to where Killigrew and Salazar stood, only ten feet away.

Two more shots sounded in quick succession from the direction of the stockade, followed by a whole fusillade, but

Salazar did not take his eyes off Killigrew for a moment. 'Mr Sampson, be so good as to send someone to find out what all the shooting is about,' he called impatiently.

'Aye, aye, sir. You heard him, Caspar. Go down to the stockade and find out what the problem is.' One of Sampson's men nodded and ran off as the alarm bell sounded. The rest of them ran out the guns and aimed them at the frigate anchored beyond the bar.

'We're ready to fire, sir,' reported Sampson.

Killigrew glanced to where Madison had thrown the revolver. It lay between him and the trail of powder leading back to the stack of cartridges outside the bunker. But Salazar stood between Killigrew and the revolver with a cutlass in his hand.

'Then what are you waiting for?' Salazar snapped over his shoulder at Sampson.

Killigrew ducked underneath the blade of the cutlass and dived for the revolver. He snatched it up, rolled over and came to a halt by the trail of gunpowder.

Salazar whirled around. He swung the cutlass but the blade met only air.

Pointing the muzzle at the charcoal-grey dust, Killigrew cocked the hammer and pulled the trigger. The cartridge in the chamber fired and spat flames down the barrel. The trail of gunpowder sparked and ignited at once.

'Look out!' shouted Sampson, as a white flame burned rapidly down the trail and the air filled with acrid smoke.

'Will someone *please* put that fire out?' Salazar snapped in exasperation, swinging the cutlass back over his shoulder to aim a blow at Killigrew's neck. Killigrew threw the revolver at his head. It struck Salazar in the middle of the forehead and he blinked once and went down.

Sampson tried to stamp out the burning trail of gunpowder as it raced towards the stack of cartridges outside the bunker;

then he thought better of it and turned and ran for his life. So did his men.

Killigrew picked himself up and ran to the wall, vaulting over it. He dropped about fifteen feet and landed heavily amongst some bushes. He clasped his hands over his head and waited for the explosion.

Seconds came and went. Nothing happened. Perhaps the gunpowder trail had not reached as far as the cartridges. Killigrew unclasped his arms and glanced up in disappointment.

On the quarter-deck of the *Thor*, Lieutenant Masterson watched as the last of the frigate's boats was swung back aboard in the davits and the men went below to man the guns. He reached for his watch for the sixteenth time in the past hour, only to remember yet again that he had loaned it to Killigrew.

'Three minutes to two bells, Lieutenant,' said Captain Crichton, seeing the motion. 'We'll be on time. We'd better pray that Killigrew, Reynolds and the others got out of there.'

'They know what they're doing,' Masterson said tightly, hoping it was true.

'And the consequences of failure,' agreed Crichton.

The ports on the gun deck were opened and the long guns loaded and run out. 'Ready when you give the word, sir,' reported the gunner.

'Very good, Mr Andrews,' said Crichton, and checked his watch again. 'One minute . . .'

There was a bright flash from the coast, and everyone turned with a gasp. A moment later there came a terrific boom as a cloud of fire mushroomed up from behind the low ridge above the beach. The roar of the explosion echoed with a rumble like thunder off the hills behind the barracoon. A vast cloud rose slowly into the night sky.

'What in God's name was that?' spluttered Masterson.

Crichton smiled. 'That, Lieutenant, I believe to have been Mr Killigrew's handiwork.'

At the foot of the wall, the flash of the explosion was blinding, as bright as the sun, and the blast was deafening. Killigrew hurriedly clamped his arms over his head once more and rolled in against the foot of the wall as the flames shot out over his head with a roar. The very earth seemed to shake around him, and then the wall crumbled and cracked. Chunks of masonry rained down on the slope of the escarpment, bouncing and spinning amongst the undergrowth, and one of the cannons crashed down inches from where Killigrew was huddled.

The roar faded slowly as dust sheeted down from above and thick smoke filled the still air. As it slowly disseminated, Killigrew glanced up and saw only flaming wreckage where the battery had previously glowered over the beach. It took him all of his self-control not to whoop with exultation in an undignified manner.

But it was not over yet. Out at sea, he could see the *Thor* waiting to do its share of the destruction. He glanced at his watch. One minute to one: and Miss Chance was still locked in her room in the *palazzo*, right at the heart of the barracoon. He scrambled up the rubble of the shattered wall to where the battery had stood. A huge, charred crater marked where the cartridges had been stacked, and the bunker had been completely flattened. There was no sign of anyone except for one or two grisly remains of those who had not managed to get clear of the explosion.

An echoing boom sounded from the *Thor*, and he turned to see a great bank of cloud rising from her side. A split second later the scream of a dozen shells hurtling through the air filled his ears. He threw himself flat on the ground as the shells screeched overhead, and a moment later a vast wall of flames burst out of the ground, completely obscuring the rest of the barracoon from his sight. The multiple explosions seemed even louder than the stack of cartridges going off, and chunks of soil and mud rained down all around him.

He did not wait for the dust to settle but at once got up and ran into the cloud of smoke. If the *Thor*'s gunners were up to snuff – and he had a feeling they would be – then he had about one minute before they reloaded and fired again.

The first shells had left no trace of the bridge which led to the central island, and precious little trace of the watercourse it had crossed. Killigrew stumbled through the mud and sprinted across the grass to the *palazzo*. The door was wide open. He dashed up the steps and inside. A moment later a blade swung at his head. He ducked down, rolled over on the marble floor, and twisted in time to see Salazar standing there with the cutlass still in his hand. The slaver's clothes were torn and scorched and his face was blackened, but he did not appear to have suffered any kind of serious injury; he had the devil's own luck, Killigrew mused grimly.

'I hope you weren't thinking of depriving me of my guest,' said Salazar, swinging the cutlass as he advanced.

In the distance, Killigrew heard the sporadic boom of the *Thor*'s guns as her men fired independently, as soon as they were ready. Once again the air was filled with the screech of shells. One landed on the lawn in front of the *palazzo*. There was a blinding flash followed by a roar, and the windows all exploded inwards. Killigrew flinched as shards of glass flew across the room.

Salazar, who had instinctively ducked, straightened and resumed his advance. He charged forwards suddenly, hacking at Killigrew's head, and Killigrew barely ducked aside in time. Salazar slashed at Killigrew, the point of the cutlass slicing through his shirt and scoring a line of blood from his shoulder.

* * *

Molineaux and Khari broke off their desperate struggle for a moment to gape in astonishment at the great plume of flame which rose up from where the battery had been.

Molineaux was the first to recover from the initial shock. He lunged forwards and seized Khari by the wrist. Khari stumbled under the onslaught, his feet slipping on the mud-bank, but he quickly rallied and twisted Molineaux this way and that. The leopard prince was easily the stronger, and he grinned as he forced Molineaux over backwards. Molineaux sprawled in the mud and Khari fell on him, plunging the Bowie knife down towards his chest. Molineaux rolled to one side and managed to kick Khari in the ribs, but without any appreciable result.

As Molineaux tried to crawl away, Khari picked himself up and stood over him. Molineaux rolled on to his back and seized a fistful of mud, staring up at where Khari towered over him and feeling like David facing Goliath. He flung the mud at the giant's face.

Blinded, Khari grunted and raised an arm to wipe his eyes. Molineaux jumped to his feet and leaped into the air, delivering a flying kick to Khari's chest. As Molineaux fell to the mud once more, Khari staggered backwards. His feet scrabbled for purchase in the slippery mud and he fell into the water with a terrific splash. The low profiles of crocodiles cruising through the channel at once changed direction.

Molineaux would have liked to stay around to see Khari's grisly demise – if only to make sure the crocodiles did not turn their noses up at him – but at that moment the *Thor*'s first salvo landed. The sky lit up orange, and he felt the ground tremble beneath his feet.

A crackle of muskets sounded behind him: not the sporadic firing of the guards, but a well-disciplined volley. He turned and saw a squad of ten marines there, giving the slaves covering fire as they ran for the canoes. The slavers turned and ran, only to find themselves face to face with another squad of marines. They threw down their muskets and raised their hands.

Feeling a wave of relief wash over him, Molineaux stumbled down towards the stockade. It was the first time he had been glad to see marines. So it was Killigrew who had come back, and he had brought some friends with him.

He had barely got as far as the alarm bell, however, when he felt burning pain explode through his right thigh. His leg crumpled beneath him and he fell against the wooden posts supporting the bell. Sobbing with agony, he glanced down and saw the haft of the Bowie knife embedded in his leg. He turned and saw Khari advancing once more. The leopard prince leaned over him, grabbed the haft of the knife and twisted it in the wound. Molineaux screamed in torment. Khari pulled the knife out with one hand, grabbed Molineaux with the other, hoisted him to his feet and slammed him back against one of the posts. He raised the knife above his head to plunge it into Molineaux's chest.

With one final effort, Molineaux lifted his knee into Khari's crotch and broke free. Khari grunted and brought the knife arcing down. The tip slashed across Molineaux's shoulder blade, and then his leg gave way beneath him and he fell. He reached out to grab something and caught hold of the bell-rope. But the pin supporting the bell had not been designed to take the weight of a man. The bell gave a half-hearted clang which broke off, along with the bell itself. Khari frowned at the sound and looked up. Molineaux stared in horrified fascination as the heavy brass bell crushed Khari's head like an eggshell. He winced.

Then the shells of the next salvo began to fall across the barracoon, shooting great plumes of fire into the night sky and hurling clumps of earth through the air. One shell landed in a nearby mud-bank and Molineaux was spattered with mud.

He started to crawl towards the landing stage where the marines were rounding up the slavers beyond the extreme range of the frigate's guns.

But his progress was agonisingly slow. He was not even halfway when the shells of the third salvo rained fire on the barracoon. He wondered if Madison was able to see this; if he had been, the slave captain would doubtless have had some pithy Biblical quote about a hail of brimstone and fire on Sodom and Gomorrah.

He felt footsteps pounding the earth behind him and twisted in panic, wondering if Khari had somehow managed to survive having his skull smashed in, but it was only a Kruman wearing a top hat. Molineaux recognised him from somewhere, and after a moment's thought placed him as the interpreter who had arrived at the village with the witch doctor the day Prince Khari had attacked.

In the darkness the Kruman almost ran straight past Molineaux on his way to the stockade. 'Hey!' Molineaux called out after him. 'Don't leave me!'

The Kruman twisted and skidded to a halt. 'You Killigrew friend?'

Molineaux nodded, and ducked his head as another shell burst nearby. 'Was it Killigrew who arranged the fireworks?'

The Kruman grinned and nodded, and helped him to his feet. 'Come, we go, plenty quick.'

'Wait a minute, what about Miss Chance?'

'White puss in big house. Mas'er Killigrew, he go fetchee. Come, we go!'

'What about Killigrew? Will he be all right?'

'Mas'er Killigrew worry 'bout Mas'er Killigrew. You, me, worry 'bout me, you. He be fine.'

Molineaux allowed Tip-Top to help him down towards the

landing stage. 'Yeah,' he sighed. 'He certainly seems to have a talent for survival.'

The whole house shuddered as one of the shells scored a direct hit on the roof. The chandelier over the receiving room shivered and tinkled, and the ornate rococo moulding fell in pieces from the ceiling. A big chunk of plaster hit the marble floor between Killigrew and Salazar.

Killigrew still backed away before the relentless sweeps of the cutlass in Salazar's hand. He looked around in desperation for something he could use as a weapon, but there was nothing. He bounded on to the mahogany table and kicked the candelabra at Salazar's head.

Salazar ducked to one side and the candelabra crashed against the wall before falling to the floor. 'I should have finished you off when I had the chance,' he snarled, and swung at Killigrew's knees. 'This is all your doing.'

Killigrew jumped over the slashing blade. Salazar leaped on to the table. Killigrew backed away until he came to the far end of the long table and almost stepped out into space. He teetered and barely managed to regain his balance.

Salazar laughed. 'No place left to run to, Mr Killigrew.'

'Then come and get me.'

Salazar lifted the cutlass and flexed his fingers around the hilt, clearly wondering if Killigrew had any more tricks up his sleeve. Then he charged the length of the table, swinging the blade of the cutlass behind his head. Unarmed, Killigrew waited to receive the attack.

Salazar swung. Killigrew ducked at the last moment and the blade swished above his head.

Salazar's momentum kept him going until he careered into his opponent. Killigrew caught him around the waist and straightened, flinging him over his shoulder. Salazar screamed, and abruptly fell silent.

Killigrew turned. It had been his plan to throw Salazar into the fireplace, but his aim had been too high. Instead Salazar's rhinoceros head had killed its killer five years too late, its horn piercing his throat underneath the jaw. Now Salazar hung grotesquely over the fireplace, the final trophy in his own collection. His arms hung limply by his sides. After a few seconds' pause the cutlass finally slipped from his lifeless fingers and clattered to the floor.

Another shell burst outside. Killigrew jumped down from the table and sprinted up the stairs. 'Suzannah!'

'In here!' She hammered against the door. 'The door's locked, I'm trapped inside!'

'Stand back!' He lashed out at the edge of the door with his foot, just below the lock. Agony exploded in his ankle, but the door snapped open. Miss Chance ran out into his arms.

Another shell smashed into the house and a huge chunk of masonry crashed to the landing. The shuddering impact hurled them both to the floor and showered them with dust. 'Are you all right?' Killigrew asked her.

She nodded. They got up and made for the stairs. 'What happened to Salazar?' she asked.

'Don't ask,' he told her. But she glanced to her left as they went down the stairs. The lawn in front of the *palazzo* seemed to be on fire, and the flames cast a hellish glow over the grisly scene of Salazar's death.

He tucked her head against his shoulder. 'Don't look.'

'I already did.'

'Come on. We'll go out the back.' He pushed her through the door to the dining room. They left the house as the last echoes of the bombardment died away and made their way down to the beach where Masterson and a squad of seamen were landing in one of the launches to help the marines round up any surviving slavers.

# Epilogue:

## The Final Hurdle

JULY 6 – HMS *Thor* (26 guns, Captain C. Crichton) was instrumental in the destruction of a slave trader's barracoon on the Guinea Coast. A large number of slaves is known to have been freed. There were a number of arrests, although many of the slave traders are believed to have been slain in the attack. None of the marines taking part in the action were killed. The site has been razed. Lieutenant C.I. Killigrew of Her Majesty's Royal Navy was mentioned in despatches.

This small snippet at the bottom of the 'Naval Intelligence' column was the only mention of the affair in any of the London newspapers. Rear-Admiral Napier folded his newspaper and glanced across to where Killigrew sat opposite him in the carriage, staring moodily out of the window as they rattled down Pall Mall. 'Well, the newspapers have decided that you should have your commission restored, at any rate.'

'Will that cut any ice at the Admiralty?'

'Public opinion is a powerful weapon, Mr Killigrew. More powerful even than the shell guns of HMS *Thor*, perhaps. I've spoken to the First Lord. He scowled a good deal, of course, but he muttered something about seeing what he could do. Cheer up. You mark my words, you'll be back in uniform before you know what's hit you.'

'I just wish I could have found out who was behind Salazar and the Bay Cay Trading Company.'

'Ah. Yes, well, we'll come to that presently. Here we are,' he added, as the carriage pulled up outside the Reform Club. He took a pinch of snuff, sneezed explosively, and then preceded Killigrew out of the carriage, limping up the steps. 'Rear-Admiral Sir Charles Napier and Mr Christopher Killigrew to see Sir George Grafton,' he told the porter.

'You're expected, gentlemen. Sir George is waiting for you in the smoking room.'

Sir George rose to his feet as Napier and Killigrew approached, and glanced pointedly at his watch. 'I don't know what this is about, Rear-Admiral, but you'd better be brief. I have an appointment with the Earl of Auckland at three.' He plumped himself back down in his chair and motioned for Napier and Killigrew to likewise be seated.

'We shan't keep you any longer than is absolutely necessary, I assure you, Sir George,' said Napier, lowering his bulk into a chair. 'By the way, you've met Mr Killigrew, haven't you?'

'Ah, yes. The young man who helped to destroy Owodunni Barracoon. If you want me to press the Lords of the Admiralty to overturn the verdict of your court-martial, young man, you can put aside any such hopes. As far as I'm concerned that trial was properly convened and carried out. The navy can hardly be held responsible if you saw fit to give a false admission of guilt.'

'That's all in hand,' said Napier. 'I think Mr Killigrew has proved his value to the navy, and I'm currently trying to come to an agreement with the First Lord regarding his reinstatement.'

'More than the blighter deserves,' muttered Grafton.

'I think you do Mr Killigrew an injustice, Sir George. But

then, you may not know exactly how much he achieved by his adventure. You see, the aim was not just to find one single barracoon and destroy it, although that was what you might call by way of an added bonus. No, indeed. What our colleagues at the Slave Trade Department wanted to know was: who was the man who financed the ships that carried the slaves to the Americas? And thanks to Mr Killigrew here, I think I can point the finger at that man right now.'

'Oh?' Grafton said cautiously. Killigrew was equally surprised, but he held his peace, suspecting that Napier knew what he was doing.

'Yes. You see, someone tipped off Salazar that Mr Killigrew was working for me. And that was a secret very few people were in possession of. I'd made sure of that; that was the very reason I arranged the whole thing without getting the Admiralty's approval first.'

'How many people knew?' asked Grafton.

'Well, just myself and Mr Killigrew. And two soldiers of the Royal Marines who helped us could have guessed, of course, but they're above suspicion. Oh, and yourself, Sir George. Or had you forgotten our little conversation of the twenty-fifth of June?'

Grafton rose to his feet angrily. 'Sir Charles, I sincerely hope you are not insinuating what I think you are.'

'Oh come now, Sir George. Do you take me for a child? I've suspected you were behind the slavers for years. Now Mr Killigrew – not to mention yourself – has kindly provided me with the proof I need to secure a conviction—'

'Call that proof?' roared Grafton. 'By God, that's the grossest slander . . . !' he spluttered apoplectically. 'Sir, I demand you retract that last statement at once, or else I shall have no choice but to . . . but to . . .'

'Call me out?' Napier suggested hopefully.

'No. To litigate, damn your eyes! I'll sue you for every blasted penny you've got!'

'I must compliment you, Sir George. I had no idea you were such a fine actor. But you're wasting your breath. Dead men cannot litigate, and you know as well as I that the penalty for slaving in this country is death . . . For heaven's sake, Mr Killigrew, what on earth are you counting on your fingers? That's very distracting, you know.'

'Excuse me, sir, but could I have a word?'

'Not now, Killigrew! When I've finished with Sir George here—'

'No, sir. *Now*.'

Napier smiled thinly at Grafton. 'You must excuse me for a moment, Sir George.' He rose to his feet and allowed Killigrew to take him to one side, leaving Grafton fuming in his seat. 'Now what is it, Killigrew?' he demanded irritably.

'You did say you told Sir George on the twenty-fifth, didn't you?'

'The twenty-fifth of June, yes. What's that got to do with it?'

'It's just that Salazar knew when I arrived at the Owodunni Barracoon on the first of July. Which means that if Salazar learned it from Sir George, then his messenger travelled from London to the Guinea Coast in less than a week.'

Napier stared at Killigrew. 'Why on earth didn't you say something before?'

'Because I didn't even know you'd said anything to Sir George.'

Napier turned back to Grafton. 'My apologies, Sir George. I seem to have made a terrible mistake.'

'A mistake? A *mistake*! I'll say you've made a mistake, you slanderous poltroon! You're finished, d'ye hear me? The pair of you! I'll have you thrown out of the navy, I'll have you blackballed from every club in town, why, I'll have you hung, drawn and quartered . . . !'

'Shouldn't that be "hanged", sir?' said Killigrew.

'*Get out!*'

Napier fled as fast as his gammy leg would carry him, followed by Killigrew.

The two of them drew breath on the pavement outside. 'I'm awfully sorry about that, Mr Killigrew. I'm afraid I made rather a fool of myself there. Still, it's not the first time and I dare say it won't be the last.'

Killigrew smiled ruefully. 'It was a good plan, sir. It would have just worked better if we'd compared notes before our meeting with Sir George.'

Napier shook his head. 'I don't understand it. I was certain it must be him . . . Oh, well, never mind. Some you win, some you lose, eh, Mr Killigrew? Can I offer you a ride somewhere?' he added, climbing back into his carriage.

'Thank you, sir, but no thanks.' Killigrew was seething that Napier had risked his life by using him as human bait and did not trust himself to hold his tongue during the ride. It had probably never occurred to the old fool that he might get killed. The Rear-Admiral had probably thought he had been doing Killigrew a favour by adding that extra touch of peril. It was flattering that Napier seemed to think him so indestructible, but that did not alter the fact he might well have been killed. Besides, he had another matter to attend to. 'There's a personal call I'd like to make,' he told Napier.

'A young lady, eh, I'll warrant! Wedding bells in the air soon, perhaps? Well, good luck to you.'

'Thank you, sir.'

'Driver! Drive on!'

Killigrew watched the carriage until it disappeared down a side street, and then hailed a passing hansom. 'Knightsbridge,' he told the driver.

The hansom dropped him off outside Sir Joshua Pengelly's house. He walked slowly down the drive to the front door and pulled the doorbell. A footman answered.

'Yes?'

Killigrew handed him his card. 'Mr Christopher Killigrew calling for Mrs Fairbody.'

'I'll see if the young lady is at home, sir,' said the footman, and closed the door in Killigrew's face.

A moment later it was flung open and Eulalia ran out. 'Kit!' she exclaimed, and embraced him shamelessly on the doorstep. 'When did you get back? I was so worried for you . . . and then I saw the piece in this morning's paper! Come in, come in! Fleming, would you ask Cook to make some tea for myself and Mr Killigrew? We'll take it in the parlour.'

Killigrew followed her into the parlour. 'Actually, Eulalia, it was your father I wanted to see.'

'My father? You go swanning off risking your neck on the high seas for absolutely *weeks*, and when you finally get back and show up on my doorstep, it's my father you want to see instead of me? Shame on you! And after the things that passed between us the last time we saw one another,' she added coyly, toying with the lapels of his frock coat.

When he did not reply, she looked up at his face. 'Kit, what's wrong? You're acting very strangely. Did . . . did you have a bad time in Africa?'

'The slavers found out about my being a spy for the Slave Trade Department.'

She gasped, and her hand flew to her mouth. 'My word! They didn't try to harm you, did they?' she asked, and then her features softened into a smile. 'But so what if they did try? Nothing could hurt my Kit.'

He shook his head. 'You're wrong there, Eulalia. I can be very, very deeply hurt indeed. By something like betrayal.'

She knitted her brow. 'Betrayal? What on earth are you talking about?'

'Only five people knew of my mission, or even knew enough to guess what it was, in time to get word to the slavers. Three of them were above suspicion. The fourth was myself.'

'And the fifth?'

'Was you, Eulalia.'

She shook her head. 'No, Kit. You're mistaken. I wouldn't do anything to harm you, you know that. I love you.'

'But you love your father more. Is he in?'

Her eyes flickered up towards the ceiling, and she bit her lip.

'I'd better go and have a word with him.' He went out into the hallway once more.

She caught up with him halfway up the stairs and grabbed him by the arm. 'Please, Kit. You're wrong about this, I promise you. If you love me, you'll forget about my father and leave him out of it. What's done is done. You're here and in one piece and that's all that matters. No one else was hurt.'

He turned to face her. 'No one else was hurt?' he echoed incredulously. 'What about all the Africans that have been enslaved and carried off to the Americas?'

'What about them? For heaven's sake, Kit! They're only niggers.'

He raised a hand to strike her in a sudden access of rage. She stared at him in horror, but he caught himself. He had never struck a woman in his life and he did not intend to start now. Instead he looked down at her, not with pity but with loathing and contempt. Then he turned and continued up the stairs.

She ran after him and caught him at the halfway landing. 'No, Kit. Please. Not my father. Whatever it is you think him guilty of . . . Please, Kit, no. Don't do this . . .'

Killigrew continued implacably up the stairs. He glanced

up and saw Sir Joshua standing there, gazing bleakly down at him. Then Pengelly turned abruptly and disappeared into his study, slamming the door behind him.

Killigrew broke free of Eulalia and ran up to the door, but Pengelly had locked it. Killigrew threw his shoulder against it, once, twice, and then stood back to kick it open.

A shot rang out on the other side. Killigrew flinched, half expecting a bullet to come flying through the planks, but this was Knightsbridge, not the Guinea Coast.

He kicked the door open and at that moment Eulalia reached his side. She took one look through the door and turned away with a sob.

'Christ!' whispered Killigrew. He was used to bloodshed, but that was on active service, not in a genteel suburb of London.

Eulalia suddenly flung herself at him, clawing at his eyes. 'You . . . you bastard! You killed him, you bastard! You did this! *You did this!*'

He caught her by the wrists and held her at bay, alarmed by her fury. The servants came rushing up the stairs. The footman and the butler took Eulalia between them while the housekeeper glanced into the study. 'Holy mother of God! Is it the master?'

The butler glanced at the body. 'It looks like it.'

Eulalia was still struggling in the footman's arms, screaming and lashing out at Killigrew with her legs. 'You'd better leave, sir,' the footman said disdainfully. 'I've got your card for when the police get here. I dare say they'll want to speak to you about this.'

'I dare say,' agreed Killigrew.

He wandered out of the house in a daze, crossed the road, and entered the park opposite. He sat down on a bench overlooking the Serpentine, buried his face in his hands, and wept.

Before he had set out on his mission, he had told Napier he would give anything to see the slave trade stopped. Now he realised just what that had meant.

'I still can't believe you used me as human bait to draw out Sir George Grafton,' Killigrew said bitterly. He had to raise his voice above the clamour of the engine and the plashing of the paddle-wheels as the ferry steamed east past the Naval Dockyard at Woolwich, bound for Gravesend and Chatham. 'I could have been killed!'

'Oh, don't be like that! I knew you'd pull through somehow. Besides, I made sure Able Seaman Molineaux was in place to watch your back, didn't I? How is Molineaux, by the way?'

'Doing well. Mr Strachan says he'll have full use of his leg again in no time. And he did save my life. In fact I couldn't have done it without him.'

'There you go then. I knew I could rely on that fellow. Just goes to prove that a blackamoor can be just as clever and stout a chap as any, eh? Must make sure I get Molineaux a berth on a decent ship, come to think of it.'

'Come to think of it, you should make sure *I* get a berth on a decent ship.'

'One thing at a time, Lieutenant. I got you back your commission, didn't I? So where would you like to go next? Another crack at the slavers? We may have rooted out one nest of the vile scum, but I suspect there are plenty more where they came from.'

Killigrew shook his head. 'I think I can rest contented that I've done my share against the slavers, sir.'

'So, which cause do you wish to turn your attentions to now, eh?'

'Now that you mention it, sir, I did hear that they're having problems with pirates in the China Seas.'

'China,' said Napier, and sighed. 'I'll see what I can arrange.'

'You might also care to pay me that one hundred guineas you owe me.'

'Good heavens! I'd forgotten all about that. Will you take a cheque?'

Killigrew nodded. 'Better make it out to Sir Andrew Strachan, QC. By an unfortunate coincidence, one hundred guineas just happens to be the retainer he's demanding before he'll act as my counsel in the Videira action.'

'You haven't heard, then?'

'Heard what?'

'It seems Videira's new ship got stopped off the coast of Liberia with a hold full of slaves by the USS *Narwhal*. Apparently the testimony of one Lieutenant Lanier went a long way to convincing the court of his guilt.'

'Good old Lanier,' said Killigrew. Since slavery was equated with piracy, the captain could only have received one punishment for his crime. 'But what about his family? Don't they want to take up the case?'

'Videira didn't have any family, so his lawyers will have to drop the action.'

'Thank God for that,' sighed Killigrew. 'Lord knows how I'd've paid Sir Andrew's fees. My agent tells me that my share of the head money for all those slaves we rescued at the Owodunni Barracoon comes to precisely sixteen pounds, three shillings and six pence.'

'You never were in it for the money.'

'It's just as well,' Killigrew said bitterly. It was reassuring to know there was some justice in the world, but that was small compensation when he remembered Eulalia and thought of what he had lost. But that was just the price he had to pay for being a slave to his principles.

'Oh, buck up, man!' said Napier. 'I know we never did

find out who was behind the slavers. But we'll get him one day.'

'I wasn't thinking about that, sir.'

'What, then? No, wait: let me guess. It wouldn't have something to do with that young lady you went off to see after we spoke with Sir George, by any chance?'

Killigrew smiled sadly. 'I think you can safely say that.'

Napier glanced to where Miss Chance stood in the bow of the ferry, gazing with the rapture of an excited schoolboy at the ships in the docks. 'It wasn't . . . ah . . . ?'

'Miss Chance? No, it wasn't her.'

'Well, when I was your age and I was jilted, I used to say that being in love was like steeplechasing. Ever done any steeple-chasing, Killigrew? Capital sport. If you take a tumble, the important thing to do is not let the experience put you off. Got to get straight back in the saddle, eh?' Napier winked, and nudged him in the ribs.

Killigrew smiled. 'Miss Chance will make someone an admirable wife one day, if she chooses to,' he admitted. 'But I fear our paths go separate ways. We had a good heart-to-heart over dinner at Rules last night. She's determined to go back to Africa to do missionary work in Liberia.'

'After all that she's been through?'

Killigrew nodded. 'Now more than ever. And it wouldn't be fair for me to expect her to marry a naval officer.'

Napier sighed, doubtless thinking of the family he was leaving behind as he returned to the flagship of the Channel Fleet. 'You're right. It's a hard life for the womenfolk, being married to us naval officers. A crotchety old fool like me in particular. Oh, by the way, did you hear about Sir Joshua Pengelly? Terrible business. Something to do with irregularities in his financial affairs. Still, I dare say there'll be plenty left in the coffers for his daughter to get by on. What's her name? Euphemia?'

'Eulalia.'

'That's it. Eulalia. You used to be a friend of the family, didn't you?'

'Used to be. Excuse me a moment, sir.' Killigrew moved aft to where one of the hands was lowering the accident boat in its davits. 'Good morning,' he said, talking to the boatman more as an excuse not to talk to Napier than because he was particularly concerned about what the man was doing.

The man was bent over the taffrail with his back to Killigrew. When he turned, Killigrew found himself staring into Eli Coffin's venomous eyes and the muzzle of a pistol.

'*Don't* put your hands up,' snarled Coffin. 'Just put 'em in the pockets of your pants nice and easy, as if we're shooting the breeze. That's it. Now let's go down below and I'll show you the engine room.'

The engine room was noisy, even by engine-room standards. The piston arms were a blur, and the whole engine seemed to be working much too quickly for its own good, shuddering and vibrating. Killigrew glanced at the pressure gauge and saw that it was way too high.

'Keep moving,' ordered Coffin, and prodded him in the back with the pistol. He had to shout to make himself heard above the din of the engine.

As Killigrew moved around the back of the engine space he found the ferry-boat's engineer. His throat had been slit from ear to ear. 'Your handiwork, I suppose?' he shouted.

With his left hand Coffin reached into the pocket of his coat and pulled out a pair of manacles, tossing them to Killigrew. 'Attach one cuff to your wrist and the other to that pipe there,' he bellowed into Killigrew's ear.

Playing for time, Killigrew clipped the first bracelet over the pipe, removing the key from the cuff to lock it in place. 'You do realise that the pressure is far too high, don't you?'

he roared. 'If you don't open the release valve soon, the boilers will explode.'

Coffin grinned. 'That's the general idea. Mr Salazar asked me to kill the rear-admiral, and to make it look like an accident. That's exactly what I'm going to do. And as an added bonus I get to kill you and that bitch Miss Chance.'

'Salazar's dead,' shouted Killigrew. 'And Madison.'

'Oh, I heard all about that, you Limey sonuvabitch. This here's what you might be calling my revenge.'

Light fell on them both as the door leading up on deck opened and Napier stood there. 'Hullo, Killigrew. Come to look at the engines? Mind if I join you?'

Coffin started to turn the pistol on him. Killigrew reached up and pulled down the handle on one of the release valves. A jet of steam shot out and Coffin screamed as his face was scalded. Killigrew grabbed him by the wrist and forced the gun to one side. They struggled chest to chest for a moment in the cramped space alongside the machinery, Killigrew slowly forcing the muzzle of the pistol towards the blur that was the piston arm. There was a clang and the pistol was snatched from Coffin's grip.

Killigrew at once broke free and grabbed hold of an overhead beam, pulling himself up to kick Coffin in the chest. The American was thrown back against the bulkhead and cracked his head. Killigrew grabbed him while he was still dazed and clipped the second bracelet of the manacles over his wrist.

Napier hobbled down the steps. 'What in the world . . . ?'

As Coffin pulled frantically on the manacle, glaring and spitting at them both, Killigrew backed away, wiping his mouth on his sleeve. 'One of the slavers, sir,' he shouted to Napier. 'He came here to kill us both in revenge.'

He turned his attention to the engine, pulling on the handle of the main release valve, but it was jammed. 'The swine's sabotaged it!'

'Can you fix it?' shouted Napier.

'Not enough time. Tell everyone to abandon ship!'

Napier hurried up the steps to the door, and Killigrew was about to follow him when Coffin shouted after him.

'Killigrew! Shipmate! You ain't gonna leave me here, are you?'

Killigrew glared at him, and then noticed a toolbox at his feet. He gave it a kick so that it slid along the floor and came to rest by Coffin's ankles. 'You broke it. You fix it.'

By the time he emerged on deck everyone was leaping over the sides without bothering to lower the accident boats; they were only a hundred yards from the river bank. Only Miss Chance dithered by the rail.

Killigrew charged towards her along the length of the deck. 'Jump! She's going to blow!'

'I can't swim!' she wailed.

'I won't let you drown!' he shouted, and launched himself at her. He caught her around the waist. The two of them went over the side and hit the water with a splash. At once Killigrew supported her, keeping her head above water as he towed her clear of the paddle-wheel which bore down on them. The ferry had just passed them when there was a loud clang and a moment later there came a sound like a huge bell cracking followed by an ear-splitting roar. The midships section of the paddle-boat disintegrated in a sudden bloom of steam, while jagged fragments of iron hurtled in every direction, raining down on the water like a thousand musket balls. The twin smoke stacks shot straight up into the air, and then dropped down once more, spinning lazily until they splashed into the river to windward.

'Are you oh-kay?' Killigrew asked Miss Chance.

'Yes,' she gasped.

The ferry had been ripped in two as if it were no more than a flimsy child's toy which had been smashed in a childish fit of temper. The two halves rapidly began to sink, bows and stern tilting up towards the sky. The accident boat still floated, attached to the taffrail by its painter. Killigrew swam across to it and got Miss Chance to hold on to the boat's gunwale while he took out his clasp knife and sawed through the painter moments before the stern sank.

Soon there was no trace that the ferry had ever existed except for people swimming in the water and Killigrew and Miss Chance clinging to the accident boat. Fortunately they were in the middle of the busiest waterway in the western world, and within seconds a coal lighter was adjusting course and heaving to in order to rescue the survivors.

Killigrew held the accident boat steady so that Miss Chance could climb in. He scrambled over the gunwale after her and glanced to where Napier and several others were being helped aboard the lighter. 'Did everyone get off in time?'

'I think so,' she told him. 'What happened?'

'It was Coffin. Are you all right?'

'Well, this dress is ruined and my hair's a mess, but I think I'll survive. And I expect I'll miss the packet to Monrovia now.'

'Don't worry. There'll be another one in a month.'

'A month,' she echoed, and lay back on the bottom boards. She smiled up at him archly. 'Whatever shall I do for a whole month?'

He grinned. 'Have you ever tried steeplechasing?'

# Afterword:

## Larger Than Life?

This story may seem far-fetched, but ninety per cent of it is based on historical fact. The Royal Navy never – as far as I am aware – used undercover spies to provide information about the slavers (although they did benefit from many ex-slavers who turned informer), but otherwise the methods used by the Royal Navy in the suppression of the slave trade, and those of the slavers they pursued, are authentic.

The climax of the story is inspired by a true incident which took place in 1847, when a slaver's barracoon was destroyed by an alliance of the Royal Navy and local people with the connivance of the captain of the USS *Dolphin*; as Hugh Thomas points out on page 692 of his authoritative work *The Slave Trade* (Simon and Schuster Inc., New York, 1997), this was 'an unusual example of British–North American collaboration'.

Francisco Salazar is fictional but he is based on Pedro Blanco, a slaver whose barracoon at the mouth of the Gallinas River was destroyed by Captain Joseph Denman of HMS *Wanderer* in 1841, although by then Blanco had already retired a millionaire. Very few of the men who profited from the slave trade were ever brought to justice. Although slave trading warranted the death penalty under British law, there is no record of it ever having been carried out.

The Owodunni Barracoon is based on Blanco's barracoon, harem and all. When Denman heard that two British subjects – a black woman named Fry Norman and her child – were being held prisoner by the King of Gallinas, who was probably supplying slaves to Blanco's successor, Denman used this as an excuse to attack and destroy the barracoon. One of the slave traders found at the barracoon, a Señor Buron, although not a British subject and not therefore subject to British law, begged Denman to take him away with him for fear of what the natives would do to him if he was left behind. Denman agreed, and in return for his kindness Buron sued him for the destruction of his goods which had been at the barracoon. The case dragged on for years, Denman having to defend himself as the navy did not support its officers when they were subjected to such legal attacks; fortunately Denman's father was a Chief Justice and he won the case in the end. It was while he was in England fighting the case that he wrote and had published his *Instructions for the Guidance of Her Majesty's Naval Officers Employed in the Suppression of the Slave Trade*, presumably to help his fellow officers avoid falling into the same legal snare as himself.

In the meantime, sad to say, the Gallinas barracoon was rebuilt and resumed its slave-trading operations; it was destroyed again in another attack by the Royal Navy in 1849. Other barracoons, at the mouths of the Sherber and Pongas Rivers, likewise received the attention of the Royal Navy.

Three of the characters featured in this book were real characters. Neither Isambard Kingdom Brunel nor William Ewart Gladstone need any introduction from me, although it is only fair to say that while Gladstone did speak out against the maintenance of the West Africa Squadron, he was a lifelong opponent of the slave trade. The third, Rear-Admiral Sir Charles Napier, is less well known, which is a pity. Napier was a popular hero, something of a legend in his own lifetime.

He had been promoted to post-rank after taking on three French ships of the line in nothing more than a brig during the Napoleonic Wars. In 1828 Dom Miguel usurped the throne of Portugal from the rightful heir, his niece Maria da Gloria. Captain Napier was employed as a sailor of fortune to command Queen Maria's fleet. To the despair of the British Foreign Office and the concomitant delight of the British public, Napier not only thrashed Dom Miguel's fleet but, fancying himself a general as well as an admiral, helped to trounce the Miguelites by land as well.

Napier's greatest moment came in 1840, after Ibrahim Pasha, the Viceroy of Egypt – a vassal of the Ottoman Empire – rebelled against the sultan in Constantinople and invaded Syria. The people of Syria, Christian and Muslim alike, preferring the less exacting regime of the Ottomans, in turn rebelled against the Egyptian invaders. Fearing the break-up of the Ottoman Empire – if only because its fall would give the Russians free access to the Mediterranean – the British government sent a fleet to the Levant to support the Ottoman sultan and his oppressed subjects in Syria. Napier was promoted to commodore and was appointed second-in-command of the fleet. But if the Admiralty hoped that the years might have mellowed him to the point where he would be prepared to take orders from someone as cautious as the commander-in-chief of the fleet, Admiral Stopford, they were disappointed. Before long Napier was playing at being a general again – and just as successfully as before – leading a naval brigade in action in the Lebanon fighting alongside the Turks.

The British government was not entirely happy with the high-handed way in which Napier imposed a peace settlement on the viceroy, which was far more exacting than the one they had intended. When the viceroy asked him what his authority was, he is said to have replied: 'My credentials are the double-shotted guns of the *Powerful* and the honour of an Englishman.' But the British public welcomed Napier back as a hero once more, and if there was one thing the government was not prepared to do, that was fly in the face of public opinion. Becoming the independent member of parliament for Marylebone in the general election of 1841, Napier was effectively kicked upstairs by his appointment as naval aide-de-camp to Queen Victoria until his promotion to the rank of rear-admiral in 1846 and his appointment as commander-in-chief of the Channel Fleet in 1847.

If Napier is less well known today than even Admirals Rodney, Hood or Cochrane, despite having been a national hero in his day, it is because his career effectively came to a dead end in the Baltic during the so-called Crimean War, where Napier was in command of the British Fleet. The British public expected great things of a man with Napier's reputation for succeeding in what most other people would not even have bothered to attempt, and he disappointed them. But it was not his fault if the Russian Fleet refused to come out of harbour to fight. He certainly did the best he could . . . but that's another story.

Men like Napier, larger-than-life characters who were prepared to risk everything out of motives that were one hundred per cent pure and noble, simply don't seem to exist any more; they are relics of a bygone age, which is a great pity. I for one have always had an admiration for the early Victorians – the more liberal sort of them, at least – and can only lament that their reputation has been dragged into the mire by certain scurrilous politicians who have sought to identify themselves with Victorian values.

Nowadays when we think of the Victorian era we tend to think of the child labour, the appalling working conditions, the poverty and squalor; we forget that it was an era of social reform, and that the Britain they left behind them in 1901 was a far better place than the one they found in 1837. In enforcing the *Pax Britannica*, the Royal Navy made the seas safer for trade. Their main aim, of course, was to make the seas safer for *British* trade; but making it safer for all trade was a side effect of which they could be justly proud. And if that most hated of bugbears, the British Empire, reached its zenith under the Victorians, then it must be remembered that the great age of colonialism and the scramble for Africa belonged to the later Victorians. Men like Napier and Killigrew, students of Adam Smith, believed in fair and equal trade, and in respecting all nations and races; they would not have approved of what was to come. It is true that sailors in the Royal Navy received head money for each slave they helped to free, but the more active members of the West Africa Squadron were undoubtedly motivated by idealism rather than greed.

And what of Killigrew himself? He is a fictional character, of course, but inspired by extraordinary characters who nonetheless lived and served in the Royal Navy during this era: men like Denman, Henry Keppel and Astley Cooper Key – gentlemanly swashbucklers who fought with revolvers in one hand and cutlasses in the other and carried the day against pirates and slavers because they never worried about the consequences of failure. Such men and their deeds are largely forgotten today, perhaps because in the public's consciousness they – along with everything else to do with the Victorian Age – are inextricably and unjustifiably bound up with the atrocities of imperialism. They were the last of a dying breed and could not exist in a world where old-fashioned virtues like courage, idealism, fair play and good manners have been replaced by arrogance, selfish ambition and unthinking political correctness. We shall not see their like again, which is a great pity.

# Killigrew and the Golden Dragon

For Sam

# *I:*

# *Pilongs*

Commander Robertson gazed up to where Mr Strachan scanned the seas from the maintop of Her Majesty's paddle-sloop *Tisiphone* with a telescope pressed to his eye. 'Will someone please tell me what my assistant surgeon is doing?'

'Looking for the sea serpent, sir.' A faint smile played on Killigrew's lips.

Robertson gave his second lieutenant a withering glare. 'The sea serpent?' Sightings of a monstrous serpent had frequently cropped up in the press over the past two years, but few educated men took them too seriously.

'Yes, sir. He thinks it might be some kind of aquatic dinosaur, a species which wasn't wiped out by the Great Flood. If he can prove it he's going to name it *strachanosaurus*.'

'I'd've thought that *mass hysteriasaurus* would be a much better name,' snorted Robertson. A tall, burly man with a leonine head, he was old enough – and able enough – to have been promoted to captain long ago, but he lacked the necessary political connections; although rumour claimed he had been offered a promotion and turned it down. A captain could command nothing smaller than a frigate, and since the Royal Navy did not have nearly enough ships to go round all its captains, such a promotion would have seen Robertson beached on half-pay. 'Don't tell me *you* believe in this dinosaur hoax, Second?'

'I've seen the skeletons in the Egyptian Hall, sir. I'm no expert, but they looked genuine enough to me. And Strachan tells me these things are taken very seriously indeed by both the Royal Society and the British Association for the Advancement of Science.'

'I suppose next you'll be telling me you believe in dragons?'

Killigrew grinned. 'Only the one my grandfather employs as a housekeeper, sir.'

Lean and tall, Kit Killigrew wore his peaked cap at a rakish angle, the hair beneath thick and dark. His saturnine complexion was the legacy of a Cornish father and a Greek mother who had met during the Greek War of Independence: Captain Jack Killigrew, an officer of the Royal Navy on half-pay, looking for adventure and a noble cause to serve, and Medora Bouboulina, a daughter of the great Laskarina Bouboulina, the lady admiral who had been the scourge of the Ottoman Navy. Killigrew's parents had died when he was three, and he had been brought up in Falmouth by his grandfather – another admiral in the family – until he was old enough to go to sea as a first-class volunteer. He had served against Barbary Corsairs, fought in the Syrian Campaign, and distinguished himself at the taking of Chingkiang-fu in the Opium War. Since then he had been fighting slavers on the Guinea Coast, but he had never been able to get the Far East out of his heart. He was happy to be returning, and happier still that he was doing so in peacetime.

It was a glorious day, with hardly a cloud to be seen, and the breeze lifted the sea into a strong but steady swell. The *Tisiphone*, six days out of Singapore and bound for Hong Kong, sailed close-hauled on the starboard tack. The brig-rigged paddle-sloop was eight-score feet from stem to stern and thirty-two in the beam. Her figurehead, a representation of the snake-haired scourge of the damned, glowered beneath the bowsprit. A single black funnel rose between her two masts, and her armament consisted of two thirty-two-pounders abaft the paddle-boxes and a sixty-eight-pounder pivot gun on the forecastle. She was a relatively small ship, intended for inshore work rather than fleet actions, with a crew of a hundred. It was nearly three months since she had sailed from Portsmouth to join the South China Seas squadron in the suppression of the pirates who infested these waters.

At the maintop, Strachan stiffened as he peered through the telescope. For a moment Killigrew – who tried to keep an open mind – wondered if his friend had actually spotted the sea serpent. The assistant surgeon snapped the telescope shut and reached for the speaking trumpet, but in his excitement he merely knocked it off the platform. It fell to the deck with a clang, narrowly missing a seaman, who jumped aside with a yell.

'Hey! Watch what you're doing, you big, clumsy . . . assistant surgeon, sir.' The seaman concluded more respectfully than he had started out when he realised whom he addressed.

'Sorry!' Strachan called back. He was in his mid-twenties, the same age as Killigrew, with blue eyes behind wire-framed spectacles and a tangle of light brown hair. 'But I see some ships!' He peered through the telescope again. 'Three of them!'

The seaman reported to the quarterdeck with the speaking trumpet which Strachan had dropped and held it out for Killigrew to inspect. There was a big dent in it where it had hit the deck.

'God preserve us from civilian officers!' Robertson snapped his fingers at the seaman and motioned to be given the trumpet, which he then raised to his lips. 'If you're going to stand in for my look-outs, Mr Strachan, be so good as to use the correct hails! In this case you should call: "Sail ho!" '

'Sorry, sir.' Strachan cupped his hands around his mouth. 'Sail ho!'

'Where away?' asked Robertson.

'What?'

The commander closed his eyes as if in pain. 'In which direction, Mr Strachan?'

'Oh! Over there.' The assistant surgeon pointed.

'Two points off the starboard bow,' deduced Robertson. 'I hope your friend knows more about dispensing medicines than he does about seamanship, Mr Killigrew. Be so good to lend him the benefit of your more expert eye.'

'Aye, aye, sir.'

Killigrew ascended the weblike ratlines and swung himself on to the maintop. Strachan was so startled he almost fell from the narrow platform, but Killigrew seized him by the arm with one hand and, with the other, caught the telescope as Strachan dropped it.

Killigrew balanced the heavy telescope with practised ease and held it to his eye, sweeping the horizon in the direction which Strachan indicated. He could see the sails of a three-masted clipper, hull-down below the horizon, and the mat-and-rattan sails of a large junk immediately alongside it, so close it was hard to tell where the junk ended and the clipper began. It took him a little longer to make out the sails of the second junk, on the far side of the clipper.

'Pilongs,' Killigrew said with gut certainty.

'Pilongs?' echoed Strachan. This was the first time he had visited the Orient.

'Chinese pirates,' explained Killigrew. He collapsed the telescope and handed it to the look-out, who had joined them on the maintop. 'Looks as if we've caught 'em in the act this time. Better get to the sick berth, Strachan.'

'All right.' Strachan climbed down through the lubbers' hole and descended the ratlines to the deck while Killigrew took the more flamboyant route of sliding down a back-stay.

'Two small junks grappled to a clipper, sir,' he reported. 'Pilongs at work, without a doubt.'

Robertson ordered the boatswain to beat to quarters and sent a midshipman below to order the engineer to get steam up. As the hands cleared the decks for action, Lieutenant Lord Endymion Hartcliffe joined Robertson and Killigrew on the quarterdeck. The younger son of the Duke of Hartcliffe, the first lieutenant was a stout, moon-faced man in his late twenties with curly hair and watery blue eyes.

'What've we got, Killigrew?' he asked, rubbing his hands together, more for something to do with them than as a show of eagerness.

'Two pilong junks grappled alongside a clipper.'

A call from the look-out at the masthead alerted them that the three ships were separating. Killigrew glanced through the telescope that Robertson handed him and saw that the two junks were indeed slipping away from the clipper. Even as he watched, smoke billowed up from the clipper's deck, already visible over the horizon, and a moment later the sails and rigging were ablaze.

He handed the telescope back to Robertson. 'The fiends have fired her.'

The commander nodded. 'They must've seen us.'

The clipper soon blazed fiercely. Killigrew guessed they had caught the pirates in the act of transferring the clipper's cargo of opium into the junks. It was all one to him if the opium was smuggled into China by Western traders or Chinese pirates; his main concern was the safety of the clipper's crew. They were probably dead already, he thought grimly. All that he and his colleagues could do was make sure that these particular pirates had hunted their last quarry.

Even with all sail crammed on her yards, the *Tisiphone* could manage no more than four knots in such light airs, barely enough to keep the two junks in sight. They were still barely halfway to where the clipper had burned down to the waterline and was already sinking, before a blast from the whistle signalled that steam was up, and a moment later the deck vibrated as the paddle-wheels churned into action. The sloop's speed trebled almost at once.

'Deck!' called the look-out. 'They're separating!'

'Clever,' said Killigrew, as Robertson levelled the telescope again. The junks could not hope to outrun a paddle-sloop under steam, but if they went their separate ways then at least one of them had a chance of escape.

'The larger one's holding her course,' said Robertson. 'Probably headed for the China coast. The other's veering off to starboard. The Paracels?'

Killigrew nodded. The Paracels were an archipelago of tiny islands and reefs, a deathtrap for any ship that did not know those waters. It was a fair bet that the master of the smaller junk knew them like the back of his hand.

'How far, Mr Yelverton?' Robertson asked the ship's master.

'To the Paracels?' As the *Tisiphone*'s master, Yelverton was responsible for navigation and was the most important officer on the ship – if not the most senior – after the commander. 'Eight miles, sir. If we go after them, we may just catch them first.'

'We ought to stop and lower a boat first,' said Killigrew, nodding to where what was left of the blazing clipper sank beneath the waves.

'I hardly think anyone is likely to have survived that fire,' snorted Robertson. 'Still, I suppose you're right, Second. It's our duty to check for survivors. Make ready the whaler, Bosun.'

The whale boat was the largest boat carried by the

*Tisiphone*, apart from the thirty-foot pinnace stowed on deck above the engine room. The boatswain ordered the whaler's crew to assemble while one of the mates prepared to take command. It was swung out in its davits and lowered until it was just above the waves. Then the *Tisiphone* stopped just long enough for the hands to shin down the lifelines into the boat. The clipper's masts were the only part of her showing above the waves, now thick with flotsam: charred timbers, a sailor's sennit hat, a few cargo chests bobbing up and down forlornly.

Killigrew stood at the bulwark as the whaler's crew cast off. Here and there he could see bodies floating amongst the flotsam. Sharks' fins circled already. 'Remember, if you can't find any survivors, at least get a piece of wreckage; something to identify the clipper,' he said.

The mate saluted. 'Aye, aye, sir.'

The oarsmen pulled away from the *Tisiphone* and the engineer started up the sloop's paddle-wheels once more.

Lowering the boat had taken only minutes, yet the *Tisiphone* had lost more time in slowing down and speeding up again. But now the engines were at full steam the sloop quickly gained on the smaller of the two junks, which was only five miles away.

'Land ho!' cried the look-out at the masthead.

The boatswain lifted the speaking trumpet to his lips. 'Where away?'

'Dead ahead! Looks like an island . . . no, several islands.'

'The Paracels,' said the master. 'If they make it to the reefs, we'll never catch them.'

'We might stand a chance if we went for the other junk,' said Hartcliffe. The larger junk was still visible on the horizon off the port bow. 'Nothing but clear water between here and China . . .'

'I think we should stick to our guns and stay with this one, my lord,' said Killigrew.

'Any particular reason, Second?' asked Robertson.

'They know we can catch the smaller junk, sir. So the larger one has to be the decoy.'

'Don't pilong chiefs always sail on their largest vessels?'

'That's what they want us to think, sir. If there's a pilong chief on board one of those junks, he'll be on the smaller one.'

'Is that what your ancestors would have done, Second?' In his gruff, sardonic way, Robertson liked to tease Killigrew about his piratical ancestors: his Cornish forebears had been notorious pirates in the sixteenth century.

The second lieutenant refused to give him the satisfaction of rising to the bait. 'It's what I'd do, sir.'

'*À bon chat, bon rat*, sir,' offered Hartcliffe.

'What's that?' demanded Robertson. Someone must at least have *tried* to teach him French once, as befitted the position of navy officer, but Robertson refused to admit it now. If he possessed any social graces, Killigrew had seen no sign of them since he had rejoined the *Tisiphone* with her new commander. The hands called him 'Tommy Pipes' behind his back, a nickname usually reserved for the boatswain's mates whose bellows were relied upon to keep everything on board shipshape and Bristol fashion. There was little work for the boatswain's mates to do on board the *Tisiphone* now that Robertson was captain: he had a booming voice of his own and was never slow to use it.

'A loose translation would be: "Set a thief to catch a thief", sir,' explained Killigrew.

'I see,' Robertson remarked gruffly. 'And a descendant of pirates to catch pirates, I suppose?'

'I'm an officer of the Royal Navy first and foremost, sir.'

'That isn't good enough, Mr Killigrew. In my command I want only officers who are Royal Navy officers first, last and everything in between. I suppose you think we can catch the smaller one before she reaches the Paracels, and then go after the other?'

'In an ideal world, sir, yes.'

'In an ideal world, eh? It may have escaped your notice, Second, but we don't live in an ideal world. Don't fall into the trap of thinking these pilongs are nincompoops. They may be unenlightened heathens without the benefits of steam and shell, but that doesn't make them imbeciles. While we're chasing the second junk, the first one will run for the horizon and change course the moment she's out of sight. We'll never catch her then.'

'Yes, sir. Shall I order the quartermaster to change course?'

'Never change horses in mid-stream, Second. We'll stand by your decision and see where it leads us.' He slapped the telescope against Killigrew's chest, his way of asking the lieutenant to hold it. 'Of course, if that junk reaches the Paracels before we can catch her and we end up losing both junks, you know I'll hold you responsible, don't you?'

'The thought had crossed my mind, sir.'

'We'll see,' harrumphed Robertson.

Killigrew checked on the junk they were chasing. She was barely five miles away now, but had less than three to cover before she reached the safety of the Paracels. He calculated the pilongs would be within range of the bow-chaser long before that; within the next twenty minutes, as things stood.

The *Tisiphone* rapidly gained on her quarry. A junk – even a pirate junk armed to the bulwarks – was no match for a Western ship in a fight, not even a mere sloop of war. A direct hit from a shell would blow a junk out of the water. Nonetheless there was a palpable air of excitement on board, as there was in any stern-chase; excitement, and tension. If it came to a fight the junk had no chance of winning, but there would always be a chance she would get a lucky hit before she went down, and even one round shot amidships would be enough to sweep the deck with splinters of wood and wreak bloody havoc amongst the crew.

'Attend to the bow-chaser, Second,' ordered Robertson. As second lieutenant, Killigrew was responsible for the guns, although the gunner – an officer by warrant rather than commission, and therefore subordinate – was perfectly capable. 'Give them a warning shot to begin with, if you please, though I doubt they'll pay it much heed. As Christians we owe them the chance of mercy, if nothing else.'

'Aye, aye, sir.' Killigrew made his way to the forecastle. 'Sixty-eight-pounder's crew close up,' he ordered. 'Call for silence!'

The boatswain's mate made the call to pipe down on his whistle and everyone stopped talking; not that there had been much chatter during the tense chase.

'Make ready!' ordered the gunner.

The gun crew slid the gun carriage on its racers towards one of the four gun ports in the prow. Every man of the gun crew had his number and his duties, and Killigrew had drilled them time and time again on the voyage from England. These were all able seamen who could do it blindfolded.

'One blank shot if you please, Guns,' Killigrew told the gunner.

'Aye, aye, sir. Remove tompion and search!'

One of the men checked that the gun had not been left loaded. It should not have been, but one could not take any chances.

'Load!'

A flannel cartridge was passed up from the magazine, slipped into the muzzle and rammed home.

'Run out!'

The gun crew hauled on the ropes to push the muzzle out through the gun port.

'Prime!'

A friction tube was inserted into the breech. There was

no need to aim. The captain of the gun grasped the wooden toggle on the lanyard. Everyone else backed away. 'Ready!'

The gunner glanced at Killigrew, who nodded once.

'Fire!'

The captain of the gun jerked back the toggle. The gun boomed deafeningly and spewed a great plume of pale grey smoke from its muzzle.

'Are they heaving to?' Killigrew called to the look-out at the masthead.

'No, sir . . . they're changing course, veering to port!'

'Running for the reefs,' snorted Killigrew. 'Range?'

''Bout a thousand yards, sir.'

'Right. We'll fire a shot across their bows. Round shot if you please, Guns.'

'Sponge!'

The barrel was wormed and sponged to clear the bore of any smouldering remains from the previous charge while one man went to fetch the next cartridge, along with a sixty-eight-pound round shot. The gun was loaded, primed once more and run out again.

'Point!' ordered the gunner. The captain of the gun lined up the bow-chaser until it pointed to a spot perhaps fifty yards ahead of the junk, to let its crew know they were within range. The *Tisiphone* was well out of range of the junk's archaic cannon.

'Elevate!'

The gun crew lifted the breech from the carriage and the number two of the gun crew slid the wedge back as far as it would go, to give the gun maximum elevation. 'Down!' he called.

'Ready!' said the captain of the gun.

The gunner waited until the pitching of the deck reached its zenith, and fired just before the gun was lined up with where he wanted the ball to fire. The gun boomed and shot back on its carriage. The shot screeched through the air and threw up a huge white plume close enough to the junk to drench the men standing on deck.

'Capital shooting, Guns,' said Killigrew. 'Any sign of them heaving to?' he called up to the look-out.

'No, sir! They . . . they're putting out sweeps, sir!'

Killigrew could see that for himself as the crew of the junk lowered the large oars into the water, trying to give themselves that extra burst of speed they needed to carry them to safety.

'They've got sand, I'll say that for 'em,' opined the gunner.

'That's because they know we'll hang every last one of the jackals if we catch them,' said Killigrew. These men had murdered the crew of the clipper and he intended to see to it that those who were not killed in this fight would be hanged for their crimes. 'Reload.'

'Aye, aye, sir. Chain shot?' Chain shot to dismast them, slow them down enough to overhaul them before they reached the reefs, and then get in close and pummel them into submission with round shot.

Killigrew was about to nod his acquiescence when he changed his mind. 'No, damn it. A shell. We'll blow the bastards out of the water.' If they could destroy this junk with one shot, they might still have time to catch the second junk.

'Aye, aye, sir!'

As the gun crew reloaded the bow-chaser, Killigrew studied the foe through a telescope. He could see them sweating at the sweeps, two men to an oar, pulling for their very lives. He knew the back-breaking agony of that kind of work over an extended period, and could have felt sorry for them if they had not been pirates, the scum of the seas. He had met Chinese the last time he had been in these waters and bore the race no ill will. He had been taught to treat all men as individuals, regardless of race, colour or creed. Indeed, of all the races he had encountered he had a particular fondness for the Chinese, with their fine art, cheerful nature and impeccable manners. But these men were criminals according to the Manchu Code as much as in British law. He would take as many alive as he could, to stand trial in Hong Kong as justice demanded, but he would not lose a wink of sleep over any that he had to kill in the process.

'Ready!' the captain of the gun announced.

Killigrew heard him, but was still searching the deck of the junk with the telescope, looking for the pirate chief who commanded her; perhaps wondering what kind of a man his adversary was. Not that it mattered: in a few seconds he would go to join the great majority . . .

'Shall I give the order to fire, sir?' prompted the gunner.

Killigrew was about to say 'yes' when he saw her.

She was pinioned between two burly pilongs – burly for Chinese, at least – on the high poop deck, and stood out by virtue of her emerald-green sari with gold brocade trimmings. Killigrew had not seen her until now and could only presume that she had been brought up from below that instant. A third pilong held a cutlass at her throat; to judge from his finery – a white silk tunic, pyjamy trousers and a crimson sash – he was the *lao-pan*, as the captains of pirate junks were known. He gazed straight back at Killigrew, grinning malevolently, as though he could see the lieutenant without the aid of a telescope, even at that distance.

'Hold your fire!' snapped Killigrew.

'Sir?'

'You heard me plain enough, Guns.' Killigrew turned the telescope to where the breakers that crashed over the reefs of the Paracels could now be seen less than a mile ahead of the junk. They only had a few more minutes to catch the junk before it reached safety.

'What's keeping you, Second?' Robertson's voice, amplified by his speaking trumpet – not that it was ever in need of amplification – boomed from the quarterdeck.

Killigrew snapped the telescope shut, tucked it under his arms, cupped his hands around his mouth to reply, and then thought better of it. Instead he jogged briskly down the deck to where Robertson and Hartcliffe stood, and saluted smartly.

'Sir, it looks as if there's a hostage on board that junk. An Indian woman.'

'These pirates have doxies of all colours on board their boats,' Robertson snapped back. 'I don't care to make war on women any more than you do, Mr Killigrew, but I can't let a pilong junk get away just because there's a woman on board.'

'I agree, sir. But this one's a hostage, I'm certain of it. One of the pilongs is holding a cutlass to her throat.'

'A bluff.'

'I don't think so, sir.'

Robertson sighed. 'Very well, Killigrew. So there's a hostage on board. What do you want me to do about it? Let them get away?'

'No, sir. With your permission I'd like to take the first cutter, along with twenty men and try to board her.'

'Have you ever boarded a hostile vessel before, Mr Killigrew?'

'On occasion.' Killigrew and Robertson had been acquainted for just the few months since they had sailed from Portsmouth so the commander only really knew his Second Lieutenant by Rear-Admiral Napier's recommendation. Corsair galleys, pilong junks, Malay prahus, slave ships – Killigrew had boarded them all. But it never got any easier; if anything, the opposite. Once you had boarded a hostile vessel and thrown yourself on to a deck swarming with men intent on slaughtering you, you knew that it was only good joss that kept you alive in the confusion of the bloody hand-to-hand combat, and each new experience only reinforced that knowledge as you saw more and more shipmates felled by blows which might just as easily have felled yourself.

'Then you'll know it's a damned tricky business. Not all of you will come back. How many of my men do you want me to risk, just to save one woman?'

'There's a difference, sir. All of the men are volunteers. They knew what they were signing up for when they joined us. That woman's an innocent; a passenger from the clipper, I'd guess.'

Robertson sighed. 'Very well. But we'll do it my way, Mr Killigrew. Lord Hartcliffe will take the first cutter with thirty men. The marines will stay on board to give covering fire as we pull alongside, keeping back enough to stop the cutter from being swamped by our wash . . .'

'With all due respect, sir, Killigrew's much better at this sort of thing than I am,' protested Hartcliffe.

'Pipe down, First. I haven't finished yet. You'll take the junk from the starboard side. Mr Killigrew will be in the second cutter with twenty men and approach the junk from port. They won't be able to keep up as heavy a fire if we attack them from both sides at once: they'll have to divide their forces. Well, don't just stand about like a couple of farts in a thunderstorm! Look lively, there!'

'Aye, aye, sir!' Killigrew ordered the boatswain to pick out the men for the boats – it was no good asking for volunteers: every man on board would step forward, if only to avoid accusations of cowardice from his shipmates – and went below to his cabin. He primed and loaded one of his six-barrelled 'pepperbox' revolving pistols, attached it to his belt with the hook on the butt designed for that purpose, and fastened on his cutlass and scabbard.

By the time he re-emerged on deck the hands the boatswain had chosen to man the cutters were ready with their own weapons; a motley array of muskets, pistols, hatchets and cutlasses. Most of the crew were old hands who had served on the *Tisiphone* before, on her previous commission with the West Africa Squadron. They had rushed to sign on again when they had heard that Commander Standish would no longer be captain. What they thought of Robertson, Killigrew had not yet divined; but then, he had not made his own mind up about the new captain.

Senior amongst the ratings in the second cutter's crew was Petty Officer Olaf Ågård, one of the *Tisiphone*'s quartermasters: a tall, blond giant who had been serving in the Royal Navy for so long he had lost all trace of his native Swedish accent. Next to him, and in sharp physical contrast, was Able Seaman Wes Molineaux. Bare-footed and stripped to the waist beneath the tropical sun, with a single gold ring through one ear, Molineaux looked more like a corsair of the Barbary Coast than a seaman of the Royal Navy. His complexion was as dark as roasted Arabica coffee beans, the features beneath his shaven head Nubian. He was not tall, but he had the broad shoulders and wiry physique of a true sailor. When he balled his fists on his hips and stood with arms akimbo to throw back his head and laugh his deep, fruity chuckle in some response to a shipmate's jest, he put Killigrew in mind of the Djinn of the Lamp: to hear was to obey, but only a fool would forget what a dangerous spirit he aspired to command.

The *Tisiphone* overhauled the junk to starboard. Hartcliffe and his men climbed into the first cutter on the starboard side of the sloop; on the port side, closest to the junk, Killigrew and his men got into the second. The engine was stopped and as the sloop slowed in the water the second cutter was lowered from the davits. As soon as Killigrew judged the *Tisiphone*'s headway to be negligible enough, he ordered the falls to be let go, and ten of the hands grasped the oars, the other ten readying their muskets.

'Shove off!' Killigrew ordered from the prow of the cutter.

The boat was pushed out from the *Tisiphone*'s side, well clear of the port-side paddle-wheel. 'Out oars!' ordered Ågård. The oars were eased into the rowlocks; the fenders were taken in. 'Give way together!'

Taking their stroke from the starboard after-oar, the oarsmen began to pull towards the junk. They were now close enough to see the breakers crashing over the reef with the naked eye, even from the height of the cutter. The boat soon gathered way as the oarsmen pulled mightily. The pilongs at the junk's sweeps would be growing weary by now, while the men in the cutter were rested and fit. The boat passed the *Tisiphone*'s prow and a moment later the first cutter emerged on the other side. Killigrew saw Hartcliffe in the bow and waved to him, before turning his attention to the junk.

'Pace yourselves,' he told the oarsmen. The junk might just be a few hundred yards ahead, but the cutters only had a knot or two's advantage and it might yet be a long chase. With Ågård at the tiller, the second cutter moved out across the junk's stern to overhaul it from port. To starboard, the first cutter paced them.

The junk's stern was ornamented with intricate Chinese carvings, and brightly painted to look like the face of a highly stylised grinning demon. When both boats were within a hundred yards of the junk, one of the demon's eyes swung up to reveal a gun port behind.

Ågård saw it too. 'Should we take evasive action, sir?' he called as the muzzle of a small bronze cannon – shaped like the mouth of a dragon – protruded.

Killigrew shook his head. 'Belay that, Ågård. There's one thing you can say for Chinese gunnery: their shots fall everywhere except where they're aimed.'

The dragon's mouth belched smoke and flames, and the shot screeched over their heads to plunge into the water about fifty yards abaft. Ågård grinned, relieved that Killigrew's cool-headedness had once again proved well founded. Killigrew looked more confident than he felt: for a first shot, it had come a damned sight closer than he had expected. Unlike many pilongs, who might be fishermen or traders fallen on hard times, these knew their business.

The long barrels of *gingalls* – outsize Chinese matchlocks firing balls more than an inch in diameter – emerged through other ports, or were levelled over the bulwark on the junk's high poop. They fired in a ragged volley. Most of the shots went wide, kicking up frighteningly large spurts of water on all sides of the two boats. One of them smashed a large piece of wood from the upper strake of the second cutter's gunwales, and one of the oarsmen cried out.

'Anyone hurt?' demanded Killigrew.

'It's Dando, sir,' said Ågård.

'I'm all right,' the seaman said quickly. 'Just splinters, that be all.'

They enjoyed a few seconds' respite while the pilongs reloaded their *gingalls*. The long-barrelled matchlocks required two men to operate them and were slow and cumbersome, although if the half-pound balls found their target they could deliver a maiming wound. In the meantime the two boats crept closer and closer to the junk, while the *Tisiphone* crept by on the far side of the first cutter. The reefs were less than half a mile away now; the sloop would have to veer off if they did not catch the junk soon, or else risk ripping her keel out on the submerged rocks.

The *gingalls* fired again as soon as they were reloaded, even more sporadically than before. One of the men in the second cutter gasped and Killigrew glanced over his shoulder in time to see him slump with a great chunk torn out of his shoulder.

Seaman Molineaux levelled his musket. 'Belay that!' snapped Killigrew. 'Don't waste a shot.'

'I can get one from here, sir,' the seaman retorted truculently.

'I don't care. We'll need to make every shot tell when we get closer.'

Another shot from the cannon behind the demon's eye sent up a great plume of water only a few yards to starboard, and the men in the cutter were drenched with spray. They could only hope that the powder in their firearms had not got wet.

Then Killigrew heard the sergeant of the *Tisiphone*'s marines give the order to fire, and a smart volley crashed from the sloop's tops and bulwarks. Screams and cries sounded from the junk. Two men in the first cutter were hit by *gingalls*, one of them screaming in pain, and another man was wounded in the second. The narrower the gap became, the more the pilongs' fire told.

Killigrew's heart pounded. This was the worst time, waiting to grapple the enemy. Once they were on board there would be no time to be afraid, everything would happen too quickly; but until then all he could do was crouch in the cutter's bow and wait, while the *gingall* balls whistled past his head.

'Come on, my buckoes!' he yelled above the rattle of musketry. 'Just a few more yards . . . one last effort . . .'

The cannon behind the demon's eye boomed again, this time smattering the water between the two cutters with small shot. The second cutter's prow was level with the junk's stern, then past it. They were close against the junk's side, so close the oars almost scraped the hull on one side while becoming entangled with the sweeps on the other. Killigrew snatched up a hatchet, grabbed one of the sweeps with his left hand and hacked at it. Molineaux whirled a grappling iron above his head and flung it over the junk's bulwark, just forward of the raised stern. He pulled it tight before a pilong could snatch it up and fling it clear. Another grappling iron fell into place beside it.

‘In bows!’ ordered Killigrew. The rowers shipped their oars as the boat was pulled against the junk’s side. A figure appeared on the poop deck above them, an iron shot held above his head in both hands, poised to fling it down and through the cutter’s bottom boards. Killigrew flung the hatchet. It whirled over and over and embedded itself in the pilong’s chest. He staggered back and dropped the heavy shot on his own head. Molineaux fired his musket and a pilong who had been aiming his *gingall* at Killigrew fell back with the top of his head missing.

There was no time for the lieutenant to thank Molineaux for saving his life. The cutter bumped against the side of the junk and two of the seamen made the ropes fast to cleats. Killigrew balanced on the cutter’s gunwale while Ågård and the others covered him with their muskets. He had done this kind of thing enough times to know that hesitation could be fatal. Without pausing even for breath, he leaped for the junk’s bulwarks.

# II:

# Lao-Pan

A pilong appeared at the bulwark above Killigrew with a sword raised above his head, ready to bring it down against his hand. A musket boomed in the cutter behind him and blood splashed across the man's tunic.

Killigrew pulled himself up and found he was staring into the barrel of an antiquated swivel gun, aimed by a grinning pilong, with the fuse burning in the touchhole. Holding on to the bulwark with one hand, his feet braced against the junk's side, Killigrew slapped the swivel gun's muzzle forcefully with his palm. The gun spun round and the barrel cracked against the side of the pilong's head. His eyes rolled up in his skull and he fell to the deck. A moment later the gun boomed and swept part of the deck with lead pellets.

Another pilong ran to where Killigrew clung to the side. The lieutenant swung his legs over the bulwark and kicked the pilong in the chest. As the pilong staggered back, Killigrew landed on his feet and drew his cutlass in his right hand and a pepperbox in his left. He got off a couple of shots from his pepperbox; there was no need to aim, the pilongs were all around him. Then they closed in.

If Killigrew had stopped to think about what he was

doing, he would have realised how insane it was and panicked: a sure way of getting himself killed. He had seen that happen to other men, and it had come close to happening to him on more than one occasion. All you could do was fling yourself into the thick of it, unthinking, kill as many of them as you could as quickly as possible, and hope your shipmates were close behind you. The only advantage a man enjoyed at a moment like this was the fact that the enemy could be relied upon to be terrified. When one man with a gun faces a hundred men with guns, every one of the hundred thinks their opponent's weapon is levelled at himself. The odds were on the side of the pilongs, but they would have been less than human not to be overawed by a man who flung himself, roaring wildly, into the teeth of certain death.

Killigrew parried a sword blow with his cutlass, thrust the six muzzles of his pepperbox against a naked torso, and fired. He stabbed one man in the throat, shot another in the face, hacked and slashed again. Three more pilongs charged him. He shot one, hacked at the next and kicked the third in the crotch. There was a time and a place for gentlemanly fighting, and this was certainly not it.

Then Molineaux and the others had joined him on the deck of the junk, and Hartcliffe and the men from the first cutter swarmed over the far bulwark. Within seconds the bluejackets outnumbered the pilongs. The Chinese would not surrender, though: even when they must have realised defeat was inevitable, they fought to the bitter end, well aware that if they were captured the only fate they could expect was execution. Killigrew had heard fellow officers – men who had fought alongside him in the Opium War seven years earlier, men who should have known better – denigrate the fighting capabilities of John Chinaman. *Damned heathens*, they said; *no moral fibre*. Killigrew knew that was hogwash: the Chinese might be badly led in war, and lack modern Western armaments, but they could be as savage and courageous as the best.

He fought his way to where the halyards ran up the side of the mainmast to support the junk's mainsail. He slashed through one rope, and then a pilong thrust a billhook at him. A sweep of Killigrew's cutlass sliced the billhook from the shaft. The pilong was fast though, and strong: he slammed the shaft like a quarterstaff against Killigrew's chest and sent him staggering. As the lieutenant charged back to meet him, the pilong reached for a pistol tucked into his girdle. Killigrew slashed with his cutlass. The pilong ducked, and laughed when the blade passed several inches above his head. Oblivious to the halyard which the cutlass had parted, he pulled out his pistol and levelled it at the lieutenant with a smirk of triumph.

Killigrew backed away and glanced up. A descending shadow prompted the pilong to do likewise. A moment later the mainsail had peeled away from the mainmast to fold itself over Killigrew's opponent and another knot of half a dozen pilongs in the waist. Bluejackets swarmed over the matting sail, bashing the shapes which struggled beneath with belaying pins and cutlass hilts until they lay still.

The lieutenant looked around. There was no sign of the Indian woman, but he caught a glimpse of the *lao-pan* in the white tunic and crimson sash dashing through the portal which led into the cabin beneath the poop deck.

Killigrew went after him. He dashed into the cabin and tripped over an extended foot. His cutlass skittered into a corner as he sprawled on his front. He reached for it, but a slippered foot came down on his wrist and pinned his right arm to the deck.

He still had his pepperbox in his left hand. He shot the pilong under the jaw and blew his brains out. Footsteps sounded. Killigrew rolled on to his back as another pilong came at him, and shot him in the chest. Then he scrambled back into a corner to survey the cabin.

The *lao-pan* was in the far corner, with the muzzle of a flintlock pistol pressed behind the ear of the Indian woman, held in front of him as a human shield. For now Killigrew concentrated on the man. He was tall and blue-eyed, hinting at European blood, although there was no other trace of it in his sallow features. Even hiding behind a woman, he had a self-assurance Killigrew had never seen in a Chinese before. The most powerful mandarins carried themselves with Confucian humility, even when addressing those they clearly regarded as inferior, such as the Western barbarians. But here Killigrew could see he was facing a man who would bow to no one, neither Queen Victoria nor the Daoguang Emperor in Peking.

Killigrew pushed himself to his feet and levelled his pepperbox at the *lao-pan*'s face, visible over the woman's right shoulder.

'Drop your gun, or I'll kill her,' the *lao-pan* said in tolerably good English.

Killigrew let the pepperbox fall to the floor. 'Surrender. We've taken the ship; you're not going anywhere.'

'We shall see.' The *lao-pan* gave the woman an almighty shove so that she fell into Killigrew's arms, and snatched up his cutlass. 'Barbarian fool! My pistol is empty!'

The *lao-pan* was about to hack at Killigrew's head when Molineaux came through the portal behind him and grabbed him by the wrist, staying the blow. The *lao-pan* whirled and punched the seaman in the stomach. Molineaux gasped and doubled up, but not before he had wrenched the cutlass from the *lao-pan*'s grip.

The Chinese snatched up the pepperbox and backed away, covering both Killigrew and Molineaux.

Killigrew relaxed and turned his attention to the woman. 'Do you speak English?' he asked her. 'Are you all right?' She merely nodded.

'With all due respect, sir, this is hardly the time!' protested Molineaux, with a jerk of his head at the *lao-pan*, who still clutched the pepperbox.

Killigrew sat the woman on a chair and turned his attention back to the *lao-pan*. He started to walk across the cabin towards him and held out his hand. 'My gun, if you please.'

The *lao-pan* levelled the pepperbox at Killigrew's head. 'Stay back!'

Killigrew continued to advance.

'I warned you . . .' The *lao-pan* pulled the trigger. The hammer fell on a spent percussion cap with a harmless click.

'Did you think you were the only one who could bluff with an empty pistol?' Killigrew demanded irritably.

The *lao-pan* threw the pepperbox at his face, but Killigrew had been expecting it, and ducked. He straightened in time to see the *lao-pan* lunge for the doorway. Killigrew caught him round the waist in a flying tackle and drove him against the bulkhead. The *lao-pan* rammed an elbow into his cheek and squirmed free. Still holding the cutlass, Molineaux got to the door first to bar his path. The *lao-pan*'s foot flashed out and connected with the seaman's wrist. The cutlass flew from his grip.

Then Hartcliffe appeared in the doorway. The *lao-pan* twisted away and snatched up the cutlass. 'Barbarian fools! You think you can cage Zhai Jing-mu like a songbird?' He backed towards one of the gun ports, his eyes flickering between Killigrew, Molineaux and Hartcliffe. He paid no attention to the Indian woman behind him, which was a mistake because she snatched up a decorated porcelain vase and smashed it over his head. The *lao-pan*'s eyes rolled up in his head and he measured his length on the deck with blood weeping from a scalp wound.

The woman slumped back into the chair, trembling.

'Are you all right, miss?' Killigrew asked her. 'Or is it ma'am?'

'Miss,' said the woman. 'Miss Peri Dadabhoy.' She

stood up and bowed with her hands pressed palms together before her. Although a formal and thoroughly respectable garment among Indian women, the sari left a lot less to the imagination than the billowing gowns and blouses of Western women. Miss Dadabhoy was in her late teens or early twenties, with smooth skin the colour of *café au lait*, a straight nose, curly black hair, sensuous lips and dark brown, almond-shaped eyes above high cheekbones. Killigrew would have liked to have taken in more, but it was ungentlemanly to stare, so he returned her bow.

'Christopher Killigrew at your service, miss.' He had heard the name 'Dadabhoy' somewhere before, although he could not place it. 'And may I present Lord Hartcliffe? And not forgetting Able Seaman Molineaux, of course.'

'My friends call me Wes, miss,' said Molineaux.

'Take care of our friend there, Molineaux,' Killigrew said curtly, indicating Zhai Jing-mu, as Hartcliffe escorted Miss Dadabhoy out on deck. 'We'll take him to Hong Kong for trial.'

Molineaux found some rope and trussed up Zhai Jing-mu with a scowl which said: *Typical! The officers get to spoon with the blowers while the ratings get left to clear up the mess.*

Killigrew hesitated in the doorway. 'Molineaux?'

'Sir?'

'Well done.'

'Thank you, sir.' To judge from his truculent tone, Molineaux was unmollified.

Killigrew could not blame him. 'You know how to handle yourself in a scrimmage, I'll say that for you.'

Molineaux finally grinned. 'Maybe I didn't go to school, sir, but even a misspent youth provides an education of sorts. What about you, sir? Don't tell me they taught you the old "Ringsend uppercut" at Eton.'

'I never went to school either, Molineaux, although

unlike you I had the benefit of a private tutor. Two private tutors, if you include Jory Spargo.'

'Jory Spargo, sir?'

'A seaman on board my first ship. He taught me a few moves which might be looked down upon in polite company, but which have saved my life on more than one occasion. Well, be about your duties. We both have plenty of work to do.'

'Aye, aye, sir.'

Killigrew followed Hartcliffe and Miss Dadabhoy out on deck. The mess there was even worse, and Killigrew steered the young woman away so that she did not have to look at the carnage, leaving Hartcliffe – who was never at ease with the opposite sex – to supervise the rounding up of the other prisoners. None of the pilongs had surrendered: those that had been taken alive had been knocked unconscious, like their captain.

Some of the Tisiphones on deck had lowered the anchor and hauled down the foresail, bringing the junk to a halt barely a cable's length from where the breakers boomed over the reefs. The *Tisiphone* had pulled alongside and the first cutter was already being hauled back into its davits.

'We need a bosun's chair over here!' Killigrew called across to one of the boatswain's mates, and then turned back to Miss Dadabhoy. 'Are you injured in any way, miss? Do you require medical attention?'

She shook her head. 'There is no need for you to concern yourself on that account, Mr Killigrew. I was not subjected to "a fate worse than death".' She was almost mocking, a smile of amusement playing impishly on her lips. Killigrew found himself warming to her at once: she made a refreshing change from the simpering ninnies he usually met.

'We'll get you aboard the *Tisiphone*, you can have a cabin to yourself, some clean clothes, a brush and scrub up, whatever you require. We're headed for Hong Kong. You have family there?'

She nodded. 'My father.'

Killigrew had been trying to think of someone with the surname 'Dadabhoy'; now he remembered that Parsis did not have family names, but patronymics, taking their fathers' forenames as surnames.

'Not Sir Dadabhoy Framjee?' he guessed.

'You've heard of him?'

'Hasn't everyone in these parts?' Framjee was the foremost of the Parsi merchants engaged in the opium trade, a wealthy philanthropist so well liked he was one of the first Indians to be honoured with a knighthood. The number of schools, colleges, hospitals, Zarathustrian fire-temples, and other charitable concerns endowed by him bore testament to his generosity.

Killigrew had often heard the Parsis described as the Jews of India, succeeding in trade by dint of hard work and a reputation for honesty and integrity. The Parsis had come from Persia in the tenth century and settled in Gujerat in western India. Nowadays they spoke Gujerati, although they continued to pray in Persian. They were Zarathustrians, of the oldest monotheistic religion in the world, and the supposed similarity of their religion to Christianity, their willingness to adopt Western manners, and – Killigrew was ashamed as a European to admit it – the lightness of their skins had made them more acceptable to the British Raj, enabling them to thrive in the Bombay business community.

The son of a weaver, Dadabhoy Framjee had started out in life as a bottle-washer; half a century later, he was one of the richest men in the world, with agencies in India, China, Egypt and England, and a fleet of cargo ships. He had made his first fortune by the time he was twenty-three, lost it all when the Great Fire of Bombay had reduced his home to ashes, and worked hard to build an even larger one. But he had never forgotten his roots or his heritage. The ancient creed of Zarathustrianism demanded that the

Parsis put back into the community what they had earned from it, and there could be no denying that Framjee's generosity was in proportion to his wealth.

'Begging your pardon, sir . . .' It was Petty Officer Ågård, with a cut on his temple.

Killigrew realised he had been neglecting his duties to talk to the woman. Understandable, but unforgivable too. 'You'll have to excuse me, miss,' he told her, and turned to the petty officer. 'Better get back aboard the *Tisiphone* and get that looked at, Ågård.'

'Hmm?' The petty officer raised a hand to the cut and looked at the blood. 'Oh, that. It's not deep, sir. I'm not hurt as bad as some of the others.'

'How many dead?'

'Six, all told, sir. I reckon we got off lightly.' Ågård spoke briskly, in a matter-of-fact tone, his voice devoid of any accusation. The dead men had given their lives in a noble cause, and Miss Dadabhoy was alive and safe thanks to them. But part of Killigrew could not help wondering if it was a fair exchange: six good men for one woman. If his own life had been lost, he wondered if his ghost would have had the good grace to look down from above – or up from below – and still say he had only done his duty. He told himself they were dead, and blaming himself would not bring them back. Tomorrow they would be buried at sea, and their few personal effects auctioned before the mast at inflated prices, to raise money for any wives and children waiting for them back in Britain.

'Very well, Ågård,' Killigrew said as Molineaux emerged from the cabin, pushing the now conscious *lao-pan* before him. 'Take the second cutter and return to the *Tisiphone*.'

'What do you want me to do with this one, sir?' asked Molineaux.

'I'll take him.' Killigrew grasped the *lao-pan* firmly by the arm. 'I want you to see Miss Dadabhoy safely aboard the *Tisiphone*, Molineaux, then help Dando with the wounded.'

'Aye, aye, sir.'

The prisoners were put in irons in the sloop's lee waist with an armed guard of marines over them while the wounded went down to the sick berth for the surgeon, assistant surgeon and the sick berth attendant to tend to. It was traditional for the wounded to be treated according to the order in which they reached the sick berth, regardless of their rank, although those with minor cuts and sprains held back so that those in more urgent need of attention would be treated first.

Killigrew and Hartcliffe reported to Robertson on the *Tisiphone*'s quarterdeck.

'I suppose you expect me to congratulate you both, eh?' sniffed the commander. 'Damned young fools. Well, I'm as much to blame as you are. I gave you permission, after all. But don't think I'm going to thank you for doing no more than your duty. If you'd done any less, on the other hand . . . well, then I'd have something to say to you, of that you may be sure!'

'I don't feel like being congratulated, sir,' said Killigrew. 'We lost six men, and another dozen wounded.'

'Seven,' Robertson corrected him. 'Private Evans was careless enough to get in the way of a stray *gingall* ball.'

Losing any man was bad enough, but Evans had been detailed to act as Killigrew's 'servant' in the wardroom, keeping his glass replenished during dinner, doing his laundry, polishing his boots and bringing him a cup of tea every morning. When a man who did all that was killed, the loss became more personal.

'I'm very sorry to hear that, sir,' Killigrew said with feeling. The one consolation was that he knew Evans had been a bachelor, without a wife or child, but he had been popular amongst the crew – no easy feat for a marine – and he would be missed by his friends.

'I believe you are,' Robertson allowed grudgingly. 'But don't think that means I'm giving you permission to mope around the rest of the way to Hong Kong. You said it yourself: the men who died were volunteers who knew the risks. The Indian woman was an innocent who got caught up in this business through no choice of her own. It was a fair exchange. And if anyone should take the blame, it should be me. I'm captain of this vessel, which means I take full responsibility for anything that happens under my command. And with young rapscallions like you on my hands, that's a heavier burden than you can possibly imagine. Where is the woman, anyway?'

Killigrew noticed Molineaux loitering at the edge of the quarterdeck and remembered that he had last seen Miss Dadabhoy in his care. 'Molineaux?'

'I took the liberty of putting the blower in the captain's cabin, sir.'

'The what?' demanded Robertson, only half turning towards him.

'The lady, sir. Miss Dadabhoy, I mean.'

'I'll thank you not to use slang expressions when you address an officer, Molineaux. You're not in your London rookery now. So, you took the liberty of putting her in my cabin, did you? That's quite a liberty, I must say. You might have asked me first. Still, I don't see where else we can put her. That means I shall have to move into your cabin, First. You can share a cabin with Mr Killigrew here. I take it Miss Dadabhoy is having all her feminine wants attended to?'

Robertson's misogyny was evident in the sneering way he said the word 'feminine'. As far as he was concerned, women had no function other than to satisfy a man's sexual urges, and that was that. Since ladies of genteel families were generally unavailable for such assignations, he had even less use for them.

'Your steward's fetching her some hot water and towels

now, sir, so she can have a scrub up before tea,' reported the seaman.

'Very good, Molineaux.' Robertson turned to Hartcliffe. 'I want you to pick a dozen men from the port watch and take command of the junk, First. Search it from top to bottom, make sure there aren't any more pilongs hiding below decks. Then wait here while we go back to pick up the whaler. The other junk seems to be long gone, and I don't propose we waste any time looking for it. When we get back we'll take you in tow. At least we'll get some prize money out of this.' He gave the junk a disparaging glance. 'Perhaps even enough to buy a round of drinks at the Hong Kong Club.'

The *Tisiphone* sailed back to where the whaler waited.

'No survivors, sir,' the mate reported grimly as soon as he was back on deck. He reported to Killigrew; he was terrified of the gruff commander, and flinched every time Robertson addressed him. 'The pilongs did a dashed thorough job.'

'What are those crates?' Killigrew gestured to the chests which bobbed in the water all around.

'Tea, sir,' said the mate. 'The clipper must've had a full hold.'

'That's queer.'

'I don't see what's queer about it, Second,' Robertson said pettishly. 'The clippers bring opium from Calcutta to exchange for tea in China, and then sail back to England with their cargoes. No point in sailing home with a hold that's only half full.'

'I'm aware of that, sir,' said Killigrew. 'What I don't understand is, why did the pilongs attack the clipper when she was obviously on the return voyage? Isn't that rather like Esquimaux stealing snow?'

Peri Dadabhoy was her father's daughter. She knew many women her own age, both European and Indian, who would have had a fit of the conniptions on being captured by pirates. She did not despise such women – it was not in her nature – and she understood that they were merely products of the culture in which they had been raised. But her father believed in the rights of woman and had raised his daughter the same as her brothers, making sure she was given the education he had never had, and that she was fit for something more in life than embroidery and music. When Queen Victoria had married Prince Albert, Framjee had held a ball to celebrate the momentous occasion, inviting not only his Parsi friends but also Muslim, Hindu and Christian business associates. Although the Parsis did not believe in keeping their women in purdah, nevertheless it was unheard of for Parsi women to be present at such a heterogeneous gathering; yet Framjee had insisted that all his daughters attend alongside their brothers, to the astonishment of his Parsi friends and to Peri's secret mortification. She was proud of her heritage and she clung fiercely to her Zarathustrian beliefs, yet in spite of herself, once she had overcome her initial shyness, she had enjoyed the ball immensely.

She had not yet been born when her father had lost everything in the Great Fire of Bombay, but she had often heard the stories. Once she had asked where her father had found the courage to go on and continue in business. 'If Zarathustrianism teaches us nothing else, my child, it teaches us that life goes on and one must learn to smile in the face of adversity and have faith in the undying benevolence of God.'

A knock on the day-room door startled her out of her reverie. 'Come in,' she called.

Lord Hartcliffe entered and bowed. She returned his bow, which seemed to confuse him; he was probably more used to women curtsying, she reflected. 'My lord,' she said, smiling in a vain attempt to put him at his ease.

'Miss Dadabhoy . . . um . . . I was wondering whether

you wished to join myself and the other senior officers for supper in the wardroom tonight, or if you preferred to dine alone in here.' Hartcliffe clasped his hands together, then seemed to realise he was unconsciously aping her and thrust them in the pockets of his pantaloons. 'Of course, if you don't feel up to a formal supper we shall all quite understand . . .'

'I shall be delighted, my lord.'

'Are you quite sure?' Hartcliffe remembered that a gentleman did not put his hands in his pockets in front of a lady and took them out again, patting them together before him. 'Don't think that we'll be put out if you decline. After the ordeal you've been through . . .'

She was careful to keep a straight face as he clasped his hands behind his back. 'No, it will be my pleasure. Unless there is some reason you feel it would be unfitting . . .?'

'Good Lord, no!' He wrung his hands. 'No, no, no! We should be delighted. Ah . . . supper at five?'

'I shall look forward to it.' She held out a hand, and after some hesitation he shook it.

'If there's anything you need before then . . .?'

She shook her head. He bowed awkwardly and went out.

The wardroom was an elegantly furnished compartment seventeen feet by twelve, a mahogany table dominating the room. There were three upright upholstered chairs down either side of the table and one at either end. There were no windows: by day the light came from a skylight in the deck head, but now the blinds were drawn under the skylight, and illumination was provided by two oil lamps which swung from the deck head, and the silver-plated candelabra which formed the centrepiece on the table. Crystal decanters stood on a sideboard with the crockery. There were three doors in the bulkhead on the far side of the room, marked 'First Lieutenant', 'Second Lieutenant' and 'Surgeon'.

There were six men in the room when Peri entered at five, plus the white-coated wardroom steward. A white linen cloth had been laid on the table, and seven places set. The steward pulled out the chair at the far end, opposite Hartcliffe, who sat at the head of the table.

'Miss Dadabhoy,' said Hartcliffe, 'you've met Killigrew and Mr Westlake, our surgeon. May I introduce Mr Yelverton, the ship's master; Mr Vellacott, our purser and paymaster; and Mr Muir, our chief engineer? Gentlemen, this is Miss Dadabhoy.'

They murmured greetings and waited for her to be seated before resuming their places.

'Is Commander Robertson not joining us?' asked Peri.

'The captain usually dines alone,' explained Hartcliffe. 'As it happens, this evening he's been good enough to stand in for me as officer of the watch.'

'Have I done something to offend him?' asked Peri. 'I am sure I am mistaken, but I cannot help but get the impression he is avoiding me.'

'The captain of a vessel usually has to adopt a somewhat aloof attitude to those under his command,' said Killigrew.

'Am *I* under his command?' asked Peri, amused.

'Only in so far as the ultimate responsibility for the lives of all on board rests with him,' Killigrew replied, offhand.

Peri had known plenty of British officers, soldiers of the Honourable East India Company's army in Bombay and naval men in Hong Kong. Broadly speaking, they seemed to fit into two categories: corpulent, red-faced men who drank too much and ate too much and damned the servants and the weather continually; and quieter, more intense men, usually either on their way to or returning from the latest troubles on the North-West Frontier and determined not to discuss their experiences. Killigrew seemed to belong to the latter category, but it was an uneasy fit: the presence of a young woman did not make him uncomfortable and he seemed to accept her being there as casually as did his fellow officers. Encounters with English gentlemen in Bombay and Hong Kong had taught her they were just as frightened of her as she had been of them; she had learned to make the most of this, although tonight, out of gratitude, she was more concerned to put them at ease.

Not that Killigrew needed to be put at ease, she guessed. Here was a man who would have been as much at home at a royal garden party as he evidently was throwing himself over the bulwarks of a hostile vessel.

Hartcliffe said a brief grace and the steward started to serve the first course: crimped salmon *en matelot Normandie*. 'We tend to avoid soup at sea, for obvious reasons,' said Hartcliffe.

'Really?' Peri could not resist asking impishly. 'What are those?'

'Well, if the weather gets rough it tends to . . .' began Hartcliffe, and then realised that she was teasing him. He grinned good-naturedly, and the others chuckled. 'On a larger ship we'd each have a personal servant to serve our food – one of the marines – but in a wardroom this size, it's cramped enough with just the six of us, without having half a dozen marines clumping about the place. Mr McBride manages to do us very nicely, though,' he added as the steward made his way round the table with a bottle of Chablis. 'You, er . . . you do partake, don't you?'

'In moderation,' she replied, holding down the neck of the bottle when it looked as though the steward might only half fill the glass. She had enjoyed drinking competitions with her brothers, and usually won.

'Ah. I wasn't sure if . . . you know . . .'

'I believe you are thinking of Muslims, my lord.'

'To be sure, to be sure.' Hartcliffe stared at his plate, bit his lip for a moment, and then picked up his fish knife and fork, his tureen of small talk exhausted.

'You are on your way to Hong Kong?' asked Peri.

Hartcliffe nodded eagerly. 'Your father lives there?'

'Sometimes in Hong Kong, sometimes in Bombay,' said Peri. 'Wherever his business takes him.'

'What line of work is your father in, Miss Dadabhoy?' piped up Vellacott.

'Shipping,' Hartcliffe said quickly.

Peri smiled thinly. 'You've no need to be embarrassed on my account, my lord,' she said, and turned back to the purser and paymaster. 'My father deals in opium, Mr Vellacott. Oh, he trades all manner of things, to be fair. But the bulk of his wealth is made from shipping opium from the Honourable East India Company's estates in Bengal to China, in exchange for tea, which he ships to England. Please believe me, gentlemen, I am not proud of how my father has earned his fortune.'

'There's no law against shipping opium,' said Killigrew. 'No British law, at any rate. Speaking for myself, I've always been a believer in free trade.'

'Except where slaves are concerned,' said Hartcliffe.

'Slaves, my lord?' asked Peri.

'Killigrew distinguished himself against the slavers on the Guinea Coast a couple of years ago.'

She turned back to the second lieutenant with renewed interest. 'How was that, Mr Killigrew?'

'It's a long story.' Killigrew gestured dismissively, and Hartcliffe started in his chair, as if someone had kicked him in the shin. 'I wouldn't want to bore you. Besides, we have a strict rule in the wardroom: no talking shop.'

'Well,' said Peri, a little disappointed. 'Your free-trade principles extend to opium, but stop short of slavery. May I ask why there should be any difference?'

'People aren't goods. Opium is.'

'Yet both trades ruin lives.'

'True. But the principle is different. It's a question of liberty.'

'I am not sure I follow you.'

'The slaves are taken against their will, deprived of their liberty. That's wrong, isn't it?'

'Of course.'

'Well, opium users aren't forced to take opium . . .'

'Perhaps not to begin with,' said Peri. 'But there is new evidence to suggest that drugs such as opium are addictive.' Her father had encouraged her to learn about the family business along with her brothers; but he had not expected her to study the debilitating effects of opium quite so enthusiastically. 'Once a person starts using opiates, he finds it very difficult to live without them. Is this not so, Mr Westlake?'

'Humbug,' snorted the surgeon.

'Mr Westlake . . .' Hartcliffe said chidingly.

'I beg your pardon, miss,' said Westlake. 'But there's absolutely no evidence whatsoever to suggest that opium is addictive.'

'Mr Strachan – our assistant surgeon,' Killigrew added in an aside for Peri's benefit – 'says he refuses to prescribe any opiates on the grounds that he finds his patients become dependent on them.'

'Mr Strachan,' Westlake said scathingly, 'has a theory that malaria is somehow transmitted by mosquito bites!'

'Mr Strachan – and Miss Dadabhoy here – may be right about opium, though,' said Hartcliffe. 'Remember Lieutenant Jardine? He went down with pneumonia and the quack prescribed Godfrey's Cordial. Well, he recovered from his pneumonia, but when he tried to stop taking his medicine, he fell prey to a range of new symptoms.'

'An entirely different illness, doubtless brought about by his weakened condition after his bout of pneumonia,' insisted Westlake.

'Yes, that's what his quack told him,' said Hartcliffe. 'No prizes for guessing what was prescribed as a cure.'

'An opiate?' asked Peri.

Hartcliffe nodded. 'Godfrey's Cordial. The problem was,

every time he stopped taking the cordial, the symptoms returned.'

'Must have been something chronic,' said Westlake.

Hartcliffe ignored the interruption. 'And the more cordial he took, the less effect it seemed to have in ameliorating his symptoms, so he had to take larger and larger doses. In the end it quite debilitated him, until he was unable to carry out his duties and dismissed the service. A terrible shame: he was a promising young officer.'

'People should be informed of the dangers of taking opiates before it's prescribed,' said Killigrew. 'If they still want to wreck their lives, that's their look-out. The freedom to ruin oneself is merely the other side of the coin which is the freedom to get on in life. You can't have one without the other.'

'That's all very well for educated people like us, Mr Killigrew,' said Westlake. 'But the Chinese are ignorant—'

'*If* that is so, then we should educate them. Those who sneer at the people of China for smoking opium might do well to take a glance inside the gin palaces of Britain.'

'Then perhaps we should stop the gin trade, too.'

'Why stop the gin trade and not the wine trade? Because the people who drink gin are poor and therefore too ignorant to know any better? I find that a rather patronising attitude, Westlake. Just because a man was born into a poor family that does not make him a fool, no more than a man born into the gentry can be assumed to be a genius.'

'Then why do the poor ruin their lives through drink?'

'Their lives were already ruined the day they were born in poverty. They drink gin to help themselves forget that fact. Perhaps if you found yourself living with that kind of despair you too might take to drinking gin. That would be your choice. Take port, for instance. No one likes a glass of port or two after supper more than I. Perhaps I'm condemning myself to the misery of gout in later life, but that is my decision. Do you think it would be right for the government to forbid people to drink port?'

The surgeon shrugged. 'If it were for their own good.'

Killigrew shook his head. He turned to Peri, as if he had higher hopes of making her understand his principles than he did of Westlake. 'I believe in a little thing called liberty, Miss Dadabhoy, the freedom to make my own choices in life. I do not believe it is the duty of the government to tell me what I may and may not do, so long as my actions harm none but myself. And if I have the right to make such decisions for myself, then so should the labouring classes be permitted their gin and the Chinese their opium. Instead of worrying about the fact that these people indulge in such vices, perhaps we should concern ourselves with the conditions that drive them to seek oblivion. If your father did not smuggle opium into China, there are plenty of others who would be keen to get their hands on his client list. At least Sir Dadabhoy spends much of his profits on philanthropic works in Gujerat, putting money back into the community. I suspect there are plenty of other China traders who are less charitable.'

'It is kind of you to say so.'

He shrugged. 'It's only the truth. And at least your father didn't put pressure on the British government to go to war with China. Selling opium to a willing client is one thing. Forcing him to buy it at the point of a gun is another.'

'Steady on, Killigrew,' said Vellacott. 'The China War was fought in defence of the rights of British merchants trying to trade with the Chinese. What they buy once that trade is established is their own affair. There's a demand for tea in Britain. We've offered the Chinese our manufactures and they've turned their noses up at them. So it has to be opium.'

'Why should they buy British cotton, when they manufacture their own perfectly good silk? And it doesn't have to be opium: there's a massive deficit of silver bullion in

China. But I don't see the China traders rushing to offer it in place of opium.'

'A bullion deficit brought about because the Chinese have spent so much of it on opium.'

'Forgive me for saying so, Vellacott, but you're missing the point. Let's look at it from the point of view of the Chinese, shall we? Suppose our positions were reversed. Now let's say the British government made the selling of gin illegal. I wouldn't approve, for the reasons I've already stated: it would be an infringement of the liberties of British subjects. But there are many other laws in Britain which I consider infringements of the liberties of British subjects; yet I respect them, because they are the law.'

'Such as?' asked Peri, intrigued.

'Well, for one thing, the political franchise needs to be widened.'

'Here he goes again,' said Yelverton, rolling his eyes, and turned to Peri. 'Killigrew thinks everyone in Britain should have a vote, instead of just those who occupy a house of ten pounds' annual rental.'

'Even that's too radical, if you ask me,' grunted Westlake. 'They should never have done away with the forty-shilling freehold rule. Only the people with a property stake in the country can be judged fit to make such momentous decisions.'

'The rich look after the poor, you mean?' Killigrew asked with amusement. 'You should take a walk through Bluegate Fields some time, Mr Westlake. They're not doing a very good job of it.'

'Ha! This from a man who'd let women have the vote!'

'And why should they not, Mr Westlake?' Peri asked sweetly.

'Women's brains are smaller than men's—' began the surgeon.

'Not in proportion to their body weight,' she countered.

'That's neither here nor there. They have a lower mental

capacity. Stands to reason. Give women the vote, next thing you know, they'll be running the country.'

'With a lower mental capacity?' Peri asked, with a straight face. Glancing at Killigrew, she saw him stifle a smile, although her irony was wasted on Westlake.

'If you ask me, the country's already run by an old woman,' said Hartcliffe.

'That's no way to talk about Lord Russell!' protested Vellacott.

'Lord Russell doesn't have a mind of his own,' said Hartcliffe. 'That's why he needs Trevelyan and Grafton to do all his thinking for him.'

'Who's Trevelyan?' Peri asked Killigrew in a whisper.

'Permanent Head of the Treasury,' he murmured back. 'Not a nice man.'

'Trevelyan and Grafton say it's the Paddies' own fault they're starving – when any fool can see it's the fault of their landlords – and lo, the dead are lying in heaps in the country lanes of Ireland,' continued Hartcliffe.

'That's your free trade for you, Killigrew,' Westlake said triumphantly.

'Not free trade, Mr Westlake,' Killigrew responded tightly. 'Callous inhumanity. Where was I?'

'You were asking us to suppose the government outlawed the sale of gin in Britain, Mr Killigrew,' said Peri.

'Thank you,' he said with a smile. 'Now, suppose the Chinese started smuggling gin into Britain, ignoring our laws. Naturally our government protests. So the Chinese go to war with us – and win.'

'Not likely,' said Vellacott.

'It's merely a hypothetical supposition,' said Killigrew. 'The Chinese going to war with us to force us to accept their breaking of our laws. Hardly what you'd call a moral crusade, is it, gentlemen? Well, I put it to you that's exactly what we did to the Chinese back in thirty-nine.'

'What exactly happened in the Opium War?' asked Peri.

'I tried to follow the reports in the newspapers, but I'm afraid I could not make much sense of what was going on.'

Killigrew smiled thinly. 'Neither could I – and I was right in the thick of it.'

'Hark at him!' Hartcliffe jibed good-naturedly. 'His ship didn't arrive until the last few months. Some of us who were there from the outset, however—'

'And a proper hash you'd been making of it until then,' Killigrew retorted. 'God knows, that war should never have been started – a ridiculous, patchy affair between two arrogant empires which had failed to understand one another and failed to appreciate the merits of one another – but if it had been done when 'twas done, then 'twere well it had been done quickly.'

Hartcliffe nodded in agreement. 'We failed to prosecute the war thoroughly – I think even Rear-Admiral Elliot sensed the ignobility of our crusade – but a decisive blow early on might have convinced the Chinese they weren't dealing with barbarians but with an industrially more advanced opponent whom their junks could not match. It might even have preserved lives by bringing the war to a swift conclusion instead of allowing it to drag on for as long as it did.

'The problem was the Emperor refused to deal directly with us. When his troops suffered reverses, his subordinates were too afraid to report their failure; our reluctance to press home victories only made it easier for the mandarins to conceal their defeats from the Emperor. After nearly three years of blockades, punitive attacks, muddled negotiations, the expeditionary force finally arrived from home waters, including HMS *Dido* with a certain Midshipman Killigrew on board. We seized the city of Chingkiang-fu – on the vital crossroads of the Yangtze River and the Grand Canal – and threatened the great city of Nanking. That forced the Chinese to come to terms. You probably know the rest.'

Peri nodded. The Treaty of Nanking had opened five ports – Amoy, Canton, Foochow, Ningpo and Shanghai – to Western trade, demanded that the Chinese pay an indemnity of twenty-one million dollars, and decreed that Hong Kong be ceded to the British. As a British possession separate from the mainland, the island of Hong Kong was a safer place for Western merchants to conduct their trade, free from interference from the Chinese authorities.

An awkward silence ensued and once again it was left to Peri to break it. 'What are your politics, my lord?' she asked Hartcliffe. She recalled that the Duke of Hartcliffe was a mainstay of the Tory Party. 'Are you a Tory, like your father?'

'Good Lord, no!' Hartcliffe replied with a grin, more relaxed now he had a couple of glasses of wine inside him. 'I'm a communist. "Working men of all countries unite," what?'

'I'll drink to that,' said Killigrew, raising his glass.

'Before or after the loyal toast?' Yelverton asked sardonically.

'In place of,' Killigrew asserted with mock gravity.

'*Aux barricades!*' declared Hartcliffe. '*Les aristocrates à la lanterne!*'

Westlake turned to Peri. 'Of course, you realise they're both stark, raving mad?'

She smiled. 'Yes. I noticed that this afternoon.'

'Roll on, thou deep and dark blue Ocean – roll!
Ten thousand fleets sweep over thee in vain;
Man marks the earth with ruin – his control
Stops with the shore.'

Able Seaman Wes Molineaux was rarely happier than when he took a trick at the *Tisiphone*'s helm, and the lines of verse came almost unconsciously to his lips. As a kinchin, barely more than a toddler, he had helped to supplement his mother's meagre wages as a charlady by 'mudlarking': searching the mudflats of the Thames at low tide for salvage – a copper nail here, a lump of coal there, it all added up. On cold winter mornings he and the other river urchins had warmed their feet in the run-off from the steam-powered manufactories on the south bank, and as the sensation had slowly returned to his numbed dew-beaters he had watched the tall ships come and go from the Pool of London, bearing cargoes from exotic lands, never once imagining that one day he would make a living as a sailor and get to see such lands for himself.

In those days he had known only cold and hunger. He had been the youngest of three siblings and the harsh life of the slums around Seven Dials had inevitably forced him into a life of crime. For twelve years he had prospered, becoming the toast of the flash mob, until one day a job had turned sour and he had been forced to flee to Ireland, hiding up in Cork and eventually taking ship on HMS *Powerful* as the cook's mate.

The voice of the officer of the watch startled Molineaux out of his reverie. 'Poetry, Mr Molineaux?' asked Killigrew, lighting his first cheroot of the day.

'Byron, sir. *Childe Harold's Pilgrimage*.'

'I keep forgetting your intellectual taste in poetry. I thought you said you never went to school? Who taught you to read?'

'An old pal of mine, sir.' Molineaux had often wondered what had happened to the man who, amongst other things, had taught him everything he had ever needed to know about breaking and entering, and thought about going to Australia to see if he could find him. But from what he had heard, some who were transported to the colonies did well for themselves once they became ticket-of-leave men; besides, knowing his old mentor, he had probably made leg-bail years ago and was in lavender somewhere. 'He taught me how to read, using *The Police Gazette* as a primer.'

'*The Police Gazette?*'

'Where they print the notices of stolen goods,' Ågård said drily.

'Ah!' Killigrew was well aware of Molineaux's felonious past, and discreetly left it at that.

'Sail ho!' cried the look-out at the masthead.

'Where away?' demanded the boatswain.

'Two points on the port quarter!'

Killigrew took the telescope from the binnacle to see for himself. 'Opium clipper coming up fast astern,' he reported to no one in particular a few moments later. 'One point to starboard, Ågård. We'll exchange flags of courtesy as she passes.'

'Aye, aye, sir. One point to starboard, Molineaux.'

'One point to starboard it is.'

Staying in the service had never been part of the plan. He had only joined the *Powerful* for one commission, until the hue and cry in London had died down. But one commission had lasted three hard years in the Mediterranean. Molineaux had chafed under navy discipline, earned himself a flogging through insubordination, and had promised himself he would jump ship at the first opportunity, when the commodore had been knocked overboard by a careless hand. Jumping after him to save his life had just seemed like the natural thing to do. The commodore had rewarded Molineaux with a singularly inappropriate gift, a volume of poetry by some cove called Andy Marvell. Molineaux had been seated on the head one day, on the verge of using the pages for a purpose for which they had never been intended, when he had chanced to read some of the lines.

He had been hooked at once. Afterwards he had sometimes wondered if the gift had been so inappropriate after all. From then on he had devoured poetry hungrily. He did not always comprehend the classical allusions, but that did not matter: what was important was the beauty of the language. A seaman on a man-o'-war did not get much time to himself, but even a few hours snatched here and there added up over voyages which lasted for months. His new shipmates aboard the *Tisiphone* had mocked him when they had first caught him reading poetry, so he had started reading aloud *The Rime of the Ancient Mariner* from a Coleridge anthology: after the first five stanzas the barracking had stopped; at the end of Part the Third he had closed the book, climbed into his hammock and bid them goodnight, turning a deaf ear to their entreaties to learn what happened next. Before the week had ended every rating on board had begged him to read them the rest, and he had finally relented.

Sailing close-hauled under full canvas, it was not long before the merchantman effortlessly overhauled the paddle-sloop. With favourable winds, a fast clipper could sail from Calcutta to Canton in about three weeks. A handsome East Indiaman with a low, sleek, double-decked hull, three raking masts and delicate rigging, the clipper's sides were painted in a chequered black-and-white pattern, perhaps to fool pilongs into thinking she was a man-o'-war. The sun was just below the horizon, yet its rays struck the clipper's upper masts and made her gleaming white royals and topgallant sails glow like spun gold. The men scrubbing the *Tisiphone*'s deck before breakfast paused in their work to admire the clipper's fine lines.

Miss Dadabhoy emerged from the after hatch, looking refreshed and lovely in her emerald-green sari. Molineaux could not help thinking that she had a few lines worthy of admiration herself. Not that he entertained any ambitions in that direction; he had once been the fancy of the hour for a well-to-do lady who was curious about the negro anatomy, and he had been happy to satisfy her curiosity. Both of them had been pleasantly surprised by the experience, while it lasted: some of these well-bred ladies could be no better than they ought to be. In those days Molineaux had been young and foolish enough to fall in love, but the lady in question had had no hesitation in reminding him of his place when he had told her of his undying devotion. Now he was an older and wiser man: it was not that he was not good enough for the likes of them; his mother had raised him to believe he was just as good a man as any gentry cove. But a black raised on the back streets of Seven Dials could have little in common with a lady more used to the genteel salons of Mayfair.

'Now that's what I call a beautiful sight,' said Killigrew.

Miss Dadabhoy turned. 'Mr Killigrew!'

He met her gaze with innocent brown eyes and indicated the clipper with a nod, although Molineaux was not convinced that was the direction the young officer had been looking in when he had spoken. The seaman grinned. Some of these officers were no better than they ought to be, either.

# *III:*

## *Hong Kong*

Peri Dadabhoy climbed the rest of the way on to the quarterdeck and gave the passing clipper a cursory glance. 'I must confess I have never been able to understand why some men are so enthusiastic about sailing ships.'

'When I was a boy, I used to spend hours sitting on the quayside at Falmouth,' said Killigrew. 'I used to watch the ships come and go, and listened to the old salts spinning yarns about the wonderful things they'd seen and the exotic lands they'd visited. I think that even if my family hadn't been naval officers for generations, I'd still have gone to sea.'

'It is a dangerous way of life, though, is it not?' she asked.

'That depends how one looks at it. Only landlubbers think of the oceans as a barrier to be crossed. I've always seen the sea as a path to faraway places.'

She shook her head. 'Why do you do it, Mr Killigrew? Risk your life to save people you have never met from pirates and slavers?'

'Someone has to.'

'Why you?'

He sighed, and moved away from the two seamen who

stood at the helm. 'If you must know . . . I suppose it all goes back to when I was in my first ship: HMS *Dreadful*, a frigate on the Mediterranean station. I was twelve when I joined the navy. One grows up swiftly in the service. Hardly a day went by in the *Dreadful* without someone getting a flogging. The captain was a good man, but weak; the first lieutenant manipulated him. He ran everything, and he was a fiend.'

'Were *you* ever flogged?'

'No. They don't flog the young gentlemen; although I was caned a few times,' he added with a rueful grin. 'But that doesn't mean that the snotties have a soft life. I suppose one expects a little rough and tumble to go on in the cockpit: youthful high-spirits, skylarking – it all helps to toughen up the character. But sometimes it goes too far. The oldsters in the cockpit – the older midshipmen and the mates – used to bully us remorselessly.'

'Somehow I cannot imagine you allowing anyone to bully you.'

'Don't think of me as Lieutenant Kit Killigrew. Think of First-Class Volunteer Christopher Killigrew, twelve years old and away from home for the first time, with no one to turn to and no one to trust.' He grimaced. 'It builds character, all right. The first lesson I learned was never to cry. The more you cried, the more they picked on you. So you kept your mouth shut and knuckled down. There was one boy who never learned that lesson, so the bullies picked on him especially. I used to listen to them tormenting him as I lay in my hammock and pretended to be asleep, and do you know what I was thinking?'

' "Thank heavens it's not me"?'

He looked at her in surprise. This was the first time he had ever told anyone this story, because he had been afraid they would laugh at him or despise him. But she seemed to understand. 'Exactly.'

She reached out to him tenderly and put one of her

hands on his. 'It was a natural reaction; certainly not anything to be ashamed of.'

'Oh, but you haven't heard the best of it yet. I hated those oldsters for bullying my friend. I used to lie awake and dream about how one day I would teach them a lesson. But I never did because I was afraid that I would only bring trouble on myself. So I did nothing, while each day his spirit became more and more crushed. He was coming apart at the seams, right before my eyes, but I did nothing because I was simply glad it wasn't me.'

'Did the bullies get their comeuppance?'

'Eventually. But by then it was too late. One day as I was coming off duty, I stepped into the cockpit and there he was, swinging from a beam on the deck head. He'd decided he couldn't take it any more, so he'd hanged himself.'

'And you blamed yourself.'

'I still do. Wouldn't you?'

'I cannot say. I have never been in such a situation.'

He nodded. 'I was so upset, for a while I thought about leaving the navy at the first opportunity.'

'Why didn't you?'

It was a question Killigrew had asked himself many times in those dark days on board HMS *Dreadful*. 'Two reasons, I suppose. First, I didn't want to prove my grandfather right. He'd always said I was spineless, useless – a white-livered bookworm – and that I wouldn't last five minutes in the service.'

'Your grandfather said that?' she asked in astonishment. She had already learned from Hartcliffe that Killigrew had been raised by his grandfather after the death of his parents. Peri had never known her grandfather, but her father had never shown her anything but love and support.

'In a way I'm glad he did,' said Killigrew. 'If he hadn't, I'd never have had anything to prove.'

'Perhaps that was what he intended all along,' she suggested shrewdly.

Killigrew glanced at her, his eyebrows raised in surprise. 'Perhaps.'

'And the other reason?'

'About a fortnight after my friend hanged himself, I went into battle for the first time. I say "battle" – more of a skirmish, really – but it was terrifying enough at the time. We were patrolling off the Barbary Coast when we cornered a corsair galley in a bay. We chased them back to their fortress, there was a fight and . . . well, to cut a long story short, we won. In the dungeons of the fortress we found prisoners captured from merchant vessels. The corsairs had been planning to sell them into slavery. When we released them . . . In the days after my friend's death, I'd been asking myself what it was all for, what purpose the navy served. I had my answer in the faces of those people when they were freed. I saw a way to atone for having stood by while a friend of mine was driven to suicide.'

'And have you not yet atoned for that, after all these years?'

'That's not for me to say. But a wise man once said: "It is necessary only for the good man to do nothing for evil to triumph." ' Then, as if afraid he was sounding pompous, he grinned boyishly. 'Besides, the danger is half the appeal.'

She studied him thoughtfully. He looked very dashing in his pea jacket and pilot cap, a cheroot wedged in the corner of his mouth. He made no attempt to dispose of it in the presence of a lady. At first she wondered if he did not consider her to be a lady on account of the colour of her skin, but she dismissed the thought as unworthy. He had treated her attentively and gallantly from the moment they had met. It was simply that he was something of what Miss Fothergill – her English governess – would have called a 'fast' man.

She remembered the first time she had seen him, the day before yesterday, leaping over the side of the pilong junk with a pistol in one hand and a cutlass in the other. He had been grinning. At the time she had assumed it was a grimace of terror; now she was not so sure. 'Life is too precious to be treated lightly, Mr Killigrew.'

He blushed and looked thoughtful. 'It's difficult to explain,' he said, and wandered over to the taffrail.

She followed him. 'I should like you to try, nonetheless.'

He gave her a penetrating glance and then he looked away. 'It's the queerest thing,' he admittedly softly. 'But when one jumps over the bulwarks of a hostile ship, or over the battlements of an enemy fortress . . . when one knows one may be slain at any moment . . . that's when I feel most alive. You say that life is precious; but you can have no idea how precious life is until you've stared into Death's eyes – and stared him down.'

'Perhaps. But surely once would be enough?'

He laughed. She did not mind; she had the feeling he was laughing at himself as much as at her. 'You'd think so, wouldn't you? But after you've done it once, everything else becomes dull by comparison.'

'You make danger sound like a drug.'

'Perhaps, in a way, it is.'

A pilot cutter came out to meet the *Tisiphone* when the steam-sloop entered Victoria Harbour and guided her to her berth in the anchorage. Robertson sent the pilot back to Harbour Master's Wharf with two messages: one for Sir Dadabhoy Framjee to the effect that his daughter was on board and in good health; and another to the Hong Kong Police, explaining that they had prisoners on board who needed to be taken into custody.

On the north side of Hong Kong Island, the town of Victoria faced across the sheltered waters of the harbour to the fishing village of Kowloon on the Chinese mainland. There were far more buildings in Victoria these days compared to when Killigrew had first visited the colony seven years earlier at the end of the war, and pale stone had begun to replace the temporary wooden shelters in earnest. Most of the buildings straggled for a mile or so along the waterfront, but here and there a few bungalows and rich merchants' houses had been built amongst the steep, treeless hills which formed a dramatic backdrop to the scene, with Victoria Peak rising to a height of over sixteen hundred feet. The stone buildings were constructed in the neo-classical style, giving the waterfront an appearance that was more Mediterranean than Oriental, but there were still plenty of wooden buildings, mat-sheds and godowns belonging to the various companies which traded out of Hong Kong.

The town was dominated by the new three-storey barracks, but there were other notable buildings. Missionaries of various denominations had wasted no time in using Hong Kong as a beachhead in the Celestial Kingdom from which to convert the heathen Chinese, and already there was a Roman Catholic cathedral, a Union chapel, an American Baptist chapel, a Chinese temple, and even a Muslim mosque. Only the Church of England cathedral remained unfinished. At East Point, on the furthermost extremity of the settlement, stood the trading factory of Grafton, Bannatyne & Co., the company's golden dragon ensign flying from the roof. A two-masted paddle-steamer was anchored in the harbour close to the factory, and Killigrew studied it through his telescope and saw it had a stylised oriental dragon painted gold for a figurehead.

Amongst all the companies which traded with China, Grafton, Bannatyne & Co. was pre-eminent. George Grafton had retired to England a little over ten years previously, leaving his junior partner behind in Canton to act as general manager of the company: *tai-pan*, 'great manager', as the Chinese referred to him. In London, Grafton had purchased himself a seat in the House of Commons, using his new-found influence to defend the interests of the China traders, and it had been his lobbying which had encouraged the British government to go to war with China over the opium issue.

The bumboats homed in on the *Tisiphone* from all directions, like half-pay post-captains swarming around a flag-officer entering the waiting room at the Admiralty. The mess-cooks crowded the bulwarks, looking to purchase local delicacies that would provide some variation from the standard navy fare of salt beef and weevil-infested biscuits. There were wash-boats too, crewed by cheerful washerwomen and seamstresses who knew Jack Tar was a dandy at heart and that laundry facilities on board navy ships were primitive at best.

'I'm going across to the *Hastings* to present my compliments to Rear-Admiral Collier,' Robertson told his officers. 'Second, I want you to take the pilongs and hand them over to the local authorities. You can take Miss Dadabhoy ashore while you're about it; see to it that she gets safely back to her father's house.'

Killigrew coughed into his fist. 'With all due respect, sir, I think it would be more tactful to minimise any contact between Miss Dadabhoy and her would-be kidnappers . . .'

'Hmph? Oh, all right, I suppose so. Take the pilongs ashore in one of the cutters. Lord Hartcliffe can take Miss Dadabhoy ashore with him in the dinghy.'

The pilongs were placed in the cutter under the muskets of the marines. Killigrew climbed down after them, keeping a watchful eye on his charges, and the cutter's crew rowed them ashore.

There were already three warships in the harbour: the seventy-two-gun ship of the line HMS *Hastings*, wearing the flag of Rear-Admiral Sir Francis Collier; the paddle-sloop HMS *Fury*; and an American sloop of war, the eighteen-gun USS *Preble*. There were other vessels, too: lorchas with Western-style hulls and Oriental sails and rigging; American whalers; and Chinese 'scrambling dragons', known to

Westerners as 'fast boats' because of their speed or 'smug boats' because of their usefulness in smuggling opium on to the mainland. They looked like Venetian galleys, with banks of oars and masts bearing mat-and-rattan oblong sails three times taller than they were wide.

Perhaps the most eye-catching vessel in the harbour was a houseboat. A hundred feet from stem to stern, she was a floating palace, three storeys piled one above the other like a wedding cake, with the roof curled up at the eaves in the oriental manner and a pagoda-like tower amidships rising up two storeys more.

Innumerable sampans crowded the waterfront, along with junks of all sizes with mat-and-rattan sails and high, beautifully painted sterns, as well as countless *yolos*: small sampans, almost square, with curved matting roofs. These last were crewed by Tanka women in blue trousers and smocks, their plaited hair decorated with ribbons and flowers, sometimes with one child tied to their backs and another at their breasts, disarmingly young and cheerful, smiling with big, white, gleaming teeth. The boats served as homes and places of trade for the Tanka people. They crowded so thickly against the dockside it seemed as if one could walk a hundred feet out into the harbour without getting one's feet wet.

Yet apart from the chatter of Chinese voices and the occasional passing tramp of soldiers' boots as they marched along the waterfront, the harbour was oddly quiet and far from being a bustling port. Trade at Victoria had not yet taken off the way its founders had hoped; with the five treaty ports open now, Hong Kong had been robbed of its *raison d'être*. There were no noisy steam cranes on the wharf – what trade did come to Hong Kong was actually transshipped at the Cap-sing-mun Passage, a dozen miles or so to the west.

By the time the cutter had nosed through this crowd to the wharf, a detail of sepoys in dark green uniforms already waited amongst the bustling crowds of coolies hurrying on errands, Chinese hawkers selling goods from the panniers of their pack horses, merchants being carried on sedan chairs. Under the command of a young European officer and accompanied by a civilian in a black frock coat, top hat, and extravagant side-whiskers, the sepoys waited outside a noisy waterfront tavern to take the pilongs into custody.

Killigrew saluted. 'Lieutenant Killigrew, HMS *Tisiphone*.'

The officer returned his salute. 'Lieutenant Dwyer, Ceylon Rifles.' Dwyer was a young man, red-haired, freckle-faced and snub-nosed. 'This is Assistant Superintendent Cargill of the Hong Kong Police,' he added, indicating the whiskery civilian.

'Welcome to Hong Kong, Mr Killigrew,' said Cargill. 'Glad to see you've not wasted any time,' he added with a broad smile, indicating the prisoners.

'All right, Havildar, let's take these men into custody,' Lieutenant Dwyer told his sergeant. 'Some of Zhai Jing-mu's men, do you think, Mr Cargill?'

'Either his, or Yao Ping-han's. I don't suppose we'll be able to get them to talk, though.'

'Did you say Zhai Jing-mu?' asked Killigrew.

'Ah,' said Cargill. 'You've heard of him, then?'

'That fellow there referred to himself as Zhai Jing-mu when we arrested him.' Killigrew indicated the *lao-pan*, whose white coat was looking decidedly grubby after three days on the deck of the *Tisiphone* without a chance to change.

Dwyer stared down his snub nose at Killigrew, and then Cargill burst out laughing. 'I believe Mr Killigrew is kidding you, Dwyer. You know what these salts are like, always spinning a yarn.'

Killigrew frowned. 'If I've said something to amuse you, Mr Cargill, I fear I did so in all innocence.'

'Come now, Mr Killigrew. Don't tell me you don't know who Zhai Jing-mu is?'

'A pilong captain, I suppose . . .'

'Captain!' snorted Dwyer. 'Admiral would be closer to the mark. He's said to have a fleet of over a hundred pirate junks under his command.'

Cargill nodded. 'We've been after him for over two years now. The most notorious pirate in these waters; and believe you me, that's saying something. He's believed to be responsible for the disappearance of five clippers last year.'

'Seven,' said Zhai Jing-mu.

Both Cargill and Dwyer stared at him with renewed interest. 'Good God, Cargill . . . you don't suppose this could be him, do you?'

The assistant superintendent brushed his whiskers thoughtfully. 'He's about the right age, according to my reports. Blue eyes, too. Rare in a Chinaman.'

Dwyer put a hand under the pilong's jaw and tilted his head back to study his face. 'Speakee English, eh? You Zhai Jing-mu?'

The *lao-pan* jerked his head away with a contemptuous sneer. 'I will be a free man one week after the tiger moon is down,' he said in Cantonese. 'And you will be dead.' He turned to Killigrew. 'And you and Miss Dadabhoy – before the end of the first week in the rabbit moon, you will all have been dispatched to the Hell of Ten Thousand Knives.'

'You've got that the wrong way round,' Cargill replied in the same language. 'If you *are* Zhai Jing-mu – and I'm starting to believe it myself – then you'll be hanged along with the rest of your crew.'

'What did he say?' asked Dwyer.

'Big talk,' said Cargill. 'Just hot air.'

Dwyer's men took the pilongs in custody and led them off in the direction of the gaol. Cargill lingered on the wharf and studied Killigrew with a speculative expression.

'Aren't you curious to know what that fellow just said to you, Mr Killigrew?'

'I speak a little Cantonese. I was on board the *Dido* during the China War.'

Cargill nodded. 'Before I came out. So, you're *that* Killigrew, eh? I take my hat off to you, sir.' He raised his topper.

'You think he really is this Zhai Jing-mu?'

'After that little display of defiance? If you were here during the war then you'll know the Chinese: all grovelling humility after they've been bested, and as often as not before. But not that one. No, Mr Killigrew, I believe you've captured the man I've been chasing these past two years.' He laughed suddenly. 'I suppose I ought to resent the fact that you've succeeded where I've failed, but, by George, I can't! If you'd heard some of the stories about the atrocities he's said to have committed . . . not all of them without foundation, I can tell you. I'm just glad that devil's finally under lock and key.'

'I just hope you'll be able to keep him there.'

'Oh, don't you worry about that, Mr Killigrew. I intend to keep a very close guard on our friend. He'll be tried at the earliest opportunity, before any of his friends can effect a rescue attempt; although to tell you the truth, I rather hope they do. Then we'll snap them up, too. Zhai Jing-mu may be the worst of the pirates in these parts, but he's not the only one.'

Killigrew smiled. 'I'm glad to hear it. For a moment there you had me thinking our work in these waters was over and done with before we'd even started.'

'Ever been to Hong Kong before?'

'Not since forty-three.'

Cargill nodded. 'As you can see, it's changed a great deal in the past six years . . .'

Before the policeman could finish his sentence, the door of the waterfront tavern burst open and a Chinese in European clothes came haring out. He dodged past Killigrew and raced down the waterfront.

Another figure emerged behind him, a tall, barrel-chested man with a huge, unkempt beard. Killigrew watched in astonishment as the man raised his hand with a pistol in it – his massive fist made the gun seem puny – and fired. Already thirty yards away, the Chinese cried out and fell. He rolled in the dust of the unpaved street and clutched his wounded leg.

'Capital shot, Captain Ingersoll,' Cargill remarked to the pistoleer.

Ingersoll scowled at him. 'I were aiming for his back,' he snarled with a West Country accent. 'Sonuvabitch stole fifty dollars off me!' He pocketed the pistol and strode over to reclaim his money.

Cargill turned back to Killigrew. 'What was I saying?'

'Just that Hong Kong's changed in the past six years. It's certainly a good deal livelier than I remember.'

Cargill grinned. 'Welcome back to the Orient, Mr Killigrew.'

As the horses thundered around the oval track at the Happy Valley racecourse, Killigrew gazed through his pocket telescope. It was not the horses he was studying, however, but the other race-goers. Just about everyone who was anyone in Hong Kong society was present: Samuel George Bonham, Her Majesty's Governor, Plenipotentiary and Superintendent of Trade; Rear-Admiral Collier and the officers of the other ships in the harbour; missionaries; and the owners and representatives of all of the great trading houses.

Unlike most of the military men there, resplendent in their uniforms, Killigrew was fashionably but unobtrusively dressed in a morning coat and top hat, as befitted attendance at a race meeting. He saw Miss Dadabhoy, ravishing in a sapphire-blue sari, but there was no sign of anyone who might have been her father. Her curly black hair was done up and crowned with a garland of flowers. There were no two ways about it, she was a damned fine-looking woman. And intelligent, too, unafraid to speak her own mind.

He had been thinking about her a great deal in the week since the *Tisiphone* had arrived at Hong Kong. That worried him. He had had plenty of female friends, and while it would not have been fair to say they meant nothing to him, certainly they meant no more to him than he did to them. Usually it was an equitable arrangement. Only once had he made the mistake of becoming emotionally attached to a woman, and it had turned out unhappily for both of them. He could not blame the woman in question for that: he had put her on a pedestal and built her up in his mind into something she had not been. The disappointment had been inevitable, but hurtful nonetheless. He had promised himself he would never make that mistake again. But that did not mean that he should never fall in love; he would just have to be more careful.

He was about to go and talk to Peri Dadabhoy when a half-familiar voice called out behind him. 'Kit? Long time no see!'

Killigrew turned and saw a handsome young man of roughly his own age, dressed in civilian clothing. There was something vaguely familiar about the man's face, but Killigrew could not instantly place it. But since only a select band was accorded the honour of being allowed to address him as 'Kit', he pasted an uneasy smile on his face as he struggled to remember where he had met this fellow. 'Good afternoon!' he said with false enthusiasm.

The man grinned. 'You don't remember me at all, do you?'

Killigrew shook his head. 'I'm sorry . . .'

'Well, it *was* over nine years ago. In those days you

couldn't see my face for the pimples.' He thrust out his hand. 'Jago Verran.'

The name was the trigger which brought all the memories back. Jago Verran had been one of his fellow midshipmen on board HMS *Dreadful*. They had been shipmates for four years, and looking at him again Killigrew was amazed he had not recognised his old friend earlier. He clasped Verran's hand and pumped it vigorously.

'Jago! Look at you, you old sonuvagun!'

'And you're looking as well as ever. When did you arrive?'

'A week ago. What about you? What have you been doing since we parted?'

'I spent three years on the *Alecto*, mostly cruising in the Med., but things were much quieter after Syria. I made it to mate but when I saw my career wasn't going anywhere I quit the Andrew Miller and joined the merchant service. I've got my own vessel now.'

'I'd heard that the problem with the merchant service was that the mess bills were even bigger than in the navy.'

Verran laughed. 'Nothing could top your mess bills, Kit. Anyway, Mr Bannatyne pays his captains well – damned well.'

'You're working for Bannatyne now?'

Verran nodded. 'That's my flapper down in the harbour now: the *Golden Dragon*.'

'What about that rather splendid houseboat opposite Governor's Wharf?'

'That belongs to Commissioner Tan. A bit of an embarrassment to Governor Bonham, actually, but it has its uses.'

'I'm not sure I follow you.'

'The Chinese still think they own Hong Kong but they're letting us use it out of the goodness of their hearts.'

Killigrew nodded. He was well aware that the Chinese believed the whole world owed obeisance to the Daoguang

Emperor in Peking, and that when the British had gone to war with China ten years earlier they had been no more than uncivilised barbarians rebelling against the celestial authority of the Son of Heaven.

'So Tan's been appointed prefect for Hong Kong?'

'Strictly unofficial, from our point of view. The plenipo' won't let him set foot on the island, except by invitation. That's why Tan lives on the houseboat. We're still trying to make the Celestials understand they've ceded Hong Kong to us in perpetuity, and their government has no authority over this island. But I suspect Bonham finds it damned useful having a representative of the Emperor so close at hand; although I dare say the Emperor finds it equally useful having one of his mandarins in a place where he can spy on everything that goes on in the colony. Still, never mind that. What about you, Kit? No need for me to ask what you've been doing these past few years: Chingkiang-fu, Borneo, the Guinea Coast . . .' Verran grinned. 'You never were one for taking it easy, were you? Even when we were snotties.'

Killigrew shrugged. 'I wear the uniform and take the pay. I've always felt I might as well earn it.'

'Earn it! What are they paying you these days? Let's see, what are you now? Still a junior lieutenant? A hundred and eighty a year?'

'Plus prize money.'

'Which is never in short supply when you're on board, I seem to recall. All the same, it's a poor reward for risking your life on a frequent basis.'

'Queen and country, Jago,' replied Killigrew, his tone self-mockingly offhand.

'Gammon! I get two hundred and fifty a year from Mr Bannatyne, and no nonsense from any damned admirals that haven't seen any fighting since the Treaty of Paris. Five hundred a year, Kit. You could be earning that. Bannatyne is always looking for captains for his clippers.'

'You've met him, then?' Killigrew had heard that the

*tai-pan* of Grafton, Bannatyne & Co. was something of a recluse.

'Of course! I take my orders directly from him. Oh, don't believe the stories you hear. He's just an ordinary chap.'

'One of the richest ordinary chaps in the world.'

Verran laughed again. 'Oh, he's a downy cove, I'll grant you that.'

'That's one way of putting it. They say he and his partner put pressure on the government at home to go to war with China, simply so they could trade more freely with the Chinese.'

'I thought a free-trader like you would approve of expanding commerce?'

'Not if the price has to be paid in human lives.'

Verran chuckled. 'You make him sound like some kind of monster. He's all right. A bit stiff-necked, I'll grant you, but if you ask me that's just because he's a little shy. He has me up at his house for dinner every night I'm in Hong Kong.'

'Sounds ghastly,' Killigrew said with a smile.

'Oh, it has its compensations. Mrs Bannatyne, for instance.'

'Good company?'

'A regular stunner.'

'Young?'

'Same age as us. She's John Keane's daughter.'

'John Keane? As in, Keane and Co.?'

Verran nodded. 'Just between the two of us – although to tell you the truth, I think everyone in Hong Kong must have guessed it – Bannatyne only married her as part of a business transaction. He got a thousand shares in Keane and Co. as his dowry, and when Keane died what he inherited through his wife made Bannatyne the majority shareholder. Within six months Keane and Co. was no more, subsumed within Bannatyne's empire.'

'I didn't think Keane was that old. What did he die of?'

'A terrible accident . . . Don't look at me like that, Kit. It *was* an accident. I was there when it happened. He was on board the *Golden Dragon*, we got caught in a typhoon and he was washed overboard . . . There was nothing anyone could have done. His body was found a week later by some Chinese fishermen. Mrs Bannatyne blamed me . . .' Verran looked glum for a moment. 'Sometimes I blame myself.' Then he pasted a smile on his face. 'Ah, well. She'll come round in due course.'

'A little dangerous, wouldn't you say? Making eyes at your employer's wife? Especially when your employer is a man as rich and powerful as Blase Bannatyne.'

'A little danger only spices things up.'

Killigrew smiled thinly. 'You always did have a penchant for mischief.'

Verran did not seem to have heard him. 'Not that there's much danger of Bannatyne noticing,' he continued, lowering his voice discreetly. 'He's completely obsessed with his work; he neglects her dreadfully. When they went on honeymoon to Macao, he took his annual accounts with him, and I can tell you for a fact that he spent as much time in business meetings as he did in the nuptial bed. No, Kit, there's something missing from Mrs Bannatyne's married life. And I intend to give it to her,' he added with a wink. Then he raised his voice again. 'Anyway, what about you? Any ladies in your life at the moment?' He nudged Killigrew and nodded to where Miss Dadabhoy was now talking to – or rather, being talked at by – another face Killigrew recognised, that of the Reverend Werner Ultzmann. 'Was Miss Dadabhoy suitably grateful to her rescuer?'

'She thanked me, if that's what you mean. Not that one expects thanks for doing one's duty.'

Verran laughed. 'You know damned well what I mean. You can't tell me you haven't boarded her?'

'There's nothing between myself and Miss Dadabhoy,'

said Killigrew, although he might have added: 'yet'.

' "I believe you, my boy!" ' Verran quoted a catch-phrase of the London stage that had been doing the rounds for the past few months; Killigrew was disappointed to discover it had reached as far as Hong Kong. 'You must be losing your touch, Kit. You'd better stick an oar in, old boy, otherwise Ultzmann might ruin your chances. Have you met the reverend? He's definitely one of the great characters of this colony.'

'Oh yes,' Killigrew said heavily. 'We've met.'

Ultzmann was somewhere in his late forties, dressed in clothes that had probably been fashionable in his native Pomerania when he had left it many years ago, including a Dutch bargee's cap of the kind worn by German students. It was not that he was unable to afford new clothes; it was widely known that the Lutheran missionary was well paid by the firm of Grafton, Bannatyne & Co. for his services as an interpreter and adviser.

The reverend had been in China for many years, and it was said that despite his bulk, the Chinese cast to his features – an accident of nature, since both his parents had been Prussians – had enabled him to travel on the mainland disguised as a Chinese, so long as he wore rose-tinted tea-stone spectacles to disguise his blue eyes. He professed a horror of the opium trade in which his employers were engaged, but had agreed to work for Grafton, Bannatyne & Co. on the condition that the company distributed free Bibles with its opium.

Ultzmann was enjoying the sound of his own voice so much that he did not notice Miss Dadabhoy give Killigrew a pleading glance over his shoulder. The lieutenant took his leave of Verran and went swiftly to her rescue. He bowed low.

'Miss Dadabhoy, may I say that you are looking exceptionally ravishing today, even by your usual standards?'

'You are too kind,' she replied mechanically, as if

bored by the commonplace gallantry. Most young women Killigrew knew either sneered at him for being too poor, or regarded him with a ridiculous adoration which only embarrassed him. There was something refreshing about the way Peri mocked him playfully. Sometimes he feared his greatest sin was taking himself too seriously; a person like Peri was just what he needed to prick his pomposity.

Ultzmann was evidently annoyed at the interruption. 'I don't believe we have been introduced, Mr . . .?'

'Then your memory betrays you, Reverend. We *have* met. The twenty-first of July 1842. Killigrew's the name, Lieutenant Christopher Killigrew. Of course, in those days I was just a midshipman.'

'I do not have much of a memory for dates.' Ultzmann's English was so accented, and if he successfully passed himself off as a Chinese Killigrew could only assume that his Cantonese was more fluent.

'Neither do I, usually. But that date is one I'm not likely to forget in a hurry. Chingkiang-fu, Reverend. Surely you remember? You told Lord Saltoun the city would be undefended.'

'Ah, yes.' Ultzmann's face became grave. 'A most unfortunate happenstance. Man proposes, God disposes. But all turned out for the best, did it not? Had we not taken Chingkiang-fu, would the Chinese have acceded so readily to the Treaty of Nanking?'

'I'm sure that thought must be a great comfort to the widows and orphans of the men who died in that attack.'

Ultzmann shrugged. 'One cannot make an omelette without breaking eggs.'

'But it shouldn't require six eggs to make a three-egg omelette.' Killigrew turned to Peri. 'Is your father here today, Miss Dadabhoy?'

'Yes, I'll take you to him. If you'll excuse us, Reverend?' She led the way across the greensward, and as soon as they were out of earshot of the missionary she turned to

Killigrew with a smile. 'Thank you for rescuing me. That is the second time now, is it not?'

He grinned. 'All in the day's work for the Royal Navy, miss.'

'You do not care for the reverend, I think.'

'Whatever gave you that idea?' Killigrew asked innocently, and she flicked her fan chidingly against his shoulder. 'I don't hate Ultzmann. You have to respect someone before you can hate them properly, and the reverend's too much of a buffoon.'

'So. Are you going to tell me what happened at Chingkiang-fu?' she asked. 'Or are you just going to put on a manly expression and tell me modesty forbids; a phrase which often leads me to wonder if it is not *honesty* which forbids?'

'It was during the war. I was serving on board the *Dido* at the time under Captain Keppel. I was a midshipman then, only eighteen. Keppel hurt himself in a fall and while he was laid up I managed to slip away and join the naval brigade which took part in the attack on the city. As I said, Ultzmann told us the city would be undefended. It wasn't. A good many men died that day finding out. But you don't want to hear about that.'

'Too grisly for a delicate lady's sensibilities, you think?'

'Too grisly for anyone's sensibilities, man or woman. You are fully recovered from your ordeal, I trust?'

'Which one? Being a captive aboard Zhai Jing-mu's junk, or being subjected to the reverend's tedious attempts to convert me from my deplorable heathenism?'

'Which was worse?'

'Oh, definitely the reverend. What do you think, Mr Killigrew? Shall I burn in Hell for eternity because of my beliefs?'

He joined in the game at once. 'Oh, indubitably. But if Heaven is full of men like Ultzmann, wouldn't you prefer Hell?'

'Was it not Machiavelli who said he would prefer to go to Hell after he died because the company would be more interesting than in Heaven?'

'Either him, or Benjamin Disraeli.'

'Is there any news on when Zhai Jing-mu will go on trial? I have been following the reports in the newspapers, but there is no word of when the trial is to take place. I had thought the chief justice would have called on me to be a witness.'

'Commander Robertson and I spoke to Admiral Collier and we agreed there was no need to put you through reliving your ordeal in the witness box.'

'I am grateful for your consideration, Mr Killigrew. But if it means I can be certain that he will be convicted . . .'

'He'll be convicted. We caught him red-handed, and the weapons we found on board his junk are material evidence of his piracy. That, and the testimony of myself and Lord Hartcliffe will be more than sufficient to convict him. You have my word on it.'

'All the same, is there not a danger his defending counsel will not dredge up some loophole through which he can escape? How did Swift put it? "Laws are like cobwebs, which may catch small flies, but let wasps and hornets break through." My father says that lawyers can be dangerous, easily twisting the words of an honest naval officer unversed in their tricks.'

'You needn't have any fears on that account. Lord Hartcliffe and I have plenty of experience of dealing with land-sharks in court from the Guinea Coast. Besides, I don't imagine they'll find a lawyer in Hong Kong who's prepared to defend Zhai Jing-mu with too much enthusiasm.'

They watched the horses pass the finishing post and Peri sighed. 'Fourth place.'

'One of your father's horses?' asked Killigrew. She nodded. 'He'll have to have a word with his trainer.'

'With me, you mean.'

'You train your father's horses?' he asked in astonishment.

'Until we can find someone better qualified. You seem surprised?'

'I was just wondering how best to extricate my foot from my mouth.'

'Blame the jockey, Mr Killigrew. I keep telling him that Shibdiz always runs best when she gets out in front and stays there, but he will hold her back in the first few furlongs. Did you have a wager, Mr Killigrew?'

He shook his head. 'I don't gamble.'

She regarded him coolly. 'Not with money, at any rate.'

'I can't get passionate about horse-racing. If I had a personal stake in the race, perhaps – if I was the jockey, for instance, or the trainer, I could feel I'd made a personal contribution to the victory – that would be another matter entirely.'

'Is winning important to you?'

'It's the second best feeling in the world. I'm not like Shibdiz, I'm afraid. I'm usually slow off the mark, but I have been known to come from behind in the final straight. Would you feel insulted if I told you that when I asked to be introduced to your father it was more than just a ruse to get away from Ultzmann?' he asked, changing the subject.

'Yes. But I might be persuaded to forgive you,' she added with a smile.

'Oh, I can be very persuasive, miss.'

'I am sure you can. There is my father. I know he wants to meet you.'

'Me? Why on earth would the great Sir Dadabhoy Framjee wish to meet a mere naval lieutenant?'

'He wishes to thank you. He seems to think you saved his daughter's life.'

'I hope you didn't give him that impression.'

'Heaven forbid, Mr Killigrew.'

Sir Dadabhoy Framjee was in his sixties, a short man with pronounced cheekbones and a thrusting, pointed jaw which seemed to dominate his whole face, even below a wide, white moustache which made him look more Turkish than Indian. He wore a white coat, *pahgris* headdress and oriental slippers which turned up at the toes. To Killigrew he looked like the fierce Sultan Schariar from the Arabian Nights, but even in those hard eyes which had built up a massive trading empire, there was a twinkle of humour and kindness which suggested even his heart might be melted by the storytelling of a Scheherezade.

Framjee was talking to a young Chinese man of average height and build, with a face that was handsome in a smooth-cheeked, effeminate way, his limpid brown eyes full of a beguiling innocence. The Chinese wore a loose-fitting sky-blue tunic and his hair was in the style that all his race were required to adopt by Manchu law: shaven at the front and tied in a long queue at the back. The Tartar Manchus had invaded China two hundred years ago and the relationship between them and China's native Han people was not unlike that between the Normans and the Anglo-Saxons must have been in the days of Robin Hood.

As Killigrew and Peri approached, Framjee turned to his youngest daughter and beamed. She bowed with her palms pressed together before her in the Indian manner. Killigrew sensed something in the formality of that greeting: not hostility, perhaps, but a sense of unease between father and daughter.

'Father, may I present Mr Killigrew, the *Tisiphone*'s second lieutenant? Mr Killigrew, this is my father, Sir Dadabhoy Framjee.'

Killigrew bowed. 'It's an honour to meet you, sir.'

'Likewise, Mr Killigrew.' Framjee's accent was pure Cambridge, although Killigrew knew the merchant had never had a formal education; that was perhaps the reason he endowed so many schools in Gujerat, so that others might gain the advantages in life which he had never had. Like many Parsi merchants Killigrew had met, Framjee was more English than the average Englishman. 'My daughter has told me a great deal about you.'

'None of it true, I hope,' said Killigrew.

Framjee chuckled. 'All of it flattering, I assure you.' Killigrew gave Miss Dadabhoy a sidelong glance as she tried to conceal her smile behind her fan. 'This is my comprador, Li Cheng,' added the merchant, indicating the Chinese, who bowed in the Oriental style, with his left fist clasped in his right hand. 'Mr Li handles the Chinese side of my business.'

Killigrew mirrored the comprador's bow. Li smiled, but Killigrew was not fooled. He was well aware the Chinese considered outward displays of emotion impolite in the presence of strangers, and often used a smile to conceal whatever they were really feeling: nervousness, anger, disgust or astonishment; all the emotions which the 'barbarians' managed to provoke in the Chinese on a regular basis.

'If you will excuse me now, Mr Li?' said Framjee. 'And remember what I told you to tell Wu-qua. Seventeen thousand cattis of gunpowder tea, but it must be of the finest quality. And do not just check the samples: make a random check from the rest of the consignment.'

'*Hai.*' Li Cheng bowed and hurried away.

'You need to tell your comprador how to do his job?' Killigrew asked in some surprise.

'He is new. But he seems jolly clever.'

'Can you trust him?'

Framjee smiled. 'Ask me again in twenty years' time. I am afraid my business is not one which engenders trust. My rivals will tell you that their word is their bond, but you should trust a cobra sooner than you should trust them. Their greed knows no bounds.'

'Whereas you are the epitome of honesty, Father,' Peri said ironically.

Framjee was unperturbed. 'Where would I be without you, my conscience, my darling daughter?'

'The very place you stand now, Father, and every bit as wealthy. If you will excuse me, Mr Killigrew? I need to talk to our jockey.' The lieutenant bowed and Peri wandered off.

'You will have to forgive my Peri, Mr Killigrew. She does not approve of the way I earn my living; though she spends the money freely enough,' he sighed.

'You surprise me, sir. She does not strike me as the kind to have extravagant tastes.'

'No, you are right. I am not being fair to her. I am jolly glad to have this opportunity to thank you in person for saving her life, Mr Killigrew. If I had to choose between her and my riches, it would be an easy decision, believe me.' He looked glum. 'Sometimes I wonder if she is not right to disapprove of the opium trade. I have tried to find alternative goods to import into China, believe me I have. But there is nothing else they will buy. They regard everything the West has to offer as inferior, the work of barbarians. Did you know that is what they call us? "*Fan kwae.*" "Foreign Devils".'

'Pardon me for contradicting you, sir, but a more accurate translation would be "ocean ghosts". It's just their way of describing us as a pale-skinned people who come from beyond the seas. The Chinese often give people nicknames based on some unusual physical characteristic; they intend no insult.'

'You speak Cantonese, Mr Killigrew?'

'I've picked up a smattering. I was here during the war.'

'A terrible business . . . oh! I do not mean to give offence . . .'

'None taken, sir, I assure you. I'm not proud of having fought in that war. When I joined the navy I thought that if I ever did have to fight in a war it would be against a ruthless tyrant like Napoleon. Instead I found myself slaughtering the Chinese because they wouldn't buy our opium.'

'You blame merchants like myself for that.' Framjee sounded as though he blamed himself.

'I blame men like Sir George Grafton, who used their influence to bring the war about. You were not such a man, as far as I am aware.'

'Perhaps not. But I still profit from the results of that war. But listen to us both, wearing metaphorical hair shirts for what happened ten years ago, when we should be putting those events behind us and trying to build a new relationship with the Chinese. Theirs is a noble culture, Mr Killigrew, with much to teach us.'

'As we have much to teach them, if only they'll admit it.'

'Ours are two very different cultures, are they not? Perhaps that is why our relations have been so troubled?'

'I sometimes wonder if the problem isn't that we're so very different as that we're so very alike.'

'I am not certain that I follow you, Mr Killigrew.'

'Two powerful empires, both convinced that we are pre-eminent in the world, and that all other cultures should bow down and accept our way of life as superior.'

Framjee laughed. 'That is very true, sir. I had not thought of it that way before.'

Killigrew lit a cheroot and offered one to the Parsi, who shook his head. 'I'm sorry about the loss of your clipper, sir.'

Framjee made a dismissive gesture. 'It was not the first clipper I have lost to Zhai Jing-mu and his pilongs. Thanks to you and your colleagues it should be the last.'

'Your own daughter played a part in capturing him, sir. I think if it had not been for her he might yet have escaped.'

The Parsi chuckled. 'I am afraid she is a spirited girl.'

'No need to apologise, sir. So many women these days are raised to be simpering ninnies, it's refreshing to meet a girl with both sense and backbone. You've brought her up well.'

'Her mother deserves the credit for that. I was always

too bound up in my work to pay much attention to either of them; until my wife succumbed to malaria in the early days of this colony. Losing her taught me to appreciate the things that really matter in this life: the ones you love. The ship I lost and her cargo were insured; what you rescued for me, no insurance company could put a price on.'

'No. But Zhai Jing-mu could.'

'I do not understand.'

'Pilongs attack clippers when they're on their way to Hong Kong with a cargo full of opium; but your ship was attacked as it was sailing for Bombay. My guess is that Zhai Jing-mu knew exactly who was on board.'

Framjee nodded. 'I would have paid any amount of money for Peri's safe return.'

'And Zhai Jing-mu knew that. Someone must have told him that your daughter would be sailing on that ship.'

'That would not surprise me. He has spies everywhere. There are many in China who are opposed to the Manchu government in Peking. Here in Hong Kong, they are safely beyond Chinese jurisdiction. Since this colony was established, it has acted as a magnet for the worst scum of China, who use it as a refuge, a base for their criminal enterprises. I am not one who believes that all the Chinese in Hong Kong are criminals – to the contrary, I would say most of them are honest, honourable, hard-working people. But there are enough criminals to make their presence felt. You have heard of the Brotherhood of Heaven, Earth and Man?'

'The Triads, you mean? I've heard rumours.'

'The Triads have close links with the pilongs. Many of the pilongs are members of the Brotherhood.'

'I thought the Triads were political organisations rather than criminal ones? Doesn't their watchword – *fan Ch'ing, fu Ming* – translate as "overthrow the Ch'ing dynasty and restore the Ming"?'

'Treason is as much a crime in China as it is in England,

Mr Killigrew. Revolutionaries need money, and rarely have scruples about how they get it. The Triads are happy to work with the pilongs, as long as the pilongs restrict their attacks to Western shipping.'

'All the same, the attack on your daughter's ship took planning, foreknowledge. Could the Triads have provided the pilongs with that kind of information?'

'The Brotherhood of Heaven, Earth and Man has spies in all sorts of surprising places,' warned Framjee. 'That is the key to its power.'

# *IV:*

# *Triads*

Hollywood Road was all hustle and bustle when Killigrew, granted a couple of hours leave by Robertson, made his way to the Chinese shantytown of Tai-ping-shan the next day. Pale-faced, languid Chinese gentlemen fluttered fans at their faces as they were pushed on wheelbarrows, seated on one side of the huge wheel while their luggage acted as a counterbalance on the other. Wealthier merchants were carried on palanquins, covered litters, which on mainland China were reserved for the use of mandarins. Coolies hurried back and forth carrying buckets of water slung from bamboo poles on their shoulders. A pair of grubby, cheerful children rode through the crowd on the back of a water buffalo.

When the British had colonised Hong Kong in 1842 it had been little more than a rock with a few small fishing villages on it. A census taken five years ago, not counting the troops of the garrison, had put the island's population at 23,872. Of these, 618 had been European. The vast majority of the rest were Chinese. Many of them were opponents of the Ch'ing Dynasty who had come to the island to be beyond Manchu jurisdiction, but that did not mean they had any great love for the British; others were merely criminals with a price on their heads. Europeans generally avoided Tai-ping-shan, so it was with a devil-may-care sense of recklessness that Killigrew wandered down the narrow, crowded streets.

In fact there was surprisingly little sense of menace in the shantytown. The Chinese avoided his gaze, but then they found casual eye-contact abhorrent so he did not take it personally. Certainly there were no menacing glares. Killigrew had found that a little politeness went a long way with the Cantonese.

He wandered about aimlessly – keeping a weather eye open for trouble, but needlessly so – losing himself in the atmosphere: the pleasantly exotic sound of a Chinese band playing in the upper storey of an open-fronted building, the sing-song jabber of cheerful Cantonese voices, the heady aroma of unfamiliar scents and spices. There were animals everywhere – pigs, dogs, hens, goats, ducks – sometimes secured in pens, sometimes just wandering the streets every bit as aimlessly as Killigrew.

He found an eating stall and ordered *gum chen kai*: soft, succulent chicken livers and crisp pork fat eaten with wafers of orange-flavoured bread. There were plenty of places to eat in Victoria, but they provided stolidly English food. Even if it had not been in his nature to sample as much foreign culture as he could in the course of his travels, Killigrew would still have gone to great lengths to escape the monotonous fare of mutton and boiled vegetables that seemed to be the staple of every chop-house from Falmouth to Shanghai.

He sat down at one of the communal tables. The other customers – all of them Chinese – eyed him uncertainly until he wished them hearty eating and rubbed his chopsticks together to remove any splinters like a seasoned Chinese gourmet. They smiled and nodded, and returned to their conversations. He ate his *gum chen kai* with a bowl of fried rice and was washing it down with delicious rice wine when he saw a vaguely familiar face in the crowd. It took him a moment to place the man: Li Cheng.

There was no reason why Framjee's comprador should not pay a visit to Tai-ping-shan, of course – he probably had relatives there, perhaps even lived there himself – yet some instinct made Killigrew wonder. Someone had tipped off Zhai Jing-mu in advance as to which ship Peri Dadabhoy would be travelling on; who was better placed to be privy to such information than the Parsi's new and untried comprador?

Killigrew drained the last of his rice wine hurriedly and paid the chef before following the comprador. He was conscious that his Western face and clothes must have stuck out like a brig in a fleet of junks as he trailed Li through the crowds, but the comprador never once glanced over his shoulder. Wherever he was going, he was headed there with a purpose.

A short distance down the road they came to a joss house with two stone lions, carved in the Oriental fashion – with stone balls in their mouths skilfully carved from the same rock so they could not be removed – on guard on either side of the door. The only other sentinel was an old Chinese monk who smiled and bowed as Li mounted the broad flight of half a dozen steps leading up to the door. After the briefest hesitation, Killigrew followed him. The monk made no attempt to stop him, smiling and bowing just the same as he had for Li.

Killigrew paused just inside the open door until his eyes grew accustomed to the gloom. Various gaudy statues of Taoist immortals, about twelve feet high, towered along the back wall, and the air was heady with the scent of perfumed sandalwood joss sticks being burned as offerings. There was no sign of Li amongst the supplicants kneeling before the numerous altars, but a rattling sound drew Killigrew's attention to a side door. He ducked through and saw Li on his knees, shaking a porcelain canister full of bamboo sticks until one of them fell out. He picked up the stick, handed the canister to an attendant, and took the stick through another door.

The attendant saw Killigrew. 'You wantchee savvy joss, missee?'

'Why not?' He stepped forwards and the attendant handed him the canister. He kneeled down as Li had done and shook the canister until a stick fell out. It had a Chinese character inscribed on it in red ink, but Killigrew had never mastered the art of reading Chinese script.

He passed the canister back and the attendant gestured for him to go through the same door as Li. Killigrew emerged into bright sunlight and found himself in a courtyard where a paved path led between ponds full of goldfish. The courtyard was deserted except for Li, who was disappearing through a door on the far side. As soon as he was out of sight, Killigrew crossed the courtyard briskly and then peered cautiously through the door.

The room beyond was another shrine, windowless, again heavy with the scent of joss sticks. Cones formed by successions of bamboo rings, with strips of lucky red papers hung inside them, dangled from an array of bamboo poles which formed a false ceiling suspended from the real one. Before an altar where another Taoist idol glowered, Killigrew saw Li hand his bamboo stick to an elderly priest dressed in ornate brocaded robes.

'*Fan Ch'ing, fu Ming*,' said the comprador.

The priest nodded and pulled aside a silk curtain. Li passed through.

Killigrew crossed the threshold and the priest beckoned him forward with impossibly long fingernails. The lieutenant held out his bamboo stick but the priest shook his head. 'English?'

Killigrew nodded.

'When were you born?' The priest spoke surprisingly good English.

'The fifteenth of October,' said Killigrew, and grinned. 'Birth date of great men.'

The priest shook his head irritably. 'What year?'

'The year of . . .' Killigrew was about to say 'Our Lord' when it occurred to him that speaking of Christ in a Taoist temple might be considered blasphemous by the priest, and he had no wish to give offence. 'Eighteen hundred and twenty-four. I don't know what date that is in the Chinese calendar.'

The old man clearly had enough experience of dealing with Westerners to be able to work it out in his head; either that, or he was making it up as he went along. But Killigrew was not overly superstitious so he did not mind either way. 'You were born in the Year of the Monkey, in the Dog Moon. In the Celestial Kingdom, the monkey is the king of all the animals.' The priest gestured expansively. 'A man born in the Year of the Monkey is intelligent, resourceful and adaptable. He is master of many skills and greatly enjoys being busy, loves travel, and seeks difficult challenges to test himself. He takes great pride in fighting for noble causes but does not take kindly to criticism.'

'How dare you say such a thing?' snarled Killigrew. The priest stepped back in fear until the lieutenant gestured calmingly. 'It's all right, I'm joking.'

The priest scowled. 'He is also fond of teasing people. A man born in the Year of the Monkey is rarely troubled by ill health and has very powerful *yang*. He is also capable of much deceit.' Finally the priest took the bamboo stick from Killigrew and glanced at the Chinese character inscribed on it. 'There are many dangers on the path to your karma. The greatest lies within yourself. Two spirits, always opposed, like two battling dragons fighting for control of your heart.' The priest clenched his fists and knocked the knuckles together in front of his chest. '*Yin* and *yang*: two people you will never meet again but who will always be with you. When these two dragons are reconciled, you will be at one with yourself; not before.'

Which was all very interesting mumbo-jumbo, but not what Killigrew had come to learn. He decided to take another chance. '*Fan Ch'ing, fu Ming*,' he told the priest.

There was not a flicker of a reaction on the priest's face. 'The consultation is concluded,' he said with a bow.

Killigrew made for the door Li had passed through, but the priest moved quickly to block his path. 'You go through that door,' he said firmly, indicating the one the lieutenant had entered by.

Killigrew was tempted to force the issue there and then, but after what he had heard he knew he would be able to come back with a search warrant and a large contingent of the Hong Kong police at a later date. He smiled and bowed in the Oriental manner, and re-emerged into the courtyard.

Two large Chinese men dressed in black pyjamas, crimson sashes and turbans awaited him in the middle of the courtyard. One carried a large scimitar and had two shorter curved swords tucked in his sash, the other a flail made from two rods connected to either end of a third by a short length of chain.

Killigrew stopped about ten yards away. 'I don't know what the Taoist tradition is, but in the West it's considered bad joss to spill blood in a holy place.'

Smiling, the two killers bowed as one. Returning their smiles thinly, Killigrew did likewise.

Then they charged.

The man with the flail came first, whirling the iron rods skilfully about his head until they blurred. Killigrew backed up the path to receive him, forcing the man to lunge further than he had anticipated. He was already off balance when Killigrew ducked beneath the whirling rods, side-stepped as far as he could on the narrow path and extended a foot. The man tripped and fell headlong into a fishpond.

The other man came at Killigrew at once, swinging his scimitar. Killigrew caught him by the wrist, whirled him around and plucked one of the short swords from his belt. The swordsman rammed an elbow into the lieutenant's stomach and broke free. Winded, Killigrew staggered back, clutching the short sword. The swordsman advanced, grinning, while the man with the flail climbed out of the fishpond, sopping wet and cursing in Cantonese.

Killigrew backed up the path until he was between two more ponds, so they could only attack him one at a time. The swordsman came first, charging with a wild cry. He hacked at Killigrew's head. The lieutenant parried the blow with the short sword but his arm was jarred so badly he was barely able to defend himself against the next. He continued to back up until he felt one of the wooden posts supporting the veranda at the edge of the courtyard against his back.

The swordsman swung at his neck. Killigrew ducked, heard a splintering sound behind him and glanced over his shoulder to see the wooden post had been cut clean in two. The swordsman grinned. Killigrew stared at him in amazement, and then recollected himself and stabbed the man in the stomach.

As the swordsman staggered away with the short sword embedded in him, Killigrew snatched up the scimitar he had dropped and braced himself to meet the man with the flail. The killer whirled his flail until one of the chains wrapped itself about the scimitar's hilt. He pulled on the flail and Killigrew, refusing to relinquish his grip, was almost jerked off his feet. The killer flicked the other end of the flail and a blow to the back of Killigrew's head nearly robbed him of his senses. His legs crumpled and he sank to his knees. He twisted on to his back and pulled the killer down on top of him. Then he let go of the sword and gripped the central rod of the flail in both hands. The two of them rolled over and over, gripping the flail between them. The killer rolled on top and pushed the rod hard against Killigrew's throat, throttling him. As his consciousness faded, Killigrew lifted a knee into the killer's crotch.

The killer relaxed enough for Killigrew to smash the rod against the bridge of his nose and throw him off.

Gripping the flail, the lieutenant rose to his feet. The killer lunged for the fallen scimitar but Killigrew kicked it into one of the ponds. He tried to swing the flail at his opponent but his handling was clumsy and he succeeded only in clipping himself across the head. As he staggered forwards, the killer smashed a fist into his chest and tore the flail from his grip. He whirled it expertly about his head and shoulders, under one arm and over the other, creating a fence of blurred steel between himself and the lieutenant. Killigrew held up a warning finger. The killer frowned in bewilderment, and Killigrew turned and ran.

At the far side of the courtyard he jumped on to the wooden handrail at the edge of the veranda, gripping a wooden support post for balance. The killer swung the flail at Killigrew's legs. He jumped over the bar, swung himself round the support post and kicked the man in the face. Then he jumped down and retreated into the shrine.

There was no sign of the old priest. Killigrew turned back to face the door and jumped up to grab hold of one of the bamboo cones. He intended to kick the killer in the chest with both feet as he came through the door, but his weight was too great and the cone broke away from the array from which it had been suspended. Killigrew landed on his feet as the killer charged through the door, whirling the flail. The lieutenant dropped the bamboo cone over his head like a cage and side-stepped.

The killer dropped the flail and drove a fist through the hoops of bamboo. Killigrew caught him by the wrist and swung him against a wooden pillar. The hoops splintered and Killigrew rammed the killer's head against the pillar until he lost consciousness.

The lieutenant was dusting his hands off when two Sikh police constables – one with a turban, the other bare-headed – charged through the door.

'Who says you can never find a bobby when you need one?' asked Killigrew.

To his astonishment, the burly constables seized him and clapped a pair of handcuffs over his wrists.

Killigrew was taken to the police office in Victoria and made to wait, still handcuffed, while one of the constables sat across the table from him with his brawny arms folded and a grim expression on his face.

'If I'm under arrest, you have to tell me what the charge is,' Killigrew told him.

Assistant Superintendent Cargill strode briskly through the door with a sheaf of papers under one arm. 'How about murder, to be going on with?'

'I acted in self-defence. Those two men attacked me without provocation.'

'Without provocation!' Cargill laughed harshly. 'You wander alone and unarmed into Tai-ping-shan and, as if that were not foolhardy enough, you blunder into a Chinese joss house and insult them by making a mockery of their religion. My job's difficult enough as it is, without Europeans making things worse for me. I have over twenty-thousand Chinese in my jurisdiction. Half of them are Triads or criminals, and the other half have no faith in British justice. If we're ever going to win their trust they have to see that Westerners and Chinese get the same treatment. Can't have one law for Europeans and another for the yellow-bellies. What the deuce were you doing? Sight-seeing?'

'I was dining at an eating stall when I saw Sir Dadabhoy Framjee's comprador, Li Cheng. I followed him on a suspicion he was up to no good and he led me to that joss house.'

'There's no law against going to joss houses, Killigrew.'

'When he was there I overheard him say, "*Fan Ch'ing, fu Ming*" to a priest. You know what that means?'

Cargill's demeanour changed at once. ' "Overthrow the Ch'ing and restore the Ming",' he said, brushing his whiskers thoughtfully. 'The Triads' watchword. Take off the darbies, constable.'

The constable unlocked the handcuffs and Killigrew rubbed his chafed wrists. 'How come your men arrived so quickly?'

'Sheer luck,' said Cargill. 'They were patrolling Hollywood Road when some damned yellow-belly decided to play knock the topper off the peeler, Hong Kong-fashion.'

None the wiser, Killigrew arched an eyebrow quizzically.

'He stole Constable Gopal's turban,' the assistant superintendent explained. 'They chased him into the joss house, where he disappeared. They were about to give up the chase when one of the attendants reported a disturbance in the courtyard.'

'What about the man I knocked unconscious?'

'Don't you worry about him. He's being brought in for questioning too.'

'And the joss house? It's obviously a Triad lair. Aren't you going to raid it?'

'You haven't given me enough for a search warrant. But I can arrange for a watch to be maintained on it. I have Chinese informers who can be trusted. We'll see who comes and goes. Perhaps it may lead us somewhere very interesting indeed.'

'What about Li Cheng?'

'Did you see him talk to either of the men who attacked you?'

'No.'

'I can have him brought in for questioning, but there's nothing I can charge him with.'

'You could warn Sir Dadabhoy that his comprador is suspected of having links with the Triads, if not actually a Triad himself.'

Cargill grinned. 'I'll leave that to you. You seem to be in

with our Parsi friend and his daughter. Once you've done that, I want you to steer clear of this whole business, apart from coming in to identify the man who attacked you. This is police matter. You let me worry about the Triads and I'll leave you to deal with any pilongs who think they can fill Zhai Jing-mu's boots.'

'Did it ever occur to you that the pilongs and the Triads might be working together?'

'You've been talking to Framjee, haven't you? I'm well aware of his pet theories about a link between Zhai Jing-mu and the Brotherhood of Heaven, Earth and Man. But I'm a police officer. That means I deal in facts I can prove, not vague theories. If you come up with hard and fast proof of any links, let me know. Until then, I'll worry about my jurisdiction and leave you to worry about yours.'

'By all means. Before I go, do you have somewhere where I can scrub up?' He held up his bloodied right hand.

'Of course.' Cargill showed him to a back room with a washstand and ordered a servant to bring a pail of water. Killigrew washed his hand and checked his reflection in the polished surface of his tin cheroot case. He still looked dishevelled after his bout with the two Triads, but after patting his hair back into place and hoiking his high collar a couple of inches higher to conceal the bruises on his throat, he looked presentable enough.

He returned to Cargill's office to take his leave, and at that moment Constable Gopal entered, looking agitated. 'Cargill Sahib? The Triad we arrested at the joss house . . .?'

'Put him in a cell on his own, Constable. I'll deal with him in due course.'

'That is just the problem, *sahib*. He's escaped.'

Cargill closed his eyes as if in pain.

Killigrew had the good grace not to smirk. 'Since you seem to have everything in hand, Assistant Superintendent . . .'

'One moment, Killigrew. Before you go, you might like to bear in mind that if everything you've told me is true, then you killed a Triad today. They won't take kindly to that. I suggest you watch your back.'

Killigrew nodded and left.

It was a short walk from the gaol to Caine Road, on the lower slopes of Victoria Peak: straight up the aptly named Ladder Street. It was tempting to ride on a Chinese wheelbarrow, but Killigrew had not spent two years fighting slavers on the Guinea Coast only to use his fellow human beings as beasts of burden. Caine Road was the residential area for most of Hong Kong Society – a term which was understood to mean the white fraction of the island's population. The Framjee residence was set back from the main road, up a winding path through a forest of bamboo and stunted Chinese pines. The house itself was surprisingly modest for the residence of one of the wealthiest men in the world, and looked more like one of the so-called villas that were springing up all over the suburbs of London.

Killigrew rang the bell and presently the door was opened by a Sikh butler with a broken nose who looked down at him snootily. 'Yes, *sahib*?'

'I'd like to speak to Sir Dadabhoy Framjee if I may, please.'

'Sir Dadabhoy is not at home, *sahib*. If you will leave your card I shall tell him you called.'

'Who is it, Gobinda?' Peri's voice called from somewhere inside.

'A gentleman calling to see your father, *memsahib*.'

'Is that you, Mr Killigrew? Show him in, Gobinda.' Peri stood halfway down the main staircase, wearing a saffron sari and with a book held in one hand at her side. 'Did you come on foot, Mr Killigrew? It is a steep climb; you must be exhausted. Can I offer you a glass of sherbet? Or perhaps you would prefer tea?'

'Sherbet sounds perfect, Miss Dadabhoy.'

'Father will be home soon. You might as well wait. We shall take the sherbet on the lawn, Gobinda.'

'Yes, Miss Peri.' The butler closed the door behind Killigrew before disappearing towards the back of the house.

If Killigrew had been expecting the interior of Framjee's house to resemble a sultan's palace he was disappointed. The hallway was decorated very much *à l'Anglais*: oil paintings on the wall, all manner of knick-knacks cluttering every surface – Staffordshire pottery vying for space higgledy-piggledy with jade horses (Tang Dynasty, unless Killigrew was very much mistaken) – and an elephant's foot umbrella stand just inside the door.

'You'll have to forgive Gobinda.' Peri led the way into the drawing room. 'He is a terrible snob, but he means well.'

'Has he been with the family long?'

'As long as I can remember. Why do you ask?'

'Oh, just making polite conversation.' Killigrew followed her through the French windows out on to the terrace at the side of the house. He waited for her to sit down at the cast-iron lawn table before taking his place opposite her. 'May I ask what you're reading?'

She held up the volume she had placed on the table so he could read the spine for himself. '*Marmion.* Sir Walter Scott.'

'You like Scott?'

'A little. I prefer Omar Khayyám.'

'I'm afraid I can't claim to be familiar with his work.'

'I do not think it has been translated into English.'

'Perhaps you should try to translate it yourself?'

'I?'

'Why not?'

She shook her head. 'I do not think I could do it justice.'

'Have you tried? You should have more faith in yourself.'

Gobinda emerged with a jug of sherbet and two crystal goblets, poured out the fruit drink, and retreated inside. Killigrew sipped his sherbet and gazed about the garden. 'This is a lovely spot.'

Peri smiled thinly. 'My father's idea of an English country garden.'

'I'll trade him this view for an English country garden any day of the week.'

She put her elbows on the table, interlinked her fingers and rested her chin on the backs of her hands. 'And of all the places you have seen in your travels, which would you say is your favourite?'

'Oh, it depends on what mood I'm in. And the time of day, of course.'

'The time of day?'

He nodded. 'My perfect day would start in the Levant, with the cry of the muezzin calling the faithful to prayer. Much better than those damned church bells we have in Britain. Then, a morning walk in China in spring, with the mist amongst the orange blossoms. For luncheon, a table outside a Greek *taverna* overlooking the Aegean with a plate of kebabs cooked over a charcoal fire, a side salad of crisp white chopped onions and flavoursome tomatoes, and a glass of properly chilled dry white wine . . .'

'I thought one drank only red wine with red meat?'

'Only if you're a snob. In the afternoon, home to the Cornish coast in high summer, where the sea breeze takes the bite out of the worst of the sun. Then to Java to watch the sunset. Have you ever been?' She shook her head. 'You haven't lived until you've seen the sun set over the Sunda Strait.'

'And in the evening?'

'Oh, it has to be London. The theatre – something light and witty, Sheridan or Molière for preference – and a little supper at Rules with the companion of my choice.'

'And who would that be?'

'If you're ever in London, I'd be honoured if you'd let me escort you around town.'

'I think I would like that.'

The clop of horses' hoofs and the rattle of a carriage sounded from the front of the house. 'That will be my father returning,' said Peri, and the two of them waited until Framjee emerged on to the terrace.

Killigrew rose to his feet and bowed. 'Sir Dadabhoy. Peri was merely keeping me entertained while we awaited your return.'

The Parsi glanced from Killigrew to Peri. 'Mr Killigrew. To what do I owe the pleasure?'

'I was wondering if I might have a word with you?'

'By all means.'

'In private?'

Framjee joined them at the table. 'There are no secrets between my daughter and me, Mr Killigrew. Anything you consider fitting enough for my ears you must also consider fitting enough for hers.'

Killigrew resumed his seat. 'It's about your comprador, Sir Dadabhoy. Li Cheng—'

'He is no longer my comprador.'

'Meaning?'

'When I arrived at my offices this morning I found his letter of resignation waiting on my desk. Effective as of midnight last night.'

'An abrupt departure. Could he have been a spy for the pilongs?'

'It is perfectly possible. Why do you ask?'

'I saw him in Tai-ping-shan this afternoon. Some instinct made me follow him into a joss house. I heard him use a Triad watchword, and then he disappeared. I tried to follow him, but I was attacked by a couple of Chinese thugs.'

Peri's hand flew to her mouth. 'Mr Killigrew! Why did you not say something sooner? Are you hurt?'

Killigrew shook his head. 'I'm quite unharmed, miss. Fortunately for me the police arrived. There's no need for concern, I assure you.'

'If you have earned the enmity of the Triads, Mr Killigrew, I fear there is every need for concern,' said Framjee.

'It's yourself I'm concerned for, Sir Dadabhoy. You and Peri. You should know Zhai Jing-mu vowed to be avenged on Lieutenant Dwyer of the Ceylon Rifles, as well as myself, Assistant Superintendent Cargill and—'

'Me, Mr Killigrew?' Peri suggested with equanimity.

'I'm afraid so, miss.'

Framjee looked worried. 'Perhaps you should return to Bombay, my dear,' he suggested.

She shook her head. 'I will not allow myself to be ruled by fear, Father. Am I to abandon you, simply because a defeated pirate makes a hollow threat? Besides, what can he do while he is locked up in the gaol, awaiting trial?'

'Nothing, himself,' said Killigrew. 'But if he has friends in the Triads, Sir Dadabhoy, and if Li Cheng is somehow involved with them, if not actually a member of their society—'

'That is a great many ifs, Mr Killigrew,' said Peri. 'And you have not convinced me that Mr Li is a Triad. He was always very civil to me when I met him.'

'I'm sure the spider was very civil to the fly when he invited him into his parlour,' said Killigrew.

She laughed. 'I am grateful for your concern on my behalf, Mr Killigrew, but I am sure it is quite unfounded. Would you not agree, Father?'

'They *did* try to take you hostage, my child.'

'But they did not try to harm me. And they failed, and now Zhai Jing-mu is in gaol, awaiting certain execution. I do not think they would be so foolish as to try any such thing again. What could they possibly gain from it?'

'She has a point, Mr Killigrew,' said Framjee. 'Are you quite certain you are not merely jumping at shadows? With all due respect, you do have a reputation for being . . . how can I put this? Excitable?'

Killigrew grimaced. 'A legacy of my Greek mother.' He looked at them both in turn, smiling happily beneath the warm sun in the genteel surroundings of the garden. It was difficult to believe that anything so terrible as kidnapping could happen here. 'Perhaps you're right,' he admitted reluctantly. 'I just want to be cautious, that's all. At least promise me you'll be vigilant?'

'I always am, Mr Killigrew,' said Framjee, and the lieutenant saw a steely glint in the Parsi's eye that reminded him here was a man who had built up two commercial empires against stiff competition. 'And we are not entirely without protection here. All of my menservants have served the Honourable East India Company as sepoys, and they are loyal to me. If Mr Li should return here looking for trouble, I can assure you he will receive a very warm reception.'

Killigrew stayed for tiffin and then took his leave of them, feeling reassured. As he walked down to Harbour Master's Wharf he saw a vessel sailing into the harbour which took his mind off his earlier concerns: one of the biggest junks he had ever seen. Amidships she had more than twenty feet of freeboard between the waterline and the top of the bulwarks, the lowest part of the bulwark which curved up sharply towards the forecastle. The poop deck towered far higher than any three-decker of Nelson's day and the mainmast stretched so high that the yellow streamers which flew from it seemed to tickle the underside of the clouds. He took out his pocket telescope and counted a dozen gun ports in one broadside. He could tell from the three tigers' heads painted on the stern it was the flagship of an Imperial admiral. He frowned: if the Governor of Canton had sent an Imperial man-o'-war to Hong Kong it might mean trouble. He transferred his attention to the decks of the *Tisiphone* and the *Hastings*. Everything seemed quiet enough: their anchor watches were in place and there was no sign of any ships beating to quarters.

One of the guns on board the junk boomed. Killigrew saw a plume of smoke blossom from the junk's side, but there was no corresponding round shot strike. After about five seconds another gun boomed, and then another. The junk was firing blank shots in a salute. The junk fired fifteen guns in all, and after a pause the guns of the shore battery fired thirteen in response. He relaxed. Whatever the junk was doing there, it was expected by the port authorities.

Killigrew paid a Tanka woman to row him back to the *Tisiphone* in her *yolo*. When he climbed up the side-ladder he found Lord Hartcliffe talking to Yelverton on the quarterdeck.

'Hello, Kit. Pleasant day?'

'It had its moments.' Killigrew nodded to the massive junk. 'Trouble?'

'Your guess is as good as mine. Admiral Huang Hai-kwang, come to talk to Rear-Admiral Collier.'

'Huang Hai-kwang? Wasn't that the name of the only captain of a junk to get the better of a British vessel in the war?'

'For which he was duly promoted,' Hartcliffe said grimly. 'By the way, this arrived for you this afternoon.' He produced a bamboo tube about ten inches long.

Killigrew checked the seal on the end and recognised the chop of Prince Tan Dian-ning. He broke it off and extracted the tightly rolled scroll within. To his surprise, it was written in English.

'Not bad news, I hope?' asked Hartcliffe.

'That depends on the quality of Prince Tan's chef. It's an invitation to dinner.'

'Dinner?' Robertson echoed quizzically.

'Yes, sir. It's a repast quite common in most parts of the

world, often used as an opportunity for entertaining guests.'

'Spare me your feeble attempts at humour, Second. What I'd like to know is what you've done to be singled out for the honour of an invitation on board Prince Tan's houseboat.'

'I'm his son, sir. That is to say, his adopted son,' Killigrew added quickly.

'You never cease to astonish me, Second. And how did you get to be the adopted son of a Chinese mandarin?'

'We met after the Opium War, sir. I foolishly allowed myself to be enticed on board one of the flower boats on the Pearl River during a stay at Canton and almost had my throat slit for my pains. His excellency was being entertained in the next compartment and he intervened to save my life. According to Confucian ethics, if you save a man's life you become responsible for anything he does after that time.' It had been Prince Tan who had taught Killigrew so much about Chinese culture and philosophy. 'I expect his excellency is keen to know if I've done anything to disgrace him in the last six years.'

'Let's hope he never learns the truth, then! You trust him?'

'I owe him my life, sir.'

'That's hardly the same thing. I may not be an old China hand like yourself, but I've been warned the Chinese never do anything without an ulterior motive.'

'You might say the same of any race on God's earth, sir. It could be the Chinese authorities' wish to pass on a message through unofficial channels.'

Robertson looked dubious for a moment, but made up his mind with a grimace. 'Oh, very well, then. I think we can spare you for a couple of hours. Perhaps you may be able to learn something from his excellency that will be useful to the governor. Just remember that relations between ourselves and the Chinese are poised on a knife edge. It wouldn't take much to spark off another war – there are plenty of people on both sides of Victoria Harbour who think that what was begun during the last war was left unfinished – so mind what you say.'

'Aye, aye, sir.'

Killigrew made his way down to his cabin, washed and changed into his full dress uniform. The crew of the dinghy rowed him across to Prince Tan's floating palace.

As he drew near he glimpsed a face at one of the windows on an upper storey: a Eurasian beauty, with wide blue eyes and skin like porcelain stretched tight over an angular face beneath black hair piled high on her head. Her doll-like beauty was exquisite, and Killigrew found himself wondering if he would be invited to meet her once he was on board. Then a hand – too large to be hers – pulled down a blind and concealed her from view.

The guards on the houseboat's gallery had been instructed to expect him and they made no challenge when the dinghy approached. A Chinese houseboy emerged and bowed as Killigrew stepped on to the landing stage.

'Lieutenant Killigrew? His highness is expecting you.'

'You lads had better get back to the *Tisiphone*,' Killigrew told the crew of the dinghy. 'Come back for me at seven bells.' He had to be back on duty at eight, and there was no harm in letting Prince Tan's men know he would be missed. The dinghy's crew rowed away and the houseboy escorted Killigrew to one of the upper decks.

The interior of the houseboat was exquisitely decorated. There was not a single beam or bulkhead that was not intricately carved into landscapes, dragons, Chinese lions and flamingos. The houseboy ushered Killigrew into a room luxuriously furnished with silk cushions and hung with crimson silk.

'Please to wait here. His highness will join you presently.' The houseboy left and Killigrew, well acquainted with Chinese customs, kept his cocked hat on: the Chinese considered it bad manners to bare one's head. He whiled away the time by studying a hanging scroll painted with a landscape of mountains and lakes, with a written scroll on either side of it. He could hear someone plucking delicate notes from a *pipa* somewhere upstairs and he wondered if it was the Eurasian beauty he had seen a few moments ago.

'Hands up!' a voice screeched behind him in English.

Killigrew whirled round and within an instant his dress-sword was in his hand. He searched the room for his would-be assailant but there was no one, just a bird in an ornate cage which hung from the ceiling. He moved closer to investigate and saw that it was a mynah bird.

'Jobbernowl!' the bird sneered in English.

Killigrew brushed the tip of his sword against the bars of the cage, so gently that the bird was not even alarmed. ' "Who's a pretty boy, then?" is more traditional,' he murmured.

'An amusing bird, is it not?' asked another voice.

Killigrew turned to see an old man in richly brocaded robes had entered the room behind him. His face was lined with age, his long, thin moustachios shot through with silver, and there were deep bags under his eyes which gave him a soulful look. When the old man saw the weapon in Killigrew's hand, alarm showed in his features for perhaps a fraction of a second before he composed himself once more.

Killigrew quickly sheathed his sword. 'I humbly offer you my most profound apologies, your highness,' he said. He did not offer to shake hands, knowing that the Chinese considered it an unhygienic barbarian custom, but bowed in the Oriental manner. 'It was not my intention to dishonour myself by drawing my weapons in your exalted home.'

'Jobbernowl!' said the mynah bird. 'Hands up!'

Prince Tan returned the bow. 'I am to blame. The bird was a gift from a business acquaintance. I should have taught it better manners. It is only natural that you should seek to defend yourself upon hearing such importunate language.'

'Your apology is wholly unnecessary,' said Killigrew.

Prince Tan gestured to the table. 'Please be seated, my honoured barbarian son.'

They sat down facing one another at the table and an *amah* girl entered with a tea tray as if on cue, and started to go through the ritual of serving out tea.

'I'm still in your debt,' said Killigrew.

'As I told you seven years ago, in saving your life, I was trusting my own judgement in the belief that you would do nothing to dishonour that trust.'

'I hope that my actions since we last met have done honour to my Chinese father.'

'I am sure that they have; and that they will continue to do so in future. I trust my barbarian son is well?' asked the prince.

'Very well, your highness, thank you.'

'His virility undiminished?'

Killigrew smiled and exchanged glances with the *amah*, who lowered her eyes demurely. 'Not so you'd notice. And yours?'

Tan sighed. 'I am an old man now, alas. What is it you barbarians say?'

'The spirit is willing, but the flesh is weak?'

'Quite so. Have some tea.'

'Jobbernowl!' squawked the mynah bird.

Tan smiled sadly. 'Since you are here, perhaps you could explain to me what "jobbernowl" means?'

'Oh, it's a colloquialism for a fool or an idiot,' said Killigrew. 'You used to hear it all the time when I was a younker. Seems to have gone out of fashion nowadays, though. I can't remember the last time I heard someone use it.'

'You see?' Tan asked the bird. 'Every time you use that barbarian word you insult one of my guests.'

'Be quiet! Jobbernowl!'

Tan turned back to Killigrew, who grinned.

'I understand my barbarian son recently distinguished himself by the capture of the notorious pirate Zhai Jing-mu?' asked Tan.

'I had the good joss to be in the right place at the right time.'

'Such is karma. But you must beware. Zhai Jing-mu has many powerful friends; and an enemy of his is an enemy of theirs. You have heard of the Brotherhood of Heaven, Earth and Man?'

'The Triads?' Killigrew nodded. 'Yes, I believe a couple of them introduced themselves to me this afternoon.'

'So I have heard.'

'News travels fast. What can you tell me about Admiral Huang?'

'Ah. I was wondering when you would ask me that question. Admiral Huang is here to offer Rear-Admiral Collier a chance for barbarian vessels and vessels of his Imperial Majesty's navy to work together to wreak righteous destruction on the pilongs.'

'Sounds good to me. *If* that really is what the admiral wants.'

Tan smiled. 'You understand the subtleties of the civilised mind well for a barbarian. There are two factions in the Imperial Grand Council in the Forbidden City. The one which is in favour at the moment advises a policy of harmonious compromise with the barbarians. But there is another faction, foolish men who can only remember the loss of face which resulted from the barbarian affair.' The 'barbarian affair' was how the Chinese dismissively referred to the Opium War. 'These men are unable to see that a second war will be even more disastrous for the Celestial Kingdom than the first was. Admiral Huang is such a man. If he is proposing a policy of co-operation between our navies, then it would be foolish not to wonder if he had an ulterior motive for doing so. Perhaps you should ask what the price for such co-operation might be.'

Killigrew sipped his tea and studied Tan thoughtfully. 'What *is* the price for such co-operation?'

'That Zhai Jing-mu be handed over to the authorities in Canton for trial.'

Killigrew laughed. 'Governor Bonham would never agree to that. Besides, what difference does it make whether Zhai Jing-mu's tried in Victoria or Canton? The penalty for piracy is the same under British law as it is in the Manchu Code, if not the manner of its execution.'

'Admiral Huang has been pursuing Zhai Jing-mu for four years, and in that time never once came close to capturing him. Yet you captured him within days of reaching the South China Sea.'

'Sheer luck,' said Killigrew. 'The admiral thinks I made him lose face?'

Tan smiled humourlessly. 'Do you think the pilongs will sit back and allow you to execute Zhai Jing-mu without making any attempt to free him?'

'They'd never break him out of Victoria Gaol.'

'Agreed. It would be far easier to rescue him while he was *en route* to Canton.'

Killigrew was starting to see what his host was driving at. He knew Tan would never make such an accusation openly, but he was curious to see how far the mandarin was prepared to go. 'True. But the question is purely academic, as Bonham won't agree for Zhai Jing-mu to be tried anywhere but in Victoria.'

'Indeed. I was merely speculating concerning Huang's motives. Be wary of the admiral, my barbarian son. His faction may be out of favour at court at present, but that may not always be the case. And he is a dangerous man to have for an enemy.'

'That's fine by me,' Killigrew said coolly. 'So am I.'

# V:

# *Yolo*

Molineaux and Ågård put the two unconscious sailors on either side of the wheelbarrow outside the Britain's Boast, one of Victoria's many waterfront taverns.

'All right, take them down to the wharf,' Ågård told the coolie pushing the barrow.

'*Hai.*' The coolie ducked his head and pushed the barrow before him. Molineaux and Ågård sauntered along behind him. There were worse jobs in Her Majesty's navy than gathering up the drunks after a run ashore, but by and large Molineaux would have preferred to be one of the unconscious men on the barrow.

One of the boatswain's mates waited in the cutter tied up at the wharf. There was already a pile of drunk men amidships, snoring or groaning. 'Two more for you, Mr Fanning,' said Ågård, as Molineaux helped the coolie carry the drunks from the wheelbarrow to the cutter.

'We're still one shy,' said the boatswain's mate.

'Who is it?'

'Who do you think?'

'Jem Dando,' Molineaux sighed.

The boatswain's mate nodded. 'I've got to get this lot back aboard, but I don't have to report him run until the morning watch. If he's not back by then, though . . . then it'll be a matter for the corporal and the marines.'

'We could keep on looking for him,' suggested Ågård.

'If you think he's worth it,' agreed the boatswain's mate.

'We've tried everywhere. The Britannia, the Golden Tavern, the Britain's Boast, the British Queen, the Caledonian, the Eagle, the Commercial, the Waterloo . . .'

'What about Labtat's?' asked Fanning.

'Labtat's?'

'Labtat's Tavern.' The boatswain's mate laughed. 'I can tell you two ain't old China hands if you've never heard of Labtat's. A cable's length up the road, then hard-a-starboard. You can't miss it. Just keep an ear open for the sound of splintering furniture and breaking heads.'

'Labtat's it is, then.' Molineaux clapped Ågård on the shoulder. 'I'll look for him. No need for us both to lose sleep, Olly. You get back to the *Tizzy*; if I find Jem I'll hire a *yolo*.'

Ågård nodded and climbed into the cutter. As the boat pulled back to the *Tisiphone*, Molineaux paid the coolie off and made his way along the waterfront. Before he had gone a hundred yards he heard English voices and what sounded like a West Country lilt. The voices came from one of the *yolos* crowded in the harbour. Chickens clucked and squawked incongruously.

He stood at the edge of the dockside and peered into the darkness. 'That you, Jem?'

Whoever was in the *yolo* was too preoccupied to hear him. 'Hold her down, Zeke.'

'Let me go!' a Chinese woman squealed in English. 'You bloody bastard barbarian! Let me go!'

'Yeow! Damned hellspite bit me!'

The man with the West Country accent laughed. 'We'll soon learn her some manners . . .'

The woman screamed.

'Stow your gaff, bitch, or we really will give you something to scream about.'

That didn't sound like Dando. Molineaux heard the sound of material being ripped. A moment later he had jumped down on to the deck of the nearest *yolo* and was making his way across the tightly packed boats to the scene of the commotion. He was aware of dirty Oriental faces peering out at him from under awnings, but no one made any attempt to stop him. That was the problem with the Chinese: a child could get murdered under their noses, and most of the time none of them would lift a finger to stop it. Karma, they called it.

The small boats rocked under his weight, but he jumped nimbly from deck to deck until he had reached his destination. He stood in the *yolo*'s bow, next to the chicken coop where a couple of bantams clucked and flapped in agitation. Under the boat's awning, two men were holding down a young Tanka woman. One of them held a knife to her throat while the other forced her legs apart and kneeled between them.

Molineaux felt rage boil in his blood. 'Let her up,' he snarled.

The two men stared at each other and then slowly turned their heads to meet Molineaux's gaze. 'It's just some damned blackamoor,' sneered one.

'Walk away, shipmate,' growled the other.

'I ain't your shipmate,' said Molineaux. 'And as you old China hands are always so fond of saying: "no can do".'

'Get rid of him, Zeke.'

One of the men rose to his feet, hitched up his trousers, and swaggered across to where Molineaux stood, picking up a gaff-hook on the way. 'You got wax in your ears, boy? Get away from here!'

Molineaux motioned for the two men to precede him with a mockingly grandiloquent gesture. 'After you.'

'You're asking for it!' Zeke swung the gaff at Molineaux's head. The seaman ducked under the blow and drove a fist into the other's stomach. Zeke doubled up, Molineaux punched him on the jaw, and Zeke fell to the deck, dazed.

The other man left the woman and pushed himself to his feet to advance on Molineaux. 'You're making a big mistake, nigger. Do you know who I am?'

'Firstly, *you're* the one making a big mistake – by calling me "nigger". And secondly, you're asking the wrong question.'

The man furrowed his brow. In the faint glow from the distant harbour lights, Molineaux could see he was in his mid-thirties or thereabouts, with a face which was mostly covered by a greasy beard. He looked well-dressed, but he was clearly no gentleman. 'The wrong question . . .?'

Molineaux nodded. 'The question ain't: do I know who you are? The question is: do I give a fish's tit?'

The man threw a punch at Molineaux's head. The seaman ducked, but the man's punch had been a feint and he caught Molineaux with a left hook. The seaman went down and fell on the chicken coop. It splintered under his weight and a hen flapped into the air. Molineaux caught it by the legs and threw it at the man's face. The man cried out in alarm and took a step back. He tripped over the gunwale and fell into the water between two *yolos* with a splash.

'Look out!' yelled the woman.

Molineaux turned to see the dim glint of light on the six barrels of a pepperbox which Zeke had produced from somewhere. The seaman launched himself at Zeke, but even the few feet which separated them might as well have been miles.

The gun went off, but not before the woman had kicked Zeke in the wrist so that the pistol discharged itself harmlessly into the gunwale.

'Bitch!' Zeke tried to pistol-whip her, but she scurried nimbly out of the way. A moment later Molineaux caught him by the wrist and forced him back down. As they rolled over and over on the cluttered deck, Molineaux glimpsed embers glowing through a gap in the door of a small stove. He forced Zeke's arm down until the back of his hand came into contact with the hot-plate on top of the stove. Zeke yelled and dropped the pistol. Molineaux punched him in the stomach, and jumped to his feet. He grabbed Zeke by the shirt-front, hoisted him up, and punched him in the jaw. Zeke tottered back and fell over the gunwale, landing on the head of the other man who was trying to climb back aboard.

Molineaux retrieved the fallen pistol and stood over them both with one foot on the gunwale. The bearded man got one hand on the gunwale and glared up at Molineaux. 'I knows you. You'm the nigger sailor on the *Tisiphone*.'

Molineaux stamped viciously on his fingers and aimed the pepperbox at his head. 'If I hear you using that word one more time, mister, I'll blow a hole in your head so big we'll all be able to see what kind of shit you've got where most coves keep their brains.'

With a snarl, the bearded man began to swim between the *yolos* after Zeke as he made his way to the quayside. 'You bain't be hearing the last of this, matey!'

'You got me quaking in my boots,' sneered Molineaux. He dropped the pepperbox overboard and turned to the woman. 'You oh-kay, miss?' Molineaux had spent two years on a Yankee brig and his talk was laced with Americanisms; the Tanka girl must have met a few American sailors herself, for she seemed to understand him.

She nodded. '*Hai.* Yes. Thank you.' She glanced down at her torn clothes. 'Bloody bastard barbarians! They tearum my shirtee!' Unabashed by Molineaux's presence, she took off the tattered remains and tossed them aside to ferret for something else to wear. Even in the dim light Molineaux could see enough to remind him that he had not had a woman since Portsmouth.

She was fastening on a fresh shirt when she saw him

staring at her. 'What matter? You no see cow-chillo without clothe before?'

'Not one as cute as you.'

She unfastened her shirt once more to display her breasts to him. 'You takee alla look-see you wantchee. My no shamee.'

'Evidently not, miss. They're very fine.' He turned away to start tidying up the debris the fight had caused.

Pouting, she fastened her shirt once more. 'What for you helpee me?'

'I wouldn't want you thinking all barbarians are pigs.'

'You devil-slave. What for you carum?'

He stood up and rounded on her angrily. 'Hey! I ain't no devil, and I sure as hell ain't no slave.' He shook his head, and chuckled. 'First time I ever bashed a man with a chicken. Who were those coves, anyway?'

'Him Missee Ingersoll, him captainee of number-one opium hulk at Cap-sing-mun.'

'You think maybe he'll come back?'

'Him no savvy me. Alla China cow-chillo lookee alla same to barbarians.'

Molineaux grinned. 'I wish that were true. If all Chinese girls looked the same as you, I think I'd retire here.'

'Him savvy you, though. If I be you, I be plenty scarum. Him makee muchee trub for you.'

'He can try.' Molineaux became aware that he was being watched. He casually picked up the gaff-hook and whirled, but it was only the hen he had thrown at Ingersoll, perched on the gunwale with its head cocked on one side as it glared accusingly at Molineaux. 'You still here?' he asked it. 'I'm surprised you didn't make a bid for freedom while you still had the chance, before you ended up in someone's cooking pot.'

The woman picked up the chicken and carried it back to the wrecked coop. The other chickens were also running loose on deck. 'They b'long here; they savvy they catchee plenty chow. What for you b'long here, devil-slave?'

'My name's Wes,' he told her irritably, as he started to jury-rig the chicken coop with a ball of twine he found.

'My namee Mei-rong.'

'Pleased to meet you, Mei-rong.'

'You no answer my question. What for you b'long here?'

'If I thought you could cook chicken the way my mum does, maybe I'd b'long here long time.'

'That not kind of hunger my thinkee you wantchee satisfy.' She crouched down next to him to help and put one hand on his.

He was tempted to lean forward and kiss her, but he shook his head. 'You don't owe me a thing, Mei-rong. If I took advantage of your gratitude I'd be no better than them two thugs we just chased away.'

'Is plenty different when cow-chillo willing,' she pointed out.

He stood up. 'Don't think I ain't tempted. But I've got to find one of my shipmates.'

'You no likee China cow-chillo?'

'I likee you very much, Mei-rong.'

'Then what trub?' She stood up on tip-toes to put her arms around his neck. He dipped his head to kiss her and a moment later she had wrapped her lithe legs around his hips, giggling. Then the two of them fell to the deck.

'Ah, what the hell?' Molineaux growled between lingering kisses. 'Jem Dando can find his own way home.'

Killigrew was drilling the starboard watch in cutlass exercises the following morning when a boat came alongside from the shore and Assistant Superintendent Cargill climbed aboard. He conversed briefly with Hartcliffe on the quarterdeck and the first lieutenant nodded and directed one of the midshipmen to show the police officer down to Robertson's day room.

Killigrew concentrated on his work. 'Come on, Dando!

Get that blade up! You're supposed to be swapping thrusts with a pilong, not doing petit point needlework!'

'Sorry, sir. Had a run ashore last night. I'm feeling a little the worse for wear.'

'If this were for real, Dando, do you think that excuse would wash with your opponent?'

'No, sir.'

'Have a heart, sir,' said Molineaux. 'You know how difficult it is to get your weapon up when you've got gallon distemper.'

The others laughed. Killigrew smiled tolerantly, but before he could reply Hartcliffe called him across to the quarterdeck. 'Keep them at it, Fanning,' Killigrew told the boatswain's mate. 'If any of these lads have the blue devils, we'll soon sweat it out of them.' He made his way across to where Hartcliffe stood. 'Which way does the wind lie?'

'The Old Man wants to see you in his day room. Seems one of the men in your watch assaulted a member of the public last night.'

'How do they know it was one of the men in my watch? Have they got a good description?'

'Well, he was black and wearing pusser's slops.'

Killigrew sighed. 'Molineaux!'

The seaman broke off his cutlass drill and crossed to the deck at the double. 'Sir?'

'Accompany me to the captain's day room, if you please.'

'Aye, aye, sir.' Molineaux followed the lieutenant down the after-hatch. 'Am I in the rattle, sir?'

'That depends. Someone answering your description assaulted a member of the public last night.'

'Oh, that. I can explain everything, sir—'

'Save it for the captain, Molineaux.'

In the day room, Robertson stood by the window while Cargill sat in one of the chairs by the table. 'I understand you wanted to speak to me and Able Seaman Molineaux, sir?'

'Yes, Mr Killigrew. Mr Cargill here tells me that a gentleman was roughly assaulted on the waterfront last night by a black sailor. The gentleman has two fingers broken in his right hand—'

'He weren't no gentleman, Cap'n,' said Molineaux.

'Pipe down!' snapped Killigrew. 'You'll speak when spoken to. Hoist in?'

'Aye, aye, sir.'

'Well, Molineaux,' said Robertson, 'am I to take it that you are admitting to this crime?'

'I was the one what done it, sir, but it weren't no crime. It was self-defence. This cove Ingersoll and his mate were trying to do me in.'

'And why, may I ask, were they trying to do that?' asked Cargill.

'Maybe you should ask them what they were doing on the waterfront in the first place?' suggested Molineaux.

'The waterfront is a public highway, sailor,' said Cargill. 'They had as much right to be there as any man.'

'Yeah, except when I found them they weren't on the quayside itself, they was in one of the *yolos*, trying to rape a Tanka girl. I went to help her and that's when they turned on me.'

'Well!' said Robertson. 'I'd say that puts an entirely different complexion on things. Wouldn't you agree, Mr Cargill?'

'If this man is telling the truth.' Cargill nodded at Molineaux.

Killigrew could see another sharp retort welling up inside the seaman. He caught Molineaux's eye and shook his head infinitesimally. The seaman bit his tongue. 'Dismissed, Molineaux.'

'Aye, aye, sir.' Molineaux saluted Robertson and Killigrew, shot a disdainful glance at Cargill, and went out.

'Well?' said Robertson.

'Sir, barring occasional flashes of insubordination, Able

Seaman Molineaux is one of our most reliable and honest hands. I might remind you that he's been twice mentioned in Admiralty dispatches. If he says this fellow Ingersoll was trying to rape a Tanka girl, I believe him.'

'I'm inclined to agree,' said Robertson. 'So, Mr Cargill, what do you want to do now? You needn't expect me to punish one of my hands for an act of chivalry, but if you want to take Able Seaman Molineaux into custody, I can't stop you. What I can do, however, is raise merry hell with your superiors, and believe me I shall if I have to.'

Cargill grimaced. 'I'm sure that won't be necessary, sir. I'll have a discreet word with Captain Ingersoll, make it clear to him that he's only likely to embarrass himself if he pushes the matter any further. I'm sure he'll see sense and let it drop.'

'Let it drop!' exclaimed Robertson. 'Aren't you going to charge him with attempted rape? Assault?'

'It was only a Tanka girl . . .'

'I see,' said Killigrew. 'What was it you said to me yesterday about having one law for Europeans and another for the Chinese?'

Cargill squirmed. 'I'm afraid it's not that simple, Mr Killigrew. Captain Ingersoll is the master of the *Buchan Prayer*, Mr Bannatyne's receiving ship, and Mr Bannatyne is an extremely influential man in these parts.'

'You mean when he says "Jump!" you ask: "How high?" ' said Killigrew.

'That's about the long and the short of it, sir, yes,' Cargill admitted with disarming candour. 'You know Bonham's predecessor left under something of a cloud? Everyone in Hong Kong knows it was Bannatyne who swung that. The story is the two of them had a row over some matter of dealing with the Chinese and Sir John refused to take Bannatyne's advice. Six months later – as much time as it takes news to get to the Colonial Office and back – Sir John was forced to resign. And it was

Bannatyne who recommended Bonham as his replacement. Now, if you gentlemen wish to take on the *tai-pan* of Grafton, Bannatyne and Co., that's your prerogative. But I'd be obliged if you'd keep me out of it.'

'Very well, Mr Cargill,' sighed Robertson. 'I can see you're in a difficult position. If Ingersoll's prepared to drop the matter, then so am I. Sounds to me like the damned scoundrel got his just desserts. Two fingers broken, eh?' The commander chuckled. 'Good for Molineaux.'

Killigrew escorted Cargill back up on deck. 'I'm given to understand that the trial of Zhai Jing-mu has been postponed yet again. Seeing that it's over a week since we arrested him, might I ask what the delay is?'

Cargill sighed with the air of a man who was weary of having to answer the same question over and over again. 'I've been gathering evidence . . .'

'Gathering evidence? We caught him in the act. I hardly see what further proof is needed.'

'I see your point of view, Killigrew. Now please see mine: Zhai Jing-mu has slipped through our fingers too many times in the past. I want to be one hundred per cent certain of a conviction before he goes to trial. Not ninety-seven per cent, not ninety-eight per cent, not even ninety-nine per cent. One hundred per cent. Over the past three years he's done thousands of pounds worth of damage to the China trade, not to mention the loss of life he's responsible for. We don't want another three years of his reign of terror because of some legal technicality.'

'When you put it like that . . . By the way, I spoke to Sir Dadabhoy Framjee yesterday. He tells me that Li Cheng resigned as his comprador yesterday morning, and hasn't been seen at the Framjee factory since.'

'Now that *is* interesting,' agreed Cargill, stroking his whiskers. 'I shall certainly have to have a word with this fellow Li.' He climbed down into the waiting boat. 'And I expect you to stay well clear of the whole thing, Mr

Killigrew. If you see this fellow Li anywhere, send word to me. Understand?'

Killigrew nodded. 'I think I'm starting to understand how this colony works.'

For a moment it looked as if Cargill might reply, but then he scowled. 'All right, take me back ashore.'

Killigrew watched the boat for a moment and then turned to the boatswain's mate. 'Pass the word for Molineaux, Fanning.'

'Aye, aye, sir. Wes! Mr Killigrew wants a word.'

The lieutenant wandered over to the taffrail and Molineaux joined him there a moment later. 'Well, Molineaux, it looks like you managed to wriggle out of it this time.'

The seaman grinned. 'Don't I always?' he smirked, and then saw Killigrew's face. 'I mean, glad to hear it, sir. Thank you.'

As Killigrew gazed across to where Admiral Huang's junk was still at anchor, he saw a Chinese woman being lowered to a chop-boat tied up below. From her fine silk robes with rich brocade, it was obvious that she was a gentlewoman, or at least a courtesan at the peak of her career.

Molineaux saw her too. 'Cool the blower with the gammy dew-beaters, sir! She's a bit young to have gout, ain't she?'

'Golden lotus feet, Molineaux,' said Killigrew. 'The Chinese find small feet attractive in women, so they take the girls when they're young, break the bones in their feet, and then bind them tightly so they can't grow more than a few inches in length. I understand the Manchus are trying to ban the practice; you have to give them credit for that.'

Lord Hartcliffe snorted. 'Damnable savages! Subjecting their women to such an unhealthy, constricting torture merely to make them conform to some unnatural ideal of feminine beauty!'

★ ★ ★

'Pull!' urged Mrs Bannatyne. 'Pull harder!' She gripped one of the posts of her four-poster bed as her *amah* hauled on the stays of her corset. 'Tighter!'

'Is too tight!' protested the *amah*. 'I hurtee you!'

'I'll decide when it's too tight. It's supposed to be eighteen inches.'

'But your waist is not eighteen inches!'

Mrs Bannatyne glared at her.

The *amah* flushed. 'But you have got beautiful shape, Missee Bannatyne. Not like my poor, fat, pig-like lump of body.'

'Spare me your Oriental humility. I've seen skeletons with more flesh on them than you. Now are you going to pull, or do I have to get Mr Shen in here to do it for you?'

In the mirror over the dressing table, Mrs Bannatyne saw a trace of fear in the *amah*'s eyes. 'I do it, Missee Bannatyne.' She hauled on the stays again, but it was no good: any tighter and Mrs Bannatyne would be in danger of fainting halfway through the evening. Plenty of girls did, to give dashing young men a chance to catch them before they hit the floor, but at twenty-five Mrs Bannatyne considered herself too old for such games, even if she had not been a married woman. She was just going to have to accept that she was a fat and frumpy twenty-two inches around the waist and the days when she had been the belle of every ball were far behind her.

She finished dressing and the *amah* was helping her pin up her hair when there came a knock on the bedroom door. 'All right, Bai-ling,' she told the *amah*. 'You can go now. I can manage the rest.'

The *amah* bowed and went out. 'Come in,' Mrs Bannatyne called through the open door.

She expected her husband to come through the door, but it was Captain Verran. In the dresser mirror she saw him lean nonchalantly against the door lintel with his arms folded and an insouciant leer on his face. 'Good evening, ma'am. May I say you look as ravishing as ever?'

'You may,' she replied distantly, wishing she had not dismissed the *amah*. Captain Verran's attentions were all very flattering – there was no denying he was a handsome fellow – and if she had not been married she might have been tempted to encourage his advances. He had a roguish charm which both repelled and attracted her at the same time. 'Is my husband back yet?' she asked.

Verran shook his head. 'He's spending the night on board the *Buchan Prayer*. He asked me to give you his apologies.' Verran took a step into the room and kicked the door to behind him with his heel. 'So it's just you and I tonight.'

'And the servants.' She rose from her chair to face him. 'I think it would be more appropriate for you to spend the night on the *Golden Dragon*.'

'In my cramped cabin? When you have so many rooms in this big, fine house of your husband's? You could give the servants the night off, you know.'

'Captain Verran! I shan't report this conversation to my husband, but I think you had better leave at once.'

'Your husband!' Verran spat contemptuously. 'You think I don't know he neglects you?'

'If he does, that is between my husband and myself.' She did not fool herself into thinking that her marriage to her husband had been a fairy-tale romance; more in the way of a business arrangement between her father and her bridegroom. As the daughter of the great John Keane she had always been aware that she could not hope to marry for love. But her husband treated her with respect, albeit a respect marked with cold formality, even when he was fulfilling his marital duties: to him, love-making seemed a chore necessary to provide himself with an heir to his financial empire, rather than an opportunity to display any warmth or affection towards his wife. But as the wife of the *tai-pan* she lived in a state of luxury comparable with that of the lesser European royalty. She knew she had no cause for complaint. Besides, she had sworn to love, honour and obey her husband, and it was a vow she meant to keep.

Verran moved closer to her. 'I could make you happy. Happier than he's ever made you.'

'You could ruin us both. Please, Captain Verran. Do not make me ask you to leave a second time.'

He stared intensely into her eyes with a fervour that sent a chill down her spine – a chill which had nothing to do with desire and everything to do with fear – and for a moment she feared he might try to force himself on her there and then. She reached behind her and picked a brooch with a long pin off the dresser. But then his customary smile slipped greasily across his face and he backed off.

'You need time to think about it, I can tell. That's fine by me. You'll come round to my way of thinking sooner or later. You know you want it.'

'I think I am a better judge of what I do or do not want, Captain Verran,' she said tightly. 'Good night to you, sir.'

He grinned and touched the peak of his cap to her, before turning on his heel and heading for the door. He was halfway through it when he stopped and turned. Her heart pounded with fear, but he stayed with one hand on the doorknob. 'Oh, I forgot to mention. Your husband asked me to tell you he wishes you to throw a ball at the factory next month. On the twenty-fourth.'

'A ball?' she echoed in astonishment. Her husband never threw balls.

Verran nodded. 'The finest this colony's ever known.'

'It's short notice, I must say. The twenty-fourth . . . that's less than four weeks away!'

'The invitations are to go out before the end of the week.'

'Who's to be on the guest list?'

'Why, everyone who's anyone. Mr and Mrs Bonham, naturally, and General Staveley and his family. The other traders, of course, and the officers of the garrison. Oh, and the officers of any navy ships in the harbour. I dare say Mr Bannatyne will let you have the full guest list at his earliest convenience.' Verran touched the peak of his cap again, and went out.

Mrs Bannatyne sat down with her head swimming. The news that her husband intended to host a ball had put all thoughts of Verran's unwelcome advances from her mind. When she had been a child, in the old days before Sir George Grafton had retired to Britain, the balls at the factory in Canton had been the finest in all Hong Kong. Social entertainments were a vital part of the China trade, a chance for the tea merchants to show off their wealth and opulence. In China, appearances were everything. Perception was more important than reality. If a man appeared to be bankrupt, then he might as well *be* bankrupt. But since Bannatyne had taken over the day-to-day running of the company, balls had become a thing of the past. It was Bannatyne's way of saying that Grafton, Bannatyne & Co. was far too successful to need to impress anyone.

She wondered if her husband *was* bankrupt. If he was, she would be the last person to find out. He never let her know anything about the business. At the beginning she had wanted to become involved, not for power or for riches, but simply so that she would have something to talk about with a man with whom she had nothing in common. She had chosen his work because nothing else seemed to interest him, but he insisted on keeping her at arm's length.

She sighed. As the hostess, she would be expected to make all the arrangements. Until now she had often wished they would hold balls again at the Hong Kong factory, if only so she had something to do with her time.

She had never hosted a ball in her life, but she suspected they required a great deal of organising.

'Have I done something to offend you?' Peri asked in a low voice, so that none of the others would hear.

'To upset me?' Killigrew was genuinely astonished. 'No. What makes you think that?'

'I cannot help thinking you have been avoiding me over the past month. Turning down my father's invitations. Turning down *my* invitations.'

'Please don't take it personally. My duties on board the *Tisiphone* have kept me busy.'

'Lord Hartcliffe has had plenty of time for social occasions.'

He smiled. 'Ah, well, that's seniority for you.'

She was not convinced. It was obvious something was troubling him, but he did not elaborate, pretending to concentrate on turning the mutton chops on the barbecue he and Hartcliffe had built.

It had been Prince Tan's idea to hold a picnic on the south coast of Hong Kong, on the rocky beach at Chek-py-wan where the off-shore island of Ap-li-chau provided shelter from the sea breezes. The gathering was mixed, but predominantly young: Prince Tan and Framjee were the oldest ones present, sitting some way off and talking confidentially. Peri's father had told her he wanted Prince Tan's help in setting up a school for the children of destitute Chinese families on Hong Kong, and he was obviously making the most of this opportunity. Mr Strachan had already erected the tent he used as a darkroom and was setting up his camera on a tripod to take some photographic pictures. Elsewhere young clerks and military officers flirted with the daughters of traders and senior officers and diplomats. Only Hartcliffe seemed aloof from such flirtations, sitting with Mr Cavan, one of the young midshipmen from the *Tisiphone*.

Peri glanced at Killigrew again, but his attention had strayed to where the Reverend Ultzmann was talking with a conspiratorial air to a young Eurasian beauty. Peri instantly felt jealous. 'You think she is attractive?' she asked Killigrew challengingly.

'The Eurasian girl? Don't you? Who is she?'

'I do not know, I am sure. She came with Prince Tan.'

He nodded. 'I saw her on his houseboat when I dined with him last month.'

'Your chops are burning.'

'Hm? Oh, Lor'!' He quickly lifted one of the chops from the griddle with a toasting fork and she held out a plate from one of the picnic hampers for him to drop it on. A moment later the second chop had joined it, and she handed the plate to Lieutenant Dwyer, the young officer of the Ceylon Rifles who had helped Cargill take Zhai Jing-mu into custody.

'Thank you, Miss Dadabhoy,' said Dwyer. 'Has anyone told you how ravishing you look today?'

'No.' She gave Killigrew a hard look, but he was oblivious, staring after Ultzmann and the Eurasian girl as they wandered out of sight behind a rocky outcrop further down the beach. 'They haven't.'

'You've been invited to this ball at the Bannatynes' next week?'

She nodded. 'Who has not?' The forthcoming ball was the talk of all Hong Kong. Balls were common enough, but this one was different: this was the first ball at the Grafton, Bannatyne & Co. factory in over a decade.

'I was wondering if I might be so bold as to ask for the honour of a dance with you?' asked Dwyer.

'But of course,' she said, giving Killigrew a sidelong glance to see how he would react. He was not even listening, curse him. 'Which one? You're the first man to ask me, so you may have your pick.'

'You astonish me, Miss Dadabhoy. I would have thought

that young beaux would be queuing up to partner you.'

'Apparently not.'

'Then, since etiquette demands I dance with you no more than three times in one evening, I should like the first waltz, the last waltz, and any polka you care to choose.'

'I fear a polka might prove to be a little too strenuous for me, but you may have one of the waltzes.'

'I shall look forward to it.' Dwyer took one of her hands and kissed it gallantly. As he leaned forward, his chops slid off his carelessly tilted plate. They plummeted towards the hem of Peri's sari and she jumped back instinctively, tripping over. She felt herself falling backwards, and then a strong pair of arms had caught her.

'Are you all right?' asked Killigrew.

'Yes. Thank you,' she said breathlessly.

'My pleasure.'

'Oh, gosh, I'm sorry,' said Dwyer. 'That was clumsy of me.'

'Yes,' Peri agreed a little impatiently. 'Thank you, Mr Killigrew, but you don't need to hold me now.'

'Sorry.' He set her back on her feet.

Dwyer looked mournfully at the chops on the ground at his feet. 'Oh, rot it! I say, Killigrew. Any chance of some fresh chops?'

Killigrew sighed. 'By all means . . .' He made as if to fetch some more from the food hamper, but Peri caught him firmly by the arm and pulled him away.

'Help yourself,' she told Dwyer, linking her arm through Killigrew's and leading him away.

'Where are we going?' asked Killigrew.

'For a walk.' She led him down the beach, in the opposite direction from which Ultzmann and the Eurasian girl had headed. 'Lieutenant Dwyer has asked me to dance with him at the Bannatynes' ball.'

'Good for him.'

'He is rather handsome, do you not think?'

'He's not my type,' Killigrew responded, deadpan.

She released his arm with a gesture of frustration. She had been planning what she was going to say to him today ever since she had learned he would be attending the picnic, and he was ruining it all, confusing her with his flippancy and apparent indifference. She took a deep breath and told herself to start again. 'Mr Killigrew, it may have escaped your attention, but I have a great deal of regard for you.'

'And I for you, Miss Dadabhoy.'

'You do not show it.'

'What would you have me do?'

She glanced back down the beach to where the others sat laughing and joking amongst themselves. No one was watching them. 'You might kiss me.'

He opened his mouth as if to respond, and for a moment it looked as though he might do exactly as she wished, but he just set his jaw, shook his head sadly and strode on.

She lifted the hem of her sari with one hand and hurried after him. 'Mr Killigrew, I had hoped that you held me in higher regard than to be completely indifferent to my feelings . . .'

'Your feelings are irrelevant to me, Miss Dadabhoy.'

It felt like she had been kicked in the stomach. She stared after him for a moment, feeling humiliated, and was tempted to let him stride away. But she was not going to let him get away so easily. 'Do you really think so little of me?'

'Miss Dadabhoy . . .'

'Peri, please.'

'Peri. Please believe me, I hold you in the highest regard. But it can lead nowhere. If I cared nothing for you, it would be the easiest thing in the world for me to seduce you. But I respect you, very much, and I can see no benefit to either of us if we pursue this. We'll only end up hurting each other.'

'So proper! So formal! So cold!' she sneered. 'You have never been in love, have you, Mr Killigrew? You have no idea of what it feels like to be . . . to be overwhelmed by such a consuming passion, to have it rob you of all your senses . . .' She was hurrying after him so that when he stopped and turned abruptly she tumbled into his arms. He held her close and kissed her with a flood of pent-up passion. She did not know whether to be delighted or terrified, but delight won out and she responded. Then he broke off the kiss and stepped back, staring at her as if he were just as astonished at himself as she were.

'Mr Killigrew!'

'I'm sorry—'

'Do not apologise!'

'Miss Dadabhoy – Peri – don't imagine that it's any easier for me than it is for you. Don't imagine that ever since I first saw you on Zhai Jing-mu's junk you haven't been in my thoughts day and night, that I haven't wanted to sweep you into my arms and kiss you as I did just then, that I haven't spent every minute away from you longing for the next time I saw you . . .'

'Then why did you turn down all my invitations?'

'Because you know as well as I that it is impossible for there to be anything between us.'

She sighed and turned her head away. 'You could never marry an Indian girl, could you, Kit?' she said disdainfully. 'Whatever would your colleagues say?'

'The devil take my colleagues. It's *you* I'm concerned about. If you married me, you'd have to renounce your religion, your people, everything you believe in.'

'I believe in you.'

'I'm sorry.'

'For what?'

'For putting you in such a position. Forcing you to choose between me and your religion was the last thing I ever wanted.'

'I am not blaming you, Kit. It is not your fault I am a Zarathustrian. If anyone is to blame, it should be me.'

'For being born into a particular culture? No one can be blamed for that.'

'What about your religion, Kit? *Are* you religious?'

'Not really. I'm an Anglican.'

'But you go to church?'

'Regularly. Once a year, for the Christmas carol service.' He could hardly count divine service on deck every Sunday: attendance was compulsory. 'If I could become a Parsi I would, Peri. I've been reading up on Zarathustrianism. All that stuff about an eternal conflict between good and evil. It makes as much sense as any religion I've encountered.'

'There is not much comfort in a religion which forbids me to marry whom I please. Perhaps I could become a Christian, start a new life in England . . .'

He shook his head. 'And then what? Settle down in a country cottage as the wife of a naval officer? Have you any idea of what that's like? Being left on your own for years at a time? It just wouldn't work, Peri. It wouldn't be fair to you.'

'Do you not think I have the right to make that decision for myself?'

'Certainly. If you could be certain you were thinking straight.'

'You think I am making no sense?'

'All I know is that when *I* look at *you*, common sense goes by the board.'

'Why not go with it?' she suggested, taking a step towards him.

He moved away, shaking his head with a sad smile. 'Have you ever noticed that man is an inveterate categoriser?'

'What do you mean?'

'It's like Strachan with his notebooks, looking for new

species so he can decide which phylum, order, and class they belong to. Everything has to be battened down and pigeonholed. Every*one*, too. I'm a British naval officer, you're a Parsi lady, and never the twain shall meet. And we all go along with it because we're terrified of not fitting in.'

'You do not strike me as the kind of man who worries about fitting in.'

'Don't be fooled. I'm as susceptible as the next man. When I was on board the *Dreadful* the oldsters used to sneer that I have "a touch of the tar brush". My mother was Greek; and, what's more unforgivable, it shows in my colouring.'

'I think it makes you look very handsome.' He accepted the compliment with an inclination of his head. 'Nevertheless, the gulf between two different European countries is hardly the same as that between Britain and India, Kit.'

He shrugged. 'There've always been those who've treated me as . . . I don't know, somehow inferior. Even when they meant well. When they say things like, "Good work, Killigrew," I can't help wondering if what they're really thinking is: "Not bad, for a dago." '

'Are you sure it is not simply your imagination?'

'No, I'm not,' he admitted. 'But the uncertainty only makes it worse. A true English gentleman never doubts himself. So I think I have some idea of what it must be like for your father, trying to be something he can never really be, losing touch with his heritage and ending up being neither one thing nor the other.'

'You do not strike me as the kind of man who is troubled by self-doubt, either.'

He smiled. 'I've learned to conceal it.'

She moved closer to him and this time he did not move away. She encircled his neck with her arms and felt his arms around her waist. This time the kiss was more relaxed, but nonetheless passionate, as they both allowed it to last. Finally she broke off. 'Kit! I had no idea Englishmen could be so passionate.'

'That's the Greek half of me.'

'And that is the half you wish to deny?' she asked incredulously.

'We'd better get back to the others,' he said. 'If we're gone too long, someone will notice, and you know how tongues wag.'

'I do not care.'

'You should. What will happen to you when the *Tisiphone* is ordered away from here?'

She looked grave. 'I would prefer not to think of that.'

'So would I. But we can't afford not to think about it, either.'

They strolled back to where the others were still chatting merrily amongst themselves. No one remarked upon their return, except for Strachan, who gave Killigrew a quizzical look, which was ignored. Peri was about to walk away from the lieutenant to talk to her father, for form's sake, when the Eurasian girl Killigrew had been so fascinated by earlier reappeared around the headland at a run. A moment later Ultzmann appeared behind her, breathlessly trying to keep up.

'Ai-ling! Wait!'

One of Prince Tan's attendants intercepted her. He took her firmly by the arm and led her back to where Tan stood watching expressionlessly. Ultzmann tried to follow them, but Killigrew blocked his path.

'You should be ashamed of yourself, Reverend,' Peri heard him hiss under his breath.

Ultzmann glared at him. 'I advise you to keep your nose out of affairs which do not concern yourself, young man.' He pushed brusquely past Killigrew. The lieutenant turned as if to follow as Ultzmann continued after the girl. 'Ai-ling!'

Prince Tan was already helping her into a palanquin, but

at the sound of Ultzmann's voice she paused and glanced over her shoulder at the reverend with tears glistening on her cheeks. Another of Tan's attendants stood firmly in Ultzmann's path and this time the reverend stopped. Tan pushed the girl into the palanquin and it was lifted on to the shoulders of two coolies and carried back up the bridle path to Victoria. Ultzmann turned away with his shoulders slumped.

Everyone had stopped talking to watch this tableau. 'Well I never!' huffed a dowager in a stage whisper that could have been heard on mainland China. 'And him a man of the cloth!'

Strachan stood up and nudged Killigrew in the ribs. 'The dirty scoundrel, eh? She's young enough to be his daughter!' The assistant surgeon's voice was amused and envious.

The picnic started to break up shortly after that. As everyone climbed into the waiting calashes and landaus, Peri sought out Killigrew one last time as he was about to climb into the hackney the officers of the *Tisiphone* had clubbed together to rent for the afternoon. 'Shall I tell Lieutenant Dwyer that my last dance at the Bannatynes' is bespoken?'

He clasped her hand in such a way that no one else would notice. 'That would be ungallant.'

'But you will be there?'

He nodded.

'Peri!' called her father, standing at the door to his victoria. She hurried to obey, but she could not stop herself from glancing over her shoulder at Killigrew as she climbed into the carriage. He was still staring after her with a smile on his face, oblivious to the impatient calls of his fellow officers.

[illegible] silence. [illegible]

[illegible] a ripple of [illegible] [illegible] [illegible] [illegible]

[illegible]

Everyone had stopped talking [illegible] [illegible] [illegible] [illegible] [illegible] the world.

[illegible]

[illegible]

[illegible]

[illegible]

[illegible]

# *VI:*

# *Tai-Pan*

There were already a dozen carriages parked outside the gates of the Grafton, Bannatyne & Co. trading factory at East Point when Killigrew arrived on foot with Robertson, Hartcliffe, Strachan, and the other senior officers of the *Tisiphone*. The naval officers were in their full-dress uniforms: epauletted navy-blue tail-coats, cocked hats and white kid gloves. In place of the two sentries who usually stood at the factory gate there were two turbaned footmen in high-collared coats of salmon and gold brocade. Glancing up, Killigrew saw the usual guards patrolling the wall above, thrown into shadow by the bright lights which illuminated the compound. Presumably the last thing Bannatyne wanted was for his ball to be disrupted by Triads.

The footmen ushered the officers through. The compound had been brushed clean and paper lanterns had been hung all the way around the perimeter; a seven-piece band was tuning up in one corner. This would be where the company spent the evening dancing, but first they were escorted to the reception room where another footman relieved them of their hats. They were greeted by a handsome woman in a ball gown of rich green velvet which set off her emerald eyes and auburn hair to perfection: their hostess for the evening. Killigrew saw at once what Verran had been talking about, and could no longer blame his friend for risking dismissal – and perhaps worse – by seeking to seduce his employer's wife. As he waited his turn to be presented to Mrs Bannatyne, he wondered how his friend was getting along on that score, and felt unaccountably envious at the possibility that Verran might have succeeded by now.

Rear-Admiral Collier did the honours. 'Mrs Bannatyne, permit me to introduce the officers of Her Majesty's sloop *Tisiphone*: Mr Robertson, Lord Hartcliffe and . . . uh . . .'

'My second lieutenant, Mr Killigrew,' Robertson continued on his superior's behalf.

'Ah, yes,' Collier said heavily. '*Killigrew*.'

Killigrew smiled wryly. He had never met the admiral before tonight; evidently a reputation of some sort had preceded him.

'Mr Westlake and Mr Strachan, my surgeon and assistant surgeon respectively,' said Robertson. 'Mr Vellacott, my purser and paymaster; and Mr Muir, my chief engineer.'

Collier nodded. 'Gentlemen, I give you: Mrs Epiphany Bannatyne.'

Robertson bowed stiffly. 'A pleasure to meet you, ma'am.'

'You are the gentlemen we have to thank for preserving Miss Dadabhoy's life?' asked Mrs Bannatyne.

'I don't believe she was in any real danger, ma'am,' said Killigrew. 'For all their villainy, the pilongs have a kind of twisted code. When they take hostages at all, they generally treat them well.' Of course, if a certain pilong held a grudge towards someone, as Zhai Jing-mu's little speech when Killigrew had handed him over to Dwyer and Cargill seemed to indicate, then that was another matter entirely. But Zhai Jing-mu was safely locked behind bars, soon to be executed, and Killigrew saw no need to alarm the ladies with such thoughts.

'I didn't catch your name earlier, Mr . . .?'

'Killigrew, ma'am. At your service.' She gave him a brief, cold, appraising gaze, and nodded. He glanced about pointedly. 'Is Mr Bannatyne not joining us?'

She smiled thinly. 'My husband will be with us presently. He's just finishing off some paperwork in the study.'

'Probably planning a dramatic entrance,' muttered Strachan.

Drinks were handed out by footmen, and the gathering stood around and made polite small talk while they waited for the other guests to turn up. Strachan turned his attention to one of the paintings on the wall, a view across Victoria Harbour from Kowloon.

'Any good?' Killigrew knew enough about art to know how little he knew, and happily deferred to Strachan – an amateur artist before he had taken up photographic portraiture – in such matters.

'Very. By Mr Chinnery, a local artist. Not as good as Mr Turner, of course, but then who is?'

They both turned away from the wall, and Strachan nodded to where Commander Robertson was talking to General Staveley, the commander of the Hong Kong garrison. 'I didn't think the Old Man would come tonight,' murmured Strachan. 'I thought he loathed social functions?'

'Did you think he would turn down a chance to meet the great Mr Blase Bannatyne himself?' asked Killigrew, smiling. He nodded to where a white marble bust of Genghis Khan stood on a pedestal in a niche. 'Take that fellow there, for example. He may not have been everyone's cup of char, but if you had a chance to meet him, would you turn it down?'

'Rubbing shoulders with barba—' started Strachan, but he was interrupted by a new voice.

'Is that how you see me? A Genghis Khan of commerce?'

Killigrew turned and saw a man dressed soberly in a black neckcloth, frock coat and trousers, more like a clergyman than a China trader. His lank hair, still untouched by grey, was parted down the centre and slicked tightly against his skull with Macassar oil. If he was a day over forty, he looked good on it. His face was plain enough, almost boyish except for the blue-tinged jowls of a permanent five o'clock shadow, the features too regular to be handsome; a little lacking in character, but perhaps women might consider him attractive.

'Mr Bannatyne, I presume?' said Killigrew.

The *tai-pan* of Grafton, Bannatyne & Co. inclined the head which launched a thousand cargoes of opium. 'I have that honour. And you are . . .?'

'Lieutenant Killigrew, HMS *Tisiphone*. And this is Mr Strachan, our assistant surgeon.'

Bannatyne nodded to the bust of Genghis Khan. 'Mrs Bannatyne's handiwork. A woman should have a hobby, don't you think?'

'Keeps them out of trouble,' agreed Strachan.

'I've always found women more interesting when they're *in* trouble,' said Killigrew, and turned back to the bust. 'Your wife has a rare talent, sir.'

Mrs Bannatyne came across to join them. 'Is everything all right?' she asked her husband.

'We were just admiring your handiwork, ma'am,' said Killigrew. 'It's a magnificent piece. Have you had any formal training?'

She blushed. 'No. I don't know how I got into it. I needed some way to spend my time. I tried my hand at watercolours, but I wasn't very good. Then one day I found a block of marble in the potting shed left over from when the house was built, and some sculpting tools, and thought I'd try my hand. My early efforts were horrendous, but Mr Chinnery had a look at them and encouraged me to persevere.'

'Good for him,' said Killigrew. 'I should like to see the rest of your body of work, if I may.'

'It's really not all that good.'

'Perhaps later,' Bannatyne said gruffly, in a tone which said: *Over my rotting corpse*.

'If they're all as good as this one, you really ought to hold an exhibition, see if you can't sell some of your work,' said Strachan. 'It really would be a shame to hide such a talent under a bushel.'

'Mrs Bannatyne merely sculpts as a hobby,' Bannatyne said firmly. 'It would be unseemly for the wife of the *tai-pan* of Grafton, Bannatyne and Co. to be a professional artist.'

'Nonsense,' said Killigrew. 'Why, one only has to look at this piece here to see what a talent your wife has. Look at those beady eyes, that sneering, supercilious expression. It's easy to imagine this rapacious swine riding roughshod over all who stand in his way, with scant regard for human life. Where did you find such inspiration, ma'am?'

She looked bewildered. 'I really couldn't say. It just . . . came to me.'

'I keep it there to remind me of whom I am dealing with whenever I have contact with the Chinese,' Bannatyne said in a calm, unruffled voice which was belied by the glare he gave Killigrew. 'Genghis Khan was a Tartar, just like the Manchu rulers of present-day China. "Know thy enemy and know thyself," Sun Tzu says in his *Art of War*, "and thou shalt be victorious a hundred times out of a hundred." '

'Doesn't he also say: "Those who win every battle are not truly skilled; those who render the armies of others helpless without fighting are the best of all"?'

'You are familiar with the Chinese classics, Mr Killigrew?'

'Only the ones I can obtain in translation. I'm afraid I haven't mastered Chinese script yet.'

'Yes, I found it rather difficult at first,' Bannatyne said airily. As Robertson and Hartcliffe approached, he turned to greet them, and behind his back Strachan mouthed: *Touché*. Killigrew did not smile. 'You must be Commander Robertson?'

Robertson nodded. 'And you are Mr Bannatyne, I presume? I've heard a great deal about you, sir.'

Bannatyne smiled, almost bashfully. 'Don't believe above half of it, sir. And this gentleman is?'

'Lord Hartcliffe, my first lieutenant. I see you've already met Mr Killigrew and Mr Strachan. I'll introduce you to Mr Westlake, Mr Vellacott and Mr Muir later if the opportunity arises. My other officers send their apologies, but we could not leave the *Tisiphone* without someone on duty.'

'Very wise, sir. You heard about the salt boat that was cut out of the harbour by pilongs the other day? It must be very embarrassing for you gentlemen of the Royal Navy to have a boat with such a valuable cargo stolen right from under your noses.' Bannatyne watched Killigrew as he spoke, as if trying to gauge his response to this provocation. The lieutenant met his gaze and kept his face expressionless.

'I don't see what's so valuable about a cargo of salt,' snorted Strachan. 'I can only assume that the pirates must have been greatly disappointed.'

'You're new to China, aren't you, Mr Strachan?' said Bannatyne, without taking his eyes off Killigrew. 'If you had been here for any length of time, you would be aware that the Manchus maintain a monopoly on salt, which makes it a highly valuable commodity on the mainland.'

'Shouldn't we go through to the compound now?' Mrs Bannatyne asked her husband.

He smiled tightly. 'You know it would be rude of us to proceed before the rest of our guests have arrived, madam. We're still waiting for Admiral Huang.'

For all his years in the Far East, the governor had not yet learned the Chinese art of masking astonishment. 'You invited Admiral Huang? And he *accepted*?'

Bannatyne nodded.

'He hasn't accepted any of my invitations to meet face to face,' spluttered Bonham. He was in his mid-forties, a dark-haired, thick-set man with a stiffly waxed moustache. 'Damn me, Bannatyne, how on earth did you winkle him out of that junk?'

The *tai-pan* smiled faintly. 'You have your ways of influencing people, Governor. I have mine.'

Killigrew did not doubt that Bannatyne's methods included bribery, corruption and even threats, but he was not convinced those were the methods that had induced the Chinese admiral to attend the ball. Huang might well be as corruptible as any government officer anywhere in the world, but no Chinese mandarin would ever have allowed himself to fall into the pocket of a Westerner, not even one as powerful and influential as Bannatyne.

'If we're waiting for a Chinaman to arrive, we'll be here long after the food's gone cold,' said General Staveley. 'Their mandarins always make a point of turning up late, and the more important they consider themselves the later they arrive.'

'Indeed,' said Bannatyne. 'Which is why I took the precaution of inviting the admiral to arrive two hours earlier than everyone else. Ah, and here he is now . . .'

A footman's voice boomed across the ballroom: 'His excellency Admiral Huang Hai-kwang of the Imperial Chinese Navy.'

Killigrew glanced up as Admiral Huang entered, wearing the traditional silk robes, thick-soled satin boots and conical hat of a mandarin. One could tell a great deal about a mandarin if you knew what to look for: Huang wore the red coral button, the yellow girdle, and the coveted double-eyed peacock's feather in his cap, while the image on his *buzi* – the 'mandarin square' embroidered on the front of his gown – was that of a highly stylised lion. In

Chinese military official's insignia, the lion was the second rank, inferior only to the mythical *qilin*. All in all, Huang's robes proclaimed him to be a person of some substance.

He was a man of substance in terms of his build as well. His face had the characteristic Mongoloid features of the Tartar Manchus, the rolls of flesh emphasising the narrowness of the eyes which twinkled with mischief above cheeks so podgy they made it impossible to determine his age with any degree of certainty. He greeted everyone in turn in the Oriental manner, bowing with his hands clasped before him.

At a signal, two more footmen opened a pair of double doors leading back out to the compound. As the band struck up a quadrille the governor and Mrs Bannatyne started off the figures. Killigrew preferred waltzes, so he helped himself to a glass of champagne from the tray of a passing flunkey and sat the first dance out.

The quadrille ended and the first waltz began. Once again Killigrew stood on the sidelines, feeling envious as he watched Lieutenant Dwyer, resplendent in his bottle-green full-dress uniform with a crimson sash, lead Peri Dadabhoy around the floor. When the waltz ended, the men promenaded halfway round the floor with their partners, and Killigrew was about to go to where he guessed Peri and Dwyer would end up, but Bannatyne intercepted him, leading Admiral Huang.

'Not dancing, Mr Killigrew?' asked Bannatyne.

'Why? Are you offering?' Something about the *tai-pan*'s staid, dour manner brought out the lieutenant's flippant side.

Bannatyne frowned. 'Ah. I was warned you were something of a humorist. Perhaps I can introduce you to a fellow naval officer: Admiral Huang Hai-kwang. Admiral, this is Lieutenant Killigrew, one of the officers of Her Majesty's paddle-sloop *Tisiphone*.'

'Ah, yes,' said Huang. 'The young officer who was first

over the wall at Chingkiang-fu.' His English, though thickly accented, was excellent.

'The first one who lived to tell the tale, at any rate,' admitted Killigrew. 'I'm surprised you've heard about that.'

'Your exploits in the late war are much spoken of by officers of the Imperial Navy.' Something about Huang's tone suggested that those officers would dearly love to avenge those exploits.

'As is your feat in getting the better of one of our gun-brigs.'

'The goddess T'ien Hou saw fit to smile on my endeavours.'

'In the Royal Navy we put our faith in steam engines and shell guns as much as in divine intervention.'

'Steam engines and shell guns are no match for karma.'

'Well, the proof of the pudding is in the eating.'

'Indeed, Lieutenant. But one pudding remains half baked.'

'Beware of what you wish for, Admiral. You might just burn your mouth.'

Huang smiled thinly. 'I understand you were one of the officers who captured the notorious pirate Zhai Jing-mu. You are to be congratulated. Many have tried to bring him to justice before.'

'Yourself included? You haven't had much luck there, either. Presumably T'ien Hou didn't see fit to smile on your endeavours?'

'Another pudding which is yet uneaten. While Zhai Jing-mu still breathes he remains a threat. It is more than a month since you captured him, and still we await his execution.'

'You'll have to accept our apologies. In Britain we believe in giving a man a fair trial before we hang him.'

'In China we also have proper legal procedures.'

'Judicial torture, you mean?'

Huang inclined his head. 'You are a clever man, Lieutenant Killigrew. I hope for your sake you are clever enough not to fall foul of it.' Huang turned to Bannatyne. 'Perhaps now you should introduce me to Mr Bonham, Bannatyne-qua?'

'Of course. If you'll excuse us, Mr Killigrew?' The *tai-pan* led Huang across to where the governor stood talking to Mrs Staveley.

Killigrew was still pondering his encounter with Huang when Peri appeared at his side. 'You promised me the second waltz, Kit.'

He turned with a smile. 'Have I missed it already, Peri? I'm sorry. Perhaps the next?'

'I have already promised that to Captain Verran.'

Killigrew glanced across to where Verran had cornered an uncomfortable-looking Mrs Bannatyne. 'From where I'm standing, I'd say Jago's got his hands full as it is.'

'You are a fine one to talk, Kit. I saw you fawning to our hostess in the reception room earlier.'

'I was merely admiring her bust.'

'So I noticed,' Peri said coolly. She gazed around at the gathering. 'It is strange. The last time I attended a ball at the Grafton, Bannatyne and Co. factory here I was only a child. That was when Sir George was *tai-pan*, of course, when we were based in Canton. Tell me, is Sir George as renowned for his balls in London as he was here in Hong Kong?'

'Only the ones he talks in the House of Commons,' Killigrew murmured absent-mindedly.

'What were you discussing with Admiral Huang?'

'Talking shop, I'm afraid. I wouldn't want to bore you.'

She smiled. 'I would rather be bored by you than fascinated by any other man.'

They danced the next waltz together, and when they had finished promenading the band struck up a lively polka. 'Shall we?' suggested Killigrew.

'Oh, no, I could not!'

'You don't know until you've tried. Come on . . . just follow me . . . and *one* two, *one* two . . .'

She struggled at first in her sari, but he supported her. Eventually she fell into the rhythm of the lively step and relaxed enough to enjoy it, laughing with delight as he whirled her round and round. When the polka ended, it was too soon for both of them, although both were breathing hard.

'Oh, Kit! That was wonderful!'

'Aren't you glad I persuaded you to change your mind? You see? You should never close your mind to new experiences.'

'You dance superbly.'

'Better than Dwyer?'

'Why? Are you jealous?'

'Should I be?'

She shook her head, making her curls dance prettily. 'No,' she said, and lowered her voice to a whisper. 'He kept treading on my toes.' She wafted her face with her fan.

'Warm?' he asked her. She nodded. 'Come on.'

He took her by the hand and they slipped through a door. He was unfamiliar with the layout of the factory but he had a good sense of direction and it did not take him long to find the verandah overlooking the landing stage at the back.

It was a warm night for February, even in Hong Kong, and the clear sky above was peppered with stars. The rainy season would not start for a few weeks yet. Across the harbour, the lights of the fishing station at Kowloon glittered in the shimmering waters. A long, low shape glided into the harbour from the direction of the Cap-sing-mun Passage.

'There's a smug boat over there without any lights on,' remarked Killigrew. 'Can't be smugglers . . .'

Peri took him gently by the lapels of his tail-coat and

turned him to face her. 'Are you a customs and excise man now?'

He slipped his hands around her waist and drew her closer. 'Why? Are you carrying any contraband?'

'You will have to search me to find out,' she teased archly.

He drew her closer to him and at the touch of their bodies felt desire well up within him. She pushed back against him so forcefully he had to brace himself against the balustrade. He felt the thrill of mutually recognised need and was about to suggest that they find a more secluded nook where he could carry out his search more fully when he became aware of someone standing in the doorway.

'I came out to tell you that dinner is served,' said Mrs Bannatyne. 'I can see that you're both hungry,' she added drily.

'Pardon me.' Blushing furiously, Peri squeezed past Mrs Bannatyne and went back into the ballroom where the other guests were already filing through to the dining room.

'Your timing *could* be more perfect, ma'am.' Killigrew was about to follow Peri inside when Mrs Bannatyne moved to block his path.

'From whose point of view, Mr Killigrew? Yours? Or Miss Dadabhoy's?'

'I'd rather got the impression that in this instance they were one and the same thing. Or are you concerned that my intentions towards Miss Dadabhoy might not be strictly honourable?'

'It's difficult to see where a romance between a naval officer and the daughter of one of the richest Parsi merchants in the world can go.'

'It's early days yet, but a short walk down the aisle hasn't been ruled out.'

'You think her father would approve of you?'

Killigrew smiled. 'Why? Do you think he'd object to the colour of my skin?'

'I think it's the colour of your money he'd be more concerned about.'

'You do both myself and Miss Dadabhoy an injustice if you think I'd marry her for her money.'

'Then perhaps you should think about how Society back in England would view a naval officer who married an Indian girl.'

'If you knew the first thing about me, Mrs Bannatyne, you'd know I'm not the kind of man who gives a damn what other people think.'

'I'll try to bear that in mind.'

'Hadn't we better go in ourselves, ma'am? The turtle soup will be getting cold. Besides, if we stay out here unchaperoned much longer, it will be *us* people start to talk about.'

'You needn't concern yourself on that account, Mr Killigrew. If they do, I shall be the very first to correct any misapprehensions they may entertain on the subject.'

With a thin smile, Killigrew gestured for her to precede him into the banqueting hall.

Bannatyne might not do much entertaining at the factory, but that had not stopped his architects from building an impressive dining hall, which probably doubled as a boardroom during the day. The grandiose proportions of the pillars which lead up to the vaulted ceiling were clearly designed to awe.

Most of the other guests had already found their places at the immense, damask-covered dining table. A massive silver candelabra dominated as the centrepiece. Footmen were lined up on either side of the hall, as precisely arrayed as guardsmen on parade. Footmen the world over tended to be chosen for their imposing size rather than their competence, but there was something about these which suggested the muscles beneath their uniforms were very real indeed. A broken nose here, a scarred face there, their ramrod-straight backs all hinted that these were veteran sepoys of the Honourable East India Company's army.

Killigrew easily found his place with the other officers of the *Tisiphone*, near the bottom of the table, a long way away from the Framjees who sat with Governor Bonham, General Staveley and Prince Tan near the head of the table, where Bannatyne himself sat. Peri avoided Killigrew's gaze.

The small talk was stilted, as it tended to be at such functions. 'So, you were at Chingkiang-fu, Mr Killigrew?' Bannatyne remarked as the main course – stewed beef *à la jardinière* – was served. He spoke loudly to make himself heard at such a great distance, and the lieutenant had to respond with equal volume, conscious that the conversation was being listened to by everyone at the table, from the governor of Hong Kong down to . . . well, probably himself and Strachan, in order of social rank.

'Yes.' The monosyllable was intended to deter further enquiries.

'You should be more proud of having done military service for your country.'

'You've never done military service, have you, sir?'

Bannatyne smiled. 'My goodness, no. I'm a man of peace. Why do you ask?'

Killigrew shook his head. 'If you had, you would know that military service is nothing to be proud of.'

'A strange thing to say for a young man who has chosen service in Her Majesty's navy as a career.'

'There's more to active service than waging war, sir. Think of all the good work the navy does against slavers and pirates.'

'Making the seas safe for trade,' said Rear-Admiral Collier. 'You should be grateful for that, Bannatyne,' he added, trying to keep his tone jovial.

'When the pilongs cease to be a threat to my shipping, I'll be grateful.'

'That's something we intend to take care of in the very near future, sir, I can assure you,' said Collier.

'I'm glad to hear it,' said Bannatyne. 'But tell me, Mr Killigrew: do you not feel that war can also be an honourable enterprise?'

'It's conceivable, I suppose, though I cannot think of any recent examples in history.'

'What about the war against China? After all, that too was in defence of British trade.'

'Perhaps you should ask Admiral Huang here how *he* feels about having opium smuggled into his country.'

'Are you not a believer in free trade, Mr Killigrew?'

'Oh, I'm a staunch defender of free trade. What I don't approve of is extraterritoriality.'

Bannatyne arched his eyebrows at that and a few of the other European men present looked shocked. 'British law for British subjects? Surely you can have no quarrel with that, Mr Killigrew?'

'British law in British *jurisdiction* would be a more reasonable policy. If a Chinaman were to murder an Englishman in London, would you think it reasonable if the Chinese insisted he were tried by a court of law in Peking?'

'Of course not!' spluttered General Staveley.

'Yet that is exactly the principle we insist on applying when British sailors cause trouble in Canton,' Killigrew pointed out.

'We make sure that justice is done,' asserted a justice of the peace. 'There's no favouritism in my court on account of nationality.'

'Yet we do not trust the Chinese courts, when anyone who has taken the trouble to study the Manchu penal system knows it is much less harsh than our own.'

'To their own people, I dare say . . .' snorted Staveley.

'Interesting that you should express righteous dissatisfaction with the terms insisted upon by your own people in the Unfair Treaties,' said Huang, speaking for the first time during the course of the meal. 'However, I trust that we will all get a fairer picture of British justice when Zhai Jing-mu is put on trial in your admiralty court tomorrow.'

'You may be assured of that,' said Bonham. 'Is it your intention to attend?'

'Regrettably, my own work will keep me in Canton. But I shall follow the law reports in the *Hong Kong Register* most closely. So too, I suspect, will the unrighteous Brotherhood of Heaven, Earth and Man.'

'Who's that?' asked Strachan.

'Triads,' growled Staveley. 'Chinese thugs.'

Bannatyne shook his head. 'The Triads are more than mere criminals, general. You must remember that to many Chinese the Daoguang Emperor, as a member of the Ch'ing Dynasty, is still seen as a foreign invader. The Triads are a political movement, a ruthless, sinister organisation whose tentacles reach into every quarter of society, intent on overturning the social order with no regard for the anarchy into which their own country might subsequently fall.'

'Rather like the Whigs,' elucidated Killigrew, well aware that Bannatyne was the president of the Hong Kong Chapter of the Reform Club.

The *tai-pan* was unamused. 'A good deal more dangerous than the Whigs, Mr Killigrew.'

'Oh, I don't know. Why don't you ask the victims of Lord Palmerston's foreign policy what they think?'

Bannatyne smiled thinly. 'Laugh if you will, Mr Killigrew. But I tell you this: if you intend to testify against Zhai Jing-mu you should watch your step very carefully. The Triads are dangerous and vengeful enemies, and their reach is long.'

'If they try anything here on Hong Kong they'll soon

have cause to regret it,' asserted the justice of the peace.

'You seem to be singularly well-informed about these Triads, Mr Bannatyne,' remarked Killigrew.

'Information is power, Mr Killigrew. In my business it pays to be well informed.'

'I regret to have to contradict what you say,' Huang told the justice of the peace. 'But my information is that since Hong Kong was stolen from the direct control of the Imperial Government by the Unfair Treaties, the island has become a refuge for the worst dregs of the Brotherhood of Heaven, Earth and Man.'

'There was nothing unfair about those treaties!' snapped Staveley. 'If the Chinese weren't so damned arrogant and had accepted the not unreasonable demands of Western trade, then there would have been no need for the war in the first place.'

'There would have been no need for war if the rebellious high-nosed barbarians had not persisted in defying the edicts of the Occupant of the Dragon Throne by perfidiously smuggling their foreign mud into the Celestial Kingdom.'

'Rebellious!' Staveley ignored Bonham's attempts to calm the situation. 'Damn your eyes! Great Britain is a sovereign nation, and not part of your heathen, degenerate, so-called Celestial Empire!'

Huang was on his feet in an instant. 'It is your barbarians who are the degenerates, profaning the Celestial Kingdom with your opium, your war and your missionaries!'

'All right, William,' Bonham told Staveley. 'That will do.'

'Damn it, George, they make me sick!'

'For heaven's sake, General! There are ladies present.'

'I can't help that! Yellow-belly scum, calling us high-nosed barbarians! They're the arrogant ones . . .'

Killigrew glanced at Bannatyne. The *tai-pan* sat back in his seat with a faint smile playing on his lips, as if he was enjoying it all immensely.

‘Oh!’ Mrs Bannatyne threw a faint, doubtless with the specific intention of trying to claw back some semblance of decorum from the shambles of the evening. Verran caught her before she fell from her chair – her cry gave him plenty of warning – and was all gallantry as he wafted a napkin in her face to give her air. The sight of a woman in a sorry plight was enough to make even the general realise he had gone too far, and he sat down, his face as scarlet as his tunic with anger and embarrassment.

Admiral Huang had risen to his feet. ‘I humbly apologise, but I fear this assault on my dignity tonight is beyond harmonious toleration.’

The *tai-pan* stood up and bowed. ‘Please accept my sincerest apologies on behalf of the general—’

‘You’ll do no such thing!’ snarled Staveley.

‘For God’s sake, William!’ hissed Bonham. ‘Haven’t you done enough damage for one night?’

‘I do sincerely regret that this most unpleasant scene should have occurred under my roof,’ Bannatyne told Huang gravely. ‘I must humbly accept all responsibility for what has happened here tonight, and offer my apologies.’ He made a half-hearted attempt to persuade Huang to stay and, when he saw the Chinese admiral was implacable, escorted him to the door.

‘Well done, William,’ Bonham muttered while Bannatyne was out of the room, mopping his brow with his napkin. ‘Another startling diplomatic coup.’

The general was all contrition, but it was too late. Bonham was going to have to spend weeks repairing the damage that had been done in a few short minutes.

The ladies had withdrawn to leave the men to their port and cigars by the time Bannatyne returned. ‘I think I managed to calm him down a little,’ he told Bonham. ‘You know what the Chinese are like. So worried about losing face. No need to be concerned. I’m certain this will all blow over.’

'I wish I shared your optimism,' said Bonham. 'I suppose I shall have to send his excellency some particularly generous gift to smooth it over.'

'You know, sometimes I wonder if we don't bend over backwards a little too far when it comes to handling Chinese sensibilities,' Bannatyne said airily. 'It's not as if we have anything to fear from another war with them. We beat them easily before, we can beat them easily again.'

'Do you think so?' said Killigrew, lighting a cheroot. 'It didn't seem so easy from the battlements of Chingkiang-fu.'

'You're missing the point, Mr Killigrew,' said Bannatyne. 'The fact is that the Chinese have no grasp of reality. Do you know their philosophy of the world? They believe that Heaven is circular, and the world is square. China is that part of the square which benefits from the celestial influences of being directly beneath that circle. All the rest of the world – the corners – are uncivilised in their eyes. To them we're no more than barbarian states which should bow down before them. We'll never be able to trade with them on equal terms until they realise that China isn't the centre of the world.'

'Neither is Great Britain. If we wish to trade with them on equal terms, perhaps we should find something they actually want to buy.'

'There's no question that the Chinese wish to buy opium, Mr Killigrew. The profits of Grafton, Bannatyne and Co. prove that beyond a shadow of a doubt.'

'I was thinking of something more beneficial than opium, Mr Bannatyne. If opium is the best merchandise our culture can offer the Chinese, then perhaps we should accept their view of us as barbarians.'

'You do not consider opium to be beneficial, Mr Killigrew? You would do well to consider that it is the wealth made by men such as myself which makes Britain great. And it is that wealth which pays for the Royal Navy.'

'As it should, since the Royal Navy keeps the seas safe for your opium clippers.'

'I haven't seen much evidence of that recently, Mr Killigrew. Nine opium clippers disappeared between Singapore and Hong Kong last year, three are missing already this year, not counting the one you found attacked by Zhai Jing-mu.'

The carriage clock on the mantelpiece chimed ten. 'Time to rejoin the ladies for coffee, I think,' said Rear-Admiral Collier, shooting Killigrew a warning look. Junior officers were not supposed to bandy words with respected citizens like Blase Bannatyne.

An upper-storey verandah facing across the harbour had been chosen to stand in for a drawing room. Killigrew found himself seated on the opposite side of the verandah from Peri and exchanged private smiles with her as one of the older ladies lectured on the uselessness of Chinese as servants. Peri was looking lovelier than ever tonight and as he gazed at her Killigrew reached a decision: there was no doubt in his mind that he wanted to spend the rest of his life with her. To hell with the navy, with Society, with the whole damned bigoted bunch of snobs: he would propose to her. Not tonight – he wanted to do it properly; Hartcliffe would lend him the money for an engagement ring. He would get a civil licence from the superintendent-registrar: he could not see Peri wanting to get married in a Christian church, and he had never had his heart set on a church wedding.

Assuming, of course, she accepted his proposal. Whatever she thought or said, it was a hard life for the wife of a naval officer, being left alone for years at a time. If he loved her, could he do that to her?

But the solution, he knew, was obvious.

He broke off his reverie when he realised that Bannatyne had risen to his feet and was making an announcement. 'Ladies and gentlemen, I hope you won't take exception, but in order to make tonight a particularly memorable occasion I've laid on an unusual entertainment which I hope you'll all find diverting . . .'

'Doesn't he think it's been memorable enough already?' Killigrew murmured to Strachan.

'If you'll please follow me through . . .' said Bannatyne.

Killigrew noticed that Mrs Bannatyne looked distinctly uncomfortable – he wondered if she was going to be asked to entertain them at the pianoforte – but when they all trooped back to the compound he saw at once that Bannatyne had something else in mind. Row upon row of chairs had been set up facing the stage where the orchestra had played earlier in a quarter-circle, with an aisle running through them at an angle. On the stage itself there was a scene which suggested some kind of building repairs were in progress: and there were curious arrangements of bricks, trestles and thick wooden planks.

Once everyone was seated, the biggest Chinese Killigrew had ever seen entered, dressed in some kind of white pyjama suit, his buttonless jacket fastened only with a black girdle tied around his waist, the gap above revealing a triangle of a smooth, glistening chest with well-defined muscles. It was hardly the kind of sight Killigrew expected to be offered after a meal. Instead of wearing his hair in the Manchu queue like every other Chinaman Killigrew had ever seen, this one wore a thick, black mop in the Western-style, parted to one side.

'Ladies and gentlemen, allow me to introduce my comprador, Shen Meng-fu,' said Bannatyne. 'Mr Shen has generously agreed to give us a demonstration of the ancient Chinese martial art of *wu-yi*. When you are ready, Mr Shen?'

Shen picked up three thick planks of wood and handed one each to Bonham, General Staveley, and Killigrew.

'If you would examine the planks, gentlemen, to confirm for yourselves that they are indeed ordinary pieces of timber, uninterfered with, and that there is no kind of trickery involved in what you are about to see,' said Bannatyne.

*So that's it*, thought Killigrew. *A magic show.* He stifled a yawn and examined his plank, although he did not expect to find anything. If there was anything to see, he would not have been allowed to handle it.

Shen gathered in the planks and laid the three of them one atop another across the trestles. Then he stood behind the trestle, took three deep breaths, and suddenly brought the edge of his hand down against the planks with a primeval yell which made some of the ladies present – and a few of the men – squeal in fright.

All three planks had been broken in the middle.

'Good God!' exclaimed Staveley.

'It must be some kind of trick,' said Strachan. 'There's something up his sleeve . . .'

'No trickery, I assure you, ladies and gentlemen,' said Bannatyne. 'Mr Shen, roll up your sleeves and show your arms to these people.'

Mr Shen did just that. His forearms were like hocks of ham. He crossed to where a small block of masonry rested across another trestle. He gave another cry and brought his forehead down against it sharply. There was a loud crack, and the block crashed to the floor in two pieces.

'*Wu-yi*, ladies and gentlemen,' said Bannatyne, as the audience applauded uncertainly. 'The power of mind over matter.'

The demonstration lasted about five minutes, and even Killigrew could not help but be impressed as Shen smashed thick boards, bricks and masonry blocks with no more than his bare hands and feet, apparently without injury to himself.

'For the next part of our demonstration, Mr Shen requires the assistance of someone from our audience,' said Bannatyne. As a showman, he could have given Mr P. T.

Barnum a run for his money. 'Mr Killigrew, perhaps you would care to step up?'

'That depends.' Killigrew rose to his feet. 'He's not going to put *me* across one of those trestles, is he?'

Smiling, Bannatyne shook his head. 'A demonstration of the "iron shirt", ladies and gentlemen. *Wu-yi* experts must learn the technique of receiving blows as well as giving them. Are you a practitioner of the noble art of pugilism, Mr Killigrew?'

'Not if I can help it. Fencing's more my cup of char.'

'But a young man with your widespread military experience must have some knowledge of hand-to-hand combat. I dare say you think you can deliver a powerful blow with your bare hands?'

'I have been known to, when the necessity arose.'

Bannatyne indicated Shen. 'Please demonstrate.'

'And have him chop me up like so much lumber?'

'Mr Shen will not retaliate. He will stand perfectly still and allow you to strike him wherever you will. Perhaps I can offer you a set of brass knuckles?'

'Not the sort of assistance a gentleman requires, I assure you.' Killigrew unbuttoned his tail-coat and handed it to Strachan.

'So be it.' Bannatyne gestured to Shen once more. The Chinese stood with every muscle in his body tensed, his feet braced squarely on the ground.

'And he won't hit me back?'

'You have my word on it, Mr Killigrew.'

The lieutenant squared up to Shen. Killigrew was tall, even for a European, but Shen met him eye to eye, and was nearly half as broad again across the shoulders. Killigrew half turned back to Bannatyne. 'There's just one thing I don't understand . . .' he said, and in the same breath turned back to Shen and drove his fist into his solar plexus with all his might.

As Bannatyne had surmised, Killigrew had picked up a

few pugilistic tricks, and he kept himself in good shape. He knew a blow like that should have brought even a fit young man to his knees. But it was like punching a block of rubber. Shen did not even flinch, except to crack his smooth face into a smile.

Killigrew stepped back and shook his hand before flexing his fingers. He suspected the blow had hurt himself more than it had hurt the Chinese. 'Of course, in a real fight I would be more inclined to go for the face,' he said, knowing he was just making excuses now.

'Please try it,' said Mr Bannatyne. 'Once again, I assure you Mr Shen will not retaliate.'

Killigrew drove his fist at Shen's face and put all his strength behind the blow. One of Shen's hands whipped up as fast as a cobra, caught Killigrew's fist and stopped it dead in its tracks.

As a final demonstration, Shen turned and drove a hand through a wooden board: not a fist, but his *outstretched fingertips*. The board splintered effortlessly. He turned back to Killigrew with a smile which seemed to say: *I could do the same to your ribcage*.

Killigrew returned his smile. 'Very impressive,' he said, reaching into his pocket for a guinea. 'What does he do for an encore? Sing a couple of choruses from "Oh Rest Thee, My Darling"?' He tossed the coin on the stage at Shen's feet. 'There's a shiner for your trouble.'

Shen merely folded his arms across his brawny chest with a look of disdain.

'Don't think that Mr Shen can be bought, Mr Killigrew,' Bannatyne said coldly. 'I pay him extraordinarily well.'

'If he's so strong, let him prove it by picking up the coin.'

For the first time a look of helplessness entered Shen's eyes.

Killigrew smiled. 'He can't, can he? His *wu-yi* has so toughened the skin on his hands he's lost all sensitivity in them. Such a skill is not won without great cost. One thing I have learned in the navy, Mr Bannatyne. Brute strength is no match for subtlety and intelligence.'

Shen left the coin on the ground and stomped inside.

'I don't need to employ anyone to be subtle or intelligent on my behalf, Mr Killigrew,' Bannatyne said tightly.

Killigrew took back his tail-coat from Strachan and shrugged it on. He was still buttoning it up with a sense of satisfaction when Shen returned from the banqueting hall with a dab of gravy on the tip of his finger. He bent down and pressed it against the coin. When he lifted the finger, the coin had stuck to his fingertip long enough for him to be able to pinch it between thumb and forefinger.

Some of the spectators applauded. 'Oh, I say!' exclaimed Framjee. 'That's jolly clever!'

Jago Verran grinned. 'What were you saying about subtlety and intelligence, Kit?'

Glaring at Killigrew, Shen exerted pressure on the coin between his fingers until his whole arm trembled and the veins stood out in his forehead. Just when Killigrew thought the Chinese was going to have a seizure, the coin snapped with a sound like a musket-shot. The impressive effect was marred by the way one half of the coin shot across the room, narrowly missing Mrs Staveley's head and bringing down one of the Chinese lanterns which promptly burst into flames. Two footmen hurriedly ran across to stamp it out.

'Damn it, man!' General Staveley snarled at Bannatyne. 'Your trained monkey almost had my wife's eye out! Enough of this damned tomfoolery!'

'All right, Shen, you can go,' snapped Bannatyne, his face flushed.

'I think we can all go,' said Bonham. 'We've seen enough.'

Bannatyne remained in the compound as everyone filed in to the reception room. His wife escorted them and a footman handed out hats. No one congratulated her on the ball, except Killigrew, who hung back long enough to make sure he was the last to leave. 'Capital ball, ma'am,' he said as he set his cocked hat on his head at a rakish angle. 'Are all your parties this much of a lark?'

She smiled thinly and gestured to the door. Grinning, he touched the prow of his hat in salute to her, and then strolled out after the others.

He tripped lightly down the steps into the compound. Most of the carriages had already gone. He caught up with Strachan. 'The others have gone ahead,' said the assistant surgeon.

Killigrew nodded. The two of them were about to walk through the gate when the last carriage rattled up behind them. Killigrew pulled Strachan back out of harm's way, but the Sikh coachman had seen them and reined in. Sir Dadabhoy Framjee leaned out of the window.

'Can I give you and your friend a ride, Mr Killigrew? Perhaps you would care to join Peri and I for a drink before we part? It is still quite early.'

Killigrew and Strachan exchanged glances; there was no need for anything to be said. 'We'd be delighted,' Killigrew told Framjee as he and his friend sat down opposite Framjee and his daughter. The Parsi rapped the ferrule of his cane on the floor of the victoria and they rattled off. 'Well, I don't know about the rest of you, but I've certainly enjoyed this evening,' said Killigrew.

'Indeed!' beamed Framjee. 'It is wrong of me, I know, but I certainly enjoyed watching Bannatyne's first attempt at a ball end in disaster. I wonder if tonight's events will have put him off hosting any more?'

'Only time will tell, sir. But somehow I think he'll get over tonight's humiliation.'

At length the coachman reined in the horses in front of Framjee's villa. As they climbed down from the carriage, the butler emerged from the house to greet them.

'We'll take coffee in the drawing room, Gobinda,' Framjee told him as they passed inside, and turned to Strachan. 'I understand you are an artist, Mr Strachan.'

'Well, I wouldn't go that far, sir. I used to dabble a little; sketches and that sort of stuff. These days photography's more my game, though I still do the occasional aquatint.'

'Do you think it is true that photography will replace painting altogether?'

'I don't know. I think art will have to become more innovative to stay ahead if it's going to survive. The camera can only show what it sees, but the artist can see so much more, tell the story behind the picture.' When it came to art, Strachan displayed the same enthusiasm he had towards fossils. 'In fact, I think there's a chance photography could be the saving of art. It's been getting awfully stale of late.'

'We have some of Mr Chinnery's landscapes in the upper gallery, if you would care to see them?'

'I'd be delighted.'

Framjee turned to his daughter. 'Peri, perhaps you'd care to show Mr Strachan while I have a word with Mr Killigrew here?'

Killigrew nodded to himself. He had been wondering what Framjee's motive in inviting him back here so late had been. Now he had a pretty good idea. So did Peri, if the concerned glance she gave him over her shoulder as she led Strachan upstairs was any indication.

Framjee had opened the door to his library and gestured for Killigrew to precede him. Inside, the Parsi sat down behind his desk with his fingers steepled. He did not invite Killigrew to sit. 'I wish to speak to you about Peri. And your intentions towards her.'

'Strictly honourable, sir, I assure you.'

'I do not doubt it. But I am wondering if your concept of what is and what is not honourable is the same as those accepted by most other people. You are aware, I take it, that her religion forbids her from marrying anyone other than another Parsi?'

Killigrew smiled. 'I could convert.'

'You could become a Zarathustrian. But you could never become a Parsi. Unless both your parents were Parsis, which I must confess I very much doubt.'

'She could convert.'

'She could. If she wished so. But my Peri is very proud of her heritage.' Framjee opened a drawer in his desk and took out a cheque. He dipped his pen in an inkwell and started to write.

'Don't you think that's for your daughter to decide?' Killigrew asked coldly.

'What kind of father would I be if I did not concern myself about what is best for my daughter?' Framjee dried the cheque with blotting paper and handed it to Killigrew. It was made out for five thousand pounds.

The lieutenant resisted the urge to let out a low whistle. 'A princely sum. I'm not sure whether to be flattered or insulted.'

'I am not asking you never to see her again. But I would be happier if you faced the fact that there can be no future for you and my daughter. No more unchaperoned walks together, eh, Mr Killigrew?'

The lieutenant slowly and deliberately tore up the cheque, scattering the pieces across the top of Framjee's desk. 'I can't be bought.'

The Parsi reached for another cheque. 'Every man has his price,' he said, dipping his pen into the inkwell once more.

'Don't bother. Mine isn't money.'

Framjee sighed and drained the ink from his nib before replacing the pen in its holder. 'You are a man of principle, Mr Killigrew. I respect you for that. To tell the truth, I think I would have been disappointed if you *had* accepted my cheque. Then let me conclude by asking you, as a man of honour, to bear in mind all the consequences for my daughter if you persist in your attentions towards her.'

'I don't need to be told to do that. Harming her is the last thing on my mind.'

'I appreciate that. But it is often the case that common sense does not get a fair hearing when passions rule the day.'

'The one must be balanced against the other,' allowed Killigrew. 'Now if you'll excuse me, sir, I think it's time I returned to the *Tisiphone*.'

Framjee inclined his head. The two of them went upstairs to the gallery where they found Peri and Strachan admiring a watercolour of Victoria Harbour.

'Come on, Strachan,' said Killigrew. 'We've outstayed our welcome.'

Peri looked at him with concern. 'Is everything all right?'

'Everything is fine, my child,' said Framjee. 'Mr Killigrew and I had some business to attend to. Now it is concluded, he feels it is appropriate he leaves. I am in agreement.'

'I thought we were staying for a dram?' protested Strachan.

'Come on.' Killigrew took his friend by the arm and all but dragged him back downstairs. The butler showed them out.

'Take care, gentlemen,' Framjee called after them. 'Victoria is a dangerous place at night.'

'Don't worry about us, sir,' said Strachan. 'It's only five minutes' walk to the waterfront from here. What can possibly go wrong in that time?'

'What did you say to him?' Peri demanded as her father returned inside and Gobinda closed the door behind him.

Framjee said nothing, but walked softly to the drawing room. Peri followed him. 'Father, what did you say to upset him like that?'

Her father sat down on the divan and rubbed his temples wearily.

'You tried to buy him off, didn't you?' persisted Peri. 'That is it, is it not? You offered him money.'

Framjee nodded.

She turned away, not even trusting herself to look at her father. 'Oh, how could you? You always said I could marry whom I chose, just as Mother defied her parents to marry you!'

'I never thought you would choose a penniless British naval officer!'

'Am I a chattel, to be bought and sold like a slave girl?'

'I only want what is best for you, my child. That is all I have ever wanted for you.'

'Do you not think I am able to judge what is best for me?'

'Are you not curious to know what he said?'

She turned back to face him.

'He tore the cheque up and threw it back at me.'

She stared at him, not sure if she had heard him right. 'He did that?'

Framjee nodded. 'A cheque for five thousand pounds, and he tore it up without hesitation. When I offered to write him another, made out to any amount he cared to name, he still refused. He must love you very much, my child.'

She saw down beside him and clasped his hands. 'And I love him, Father.'

'If you married him, you would be an outcast from your own people.'

'And from you, Father?'

'No, my child. You will always be my daughter. But I cannot have my daughter married to a penniless naval officer, so . . . I fear your dowry will have to be very generous indeed.'

She hugged him. 'Oh, Father!'

'Be still, my child! He has not yet asked for your hand!'

'Oh, but he will if I tell him we have your blessing.'

'I think if Mr Killigrew has it in his mind to marry you, he will do so with or without my blessing.' Framjee chuckled. 'Just as I married your mother. But I do not think it would be a good idea to tell him that I will pay any dowry. If he loves you he will need no encouragement, and he would not want people to think he had married you for money.'

'He'll ask, Father. I know he will!'

'What was all that about?' Strachan asked Killigrew as they ambled down Caine Road towards the top of Ladder Street. 'No, wait, let me guess: he was trying to buy you off, wasn't he?'

'If he was, that's between Sir Dadabhoy and myself.'

'I'll bet he was. How much did he offer you?'

'None of your damned business.'

'She's a braw lassie,' Strachan admitted. 'I hope you don't mind me asking, Killigrew, but what . . .?'

'If you're going to lecture me, please don't,' said Killigrew. 'I had enough of that tonight from Mrs Bannatyne and Sir Dadabhoy.'

'Ah. I noticed our hostess looked a little flushed when the two of you came in to dinner tonight. I wasn't sure if you'd been rowing or spooning with her.'

'I never get involved with married women.'

'More fool you. She deserves better than that smug bastard Bannatyne . . . Do you think she really sculpted that bust of Genghis Khan?'

'Why not?'

'Because it's damned good, that's why. As good as any modern sculpture I've ever seen, and better than most. You know, I rather liked her.'

'You want to bed her, you mean.'

'Please, Killigrew. Just this once could you credit me with having finer feelings?'

They walked down Ladder Street in silence. 'I'm

thinking of resigning my commission,' Killigrew suddenly announced.

Strachan stopped and turned to stare at him. 'I beg your pardon?'

'I said: I'm thinking of resigning my commission.'

'You? Leave the navy? That'll be the day!'

'Why not? My Uncle William's always pressing me to work for his company in the City. I'd get paid six times what I'm earning at the moment.'

'And you'd die of boredom within a week. How long have I known you, Killigrew? Two years? The navy's your life. You're never happier than when you're chasing slavers or crossing swords with pirates. You think you'd get the same kind of satisfaction from some sinecure in the City?'

'A City job would leave me more time for other pursuits. Charitable works. Politics, perhaps. I'm always mocking politicians for being corrupt; perhaps it's time I stood for office myself, introduced a bit of decency into the House of Commons.'

'You wouldn't last five minutes in Parliament. What, do you want to become everything you despise? Someone like Blase Bannatyne and Sir George Grafton?'

'I'm more worried I'll become everything I despise if I stay in the service much longer, Strachan. I tell myself I fight the slavers and the pirates because it's the right thing to do; but is it? I kill them as ruthlessly as they kill their victims. Am I really any better than them?'

'Yes, you are, and you damned well know it.' Strachan narrowed his eyes shrewdly. 'This isn't about pirates and slavers, is it? This is about Miss Dadabhoy.'

'I don't know what you mean, I'm sure.'

'You're going to ask her to marry you, aren't you? That's why you want to leave the service: you don't want her to live the life of a naval officer's wife.'

Killigrew sighed and thrust his hands into his pockets. 'If she marries me, she'll no longer be accepted as a Parsi.

If she's prepared to make that kind of sacrifice, isn't it fair that I make a sacrifice in turn?'

'She's a lovely girl, Killigrew. Damn me, I'm envious. But have you really considered what you'd be giving up? I mean, *really* considered?'

Before Killigrew could reply, a shot sounded nearby. 'That was a firecracker, wasn't it?' Strachan said nervously. 'It's the Chinese New Year about now, isn't it? Please tell me that was a firecracker.'

'There was no firecracker.'

'I was afraid you were going to say that. Maybe it would be best if we didn't get involved . . .'

'It sounded as if it came from the direction of the gaol. You run to the barracks and raise the alarm.'

'Good idea,' Strachan said with relief. He took a few hurried steps down Hollywood Road, and then stopped and turned back. 'Killigrew? You're not going to do anything . . . *rash* . . . are you?'

'You know me, Strachan.'

'In other words, "yes".' The assistant surgeon sighed and set off for the barracks at a sprint.

Killigrew strode towards the gaol. He was halfway there when another muffled shot sounded somewhere up ahead. He broke into a run and a moment later there came a third shot.

He rounded the next corner and saw the gaol immediately ahead of him, its barred windows a blaze of light, the door wide open. The smell of gunsmoke was heavy on the air, and he could smell something else: something sulphurous.

Conscious that the only weapon he had was his dress-sword, he drew it from its scabbard and dashed across the street to press himself up against the wall by the door. He listened for a moment. Inside, all was silent. He peered through the door and jerked his head back quickly, but in that split second he had seen enough to reassure him that no one had a gun lined up on the door. He took a deep breath and dashed through, turning as soon as he was inside to make sure that no one was lurking in wait just inside.

There was no one in sight. He took a step closer to the counter and felt something crunch under his foot. Glancing down he saw that the floor was covered in pottery shards: stink-pots.

It was a favourite trick of the pilongs to make grenades by filling small earthenware pots with a combustible mixture of brimstone, gunpowder, nitre, bitumen, rosin and other noxious substances. A fuse was inserted in the neck and lit before the stink-pot was thrown on to the deck of another vessel. The explosion was usually sufficient to daze and choke everyone within ten yards for a few seconds, and if enough stink-pots were thrown it gave the pilongs time to board the vessel unopposed. Whoever had attacked the gaol had simply used the same tactic on land.

Killigrew leaned over the counter and craned his head to look through the doorway behind. There was no one in the next room, but he spotted a puddle of blood on the floor beneath him.

Sword in hand, he vaulted over the counter. The Sikh constable whose body had been shoved under the counter had been all but decapitated by a sword-stroke.

His heart pounding, Killigrew slipped into the next room and found two more constables, as savagely murdered as the first had been. He was about to go back and wait outside for Strachan to return with reinforcements when he heard a muffled sound from the door leading to the back of the building. Still gripping his sword, he took another deep breath and dived through.

The Triad waited for him with a crossbow lined up on the doorway from the far end of the corridor. Killigrew froze, knowing he could not hope to kill the man with a sword at that distance. He braced himself for the shot – at that range there was a good chance the pilong might miss.

A moment later something connected with the back of his neck. He dropped the sword and sank to his knees. Another blow struck him on the back of the head, and the last thing he saw before the cobwebs of oblivion wrapped him in their coils was the floor rushing up to meet him.

# *VII:*

# *Wu-Yi*

---

The gig bumped against the *Tisiphone*'s side, and Robertson, Hartcliffe, Westlake, Vellacott and Muir climbed up the side-ladder to the entry port. At the top, Robertson turned to address the coxswain. 'You'd better row back to the wharf and wait for Killigrew and Strachan, Ågård.'

'Aye, aye, sir. All right, lads, you heard him. Shove off and give way together.'

There were three men in the gig in addition to Ågård: Molineaux, Dando and O'Connor. They pulled for the wharf and Molineaux jumped on to the stone steps cut in the quayside to tie the gig's painter to an iron ring.

O'Connor produced his pipe and lit it. 'All right then, Wes, what's all this I hear about you going to the rescue of some yellow-belly lass?'

'You know me, Joe. Never could resist going to the aid of a damsel in distress.'

'Is it true what they'm be saying?' asked Dando.

'About what?'

'About Chinese girls being . . . different . . . to English lasses.'

'In what way?'

'Well, you know how English lasses be . . . rigged fore

and aft . . . down below? Be it true that Chinese girls be rigged athwartships?'

'Rigged athwartships . . . Jem, where the hell do you come up with this hogwash?'

'Well? Be it true? Or didn't you find out?'

'That ain't the kind of question a gentleman answers.'

'Arr, but you bain't be no gentleman.'

'What the hell's going on over there?' asked Ågård suddenly. He was narrowing his eyes to where a group of figures had just emerged from a side-street and were dashing through the darkness to where a smug boat was tied up at the next wharf. Molineaux heard voices calling out in Cantonese.

'Trouble,' he said, well aware that the Chinese were not allowed to wander the streets of Victoria after curfew without a light and a pass from their employer.

'I reckon we'd best stay here and wait for Tom Tidley and the assistant sawbones,' O'Connor said nervously.

'You can wait here,' said Molineaux. 'I'm going to investigate.' He hurried across the waterfront followed by Ågård, Dando and a reluctant O'Connor. 'Hey!' he called out as they drew near. 'Anyone here speakee English?'

The dozen or so shadowy figures on the wharf froze. Out of the corner of his eye, Molineaux saw something fizzle on the gunwale of the smug boat. 'Swivel!' he yelled.

The four seamen threw themselves to the ground a moment before the swivel gun boomed. Molineaux felt something sting his left buttock, but he was on his feet a moment later. The Chinese on the dock made a dash for the gangplank leading down to the smug boat's deck, but Molineaux caught one around the waist in a flying tackle and brought him down. The two of them rolled over and over, until Molineaux knocked his opponent unconscious with a punch to the jaw.

He looked up. The other three seamen were getting stuck in. Molineaux recognised Zhai Jing-mu amongst the men hurrying for the boat as the mooring ropes were cast off. He went after him and got halfway down the gang-plank before one of the Triads came up to meet him: a young, rather effeminate-looking Chinese. Like most of his race, he was not tall, and he was less muscular than many of his compatriots. This one looked as though a slight breeze might be enough to blow him down.

Molineaux reached behind him and pulled his Bowie knife from a sheath he wore in the small of his back. 'Out of my way!'

'You go to hell!' the Chinese snapped back. He jumped into the air. One foot connected with Molineaux's wrist, dashing the Bowie knife from his grip, while the other smashed into his jaw. He staggered and had to seize the hand-rope to stop himself from falling in the water.

The Chinese seized his advantage and charged forwards, delivering a succession of rib-jarring blows to his chest. Molineaux managed to land a lucky punch on the Chinese's jaw. The pilong staggered back and stepped off the gangplank. Molineaux glanced down and saw the Chinese catch hold of the side of the gangplank, swinging underneath it as nimbly as an acrobat. As Molineaux bent over to try to see where he had gone, the Chinese's feet connected with his buttocks. The seaman was knocked forwards and plunged headfirst into the water.

When he surfaced he saw the gangplank being taken on board while the oars were lowered from the smug boat's sides. One of them nearly brained him. He grabbed hold of it in a futile attempt to impede the boat's progress. A figure appeared at the gunwale above him and a moment later a pistol cracked with a flash and a bullet kicked up a spurt of water only inches from where Molineaux trod water. He relinquished his hold on the oar and ducked beneath the waves.

By the time he had surfaced the smug boat was already fifty yards away, the oarsmen pulling strongly for the harbour mouth. Molineaux punched the water in frustration and swam back to the dock where Ågård helped him out. 'You all right, Wes?'

'I got shot in the bum, kicked in the nut and knocked in the drink,' snarled Molineaux. 'Do I look oh-kay to you?'

Ågård grinned. 'You'll survive.'

Molineaux reached inside his trousers to explore his stinging buttock gingerly. There was no blood: the pellet which had hit him must have ricocheted off the quayside first. He glanced about the waterfront. Dando was nursing a cut on his arm while O'Connor tied up the pilong Molineaux had knocked out. 'Well, at least we got one of them,' said Ågård.

Molineaux bent to retrieve his Bowie knife, which had fallen on the quayside. 'But we let Zhai Jing-mu get away.'

The first indication Killigrew had that he was still alive was the pain. It coursed through the very fibre of his being, through every limb and nerve-ending, but it was concentrated in a pounding ache in the back of his skull.

He lay still for a moment, listening, but heard nothing. Opening an eye fractionally, he saw only the floor of the corridor. His sword lay a foot away. He snatched it up and jumped to his feet, but there was no one else in sight. Then the intensified throbbing in his skull forced him to slump to the floor once more, his back to the wall. Feeling sick and woozy, he checked his fob watch: a quarter past midnight. He could not have been unconscious for more than a couple of minutes, but it had been enough time for the Triads to make good their escape.

He reached inside his coat, produced a cheroot and lit it. The rich taste of the tobacco helped to stimulate him enough to find the strength to rise to his feet.

'Who's there?' a voice called from one of the offices leading off the corridor.

'Lieutenant Killigrew, HMS *Tisiphone*.'

‘You! What the deuce are you doing here?’

Killigrew recognised Cargill’s voice. He staggered into the office and found the assistant superintendent braced behind a cabinet with a single-shot percussion pistol held in both hands.

‘I was on my way back from the ball at Bannatyne’s when I heard shooting. Thought I’d better come and investigate.’

‘I’m glad you did. You must’ve frightened them off.’

‘Zhai Jing-mu?’

‘Let’s check, shall we?’ Cargill produced a bunch of keys and led the way downstairs to the cells. Killigrew noticed that the policeman was limping, bleeding from a wound in his leg.

‘What happened to you?’

‘Hmm?’ Cargill glanced down at his leg. ‘Oh, that’s nothing. Just a scratch.’

Still feeling groggy, Killigrew rubbed the back of his head. ‘They knocked me out. Why the devil didn’t they kill me when they had the chance?’

They stepped into the lock-up. The cells were all empty. ‘Because they got what they came for?’ Cargill suggested bitterly.

‘The man I saw wore the same clothes as those Triads who attacked me in the joss house,’ said Killigrew.

Cargill nodded. ‘Looks like you were right, Killigrew. The Triads and the pilongs are working hand in glove. I should have listened to you.’

‘Would it have made any difference?’

‘Probably not,’ Cargill admitted ruefully, and then slammed his fist against the stone wall. ‘Damn it to blazes! How could I have let this happen?’

Killigrew remembered the smug boat he had seen from the terrace of Bannatyne’s house. ‘Maybe he hasn’t got away yet. I saw a smug boat in the harbour. That must be how they’re planning to get away from Hong Kong, while we’re still too stunned to do anything about it.’

'You're right, by George!' Cargill led the way back upstairs. They dashed out of the gaol and a moment later a musket-shot sounded. Killigrew felt the ball whip-crack through the air close to his head and flung himself down on the ground.

'Hold your fire, damn your eyes!' shouted someone. 'They're English!'

Killigrew raised his head and saw a squad of a dozen sepoys with Lieutenant Dwyer and Strachan. He pushed himself to his feet and helped Cargill up after him.

'What happened?' asked Dwyer.

'Gaolbreak,' said Killigrew. 'We think they're heading for the harbour.'

'Come on, then.'

By the time they reached the waterfront the smug boat had long gone. The only figure on the quayside was Molineaux, seated on a low shape. The seaman stood up and put one foot on the shape. Killigrew recognised it as a Triad.

'Good evening, Molineaux.' He indicated the seaman's prisoner. 'Seen any more like that?'

''Bout a dozen of 'em, sir. Our old sparring partner Zhai Jing-mu was with 'em. They jumped on to a smug boat and cut and ran. Olly, Jem and Joe went back aboard the *Tisiphone* in the gig to alert the cap'n.'

Killigrew glanced across the harbour to see that the *Tisiphone* was under sail, moving out from her anchorage. But the wind was light, the sails sagging limply from the yards, and there was no sign of the smug boat. Such vessels were also known as 'fast boats' with good reason. The *Tisiphone* would have had her fires banked, and it would be some time before she could get steam up.

'Damn it!' Killigrew rammed his dress-sword back in its scabbard with a gesture of frustration.

'But apart from that, sir, how did you enjoy the ball?' asked Molineaux.

★ ★ ★

With the *Tisiphone* off on its futile pursuit of Zhai Jing-mu, there was nothing for it but for Killigrew and Strachan to spend the night at the Hong Kong Club, where Lieutenant Dwyer signed them in as guests.

Killigrew was so tired he fell fast asleep at once, but he was troubled by nightmares. He slept fitfully until the creeping light of dawn slipped through the louvres on the window to tickle him awake long before one of the club stewards came to rouse him. He shaved, washed and dressed – back in his dress uniform – and made his way downstairs to take breakfast on the verandah. Presently Strachan joined him, yawning, blinking owlishly, his hair every which way but flat. The assistant surgeon was not a morning person.

'Is the *Tisiphone* back yet?'

Killigrew had already surveyed the ships in the harbour and he did not bother to look up from his newspaper. 'Not yet.' He was nursing a pounding headache and his neck felt as though it had been put through a wringer. Whoever had hit him the previous night had a punch like a steam-hammer.

Strachan slumped into a chair in time to order devilled kidneys for breakfast, while Killigrew preferred scrambled eggs on toast. They were reading the morning papers over a pot of tea when Lieutenant Dwyer entered.

'Good morning, gentlemen. I trust you slept well?'

'As well as can be expected,' said Killigrew. 'Will you join us for a cup of tea?'

'I do believe I shall.' He signalled for a flunkey to bring a third cup and saucer. While the tea was being poured out, one of the white-coated club porters approached the table with three envelopes on a silver salver. He placed the salver on the table. 'Hullo,' said Dwyer, shuffling the envelopes. 'One for you here, Killigrew.'

Killigrew tore open his letter. 'Ah. From Rear-Admiral

Collier. He wants me to report to him on board the *Hastings* at nine.'

'You too, eh?' Dwyer held up one of his letters, an almost exact replica of the one Killigrew held, before opening the other.

'How come I don't get invited?' asked Strachan.

'Be grateful,' Killigrew told him. 'After last night's fiasco, I don't think anything the admiral's going to have to say to us is likely to be complimentary.' He glanced across and saw Dwyer frown as he perused his other letter. 'Bad news?'

Dwyer glanced up, quickly folded the envelope and tucked it inside his jacket. 'No. Possibly good news, actually. What time do you make it?'

'Nearly eight o'clock. We'd better get underway if we're to report to the admiral on time.' Killigrew dabbed his lips with a napkin and rose to his feet, leading the way outside. Under the portico in front of the club, Dwyer seemed to hesitate.

'Not coming with us, Lieutenant?' asked Killigrew.

'Erm . . . no. Give the admiral my apologies, would you? I'm afraid I've got another appointment.'

Army officers were not at the beck and call of the navy; nevertheless, it was not done for a mere lieutenant to snub a rear-admiral. But if that was what Dwyer intended to do, that was his business, no matter how curious Killigrew might find it. 'All right. We'll see you later, perhaps.'

Killigrew and Strachan found Molineaux waiting for them outside the gates to the club grounds. 'Good God, Molineaux!' exclaimed Killigrew. 'You haven't been out here all night, have you? I do apologise for my thoughtlessness, if I'd known . . . You really should have said something . . .'

'Not me, sir. I spent the night on a *yolo*.'

'This wouldn't be the same *yolo* on which you had your little altercation with Captain Ingersoll, would it?'

Molineaux grinned. 'That'd be telling, sir.'

As the three of them made their way down to the wharf they saw the *Tisiphone* returning to harbour under steam. 'Think you can persuade your Tanka girl to take us back?'

'A dollar could do it better than me, sir.'

As Mei-rong sculled Killigrew, Strachan and Molineaux back to the steam-sloop, the signals flew thick and fast between the *Tisiphone* and the *Hastings*. Commander Robertson was likewise being summoned into the presence of the rear-admiral; it was reassuring for Killigrew that he would not have to face Collier's wrath alone.

The *yolo* bumped against the *Tisiphone*'s side and Killigrew paid Mei-rong a dollar before following Strachan and Molineaux up the side-ladder. Hartcliffe awaited them on deck.

'I'm damnably sorry, Killigrew. I'm afraid that devil gave us the slip. We spent all night looking for him, but he just vanished into thin air.'

Killigrew shook his head. 'There must be a thousand creeks and inlets within ten miles of here that haven't been charted, and I'll lay odds Zhai Jing-mu knows them all like the back of his hand.'

Robertson came up on deck and the gig was lowered from its davits to carry him and Killigrew across to the *Hastings*. The gig reached the flagship's accommodation ladder first and Robertson and Killigrew climbed up to the quarterdeck where they found the *Hastings*' commander, Captain Francis Morgan, awaiting them.

'You're a couple of minutes early, gentlemen.'

'We didn't want to keep the admiral waiting, sir.'

A dour, strait-laced, humourless man, the very antithesis of the Captain Morgan of buccaneering fame, Morgan sniffed and escorted the two of them down to the admiral's quarters. He knocked on the door.

'Who is it?'

'Morgan, sir, with Commander Robertson and Lieutenant Killigrew to see you, sir.'

'Show them in.' Collier's voice sounded deceptively mild. *The calm before the storm*, thought Killigrew.

Morgan ushered them inside. Collier sat at the table in his day room, going over some paperwork. He did not look up as the three men stood to attention before him. Collier made another note in the margin of the report he was reading before he spoke, still without looking up. 'Where's Lieutenant Dwyer?'

'Had another appointment, sir,' said Killigrew.

Collier glanced up at him. He was a choleric man and he did not look pleased. 'Oh, did he?' he said heavily. 'Well, Commander? Did you catch Zhai Jing-mu?'

'No, sir,' Robertson replied flatly.

Collier drained the excess ink from the nib of his pen and leaned back in his chair. 'There have been some great days in the annals of the Royal Navy, gentlemen. Days like the Nile, Trafalgar, the Glorious First of June. On the other hand, there have been some downright disastrous days. Days like the fall of Minorca, the sinking of the *Royal George*, and Admiral Sir Cloudesley Shovell's attempt to take a short cut through the Scilly Isles. I put it to you, gentlemen, that last night's fiasco was on a par with those.'

'An exaggeration, I think, sir,' ventured Killigrew. 'Besides, it was not the responsibility of the Royal Navy to keep Zhai Jing-mu under lock and key.'

Collier looked up at the lieutenant and glared. 'It may not have been our responsibility, Mr Killigrew, but the fact remains that you had Zhai Jing-mu in your hands, and you let him slip away! Three navy ships in the harbour, God knows how many men in Staveley's garrison, not to mention the Hong Kong Police, and against all that a handful of Triads were able to sail straight into the harbour unchallenged, break Zhai Jing-mu out of the gaol, and then escape again without let or hindrance.'

'According to one of my hands who confronted the

Triads on the wharf as they made their escape, there were at least a dozen men involved in the breakout,' Robertson said mildly. 'Not counting the crew of the smug boat. It's difficult to see what Killigrew could have done against them on his own.'

'Perhaps *not* charging in through the front door – while Zhai Jing-mu was charging out of the back, leaving only a rearguard to take care of foolhardy naval lieutenants – would have been a good start,' snorted Collier. 'Assistant Superintendent Cargill tells me you allowed yourself to be knocked unconscious, Killigrew. Might I ask how?'

'I suspect one of the Triads used *wu-yi* on me, sir. You know, like Bannatyne's comprador did at the ball last night.'

'If one more clipper is lost because you let Zhai Jing-mu slip through your fingers, Lieutenant, I'll do a damned sight worse than use *wu-yi* on you. You made a laughing stock of the navy last night. Fortunately today's papers went to press before news of last night's débâcle came out, but I'm not looking forward to reading tomorrow's. There are elements in the House of Commons – you know who I'm talking about – who'd like to see swingeing cuts in the naval estimates. The mess you made of things last night is nothing more than grist to their mill. Go on, get out of my sight, the pair of you. And don't let me see you again until you've brought me Zhai Jing-mu's head on a platter.'

Robertson and Killigrew saluted and made their way back to the gig tied up alongside. 'Thank you, sir,' Killigrew said as they were rowed back to the *Tisiphone*.

'For what?'

'Coming to my defence.'

'Hmph. Don't know why I bothered. Collier's absolutely right, Second. We made utter fools of ourselves last night.'

'There is a solution, sir.'

'Oh, please enlighten me, Lieutenant, do!'

'We find Zhai Jing-mu and his fleet and sink it.'

'Capital notion. And how do you propose we go about that?'

'Zhai Jing-mu is supposed to have a fleet of over fifty junks, sir. You can't hide that many junks easily. He must have a base of operations somewhere, a place where he can careen them, grave their hulls, ship supplies, ammunition, unload his plunder.'

'The thought had occurred to me, Second,' said Robertson. 'Just how do you propose we find this base? There are over two thousand miles of coastline between Saigon and Shanghai; not counting every island, creek, river, lagoon and inlet large enough to conceal a fleet of fifty junks. At present Collier has seven vessels under his command. Do you have any idea how long it would take to search it all?'

'We faced a similar problem on the Guinea Coast, sir. We still managed to find the Owodunni Barracoon.'

'Yes, Mr Killigrew, thanks to Admiral Napier I'm well aware of your exploits at Owodunni the year before last. I hope you're not seriously proposing to try to join the crew of a pilong junk? Somehow I can't see you passing yourself off as a Chinaman.'

'No, sir, but there are easier ways of finding something than an exhaustive search. *Someone* knows where that pilong base is. We just have to ask the right man.'

'Take your pick, Mr Killigrew. The population of China is said to number in hundreds of millions.'

'With your permission, sir, I'd like to start with the Triad Able Seaman Molineaux captured last night. If the Triads have such close links with the pilongs—'

'I hardly think he'll blurt out the location of Zhai Jing-mu's base to you.'

'That all depends on how I ask him, sir.'

'If you weren't an officer and a gentleman, Killigrew – and I confess I sometimes have my doubts – I'd say that sounded like a proposal to inflict torture on the fellow.'

'Wouldn't dream of it, sir.'

'I should hope not. All right, Second, take the rest of the day off. What you choose to do with it is your own affair. If you can find out where Zhai Jing-mu's base is, all well and good. If I hear you've been torturing prisoners awaiting trial, I'll disown you. Do I make myself clear?'

'As crystal, sir.'

Captain d'Acosta of the Royal Engineers reined in his horse on the bridle path leading south from Happy Valley, high up in the central mountains of the island. 'Dwyer!'

Lieutenant Dwyer wheeled back to where he had halted. 'Sir?'

'Show me the letter again.'

Dwyer reached inside his tunic and passed the letter he had received at the Hong Kong Club that morning to his friend.

D'Acosta scanned the single page. 'It says to come alone. Why alone, Dwyer? And why in the middle of nowhere, on the south side of the island? It's got to be a trap.'

'Of course. Why do you think I'm not going alone?'

'But why d'you have to drag me into this?'

'Because I know I can trust you. Look, maybe it isn't a trap. Shen is Bannatyne's comprador, for God's sake. He's not going to try anything against two of Her Majesty's officers. Maybe he does know where we can find Zhai Jing-mu. If he does, there are plenty of reasons why he wouldn't want to meet us in Victoria.'

'Such as?'

'Maybe he's frightened that the Triads will see him talking to us and guess he's betraying them. And even if it is a trap; well, if there's more than two of them we'll just turn tail and get the deuce out of there. Discretion's the better part of valour, after all. And if there's only a couple of them we'll take them into custody and hand them over to Cargill.'

'If you ask me we should hand this letter over to Cargill and be done with it, let the police deal with it.'

'And let them get all the glory of capturing Zhai Jing-mu

for themselves? I told you what a hash they made of things last night, ably abetted by Her Majesty's navy. Well, here's a chance for the army to succeed where everyone else has failed, and I'm not going to let it pass.' Without waiting to see if d'Acosta followed, Dwyer dug his spurs into his horse's flanks and rode down the slope towards Tai Tam Bay on the south side of the island.

The fishing station was where Shen's letter had said the rendezvous would be, on the peninsula which formed the right-hand side of the bay. The mat-shed building looked ramshackle and deserted. Dwyer reined his horse about fifty yards down the beach and swung himself down from the saddle, checking his percussion pistol while he waited for d'Acosta to catch up.

The captain of Engineers rode up and reined in. He nodded to the fishing station. 'In there?' he exclaimed incredulously.

Dwyer nodded. 'Come on, man. Show some spunk. Got your pistol?'

'And my sword.'

They tied their horses to a wooden post which might once have formed part of a breakwater, and then crunched across the shingle to the fishing station. Dwyer stepped on to the boardwalk outside and pushed the door open. It creaked eerily to reveal Shen seated in the gloom within, dressed in a white linen suit. The comprador struck a brimstone match and opened an oil lamp to apply it to the wick within, before shaking out the match. 'Come in, Lieutenant Dwyer.'

Dwyer glanced about cautiously, but it was obvious the comprador was alone in the place. Reassured, he entered. 'You said in your letter you might know where I could find Zhai Jing-mu.'

'You have brought the letter?'

Dwyer nodded. 'Captain d'Acosta's got it.'

'Call him in. He is too conspicuous standing out there.'

'Sir!'

The engineer captain entered. Seeing only Shen, he too relaxed, although not so far as to return his pistol to its holster.

Shen got up and crossed to the door, glancing out before closing it behind them. 'You made sure you were not followed?'

'Yes, yes!' Dwyer said impatiently. 'Are you going to tell us where Zhai Jing-mu is, or not?'

'I asked you to come alone.'

'I wasn't sure if this was a trap.'

'A wise precaûtion. What I have to tell you is for your ears only, however.'

'Anything you've got to say to me you can say to Captain d'Acosta as well.'

'I think not.' Shen brought the edge of his open hand down against the side of d'Acosta's neck. Dwyer heard the bone snap audibly. He whirled with the pistol in his hand. Shen's leg shot out and smashed Dwyer's wrist against the wall. The lieutenant dropped the pistol with an agonised sob. He sank to the floor and pulled his sword from its scabbard, trying to ward off the comprador.

Shen snatched the sword effortlessly from his grip. Sneering, he bent it into a U-shape before tossing it into one corner of the room. Then he picked up a rough sack.

'What's in there?' Dwyer whispered fearfully.

'Nothing. Yet. Soon it will be full of heads.'

'Heads . . .?'

'Lieutenant Killigrew's; Miss Dadabhoy's; and yours, Lieutenant. I have a message from Zhai Jing-mu.' Shen grabbed Dwyer by the front of his tunic and hoisted him to his feet. 'He asked me to tell you he always keeps his promises.'

The last thing Dwyer saw before one of his own ribs stabbed his heart was Shen's fingertips effortlessly piercing his chest.

# *VIII:*

# *The Akhandata*

---

Back on board the *Tisiphone* Killigrew made his way to his cabin, changed into his pea jacket and pilot cap, packed some things in a holdall, and got some of the hands to row him to the wharf. He made his way first to the police office and was presently ushered into Assistant Superintendent Cargill's presence.

'Killigrew!' Cargill leaped to his feet and came around the desk to pump his hand. 'Good to see you back on your feet so soon!' He clapped him on the back. 'How are you feeling?'

'Fine. How's that leg of yours?'

'Not too bad. It only needed a couple of stitches. I said it was just a scratch, didn't I? Well, what can I do for you?'

'I'd like to question the Triad who was arrested last night, see if we can get him to tell us where Zhai Jing-mu's base is.'

'Forget it. I've been questioning him all morning. He's not saying anything. Some damned fool told him his rights.'

'Perhaps you haven't been asking him nicely enough.'

'You think you might be able to get something out of him?'

'I have my methods, Mr Cargill.'

The police officer looked shocked. 'Mr Killigrew, I hope you're not proposing to torture him?'

Killigrew opened his holdall so that Cargill could see inside. 'I think this should do the trick.'

Cargill blanched. 'Good God, man! You're not serious, are you?'

'I'm in deadly earnest, Mr Cargill. You know the Chinese say that if you save a man's life, you're responsible for his actions thereafter?' Cargill nodded. 'By letting Zhai Jing-mu get away last night, I saved his life. If he attacks one more clipper before we can get to him, it will be on my head.'

'*Our* heads, Mr Killigrew. I was there too, remember? All right, we'll have a stab at it.'

They made their way to the gaol. A coolie was still washing the blood off the floor. Cargill showed Killigrew down to the cells where the sole prisoner glared at them sullenly. The assistant superintendent turned to two of his men. 'All right, let's be having him. Clap a pair of darbies on him, Constable. Knowing our luck, he'll probably turn out to be another *wu-yi* expert.'

The prisoner was dragged up to one of the offices and seated in a chair behind the desk. Cargill told the two constables to stand on guard outside, and then closed the door. 'Let's get it over with. I can't say I relish doing this to a prisoner, Triad or otherwise.'

'Ruthless men require ruthless methods,' Killigrew said firmly, and sat down opposite the Triad. 'Speakee English?'

'My no makee-tellee nothing, *fan-kwae*!' spat the prisoner.

'Oh, but I think you will,' Killigrew said with soft menace. The Triad's eyes widened in apprehension when the lieutenant opened his holdall. Then Killigrew placed a bottle of whiskey and a tumbler on the table between them. 'Care for a drink?'

★ ★ ★

'You my number-one frien',' slurred the Triad. 'What you wantchee savvy? I tellee you alla.'

'You might start by letting me know where I can find Zhai Jing-mu,' said Killigrew.

'Whiskey finishee, Missee Killigrew.' The prisoner held out his tumbler in his shackled hands.

Killigrew sighed and reached for the bottle.

'Are you sure that's a good idea?' asked Cargill. 'He looks like he's had enough to me.'

'I think we're getting close.' Killigrew topped up the prisoner's tumbler. 'Chin-chin.'

'Chin-chin.' The prisoner knocked it back in one and gasped with pleasure. 'How-how-ah!'

Cargill looked at his watch.

'My b'long Triad no longer. They makee-tellee barbarian bad, but you no bad, Missee Killigrew, you my number-one frien'.'

'Friends shouldn't have secrets from one another, should they, Chan?'

The prisoner shook his head woozily. Cargill had to move quickly to stop him from falling out of his chair. When he had propped up Chan, he glanced at his watch again.

'So, where can I find Zhai Jing-mu?'

'So sorry, Missee Killigrew. No can tellee. My tellee you where catchee Zhai Jing-mu, Triad spilum Chan.' He was clearly terrified the Triads would murder him if he betrayed them.

'Yes, but if you don't tell us, you see, you'll be put on trial, found guilty and be hanged. If you help us, on the other hand, we can protect you.'

Chan held out the tumbler once more. 'Whiskey finishee, Missee Killigrew.'

There was a knock at the door. Cargill opened it and stepped outside to take a message.

'Now look, Chan, you're not such a bad fellow,' persevered Killigrew. 'All right, so you've been a Triad. But the way I understand it, some Triads are traitors, others are no worse than Chartists. You were led astray, that's all.'

'What Chartist?'

'Never mind. You don't want to be executed because of Zhai Jing-mu, do you?'

'Zhai Jing-mu number-one hero to Han people. Him givee Manchu plenty trub.'

'He's a pirate, Chan, a common thief and a murderer. However much the Triads may try to make a hero out of him, he's only interested in himself. I've even heard that he's offered to become an imperial admiral, and to sweep all the other pilongs from the seas, in return for amnesty for all his past crimes. Is that true, Chan?'

'*Hai.* Is true. Zhai Jing-mu scarum Manchu so muchee, they wantchee makee agree.'

'And where will that leave the rest of you?'

Chan gazed into his tumbler and said nothing.

'You see, Chan? Zhai Jing-mu doesn't care about the Han people. He'd make a covenant with the Devil as quickly as with the Manchus, if it was to his profit. And if that means selling you and your friends down the river, he doesn't care one jot. Are you really willing to die to protect such a man?'

'What river?' asked Chan.

The door opened and Cargill stuck his head through, his face grim. 'Can I have a word?'

Killigrew nodded and stepped outside, leaving a delighted Chan to help himself to more whiskey. In the corridor, Killigrew closed the door behind him. 'What's wrong?'

Cargill jerked his head at the door. 'Has he told you anything yet?'

'Not yet, but I think he's ready to talk . . .'

A crash sounded on the other side of the door. The two

of them burst through to find that Chan had fallen from the chair and was fast asleep on the floor, snoring.

Killigrew sighed.

'Never mind,' said Cargill. 'It was a nice idea.'

'When he wakes up, he's going to have a number-one headache. Don't let him have anything to drink – not even a sip of water – until he talks.'

'By George, Killigrew! You really are a ruthless bastard, aren't you?' Cargill said admiringly.

'You were going to tell me something?'

The assistant superintendent's face became grim. 'It's bad news, Killigrew. Lieutenant Dwyer. He's been murdered.'

Killigrew stared at him. 'Murdered? By whom?'

'We don't know. His body was found alongside that of Captain d'Acosta at a place called Wong-ma-kok on the south side of the island.' Cargill gripped his upper arm. 'They cut off their heads, Killigrew. Those swines butchered them. They were only identified by their uniforms and the papers they were carrying on them.'

Killigrew shook his head in disbelief. It had only been that very morning that he had breakfasted with Dwyer. Then he remembered something. 'Did Dwyer have a letter on him?'

'A letter? What sort of letter?'

'I was with Dwyer at the Hong Kong Club this morning when he received a letter. He seemed fairly excited by it. Then he left suddenly, saying something about an appointment. If you can find that letter, there's a chance it will lead you to his murderer.'

'It's a slim chance,' said Cargill. 'But it's worth looking into.'

Another, grimmer thought struck Killigrew, and he suddenly felt chilled. 'What's the date today?'

'The twenty-fifth of February. What's that got to do with anything?'

'No, I mean, in the Chinese calendar?'

'Let me see . . . the year of the Rooster, the rabbit moon . . .' He counted on his fingers: 'One, two, three . . . the sixth day of the rabbit moon.' He looked up at Killigrew in horror. 'Oh Christ!'

The Sikh butler who opened the door of the Framjee residence peered at Killigrew disdainfully. 'Yes, *sahib*? May I help you?'

'I need to see Miss Dadabhoy.'

'If you'll give me your card, *sahib*, I'll see if she is in.'

Killigrew pushed him aside. 'This isn't a social call, damn your eyes, this is an emergency. Her life's in danger.' He strode across the marble-floored hall. 'Peri? Peri!' He checked the parlour and the drawing room, but both were deserted. The butler tried to grab him, but he pulled free and ran for the stairs. 'Peri!'

Framjee emerged from a door on the landing and leaned on the banister. 'Mr Killigrew! What in the world is going on?'

'I am sorry, sir,' said the butler. 'I tried to stop him, but he pushed past me and—'

Framjee made a calming gesture. 'That is all right, Gobinda.' He met Killigrew at the top of the stairs. 'Mr Killigrew, what is the meaning of this?'

'Where's your daughter, sir?'

'In the garden, I should imagine. Why? Whatever can the matter be?'

Killigrew ran halfway back down the stairs before taking a shortcut by vaulting over the banisters. He ran into the ballroom and out through the French windows on to the terrace where he found Peri relaxing on a swing-seat with Tennyson's *The Lady of Shallot*.

'Kit! You are early.'

'Are you all right?'

'Yes, of course . . .'

He pulled her off the seat and into his arms. He kissed her and held her close. 'Thank God! Thank God!'

Framjee emerged on to the terrace followed by the butler. 'Mr Killigrew! I demand an explanation.'

The lieutenant released Peri and turned to her father. 'Your daughter must leave Hong Kong, sir. Now. Do you have any ships bound for Bombay in the harbour?'

'The *Akhandata* is in the Cap-sing-mun anchorage . . . but I cannot just send my daughter away at a moment's notice.'

Killigrew gripped him by the shoulders. 'Sir, please believe me, your daughter is in deadly danger.'

'Mr Killigrew, please!'

'When the *Tisiphone* first moored in the harbour and I handed Zhai Jing-mu over to Assistant Superintendent Cargill and Lieutenant Dwyer, he said something about him being free and the rest of us being dead before the end of the first week in the rabbit moon. Well, today is the sixth day in the rabbit moon. And Zhai Jing-mu escaped last night.'

Framjee nodded impatiently. 'I heard all about the gaol-break. But if Zhai Jing-mu escaped only last night, surely he will be lying low? The last thing he will want to do is risk recapture by seeking to fulfil some threat he made.'

'That's what I thought. Until I learned Lieutenant Dwyer was murdered this morning.'

Framjee's face turned ashen.

'Zhai Jing-mu may be in hiding now, but he has plenty of friends,' continued Killigrew. 'The Triads, for one. Sir, your daughter was included in his threat. If it hadn't been for her, he might still have escaped that day he attacked the clipper. They've already got one of us, they'll be coming after the rest. They've got less than thirty hours to make good his threat, but I'm convinced they'll try.'

Framjee nodded. 'Peri, go up to your room and pack for a voyage back to Bombay.'

'Yes, Father.'

'Go with her, Gobinda,' Killigrew told the butler. Gobinda nodded and followed Peri inside. 'Can you trust the crew of the *Akhandata*?' Killigrew asked Framjee.

'Implicitly, Mr Killigrew. Once she is on board, she will be safe.'

'What if the pilongs try to stop her before she gets to Bombay?'

'They can try. But at this time of year the monsoon winds will be behind the clipper all the way to Singapore. There is not a ship in the world which can catch the *Akhandata* when she has a following wind, Mr Killigrew, not even one of your steamers.'

'All right. I'll escort your daughter to the anchorage and see her safely on board. Have you got any guns? I'm afraid I came out unarmed.'

'I keep my shotguns in a cabinet in the billiards room.'

'I'll fetch them. Tell your coachman to prepare your carriage. As soon as Peri's ready, we'll leave. If we can stay one step ahead of the pilongs, there's every chance we can beat them.'

Killigrew made his way to the billiards room. The gun cabinet was locked, but under the circumstances he had no qualms about breaking it open with a billiards cue. Ammunition was in a drawer below. He loaded and primed two double-barrelled sporting guns and stuffed his pockets with cartridges.

When he emerged into the hallway, Peri was already coming down the stairs while behind her two footmen carried a trunk between them. 'Put that on the carriage,' Framjee told them. 'Do not worry, my dear,' he added to his daughter. 'Gobinda will go with you to Bombay, to protect you.'

'Know how to use one of these things?' Killigrew asked the butler, holding up one of the shotguns.

Gobinda stood erect. 'I was a havildar in the Twenty-First Bengal Native Infantry.'

Killigrew tossed him one of the shotguns. Gobinda caught it by the barrel in one hand and checked that it was loaded. They went outside and the butler climbed on to the roof of the carriage to sit beside the coachman while Killigrew, Framjee and Peri rode inside.

'Are all these guns really necessary?' asked Peri.

'Just a precaution,' said Killigrew. He sat facing forwards, peering out of the side window in the hope of spotting any trouble ahead before it was too late. The trip to the harbour was the most dangerous time; once they were on board the *Akhandata* they would be safe.

They reached Framjee's trading factory without incident and the carriage drove unchallenged past the guards into the compound. 'Close the gates!' ordered Framjee. There was no sign of the genial, humble Parsi now: here was a man who could think and act in the same breath, the man who had built up a business empire worth hundreds of thousands of rupees. The guards stood aside as he led the way. The back of the factory overhung the waterfront, and a thirty-four foot side-wheel steam-pinnace was tied up there. A white sailor with a silk neckerchief was polishing the engine. As Framjee stepped out on to the stage, the sailor stood to attention.

'How soon can you get steam up, Mr Endicott?'

'Fifteen minutes, sir.' Endicott was a Liverpudlian by his accent, with lank, straw-coloured hair slicked to his head with a centre parting.

'Get on with it, then.'

'Aye, aye, sir.'

'Put the trunk in the pinnace,' Framjee ordered the flunkeys, and marched back into the factory. 'I shall write a letter for the captain of the *Akhandata*,' he explained to Killigrew. 'He will know what to do.'

The Parsi disappeared into an office and left Peri seated on a bench in the corridor with Killigrew. 'You're going to be all right,' he told her. 'Don't worry, Peri, it won't be for long. By the time you reach Bombay, I expect your father will be writing to tell you we've got the whole thing cleared up and it's safe for you to come home.'

'You will not be coming with me?'

He shook his head. 'I can't go absent without leave. I have my duties to attend to. And those include dealing with Zhai Jing-mu.'

As she looked up at him, her round eyes moist with tears, he was tempted to ask her to marry him there and then. But that would not have been fair: she had too much on her mind; the last thing she needed to worry about now was a marriage proposal. He kissed her instead and she held him close.

'I'm frightened, Kit.'

'Don't worry, everything's going to be just fine.'

He heard a cough behind him and broke off the embrace to find Framjee standing over him. Killigrew rose to his feet but made no attempt to apologise.

'Give this to the captain of the *Akhandata*,' ordered Framjee, holding out an envelope. Killigrew nodded and slipped the letter inside his jacket.

'Are you sure you will not come, Father?' asked Peri, as they made their way out on to the landing stage. 'I shall miss you.'

Framjee shook his head. 'I have to stay here and run the company. Do not worry, my dear, I shall be perfectly safe. The pilongs would never assassinate me. That would be killing the goose that lays the golden eggs. Is that not so, Mr Killigrew?'

'That's more or less the long and the short of it, sir.'

Peri nodded and dabbed at her eyes with a handkerchief. 'All right, Kit. I am ready now.'

Killigrew handed her down into the steam-pinnace where Gobinda already waited with the trunk. Then he untied the painter and jumped down after them. She waved her handkerchief at her father – already a forlorn figure without the company of his daughter – while Endicott opened the valve which engaged the steam engine, a miniature version of the kind on the *Tisiphone*. It hissed and rattled into life, and the paddle-wheels drove the pinnace westwards across the harbour.

'Give those other vessels a wide berth,' Killigrew told Endicott, indicating Admiral Huang's junk and a couple of sampans moored in mid-harbour. If there were Triads on board either vessel, they might try to take a pot shot at himself or Peri with a *gingall*. Endicott nodded and adjusted the tiller with a wink at Peri. She did not notice.

'Have you been working for Framjee and Co. long?' asked Killigrew.

Endicott glanced up. 'Me, sir? Nah. Only a few months. I used to work for Grafton, Bannatyne and Co., until I got my walking papers.'

They chugged past Stonecutters Island at the mouth of the harbour. Five miles away, the jagged spine of Lan-tao Island rose up through the haze which hung above the sea. Endicott adjusted the tiller and the pinnace headed for the Cap-sing-mun Passage between Lan-tao Island and the mainland. It was a pleasantly mild day, and as Killigrew sat beside Endicott in the stern he lit a cheroot, but he could not relax. It was dangerous to underestimate the Triads, and he knew Peri would not be safe until the *Akhandata* was underway. Even this close to Hong Kong, the Triads and pilongs would not hesitate to try something. The question was, what? He kept his eyes on the shore and on the other vessels that passed him: smug boats, sampans, and lorchas bustling between Cap-sing-mun and Hong Kong.

It took them the best part of an hour to reach the passage. Lan-tao was about eleven miles long, the north-eastern tip about a mile from the mainland, but the passage was divided in two by the islet of Ma Wan. As they passed through on the south side of the islet, the steep shore seemed to loom over them menacingly. But it was just Killigrew's imagination, and a few moments later they rounded the northern tip of Lan-tao and entered the Cap-sing-mun anchorage.

If Hong Kong was the head of the opium trade, then Cap-sing-mun was its heart. Here were moored the receiving ships of the trading companies, the opium hulks: ancient merchantmen with their masts taken down and their deck houses roofed over so that they looked like the prison hulks at Woolwich and Portsmouth. The holds of the hulks acted as stores for the opium brought by clipper from Bengal and Turkey to be exchanged for green tea brought down the Pearl River Estuary by smug boat. The smug boats would off-load their cargoes on to the waiting clippers and then take on cargoes of opium from the hulks to be touted along the southern coast of China.

Theoretically, importing opium into the Celestial Kingdom was forbidden, but there were plenty of buyers and, since the Manchus paid their mandarins poorly, expecting them to supplement their incomes with *cumshaw* – or 'squeeze', as bribery was known – it was easy to find a prefect who could be persuaded to look the other way when opium was smuggled through his district. Occasionally the authorities in Canton would receive an order from Peking to step up their suppression of the barbarian opium smugglers. When that happened, Imperial war-junks would be sent down the Pearl River estuary, but only after the barbarians had been given plenty of warning, and only opening fire once the barbarian clippers were out of range. The authorities in Canton had borne the brunt of the war, while the Imperial Grand Council in Peking had been relatively unscathed, so the Cantonese knew better than the Dragon-Emperor's advisers that the Celestial Kingdom could not afford to risk another war by offending the barbarians. And the China Traders made it worth the Cantonese authorities' while to turn a blind eye when necessary.

The opium hulks were moored in the lee of Lan-tao Island and another island off Lan-tao's north-shore, Chek-lap-kok. Smoke curled from beneath the conical hats of chimneys, and laundry hung to dry from washing lines, a reminder that many men not only worked on board the hulks but also lived, ate and slept there. Some of the hulks were decorated with flower pots on their roofs, an indication that there were few, if any, seamen in their crew: sailors were superstitious about having flowers on ships – they considered them too reminiscent of funeral wreaths – and would not tolerate them. All hulks bore the flag of their respective trading houses, and the golden dragon of Grafton, Bannatyne & Co. fluttered from the mast of the *Buchan Prayer*.

'There's the *Akhandata*.' Endicott pointed to where the clipper was moored a short distance away from the Framjee opium hulk, and adjusted the pinnace's tiller accordingly. The clipper rode at anchor with all sails furled and looked curiously peaceful.

Peri smiled sadly. 'I would feel a good deal happier if you were coming with me, Kit.'

'I wish I could come, too. But someone's got to stay here and find Zhai Jing-mu. Once he's been taken care of, you'll be safe enough.'

She shook her head. 'How did we get into this predicament, Kit? What did we ever do to deserve this?'

'It isn't a question of deserving, Peri. Your father worked hard all his life to get himself where he is today. Some people envy that. That's your only crime.'

At last the pinnace bumped against the *Akhandata*'s hull. The side ladder was already down and Killigrew climbed up to the entry port.

The deck was deserted.

Killigrew could feel the hairs prickle on the back of his neck. He turned back to the pinnace. 'Wait there. Something's wrong. Pass me one of those shotguns, Gobinda.

I'm going to look for the captain. Have you got a watch?'

The butler nodded.

'If I'm not back in two minutes, get out of here. Go back to Hong Kong, go to the *Tisiphone*, got that? You'll be safe there.'

'Be careful!' called Peri.

Killigrew nodded as he took the shotgun Gobinda passed up to him. 'Two minutes,' he reminded the butler, and then crossed the deck to the after-hatch.

All was eerily silent on board the *Akhandata*, except for the creaking of the ship's timbers. His finger on the shotgun's trigger, Killigrew descended the companion way to the lower deck. There was no sign of anyone. As he tiptoed along the corridor to the captain's quarters, something shot out of a cabin and ran over his feet. He almost jumped out of his skin.

The cat ran up the companionway and disappeared through the hatch. Killigrew continued to the end of the corridor and laid his left hand on the doorknob. He eased back the hammers on the shotgun, wincing at each click. Then he kicked the door open and went through, moving quickly to one side, sweeping the day room with the shotgun's twin muzzles.

The captain, a European, sat at his table.

Killigrew felt the tension flood out of him. 'For Christ's sake, Captain! What kind of a ship are you running—' He broke off. When a stranger with a shotgun burst into a room, some kind of reaction was to be expected, but the captain just sat there, staring. Killigrew crossed the deck with two long strides and pulled the captain forwards. The man slumped across the table. There was a bloody slit in his back. He had bled, but not much: the blade must have gone straight to his heart.

Killigrew swore and dashed back out of the cabin. He reached the foot of the companionway and was about to ascend when a shadow fell across him. He looked up, raising the shotgun along with his eyes, but it was only Gobinda.

'I thought I told you to stay with Miss Dadabhoy?' Killigrew demanded angrily.

Gobinda took two steps down the companionway. Then his legs crumpled beneath him and he toppled forwards. Killigrew side-stepped as the butler sprawled at his feet, a dagger planted firmly between his shoulder blades.

The lieutenant was about to launch himself up the ladder when Peri appeared at the hatch above him. And Zhai Jing-mu was beside her, holding a flintlock pistol to her head. Her face was pale and streaked with tears.

'Lieutenant Killigrew,' observed the *lao-pan*. 'I hear you've been looking for me.' He gave Peri a push, and followed her down.

'It's all right, Peri,' said Killigrew, struggling to keep the tremor out of his voice. 'Everything's going to be all right. It looks like you won't have to go to Bombay after all. I think we can settle this whole thing right here and now.'

'That remains to be seen,' said the *lao-pan*. 'Put the shotgun down, Mr Killigrew.'

The lieutenant was filled with loathing for Zhai Jing-mu, for using someone he cared about to get at him. He would kill the pilong without hesitation, if only he had not been terrified of hurting Peri. He had to get her safely out of the way; then he could deal with Zhai Jing-mu once and for all. 'The girl's done nothing to harm you. Let her go.'

'I intend to. Once you've put the gun down.'

Killigrew did not believe that for a moment. 'So you can shoot her and then kill me? No can do, Zhai. Put the girl back in the pinnace and then we'll settle this between us, just you and me.'

The *lao-pan* thumbed back the hammer of his pistol. 'Put the gun down. Or I will shoot her.'

Killigrew shook his head. 'I don't think so, Zhai. Right now she's the only thing between you and me. If you kill her, so help me, I'll tear your heart out.'

'Last chance, Lieutenant. I mean what I say.'

'Go ahead,' bluffed Killigrew. He knew that Zhai Jing-mu would not waste his only bullet on his hostage and leave himself defenceless. 'Shoot her. She means nothing to me.'

Zhai Jing-mu shrugged. 'As you will.' He pulled the trigger.

# IX:

# *Pipe Dreams*

The sound of the shot was deafening in the confined space below decks. Peri Dadabhoy's face exploded outwards, her blood spattering the bulkheads. Her lifeless body toppled down the companionway.

The horror hit Killigrew like a physical blow. He stared down at her corpse, not believing the evidence of his own eyes. He had killed her.

'That is what you wanted, is it not?' Zhai Jing-mu asked with a smirk.

Killigrew raised his brown eyes to meet the pilong's blue ones. His guts seethed with hatred. He brought up the barrels of the shotgun, determined to wipe the smile off the pilong's face for ever. As his finger tightened on the first trigger, however, a hand shot out from his left and grabbed the barrels. The gun was tugged aside and the shot blew a hole in the bulkhead beside the *lao-pan*.

A moment later something smashed into Killigrew's jaw. He had been concentrating on Zhai Jing-mu and it had never occurred to him that the *lao-pan* might have an accomplice creeping up behind him. He staggered to his right and felt the shotgun pulled from his grip. As the accomplice tried to reverse the weapon, Killigrew kicked him in the stomach. The man doubled up and the second barrel discharged itself into the deck.

Killigrew turned and ran, determined to stay alive long enough to avenge Peri.

'Don't let him escape!' shouted Zhai Jing-mu.

The lieutenant reached the door to the captain's quarters. A bullet spanged over his head and smashed a hole in the glass of the stern window. He slammed the door behind him and looked about the day room. He dragged the chair from beneath the dead captain, letting the corpse sprawl on the floor, and positioned it with the back rest wedged under the doorknob. A moment later the door shuddered as someone on the other side threw his shoulder against it.

Killigrew grabbed the table and pushed it into the middle of the room, beneath the skylight. By standing on top of the table he was able to reach the catch. He threw the skylight open and hauled himself up on deck. He crossed to the after-hatch, slammed it shut, and quickly battened it down so that no one could get up from below. He hoped it would hold long enough for what he had to do.

He crossed to the entry port and glanced down. There was another pilong in the boat, holding a shotgun at Endicott's throat. As Killigrew's shadow fell across him, he glanced up and took the gun off the sailor to aim it at him. Killigrew ducked back and a moment later shot peppered the bulwark. Then he heard a groan.

'Lieutenant!' called Endicott.

He glanced cautiously over the bulwark. The pilong was dead, a dagger thrust between his ribs. Endicott threw the shotgun up to him.

He caught it in both hands. 'Good work! Now get the hell out of here!'

'What about you?'

'I've got someone to take care of first. Go on, go!'

As Endicott got the pinnace's steam engine going again, someone hammered on the underside of the after-hatch. Killigrew ran across to the forecastle. He could see Framjee's opium hulk less than three cables away. He waved his head above his arms, trying to get someone's attention. Surely they had heard the shooting?

He heard a sound behind him and saw two pilongs come up through the after-hatch. He emptied the shotgun's other barrel at them – next to useless, at that range – jumped down the fore-hatch and found himself in a charnel house.

There were bodies everywhere: the crew of the *Akhandata*, slaughtered to a man. The deck was awash with blood.

Choking back the bile, Killigrew fumbled in his pockets for a couple of fresh cartridges. He had just snapped the breech shut when a figure appeared at the hatchway above him. He thumbed back one hammer and let the pilong have it in the chest.

Killigrew ejected the spent cartridge, reloaded that barrel and thumbed back both hammers. How many pilongs were there on board the clipper? Enough to slaughter the entire crew. More than enough to slaughter him.

Gasping for breath, he made his way down to the lower deck. He found what he was looking for amidships: the magazine. Even clippers needed a powder room, to supply the guns they carried as protection against pilongs. There were only three barrels of gunpowder in there: Killigrew hoped it would be enough. A kind of Viking funeral for Peri, one that Zhai Jing-mu would not live to forget. He hoped Framjee would understand.

There were no fuses, so he had to do it the old-fashioned way, breaking open one of the barrels of powder and tipping it on its side. He could hear footsteps on the deck above him, the pilongs searching the ship for him. They had not got to the lower deck yet, but they would. He found a small pail and scooped it full of gunpowder, using it to lay a long, winding trail out of the powder room, glancing fearfully over his shoulder every few seconds.

A footfall sounded on the deck behind him. He whirled and brought up the barrels of the shotgun. There was a pilong behind him with a crossbow.

Killigrew fired first. The pilong fell to the deck.

Then he heard a pistol being cocked behind him.

He turned. Twenty feet away, Zhai Jing-mu crouched halfway down the companion ladder leading up to the next deck. He had a pistol in each hand, both levelled at Killigrew.

'Drop the shotgun, Mr Killigrew. It is useless at this range.'

'Those peashooters of yours aren't going to be much better, unless you're a damned fine shot.'

'Is that a chance you are willing to take?'

Killigrew lowered the muzzles of the shotgun to the deck, and shrugged. 'You're going to kill me anyway.'

'Precisely so.' Zhai Jing-mu fired.

A searing pain lashed through the side of Killigrew's head. He pulled the trigger of the shotgun. The muzzle flash sparked the trail of gunpowder. The powder flared and the flame raced back along the trail towards the magazine. He had the satisfaction of seeing Zhai Jing-mu's eyes widen in horror as he realised what he had done.

Then the pilong fired the other pistol, but in his panic the shot went wide. Zhai Jing-mu dropped both pistols and scrambled back up the companion ladder. He was halfway through the forward hatch when Killigrew caught him by the sash and pulled him back down.

'Oh no you don't, you sonuvabitch! You're going down with the ship. Or rather, up.'

The two of them grappled at the foot of the companionway. Killigrew grabbed hold of one of the rungs and pulled himself up to kick the pilong in the face with both feet.

'When you get to Davy Jones' locker, you can pay your respects to Peri!'

Zhai Jing-mu staggered back and tripped over the coaming of the hatch leading down to the lower deck. As he fell out of sight, Killigrew ascended the last few rungs to the upper deck. He ran across the forecastle and dived over the bulwark. A moment later the *Akhandata* blew up.

'Here it comes.' As the men of the *Tisiphone*'s starboard watch took on board barrels of water from a harbour lighter, Ågård nudged Molineaux and nodded to where Captain Morgan was being rowed out to the sloop in a gig from HMS *Hastings*. Rear-Admiral Collier had been laid low by an apoplectic stroke two weeks earlier and Morgan was now the senior naval officer in Hong Kong. 'From the look on his face, someone's going to catch it now.'

'Yur,' said Molineaux. 'And I think I can guess who.'

'Boat ahoy!' challenged the marine sentry at the gangway.

'*Hastings*!' returned the gig's coxswain.

'Molineaux!' called the boatswain's mate. 'Run below like one o'clock and inform Commander Robertson that Captain Morgan is coming on board.'

'Aye, aye.' Molineaux went down the after-hatch and approached the marine on duty outside Robertson's door. 'Message for the cap'n. Cap'n Morgan coming on board.'

The sentry crashed the stock of his musket against the deck. 'Message for the captain! Captain Morgan coming on board.'

'Tell him I'll be up directly,' Robertson's voice called out.

'Tell him he'll be—' began the sentry.

'Yur, all right, Barnes, I think I got that,' Molineaux replied sarcastically. He went up on deck and relayed the message to the boatswain's mate.

'All right, Molineaux, back to work.'

Fanning piped Morgan on board and Commander Robertson met him on the quarterdeck. Neither of them smiled. 'An unexpected pleasure, Captain,' said Robertson.

'Hardly unexpected,' Morgan said coldly. 'And unlikely to be a pleasure. For either of us.'

Robertson nodded. 'Shall we go down to my day room?' he suggested, and shot a glance at where Molineaux was pretending to check a cask for leaks. 'Fewer prying ears.'

Morgan nodded and the two of them descended through the after-hatch.

'I wouldn't mind being a fly on the wall in Tommy Pipes's day room right now,' said O'Connor.

'Looks like you're not the only one.' Molineaux nodded to where two of the *Tisiphone*'s landsmen scrubbed the quarterdeck. The skylight over the captain's day room was ajar and the two landsmen were taking an inordinately long time to scrub the adjacent deck.

The boatswain's mate saw them. 'If you scrub that patch of deck any longer, gentlemen, you'll fall through it!' he snarled. 'All right, you can leave that for now. Go and clean the head.' He watched the two landsmen until they had reached the forecastle, and then got down on his hands and knees by the skylight. A moment later Ågård, Molineaux and O'Connor had joined him. The boatswain's mate scowled at them, but could not tell them to leave without the captain hearing him and spoiling the game for all of them.

'. . . don't mind if I have one, do you, sir?' Robertson was saying.

'No, go ahead,' replied Morgan, and crystal clinked as Robertson poured himself a drink from a decanter.

'This is a very painful duty for me,' said Morgan, when Robertson had settled down. 'Now I know that Lieutenant Killigrew has done good work on behalf of the navy in the past, but . . . well, to be frank, his methods have increasingly begun to raise eyebrows in certain quarters, if you know what I mean.'

'*Who* you mean, more like.'

'And his latest escapade only seems to confirm what they've been saying. Frankly, Robertson, to me it looks like the proverbial last straw. The question is, what are we going to do about it?'

'*Do* about it, sir? I'm not sure that we need to *do* anything about it. I've read Killigrew's report, questioned him closely and found that he behaved perfectly satisfactorily.'

'Perfectly satisfactorily! For pity's sake, Robertson! He blew up a clipper! Right in the middle of Cap-sing mun anchorage!'

'I'm sure Sir Dadabhoy is fully insured.'

'Against acts of God, Commander. I believe that acts of Lieutenant Killigrew are something of a grey area as far as insurance companies are concerned.'

Robertson chuckled. 'Yes, I'd been warned that he had a callous disregard for the safety of property. I'm amazed that no enterprising marine insurance company has yet offered a policy with our indomitable lieutenant in mind.'

'This is no time for levity, Robertson. Aside from the destruction of the *Akhandata*, there's also the question of loss of life to be taken into account.'

'I'm fully aware of that, sir. My people spent most of last Sunday afternoon pulling bodies out of the anchorage. We can hardly blame Killigrew for the slaughter of the crew of the *Akhandata*; and as for the pilongs, he was only doing his job.'

'And Miss Dadabhoy? The daughter of Sir Dadabhoy Framjee, an extremely influential man in these parts?'

'How much influence Sir Dadabhoy has is hardly the point, a fact which I'm sure – if he was here to speak for himself – he would be the first to point out.'

'*Au contraire*, Commander Robertson, that is *precisely*

the point. How am I to explain to the other traders that the daughter of one of their associates was killed because Lieutenant Killigrew thought he could play games with the girl's life?'

Molineaux, Ågård, O'Connor and the boatswain's mate jumped as something slammed in the cabin below: Robertson's glass against the table, by the sound of it. 'With all due respect, sir, bearing in mind the particular regard in which Killigrew held Miss Dadabhoy, I would imagine he did everything in his power to save that poor girl.'

'And I put it to you, Commander, that he allowed his personal feelings to cloud his judgement.'

'We've all made mistakes in our youth, sir. Killigrew's a damned fine officer and I believe he did everything he could. The sad fact of the matter is that sometimes everything simply isn't enough. It's a tragedy, but there it is. You didn't see him after Mr Endicott pulled him out of the harbour. I did. I know that young man, and believe me, if he could turn the clock back and exchange his life for hers, I truly think he would do just that.'

'Hmph. Well, he *can't* turn the clock back. Where is he? I think it's high time I had a word with him myself. I'm sure he's had plenty of time to recover from his injuries.'

'Ah. I'm afraid he isn't on board at the moment, sir. I told him to take a fortnight off to rest and make sure he was fully recovered.'

'Is that so, Commander? I was informed you'd given him a week. That was twelve days ago.'

'Who told you that, sir? No, don't tell me, let me guess: that priggish little squit Norris.'

Norris was one of the *Tisiphone*'s mates, a devout, self-righteous Christian, and thoroughly disliked by the hands. It was news to Molineaux that Robertson shared their dislike.

'Well, it hardly matters, does it?' continued Robertson.

'Lieutenant Killigrew is my officer. If I choose to extend his leave indefinitely, that's between him and me.'

'Her Majesty's government does not pay its officers to keep their feet up in Hong Kong, Commander. I expect to see Lieutenant Killigrew back on duty by Monday morning, is that understood?' Chair legs scraped against the deck.

'You have to make allowances. Killigrew was deeply upset by what happened to Miss Dadabhoy. I may not blame him for what happened to her. That does not mean he doesn't blame himself. I think under the circumstances—'

'Monday morning, Commander. I shall expect to see him in my cabin in *Hastings* at nine a.m. on Monday. If he does not appear, I shall have no option but to recommend that Lieutenant Killigrew be court-martialled for gross dereliction of duty and desertion. Do I make myself clear?'

'Abundantly so, sir.'

The door slammed. Molineaux and the others stood up and quickly tiptoed away from the skylight so that when Morgan emerged on deck they were back at their duties. The boatswain's mate piped the captain over the side.

As soon as Morgan's gig was on its way back to the *Hastings*, O'Connor turned to Molineaux and Ågård. 'Hear that, lads? Tom Tidley's gone adrift!'

'Don't you believe it!' snorted Ågård. 'If I know him, he's probably off doing secret work somewhere, tracking down the rest of them yellow-belly pilongs. You mark my words, lads, he'll turn up just as the ship's bell's chiming the end of the middle watch on Monday morning, ready to present his compliments to Cap'n Morgan, along with the exact whereabouts of a pirate lair!'

One of the marines emerged from the after-hatch and faced the boatswain's mate.

'Fanning? The Cap'n wants to see you in his day room. Along with Ågård, Molineaux and O'Connor?'

The four seamen presented themselves in Robertson's day room and stood to attention in a line. The commander paced up and down in front of them. 'I'm sure I don't have to remind you four that eavesdropping at skylights is an extremely nasty habit, and I won't tolerate it on board this vessel. I hope I don't ever catch any of you at it.'

The boatswain's mate exchanged glances with the others. 'No, sir.'

'Glad to hear it. Dismissed, gentlemen.'

As soon as the afternoon watch was over, Molineaux made his way forward to the sick berth and knocked on the door.

'Come in,' called Mr Strachan.

Molineaux entered and closed the door behind him. The surgeon, Westlake, avoided the sick berth if at all possible as a consequence of which it had become the domain of Mr Strachan. The young assistant surgeon kept everything in neat and pristine condition, if only so he could use the place as a developing room for his photographic plates. He had stretched lines across the deck head and pictures of the local flora and fauna hung side by side with surgical appliances.

'Drop your breeks,' said Strachan, his nose buried in Knox's *Anatomy*.

'Sir?'

'You want me to inspect you for social diseases, don't you?' Strachan turned a page with a sigh. 'It's always the same with you fellows. When are you going to learn that prevention is far better than cure? Wash your parts with coal-tar soap and I'll put you down for a course of mercury treatment—'

'This isn't about my parts, sir,' interrupted Molineaux. 'It's about Mr Killigrew.'

Strachan looked up. 'Killigrew's contracted a social disease? I'd've thought he'd know better.'

This was a possibility which had not occurred to

Molineaux. 'I don't know about that, sir. He's gone missing.'

'Well? What do you want me to do about it?'

'You're his friend, aren't you?'

'I'd like to think so. Not that it's any of your business, Molineaux.'

'Aren't you worried about him, sir?'

'Damn your impertinence! Killigrew can look after himself.'

'What if he can't?'

'You think he might be in trouble?'

'He already is. He's gone adrift, hasn't he?'

'Killigrew wouldn't go absent without the captain's permission unless he had a good reason.'

'Wouldn't he, sir?'

'What are you suggesting?'

'He was sticking it away prettily heavily the other Sunday evening, wasn't he?'

'Damn your eyes, Molineaux! How much Mr Killigrew chooses to drink is no concern of yours!'

'Sir, I'd like to think that Mr Killigrew is a friend of mine, too. Now if he *has* got a good reason for being adrift, then it probably means he's in danger and needs our help, if he isn't already dead. If he hasn't got a reason, then don't you think it would be better if his friends found him drunk in a tavern before his superiors did?'

Strachan stared at him for a moment. 'Be so good as to have the dingy lowered, Molineaux,' he said, closing his book. 'I'm going ashore.'

'It would be more discreet if we got one of the *yolos* to take us ashore.'

'Us?'

'A gentry cove like yourself can't be seen frequenting the waterfront gatherings, any more than I could get into the saloon of the Hong Kong Club or the Victoria Hotel.'

'All right.' Strachan reached for his hat and coat.

On deck, Molineaux crossed to the entry port and looked about. He recognised Mei-rong's *yolo* amongst the bumboats and waved her across. She started to scull towards the foot of the side ladder.

A voice in Molineaux's ear almost made him jump out of his skin. 'Going somewhere?' asked the boatswain.

Strachan intervened. 'Ah, Bosun. I'm just going ashore to pick up some medical supplies from the naval stores. I've asked Able Seaman Molineaux to assist me.'

'Very good, sir,' the boatswain said obsequiously, and turned to Molineaux with a snarl. 'Now you behave yourself ashore, Molineaux. I don't want to hear from Mr Strachan here you've been giving him any trouble.' He turned back to Strachan. 'If he gives you any jaw, sir, you just let me know. I'll sort him out.'

Strachan smiled nervously. Molineaux had noticed that the assistant surgeon was as frightened of the boatswain as any of the ratings. 'I shall, Bosun. Don't worry, I'm sure Molineaux will be on his best behaviour.'

'That ain't saying much,' sniffed the boatswain. 'Er . . . would you like me to have the dinghy lowered, sir?'

'That's all right, Bosun. We'll take a *yolo*.'

'As you will, sir.'

Molineaux and Strachan climbed into the *yolo* and Mei-rong sculled them across to the wharf. 'Give her a dollar, sir,' Molineaux told Strachan when they reached the quayside.

'A dollar!' protested Strachan, horrified. 'Just for rowing us across the harbour?'

'Got to keep the natives friendly,' said Molineaux, deadpan. Strachan sighed and reached into his pocket while Molineaux kissed Mei-rong goodbye and told her not to wait for them.

'Won't we need a boat to take us back?' asked Strachan as they watched her row back out to the *Tisiphone*.

'No shortage of boats round here, sir,' he said, gesturing

at the sampans and *yolos* which crowded the waterfront. He cast his eyes over the town: it was still not that large, but there were plenty of nooks and crannies into which a drunken sailor might crawl, and the setting sun was spinning a web of darkness over the rooftops. 'Hadn't we better start searching?'

Strachan nodded. 'You try the waterfront taverns, I'll check the Hong Kong Club and places like that.' He checked his watch. 'We'll meet outside the post office on Queen's Road in three hours, at half-past nine.'

While Strachan glanced under newspapers draped over sleeping gentlemen in the rooms of the Hong Kong Club, Molineaux lifted sailor's faces out of puddles of their own vomit in the gutters of alleys behind taverns. When the seaman reached the post office shortly before nine, Strachan already awaited him. 'Any luck, sir?'

Strachan shook his head. 'You?'

'I spoke to a Portuguese sailor who things he saw someone answering Killigrew's description heading off towards Tai-ping-shan.'

They both glanced down Queen's Street to westward. 'Why would he go down there?'

Molineaux shrugged. 'You tell me, sir.'

'Maybe he picked up a trail that might lead him to the pirates,' said Strachan. 'How long ago did this fellow see Killigrew going towards Tai-ping-shan?'

'Sunday evening, sir.'

'Five days ago?' spluttered Strachan.

Molineaux coughed. 'A week ago on Sunday evening, I mean.'

'*Twelve* days! And no one's seen him since?'

'Doesn't sound too good, does it? You want me to go in after him?'

'On your own? By jings, no! Naturally I'll come with you.'

Molineaux gave him a funny look. 'You ever been into Tai-ping-shan, sir?'

'Have you?' countered Strachan.

'No, sir. But from what I hear, it's not all that different from a rookery. You ever been in a rookery?'

Strachan looked bewildered. 'What, you mean like, where rooks live?'

Molineaux took a deep breath. Strachan might know all there was to know about scurvy and yellowjack – although sometimes Molineaux had his doubts – but when it came to the flash world Strachan was greener than an Irish pasture in spring. 'Not rooks, sir. Crooks. The kind of places where the crushers daren't go because they know what the locals will do to them.'

'Oh! I see. Well, I can't very well let you go into a place like that alone,' Strachan said staunchly.

Molineaux was not convinced that Strachan would be more of a help than a hindrance, but he decided to say nothing. His main objection was that Strachan would stick out in a rookery anywhere in the world like a man wearing a sandwich board with the slogan: 'prime plant'; but Molineaux had to acknowledge that he himself was not likely to pass unnoticed through the streets of a Chinese shantytown.

'Stick close to me, sir. And try to look as though you've got every right to go where you're going.'

'Well, haven't I?'

Molineaux sighed. 'Yes, that's right, sir. You just remember that.'

Tai-ping-shan was less than a mile down Queen's Road, but it was a thousand leagues from the broad, elegant streets of Victoria. It was every bit as filthy and poverty-stricken as the back streets of Seven Dials parish in London, but while the tumbledown shacks were even more precarious than the ancient tenements of the slums back home, at least here one could see one's hand in front of one's face in a town where there were no factory chimneys to enhance the fog. An Oriental band played music somewhere in the distance, while Chinese voices jabbered excitedly inside a gaming den the two Britons passed. Children peered out of the gloom at them, eyes a thousand years old set in faces that were barely past puberty.

'You wantchee suckee-fuckee?' asked one girl who looked young enough to be Strachan's daughter. 'My givee good suckee-fuckee, only twenty cash!'

'What's suckee-fuckee?' Strachan asked Molineaux.

'It's a local delicacy. Come on, sir, let's keep moving. And for God's sake keep your watch chain covered and one hand on your pocket book.'

It was too late: three shadows moved out of the gloom to block their path. Molineaux glanced instinctively over his shoulder and saw two more men behind him. He was glad he had brought his 'persuader' – a brass belaying pin – tucked up his sleeve.

'You givee money!' hissed one.

'What's the cause?' asked Molineaux, allowing his persuader to slide down into his hand.

The first robber looked puzzled. 'Cause?'

'Sure. I can't give away money unless it's in a good cause.'

The robbers looked bewildered, and Molineaux took advantage of it to strike the first across the face with the belaying pin. Even as the first went down, he whirled and struck one of the men behind him across the cheek. The second man whirled with blood on his face, and the remaining two in front of them hesitated uncertainly.

Molineaux reached behind him, pulled his Bowie knife from its sheath and showed it to the ruffians. 'You want some of this? Come on and get it, you sons of bitches!'

They shook their heads, still hesitating. The first man Molineaux had hit groaned, but made no attempt to get up.

Molineaux glanced sideways at Strachan. The assistant

surgeon had adopted the traditional boxing stance, his guard high. Molineaux suppressed another sigh. 'Come on, sir.' He led the way forward, and Strachan followed him. One of the robbers tried to block their path, but Molineaux brandished the Bowie knife and the robber melted aside. The two Britons hurried on down the street.

Thirty yards further on, Strachan glanced over his shoulder. 'Are they coming after us?' asked Molineaux. His heart was pounding in his chest.

'Doesn't look like it.'

'Don't worry. They will.'

As soon as they were around the next corner they both broke into a run. Molineaux took care to make sure Strachan did not get away from him; the assistant surgeon would not last five minutes on his own in Tai-ping-shan. Molineaux was not even convinced that he himself could last ten.

Around another corner they paused to catch their breath. 'Oh-kay, I think we lost them.'

'It's a damnable disgrace!' said Strachan. 'Someone ought to call a constable.'

'Whatever you say, sir.' Molineaux looked around. There was no one in sight, but that did not reassure him. 'This was a chuckle-headed idea. We're wasting our time. If Mr Killigrew is around here – and if he ain't already dead – we're never going to find him.'

'All right.' Strachan hesitated. 'Which way is back?'

Molineaux looked around him again. He was not sure.

'Are we lost?' asked Strachan.

'Of course not. All we have to do is go downhill until we get to the shore, and then turn right and keep going.'

'What's that reek? I can't quite place it . . .'

Molineaux recognised the odour, like rotting vegetables and yet somehow sickly sweet at the same time. 'Opium, sir.' He nodded to the door of a mat-shed. 'Seems to be coming from in there. Must be an opium den. No point looking for Killigrew in there. Even he's not that much of a booby . . .'

The two of them stared at one another.

'I suppose it's worth taking a look,' said Strachan.

Molineaux nodded.

The interior of the mat-shed was a noisome, poky place, the scent of opium almost overpowering. A few paper lanterns which hung from overhead beams provided enough light for Molineaux to be able to make out the trestle tables arranged all around the walls. On some of them men reclined in a state of unconsciousness, so still they might have been dead. Perhaps they were.

An old man pottered up to Molineaux and Strachan and with a toothy grin he offered them a pipe: a reed about an inch in diameter with a bowl at one end. 'Smokee?'

'No smokee,' Molineaux told him.

'We're looking for an Englishman . . .' began Strachan.

'Blissful dreamy. Plenty blissful dreamy.'

It was obvious the attendant did not understand English and had learned only a few words by rote, just those pertaining to his job.

'No, thanks,' said Molineaux. 'Come on, sir. Let's work our way around until we find him.'

A small lamp stood at the head of each couch, and by the light of those they could make out the faces of the dreamers. They appeared old and wizened, their faces drawn, pallid, haggard and skull-like. They were oblivious to the two Britons who moved amongst them.

'Molineaux!' Strachan called from the other side of the room. The seaman crossed to stand beside the assistant surgeon, and gazed down at where Killigrew lay on his back, an imbecilic grin on his ashen, unshaven face. He was dead to the world.

Molineaux swore. 'How the hell are we going to explain *this* to Commander Robertson?'

★ ★ ★

Killigrew lay on a tropical beach in Peri Dadabhoy's arms and enjoyed the warmth of the sun on his body. There was not a cloud to be seen in the azure sky, and the junks bobbing on the waves out to sea had a calm, peaceful look. On the beach all was silent but for the gentle lapping of the waves. He turned to Peri. She smiled up at him, and he kissed her.

Some instinct made him glance over his shoulder, and he gaped. A great Chinese dragon flew through the sky, twisting and turning, looping its long, slender body back and forth on itself like a crepe streamer. Its scaly body was golden, and it cracked with lightning.

He wondered if he were imagining it and turned to Peri. She saw it too, and she smiled. The next thing he knew she had risen to her feet and was walking naked across the sand towards the water, waving her arms over her head at the dragon in the sky.

But he sensed the dragon was dangerous. He called out after her, but she did not seem to hear him. She waded out into the water until she was waist deep in the surf, and then dived forward and swam out towards the fishing junks to get closer to the dragon.

The dragon stopped, beating its leathery wings as it hovered high above them in the sky. Then it swooped and dived like a hawk, plunging towards its prey.

Killigrew was on his feet in an instant. He started to run down the beach, but before he had gone a dozen paces the fine white grains beneath his feet turned to quicksand and he sank up to his waist.

As the dragon swooped low over the junks it spread its jaws wide and a jet of flame poured forth. The junks were instantly charred to a crisp and the air filled with black, sickly sweet smoke. But Peri had not seen the attack on the junks and she still swam out towards the dragon. Killigrew tried to climb out of the quicksand, but the harder he struggled the more it held him back and sucked him under.

The dragon swooped on Peri, skimming the water and rising with her caught in its talons. Killigrew tried to scream but the quicksand filled his mouth and he choked.

As the dragon flew overhead Peri's body dropped to the sand only a few feet from where Killigrew struggled in the quicksand. It landed with a thud. She too had been charred to a crisp.

The quicksand evaporated and he ran to where she lay on the deck of a tea clipper, but by the time he had climbed over the bulwark her body had vanished. He glanced across to the poop deck and saw Jago Verran at the helm. The captain laughed. 'She's not for you, jobbernowl!'

Furious, he ran across the deck and climbed the companionway to the poop after Verran, but as he reached the top of the ladder Zhai Jing-mu appeared above him and kicked him in the face. He felt no pain, but was conscious that he was falling backwards, down and down, taking for ever to hit the deck below. When he finally landed it was in something soft and sticky which broke his fall, like molasses.

He tried to swim back to the island but it was far away, and when he finally reached the sandy shore the palm trees which had fringed the beach had vanished, as had the sea behind him, and he was in an endless desert beneath a suffocating sun which blistered his skin. Then he looked up and realised it was not the sun which burned him, but the dragon. It hovered above his head and breathed black smoke over him. He watched in horror as his own skin blistered and burned.

He looked up at the dragon, pleading, but saw no mercy in its reptilian eyes . . .

His own eyes.

'Bring her back!' he roared at the dragon.

But now the dragon had his own face. It laughed at him.

He looked down at his skin. The blisters had formed into scabs, and the scabs grew four pairs of legs each and turned into spiders which ran all over his body, tearing at his flesh with their massive, venom-filled mandibles. He screamed and tried to brush them off, but at that moment the dragon swooped on him and enfolded him in its leathery wings. He fought his way out of the wings and found himself lying on a bed in a room that was ten feet wide and a thousand miles long.

At the far end of the room he could just make out three figures, a European man and woman, and a black man wearing pusser's slops and holding a sennit hat before him. They looked vaguely familiar, as if he had known them in a dream, except that each of them had a nose that was a mile long. They swung those hideous noses in his direction as they turned to look at him.

*Is he all right?* Asked the woman.

*He's having a nightmare*, said the white man. *I've heard it's not uncommon when a man's been deprived of the drug he's come to depend on.*

*He's awake*, said the black man.

Killigrew nodded. They spoke as if they cared about him, but he knew they were lying. They were plotting against him. Plotting to keep him away from Peri. They were going to murder him!

The white man came towards him. His elongated nose seemed to fly at Killigrew like a lance. Killigrew tried to crawl away with a yelp of terror. He was going to be skewered on that elongated proboscis. 'No! Stay away from me! You're going to kill me!'

*It's all right*, said the white man. *I've brought you some medicine.* He showed Killigrew a small brown bottle.

'No! It's poison! Stay away from me! You're trying to poison me! Where's my pipe? Give me another pipe, damn your eyes!'

*It's laudanum*, said the white man. *It will help wean you off the opium . . .*

Killigrew glanced at the bottle in the man's hand, but it

had changed into Peri, and she was the size of a doll. 'Kit!' she called. 'Kit!'

He sobbed. 'Peri! You bastards, what have you done with her? Give her back to me!'

*Be sure you drink it all*, said the man, and handed Peri to him. She seemed to grow back to full size in his arms. He kissed her greedily and at once a warmth seemed to spread through him. The strange room faded and he was back on the beach with Peri in his arms. He settled back in the hammock with a smile of blissful ecstasy.

# X:

## *Happy Valley*

Killigrew woke up in bed and turned to where Peri lay, but she was not there. Panic seized him at once and he cried out for her.

The door opened and Molineaux burst into the room. He took one look at Killigrew and swore irritably. 'Another nightmare, I suppose?'

'I hope so,' Killigrew said hoarsely, hoping he would wake up next to Peri and it would be all over. 'Where's my pipe? Bring me another pipe, damn your eyes!'

Molineaux rolled his eyes. 'Here we go again. No more pipes, sir. How many times do I have to tell you? You want me to ask the sawbones for some more laudanum?'

'Where's the necessary?' Killigrew's voice sounded harsh and unfamiliar to his own ears.

'Right here.' Molineaux reached under the bed and pulled out a chamber pot decorated with Napoleon Bonaparte's face on the inside. 'You mean to say you're actually going to *use* that thing for once, instead of having a jerry-go-nimble in the bed?'

'A gentleman does not excrete in his bed, Molineaux.' Killigrew was trying to get up, but his emaciated limbs responded clumsily.

'Oh, right. I suppose you're going to tell me the Triads have been sneaking in here and doing dockyard jobs on your mattress – and worse – while you slept?' Molineaux helped him up.

Killigrew felt weak and shaky all over as he relieved himself into the chamber pot. As soon as he had finished he sat down once more, exhausted. 'Where am I?' he croaked.

'The Bannatyne house.'

'The Bannatynes' . . .!' Killigrew sat up sharply, and immediately regretted it. 'How long have I been here?'

'Four weeks, give or take.'

'Four weeks!' Killigrew pushed himself up and lunged for the door. 'I have to get out of here. I have to get back on duty . . .' He only made it halfway before his legs crumpled beneath him and he sprawled on the rug before Molineaux could catch him.

'Calm down, sir.' Molineaux tried to pick him up.

Killigrew cried out. 'Don't touch me!' he snapped irritably.

'Oh-kay, oh-kay! I was only trying to help! You don't have to worry about getting back on duty just yet,' Molineaux continued as Killigrew sat back on the bed. 'It's all taken care of, thanks to your pals Wes Molineaux and Mr Strachan. Not to mention Mr and Mrs Bannatyne, who've kindly put you up until you recover from your illness.'

That worried Killigrew, but his brain was still too addled to work out why. 'What about the *Tisiphone*?' he said weakly, sniffing.

'Don't worry about that. That Strachan ain't as green as I first thought. He came up with a downy fakement and no mistake. He told Commander Robertson that you'd contracted some rare, highly infectious tropical disease with a long Latin name I can't remember. Probably made it up there and then, but even that daft old bugger Westlake didn't dare gainsay him. So instead of being kept in the naval hospital Strachan told them you'd have to be kept up here in quarantine, where the higher altitude would do you good.'

Killigrew sniffed. 'Have I contracted a rare disease?'

'Lumme, sir, try to keep up, will you? Mr Strachan says you've got a dependency on opium.'

'Opium . . .?' Killigrew had known there was something he wanted. 'Where's my pipe?'

'Oh, Lor'! Don't let's go through that again. Mr Strachan's gone down to Victoria with Mrs Bannatyne to fetch you some laudanum.'

'Who else knows I'm here?'

'Everyone. But only me, Strachan, and the Bannatynes know the real reason why. Even their servants have been kept at arm's length; though it wasn't difficult, once they heard you had an infectious disease.' He took out a clean handkerchief and held it out when Killigrew sniffed again.

The lieutenant took it from him and blew his runny nose. 'Thank you,' he said grudgingly. Suddenly feeling cold, he dragged the blankets off the bed and wrapped them around his shoulders, shivering.

He heard a door open in the next room, and Strachan's voice: 'By jings, that hill takes it out of me every time.'

'Mr Strachan?' called Molineaux. 'In here. He's awake. And making sense. Sort of.'

The door opened, but it was Mrs Bannatyne who entered, looking especially fetching in a white muslin morning gown. 'How are you feeling?'

'Damnable.'

'You look much improved.'

'Have you got a looking-glass?'

'I'll go fetch one,' said Molineaux, and went out.

A moment later Strachan entered with a small phial and a crystal sherry glass. 'And how's the patient this morning?'

'Spare me your bedside manner, Mr Strachan.'

‘I’d say he’s on the road to a full recovery,’ Mrs Bannatyne said drily.

Strachan emptied the contents of the phial into the glass and handed it to Killigrew. ‘Get that down you.’

‘What is it?’

‘Laudanum. We’ve been giving it to you twice a day, a smaller and smaller dosage each time. Do you not remember?’

Killigrew ached to toss the contents of the glass down his throat so desperately he suddenly found himself wanting not to, just to be bloody-minded and prove to himself he could do it. ‘Am I sick, Strachan? I feel like I’ve got a chill.’

‘You’re suffering from the same symptoms as a lot of patients I’ve know coming off an opium-based medication.’

‘So what am I supposed to do? Keep on taking laudanum for the rest of my life?’

‘Not a wise notion,’ said Strachan. ‘An old friend of mine from Edinburgh works as an apothecary in Manchester now. He’s often told me how a lot of his customers from the labouring classes buy opium lozenges. They keep on coming back for larger and larger doses. He thinks that the more opium one takes, the more the body becomes used to it, and the more it craves it. It’s an awful nasty vicious circle, and we’ve got to break you out of it. So we’re weaning you off it.’

Molineaux returned with a looking-glass and held it up so Killigrew could see his own reflection. It took Killigrew a few seconds before he realised that the pallid, haggard face which stared back at him was his own. He reached up tentatively to touch his cheek, and then stroked his smooth jaw. ‘I thought you said I’d been here for four weeks? Someone’s shaved me.’

‘Someone’s shaved you, bathed you, changed your soiled sheets and fed you,’ said Mrs Bannatyne.

'You?'

'Joint effort,' she said. 'Mr Molineaux's been helping cook with the food.'

'Was it any good?'

'Not according to you,' Molineaux said surlily. 'One time you hurled your plate at my head and swore blue murder at me.' He indicated a stain on the wall beside the door.

Killigrew felt ashamed. 'Sorry. That would have been the opium talking.'

'That's what Mr Strachan said, sir.'

The lieutenant glanced at the glass of laudanum in his hand, and with slow deliberation tipped it into the chamber pot. He glanced up at them and grinned sheepishly. 'I've made rather an ass of myself, haven't I?'

All three of them folded their arms and nodded firmly.

'Well, I'm glad to see your condition seems to be much improved,' said Strachan. 'There's nothing like enjoying the occasional success to renew a man's faith in his own abilities. I'd better go now. I have to get back to the *Tisiphone*.'

'What about you, Molineaux?' asked Killigrew. 'Haven't you got duties to attend to?'

The seaman grinned. 'Mr Strachan was kind enough to get me appointed to full-time nursing duties until you're fit enough to join polite society once more, sir. So take your time getting better.'

'But you could walk back down to Victoria with cook to help her with the shopping, Mr Molineaux,' said Mrs Bannatyne.

'Couldn't you have got it just now, when you were in town, Mrs B?'

She glared at him. 'I hope you're not suggesting I should go *shopping*, as if I were some common housekeeper?'

'What do *I* look like?' demanded Molineaux. 'The chambermaid?'

'That reminds me,' said Killigrew, and handed him the chamber pot. 'You can empty that on your way out.'

Molineaux sighed. 'It's a man's life in the navy.'

As soon as Strachan and Molineaux had gone, Killigrew eased himself out of bed. Mrs Bannatyne tried to stop him, but Killigrew managed to turn an attempt to push him back into an act of supporting him.

'You should be resting,' she chided.

'I've been resting for four weeks,' he told her. 'Now I have to build up my strength. Help me across to the window.'

They pushed the shutters open and saw the rooftops of Victoria laid out far below them.

'Nice view,' said Killigrew. 'So tell me, since when did you and your husband become so concerned about my welfare?'

'Ever since Mr Strachan came to tell us you were sick and needed a place to rest until you could be cured.'

'Well, at least now you've had a chance to see the pernicious effects of the drug your husband imports into China.'

'I'd heard you were in favour of the drug.'

'It's freedom of choice I'm in favour of. Instead of worrying about the fact that people smoke opium we should concern ourselves with what drives them to seek oblivion in such vices.'

'That was going to be my next question.'

He sighed and made for a chair. She tried to help him, but he shook his head. 'I need to do it for myself.'

'As you wish.'

It was touch and go, but he made it to the chair. She sat down on the bed facing him. 'You cared for her very much, didn't you, Mr Killigrew?'

'Who?'

'You know perfectly well whom I mean. Miss Dadabhoy.'

'I can't have cared that much for her,' he replied bitterly.

'I was the one who got her killed.'

'You did everything you could to save her.'

'Oh, I did everything I could, all right. I led her straight into a trap on board the *Akhandata*, and then goaded Zhai Jing-mu into shooting her. How's Sir Dadabhoy?'

'Putting a brave face on it. But her death has hit him hard. He's a broken man. All his wealth . . . I think he'd give up everything to have her back.'

'Two lives broken. I'm a veritable Jonah, aren't I?'

'You mustn't blame yourself, Mr Killigrew. You were not the one who pulled the trigger. And at least Zhai Jing-mu got his comeuppance.'

'That won't bring her back, though, will it?' Talking about Peri had brought back the craving which seemed to permeate every fibre of his being. 'Molineaux didn't . . . ah . . . empty the necessary, did he?'

'The one with the laudanum and your . . . you know what . . . in it? Oh, Mr Killigrew! Surely you cannot be that desperate? How low can a man sink?'

'Pretty low, I can assure you. Where does Strachan keep the laudanum?'

'I thought you'd decided that you didn't need it any more?'

'I don't. I just want a sip . . .'

'There's none in the house. Mr Strachan made sure there was never any more laudanum in the house than was necessary for your next dosage. He knew there would be moments like this.'

'That son of a bitch!'

'That's no way to talk about a friend who's nursed you, put up with weeks of abuse from you and made sure your superiors never discovered what a disgrace you'd become.'

Killigrew took a deep breath. 'I'm sorry. I just want a little sip, that's all . . .'

'Mr Killigrew, I would have thought that even you would have worked it out by now. It's not opium you want, it's Miss Dadabhoy. The opium's just a substitute. You have to accept that she's gone, and get on with your life.'

'My life's over. What have I got to live for, now that she's dead?'

'There are other women in the world, you know, in case you hadn't noticed?'

'Not like Peri. Couldn't you send one of the servants down to Victoria to get some laudanum? I don't need much, just a sip. You must know which apothecary Strachan buys it from.'

'No! You must find something to take your mind off it, that's all.' There was a firm rap on the door, and she stood up sharply. 'Come in.'

Bannatyne entered and regarded his wife with surprise. 'I did not expect to find you in here, madam,' he said with cold formality.

'I was just keeping Mr Killigrew company.'

Bannatyne turned his gaze on the lieutenant. 'Good to see you up and about, Mr Killigrew. How are you feeling?'

'Much improved, thank you. And I want to thank both you and your wife for your kindness in taking me in.'

'Not at all, Mr Killigrew. It's the least we could do. It would be a terrible shame if the navy lost such a promising young officer all because of one momentary and entirely understandable indiscretion.' Bannatyne turned to his wife. 'I wonder if I might have a word with Mr Killigrew in private, madam?'

She nodded and left the room without arguing. Bannatyne crossed to the window. 'I trust everything is to your satisfaction, Mr Killigrew?'

'You've been more than hospitable, Mr Bannatyne. So much so that I can't help wondering—'

'Why?' Bannatyne finished for him.

Killigrew nodded.

'You do not care for me, Mr Killigrew. I can see that. No, don't deny it. I understand from the Reverend Mr

Ultzmann that you blame Grafton, Bannatyne and Co. for the war with China. Well, I can see that we are not going to be able to agree on whether or not the war was justified. But that was seven years ago. Both Britain and China need to put the war behind them, to forge a new relationship based on trust and mutual respect.'

'You make it sound so easy.'

Bannatyne turned back from the window with a faint smile. 'I did not intend to. I have enough experience of the Chinese – and, yes, of the Foreign Office – to know it will not be that straightforward. It may also be as difficult for you and I to forge a new relationship, Mr Killigrew. But I can assure you that just as Britain and China will be best served by recognising their mutual interests, so it is with you and I. We must put the past behind us and work together.'

'And what mutual interests do we share?'

'Zhai Jing-mu may be dead thanks to your efforts, Mr Killigrew, but there are plenty of other pirates out there. Traders like myself need men like you to keep the pilongs suppressed. I scratch your back, Mr Killigrew; I expect you to scratch mine.'

*In other words*, thought Killigrew, *if I don't do what you want, Captain Morgan is going to find out the real cause of my 'illness'*. 'I'm afraid my naval training hasn't equipped me with back-scratching skills, Mr Bannatyne.'

'Oh, I certainly wouldn't ask you to do anything contrary to your sense of duty, Mr Killigrew. All I ask is that you make a speedy recovery, and then you can get back where you belong, out hunting pirates.'

Killigrew did not believe a word of it, except perhaps the implication that the sooner he was out of the house, the happier Bannatyne would be. He shivered, and not just because he still felt a little feverish.

'Good God, man!' Captain Morgan exclaimed on seeing

Killigrew. 'You look dreadful!'

'Thank you, sir. Very good of you to say so.'

Irony was wasted on Morgan. 'You know, Killigrew, I thought maybe you were malingering, feeling sorry for yourself. I must apologise. You've clearly been very ill indeed. Still, Mr Strachan assures me you're past the infectious stage. Think you'll be ready to come back on duty soon?'

'Yes, sir.' Killigrew felt embarrassed by Morgan's solicitation, especially since he was now well aware that, in effect, feeling sorry for himself was exactly what he had been doing. 'I'm feeling much stronger now.'

Bannatyne's butler entered the room. 'Dinner is served.'

They went through: Mr and Mrs Bannatyne, Jago Verran, Captain Morgan, Commander Robertson and Killigrew. Verran was a regular guest at the Bannatynes' dining table, but Killigrew did not know why the reclusive Bannatyne had taken it into his head to invite Morgan and Robertson for dinner.

Table talk at the Bannatynes' had invariably been stilted since Killigrew had been a guest there – although he suspected that it had always been like that, and his presence was not to be blamed – but with Morgan and Robertson there the atmosphere seemed even more uncomfortable than usual. The only compensation was the food, which was up to its usual standards. Whatever Bannatyne's faults, he certainly knew how to live.

'I understand another clipper has been reported missing on the voyage to Singapore,' Bannatyne remarked over the *escalopes d'agneau à la Clamart*.

'Damn it, the Royal Navy can't be everywhere,' muttered Morgan. 'We only have limited resources . . .'

'Oh, it was not my intention to imply anything to the contrary,' said Bannatyne. 'Please don't think that we China traders don't appreciate your sterling efforts against the pilongs. As it happens, I've been thinking about what was said at my ball in February, and I think I may have come up with a possible solution.'

'Oh?' Morgan asked cautiously.

'It seems to me we are on the same side, after all. That helping you to bring the pilongs to justice is in my interests as much as anyone's. So I have decided to put the *Golden Dragon* and her crew at your disposal.'

Killigrew glanced at Verran, who grinned. The *tai-pan* had obviously already discussed this with him.

'That's damned generous of you, sir,' said Morgan. Killigrew had the feeling that if Bannatyne had suggested that the captain strip naked and paint himself with woad while singing 'Buffalo Gals, Won't You Come Out Tonight?' accompanied by Ethiopian serenaders, Morgan would have agreed with alacrity.

'She's a steamer, and shallow-draughted,' continued Bannatyne. 'Just the thing for chasing pirate junks in and out of the creeks and bays on this coast. And Captain Verran here knows these waters better than any other European. I'll put him and his crew entirely at your disposal.'

'Naturally we accept,' said Morgan.

'There is one condition, however,' said Bannatyne.

Somehow Killigrew had expected as much. He reached for his wine glass and took a sip, desperately wishing it were a glass of laudanum.

'Under such circumstances you would want a naval officer on board, in command?' Bannatyne asked Morgan.

'Well, naturally.'

'Then I must insist that Mr Killigrew be given the honour.'

Killigrew almost choked on his wine. 'Me?'

'Out of the question,' Morgan said quickly. 'Do you want the *Golden Dragon* to go the way of the *Akhandata*?'

Bannatyne smiled. 'I know all about what happened on board the *Akhandata*, Captain Morgan. As far as I understand it, Killigrew acted with remarkable presence of mind and followed the only course of action open to him, other than to permit Zhai Jing-mu to escape. I've also spoken to Sir Dadabhoy and several of the other traders. We all agreed that the loss of a clipper was a price worth paying to rid the seas of Zhai Jing-mu.'

Killigrew had not seen Framjee since the day Peri had been killed. 'And what about the loss of his daughter?' he asked Bannatyne bitterly. 'Was that a price worth paying?'

'You mustn't blame yourself, Mr Killigrew,' said Mrs Bannatyne, with concern in her eyes.

Her husband reached across and took her hand. She seemed surprised by the gesture. 'Unfortunately the union of Mrs Bannatyne and I has not yet been blessed with issue, so never having had a daughter I cannot presume to imagine what it must be like to lose one. Our hearts are all with Sir Dadabhoy at this difficult time. But I think we should also bear in mind that it was Zhai Jing-mu who murdered Miss Dadabhoy, not Mr Killigrew here. The lieutenant did everything he could to save that girl's life, and I think we are indebted to him for that. And while Zhai Jing-mu is dead – thanks solely to Killigrew's efforts – I also think we should bear in mind that there are plenty of other pilongs in the South China Sea, and we all have loved ones who might one day fall prey to their depredations. If I loan the *Golden Dragon* to the Royal Navy, I do not want it to be wasted through overcautiousness.'

'There are no officers under my command who can be accused of overcautiousness,' said Morgan.

'I also have Captain Verran's sensibilities to take into account,' said Bannatyne, and Verran winked mischievously at Killigrew. Bannatyne smiled. 'I'm sure you gentlemen must know how possessive captains are about vessels which, strictly speaking, do not belong to them. Since Verran is my best captain, it is not my desire to go against his wishes in this matter. He served with Lieutenant Killigrew when he was in the navy, and he knows the two of them can work together.'

'That's as maybe,' snorted Morgan. 'But I have plenty of other officers who can do the job just as well, if not better.'

Bannatyne sat back in his chair. 'Then my offer must be withdrawn.'

Morgan smiled uneasily. 'Come now, sir. You said it yourself: we are fighting on the same side here. What does it matter which naval officer is put in command of the *Golden Dragon*?'

'To you, perhaps, nothing. But to myself and Captain Verran it matters a great deal. I gather from speaking to Mr Killigrew that he holds me responsible for the China War. While our opinions are divided on the necessity of that war, there is nothing I would like better than to put those days behind us. The colony of Hong Kong has a glorious future ahead of it, and we must look to that future. It will doubtless surprise Mr Killigrew, but his disapproval does upset me. I just want him to see that while we may not see eye-to-eye on everything, we are fighting on the same side.'

Morgan caved in. 'Killigrew is Commander Robertson's second lieutenant . . .'

'I have no objections, sir,' said Robertson. 'If Mr Killigrew accepts, of course,' he added quickly.

'Well, Mr Killigrew?'

Killigrew stared at Bannatyne while trying to make up his mind. In all his days he had never heard so much hypocrisy and cant as Bannatyne had uttered in the past few minutes and he did not trust the *tai-pan* an inch. Bannatyne was plotting something, but what, the lieutenant could not imagine. But accepting his offer seemed to be the only way out, and at least with Verran to watch his back Killigrew knew he would be safe.

'Very well,' he said at last. 'I accept.'

★ ★ ★

'Can I buy you fellers a wet?' the sailor asked in a Liverpudlian accent.

'That depends,' said Molineaux. 'What's in it for you?'

The monsoon season had arrived with a vengeance, and outside the rain hammered against the shutters of Labtat's Tavern. The wind forced it under the shingles and the landlord had put pails at strategic points about the room to catch the unending succession of drips. But the fire in the hearth was warm and Molineaux and Ågård were cosy and dry as they stood at the bar and listened to the drops plopping into the overflowing buckets.

The Liverpudlian grinned. 'Well, if your cap'n's looking to take on hands, you might mention my tally. Endicott's the name: Seth Endicott.'

'Olly Ågård and Wes Molineaux,' said Ågård. 'You haven't run from one of the clippers in the Cap-sing-mun anchorage, have you? Our cap'n don't hold with deserters.'

'Wait a moment, Olly,' said Molineaux. 'I know this feller. Weren't you the cove who pulled Tom Tidley out of the drink after the *Akhandata* blew up?'

'Tom Tidley?' said Endicott, bewildered.

'That's what we calls our second lieutenant,' explained Ågård. 'On account of how he always keeps his rig tidley . . .'

'. . . Even when he's got a bit tidley himself,' finished Molineaux.

'Your second lieutenant? You mean Mr Killigrew. Oh aye, I took him out to Cap-sing-mun, and I brought him back.' Endicott looked grim. 'Only problem is, there were three passengers on my pinnace when we left and only one when I returned.'

'If you work for Framjee, how come you're looking for a new berth?' asked Molineaux.

'Got the sack, didn't I?' Endicott said bitterly. 'Youse fellers must know 'tweren't my fault Miss Dadabhoy got herself killed. But Sir Dadabhoy didn't see it that way.'

'The poor bloke's upset,' Molineaux pointed out. 'He's just lost his daughter, for Chrissakes. Maybe when he's had a chance to recover from his loss . . .'

'Nah.' Endicott shook his head. 'I need blunt now, if I ain't going to go hungry. Besides, I'm sick of working for these jumped-up *tai-pans*: Framjee, Bannatyne, the whole bloody lot of 'em. They can all go to hell in a handcart as far as I'm concerned. No, give me a job in the Andrew Miller any day. At least you know where you stand, then.'

'Aye,' said Ågård. 'Up to your neck in it at the bottom of the heap.'

'Did you used to work for Bannatyne?' Molineaux asked Endicott.

'Oh aye. I was on board the *Arachne* until I got my walking papers.'

'What did you get the sack for?'

''Tweren't my fault—'

'No, it never is, is it?' muttered Molineaux.

'No, really. They never told us. If you ask me it was to keep crew costs down. The next time she went out she was precious short-handed. Hardly surprising she went down.'

'Typhoon?'

'Pilongs. At least, that's what they say. No survivors . . . and if you believe that, you'll believe anything.'

'What do you mean?'

'When I was on the *Arachne*, the *ghaut serang* – that's what we call bosuns on the clippers, *ghaut serangs* – name of Kneebone, Jake Kneebone. Well, the day before the *Arachne* sailed, half of us was sacked and replaced with a few yellow-bellies. The *tai-pan* trying to save himself some blunt; leastways, that's what I thought at the time. A few weeks later word comes back from Singapore: the *Arachne* never arrived. Well, I thought nothing more of it until a few months after, when who should I see walking around as large as life but Jake Kneebone? He pretended like he didn't know me, but it were him all right.'

Molineaux reached into his pocket. 'Let *me* buy *you* that drink.'

Molineaux made his way round to the back of the Bannatynes' house and knocked on the kitchen door. The Chinese parlour maid opened it and he at once seized her in his arms and gave her a kiss.

'Let go!' she protested. 'You all wet!'

'A little water never hurt anyone,' he told her, peeling off his rain-cape and tarpaulin hat and hanging them from a peg close to the cooking range. 'Is Mr Killigrew in?'

'Yes, but you no go up there,' said the parlour maid.

'Who's going to stop me?' Molineaux pointed out. He gave her another peck on the cheek and slipped upstairs.

He was wandering about in search of the lieutenant when a footman emerged from one of the rooms. 'May I help you?' he demanded disdainfully.

'Yes, I'm looking for Mr Killigrew.'

'How did you get in? I did not hear you ring the bell.'

'I can't help that. Where can I find Mr Killigrew?'

'I must ask you to wait outside until I can ascertain if the lieutenant—'

A door opened further down the corridor and Mrs Bannatyne emerged. 'What is it, Ranjit?'

'This negro is looking for Mr Killigrew, ma'am.'

'That's all right, Ranjit. Be about your duties. Come and join us in the games room, Mr Molineaux. Mr Killigrew is teaching me to play All-Fours.'

Dressed in white trousers and a linen shirt, Killigrew sat at a card table topped with green baize. He looked a good deal better than he had done of late, but not as healthy as he usually was, his eyes still sunken in his head and his complexion pallid.

'What is it you want, Molineaux? Has the captain sent you with a message?'

'Yes, sir. For your ears only.'

Mrs Bannatyne smiled thinly. 'I'll be in the drawing room,' she told Killigrew, and went out.

'Bad timing, sir?' asked Molineaux.

'I'll say. I was just teaching her to beg in All-Fours.'

'It's all right for some. How are you feeling, sir?'

'Much improved, thank you for asking. And thank you for helping Strachan and Mrs Bannatyne look after me. I'm sorry I was so unappreciative at the time.'

'That's oh-kay, sir. Still think opium should be freely available?'

'It's no good banning it: you might as well ban carving knives for fear that people will cut their fingers off.'

'Carving knives have uses other than cutting off fingers, sir.'

'And opium's a powerful medicine. But people need to be educated about the dangers before they make up their own minds whether or not to use it. I only went into that opium den for one night. If I'd known I'd become so . . . so . . .'

'Mr Strachan calls it an "addiction", sir.'

Killigrew nodded. 'My God, it's the perfect commodity – from the supplier's point of view. The more of it you sell, the more the customer needs to buy. I wonder if Sir Dadabhoy knows that?'

'I don't know, sir. But I'll wager Bannatyne does.'

The lieutenant looked thoughtful for a moment, and then glanced up at Molineaux. 'What's the message that's for my ears only? Or was that merely a ruse to get rid of Mrs Bannatyne?'

'Merely a ruse.' Molineaux lowered his voice and told Killigrew what he had learned from Endicott.

'If this fellow was dismissed from the crew of one of Bannatyne's ships, he probably held a grudge,' Killigrew said when the seaman had finished. 'He might have made the whole story up.'

'Yur, that's what I reckoned at first. So I went to the

offices of the *Hong Kong Register* and did some checking up in their library. The *Arachne* was rated A1 at Lloyd's, but from what Seth told me she would've struggled to be rated C3. She was a floating coffin, sir, fit only to be broken up or used for target practice. If the pilongs hadn't sunk her, the next big wave would have done the job twice as easily. If it *was* pilongs that sunk her.'

Killigrew took out his linen handkerchief to blow his nose. 'You think it might have been an insurance swindle?' he asked, tucking it up his sleeve.

'More than that, sir. I also did some crosschecking. Every big company that trades with China has lost at least half a dozen clippers to pilongs in the past four years. Every company except for Grafton, Bannatyne and Co. They've only lost the one ship, sir. The *Arachne*.'

'That doesn't prove anything, Molineaux,' Killigrew said carefully.

'Maybe not, sir; but it makes you wonder, doesn't it? And there's something else you should know about. I've been doing some thinking, and it doesn't make sense.'

'What doesn't make sense?'

'This whole Zhai Jing-mu bobbery. You know that Triad you were questioning on the morning that . . . you know, when the *Akhandata* went down?'

'Chan? What about him?'

'Did you know he died?'

Killigrew regarded the seaman in shock. 'Died? Good God, I never intended to—'

'Oh, don't you worry about that, sir. 'Tweren't your fault.'

'But . . . the whiskey I gave him . . . wasn't it alcohol poisoning?'

'Mr Strachan had a look-see at the stiff 'un, sir. He reckons arsenic did for him. And that only takes a quarter of an hour to take effect, he says. And it was four days after you gave the Triad whiskey that he cocked his toes.

Mr Cargill traced the poison to the bakery which provides the coop with its bread, but the trail goes cold there. Apparently one of the baker's boys mizzled that night.'

'Mizzled?'

'Cut and run, sir. Disappeared.'

'Strachan never said anything about this to me.'

'He didn't want to, sir. Thought it best not to worry you while you was on the mend. I agreed, until I got to thinking: why would anyone want to burke the Triad?'

'To stop him from talking, I suppose.'

'Talking about what, sir? Everyone knew that Zhai Jing-mu was dead by the time that poison must've gone into the toke; so who was the prisoner trying to protect?'

'His fellow Triads, perhaps?'

'Maybe. Or maybe Zhai Jing-mu ain't dead.'

'Don't be ridiculous, Molineaux. He was on board the *Akhandata* when it blew up.'

'I helped pull the bodies out of the water. But I didn't see Zhai Jing-mu's body.'

Killigrew looked thoughtful. 'Did you recover *all* the bodies from the *Akhandata*?'

'Difficult to say, sir, since we don't know how many were on the clipper to start with. But all the members of the crew were found, along with . . .' Molineaux's words trailed off when he saw the haggard look on Killigrew's face. The lieutenant might be at pains to conceal it, but there was no hiding the fact that Miss Dadabhoy's death had hit him hard. 'Well, you take my point, sir. We also found the bodies of half a dozen unidentified Chinamen, most of 'em with shotgun pellets in them. But one thing's for sure: none of 'em belonged to Zhai Jing-mu. Dead or alive, I'd know that blue-eyed bastard anywhere.'

'There could be a dozen reasonable explanations as to why his body was never recovered. It might have gone down with the ship, or else been carried out to sea with the tide.'

'You willing to stake your life on that, sir?'

Killigrew ruminated for a moment. 'Have you shared this theory with anyone on board the *Tisiphone* yet?'

'Mr Strachan and me put it to Commander Robertson, sir.'

'And what did he say?'

'The same as you: he thought it was all gammon. Only difference was, when he said it, I could tell he believed it *was* gammon.'

Killigrew found Sir Dadabhoy Framjee at Peri's sepulchre in the cemetery in Happy Valley. The Parsi looked as if he had lost a great deal of weight in the past two months, his sorrowful eyes shrunk deep into his skull, his once rubicund cheeks now hanging slack from his face. Unlike Killigrew, he carried no umbrella against the slashing rain, yet he was heedless of the fact that he was getting soaked through.

This was the first time the two of them had spoken since Peri had been murdered. Killigrew had been in two minds as to whether he should speak to Framjee at all and he braced himself for an outburst of bitterness and recrimination, but at the sound of his footsteps on the gravel path the Parsi merely looked up and smiled wanly.

'Mr Killigrew.'

'Sir Dadabhoy.' Killigrew held his umbrella to give the Parsi some shelter from the rain.

'Every morning I go into the parlour for breakfast and expect to see her, waiting to read the papers to me as she always used to. Then I come down here, in the hope it will help me to understand she is never coming back.' Framjee kneeled and laid the wreath he had brought before the sepulchre.

Killigrew laid his own wreath next to it. 'I understood the coffin was sent back to Bombay?'

Framjee nodded. 'For a traditional Zarathustrian

funeral. She was always proud of her religious heritage, so much so that sometimes she made me feel ashamed . . .'

'I suspect you're a better Zarathustrian than I am a Christian, sir.'

'You are very kind to say so.' Framjee gestured to the sepulchre. 'I wanted a memorial to her here on Hong Kong, to remind people at what cost this colony is maintained. Does that seem foolish to you, Mr Killigrew?'

Killigrew shook his head.

'Walk with me, sir.' Framjee gestured to the entrance gate, and the two of them wandered side by side down the path with their hands clasped behind their backs. 'I am given to understand that you blame yourself for what happened to my daughter.'

Killigrew smiled sadly. 'Wouldn't you, sir? I led her right into that trap, I goaded Zhai Jing-mu into shooting her . . .'

'You tried to bluff him, just as you did when you first saved her from him back in January. You did what you thought was right; you must not blame yourself. It was not your finger on the trigger.'

'It might as well have been.'

'No, Mr Killigrew. I have heard a great deal about you: the work you did against the pirates in Borneo, and against the slavers on the Guinea Coast. If anyone is to blame, it should be me. You advised me to send Peri back to Bombay back in January, and we pooh-poohed your advice. If we had listened to you, Peri would still be alive today.'

'Or her ship might have been attacked by pilongs on the way, or it might have foundered and sunk in a typhoon.'

Framjee nodded. 'So many ifs. Only one man had his finger on the trigger, and that was Zhai Jing-mu himself. Blaming ourselves will not bring her back.' He looked at Killigrew speculatively. 'I have also heard people say that you are something of a pirate yourself; is it not true? But there is one difference between you and the pilongs. They are motivated by greed and avarice: you are motivated by a strong sense of justice.'

Killigrew grinned cynically. 'Ah, yes. Good old British fair play.'

'You do yourself an injustice, Mr Killigrew. We both know that the British Empire has hardly brought the happiness to the lives of all the people it has touched in the way that some back in London might like to think. But we must never lose sight of the fact that the Pax Britannica has done *some* good. At least Zhai Jing-mu will never trouble any more innocent people.'

'I wish I could be sure of that.'

Framjee looked at Killigrew in surprise. 'You think he might still be alive?'

'I'm almost certain of it, sir.'

The Parsi shook his head sorrowfully. The two of them walked on in silence to the entrance of the cemetery. Killigrew felt uneasy, as if by allowing Zhai Jing-mu to escape yet again, he had somehow let the Parsi down; and let Peri down, as well.

Framjee seemed to have reached a similar conclusion. 'Perhaps it is wrong of me to think it, but I do not believe the spirit of my daughter will ever be at rest while her murderer is at large,' he said when they reached the gate. He looked up at Killigrew. 'You are going after him, are you not?'

'That's my intention.'

'I shall pay you one thousand pounds if you see to it that his reign of terror is finally brought to an end.'

Killigrew did not know which shocked him most: the implication that he act as a hired assassin, or the high price that Framjee put on such an act; at his current salary, it would take him over five years to earn that much money. But there could only be one answer to the Parsi's offer.

'I'm sorry, sir. It's a generous offer, but I couldn't

possibly accept. I have my duty to do.'

Framjee looked despondent. 'So you will catch him again, God willing, and bring him back to Hong Kong, and he will escape again before he can be brought to trial, and then we shall be back where we started.'

Killigrew shook his head. 'You misunderstand me, sir. I may have only one reason to want Zhai Jing-mu dead, but it far outweighs the thousand you're offering me.'

# XI:

# The Spider and the Fly

Li Cheng hurried through the muddy streets of Tai-ping-shan to get out of the pelting downpour as quickly as possible. He hated the monsoon; but also recognised that if there were no rainy season, no one would appreciate the dry season. That was *yin-yang*: no shadow without illumination, no light without darkness. He sometimes wondered if the barbarians were the *yang* to the Chinese *yin*. That would account for why the gods had seen fit to create such loathsome, uncivilised beings.

The streets were deserted except for those few people who had no choice other than to be outside in such relentless rain. Here a few wizened faces peered from windows with mournful expressions; there a coolie squatted beneath the eaves of a shack with the rain streaming off his broad conical hat.

At the eating stall opposite the joss house on Hollywood Road two men sat at one of the tables, heedless of the rain. Li Cheng did not spare them a glance, but entered the adjoining tea house. He purchased a pot of tea with a couple of copper cash from the money-string on his belt and went upstairs. At a table in one corner four old men were playing mah-jongg, shouting the calls noisily each time they slammed one of the elaborately carved bone tiles. The place was busy, but Li had no difficulty finding a table. It was perfectly positioned, beside a window overlooking the street outside. While he was waiting for an attendant to bring his tea, he took a leather pouch from his belt and emptied the pieces of a tangram on to the table.

The tangram was an ebony tile perhaps four inches square, cut into seven pieces of different shapes: a square, a lozenge-shape, different-sized triangles. The trick was to jumble the pieces up and then see how quickly one could form them back into the square. It was trickier than it looked, but Li could do it in seconds with his eyes closed. A skilled tangram player could also arrange the pieces to form pictures: a coolie, a farmhouse, whatever the imagination could conceive; the number of permutations was infinite.

Li arranged the pieces to form a representation of a barbarian devil-ship. Playing with his tangram helped him to think, to visualise problems from alternative directions.

'You are a little old to be playing with a child's toy,' snorted a familiar voice. Li glanced up and saw a bulky figure, dressed as a coolie, standing over the table.

Li Cheng concealed his irritation. Admiral Huang was a Manchu, what the barbarians called a Tartar. Not being Han Chinese, he was unable to appreciate fully the subtleties and complexities of Chinese culture. But even the Manchus could have their uses sometimes, when one needed a blunt instrument.

'Admiral,' murmured Li. 'Please accept my humble apologies for failing to kowtow as befits one of your exalted station, but I am discreetly reluctant to betray your identity.'

'Spare me the pig shit, Li.' Huang took out a silver cigarette case and lit a Russian cigarette. 'Tell me what you have managed to learn so far.'

'Did you see the two men sitting at the eating stall next door when you arrived?'

'Yes. What of them?'

'They are constables of the Hong Kong Police, disguised to look like civilians. They are watching the temple.'

'Why do they not raid it, if they know it is a Triad lair?'

'They think that watching who comes and goes will lead them to bigger fish.'

'Will it?'

'No.'

'Good. The last thing we need is for the barbarians to go clumsily blundering in and spoil everything. What about Framjee?'

'He knows nothing.'

'Pah! Then the trouble we took to infiltrate you into his employment was wasted.'

Li rearranged the pieces of the tangram and then tapped a finger on the table to indicate them to the admiral. 'What do you see?'

'A tangram.'

'A rabbit,' said Li. With one finger deftly pushing the pieces around the table top, he rearranged them. 'And yet with a different rearrangement of pieces, we see a dragon.'

'All I see is a tangram,' insisted Huang. Li knew the admiral was not stupid, but sometimes he could be deliberately, frustratingly obtuse.

'The mystery we now face is like the tangram. We have all the pieces before us, but until we can put them together the right way round we will not see what is right under our noses. We arranged them badly to start with, and that led us to see a connection with Framjee where no connection existed.'

'Very philosophical. Confucius would be proud of you,' sneered Huang, and gazed out of the window. Something seemed to catch his attention. 'Interesting . . .'

Li followed his gaze and saw a barbarian in a greatcoat and pilot cap striding through the muddy puddles with a grim expression on his pale face. 'Killigrew.'

'Ah, so you know the barbarian naval officer?'

'We have encountered one another on several occasions,' Li admitted with a faint smile. 'He followed me into that very temple four months ago. The Triads tried to kill him. I had to jump out of a window and steal a constable's turban to make him and his friend follow me, so they would intervene without the necessity of my revealing my purpose.' He watched as Killigrew entered the joss house a second time.

'It would have been easier to let the Triads kill him,' snorted Huang.

'Easier, but less expedient. If a barbarian is attacked by Triads in a temple, then the barbarian police watch the temple.' By leaning out of the window and craning his neck, Li could just see the two plainclothes policemen arguing about whether or not to follow Killigrew into the temple. He ducked back inside and sat down again. 'But if a barbarian is killed there, then the police will tear everything apart in their search for the killers. I did not think I could afford to let that happen.'

A crash sounded across the street from inside the temple. 'It sounds like everything is being torn apart anyway,' said Huang.

'It is too late now. He will learn nothing. What are the two policemen doing?'

'One of them is running up the road to Victoria. The other remains in his seat.'

Li nodded. 'They have been given strict instructions to observe, but not to reveal their presence.' He chuckled softly. 'As if every man who walks down this street does not recognise them at once as lackeys of the barbarians.'

Another splintering crash echoed from inside the temple, followed by shouts of protest, a scream and another crash.

Huang toyed with the pieces of the tangram on the table before him. 'You said you had encountered Killigrew more than once?'

Li nodded. 'When we rescued Zhai Jing-mu from the gaol. Zhai left Yeh and I to watch the front while he and the others escaped from the back. Yeh would have shot Killigrew if I had not knocked the barbarian out with a blow from behind.'

Yet another crash sounded across the street. Both Huang and Li turned their heads with mild curiosity as a young priest came flying headfirst through the splintered shutters of the temple to fall in the mud outside. A moment later Killigrew appeared in the doorway and marched across to where the priest was trying to crawl away. He grabbed the priest by the throat and hoisted him to his feet.

'Where can I find him?' the barbarian demanded in his execrable Cantonese.

The priest tried to kick Killigrew in the crotch, but the barbarian twisted aside and caught the blow on his thigh. He punched the priest on the jaw and threw him into the mud once again.

'Where?'

Huang sighed and turned his attention back to the tangram. 'These barbarians are crude and unsubtle in their methods. His blundering will spoil everything.'

'Do you want me to kill him?' offered Li, rising to his feet.

Before Huang could reply, something outside caught his attention again. Two Triad hatchet men had appeared and stood in the rain facing Killigrew. The barbarian grinned. 'Ah, at last. Just the gentlemen I'm looking for.'

'Wait,' Huang told Li. 'I want to see this.'

Li nodded and sat down again.

The Triads each drew their hatchets and circled around until they were standing on either side of the barbarian. Killigrew reached under his coat and drew his cutlass. One of the hatchet men charged with a wild shout. Killigrew dodged him and danced to one side so that he could keep an eye on both of them at once. The second attacked. Killigrew parried the Triad's hatchet and ducked, turning away, as the first came at him again. Their weapons clashed, and the head was sliced from the haft of the hatchet. As the hatchet man staggered forwards, Killigrew struck him on the back of the head with the hilt of his cutlass. Dazed, the Triad stumbled into the wall of the temple and sank into the mud.

The second hatchet man struck at Killigrew from behind but the barbarian seemed to sense it coming. He whirled away, the skirts of his greatcoat flying, and parried the Triad's next blow. A swipe from the Triad's hatchet caught the hilt of the cutlass and tore it from his grip. Then the first was back on his feet again and seized Killigrew from behind in an arm lock.

Grinning victoriously, the second advanced on Killigrew and raised his hatchet to bury it in his skull. The barbarian kicked him in the crotch. As the Triad doubled up with a howl, Killigrew flicked a boot into his face and the hatchet man sank into the mud.

'He is a meritorious fighter,' observed Huang.

'For one who knows nothing of *wu-yi*,' Li sniffed contemptuously.

Still caught in the first Triad's arm lock, Killigrew threw himself backwards across the street. The Triad's feet slipped in the mud and he was thrown across one of the tables at the eating stall. The plainclothes policeman jumped up and ran clear to stand under the eaves of the next shop along. He watched, reluctant to get involved and looking as forlorn as the last *dim-sum* at a banquet.

The Triad recovered and pushed the barbarian off, still holding one of his arms in the small of his back. He pushed Killigrew's face towards the glowing cinders of the eating stall's cove. The barbarian pushed back, but the Triad was stronger. Killigrew reached up until his fingers closed around the handle of a wok hanging from an overhead rack. A resounding clang sounded across the street and the Triad staggered back with blood gushing from his nose.

'Resourceful, too,' said Huang.

The Triad shook his head muzzily, noticed the barbarian's cutlass at his feet and snatched it up. He circled Killigrew once more, grinning wolfishly. The barbarian parried a sword-stroke with the wok and then threw it at the Triad's head, but the hatchet man ducked and the wok splashed into the mud.

The Triad charged. Killigrew fumbled on the table behind him and snatched up an implement. Holding it before him, he revealed it to be a single chopstick.

Li almost laughed out loud, but Huang was watching the fight intently.

The Triad charged, swinging the cutlass at Killigrew's neck. The barbarian side-stepped, slipped in the mud and thus by accident rather than design avoided a blow which would otherwise have decapitated him.

'He possesses that quality which even the best of us cannot survive without,' said Huang. 'Good fortune.'

'But fortune is a fickle mistress,' pointed out Li, wafting his hand half-heartedly at a fly which had buzzed in out of the rain. 'See, now he is finished.'

The Triad stood over Killigrew and tried to stab him in the chest with the cutlass. The barbarian caught him by the wrist and pulled him down. The two of them rolled over and over until Killigrew was on top. He banged a fist into the Triad's throat, and when he took his hand away Li saw a chopstick embedded there. Ironic, when one remembered that Confucius had said that chopsticks were preferable to knives because knives could be used as deadly weapons.

Staggering with exhaustion, Killigrew pushed himself to his feet. He looked around, the rain cutting rivulets through the mud which caked his face. He saw the second Triad recovering consciousness and splashed over to where he lay. Realising his peril, the Triad tried to crawl away but Killigrew caught him by one ankle and dragged him back through the mud to the eating stall. He dropped the Triad's leg, grabbed him by the tunic, and pulled him up out of the mud to throw him across one of the tables. Still holding him by the shirt front, he snarled in his face.

'Where's Zhai Jing-mu?'

Before the Triad could reply, a single shot rang out across the street and the top of his head was blown off. Killigrew looked around sharply. So did Li and Huang. Assistant Superintendent Cargill was sprinting through the mud with a pistol in one hand, the other plainclothes officer hard on his heels.

'You damned idiot!' Killigrew snarled furiously. 'He was about to tell me where Zhai Jing-mu is!'

Cargill reached down, seized the dead Triad's right arm and lifted it so that Killigrew could see the dagger in his hand. 'The only thing he was about to do was stick this between your ribs. What the deuce are you trying to do? Tackle the Brotherhood of Heaven, Earth and Man single-handed?'

'If that's what it takes.'

'I told you before. You worry about the pilongs and let me worry about the Triads.'

'And I told you: they're working together. The Triads could be the only link to Zhai Jing-mu.'

'If he's still alive.'

'Oh, he's alive, all right.'

'Then I dare say you won't have to go looking for him. He'll make his presence felt soon enough.'

Li and Huang watched the two barbarians walk away through the rain while the constables ordered a coolie to fetch a barrow to bear away the two dead Triads. The priest had crawled off shortly after the arrival of the two hatchet men.

'Do you still want me to kill him?' Li asked Huang.

'Do you think you can?'

The fly was buzzing about their heads again. Li watched it for a moment while taking out his chopsticks. A lightning-like movement, and he had seized the fly between the sticks. 'Catching that fly was difficult. Exterminating the *fan kwae* will be easy.' He released the fly and it buzzed away.

'You did not kill the fly, Li.'

'I saw no reason to.'

The admiral chuckled. 'The time you spent learning *wu-yi* at that Shaolin Temple has left you with Buddhist tendencies, Li Cheng.'

Li did not smile. 'When the propitious moment arrives, I shall do what needs to be done.'

'The barbarian is no more dangerous than that fly.'

'But he has a potentially fatal tendency to turn up in the wrong place at the wrong time,' pointed out Li.

'You were right earlier when you said that killing a barbarian naval officer would draw too much attention. If Killigrew carries on the way he has done these past few months, it is likely he will get himself killed and save you the trouble. But if he gets too close, if he becomes a threat . . . I leave it to your discretion.'

Li nodded his head. 'Zhai tells me he has set up a rendezvous with Admiral Nie to arrange for him to be granted full pardon in return for helping to suppress the other pilongs on this coast.'

The admiral's brow became clouded. 'Curse Nie's interference! He must be stopped.'

Li stared down at the pieces of the tangram. There was something not right about the way they were arranged.

Huang opened a fist to show one of the pieces nestling there. He must have palmed it while Li was gazing out of the window. 'Is this what you are looking for? Make sure you have all the pieces of the puzzle before you try to see the picture. Remember, there is too much at stake for any errors. The destiny of the Celestial Kingdom depends on us.'

'Rumour has it that the *Golden Dragon* sails next week with a fortune in silver bullion stowed in her hold. And Killigrew on board.'

'It is obviously a trap,' snorted Huang.

'Yes,' agreed Li. 'But who is the spider, and who is the fly?'

'Are you certain you're fit for duty, Second?' Commander Robertson peered from beneath his bushy eyebrows as Killigrew stood to attention before the table in his day room.

'Never felt better, sir.' Even four weeks after moving out of the Bannatyne residence, the lieutenant still felt dreadful, his craving for laudanum as strong as his craving for opium had ever been, but at least he had strength enough to conceal the shakiness he felt. 'I've been taking plenty of exercise, trying to get myself back in shape.'

'Yes, Mr Cargill told me about your jaunt into Tai-ping-shan last week,' Morgan said drily. 'I can't say I approve of this plan you've drawn up with Captain Verran,' he snorted. 'Why not put more guns on the *Golden Dragon*? Or take more men? You'll be helpless if the pilongs attack.'

'No, sir. The pilongs must have plenty of spies here in Victoria. If they see us cramming men and guns on to the *Golden Dragon*, they'll know it's a trap. The only reason the pilongs have never attacked her before is because they've never had incentive enough to do so.' Verran had put word out that the steamer was carrying a fortune in silver bullion, although if an attack on the *Golden Dragon* was successful, the pilongs were going to be sorely disappointed: her cargo consisted of nothing more valuable than several strongboxes packed with bars of iron ballast.

'At least let me follow in the *Tisiphone*,' urged Robertson.

'That way, if the pilongs do attack, we'll be there almost at once, to even the odds . . .'

'No, sir. The pilongs will see the *Tisiphone* leave in our wake and again know it's a trap.'

'I suppose it makes sense,' said Morgan. 'I'm just worried that in your eagerness to make the *Golden Dragon* look like a temptingly helpless target, you might make her too helpless in reality.'

'Captain Verran's confident that the *Golden Dragon* can hold her own against a pilong attack, sir, and I trust him to pick a crew he can rely on utterly.'

'On your own head be it, Lieutenant,' said Morgan. 'But bear in mind that if things go wrong this time, it won't be a question of what I'll do to you: the pilongs will make any punishment I can cook up for you a purely academic question.'

They stood up and left Robertson's quarters. 'You still haven't told me which four men you want to take,' the commander remarked to Killigrew as they headed for the companionway.

'I thought I'd take O'Connor, Dando, Firebrace and Gadsby.'

'Firebrace and Gadsby!' exclaimed Morgan. 'Aren't those the two you recently had flogged for desertion, Commander?'

Robertson nodded.

'They've been punished for their crime, sir,' said Killigrew. He had been the one who had dragged the two absconders from their hiding place in a brothel in Tai-ping-shan back in January, only to see them subjected to the barbarity of the lash. It had not made him feel proud.

'That's debatable,' snorted Morgan. 'If it were up to me, I'd've hanged the swine.'

'I thought it would help restore their self-esteem if we showed we had some trust in them. A sailor without self-esteem is no good to anyone.'

'I understand your thinking, Killigrew,' Robertson said as they ascended the companionway. 'But are you sure that on a voyage as perilous as this one, you wouldn't prefer to have someone more experienced at your back? I understand that Molineaux has already volunteered, and I'm sure I could spare Ågård.'

'I wouldn't want to be accused of favouritism, sir,' Killigrew replied as they emerged from the after-hatch on to the quarterdeck. Heavy raindrops pattered noisily against the awning spread over the deck and churned the waters of Victoria Harbour into an unending dance of bouncing droplets. 'Besides, Firebrace and Gadsby will never get any experience if we keep relying on the experienced men. Dando and O'Connor are both stout hands; and I'm gambling that Firebrace and Gadsby will be seeking to redeem themselves.'

'I suppose you know what you're doing,' Robertson sighed in a tone of voice which suggested he did not believe a word of it. He turned to the boatswain. 'Have Able Seamen Dando and O'Connor, and Landsmen Firebrace and Gadsby, report to me at once.'

'Aye, aye, sir.'

Killigrew pulled the brim of his cap down over his eyes against the rain and buttoned his greatcoat, tying the belt in a casual knot. 'Go to my cabin and fetch my dunnage,' he told Dando when the four sailors reported on the quarterdeck. 'Then fetch your kit bag. Same goes for the rest of you. We'll be spending a few weeks on detached service on board the *Golden Dragon*.'

The four seamen exchanged puzzled glances. Of all the ratings on board the *Tisiphone*, only Ågård and Molineaux knew about the proposed plan to use the *Golden Dragon* to trap the pilongs, and Killigrew knew they could both be trusted to keep their mouths shut. Scuttlebutt being what it was, what became known amongst the hands would soon be common knowledge ashore, and that would ruin everything.

He hoped that Verran had shown a similar discretion with the hands aboard the *Golden Dragon*.

They went down into Morgan's waiting gig with the captain and were rowed through the driving rain to where the *Golden Dragon* was anchored, loading supplies for the coming voyage from a harbour lighter.

Morgan cast his gaze across the harbour to where some Chinese were laying the keels of some large canoes on the stocks. 'What are they building over there?' he wondered out loud. 'Fishing boats?'

Killigrew took out his pocket telescope and levelled it briefly. 'Dragon boats, sir.'

'Dragon boats?'

'Yes, sir. For the festival next month. The Chinese hold the dragon boat festival every year around the fifth day of the fifth month of their lunar calendar. It's supposed to commemorate an ancient Chinese poet and statesman who drowned himself in a river. The people set out to find his body, but to no avail, so they made offerings to the gods of the river. The dragon boat race commemorates it. The different Chinese trade guilds each build their own dragon boat and race against one another. It's quite a spectacle to see.'

They were drawing closer to the *Golden Dragon* now. A hundred feet from stem to stern, the steamer was even smaller than the *Tisiphone*. Like the *Tisiphone*, she was a 'flapper' – a paddle-steamer; what the Chinese referred to as an 'outside-walkee' – with two masts straddling the single funnel.

By the time they climbed up the accommodation ladder, Captain Verran awaited them at the entry port with Assistant Superintendent Cargill. For once Verran's characteristic insouciant grin was in abeyance. 'Welcome aboard, Kit.' He ignored Captain Morgan for the moment, clearly enjoying the chance to snub a man he would have to have shown deference to in his navy days.

'These your lads?' He indicated Dando, Firebrace, Gadsby and O'Connor.

Killigrew nodded, dusting rainwater from his cap with the back of his hand.

'Hassan!' Verran waved across one of his petty officers, a brown-limbed Malay. 'This is Abdul Hassan, my *ghaut serang*,' he added to Killigrew. Verran turned back to Hassan. 'This is Lieutenant Killigrew; he's going to be in command of the *Golden Dragon* for our next voyage. As long as he's on board, you'll obey one of his own orders as if it were my own.'

Hassan bowed before Killigrew. '*Tuan.*'

'Have Mr Killigrew's dunnage taken below to his cabin and see his men to their berths in the fo'c'sle.'

'Aye, aye, sir.' Hassan snapped his fingers at a couple of Filipino sea-cunnies and issued orders to them in rapid Malay.

Studying the upper deck, Killigrew saw that the *Golden Dragon* was well run, the decks not unnecessarily cluttered, all ropes ends squared off, the rigging taut and in good condition. He also noticed that she had her own cannon: a thirty-six-pound bow-chaser and an eight-inch pivot gun in the stern, which made her armament only slightly inferior to that of the *Tisiphone*. He hoped it would be enough to defend the steamer against any ambush that Zhai Jing-mu might be planning for them.

Morgan cast a disdainful eye over Verran's crew, a mixture of Lascars, Malays and Filipinos, most of them carrying daggers, swords and wavy-bladed krises in their sashes. One or two even carried ancient flintlock pistols which looked as if they might be as hazardous to the firer as to the target. They scuttled about the rigging with all the agility of spiders negotiating their own webs. 'Are all your crew natives, Mr Verran?' asked Morgan.

'All except my two *tindals* . . . mates, I mean.'

'I know what *tindals* are, Mr Verran.'

'They're both Yankees. I'll introduce you to them later, Kit.'

'They're a piratical-looking bunch,' said Morgan.

Verran grinned. 'I suppose so. I dare say some of them have been pirates, at some point in their lives. But there isn't a man on board who isn't one hundred per cent loyal to me. And these sea-cunnies are some of the best sailors in the world, Cap'n Morgan.'

'Except the British sailor,' sniffed Morgan.

'And the Krumen,' added Killigrew.

Verran bowed mockingly in deference to Morgan's superior wisdom.

'Before I can send you off on this voyage there are certain formalities to be attended to,' said Morgan, and indicated his clerk. 'Taylor has the paperwork with him. May we use your day room?'

'But of course, Cap'n.' Verran ushered Morgan and his clerk down the after-hatch, winked at Killigrew, and followed them below.

Killigrew was about to go after them, but Cargill stopped him. 'Wondered if I might have a word?' he asked, stroking his whiskers.

'By all means.' Killigrew guided the assistant superintendent over to one corner of the quarterdeck where they could talk with some degree of privacy.

'I'm sorry about what happened to Miss Dadabhoy. I know you were fond of her. Her murder shocked us all. I think you should know that no one blames you for what happened.'

'Except myself,' Killigrew said tightly. He did not like to talk about what had happened, but every night he lay awake, wondering if she might still be alive if he had played things differently.

'It was Zhai Jing-mu who killed her. Now you know what kind of men you're up against, Killigrew. It's all very well the lawyers talking about due process and prisoners' rights; that's what allowed Zhai Jing-mu to escape in the first place. But I'm sure I don't have to tell you that what answers in the Admiralty Court doesn't necessarily answer on the South China Sea.'

'I hear that someone poisoned the prisoner we had in the gaol.'

Cargill nodded grimly. 'My fault. I should have known that someone would try to hush him. But it only shows what ruthless villains we're dealing with. You can't afford to take half-measures. This is war, and the only good pilong is a dead pilong.' Cargill clapped Killigrew on the shoulder as Verran, Morgan and his clerk re-emerged from the after-hatch. 'I'm going ashore with Captain Morgan. Good luck, Killigrew. I only wish I were coming with you. Next time, perhaps, eh?'

As Verran stood at the entry port to see Morgan off, Cargill had a word with him before he descended the accommodation ladder. Something he said made Verran glance back at Killigrew. When he saw the lieutenant watching them, Verran smiled and waved before turning back to Cargill.

'Loo-tenant Killigrew?'

Killigrew turned and saw a young man of about twenty. He was snub-nosed, and although he had obviously grown a beard to make him look older, it actually had the opposite effect. 'Hayes is the name, sir. Billy Hayes. I'm the number-one *tindal*.' He grinned. 'What you'd be calling the first mate. Welcome aboard, sir. The cap'n asked me to show you to your cabin.'

'Much obliged.' Killigrew allowed the *tindal* to show him below decks. 'So tell me, Mr Hayes, how does a son of Columbia come to be serving on a British steamer in Chinese waters crewed by sea-cunnies?'

Hayes grinned. 'When I was a kid I used to work on my pa's barquentine on Lake Erie, running furs down from Canada. Then I got a job on the brig *Pilgrim*, out of

Boston, sailing around the Horn to fetch bullocks' hides from California. I met Cap'n Verran in San Diego and he offered to pay me twice what I was getting on the *Pilgrim*.'

'What was Verran doing in San Diego?'

Hayes turned away to open the door to one of the cabins for him. 'Running mails across to the States for Mr Bannatyne. This here's your cabin, sir. Hope it suits.'

Killigrew took in the accommodation. The cabin was marginally smaller than the one he enjoyed on the *Tisiphone*, which was small enough. But what this one lacked in space it certainly made up for in comfort and style, with polished teak fittings and plush velvet furnishings. 'Don't worry,' he told Hayes with a faint smile. 'It won't be the first time I've had to rough it.'

Hayes grinned. 'Yeah, the cap'n's told me all about you, sir. Syria, Borneo, China, the Guinea Coast . . . Reckon if your navy had had a few more boys like you back in 1812, things might have been real different. Good to have you aboard, sir. We'll soon bring them pilongs to heel. Cap'n says to let you unpack and then you can join him on the quarterdeck. We'll be setting sail on the afternoon tide.'

'Thank you, Mr Hayes.'

'Call me Bully.'

Killigrew waited until the *tindal* had gone out before opening his sea chest. Then he took out his pepperbox, checked it was loaded and slipped it into one of the capacious pockets of his greatcoat. He was unpacking his shirts into a drawer when he found a full bottle of laudanum. He took it out and stared at it for a moment.

'Thanks, Jago, but no thanks.'

He crossed to the porthole and was about to throw the bottle out when instead he pulled out the stopper, took a sip, and smiled. He had forgotten how good the taste was. He took a longer pull, and at once a warm feeling of contentment spread outwards from his stomach. He replaced the stopper and put the bottle back in the drawer.

# *XII:*

# *Wheel of Death*

Killigrew and his opponent circled one another on the quarterdeck of the *Golden Dragon*, where the awning stretched overhead protected them from the heavy rain. Both of them were out of breath from wielding their heavy cutlasses. Killigrew aimed a slash at his opponent's head and the man brought his own blade up to parry, but the blow was a feint and Killigrew tried to slide in under his guard. His opponent was as fast as lightning, though, and managed to knock the thrust aside before it went home. He took a step back, drawing the lieutenant on. Killigrew lunged but his opponent side-stepped, caught him off balance and slashed at him as he staggered past. His razor-sharp blade sliced through the fabric of Killigrew's sleeve and drew blood from his upper arm.

'*Touché!*'

'*Pax!*' responded Killigrew.

Verran grinned. 'You're slowing up in your old age, Kit.'

'And you've learned a few tricks since we were in the *Dreadful*.' Killigrew parted the rent in his sleeve to study the cut below.

'Gosh, did I do that?' Verran exclaimed as they both

slotted their cutlasses into their scabbards. 'Sorry. I just got carried away . . .'

'Lack of control, Jago. Didn't I always tell you control was paramount?'

'Yes, but that was in another context, I seem to recall.'

'Never mind. It's just a scratch,' Killigrew said truthfully enough. 'I think you won that bout.'

'And the match. Well! I never thought the day would come when I could get the better of Kit Killigrew with a cutlass! This deserves an entry all of its own in my journal.' Verran turned to his steward. 'Fetchee two-piecey char, Muda.'

The Malay grinned. '*Hai*, Missee Verran.' He scurried below.

The *Golden Dragon* was two days out of Victoria, having touched at Macao before turning south for Cape Padaran on the coast of Cochin China. The rain continued ceaselessly, falling from a leaden sky which stretched from horizon to horizon, so dark there was little to choose between day and night. The steamer's engineer, a cheerful Scot named MacGillivray, had kept steam up in the boilers in case they needed to manoeuvre quickly if and when the pilongs attacked, but so far they had been able to run before a soldier's wind from abaft and they had made an average of seven knots under sail alone. The steamer pitched roughly over the steep, foam-veined waves, but two seasoned sailors like Killigrew and Verran had little difficulty maintaining their balance. They had been overhauled by a couple of clippers and passed a Peninsula and Oriental steamer bound for Hong Kong, but had yet to sight any pirates.

'The wind's freshening,' remarked Verran. 'Better take in the t'gallants, Mr Boggs.'

'Aye, aye, sir!' Verran's number-two *tindal*, a handsome youth with a girlish face and delicate hands, turned away to issue orders to the hands. Killigrew watched as Dando,

Firebrace, Gadsby and O'Connor ascended the rigging with the sea-cunnies to furl the topgallant sails.

'What do you think of my crew, Kit?' asked Verran.

'Morgan was right about one thing: they *are* a villainous-looking bunch of pirates. But they know what they're about, I'll say that much for them. What about my lads? I trust they're pulling their weight?'

'I've had no complaints.'

Killigrew watched as Boggs played a rope's end against the backs of some sea-cunnies who were not hauling on the clew lines fast enough for his taste. 'Your number-two *tindal*'s a little on the young side, isn't he?'

'Boggs? Perhaps. But this is a young man's game; you know that, Kit. Besides, he's got a sharp mind, a firm hand and the ambition to go places. You mark my words, one day Mr Boggs is going to make a name for himself in these waters.'

'Light off the port bow!' called the look-out at the masthead.

Killigrew and Verran exchanged glances. 'Want to go and see what it is?' suggested Verran.

Killigrew nodded and took the telescope from the binnacle. He climbed a short way up the ratlines, hooking one elbow around a shroud to secure himself, and pointed the telescope with one hand over the lens to try to keep the rain off it. It was almost impossible to make anything out through the sheeting downpour, yet he could see not one but two blazing fires about a mile away.

He closed the telescope and climbed back down to the deck. 'Looks like a couple of junks on fire.' He remembered that they were approaching the reefs and islands of the Paracels, where he had first encountered Zhai Jing-mu.

'Looks like there's mischief afoot,' said Verran. 'Must be the work of pilongs. Two points to starboard, Suleiman. Better bring in the flying jib and have the leadsman in the chains, Hassan.'

'*Tuan*, Missee Verran. All hand to quarter!'

'There could be men dying on those junks, Jago,' Killigrew murmured as the *Golden Dragon* nosed her way forward, the leadsman calling the soundings from the chains.

'I know, Kit, but there are dangers in these waters other than pilongs. I don't want to go steaming in only for us to tear our bottom out on a reef. Mr Boggs, go below and tell Mr MacGillivray to have the engines ready to turn full astern when I give the word. If this turns out to be a trap, I want us to be ready to pull back in a hurry.'

'Aye, aye, sir.' Boggs went below to the engine room.

At length the *Golden Dragon* crested another steep wave and suddenly the junks – there were three of them – leaped into clear view through the sheeting rain, less than two cables away. All three were on fire, but only one was fully ablaze. Another had sunk with only its topmasts showing above the waves, but the fire had never really caught hold of the largest and now the spume and the rain had conspired all but to extinguish its charred timbers.

'Imperial men-o'-war,' said Verran.

Killigrew nodded. He had already seen the three tigers' heads painted on the stern of the largest. He knew it could not be Admiral Huang's junk; that had still been moored in Victoria Harbour when the *Golden Dragon* had sailed, and while junks were deceptively swift there was no way Huang could have got here ahead of them.

There was a regular booming crash, the sound of breakers on a reef, and the next time a wave lifted the *Golden Dragon* out of a trough they could see the white horses pounding over the rocks about half a mile away beyond the junks. Hassan, the *ghaut serang*, ordered the sails boxed, and the steamer hove to.

Killigrew studied the flagship through the telescope. It was massive, as big as Huang's. There was no sign of life on deck, but even at that distance the high-sided junk seemed to tower over the steamer.

'I'm going on board the flagship,' Killigrew said in a firm voice. He half expected Verran to argue – they both knew it would be madness to try in these conditions – but the captain merely nodded.

'Mr Hayes! Prepare the jolly boat. We're sending a search party on board the big junk.'

The jolly boat was swung out in its davits. Killigrew and the boat's crew went below to put on their oilskins before they emerged from beneath the *Golden Dragon*'s awning. 'Watch yourself, Kit,' Verran warned Killigrew as he prepared to join Hayes and the others in the boat. 'It could be a trap.'

'I don't think we'll find any pilongs lying in wait. They're bold fellows, but not bold enough to linger on board a junk which is being carried towards a reef while they're waiting on the chance that we might turn up.'

'Perhaps. But don't you linger too long, either. I reckon you've got less than an hour before she strikes. And leave one man on deck, watching this ship. If I see any other vessels put in an appearance, I'll send up a blue light. When that happens you come straight back, all right? I don't care if you find the Crown Jewels on board, you leave them.'

'I just want to take a look-see, to try to find out what happened here.'

Killigrew climbed down the side ladder to where the jolly boat bobbed up and down in the *Golden Dragon*'s lee quarter with Hayes and half a dozen seamen in it. He waited until the boat neared the zenith of its next rise, and then jumped down, when the drop was shortest. Then the wave slipped away from beneath them and the boat dropped sickeningly away from the steamer's side.

'All right, pull!' roared Hayes. 'Every mother's son of you! Pull, damn you!'

The rain lashed them as the boat was tossed up and

down by the heavy seas. In less than a minute every man in the boat was drenched through in spite of their oilskins. Killigrew knew that even if he had been able to get at the pepperbox he wore beneath his rain-cape, it would be useless, the powder soaked through.

The brightly painted junk towered over them, its open gun ports dark and forbidding. A rope ladder hung down its side from the entry port in the lee waist, twenty feet above them. Killigrew stood up in the boat's prow and prepared to jump.

'I sure hope you know what you're doing, mister!' Hayes had to yell to make himself heard above the noise of the wind and the rain.

Killigrew took a deep breath, waited for the next wave to bring the ladder closer, and jumped. He hooked both hands over the second-from-bottom rung, but his fingers slipped on the wet board and left him dangling from one arm. He gripped the rope and hauled himself up until he could get one foot on the lowermost rung.

Gasping for breath, he tilted his head back and felt the heavy rain sting his face. There was no point in hanging around. Wondering what would be waiting for him on deck, he began to climb. Once he was immediately below the entry port, he hooked one arm around a rung and reached under his rain-cape to draw his cutlass. He took a deep breath and scrambled up the last couple of feet.

Whenever he remembered Chingkiang-fu, he was always at a loss to decide which was the greatest horror: the terrible hand-to-hand conflict on the battlements of the walled city, or the sights which had greeted him within the walls once the city had fallen. After one last desperate defence at the centre of the city, the Tartar soldiers had gone back to their homes, slaughtered their wives and daughters rather than let them be raped by the barbarian invaders, and then committed suicide. Killigrew would never forget wandering through those streets, where every house concealed the bodies of women hanged from the roof-beams with silken scarves in nooses about their necks, and children of all ages – even tiny babies – with their throats slit, their bodies tumbled into wells and fishponds. The stench of death in his nostrils, the blood of innocents wherever he turned, innumerable flies buzzing around the fast-rotting corpses on that stiflingly hot day. The memory was as fresh in 1849 as it had been seven years earlier.

As soon as he pulled himself through the entry port and crouched in the lee of the bulwark, sweeping the deck with his eyes for danger, Killigrew knew he had a new memory to add to the album. As horrific as the aftermath of Chingkiang-fu had been, it had been meant – in the eyes of the perpetrators, at least – as an act of kindness.

There was no evidence of any kindness on the junk. The lucky ones had died swiftly from sword-slashes. Each time the deck rolled, half a dozen decapitated heads tumbled from one side to the other. Even the slicing rain could not wash away all the blood. Others had died harder, tortured by men who took pleasure in suffering, then roasted alive. One man had been pinned to the door leading into the poop, skewered on a bamboo spear, his curved sword still hanging from his wrist by a leather thong. Another – a mandarin, from what Killigrew could see of his charred robes – had been hung by a long rope tied about his ankles from a crossbeam slung from the truck of the mainmast, high above. A fire had been lit below him, so that each roll of the junk's deck had swung his head through the flames.

Killigrew bit back the bile which rose to his gorge.

'Sweet Jesus!' gasped Hayes, appearing at the entry port beside him. Both of them were too stunned to say anything for a few moments. They gazed at the grisly scene with horror and revulsion as four of the sea-cunnies climbed up the side ladder behind them, leaving two in the boat.

Hayes was the first to find his tongue again. 'God-damned heathens! Zhai Jing-mu's work?'

'Who else would do such a thing?' Killigrew's hoarse voice cracked. 'Come on. Let's see what we can find.'

'What are we supposed to be looking for?'

'I don't know,' Killigrew said irritably. It was not the slaughter he found so offensive. He himself had had recourse to killing enough times in his career not to condemn it out of hand, and these poor devils had been sailors of the Imperial Chinese Navy who, like the men on board the *Tisiphone*, had known what they were signing up for when they had joined. What was so sickening was the relish that had obviously gone into this atrocity. Killigrew bottled up his anger; he swore to himself he would uncork it at a later date, and let Zhai Jing-mu have a taste of the vintage. 'There may be survivors.'

''Vast heaving, Killigrew! Seems to me the pilongs have done a goddamn thorough job.'

'Nevertheless, Mr Hayes, we must be certain.' Killigrew picked his way between the corpses and headed aft to the cabin beneath the poop. Much of the raised stern had been burned away, the charred timbers steaming slightly in the incessant rain. There was more blood here, another body, huddled in a shapeless mass at the foot of a bulkhead.

He found a hatch and descended. The rainwater which gathered on deck trickled steadily from the corners of the hatch and made crazy patterns on this lower deck. The paper lanterns which illuminated the 'tween decks still burned, and as they swung with the rolling of the junk they cast eerie shadows back and forth. The rain hammered down above, and the timbers creaked, but even so it was quiet enough for Killigrew to be aware of his own breath rasping raggedly through his teeth.

Below decks, the junk's hull was divided up into a series of watertight compartments which could be sealed off in the event of the hull being breached; another ingenious Chinese innovation. Killigrew stepped up to one of the doors and listened. Was it his imagination, or could he hear sobbing on the other side of the door? He flexed his fingers around the grip of his cutlass, balanced on one foot, and kicked the door. It swung open, stopped short before it reached the bulkhead as it struck something with a thud, and then swung back. In the same instant he heard a yelp of pain.

He pushed the door open once more and barged through, whirling to face the young Chinese who had been hiding behind the door. The man looked dazed – a massive bruise already swelled on his forehead – but his eyes widened when he saw Killigrew and he snatched up the curved sword he had dropped. He was dressed in the sky-blue uniform of an Imperial soldier, a black silk cap with an upturned brim and two squirrels' tails hanging down behind, and a yellow patch on his chest embroidered with the Chinese character for 'brave'. He was clearly terrified as he pointed his sword at Killigrew with trembling fingers. Killigrew could hardly blame him. The brave must have hidden down here when the pilongs had attacked the junk. He must have heard the screams of his comrades as they had been tortured to death, knowing that a similar fate must await him if his hiding place was discovered. And now, after being stranded on this drifting junk with no company but corpses, the vessel which had come to rescue him was crewed by 'ocean ghosts'.

Killigrew backed away from the terrified brave. 'Do not be alarmed,' he said in Cantonese. 'I mean you no harm. I will try to help you, if I can. See, I am going to put my sword away.' He slotted his cutlass into its scabbard. The brave regarded him with suspicion, but lowered his sword after a moment.

'What have you got?' demanded Hayes, coming through the door behind him.

The brave immediately brought up his sword once more. His grimy face was streaked with tears, but his expression was grimly determined.

'Tartar brave,' Killigrew said in English, and switched back to Cantonese for the soldier's benefit. 'It is all right, he is a friend. We are not going to harm you. What is your name?'

The brave cuffed the tears from his cheeks. 'Yan.'

'All right, Yan. My name is Kit Killigrew; I'm an officer of the British navy. You understand British navy?'

Yan nodded. 'High-nose barbarians enemies of Celestial Kingdom.'

Killigrew shook his head. 'Not enemies. Friends. Britain and China are at peace now. We're going to help you. But you must come with us. This junk is adrift and being carried towards a reef. In a few minutes, the rocks will tear out her keel. Then she will either sink or be pounded on the reef. Understand?'

Yan nodded, and sheathed his sword.

The boarding party made a cursory search of the rest of the junk but found no one else. They put Yan in the boat and rowed back to where Verran awaited them on the deck of the *Golden Dragon*. Yan had never been on a barbarian devil-ship before and was apprehensive, but Killigrew managed to reassure him. He took Yan down to the saloon, gave him a towel to dry himself and a shot of brandy to steady his nerves. He poured himself a generous measure, too. He felt he needed it after the sights he had seen on the deck of the junk. There was still some laudanum in the bottle Verran had left in his cabin; he would need it to help him sleep tonight.

Yan gasped as he swallowed the fiery liquor. 'How-how-ah!'

'Good?'

'Very good!'

Killigrew smiled and sat down facing the brave. 'Yan, I need you to tell me what happened. Most importantly, I need you to tell me how much time passed between the pilongs leaving the junk and our arrival. Do you have any idea?'

Yan shook his head. 'I know they attacked at the Hour of the Snake. After that I lost track of the time.'

Killigrew knew that the Hour of the Snake could mean any time between nine and eleven o'clock in the morning. He glanced at the chronometer on the sideboard. It was twenty-three minutes past one. 'So there was not much time between the pilongs leaving and our arrival?'

Yan grimaced. He seemed much more relaxed now. 'It felt like much time.'

'I know, Yan, I'm sure it did.' Killigrew's mind was racing. Even if the pilongs had attacked the junks at nine, they could not be more than a couple of hours away. 'Did you see which direction they sailed in?'

Yan shook his head. 'No. I was hiding below decks. I stayed there until all was quiet, and then I waited longer. I thought it might be a trick, to make me come out of hiding.' He hung his head. 'I was very afraid.'

'That's only natural. Amongst my people I am considered very brave, but I am frightened sometimes too. I know if I had been through what you have endured today, I would have gone out of my mind with terror.'

Yan looked morose. 'I am a coward. I hid and left my comrades to die.'

'Listen, Yan. You followed the only sensible course of action. If you had come out of hiding, you too would have been killed, and there would have been no benefit. But now you can help us catch the pilongs who attacked your junk, and avenge the deaths of your comrades.'

Yan did not look much cheered by this prospect. Before Killigrew could urge him to try to remember some clue which might give them an indication as to which direction the pilongs had sailed in, there was a knock at the door. Still jumpy, Yan looked up in alarm.

'It's all right, Yan. You stay there.' Killigrew stood up and opened the door a crack.

It was Muda, the *Golden Dragon*'s Malay steward, with a

tray of food for the prisoner. 'Captainee wantchee savvy if Chinee man tellee alla yet?'

'Not yet, Muda.' Killigrew took the tray from the steward and closed the door behind him with his heel. He put the tray down in front of Yan. 'Are you hungry?'

Yan nodded. 'Very.'

'The ship's cook prepared this for you.' The tray bore a bowl of stewed pork, another of fried rice, and a pair of chopsticks: a reassuringly Oriental meal for their Chinese guest. Yan thanked Killigrew and tucked in eagerly.

The lieutenant sat back in his chair and lit a cheroot. He was impatient to get in pursuit of the pilongs, but he knew that pressing the brave would only make him panic, and a man who was panicking could not think clearly.

Yan was almost halfway through the meal when he looked up suddenly. 'I heard! I heard the pilongs talking. They said something about "the brothers".'

For a moment Killigrew wondered if he was talking about the Brotherhood of Heaven, Earth and Man, and then it clicked. There were two islets off the coast of Lan-tao Island known as 'the Brothers'. But that was in Cap-sing-mun anchorage, right beneath the noses of the barbarians, and seemed an unlikely rendezvous for pilongs. Dredging his memory he remembered there were two more islets, also named 'the brothers', off the coast of Hainan Island.

'Did they mean the ones off the south coast of Hainan?' he asked.

'I do not know. I suppose that might be what they meant.'

'All right, Yan. You stay here and finish your dinner. I'll tell Captain Verran.'

Even as Killigrew made his way from the saloon to Verran's quarters, his initial elation was overhauled by suspicion. He did not doubt Yan was telling the truth, but it was all too easy. Could it be the pilongs had known that the *Golden Dragon* was coming, and they had deliberately let Yan overhear them talking about the Brothers as the bait to an elaborate trap?

He knocked on the door to Verran's day room.

'Who is it?'

'Killigrew.'

'Come in, Kit.' Verran's day room was decorated like any English parlour, with chintz antimacassars over the easy chairs and lace curtains as delicate as cobwebs stretched over the stern window. Verran was sitting down to dinner. 'Close the door behind you. Has your new pal told you anything yet?'

'He overheard the pilongs say something about the Brothers.'

'Off Hainan?' Verran was on his feet in an instant. He crossed to the door and called up. 'Mr Boggs!'

'Sir?'

'Set a course north by north-west for the Brothers, off Hainan Island. Tell Mr MacGillivray full speed ahead.'

'Aye, aye, sir.'

Verran closed the door and sat down again. 'We can reach the Brothers in a day's steaming,' he told Killigrew enthusiastically. 'If we're only a few hours behind the pilongs there's every chance we'll overhaul them on the way.'

'Perhaps that's what they want.'

'What do you mean?'

'It's all too convenient, Yan having overheard a vital clue like that.'

'You think your new pal might be a plant?'

'Even William Macready isn't that good an actor. But it could be they deliberately let him escape detection, and then let him overhear their intentions.'

Verran stared at him, and then laughed. 'By God, Kit, you're a suspicious son of a gun, aren't you?'

'Doctor's orders. He says I'll increase my life expectancy

so long as I don't accept anything at face value.'

Verran chuckled. 'I'm surprised your doctor didn't recommend you swallow the anchor and take a job in the City, if he's so worried about your life expectancy.'

Killigrew grinned. 'He did. I told him it was out of the question.'

'He's probably worried about whether or not you'll live long enough to pay his bills. Don't worry, Kit. If it *is* a trap, the pilongs are going to discover that this dragon has sharp claws.'

Killigrew almost choked when Yan told him that the three Imperial junks had sailed to the Paracels not to catch Zhai Jing-mu, but to parley with him. 'Admiral Nie wanted to offer him an amnesty for all his crimes and a post in the Imperial Navy, in return for his helping to sweep the other pilongs from the seas,' explained Yan.

'Was Admiral Nie acting on Imperial authority? I mean, did the Imperial Grand Council *know* what Nie was doing?'

'I do not know. I am only small fry; humble soldiers like me are told nothing. But I got the impression that negotiations had been going on between Admiral Nie and Zhai Jing-mu for many months. That is why the admiral thought it would be safe to meet Zhai at the rendezvous, why we let him and his men on board the flagship. We only allowed a few to board. We did not know that Zhai had other agents amongst our crew.'

'What happened? Did the negotiations fall apart?'

'I do not think so, Killigrew-qua. As soon as the pilongs had a foothold on board the flagship, the shooting began.'

'So either something changed Zhai's mind about accepting the amnesty, or he had been planning this for months, stringing Admiral Nie along with the attack in mind.'

'I suppose so.'

Killigrew wondered what Zhai Jing-mu hoped to achieve

by attacking three Imperial men-o'-war, apart from annoying the Imperial authorities even further. 'Was there any treasure on board any of the junks in the flotilla?' he asked Yan.

'I do not think so, but after the slaughter, I heard the pilongs taking armaments and ammunition from the junk: cannon, gunpowder, shot, *gingalls*, swords.'

'A valuable haul to a man like Zhai Jing-mu, but at a devilish price: I can't imagine anyone being foolish enough to offer him another chance at amnesty after this. He made the Imperial authorities lose 'face'. They'll go all out to catch him now. As long as the Ch'ing Dynasty rules in Peking, he'll never be safe.'

It was the morning of the day after they had found the three junks stricken off the Paracels. The monsoon was over, the rain had stopped abruptly and the heavy swells of the sea had given way to a light chop. The *Golden Dragon* steamed along the coast of Hainan Island, off the south coast of China, the sails close-hauled to give the steamer an extra few knots.

Killigrew had taken Yan on a tour of the steamer, explaining to him as simply as possible how the steam from the boilers powered the pistons which drove the paddle-wheels, and showing him the thirty-six pounder in the forecastle and the eight-inch shell-gun in the stern to reassure him they had nothing to fear from the pilongs they were sailing to meet. 'One hit from a shell can sometimes be enough to blow a junk clean out of the water,' he had told Yan. 'I know: I've seen it happen.' Sensible to the fact that if these barbarians meant him harm they had already had every opportunity to kill him, Yan was much more calm than he had been the day before.

'On deck there!' cried the look-out at the masthead. 'Sail ho!'

'Where away?' demanded Hayes.

'Dead ahead!'

Killigrew took the telescope from the binnacle and ascended to the top of the starboard paddle-box. Bracing his legs on the flat keel of the upturned paddle-box boat there, he extended the telescope and peered through the rain. Almost at once he picked out the mat-and-rattan sails of two three-masted junks sailing abreast before the wind. He descended to the quarterdeck once more.

'What's their heading?' asked Verran.

'West by north.'

'Coming straight towards us, you mean.'

Killigrew nodded. 'Or sailing along the coast in the opposite direction to us, depending on which way you look at it. You think it could be Zhai Jing-mu?'

'I doubt it. He's supposed to be sailing away from us, not towards us, remember?' He took the telescope from Killigrew and lifted it to his eye. 'It's probably just a pair of fishing junks.'

'All the same, if he was only a couple of hours ahead of us we should have caught him by now. You don't suppose we passed them in the night, do you?'

'It's possible. My people would have kept a pretty sharp look-out for them, but we could have passed them as they tacked miles to one side of our course.' He snapped the telescope shut and handed it to Hassan to replace in the binnacle. 'Still, at least we know where they're going. And if it's a trap, I'm sure they'll make certain we find them.'

'I still don't like it.' Killigrew lowered his voice. 'The most powerful shell-gun in the world can only shoot one junk at a time, and you know how these pilongs rely on force of numbers. If we find ourselves heavily outnumbered . . .'

Verran stared at him in astonishment. 'Kit! Surely you're not suggesting we turn tail and run back to Hong Kong?'

'Christ, no! But I want to make sure we give ourselves every possible advantage. If it *is* a trap, the pilongs will be expecting us to sail for the Brothers, correct?' Verran nodded. 'Why make it easy for them? The Brothers could be where their ambush is laid. I say we heave-to in Galong Bay, a couple of miles to westward. We'll stop the engines so the smoke from our funnel doesn't give them advance warning of our approach, anchor in the bay and send a boat ashore. A landing party can approach the Brothers from landward, and see what the pilongs have got in store for us.'

'Sounds like a first-rate plan to me. Let's go below and work out the details.'

'Later.' Killigrew nodded to where they were fast coming up on the two junks. 'These may not be Zhai Jing-mu's junks, but there's no reason why we should limit ourselves to him. There are plenty of other pilongs in these waters. We'll stop these two and search them. If they're not pilongs, they may be able to give us some information about where the pilongs are.'

'All right,' Verran said cautiously. 'We'll hail them as they pass us, then come about and overhaul them from astern. Hassan, call all hands to quarters.'

As the *Golden Dragon*'s crew scuttled to their action stations, Killigrew took out his pepperbox and checked each of the barrels was primed and loaded. He had cleaned it out after the soaking it had got the previous day; as long as he stayed under the awning which kept the worst of the rain off the steamer's deck, it should be all right.

He glanced up at the two junks again, so close now that all but their masts and sails were hidden beneath the *Golden Dragon*'s prow from where Killigrew stood on the quarterdeck. Both junks were less than half the size of Admiral Nie's flagship and if they were not careful they were going to be run-down by the steamer.

'Hadn't you better put the helm over?' asked Killigrew.

Verran grinned. 'The hell with them. They can move for us.'

For a moment it looked as though the two junks would

sail under the steamer's prow, but when they were less than two cables away they suddenly parted so that they would pass on either side of the *Golden Dragon*. Killigrew relaxed.

When the two junks were a hundred feet apart, a cable suddenly rose up out of the water between them, running between the sterns of the two junks.

It came to Killigrew in a flash: this was how they were able to catch and board faster vessels, meeting them head on; the cable would catch across the *Golden Dragon*'s prow, and the two junks would be swung in towards the steamer's sides, coming against her bulwarks fifty feet abaft of the prow. The pilongs would be perfectly placed to throw grappling irons over the steamer's bulwarks.

They meant to board the *Golden Dragon*!

Killigrew crossed the deck to where Dando, Firebrace, Gadsby and O'Connor stood on the forecastle with the rest of the bow-chaser's gun crew. 'Push her over to the aftermost port-side gun port! We'll knock out the one to port first as she comes under our prow; then we'll have only one left to worry about . . .'

Dando and O'Connor put their shoulders to the thirty-six-pounder and tried to slide it on its brass racers, but it was too heavy for just the two of them.

Killigrew rounded furiously on the two landsmen, Firebrace and Gadsby. 'Don't just stand there, you horse-marines! Bear a hand!' Swearing, Killigrew joined Dando and O'Connor at trying to move the bow-chaser.

A couple of pistol shots sounded and O'Connor gasped. Next to him, Dando slumped over the gun. Killigrew stared at them both in astonishment. O'Connor slid to the deck, dead, and Killigrew saw a bloody wound in Dando's back. He realised the shots had come not from the junks, but from behind him. As the two junks sailed past the prow on either side, he glanced over his shoulder and saw Firebrace with a pair of smoking pistols in his hands.

'Are you insane?' he spluttered.

Gadsby also had a pistol in one hand and he levelled it at Killigrew. 'Never saner, you sonuvabitch. Hand over the pepperbox.'

Killigrew stared at him for a moment. The two junks bumped against the steamer on either side, just ahead of the paddle-boxes. The rest of the *Golden Dragon*'s crew, far from preparing to repel boarders, were making fast the ropes which the pilongs threw up to them. A moment later the paddle-wheels stopped turning and Hassan ordered the sails boxed.

Realising that he had been betrayed on all sides, Killigrew put his hand on the grip of his pepperbox.

'Uh-hunh!' growled Gadsby. 'Handsomely does it, Mr Killigrew. Cap'n Verran says he wants you taken alive, but I'll put a bullet in your skull before I risk my own skin.'

Pinching the pistol between forefinger and thumb, Killigrew slowly unhooked his pepperbox from his belt. Gadsby grinned victoriously.

Killigrew tossed the pistol at him. 'Catch!'

Caught off guard, Gadsby dropped his own gun instinctively to clutch at the pepperbox. Killigrew kicked him in the crotch, and threw a left cross at Firebrace's jaw.

Hayes appeared behind them with a pistol in either hand. 'Not smart, Loo-tenant. You don't know when you're whupped, do you?'

Killigrew backed away. 'I'm a fast learner.'

Hayes smiled. 'Glad to hear it. Clasp your hands behind your head. Get his sword, Boggs.'

The number-two *tindal* dragged Killigrew's cutlass from its scabbard and backed away as the pilongs swarmed over the *Golden Dragon*'s sides. Somehow Killigrew was less than surprised to see Li Cheng amongst them, along with the Triad who had almost shot him the night of the gaolbreak. Li met his eyes with a penetrating glance, but it was impossible to tell what he was thinking. There was no sign of Zhai Jing-mu himself.

'Turn around.' Hayes gestured with one of his pistols. Killigrew had no choice but to obey. A moment later Boggs had thrown him against the thirty-six-pounder – for such a slight-looking youth, he was surprisingly strong – and Killigrew's wrists were bound behind his back.

Then a new voice cut across the words of command being given on the *Golden Dragon*'s deck. 'Everyone throw down their weapons!' a voice commanded in Cantonese. 'Or Captain Verran is the next to die!'

All eyes turned to the quarterdeck, where Yan stood behind Verran with a sword at the captain's throat. Verran did not look particularly troubled by this new development.

'He did his job well,' the *lao-pan* of one of the junks said in Cantonese. Killigrew recognised him as the Triad who had menaced him with a crossbow at Victoria gaol. 'Unwitting fool!'

'Yes,' Verran agreed in the same language. 'But we no longer have any purpose for him.'

Killigrew saw what was coming next. He looked about to see if there was some way he could forestall the inevitable, but with his hands tied behind his back he was helpless.

'Muda!' snapped Verran. Seated astride the main yard, the *Golden Dragon*'s steward raised an eight-foot-long bamboo blowpipe – Killigrew recognised the Malay sumpitan – to his lips.

'Look out, Yan!' yelled Killigrew.

It was too late: one puff from Muda, and a moment later Yan had released Verran to stagger back with his throat skewered by a long dart; tipped with deadly *radjun* venom, Killigrew had no doubt.

As Yan dropped to the deck, Verran nonchalantly flicked a piece of fluff from his shoulder, raised a hand in acknowledgement to Muda, and then exchanged bows of greeting with the *lao-pan*. Then he beckoned for Hayes to approach.

Hayes turned to Firebrace and Gadsby. 'Bring him,' he ordered curtly, indicating Killigrew.

The lieutenant was dragged across the quarterdeck. 'Running with the hare and hiding with the hounds?' he asked his one-time friend bitterly.

Verran grinned. 'I find life so much more exhilarating this way.'

'How much is Bannatyne paying you, Jago?'

'You think I'm in it for the money? Kit! I thought you knew me better than that.'

'Then why? Surely you don't find common cause with Zhai Jing-mu and the Triads?'

'Sheer devilment, old boy. Who'd've thought that pimply little Jago Verran would one day help to make history? I'd've asked you to join us if I'd thought you'd say yes, but you always were an utter prig, weren't you?'

'Better a prig than a murderous fiend. How can you work with a man like Zhai Jing-mu, damn you? He killed Peri in cold blood!'

Verran tutted. 'You were the one who took her to the *Akhandata* that day, Kit, not me.' Killigrew lunged for him furiously, but Firebrace and Gadsby held him back. After a moment he stopped struggling. 'As hot-blooded as ever, eh?' Verran continued. 'Perhaps if you hadn't been so fired up about avenging her death, Zhai Jing-mu wouldn't want your head on a plate for blowing him up.'

'You're going to burn in hell for this, Jago.'

'Oh, I dare say. But not for a very long time.'

Killigrew turned to Firebrace and Gadsby. 'I might have known this humbug would turn traitor, but what about you two?'

'Cap'n Verran here made us a better offer,' sneered Gadsby. 'Did you think that by showing you still had faith in us in spite of everything, you'd win our eternal loyalty?'

'That was the general idea,' Killigrew admitted ruefully.

Gadsby laughed. 'Your faith in human nature is touching, Killigrew, but sorely misplaced.'

'Jago and I were friends once,' Killigrew told them. He glared bitterly at Verran, who shrugged indifferently. 'Not too long ago, I might add. It didn't take long before he sold me down the river. If he can throw so many years of friendship away in a brace of shakes, how long do you two expect to last?'

'You'd say anything to save your own neck,' spat Firebrace.

Boggs handed Killigrew's pepperbox to Verran. The captain turned the revolving pistol over in his hands. 'Actually, Mr Firebrace, I'm afraid Mr Killigrew is absolutely right.'

Firebrace and Gadsby turned to stare at him with uneasy smiles. 'You wouldn't, would you?' pleaded Gadsby. 'We did everything you told us to. We had a deal . . .'

Verran rubbed his cheek with the muzzles of the pepperbox. 'What was it you said to Mr Killigrew just now? Ah, yes, that was it . . .' Verran levelled the pepperbox at Gadsby's head. ' "Your faith in human nature is touching, but sorely misplaced." '

He blew Gadsby's brains out. Firebrace turned and ran for the side. Verran's second shot took him between the shoulder blades before he got halfway across the deck. He sprawled on his face and lay motionless.

Verran turned to Li Cheng. 'Weigh the bodies down with chains and send them to Davey Jones' locker.'

Killigrew felt sick as he watched the bodies of Dando, Firebrace, Gadsby, O'Connor and Yan being tipped unceremoniously over the side. Perhaps Firebrace and Gadsby had got no more than they deserved, but Killigrew had served with Dando and O'Connor for nearly four years now and they had been loyal, while Yan had been an innocent pawn in all this, and had proved himself worthy of the title 'brave' in the final analysis, even if it had achieved nothing.

'I suppose a similar fate awaits me?' he asked Verran.

'Nothing so quick and painless, I assure you. It's nothing personal, you understand, but I have my orders.'

'So you take your orders from Zhai Jing-mu now?'

'For as long as it serves my purpose,' admitted Verran. 'He's very keen to renew his acquaintance with you, Kit. He said something about "an eye for an eye". I'm sure he'll explain it better than I can when we get where we're going.'

'And that would be . . .?'

'His lair, of course. What, did you think I would blurt out the location, so you could escape and then lead a flotilla of navy ships there? What is it my namesake says in the play? "Demand me nothing: what you know, you know." ' Verran shook his head and tutted. 'You never do give up, do you, Kit?'

'Not while there's breath in my body.'

'A circumstance which Zhai Jing-mu will not hesitate to rectify, I assure you.' Verran turned to the second *tindal*. 'Put him in irons in the lazarette, Mr Boggs. And watch him – he's a tricky devil.'

Boggs nodded and started to drag the lieutenant towards the forward hatch. Killigrew went willingly at first, then stopped abruptly. He pulled Boggs off balance, and then tripped him up with a sweep of one leg. Boggs hit the deck before anyone had a chance to realise what was happening. Killigrew ran on to the forecastle, got one foot on the carriage of the thirty-six-pounder and the other on the gun itself. A bullet whistled past his head. Balancing with difficulty because of his hands tied behind his back, he ran down the barrel towards the muzzle and then launched himself head-first over the side.

He plunged straight under, then jack-knifed his body under the prow and allowed the air trapped inside his clothes to buoy him up against the hull until he felt the keel between his shoulder blades. The keel was hardly sharp, but it was encrusted with barnacles which provided a rough, abrasive surface. He sawed the rope binding his hands against it, while the air in his lungs rapidly ran out.

A dark shape loomed through the water towards him: a shark. It zoomed straight at him, then seemed to change its mind and darted off in another direction. Another shark drifted past, further away. The blood from the bodies of the men tossed overboard would bring every shark for miles around: the sooner he got out of the water, the better.

The tightness in his chest was almost unbearable and for a moment he thought he was going to drown. The water had seeped through his clothes and he was losing his buoyancy, drifting down from the hull of the *Golden Dragon*. He pulled on his bonds in desperation and they snapped. Feeling a dark mist sweep over him, he kicked and clawed his way to the surface. He came up beneath the square-cut prow of the junk grappled to the starboard side of the steamer and whooped a great gulp of air into his lungs as he trod water.

He could hear footsteps pound the decks above him, and voices cried out confused orders in English, Malay and Cantonese. 'Find him, and kill him! Do whatever you have to do, but don't let him get away!'

'Over here!' shouted a voice immediately above Killigrew's head. 'I think I heard him surface!'

'Lower the jolly boat, chop chop!' shouted Verran. 'A hundred dollars to the man who brings me his head!'

A couple of bodies splashed into the water in quick succession and two pilongs surfaced, grinning savagely as they gripped daggers between their teeth. Killigrew ducked back under the water and swam beneath the *Golden Dragon*'s keel. No sooner had he surfaced in the lee of the other junk than a shot sounded from the deck of the steamer and a *gingall*-ball kicked up a spout of water close by. He swam in towards the *Golden Dragon*'s side, sheltering beneath the rear overhang of the paddle-box where the wheel itself gave him some cover from the deck of the second junk.

Something grabbed his ankle. He kicked instinctively with his other leg, hoping it was a pilong rather than a shark, and felt the sole of his foot connect with something. The other pilong had surfaced a short distance away.

Killigrew duck-tailed beneath the waves once more. Dazed, the first pilong was striking for the surface. Above Killigrew, the lower-most boards of the paddle-wheel hung motionless in the water. He pulled himself up between two of them. They were six feet across but only two and a half feet apart: a tight fit, but not too tight. He climbed up until he was inside the paddle-wheel. If the engines were started now, the barnacle-encrusted boards would slice him up like a Chinese cook preparing Peking duck.

As he stood on the inner-edge of the lower-most board, the axle was two feet above his head, but stanchions running across the wheel from side to side connected the spokes at chest height. The stanchions were slippery with marine slime, but by gripping on to one of the spokes he was able to balance enough to haul himself up until he could get both his feet on to the stanchion while wrapping his arms about the greasy axle.

Both the pilongs climbed into the wheel below him. 'We have him trapped!' once of them shouted in Cantonese. 'He's in the port-side paddle-wheel!'

'We could get at him if we lifted the paddle-box boat,' offered Hayes, somewhere above Killigrew's head.

'Why bother?' Verran called back. 'Have Mr MacGillivray start the engines: full ahead. I've always wondered what would happen if a man was inside the wheel when the engines were started,' he added sadistically.

# XIII:

## *Give a Dog a Bad Name . . .*

The two pilongs in the paddle-wheel must have understood English, for they exchanged shocked glances when they realised that they were expendable in Verran's eyes – and about to be expended. Killigrew was less shocked – it no longer came as any surprise to him that Verran wanted him dead – and he recovered first, kicking one pilong in the mouth in which he gripped his dagger. The pilong screamed as blood spurted. Moaning, he gave up trying to catch Killigrew and instead began to ease himself through the boards to get out of the wheel before it started to turn.

Killigrew was already climbing. It would take only a few seconds for the order to be relayed to MacGillivray in the engine room. The other pilong tucked his dagger in his sash and climbed nimbly up after him. He got his arms over the axle and grabbed one of Killigrew's ankles. The lieutenant kicked him in the wrist and continued climbing until he was able to reach up through the upper boards and pull himself up. There was not much space above the wheel, where the paddle-box boat formed the ceiling, but he squeezed through. He tried to climb through the thwarts of the upturned boat and still had his feet on the boards when the wheel started to rotate.

The pilong was climbing up and had his feet on the axle and his arms on one of the stanchions. He cried out. Killigrew stepped on to the next board, and then the next, struggling to keep from falling as the boards moved beneath his feet with increasing speed.

The wounded pilong was only halfway between two of the boards when the top half of his body was smashed against the edge of the paddle-box. One of the boards snapped against his torso, and his body flopped free. It got caught on the paddles below and was swept up on the outside edges of the boards.

Killigrew kicked off with one final effort and pushed himself through the thwarts, lifting his feet clear before he missed his footing on the broken board. A moment later the sodden corpse of the first pilong was carried past inches from his face.

The second pilong still had his feet on the axle and gripped the stanchion, but now the stanchion was below the axle rather than above it and the pilong was upside down. His screams of terror were almost drowned out by the churning of the waters as the boards thrashed down against the waves. The first pilong was deposited in the water which churned in the wheel's wake.

The second pilong was brought upright again, and as Killigrew glimpsed his horror-stricken face through the speeding boards he felt only pity. As a pilong he deserved to die, but not like that. No one deserved to die like that. As the water churned and dripped the spokes and stanchions became even more slippery until the pilong lost his grip. He bounced off one of the stanchions below. Another stanchion came up to meet him and Killigrew heard a bone snap sickeningly. Then the pilong landed on the boards at the bottom of the wheel. They quickly dragged him to the top and dropped him down through the whirling stanchions once more. Killigrew could only squeeze his eyes shut. After what seemed like forever, the throb of the engine faded and he opened his eyes once more. There was nothing left of the pilong, nothing that was too large to slip between the boards at least, and as the wheel's rotation slowed he saw that the water which dripped down from the boards was tinged vermilion with blood. Abaft, the sharks snapped at chunks of meat which floated in the water.

Outside the wheel, he glimpsed the prow of the jolly boat. 'Bring me his body!' Verran ordered from the steamer's deck.

But the men in the boat were going nowhere near that feeding frenzy. 'Sorry, Cap'n!' Killigrew heard Boggs call. 'Looks like the sharks beat you to it!'

'I wonder . . .' Verran did not sound convinced. Killigrew knew what was coming next. 'Let's have the port-side paddle-box boat up, Mr Hayes, just to make sure.'

Feet sounded on the deck as the hands attached the cradle supporting the paddle-box boat to the inboard davits. Ropes creaked and a moment later light flooded through the gap beneath the boat as it was hoisted up an inch at a time. Unarmed, pinned above the thwarts of the upturned boat, there was nothing Killigrew could do to defend himself. Six inches, seven inches, eight inches . . . The boat was lifted inexorably higher. Sooner or later someone was going to look underneath and his hiding place would be revealed.

Twelve inches, thirteen inches, fourteen inches . . . A shadow appeared, and a moment later a head was thrust through the gap between boat and paddle-box. Killigrew saw a Manchu queue. Then the head rotated as the man craned his neck to glance into the boat above him.

Killigrew looked around for something he could use as a weapon, but there was nothing.

His eyes met those of the man with the queue, and he recognised Li Cheng. The two of them stared at one another for what seemed like an eternity. All Li had to do was call out 'He's here!' and Killigrew would be a dead man.

Instead, the Chinese merely winked and withdrew his head.

Killigrew blinked. He had never seen a Chinese wink before.

'It is clear, Captain Verran,' he heard Li Cheng say. 'The sharks must have got him.'

'All right. Lower the boat back in place and let's get underway again.'

Killigrew wondered why the Chinese had helped him. What did he have to gain? It was impossible to guess. Perhaps this was someone's idea of a joke: as soon as Li was out of earshot he would tell Verran exactly where Killigrew was hiding, and they could both have a good laugh about it, safe in the knowledge that the lieutenant was right where they wanted him and in great discomfort to boot.

But he did not have to stay there. Indeed, if they were going to use steam to get underway, he had only a few seconds to climb back down into the water or else be trapped until the next time they stopped the engines.

The men in the jolly boat were rowing back around the stern, but they would have their faces turned towards the paddle-wheel. This was going to have to be timed to a nicety, if it could be timed at all. Killigrew could not wait until the jolly boat was out of sight: he eased his legs between the boards and lowered himself until he dangled at the fullest extent of his arms from one of the thwarts. He moved his grip from the thwart to one of the boards, one hand after the other, until he was able to get his feet on one of the stanchions. He just glimpsed the stern of the jolly boat as it disappeared from view.

He dropped to the axle. His feet slipped and he fell face-down across one of the stanchions. The wind was pounded from him and tears came to his eyes as he choked back a gasp of agony which would have given the game away. The sharks still fought for the last few shreds of pilong, but Killigrew knew he would be safer in the water with them than he would up on deck with Verran and his murderous crew.

He pushed himself back off the stanchion and eased himself feet first into the water. The broken board was immediately below him and he slipped into the water with barely a ripple. The sharks were too busy fighting amongst themselves to pay him any heed. He swam under the hull of the junk grappled to the *Golden Dragon*'s port side, out of sight of anyone on deck. He was too far away to be able to hear what was going on on the steamer's deck, but all seemed quiet enough on the junk. He trod water for a minute or two, using shallow, controlled breaths until he had got his wind back.

The shore was visible about half a mile away. As soon as his breathing was more even, Killigrew ducked under the water and swam for the stony beach until the tightness in his aching lungs forced him to surface once more. He flipped on to his back and allowed himself to float to the surface until his face kissed the air. He could see the two junks casting off from the *Golden Dragon* now, hoisting their sails. Everyone on board was too busy to spy him in the water, perhaps a cable's length from the nearest junk. He took a couple of deep breaths and submerged once more. When he next surfaced, he was too exhausted to swim underwater any longer. He was closer to the shore than to the three vessels now, and besides, the *Golden Dragon* was getting steam up. Killigrew rolled on to his front and struck out for the shore with a gentle breaststroke. A few minutes later he crawled up through the surf on to the stony beach, and reflected that there had to be easier ways of earning a hundred and eighty pounds a year. Suddenly the prospect of a tedious sinecure in the City of London did not seem so awful after all.

Verran watched the shore astern through his telescope.

After a moment, he chuckled softly to himself and snapped it shut.

'Something amusing, Captain Verran?' asked Li Cheng.

'He made it. The sly son of a gun actually made it ashore.'

'Who made it?' asked Hayes.

'Killigrew. Here – ' Verran handed the *tindal* his telescope – 'see for yourself.'

Hayes peered through the telescope. 'I see a figure, but you must have the eyes of a hawk if you can tell who it is from here.'

'It's Killigrew, all right. Who else would it be?'

'How the hell could he have escaped?' demanded Boggs. 'The paddle-wheel, the sharks . . .'

'You should never underestimate a man like Kit Killigrew, Mr Boggs.'

'We got to turn back and go after him.'

'Do you want me to kill him?' offered Li Cheng. Not betraying the barbarian's hiding place underneath the paddle-box boat had been an unnecessary risk; Li's mission was of far greater importance than the life of a barbarian. But he was starting to wonder if the lieutenant might not prove useful. Nonetheless, if Verran suspected Killigrew had escaped with Li's help, he would be as good as dead.

Verran gestured dismissively. 'What's the point? By the time we've put about, steamed back and put a boat over the side, and the boat's rowed to shore, he'll be long gone.'

'If he makes it back to Hong Kong and tells everyone we've been working with the pilongs, then we'll all be up the creek,' warned Hayes.

'Then we'll have to see to it he isn't believed, shan't we?'

'And how the hell do you intend to do that? Who's going to take the word of a merchant captain over that of a naval officer?'

Verran checked his watch. 'The Hoi-how fleet should

reach the fishing grounds off Saddle Island in a couple of hours, shouldn't it?' he asked Yeh, the *lao-pan* of the pilong junk which had brought Li Cheng to this rendezvous. Yeh nodded. 'Set sail for Saddle Island,' Verran ordered Hayes. 'Full ahead.'

'Aye, aye, Cap'n.'

Verran turned to Li Cheng and Yeh. 'You two come with me.'

They followed him down to his day room. He reached for a bottle of rum. 'Drink?'

Both Yeh and Li Cheng shook their heads. Verran poured himself a generous measure. 'I know Zhai Jing-mu had his heart set on dealing with Killigrew personally, but I'm afraid that's not going to be possible now.'

'Because you let him get away,' Yeh said coldly.

Verran shook a warning finger. '*We* let him get away, remember?'

'If he gets back to Hong Kong and warns the authorities . . .'

Verran laughed. 'Warns them about what? He knows nothing.'

'He knows you are in league with Zhai Jing-mu.'

'You let me worry about that. In a few hours he can tell them the sky is blue and no one's going to believe him. He's already got a reputation with his superiors for being reckless and unstable. I'm going to make sure that reputation is trebly confirmed.'

'What do you intend to do?'

'Give my men some target practice.'

It took them seven hours to sail around the south-east coast of Hainan Island to where Saddle Island rose up four and a half miles off shore. The small junks of the Hoi-how fishing fleet were there, their lights coming on as the sun set over the shore. Li Cheng counted about two dozen of them. Seeing the junks reminded him of his own childhood at Canton, where his father had worked as a fisherman amongst the islands of the Pearl River estuary; until he had been killed by the barbarians.

'Well, there's the fishing fleet,' Hayes remarked when Verran came up on deck. 'What do you want us to do now?'

'Sink it,' Verran said simply.

'What, sink them all?'

'No, no! Leave one. We want a witness to return to Hoi-how and report what was done.'

'Have you got a screw lose? The yellow-bellies may be crazy, but they ain't stupid. They'll have no problems identifying the *Golden Dragon* . . .'

'A ship which is under the command of Lieutenant Kit Killigrew of Her Majesty's navy, as far as the authorities in Hong Kong are aware.'

'Until this morning.'

'After this evening's work I expect tensions in Hoi-how will be running too high for anyone to worry about a discrepancy of a few hours. It will take Killigrew days to travel overland from the south coast of the island to Hoi-how. By then all anyone in the city will remember is that the fishing fleet was attacked by a barbarian devil-ship, and Killigrew will be a barbarian from that same ship. When he realises the magnitude of his crime, what more natural than he should lie about the time he swam to the coast of the island?'

Boggs grinned. 'I get it,' he said, and ran to the bow-chaser on the forecastle calling for the gun crew.

'You ain't making a heap of sense, Cap'n,' protested Hayes.

'Do try to keep up, Hayes. It's perfectly simple. Killigrew went insane and ordered his men to start shooting at the fishing junks. He insisted they were pirates, though Heaven knows we tried to tell him otherwise. He was crazy for opium – the *tai-pan* and his wife will confirm that he was recovering from being an opium user, and I've got an empty laudanum bottle below which he polished off – and thirsting for revenge against the yellow-bellies after the murder of his lady love.'

Hayes stared at Verran and a smile spread slowly across his face. 'Sweet Jesus, Cap'n. It's perfect!'

' "We tried to stop him, Captain Morgan." ' Li realised that Verran was already rehearsing what he would tell the barbarian authorities when they got back to Hong Kong. ' "But his men wouldn't listen to us. They just kept blasting away, while Killigrew kept us covered with a pepperbox, frothing at the mouth and calling us mutineers while urging his men on to greater slaughter. God knows what they thought they were doing: maybe they really believed they were firing at pilong junks, maybe they were just trained to obey orders, or maybe they just didn't give a damn . . . in the end, I could bear it no longer. I tackled Killigrew, tried to wrest the gun from him . . . there was a scuffle . . . his men came to his aid, they were killed . . . Killigrew jumped overboard and swam for the coast of Hainan. There was nothing we could do but pull a couple of survivors from the water and head home to report this sorry tale." '

'Survivors?' asked Hayes.

Verran indicated Yeh and Li Cheng. 'I'm sure these gentlemen will have no hesitation in playing the part of fishermen from Hoi-how when they testify in Victoria to Killigrew's moment of madness.'

Li Cheng shook his head. 'I cannot go. I am known in Hong Kong. If I am recognised the whole calumny falls apart.'

Verran turned to Yeh. 'What about you?'

'I will do it. If we stop off at Liu-chu on the way back, I can pick up some friends who can testify also.'

'Excellent! So you see, I don't think we need to worry about Mr Killigrew any more.'

Hayes nodded. 'As you say, he'll head for Hoi-how: it's

the shortest route to the mainland, and the likeliest place he'll get passage back to Hong Kong. If the crowd doesn't tear him to shreds, the authorities will execute him for piracy. And even if they don't – even if they choose to abide by the Treaty of Nanking and hand him over to the British in Hong Kong – we'll have arrived days ahead of him to spread the bad word. Cap'n, you're a goddamned genius.'

Verran beamed. 'I know.'

The bow-chaser boomed, startling Li Cheng, and a moment later a fishing junk was lifted out of the water by a direct hit from a shell. Boggs and his gun crew worked quickly to reload the thirty-two-pounder. Within a couple of minutes, the gun boomed again and another junk was destroyed. Some of the fishermen on the deck were hurled screaming through the air. Verran laughed to see them.

The third shot and the explosion of the third junk finally snapped Li Cheng out of his awed reverie. Until then he had stood as a helpless spectator, knowing he could not betray himself by revealing the slightest weakness, and there was nothing he could do against so many men. It was nothing to him if the barbarian Killigrew was lynched by the people of Hoi-how, but he could not stand back and allow these fishermen to be slaughtered.

Perhaps there was something he could do after all.

He made his way down to the orlop deck where he found a storeroom. There were kegs, ropes, boxes, sacks. He ran his finger over the writing on one of the canisters. He spoke English fluently, but struggled with the barbarian method of spelling, using a small number of characters to represent different sounds, and using those sounds to spell out words.

'P . . . en . . . jellee's p . . . pa . . . te . . . patent la . . . lamp oh-ill. Penjelly's patent lamp oil.' He took the canister down from the shelf, unscrewed the lid and took a sniff. This was what he was looking for.

The thirty-two-pounder two decks above boomed again, reminding him he had no time to waste. He picked up a box of matches and carried them aft with the canister of lamp oil. A constant succession of crewmen ascended and descended the companionway between the upper deck and the magazine, but everyone was too busy to pay any attention to Li. The rest of the ship seemed deserted. To avoid MacGillivray and the stokers in the engine room he ascended to the lower deck and headed aft to Verran's day room. He closed the door, took the cap off the canister and splashed lamp oil everywhere: over the deck, the bulkheads, the furniture. He had almost finished when the door burst open. It was Yeh.

'Li Cheng, what are you doing in here? Every hand is needed on deck—' He broke off when he saw the empty canister of lamp oil in Li's hands.

Li threw the canister at his head. Yeh swatted it aside and drew his sword. Li leaped on to the table. The *lao-pan* slashed at his ankles, but Li jumped over the arcing blade and caught hold of the rim of the skylight above his head. He kicked the *lao-pan* in the chest with both feet, and then dropped to the floor. As Yeh came at him again, he kicked the sword from his hand.

Yeh stared at him. 'So, you know *wu-yi*, eh?' He adopted the classic martial arts fighting stance. 'Well, I am a master of the black belt!'

As the two of them circled, Li shook his head. 'You are mistaken. Once you were a master of the black belt. Now you are dead.' He took out the matches, and as the *lao-pan* stared at him in horror, Li struck one and dropped it to the floor.

Yeh cried out as the flames spread quickly through every part of the room. Li snatched up a chair and threw it at the stern window. The panes of glass between the leading shattered. The flames blazed all around Li now and his left sleeve was on fire. He smashed the chair against the leading until it fell out, then used the legs to sweep away the last jagged shards of glass around the frame. Then he dived out.

The water extinguished his burning clothes. He surfaced in the wake of the *Golden Dragon* and looked around, treading water. The nearest junk was a hundred yards away, but it was in flames. He struck out for one further off while the steamer's bow-chaser continued to sink the fishing boats remorselessly.

After he had swum a few hundred yards Li found himself surrounded by men and women from junks which had already been sunk, some of them horribly injured. He heard a woman scream and twisted in the water to see a shark's fin angling towards her. He grabbed her and pulled her out of the way.

'Don't struggle!' he hissed.

The shock of being seized paralysed her with fear, and it saved her life. The shark swam past only inches away and another man struggling in the water was abruptly dragged under.

A piece of wreckage drifted past. Li grabbed it and helped the woman cling on to it beside him. 'Rest now. Kicking in the water only attracts the sharks.'

She nodded. The mass of struggling bodies in the water became the focus of a feeding frenzy about twenty yards from Li Cheng and the woman.

He turned to where the *Golden Dragon* steamed on, glowing sparks flying from the funnel in the gathering dusk. Her bow-chaser had fallen silent: the men on deck were too busy fighting the fire in the day room to have any thought for pressing home their attack on the fishing fleet.

A junk altered course to pick up the men in the water. Li waved a hand above his head to attract the attention of her crew. She hove to close by and Li and the woman risked a few kicks to bring them close to her hull. Fishing nets were thrown over the gunwales to help the men and women in the water climb aboard. Li Cheng helped the woman on board and then climbed up after her. He stayed at the gunwale to help everyone else climb out of the water – after the sharks had finished with them, there were few survivors – but even so the deck of the small junk was crowded. Out of a fleet of about two dozen, only eight still floated.

Exhausted, Li collapsed in the lee of the bulwark in the junk's waist. He looked at the faces of the men and women on deck: tired, bedraggled, stunned and shocked. How many loved ones had they lost?

One of the fishermen shook a fist at the departing steamer. 'Cursed barbarian devil-ship! May the goddess T'ien Hou condemn you to an eternity in the Hell of Ten Thousand Knives!'

'What I don't understand is, why?' sobbed the woman Li Cheng had rescued from the water. 'Why did they attack us? What did we do to harm them?'

'The barbarians need no excuses. They are cruel savages who kill for the pleasure of it.'

Li Cheng was starting to think that the fisherman was right. So many people killed, just to destroy the reputation of one barbarian naval officer. Captain Verran was deranged; and so were the men who had gone along with it.

One youth had been pulled out of the water with his legs bitten off above the knees by a shark. The fishermen did what they could for him, but his life poured out on to the deck with his blood. The woman Li had pulled out of the water cradled the youth's head and shoulders in her arms. 'It is all right, Bao. Everything is going to be all right. Do not die, please do not die . . .'

She was the only one who could not see what was obvious to everyone else: the youth was already dead. Finally one of the men pried her away from the corpse.

'The men who did this will be made to pay dearly,' snarled Li.

The fishermen all turned to stare at him. 'Who are you?' demanded one. 'I do not recognise you.'

'Yes. Where did you come from? You're not one of us.'

'He must have come from the barbarian devil-ship!'

'What is your name?' demanded the skipper of the junk.

'My name is Li Cheng and I am an Imperial spy. And it is of vital importance that you take me to Hong Kong at once. I have to report to Admiral Huang.'

'No . . . no . . . no . . .' With a growing sense of weariness, Strachan sorted through the bones Mei-rong had brought him in her *yolo*. There were dog bones, cat bones, pig bones, cattle bones, even – rather disturbingly – human bones; but none of them was what he was looking for.

'What for you no likee bones?' asked Mei-rong.

'They're bonny bones, but I wanted dinosaur bones.'

'What is dinosaur?'

'Dragon. Dragon bones.' The dragon was such a prominent motif in Chinese art and culture, he was sure that at some point in Chinese history an entire dinosaur skeleton had been found by some imaginative peasant, sparking off the whole dragon culture. Perhaps more than a skeleton. An iguanodon, maybe, or a megalosaurus, or even a species of dinosaur as yet undiscovered by man.

*Strachanosaurus.*

But if strachanosaurus were out there, there were no traces of it amongst the bones in Mei-rong's boat.

She said something to her sister, and the two of them fell about laughing hysterically. 'That's the way to do it, Mr Strachan,' Molineaux called from the entry port of the *Tisiphone*. 'Get 'em laughing. Works for me every time.'

Strachan scowled up at him. 'Now really, Molineaux! For your information I'll have you know I'm engaged in serious scientific research.'

Before Molineaux could reply, a hubbub arose from the bumboats crowded round the far side of the stern, which quickly spread through all the boats there. 'What is it?' Strachan asked Mei-rong. 'What's going on?'

'My go now. You wantchee bones or no?'

'No . . . er . . . look, here's a shilling for your trouble . . .'

'Ahem!' said Molineaux.

'Half a crown, I mean.'

'*Ahem!*'

'All right, a crown.' Strachan paid up and Mei-rong hurried up out of the boat and back up the side ladder. 'I don't mind you driving a hard bargain, Molineaux, but do you have to do it on behalf of others? At my expense?'

'Have a heart, sir. I'll bet she spent hours collecting all those bones.'

'She probably just rifled through a rubbish heap outside a butcher's shop.'

'And how much would I have to pay you to get *you* to rifle through a rubbish heap outside a butcher's shop, sir?'

'When you put it like that . . .'

From the deck of the *Tisiphone*, Strachan could see what had excited so much interest amongst the bumboats: the *Golden Dragon* had rounded Belcher Point and was entering Victoria Harbour. She anchored a short distance away and the bumboats swarmed round her like beaux abandoning the prettiest belle at the ball when an even prettier one arrived. 'Looks like Mr Killigrew's back,' said Molineaux, and grinned. 'What do you think, sir? Reckon he's got Zhai Jing-mu chained up in the hold?'

'News of that hempie's death will be more than sufficient for me,' said Strachan. He gazed across at the steamer and had the unaccountable feeling that something was not right. Perhaps it was the sails and rigging: he did not know about such things to be able to say when they were not shipshape and Bristol-fashioned. Perhaps there was something else. If he had not been a scientific man, he might have said he was feeling fey.

The *Golden Dragon* lowered its jolly boat and the crew

rowed it across to the *Tisiphone*. As it approached, Strachan saw Killigrew's friend Captain Verran in the stern, but there was no sign of Killigrew himself, or of Dando, Firebrace, Gadsby, or O'Connor.

Molineaux had noticed that too. 'Maybe he's asleep in his cabin,' he said dubiously. There was no need for him to say who 'he' was. 'Tiring work, fighting pilongs all day long.'

'Maybe,' allowed Strachan.

By the time the *Golden Dragon*'s jolly boat bumped against the *Tisiphone*'s side, Robertson had come up on deck. 'Permission to come on board, Commander?' Verran, grim-faced, called up from the jolly boat.

'Permission granted, Mr Verran. Where's Killigrew?'

'We need to talk, sir. In private.' Verran climbed up the side ladder and went below with Robertson without another word.

'Something's wrong,' Molineaux said with certainty.

Verran and Robertson were closeted in the commander's day room for an hour, during which speculation ran rife on the decks of the *Tisiphone*. Voices were raised in the day room, but this time Robertson had made sure that the skylight was closed, in spite of the heat of the day, and it was impossible for anyone on deck to make out what was said. After a while, Robertson and Verran emerged on deck. 'Prepare my gig, Bosun,' ordered the commander. 'We're going across to the *Hastings*.'

'Aye, aye, sir.'

While the gig was being lowered, Verran climbed down the side ladder to where his men waited in the *Golden Dragon*'s jolly boat and had a quiet word with the coxswain. The coxswain nodded, and as Verran climbed back on the *Tisiphone*'s deck the jolly boat rowed for the wharf. When the gig was lowered, Robertson and Verran descended the side ladder and were rowed across to the *Hastings*.

All this only intensified the speculation. 'What the deuce is going on, do you think, Mr Strachan?' asked Hartcliffe.

'I don't know, my lord. But I don't like this one little bit. Why hasn't Killigrew shown himself yet?'

'Maybe he's not on the *Golden Dragon*,' said Molineaux. 'Maybe he's in trouble.'

'Then why hasn't the cap'n given orders for us to get under way?' asked Ågård.

'Maybe Tom Tidley's dead,' said Fanning.

'Killigrew dead?' scoffed Molineaux. 'He'll out-live us all, that one. What about the others? That's what I want to know. Dando and O'Connor, and those two fat-heads Gadsby and Firebrace?'

Robertson and Verran had been on board the *Hastings* for nearly half an hour when Strachan saw one of the petty officers on deck call instructions down to the coxswain of the gig. It rowed back to the *Tisiphone*. 'Captain Morgan presents his compliments and requests that Mr Strachan attend him on board the *Hastings*,' the coxswain called up.

Strachan crossed to the entry port. 'Me?' he asked in astonishment. 'What does he want with me?'

'He didn't say, sir, but if I'm any judge it wouldn't do to keep him waiting.'

It did not do to keep Morgan waiting at the best of times, and Strachan had the feeling that this was not the best of times. He climbed down the side ladder and was rowed across to the *Hastings*, where a marine showed him below decks and knocked on the door of Morgan's day room. 'Mr Strachan to see you, sir.'

'Then send him in at once!' snapped Morgan.

The marine opened the door for Strachan and closed it behind him.

Morgan, Robertson and Verran all sat around the table in the middle of the room, their faces bleak. The assistant surgeon was not invited to sit.

'Mr Strachan, when Mr Killigrew was ill and you

attended him at Mr Bannatyne's home, what was it you said he was suffering from?' asked Robertson. He checked some notes he had made at the time. ' "Temporomandibular amenorrhoea"?'

'That was it, sir.'

'Are you sure you wouldn't like to revise that statement, Mr Strachan?'

'May I ask what all this is about, sir?'

'Answer the question, damn your eyes!' snapped Morgan.

Robertson, maintaining a tight grip on himself, held up a hand for calm. 'According to Captain Verran here, Mr Killigrew went insane and ordered his men to open fire on a fleet of fishing junks. When Verran and his crew tried to stop him, there was a scuffle in which Seamen Dando and O'Connor, and Landsmen Firebrace and Gadsby, were killed. Mr Killigrew then jumped overboard and swam ashore, where he evaded the attempts of Captain Verran and his men to recapture him.'

Stunned, Strachan stared at Verran. 'I don't believe it, sir.'

'I'm afraid it's true,' said the merchant captain. 'Any member of my crew will confirm it. As will the three men I have on board the *Golden Dragon* whom I pulled out of the water after their junk had been sunk. They were amongst the lucky ones. I think some of the junks got away; I expect we'll be hearing from the Chinese authorities soon enough. They'll confirm everything I've said.'

'What's your man Killigrew trying to do, Robertson?' snarled Morgan. 'Start another war with the Celestials?'

'But why would he do such a thing?'

'We thought you might be able to enlighten us on that score, Mr Strachan,' said Robertson. 'Perhaps he had not fully recovered from his bout of . . .' he checked the log again, '. . . temporomandibular amenorrhoea.' He said the term in a tone of voice which implied that at some point he had gone ashore, consulted a medical dictionary in a bookseller's and discovered that amenorrhoea – temporomandibular or otherwise – was an ailment which troubled only the fair sex. 'Perhaps it had affected his state of mind in some way?'

'Mr Killigrew was as sane as you or I when he boarded the *Golden Dragon*, sir,' Strachan said stoutly.

'I'm afraid that's not entirely true, sir.'

Strachan turned to see Blase Bannatyne enter behind him.

Everyone rose to their feet as the *tai-pan* doffed his top hat. 'I came as soon as I heard, gentlemen. No, please, don't stand.'

Morgan pulled out a chair for Bannatyne. 'Please be seated, sir. Can I get you a drink?'

'No, thank you.'

'You were saying, Mr Bannatyne?' Robertson demanded impatiently.

'I'm afraid I'm partly to blame for this. You see, it was my idea to try to conceal the truth of Killigrew's illness. Mr Strachan here wanted to report it to you, but I was the one who pointed out that by doing so he would be in danger of ruining Mr Killigrew's career. Gentlemen, it grieves me to have to inform you that Lieutenant Killigrew had become an opium user.'

Morgan rounded on Strachan. 'Well, sir? What do you have to say for yourself?'

Strachan knew when he was beaten. 'All right, it's true up to a point. He started smoking opium after Miss Dadabhoy was killed. But we'd weaned him off before he went aboard the *Golden Dragon*. I would never have permitted him to return to active duty if I hadn't thought he was fit enough.'

'I'm afraid he must have had a relapse, Dr Strachan,' said Verran.

'*Mr* Strachan, actually,' the assistant surgeon corrected him tersely.

Bannatyne regarded him in surprise. 'Oh, so you're not a fully qualified doctor, then?' he said, as if this were the first he had heard of it.

Strachan blushed. 'I'm a Licentiate of the Society of Apothecaries.'

'But not an MD.'

'Neither is Mr Westlake, my surgeon,' pointed out Robertson. 'Calm down, Mr Strachan. No one is calling your medical competence into question.'

'To the contrary, Robertson,' said Morgan. 'I think Strachan's medical competence is exactly the question here. He certified Killigrew as fit for duty when clearly the lieutenant was not.'

'He had a relapse,' said Verran. 'It wasn't until we'd gone to sea that I noticed he was swilling back the laudanum pretty heavily. I didn't like to say anything. I suppose I should have realised; in some ways it was my fault . . .'

Strachan could not believe any of this. 'Oh, but this is utter gammon! Opiates calm people down, they don't overstimulate them. The behaviour which Mr Verran here has described is hardly symptomatic of a man taking laudanum.'

'How about a man undergoing withdrawal symptoms after his laudanum ran out?' suggested Verran. 'He was fine for the first couple of days, but after that he grew increasingly irritable.'

'Irritable perhaps,' said Strachan. 'I get irritable if I have too many cups of coffee in the morning. But I don't go murdering dozens of innocent Chinese fishermen!'

'But if he mistook them for pilongs,' said Verran. 'If he was thirsting for vengeance after the murder of the woman he loved . . .'

'I always said that Killigrew's buccaneering ways would lead him to a bad end,' said Morgan. 'I'm afraid none of this comes as a surprise to me. Knowing Killigrew, I think something like this was bound to happen sooner or later.

Forgive me, Mr Bannatyne, but you cannot say I did not warn you.'

Bannatyne shook his head sorrowfully. 'I know, Captain. You're perfectly right, I fear. I should have listened to you.'

'I think we should hear what Killigrew has to say for himself before we condemn him,' Robertson said mildly.

'*If* we see him again,' said Morgan. 'Oh, he'll be given a chance to explain himself, all right. At his court martial. And as for this scoundrel,' he indicated Strachan, 'it's my recommendation that you dismiss him at once. And I shall be writing a very strongly worded letter to the medical director-general regarding his conduct. As far as I can see there is nothing further to be said. Commander Robertson, Mr Strachan, you may consider yourselves dismissed.'

Robertson and Strachan took their leave and made their way up on deck. They were followed a moment later by Bannatyne and Verran.

The *tai-pan* gestured helplessly. 'I cannot tell you how much I deeply regret all this, Commander Robertson. I blame myself . . .'

'I'm sure you did what you thought was right, sir.'

Bannatyne and Verran climbed into the flory boat that had brought the *tai-pan* out from the quayside, as soon as they were heading out of earshot, Strachan turned to Robertson. 'If you want my letter of resignation from the service, sir . . .'

'. . . I shall ask for it,' Robertson concluded for him gruffly, and gestured for him to follow him down to the gig. 'What do you make of all that, Mr Strachan?' he asked as they were being rowed back to the *Tisiphone*.

'I don't know, sir. It seems awful suspicious to me. But I do know one thing: Killigrew wouldn't have attacked an innocent fishing fleet, not without good reason.'

'I'm inclined to agree with you there. I must say, I'd feel a good deal happier if Dando or O'Connor were alive to confirm or deny these accusations. Deuced rum that all four of the sailors we put on board the *Golden Dragon* with Killigrew should have died in that scuffle. You'd think that Verran and his men would have been able to subdue at least one of them without killing the poor devil.'

'Yes, sir.'

'And another thing. You as good as accused Verran of lying.'

'I did?'

'Yes indeed, Mr Strachan. And a man like that would not normally allow his honour to be impugned. He'd've called you out.'

'Perhaps he was frightened I might be a better pistol shot than he, sir?' Strachan had never fired a pistol in his life, but Verran did not know that.

'As the injured party he'd've had choice of weapons. He'd've chosen swords. And from what I've heard of Verran, he's got nothing to fear from anyone in that field. No, Mr Strachan. Verran *was* lying. What I don't understand is: why?'

'I've a feeling only Killigrew will be able to tell us that, sir.'

'Then we'd better hope that Morgan gets to him before the Celestials do. Because at least that way he'll get a chance to defend himself.'

It took Killigrew the best part of a week to cross the south side of Hainan Island to Hoi-how, the main settlement of the island, on the north. From there he hoped to cross to the mainland and continue his journey overland, or better still to get passage on a ship to Hong Kong, nearly three hundred miles away.

Food was no problem. Killigrew always carried a couple of gold sovereigns on him in case of situations like this. Queen Victoria's head might not be known in a humble tavern on the south side of Hainan – one of the few places where it was not – but gold was recognised everywhere. Unable to provide Killigrew with enough copper cash to cover the change for a bed for a night, a hot meal of fish stew and rice, and several cups of rice wine, the innkeeper had gone through the rigmarole of refusing to accept a bargain so profitable to himself, like a priest refusing a bishopric three times before accepting. Killigrew reckoned that he paid the equivalent of ten shillings for that warm but hard, louse-infected bed, but when he woke up his clothes had been dried over a smoky fire and he had enough copper cash in change to take him to Hoi-how. The next day he was offered a ride on an ox cart to the next village on the road, but climbed down and walked when he realised he would make better time on foot.

Wherever he went, the people were a little afraid of him. They had heard of barbarians, but he suspected that most had never seen one in these remote parts, and he was aware – not of stares, the Chinese thought it rude to stare – but of a distinct *absence* of stares, as everyone pointedly averted their gazes. But they were hospitable enough, and polite, and grateful when he paid them. When they saw that for all that he was a barbarian, he was still a human being like them, they were warm and friendly.

The journey reminded him how much he loved China. Nothing was ever too much trouble for the people. Most of the time they seemed to be able to anticipate everything he wanted, and when they could not provide it their apologies were excruciating. When he thought of the treatment a shipwrecked Chinese would have received in Europe, he cringed inwardly with shame for his own race, and he cringed even more when he thought of the ghastly war he had taken part in against these people, when he had been young enough to believe the nonsense he had been fed about the Chinese being an evil race with no sense of morality. The years had taught Killigrew that a different system of values was not necessarily a worse one; he only wished he could make other people see that.

He did not blame the ignorant people of Great Britain, who clamoured for war against the Chinese when they heard of the atrocities which had been committed against the China traders. They could only believe what they heard, and all that they heard was told to them by men who should have known better, but found it in their own interests to whip up such hatred against an alien race. Men like Sir George Grafton and Blase Bannatyne, who manipulated public opinion for their own ends.

Chinese hospitality came to an abrupt end when Killigrew reached Hoi-how, however. He could not blame the people, of course; they seemed to have enough problems of their own. Everyone was dressed in white – the funereal colour in China – and in the harbour he saw dozens of coffins being brought ashore. Some terrible disaster at sea, it seemed.

'What happened?' he asked one mourner, amidst the wailing and sobbing that was going on all around them.

The man merely turned, scowled, and spat in his face. 'Barbarian devil! Go back to your own country!'

A Chinese constable, dressed in blue robes and a red cap, and armed with a rattan cane and a whip, stood nearby. He also scowled when he saw Killigrew, who bowed in the Chinese manner to mollify him. 'Can you direct me to the *yamen*, please?' The *yamen* was the centre of local administration, where Killigrew hoped to find a mandarin who would arrange to ship him back to Hong Kong in return for a generous promise of *cumshaw*.

'The *yamen*?' The constable looked Killigrew up and down. 'I'll escort you there myself.'

'That is very kind of you, but it isn't necessary—'

The constable ignored him and signalled for three of his colleagues to assist him by holding up a hand, palm-down, and beckoning with his fingers. From the grim looks on their faces, Killigrew had the feeling that a rejection of their assistance might create trouble, and that was the last thing he needed. 'Since you insist . . .'

They escorted him to the imposing gate of the *yamen* where half a dozen guards were on duty. 'A barbarian!' exclaimed one of them. 'Where did you find him?'

'He approached me in the street,' said the first constable. 'He wanted directions to the *yamen*.'

'Did he, indeed!'

'Yes,' said Killigrew, and bowed again. 'I would be humbly grateful if the magistrate showed the generosity of spirit to grant a barbarian such as myself the honour of an interview. I am a British naval officer who has been marooned on this island, and I only wish to return to Hong Kong. Naturally anyone who helps me will be generously rewarded.'

'Marooned, you say?' asked the chief guard.

'Yes.' Killigrew bowed again, buying himself more time while he tried to make up his mind about how much of his story he wanted to explain to these minions, when he knew he would only have to repeat himself when he was taken before the magistrate. 'I was on the devil-ship *Golden Dragon* when it was seized by pilongs and . . .'

Killigrew's words trailed off as he found his neck surrounded by a ring of razor-edged swords. 'So sorry, is my pronunciation at fault?' he asked nervously.

# XIV:

## Tuen Ng

'Do you honestly expect me to believe that?'

Hearing her husband's voice in the hall, Mrs Bannatyne rose from the writing desk in her boudoir and went out to greet him. She was curious to know why he had been called away so suddenly. She emerged on to the landing, and as the two of them crossed the hall below she heard Jago Verran reply.

'It's the truth, sir. He jumped overboard and swam under the keel—'

'With his hands tied behind his back.'

'He must've got them undone, somehow.'

'Perhaps he persuaded one of those sharks to gnaw through his bonds,' said Bannatyne. What her husband did not know about sarcasm was not worth knowing. She paused on the landing without showing herself, curious to know what they were discussing.

'He's a downy fellow, sir. You can't overestimate a man like Kit Killigrew.'

'*I* don't intend to. *You* were the one who let him escape.'

'I've seen to that . . .' The two of them went into the parlour and their voices became muffled. Mrs Bannatyne tiptoed downstairs and stood close enough to the door to listen.

'Verran, you're a damned fool!' Bannatyne's tone, imperturbable as ever, was a good deal more temperate than his words.

'You wanted the Royal Navy and the Chinese at each other's throats, didn't you?'

'Leave that part of it to me. Your job was to deliver Killigrew to Zhai Jing-mu . . .'

Mrs Bannatyne felt as shocked as if she had been punched in the stomach. She reached for the doorknob to enter and protest, then caught herself and continued to listen instead.

'The *Golden Dragon* is well known as a vessel of the house of Grafton, Bannatyne and Co.,' her husband was saying. 'It will be my throat the Chinese will be at, not the Royal Navy's. And what am I to say to Zhai Jing-mu? He'll think I've humbugged him. And men like Zhai Jing-mu do not care to be humbugged.'

'Yeh was there. He saw what happened. He'll explain everything to Zhai.'

'And if Killigrew somehow eludes the Chinese and makes it back to Hong Kong? If he tells Captain Morgan that you're working with the pilongs? That will immediately point the finger of suspicion at me.'

'He won't be believed. You saw Morgan just now. He was only too willing to believe Killigrew ran amok and attacked a fishing fleet. So if the yellow-bellies don't kill him, his own navy will. Rather clever of me, I thought.'

'Leave the thinking to me in future, Verran. Have you any idea what kind of hornets' nest your antics have stirred up? If his navy *does* get hold of Killigrew, they'll court martial him. He'll be able to tell them everything he knows. He may not be believed, but a great deal of mud will get thrown around and some of it may stick to me. I can't afford that, not with the *Tuen Ng* so close. So you get back on board the *Golden Dragon*, return to Hainan, find Killigrew, and kill him.'

'We haven't finished repairing the fire damage in my day room yet,' protested Verran.

'Get in done *en route*. I don't care what it takes: I want Killigrew dead.'

The door opened abruptly and Mrs Bannatyne found herself face to face with her husband. It was difficult to say which of them was more surprised, but she recovered quickly.

'Oh, hello, Blase. I didn't hear you come in. Did I leave my parasol in there?'

'Your parasol?'

'Yes, I'm going to take tea with Mrs Dent this afternoon. Unless you have any objection?'

Bannatyne smiled. 'But of course, madam. You do as you please. I'll have Amrish prepare the carriage.'

She went back upstairs and changed quickly into her afternoon dress in time to meet the carriage as the coachman drew up outside the front door. 'Harbour Master's Wharf, please, Amrish.'

The coachman opened the door for her and she was astonished to find her husband already seated there with Verran. Bannatyne had a calfskin holdall at his feet. 'Get in,' he snapped at her.

She stared at him.

Verran reached inside his coat, pulled out a pistol and levelled it at her. 'Do as your husband says, ma'am. Didn't you once promise to love, honour and obey him?'

'This is ridiculous!' she protested. 'Blase, how dare you let him sit there and wave that thing at me?'

'Get in,' Bannatyne repeated tersely. 'We have a lot to discuss.'

She climbed into the carriage and the coachman closed the door behind her. Faced with a choice of sharing a seat with her husband or Verran it was a difficult decision, but in the end she plumped for her husband.

Bannatyne rapped his cane on the ceiling of the carriage. 'The factory, Amrish.'

'Yes, *sahib.*' The coachman whipped up the horses and the carriage started down the drive.

Bannatyne turned to his wife. 'How much of my conversation with Verran did you overhear earlier?'

'Conversation? What conversation? I don't understand—'

'Oh, come now, madam. You know as well as I do that the Dents' house is not on Harbour Master's Wharf. Who were you going to see? Captain Morgan? Commander Robertson? Since when did your social activities include taking tea with naval officers?'

'For Heaven's sake, Blase! I'm sure I don't know what you're talking about.'

'Really, madam. Do you really take me for a fool, after all these years?'

'Why not? It's now patently clear that you've always taken me for a fool—'

Bannatyne slapped her viciously. 'What were you going to tell Robertson? Come along, speak up. I haven't got all day.'

Stunned with shock as much as pain, she shrank into the corner of the carriage and stared at her husband in disbelief. 'I'm sure I don't know what any of this is about,' she said dully.

'Give her to me for half an hour, sir,' leered Verran. 'I'll make her talk.'

'Yes, you'd like that, wouldn't you?' she spat.

The carriage passed through the gates of the Grafton, Bannatyne & Co. trading factory at East Point and the coachman reined in in the compound. 'Put her in my cabin on board the *Golden Dragon*, and take her to the Cap-sing-mun anchorage,' Bannatyne ordered Verran. 'I'll deal with her in the fullness of time.'

'But if she knows too much about our plans . . .' warned Verran.

'She knows nothing of our plans. We did not discuss them this morning. And . . . Verran?'

'Sir?'

'If Mr Shen tells me you've harmed Mrs Bannatyne in my absence, I'll kill you myself. She is still my wife. Do you understand me?'

'Yes, sir,' Verran said surlily.

'What are you going to do with me?' Mrs Bannatyne demanded fearfully.

'Just put you out of the way for a while. There won't be any visits to officers of Her Majesty's ships, not until it's too late. By then the Royal Navy will have enough problems of its own, without having to concern itself with any far-fetched rumours about the *tai-pan* of Grafton, Bannatyne and Co.' Bannatyne reached down and took a bottle and a gauze pad from the holdall at his feet. He tipped some of the clear liquid in the bottle on to the pad.

'What's that?' asked Mrs Bannatyne.

'A new discovery from Europe, my dear. It's called chloroform. Doctors use it as an anaesthetic in operations, so their patients don't feel any pain.'

Mrs Bannatyne did not feel reassured. She struggled as he clamped the pad over her nose and mouth.

'. . . Just breathe normally, my dear . . .'

Killigrew was woken by the tramp of marching feet and the jingle of arms. He stood up and crossed to the door of his cell in the *yamen*. Peering out through the bars, he saw a troop of Imperial bannermen crossing the courtyard to his cell.

He knew they were coming to drag him to his place of execution. If he was going to think of a way to escape, now would be a good time to do it.

He had been kept in the cell for over a fortnight before the trial. He had been bedraggled and lousy enough after his trek across Hainan Island. Now what was left of his uniform was filthy and ragged, the kerseymere trousers and linen shirt now nearer black than their original white, his hair long and matted, three weeks' growth of beard on his chin, his underclothes crawling with lice.

The trial had been conducted in Mandarin Chinese, too swift for his understanding of the Cantonese dialect to be able to keep up with. Only the occasional phrase had filtered through: 'piracy', 'mass murder', and 'death by strangulation' had been common themes. There had been no jury: the magistrate had weighed up the evidence and assigned the punishment according to the Manchu Code. All Killigrew knew was that he had been set up somehow by Verran and his crew.

His craving for laudanum was gone, thanks to enforced deprivation, but it had been a hard two weeks: a fortnight of nightmares both sleeping and waking, almost driving him to the verge of insanity. But now the craving was gone, and he was starting to feel himself once more. In fact, he felt better than he had done since Peri had been killed.

And the men who were responsible for her murder were going to get away with it, while he was executed for a crime he had not committed.

He looked desperately about his bare, filthy cell for something he could use to defend himself, but there was nothing. With the heavy wooden cangue locked about his neck and wrists, like a portable set of stocks, he was hardly in much of a position to defend himself anyway.

One of the bannermen unlocked the cell, flanked by men who kept Killigrew covered with drawn bows. The bannerman entered, unfastened the chain which shackled the cangue to the rear wall of the cell, and then led Killigrew outside like a dog on a leash. He indicated the wooden bamboo cage they had brought with them.

'Get in,' he growled.

'You know that if you execute a barbarian, China will be breaching the Treaty of Nanking. It will mean war between your people and the barbarians, and China will be humiliated again.' For all that Killigrew did not approve of the treaty and the principle of extraterritoriality enshrined in it, he could not allow an innocent man to be put to death. Especially not when the innocent man was himself.

The bannerman tugged on the chain, pulling Killigrew off balance so that he fell painfully on his knees. 'In!'

Killigrew was manhandled into the cage. It was so cramped, he had to sit with his thighs against his stomach and the edge of the cangue hooked over his knees. It was excruciatingly uncomfortable. The door was closed and locked, and then four coolies hefted the cage on to their shoulders. Then they proceeded to the main gate of the *yamen*, with six bannermen before the cage and six more behind it.

There was a crowd outside the *yamen*, a hundred faces twisted in scowls of hatred and rage, spitting, throwing rotten fruit and eggs, chanting: 'Death to the *fan kwae*! Death to the *fan kwae*!' The guards struggled to clear a passage, and for a while Killigrew feared he might be lynched before he reached the place of execution, wherever that might be.

The uncomfortable journey took him down to the docks, where a massive war-junk seemed to tower over the small, single-storey hovels and godowns which lined the waterfront. At the foot of the gangplank, the senior bannerman read out a proclamation.

'By the order of his Imperial Excellency Governor-General Xu Guang-jin, it has been decreed that the high-nose barbarian will be taken to Canton to be executed before the barbarian merchants in Canton, as a warning to their people.'

There was a roar from the crowd – part approval that the

barbarians would be made to lose face, part disappointment that the crowd would not get to see a malefactor executed for their edification and entertainment (just like any crowd outside Newgate, Killigrew could not help thinking) – and for a few seconds the rain of rotten fruit and eggs being pelted at him seemed to intensify. Then the bannerman signalled the deck of the junk, where the Chinese sailors were already making preparations to get under way. The cage was manhandled below decks, through a series of ill-lit compartments like a rabbit warren. Eventually it was put down in a pitch-black chamber.

'Leave him here,' ordered the senior bannerman. Footsteps sounded on the deck as the coolies withdrew from the chamber, and Killigrew heard the door being locked and closed. Everything was silent but for the creak of the timbers and the slop of water close by.

In the pitch-darkness, Killigrew had no concept of how long he was kept there. His limbs were already numb from being cooped up at such an awkward angle, and if he were kept like this all the way to Canton, he would be unable to walk once they arrived. Not that he would need to be able to walk to be executed.

After a while the creak of the junk's timbers changed, and the motion of the rolling deck seemed to increase. They were sailing out to sea. It was over three hundred miles to Canton; with fair winds, the junk would arrive within a few days.

He heard the door open and saw a glimmer of light in the darkness, a taper jogging along unsteadily as if carried in someone's hand. He heard footsteps: two people, but lighter of foot than bannermen or coolies. The door was closed behind them, and he heard a wooden bar slide into place from outside. The taper circled the compartment, lighting a number of lanterns, until there was enough light for Killigrew to see that, far from being in a fetid orlop deck, he was in a chamber luxuriously hung with crimson silk and furnished with soft cushions. Beside the cage was a large tub of steaming, soapy water.

The two people in the room were a couple of pretty *amah* girls. The one holding the taper blew it out, and then they both bowed to him. The other had a set of keys which she promptly demonstrated fitted the lock on the cage, and the cangue about his neck. Having set him free, they stepped back and bowed again, apparently unaware they were locked in a chamber with a barbarian convicted of piracy and mass murder. There was a shaving razor and a pair of scissors on a tray close by, but there seemed little point in using them as weapons to hold these girls hostage so he could bargain for his freedom: they would be slaves, expendable, otherwise they would not have been put in this situation.

Killigrew rubbed his chafed wrists, stretched aching limbs, scratched his louse-bites as discreetly as possible in the presence of ladies, and eyed them warily. 'Perhaps I'm looking a gift horse in the mouth,' he remarked in Cantonese, 'but to what do I owe the special treatment? I'm sure not all convicted criminals are treated like this.'

The two girls giggled. 'You are to refresh yourself before you take dinner with Admiral Huang.'

'Refresh myself?'

'We have been ordered to fulfil your every desire,' said the girl, and the two of them giggled again.

He eyed them appraisingly. 'Well, let's start with a bath and a shave, shall we?'

One bath, shave, haircut, massage, manicure and change of clothes later, Killigrew found himself dressed in a black silk tunic, pyjamy trousers and silk boots. He was ushered on to the poop deck, where Admiral Huang sat at a table beneath a silk awning to protect him from the heat of the sun. He rose to his feet and bowed. Dazed by all this fine treatment, Killigrew bowed back.

Huang indicated a chair. 'Please be seated, Lieutenant,' he said in English.

They sat down facing one another. A servant brought a tureen of soup on to the poop deck and started to ladle it into their bowls. 'Shark's fin?' Killigrew asked his host.

Huang nodded. 'You must be hungry. I do not imagine that gaol food is particularly sustaining.'

'No worse than you'd get in a British gaol, I'm sure.'

'I am sorry we are unable to provide you with barbarian food. My cook has prepared the finest banquet he could, under such circumstances.'

'Oh, I like Chinese food.'

His host nodded approvingly and tucked in. After a few moments, Huang looked up. 'You are not eating, Lieutenant Killigrew. I trust you do not fear the food is poisoned?'

'No. I'm just curious to know why I'm getting the mandarin treatment. Two hours ago I was being conveyed to my execution. Or is this the hearty meal for the condemned man?'

'Please forgive the subterfuge, Lieutenant. I hope the manner of your being brought aboard this vessel did not incommode you unnecessarily. Feelings are running high in Hoi-how. There are few families who did not lose a loved one in the perfidious attack on the fishing fleet. If we had announced that you were to be handed back to your people in Hong Kong, then there would have been severe disturbances.'

'So you intend to abide by the treaty?'

'May demons wipe their backsides on your unfair barbarian treaties!' snarled Huang. 'If I thought you were the man who had masterminded the attack on the fishing fleet, then I would kill you myself, with my bare hands!'

Killigrew refused to be flustered by the admiral's sudden rage. 'Since you haven't, I can only suppose that you believe in my innocence.'

'We Chinese are not fools, Lieutenant. Why would a man on board a ship attack a fishing fleet, and then jump overboard and swim to an island where he could expect to encounter only hostility for his crime? The ways of you barbarians are curious, but not suicidal. I learned from an informant that you jumped off the *Golden Dragon* seven hours before it attacked the fishing fleet.'

'An informant?' Killigrew thought for a moment. 'Li Cheng?'

Huang nodded. 'I had the matter looked into. One of my men found the inn where you had dinner on the afternoon that you landed.' He tossed a gold sovereign on the table. 'Yours, I believe. At the hour of the rooster – when the *Golden Dragon* attacked the fishing fleet – you were eating fish stew and rice, and doing your best to drink up the innkeeper's entire stock of rice wine.'

'If you'd been through what I'd been through that day, you'd've needed a drink, too.'

Huang lit a Russian cigarette and took a long drag. He breathed smoke out through his nostrils and fixed Killigrew with his gimlet eyes. 'What do you know of a plot to overthrow the Ch'ing Dynasty, Lieutenant?'

'I didn't know there was one. Who's behind it?'

Huang smiled, the corners of his eyes crinkling into crow's feet. 'Ah. You think perhaps it is me, working to overthrow the dynasty from within?'

'The thought had occurred to me,' Killigrew replied sardonically. 'But I dismissed it.'

'Oh? May I ask why?'

'You're a Tartar – a Manchu. What would you have to gain by allying yourself with the pilongs and Triads?'

Huang chuckled. 'Well done, Lieutenant. I am pleased to see you are not as ignorant of civilised politics as many of your compatriots. You are absolutely right. I am loyal to my emperor. But I am also loyal to my country, and that country is China. As an admiral in the Imperial Navy I must serve both my emperor and my people as I think fit, and as long as the Ch'ing Dynasty rules in the Forbidden City then the people I am responsible to include both the Manchus and the Han.'

'All right. So if not you, then who?'

'That is what I am trying to find out. A barbarian, perhaps?'

'What would a barbarian have to gain?'

'Plenty, if he were the *tai-pan* of one of your trading companies. I am well aware that these merchants complain of what they consider to be the restrictive trade practices of my country.'

'Can you blame them? The West has a great deal to offer China, just as China has a great deal to offer the West. But if your people insist on sneering at the industrial produce of the West and refuse to buy it, can you blame the China traders if they're forced to sell opium to purchase tea?'

'It is not for me to criticise Imperial policy. But if there is a threat against the state then it is my job to expose it and crush it. Zhai Jing-mu has grown as powerful as any pirate chief can, but he wants more. He wants legitimacy.'

'You're thinking of the deal he tried to cut with Admiral Nie? No, Zhai must have changed his mind. You'll find what's left of Nie's flotilla floating amongst the Paracels.'

'So I have been informed. I tried to stop Nie from going to that rendezvous, but he would not listen. He paid the ultimate price for his foolishness. What I must now ask myself is, what made Zhai Jing-mu change his mind? The terms proposed by Nie were generous.'

'Zhai must have got a better offer.'

Huang nodded. 'He believes that the Triads must be close to their aim of overthrowing the Ch'ing Dynasty, otherwise he would not ally himself to them. But the Triads have been trying to overthrow the Manchus ever since my ancestors invaded China over two hundred years ago. What makes Zhai think that now they may finally succeed?'

'The Triads must be getting help from a new source,' deduced Killigrew. 'Someone outside China.'

'Very good, Lieutenant. Keep going.'

'A foreign power?' Killigrew tried to think of all the nations who envied Britain's position at the forefront of trade with China. 'France? The United States? Russia?'

Huang shook his head. 'You disappoint me, Lieutenant. Think of someone closer to home.'

'Sir Dadabhoy Framjee?'

'My first thought. But an agent I infiltrated into Framjee's company managed to eliminate the Parsi from his enquiries.'

'Mr Li has been a busy little bee, hasn't he?'

Beaming, Huang inclined his head.

'All right, not Sir Dadabhoy. Zhai's murder of his daughter ruled him out anyway. Who does that leave? There are dozens of China traders to choose from.'

'You are not thinking, Lieutenant. Which of the companies is large enough to provide the Triads with the resources to overthrow the Ch'ing Dynasty? Which *tai-pan* held a ball at his factory on the night that Zhai Jing-mu was freed from his gaol, thus ensuring all the senior officers of Hong Kong were elsewhere at the time? Who had Sir John Davis – a man renowned for his conciliatory attitude towards China – dismissed as Governor of Hong Kong, and replaced by the more aggressive Mr George Bonham? Who do you think gave the order for you to be handed over to Zhai Jing-mu?'

Killigrew nodded. He felt as if he were finally awakening from a dream. When the admiral laid all the pieces on the table, it fitted perfectly. 'Bannatyne.'

'Yes. Blase Bannatyne.'

'Have you thought of explaining this to the British authorities?'

'Which British authorities? Mr Bonham? I am not suggesting the plenipotentiary is in Bannatyne's pocket, but you have seen how he acts in Bannatyne's presence. Bonham cannot govern Hong Kong without the support of the China traders, and Bannatyne is their leader. Besides, what would I tell Bonham? That I suspect that Bannatyne is behind some plot to overthrow the Ch'ing Dynasty, but I do not know what the plot is and I have no proof of Bannatyne's involvement? That is where you come in, Lieutenant.'

'You want me to spy on Bannatyne?'

'You are the only barbarian I can trust. Perhaps the only man I can trust.'

'What makes you think you can trust me?'

'Zhai wants you dead. So does Bannatyne. Whichever side you are on, it is not theirs. Besides, your persistent bumbling has damaged Bannatyne's plans as much as it damaged my own.'

Killigrew almost choked on his soup. 'My bumbling . . .?'

'I successfully infiltrated one of my spies into the Tai-ping-shan chapter of the Triads. He was on a junk which would eventually have led him to Zhai Jing-mu's lair and perhaps provide proof of a link between Bannatyne and the Triads. Your escape from the *Golden Dragon* scotched that plan and forced him to compromise himself in order to mitigate the severity of the attack on the fishing fleet.'

'Well, of course if I'd known Li was one of your spies, I'd happily have let Verran take me to Zhai Jing-mu to be tortured to death,' Killigrew said sardonically.

'Li Cheng is a good agent, but sometimes he lets his heart rule his head.'

'I still don't understand. You talk of a plot to overthrow the Ch'ing Dynasty. But you don't know what it is and you're not sure who's behind it. Forgive me for saying so, but what makes you think there's a plot at all?'

'Li's predecessor. His instructions were much simpler: infiltrate the Triads in Tai-ping-shan as a stepping stone to locating Zhai Jing-mu's lair. That was a year ago. Six months ago he stumbled into the *yamen* at Canton, mortally wounded. Fortunately he managed to get past the guards and gain entry to the private chamber of Xu Guang-jin. He knew he could not trust the information he had discovered to anyone of a lesser rank than the governor-general. With his dying breath he warned his excellency of a plot to overthrow the Ch'ing Dynasty that would take place in Hong Kong at the time of the *Tuen Ng*.'

'The *Tuen Ng*?' Killigrew had heard that phrase before somewhere, although it took him a moment to remember what it signified. 'The dragon boat festival.'

Huang nodded. 'Four days from now.'

'Oi! And where do you think you're going, slanty-eyes?'

As Killigrew climbed the side ladder to the deck of the *Tisiphone*, he tilted his head back so that his face was no longer hidden from the boatswain by the conical hat he wore. 'I may be out of uniform, Bosun,' he said tightly, 'but nonetheless I must insist you address me as either "sir" or "lieutenant".'

The boatswain's eyes bulged out of his head. 'Lieutenant Killigrew! Sir! Sorry, sir, didn't recognise you in them chinky-chonk clothes.'

All the hands on deck crowded round to stare. 'That you, sir? We heard you was dead!' said Molineaux.

'Or captured by the yellow-bellies,' said Ågård.

'I was.' Killigrew gestured to where Huang had moored his junk a short distance away. 'Fortunately, Admiral Huang was kind enough to bring me back to Hong Kong.'

'You may not want to stay put, sir,' warned Ågård. 'They're saying you went nuts and attacked a fishing fleet. Not,' he added loyally, 'that any of us believed it for a moment.'

'I'm glad to hear that, Mr Ågård.'

'All right, all right, get back to work, you lot!' growled the boatswain. 'Begging your pardon, Mr Killigrew, sir, but

Commander Robertson left instructions that if you was brung back on board you was to be taken to him at once.'

Killigrew gestured to his Chinese clothes. 'Don't I get a chance to change into my spare uniform first?'

'He was very specific about the "at once" part of the order, sir.'

Killigrew allowed the boatswain to escort him down to Robertson's day room, where the commander was in conference with Lord Hartcliffe. Both of them leaped to their feet when the marine sentry ushered Killigrew in, and Hartcliffe pumped his hand vigorously.

'Kit! By all that's wonderful! I was starting to fear the worst!'

'All right, First, that will do,' snapped Robertson. 'You can try to dislocate his arm later. Killigrew, you do realise that Captain Morgan has had a warrant put out for your arrest, don't you?'

'No, sir. But if I can convince Admiral Huang of my innocence, sir, I'm sure I can do the same for Morgan.'

'Huang?' Robertson glanced out of the window to where the admiral's junk rode at anchor. 'So, he brought you back, eh? And I suppose he provided you with those ridiculous clothes as well?'

'After a fortnight in a gaol cell, sir, I'm afraid the uniform I was wearing was only fit to be burned.'

'All right. You can change later. Word of your return has probably reached the shore already. I dare say we haven't much time before Morgan arrives with Mr Cargill and demands that you be clapped in irons, so make your explanation short, and don't leave out anything pertinent.'

'I'll start at the beginning, sir, and you'll have to bear with me. I'm still trying to get all this straightened out in my mind. A lot of what I have to say is supposition, but if you'll bear with me you'll see it fits. Bannatyne is in league with the pilongs.'

'Capital idea, Killigrew,' Robertson said sarcastically.

'Get the supposition over and done with. Do you have any proof of that?'

'No, sir. But Grafton, Bannatyne and Co. have lost fewer ships to pilongs than any other company trading with China. One, to be precise, and it looks like even that may have been an insurance swindle. Bannatyne provides Zhai Jing-mu with all the information he needs about shipping movements to and from Hong Kong: not just which ships are sailing when – Zhai could pick up that kind of information from the *Hong Kong Register* – but what cargoes they're carrying. He's a sharp one, I'll lay odds he has had at least one spy in each of his rivals' factories. So Zhai Jing-mu gets information and in return Bannatyne has his ships left alone; at the same time as his rivals lose millions from Zhai's depredations.'

'It's a little far-fetched, but it does make a kind of sense,' Robertson admitted grudgingly. 'Go on.'

'All right. Let's suppose that Zhai Jing-mu wasn't killed when the *Akhandata* went down. Even if he wasn't badly injured, he must have been upset. He laid a trap for Peri and me, but he only got half of what he was after. I escaped and killed several of his men into the bargain. Zhai Jing-mu lost face that day. He's only a man, surrounded by other men just as ambitious as he is. Each time one of his schemes goes awry he loses a little of the mystique which gives him such a powerful hold over his followers. The only way he can remedy that is to correct his earlier mistake, make it clear to all that anyone who stands in his way will die horribly. So he lays another trap, this time with the help of his friend Bannatyne.'

'So that was why Bannatyne lent us the *Golden Dragon*? As a ruse to capture you?'

'Verran knew it was the perfect bait. Every man has his weakness. With some it's women, with others gaming.' Killigrew grinned ruefully. 'With me I'm afraid it might be the chance of an independent command and an opportunity to take a crack at the pilongs.'

'All right, what exactly happened?'

Killigrew told him quickly about the 'attack' on the *Golden Dragon*. 'They tried to take me prisoner, but I managed to jump overboard and swim ashore,' he concluded briefly. 'It took me the best part of a week to walk across Hainan to Hoi-how. When I got there I reported to the magistrate at the *yamen* and was promptly arrested for the attack on the fishing fleet. That seems to have been genuine enough. Verran must have opened fire on those junks just to make it look as if I'd run amok, so that no one would believe me if I came back here to tell you he was in league with the pilongs.'

'Frankly, Second, I'm still not sure that I *do* believe you. But I believe Verran even less. Yet even if what you've told me is true, that hardly proves your wild allegations about Bannatyne. Solid proof is what we need.'

'We'll get it,' said Killigrew. It might have been Zhai Jing-mu who had pulled the trigger when Peri had been murdered, but it was obvious that Bannatyne had been behind it all, pulling the strings. 'When I catch up with Verran, he'll tell us all. His only chance now is to turn Queen's evidence. He's just a pawn in this whole thing. Bannatyne's the spider lurking at the middle of this web, and it's him I want.'

There was a knock at the door. 'Begging your pardon, sir,' called the marine sentry. 'But apparently Assistant Superintendent Cargill of the Hong Kong Police wishes permission to come on board.'

'That's all right, Barnes. Have him shown down here at once.'

'Very good, sir.'

Robertson checked his watch. 'Ten minutes: remarkably swift work for a policeman.'

'That Cargill's no fool,' allowed Killigrew.

While they were waiting, the sound of sawing and

hammering from the waterfront drew his attention out of the stern window, open to let some air flow through the room on such a stifling day, and he saw some kind of scaffold being built on the open space in front of the barracks. Wherever he looked preparations were underway, strings of paper lanterns being hung from buildings and across streets, and temporary spectator stands being built wherever there was space on the waterfront. 'What's going on out there?'

'Preparations for the dragon boat festival on Tuesday night,' explained Robertson. 'They're making a big thing of it this year.'

Killigrew nodded. Westerners usually looked down their noses at Chinese festivals, but entertainment was so difficult to come by in the colony that anything which could be used as an excuse for a celebration was usually seized upon. He wondered if what Huang had told him about a possible plot taking place at the festival was true. It was now Sunday afternoon, which meant that if there was a plot he had just over two days to expose it. He hoped that if he could find proof to convict Bannatyne of aiding and abetting pirates that would scupper whatever scheme was being hatched.

Cargill was shown into the day room. 'Come in, come in, Mr Cargill,' said Robertson. 'I believe you already know Lord Hartcliffe and Mr Killigrew?'

Looking flushed, Cargill nodded. 'Yes, sir. I'm sure you know why I'm here.' He took a piece of paper from inside his coat and unfolded it. 'I have a warrant for the arrest of Lieutenant Christopher I. Killigrew, suspected of having—'

'Yes, yes, yes!' Robertson said impatiently. 'We know all about that. Stow it, Cargill. That's fine, except you need to cross out Killigrew's name and write Captain Jago Verran's in its place.'

Cargill looked at them in surprise. 'Captain Verran!' He

brushed his whiskers thoughtfully. 'That would explain it . . .'

'Explain what? Explain yourself, man!'

'I've got a missing person's report on Captain Verran. In fact, I've got a missing ship report. He's disappeared, along with the *Golden Dragon* and her crew. Mr Bannatyne only informed me this morning. The *Golden Dragon* left for Macao a couple of days ago with Mrs Bannatyne on board, but it never arrived. I'd assumed it must've been attacked by pilongs.'

'Damned inconvenient,' said Hartcliffe.

'Not from Bannatyne's point of view,' said Killigrew. 'All too convenient, if you ask me. I've a feeling Mrs Bannatyne is in deadly danger.'

'How so, Second?'

'I should have expected Verran to disappear with the *Golden Dragon.* Bannatyne knew his story wouldn't hold water if I made it back here. If Verran's gone adrift he can't be made to answer any awkward questions.'

'But what about Mrs Bannatyne?' asked Hartcliffe. 'Why should she disappear? Unless she was involved in some way . . .'

Killigrew shook his head grimly. 'No. That's just it. She wasn't involved at all. She must've stumbled across something proving her husband's collusion with the pirates. She's not the first member of her family to disappear while sailing to Macao on a vessel captained by Verran.'

'You're referring to her father?' Cargill drew himself up to his full height. 'I conducted the inquiry into his death personally. The coroner's verdict was death by misadventure. Gentlemen, I'm afraid I'm a little behind you all here. Are you suggesting that Mr Bannatyne is in league with the pilongs?'

'Isn't it obvious?' asked Killigrew.

'That's an extremely serious accusation, sir. I know it's not my place to give you advice, but nevertheless I feel I must remind you that Mr Bannatyne is an extremely influential man. Both here and back in England.'

'We're well aware of that,' Robertson said tersely.

'I trust you have some proof of what you suggest?'

'If I had proof, Mr Cargill, we wouldn't be standing here jawing, we'd be on our way to Bannatyne's house to put that devil under arrest.'

'Are you absolutely sure you're not misconstruing this, sir? I mean, I know it's not my place to speculate, but from what Mr Bannatyne said to me this morning . . . well, I rather got the impression he thought his wife might have run away with Captain Verran.'

'Perhaps,' Killigrew said dubiously. 'But it doesn't alter the fact that Verran's guilty of piracy and murder.'

'It's still a case of your word against his,' pointed out Cargill. 'And the word of his crew, and three Chinese fishermen Captain Verran pulled out of the water after you sank the fishing fleet.'

Killigrew was on his feet again in an instant. 'Jesus Christ! You don't honestly believe that, do you?'

'It's not a question of what I believe. It's a question of what the jury's going to believe. And I'm afraid the word of an opium smoker isn't going to count for much.'

'An opium smoker? Who told you that?'

'It wasn't Strachan, if that's what you're thinking,' said Robertson. 'Bannatyne told us.'

Killigrew grimaced. 'I should have seen that one coming.'

'Do you deny it?'

Killigrew sighed. 'No. But I'm off the filthy stuff now. And I certainly didn't order an attack on any damned fishing fleet.'

'I never believed *that* for a moment,' said Robertson. 'But you must take Mr Cargill's point. You're batting off a sticky wicket here.'

'I'm sorry, sir,' said Cargill. 'But until this whole matter has been cleared up, I'm going to have to take Mr Killigrew in for questioning at the very least.'

'Now hold on a moment, Assistant Superintendent. I'm sure we can come to a mutually satisfactory arrangement here. I'm going to speak to Captain Morgan immediately to try to get him to see this business isn't as clear-cut as it first appears. While I'm doing that, would you have any objections if Mr Killigrew were to stay on board the *Tisiphone*? I'm sure he'll give you his word of honour as an officer and a gentleman that he won't go anywhere.'

Killigrew stuck his hands in his pockets and nodded.

'I suppose that's all right,' mused Cargill.

'Very well, then,' said Robertson. 'That's settled. You and I shall go and see Captain Morgan while Killigrew remains here.'

Killigrew and Hartcliffe went up on deck to see Robertson and Cargill off.

As soon as the gig was out of earshot, Killigrew turned to Molineaux. 'Fancy a jaunt to the *Buchan Prayer*?'

Molineaux raised an eyebrow. 'I take it we don't have an invitation, sir?'

'That's why I'd like you to come with me. I need your skill at picking locks and breaking and entering.'

'I came to sea so I could get away from a life of crime,' Molineaux said huffily.

'Just one last time. Remember, you're on the side of justice now.'

'Tell it to the beak when he has me lagged for breaking and entering.'

'Actually, in law I don't think you can be transported to Australia for trespassing on a private vessel.'

'No?'

Killigrew shook his head. 'This will count as piracy. You know what penalty that carries, don't you?'

Molineaux sighed. 'I wish you'd kept your trap shut, sir. I was just starting to think this might not be such a daft idea.'

'It would hardly be fair to ask you to do this without letting you know the risks involved. If you want to back out, I shan't think any the less of you.'

'In a pig's eye!'

'I can't order you to do this.'

'Oh-kay, oh-kay. I'll help.'

Hartcliffe was horrified. 'Killigrew, what are you talking about? I thought you were going to stay here?'

'While Cargill and Morgan prepare the case for the prosecution? No can do, my lord. We have to find the *Golden Dragon* before it's too late. Verran hasn't got the sand to disobey Bannatyne. Our friend the *tai-pan* knows exactly where his missing steamer is, and it's my guess we'll find the information we're looking for on board Bannatyne's receiving ship. We may even find proof of Bannatyne's involvement with the pilongs.'

'Please, Killigrew, I'm begging you. The Old Man's going to have me strung up from the yardarm if he gets back and finds I've let you cut and run. Besides, you promised Cargill on your word of honour. As an officer and a gentleman.'

Killigrew grinned boyishly. 'I had my fingers crossed.'

# XV:

## *The Buchan Prayer*

Killigrew was still dressed in his Chinese clothes – conical hat and all – when he climbed into Mei-rong's *yolo* with Molineaux. If one of Cargill's constables – or one of Bannatyne's spies, for that matter – saw a man in the uniform of a naval officer being sculled away in a *yolo*, that would give the game away; the black silk tunic and pyjamy trousers would also provide better camouflage than his white pantaloons and shirt when Killigrew climbed aboard the *Buchan Prayer* at night.

'I hope you know what you're doing, Killigrew,' Hartcliffe called down softly from the entry port.

'That makes two of us,' Killigrew heard Molineaux mutter under his breath. The seaman was dressed in his pusser's slops, just another sailor and hardly likely to arouse any suspicions on shore. Both Killigrew and Molineaux quickly sat down beneath the matting awning while Mei-rong sat cross-legged in the stern, sculling the boat towards Possession Point and beyond, swirling figures of eight in the water with well-practised motions.

'How long will it take us to reach Discovery Bay, Mei-rong?' asked Killigrew. They were headed for Lan-tao Island, and Discovery Bay would make a good place to land, on the far side from the Cap-sing-mun anchorage but at the narrowest part of the island.

'Four hour.'

Killigrew nodded. It would be twilight by then; they would have a bite to eat, and then walk across the island. Then it should be dark enough to swim out to the *Buchan Prayer* unobserved. 'Once we get out of the harbour, Molineaux can scull,' he said, and the Able Seaman nodded eagerly.

'No can do!' hissed Mei-rong. 'My boat, my rowum. My no trustee barbarian rowum.' She grinned. 'You no worry; my plenty strong, my gettee you there in plenty good hour.'

Killigrew shrugged and made himself comfortable amongst the rough cushions and bolsters. 'I'm going to get some sleep, Molineaux. Wake me in a couple of hours and then you can take a spell.'

'Aye, aye, sir.'

Killigrew tipped his conical hat over his eyes and went to sleep. The sea was no place for insomniacs; one soon learned to sleep when and where one could.

Twilight was descending when he awoke. Glancing out from beneath the awning, he could see the shore of Lan-tao only a couple of cables' lengths away. He heard a low murmur of voices behind him and twisted to see Molineaux seated at the rear of the awning, talking to Mei-rong as she continued to scull them as tirelessly as ever towards the island. 'I thought you were going to wake me when we got halfway?'

'Is that the time already, sir? I had no idea it was so late.'

'You need your sleep just as much as I do, Molineaux.'

The seaman grinned. 'You looked so peaceful, sir; seemed a shame to wake you.'

Killigrew joined them in the stern and indicated a cove to the east of Discovery Bay. 'Can you put us ashore there?' he asked Mei-rong.

She nodded and sculled the boat in through the surf.

Killigrew and Molineaux jumped overboard and dragged the boat over the shingle into a place of concealment between two boulders. Mei-rong had cooking utensils and a stove on board and she prepared fish stew and fried rice for them.

'There's something I don't understand, Mei-rong,' said Molineaux. 'You Chinese are s'posed to be an ancient and wise people, right?'

She nodded. '*Hai.*'

'You invented paper, printing, gunpowder, the compass and all kinds of useful stuff like that, right?'

'*Hai.* What you wantchee savvy?'

'So how come you never invented bloody forks?'

She laughed. 'Chopstick plenty good for civilised Chinee. Missee Killigrew, him eatee with chopstick, can. Only barbarian needee fork.'

Molineaux produced his Bowie knife and used the blade to balance his food on as he scooped it into his mouth.

'Where did you get that?' asked Killigrew. 'I've seen cutlasses with smaller blades.'

'Took it off a slaver at the Owodunni Barracoon, sir. It's called a Bowie knife. Invented by some Yankee cove who got cramped at the Alamo.'

'If that's the kind of weaponry the Texans had at the Alamo, it's hardly surprising they held out for so long.'

'You got any weapons, sir?'

Killigrew shook his head. 'Remember, if we bump into any guards, they may just be innocent employees of Grafton, Bannatyne and Co.'

'Innocent!' scoffed Molineaux, who did not share Killigrew's free-trade principles. 'Don't see as how anyone who works smuggling opium can be called "innocent", sir.'

'All the same, they're not guilty of anything under British law.'

'Is it oh-kay to scrag them in self-defence?'

'If you must,' sighed Killigrew. 'But *only* if you must. If all goes well we won't need any weapons.'

'And if all *doesn't* go well?'

'I'd rather not think about that.'

'You needn't worry, sir. If the worst comes to the worst and they catch us, somehow I don't think it will ever come to a trial.'

They washed down their food with some rice wine and Killigrew glanced about at the gathering dusk. 'Time to go,' he decided.

'You be plenty careful!' Mei-rong warned them.

Molineaux nodded. 'Remember, if we're not back by sun up, you head back for Victoria Harbour and pretend you never even heard of us.'

Killigrew and Molineaux set off walking across the island. Complete darkness had fallen by the time they reached the far side, but paper lanterns lit up the decks of all the receiving ships. They could just make out the guards patrolling the decks. The opium-stuffed hulks were prime targets for pilongs, and they were well defended with cannons and swivel guns.

A strong sea ran through the Cap-sing-mun Passage and it was hard work just to swim out to the *Buchan Prayer*. They reached the hulk without anyone on deck raising the alarm, and swam round to the stern. Both stern ports were barred shut: somehow Killigrew had not expected getting aboard to be easy, but it had been worth a try.

They swam the length of the hull to the anchor chain, using a gentle breaststroke that caused hardly a ripple. On the deck above them there would be a watch on duty, but no one was gazing over the bulwarks. 'I'll go up first,' whispered Killigrew. 'When I signal the coast is clear, you follow.'

Molineaux shook his head. 'Better leave this to me, sir. I've done this kind of thing before. On land, at any rate.' Before Killigrew could protest, Molineaux was climbing nimbly up the taut anchor chain. He reached the hawse hole and from there he could get one foot on the cheeks of the port bow. He scrambled over the rails on to the beak over the prow and was gone from sight.

A moment later his head appeared at the rail, peering down to where Killigrew still trod water by the anchor chain. Molineaux pointed to something, and in the dim illumination of a paper lantern Killigrew could make out a sentry armed with a musket standing on the forecastle. The sentry faced forwards; the only reason he could not see Molineaux was because the seaman was in shadow. If Molineaux tried to climb on to the forecastle he would be spotted and the alarm would be raised. Killigrew saw Molineaux stick two fingers in his mouth, and for a moment he thought the seaman was going to whistle. Then he understood: Molineaux wanted a distraction, something to make the sentry turn away from the prow.

Killigrew had a better idea. He slapped the water beside him with the flat of his hand to make a splashing noise.

The sentry crossed to the starboard-side rail of the forecastle and glanced down. He carried a bull's-eye lantern and suddenly opened the shutter so that the beam fell on Killigrew. Still treading water, the lieutenant smiled and waved. A moment later the sentry crumpled as Molineaux stepped up behind him and hit him on the back of the neck with the haft of his Bowie knife. The seaman caught him before he could hit the deck with a noisy thump and then signalled that the coast was clear.

Killigrew shinned up the anchor chain and was about to climb over the rail to join Molineaux on the forecastle when he heard a voice as another sentry appeared from behind a deck house. 'You all right, Zeke?'

'He just collapsed,' Molineaux called softly. He was no fool: he must have known that all the second sentry could see was one figure crouched over another slumped on deck. He motioned for the other sentry to approach.

The second sentry hurried forward, reassured by Molineaux's distinctly non-Chinese accent. 'Is he all right?'

Molineaux stood up and punched the man in the throat. He gave a strangled gasp, and Molineaux hit him again. This time he went down. 'No worse than you,' he told the second sentry's unconscious body.

Killigrew climbed over the rail. 'Everything all right?' he whispered.

'Nothing I couldn't handle,' Molineaux assured him. 'Help me get this one trussed up and we'll lower them on to the head. They'll be out of sight there.'

Killigrew nodded. 'All the same, someone's bound to notice their absence. We may not have much time.'

'We'd best look lively then, sir.'

Molineaux had already gagged and bound the first sentry with his own belt, bootlaces and musket-sling. They did the same for the second, and gently lowered both to the grating of the head, more so as not to make any unnecessary noise than because they did not want to hurt the men.

'Now what?' asked Molineaux.

'We'll search the ship separately. You try the offices in the stern deck-house; see what papers you can find in the safe. I'll check the accommodation below decks, see if Mrs Bannatyne's being held on board.' Killigrew was hoping against all common sense that the *tai-pan* would not have it in his heart to murder his own wife in cold blood; but if Huang's theories were correct, Bannatyne was a ruthless man who would stop at nothing, and Mrs Bannatyne was probably at the bottom of the South China Sea. But until he knew that for certain, Killigrew had to do everything in his power to rescue her; after the way she had cared for him during his sickness, he owed her that much at least. 'If someone raises the alarm, it's every man for himself. If either of us doesn't make it back to where we left Mei-rong with the *yolo*, then he takes his own chances.'

Molineaux nodded. They both crept along the deck, leaving a trail of wet footprints that would lead anyone who stumbled across them straight after the two trespassers, but that could not be helped. Molineaux opened the door to the aftermost deck house and peered through for a moment before stepping inside and closing the door behind him.

As soon as the seaman was out of sight, Killigrew glanced about until he found the after-hatch. He descended a companionway to a narrow corridor with doors leading off on either side. He listened at the first, heard nothing, and gently rapped his knuckles against it. There was no reply, but he opened it anyway, to find an empty cabin with linen folded on the bare mattress of the bunk. He was about to try the door of the next cabin when he heard sounds coming from the door behind him. Creaking and moaning. He glanced at the sign on the door – 'Captain Ingersoll' – and smiled. He grasped the handle and slowly eased the door open.

Ingersoll lay on the bunk with his head thrown back on the pillows, his eyes closed in ecstasy. A Chinese girl sat astride his hips, her head thrown back, her back to the door. A percussion pistol lay on a chair next to the bed: Ingersoll was clearly not a man who liked to take chances.

Both were too focused on what they were doing to notice Killigrew enter the cabin and close the door behind him. He tiptoed across the deck, picked up the pistol, encircled the girl's neck in the crook of an elbow and clamped a hand over her mouth while he levelled the pistol at the man's head.

The girl writhed in panic and moaned. 'Oh, yes!' gasped the man. 'Yes! That's it! Yes!'

Killigrew tapped him on the chest with the cold muzzle of the pistol. Ingersoll's eyes opened and his hand shot out towards the chair, fumbling for the pistol which was no longer there. He stared at Killigrew in shock. 'What the . . .? Who the hell be you?'

'The questions you should be asking at this juncture are: what do I want, and what's going to happen to you if I don't get it? Speakee English?' he asked the girl.

She nodded as best she could.

'I'm going to take my hand from your mouth in a moment. If you scream, he dies. Then you. Savvy?'

She nodded again.

He took his hand away. 'Put on that robe.' He jerked his head to where a scarlet silk robe, the kind of thing Chinese prostitutes wore, was tossed on the deck.

She climbed off Ingersoll. 'You him spilum, my no care,' she said with defiant truculence, but she was trembling and did as she was told.

Killigrew kept the pistol levelled at Ingersoll. 'You be Killigrew!' the captain exclaimed in shock.

'I'm honoured that my reputation has preceded me. Get up.' Killigrew backed away and gestured to the girl with the pistol. 'Tie her up and gag her. No snowball hitches.'

Ingersoll scowled. 'All right, missy. On the bunk, face down. You won't be tied up for long.'

'Most time my makee payee plenty extra for this.'

Killigrew picked up a silk scarf with his left hand and passed it to Ingersoll. 'Gag her. I think we've both had enough from her for one night.'

'Speak for yourself,' scowled Ingersoll. 'What do you want?'

'Where's the *Golden Dragon*?'

Ingersoll grinned. 'You best be asking Cap'n Verran that, matey.'

'It's Verran I'm looking for. Go to the porthole and put your hands behind your back.'

He had to put the pistol down to tie Ingersoll's hands. The captain launched himself backwards off the bulkhead and cannoned into Killigrew's body. He was bigger and stronger than Killigrew, and when they crashed into the door it was the lieutenant who bore the brunt of it.

Then Ingersoll threw himself across the room and snatched the pistol from the chair. Killigrew caught him by the wrists before he could level it, but Ingersoll managed to squeeze a shot into the deck head. It was deafeningly loud in the confined space of the cabin. The lieutenant rammed a knee into Ingersoll's dangling scrotum and the captain dropped with a strangled scream. Killigrew prised the pistol from his grip and hit him with it.

While Ingersoll was still dazed, Killigrew gagged him and bound his hands behind his back. He could hear feet pounding the deck above his head. By the time he opened the door and pushed Ingersoll out before him, two guards were descending the companionway at the far end of the corridor.

Killigrew held the pistol to Ingersoll's head. 'Put down your muskets and back away, or I'll shoot your captain!'

Ingersoll made moaning sounds behind the sock Killigrew had gagged him with. The guards lowered their muskets to the floor and backed up the companionway. Killigrew pushed Ingersoll before him until he could pick up one musket in his left hand and hold the muzzle to Ingersoll's head. Then he dropped the pistol and picked up the other musket, slinging it across his shoulder. He goaded Ingersoll up the companion ladder and they joined the two guards on deck.

'Much obliged,' said Killigrew. 'I think your captain was trying to tell you the pistol was empty.'

'That's all right, matey,' said one of the guards, grinning. 'So were our muskets.'

Still holding the musket's muzzle to Ingersoll's head, Killigrew pulled the trigger. The hammer fell with a hollow snap.

One of the guards punched him in the face. He felt his knees crumple beneath him and then the empty musket was snatched from his grasp. A moment later the butt was rammed into his stomach.

The other guard took out a clasp-knife and sliced through Ingersoll's bonds. The captain tore off the gag. 'That be right good work, lads,' he said as more guards arrived. 'Let's drag him in the office, afore I be freezing to death.'

Killigrew's arms were seized and he was hoisted to his feet. They manhandled him through a door into one of the deck houses: the same deck house Killigrew had seen Molineaux enter a few minutes earlier. There was no sign of the seaman now except for the last traces of some wet footprints which faded on the way to the safe. Ingersoll and his men did not seem to notice them.

The captain reached behind the door and produced a greatcoat which he quickly put on to cover his nakedness. Killigrew was thrown into a chair. 'Shall we tie him up, Cap'n?' asked one of the guards.

'Why bother?' Ingersoll took a musket off one of the guards. 'Be this primed and loaded?'

'Aye, aye, Cap'n.'

'Good.' Ingersoll raised the stock to his shoulder and levelled it at Killigrew's face from almost point-blank range. There was murder in his eyes. 'There be only one way to deal with scum like this . . .'

Molineaux slipped into the office on board the *Buchan Prayer* and closed the door behind him. Everything was dark. He squeezed his eyes shut and counted slowly to ten in his head. When he opened them again, he was able to see the safe which stood in one corner. He crossed for a closer examination. A Chubb safe with a combination lock: a cracksman's worst nightmare.

But, as his mother never tired of reminding him, he could do anything if he put his mind to it. He looked about the office, his eyes growing more and more accustomed with every passing moment to the faint light which filtered through the portholes. He found a pencil on the desk and some papers. Looking at the top sheet, he saw it was a receipt for an eight-inch shell gun. That meant nothing: all tea clippers carried cannon to defend themselves from pilongs, and a man like Bannatyne would want his ships to have the biggest and best guns money could buy. Searching in the drawers he found a bottle of rum and a tumbler. He took the tumbler and, on second thoughts, took a fortifying nip of Nelson's blood straight from the bottle. Then he sat down cross-legged beside the safe. Chubb offered a reward of a thousand pounds to any man who could crack one of these things. Molineaux wondered if he would ever be able to claim the prize if he succeeded tonight.

He pressed the tumbler to the door of the safe and his ear to the tumbler. Then he slowly turned the dial until he heard the first, faint click. Left six. He made a note on the back of the piece of paper and then turned the dial clockwise until he heard the next click. Right eleven. Click. Another note. Left nineteen. Click. Right sixty-nine.

He grasped the handle, took a deep breath, turned it, and . . .

The safe stayed locked.

'Bugger.'

He was about to start again when he heard what sounded like a pistol-shot. He thrust the paper inside his shirt and put the pencil and tumbler back where he had found them. Then he crossed to the door and opened it a crack. Two guards charged down the deck towards him. He quickly pushed the door to and reached for his Bowie knife, but the footsteps on the deck turned outside the deck house and clattered down a hatchway. He heard tense, muffled voices, and then the footsteps came back up the companionway, more slowly now.

'Much obliged.' Molineaux recognised Killigrew's voice immediately outside the door. 'I think your captain was trying to tell you the pistol was empty.'

Molineaux heaved a sigh of relief. It sounded as though the lieutenant had everything under control. He was about to go outside and help him when another voice spoke.

'That's all right, matey. So were our muskets.'

There was a pregnant pause, followed by a snap. Then there was a thump, a gasp, and another thump. Someone – Killigrew by the sound of it – groaned.

'That be right good work, lads,' a third voice declared a moment later. 'Let's drag him in the office, afore I be freezing to death.'

Still clutching his Bowie knife, Molineaux pressed himself up against the bulkhead beside the door and a moment later it was thrown open, partially concealing him. A hairy hand came round the door and reached for a greatcoat which hung on a hook an inch from Molineaux's face. The hand was as likely to find his nose as the greatcoat. He took the coat off the peg and held it where the groping hand would find it. The coat was accepted and a moment later Captain Ingersoll, as naked as the day he was born, stepped into sight. He had his back to Molineaux as he shrugged on the coat. Beyond him, Molineaux saw a dazed-looking Killigrew being thrown into a chair.

'Shall we tie him up, Cap'n?' asked someone out of sight on the other side of the door.

'Why bother?' Ingersoll stepped out of sight again. A moment later he reappeared with a musket in his hands. 'Be this primed and loaded?'

'Aye, aye, Cap'n.'

'Good.' Ingersoll raised the stock to his shoulder and levelled it at Killigrew's face from almost point-blank range. 'There be only one way to deal with scum like this . . .'

Molineaux realised that in another second Killigrew would be dead. He had no way of knowing how many other people were in the room, but it seemed reasonable to suppose that Ingersoll was not the only one holding a musket. And Molineaux was armed only with a Bowie knife: intimidating enough to look at, but not when the other cove had a barking iron.

The sensible thing to do was to stay concealed and hope for the best. Killigrew had known what risks he was taking when he had suggested this hare-brained scheme, the same as Molineaux. Staying put was what Molineaux reckoned Killigrew would have done.

*No*, Molineaux told himself. *That's what you'd like to think Killigrew would do if your places were reversed. But he'd think of something, so think fast.*

But he could not think of anything, except leaping out from behind the door and hoping that there were not too many of them, hoping that Killigrew was not as dazed as he seemed and would come to his aid, hoping that he would have the element of surprise.

Too much to hope for, but he was not going to stand there while they murdered Killigrew. He steeled himself to leap out and . . .

'*Scheisse!* What do you think you're doing?' snapped a new voice.

'Rat-catching, Reverend,' said Ingersoll. 'I caught this sonuvabitch . . .'

'I can see that. Do you know who that is?'

'Right enough. This be Killigrew. And if you think I be going to take any chances with him . . .'

The newcomer stepped into the room and Molineaux recognised him as the Reverend Werner Ultzmann. The missionary knocked the barrel of Ingersoll's musket up. '*Dumkopf!* Don't you know that Zhai Jing-mu wants this one alive?'

'That be Zhai Jing-mu's problem.'

'It will be *our* problem if you kill him now. After Herr Verran so carelessly let him get away, Zhai already suspects we humbugged him. We need Zhai's goodwill if the plan is to work out to our benefit; otherwise all the work we have done will have been for nothing!' Ultzmann turned to someone out of Molineaux's line of sight. 'Tie him up.'

Another man stepped into sight and set to work binding Killigrew's hands behind his back.

'What do you intend to do with him?'

'The next smug boat is due to arrive any moment now. When we've unloaded the tea and put the opium on board, I will take him with me. We'll stop off at Zhai's lair on our way to Swatow and I will hand him over to the pilongs. That way we regain the Triads' trust and we will all be rid of Killigrew. Do not concern yourself, Captain Ingersoll. I shall make sure the *tai-pan* knows who it was that captured Killigrew.'

'And if he escapes? Will you let him know whose fault *that* were?'

'He won't escape. Leave us. I wish to have a word in private with Herr Killigrew here.'

Ingersoll shooed his men out of the office and followed them out. He pulled the door to behind him, exposing Molineaux. Ultzmann had his back to the seaman, but Killigrew was fully conscious now and his eyes met Molineaux's for a fraction of a second. The seaman had to give the young officer credit: his face registered no surprise and he quickly shifted his gaze to the missionary.

'Zhai Jing-mu can kill me if he likes, but he'll be wasting his time,' said Killigrew. 'You think we don't know what the *tai-pan*'s up to? Feeding Zhai Jing-mu all the information he needs about shipping movements, and in return Zhai leaves his shipping alone. Oh, except for one overinsured floating coffin, for form's sake.'

'You blundering young idiot! I warned you once not to interfere in things which were no concern of yours, but you did not listen. Now you will die, and you have done nothing to halt Bannatyne's plan.'

Molineaux still had his Bowie knife in his hand. He

started to tiptoe across the deck towards Ultzmann's back.

'What plan would that be?' asked Killigrew.

'You think you'll escape and foil it? Sorry, my friend. I am not a fool.'

Molineaux raised the knife, ready to strike Ultzmann on the back of his head with the heavy haft.

'Whatever it is you're planning to do, I beg you not to,' said Killigrew.

Molineaux froze. Killigrew begging? That did not sound right.

'I'm going to be taken to Zhai Jing-mu's lair?' asked the lieutenant.

'I already said as much, didn't I?' Ultzmann said impatiently, still oblivious to Molineaux's presence.

Molineaux realised that Killigrew was speaking for his benefit rather than Ultzmann's. But at any moment the missionary was going to turn and see him. *What the hell am I supposed to do, then?* Molineaux mouthed at Killigrew.

'You want my advice?' asked Killigrew, his gaze fixed steadily on Ultzmann. 'If I were you, I would lie low until all this is over. Better still, go to the British authorities in Victoria and tell them I'm being held prisoner.'

'I . . . I cannot,' said Ultzmann.

Molineaux tiptoed back to the door and laid his hand on the knob.

'How much is Bannatyne paying you?'

Molineaux turned the doorknob and opened it a crack, praying no breeze would alert Ultzmann.

'You think all I care about is money?' Ultzmann demanded bitterly. 'I am a man of the cloth!'

Molineaux glanced outside. There were no guards in view. He slipped out on deck.

'A man of the cloth who's been aiding and abetting piracy and murder! What sins is Bannatyne using to blackmail you, Reverend?'

Molineaux was curious to know himself, but he closed the door softly. Even then he hesitated, still tempted to go back in and deal with the missionary. Did Killigrew know what he was doing? Molineaux hoped so, for his sake.

He was about to make his way back to the anchor-chain when a door from one of the deck houses opened and light flooded across the deck. Molineaux climbed the companion ladder to the poop deck, grabbed the eaves of the aftermost deck-house and swung himself up on to the roof. A moment later two guards emerged from a door and took up position outside the office where Ultzmann was speaking to Killigrew. There was no way Molineaux could get past them to the forecastle, and if he jumped overboard the splash would alert the guards. He lay flat and waited to see what would happen next.

'Smug boat coming in, Cap'n . . .' called a voice.

Molineaux glanced to the other side of the ship and saw a boat approaching from starboard.

'They be late,' said Ingersoll. 'All right, the starboard watch can start unloading the opium and bringing the tea on board.'

The oarsmen on the smug boat shipped oars downwind of the hulk and moved into position alongside under sail power alone. When the boat was close enough, ropes were thrown across and it was made fast. Two gangplanks were lowered to the smug boat and several figures ascended to the opium hulk. Molineaux shifted position so he could see what was going on.

'Shall we go inside?' Ingersoll suggested to the two Chinese who had ascended from the smug boat. He gestured to the door of the deck-house and the three of them joined Ultzmann and Killigrew in the office. The door was closed.

Molineaux stood up and tiptoed forward across the roof. He cut loose a backstay and used it to swing across to the next deck house, his feet making barely a sound when he touched down. He spun round and crouched down, expecting men to come pouring out of the deck house and surround it.

'All hands on deck!' A bell was rung, and men came rushing up from the forward hatch to crowd the deck. But they were not looking for Molineaux. They formed two human chains, one down each of the gangplanks. As sacks of opium were passed down one gangplank to the smug boat, sacks of tea were handed up to the opium hulk and thrown down the main hatch. English clerks and Chinese schroffs kept a careful count of the number of sacks passing in each direction.

Molineaux could not move from the roof of the deck-house while the exchange was carried out. He tried to get comfortable. He had a feeling he was in for a long wait.

The men worked quickly and cheerfully, as they might do on a public dockside. They might be working at night, but no one was making any attempt at secrecy: they sang shanties as they toiled in the full glare of the deck lights. And why shouldn't they? They were not doing anything illegal as far as the British were concerned, and the Chinese had already shown a willingness to turn a blind eye time and time again, as long as they received their *cumshaw*.

Bannatyne's massive comprador, Shen, emerged from one of the deck-houses to watch. After a while he called for the proceedings to halt while he weighed a few sacks of tea chosen at random, and opened a couple to examine the quality of the dried leaves. With a nod of approval, he signalled for the sacks to be sewn up once more and the work continued.

The exchange took nearly three hours. Molineaux had to keep shifting his position during this time to stop himself from getting pins and needles. But he could not move while so much activity was taking place on deck.

Eventually all the opium had been brought up from the

*Buchan Prayer*'s hold and the smug boat was packed to the gunwales. One of the Chinese called up from the boat in Cantonese, and a guard knocked on the door to Ingersoll's office. 'Laded and ready to go, Cap'n.'

A few moments later the door opened and Ingersoll emerged with Ultzmann and the two Chinese, escorting Killigrew at pistol-point between them.

'Hope you know what you be doing, Reverend,' Ingersoll said as the two Chinese escorted their prisoner down one of the gangplanks to the smug boat. 'Remember: the *Golden Dragon* sails at midnight the night after tomorrow. If you're late, you'll be left behind.'

'You think it wise to use the *Dragon* in this anchorage so publicly?' asked Ultzmann.

'*Tai-pan*'s decision, matey,' said Ingersoll. 'She's got two knots on the *White Tiger*. Don't worry, she'll be disguised. Besides, by that time everyone will have too many problems of their own to worry about the *Dragon* any more.'

Ultzmann took his leave and made his way down to the smug boat. The mooring ropes were cast off and Molineaux watched helplessly as the crew pushed off from the side of the hulk and dipped their oars. As they rowed it towards the Cap-sing-mun Passage, Molineaux wondered where they were going, and what Killigrew's chances of escaping were once he had found Zhai Jing-mu's lair.

Ingersoll and Shen turned and went back inside the deck house while the rest of the crew went below, leaving only one or two guards out on deck. Molineaux realised that the sky had lightened considerably: dawn was less than an hour away.

He crawled across to the forward edge of the roof. A sentry stood immediately below. Molineaux reached down, grabbed the man's neckerchief, and pulled it tight. The man struggled, but the neckerchief which dug into his windpipe choked off his cries. After a moment he stopped struggling. Molineaux jumped down and lowered his body to the deck. The man was still breathing and would wake up in a while with a splitting headache and a very sore throat.

Molineaux climbed back the way he had come on board, shinning down the anchor chain until he was up to his neck in water. He struck out for the shore. His limbs protested agonisingly after the first few strokes: cramp. Hardly surprising: he had been lying more or less motionless on the roof of the deck-house for the best part of five hours. Resisting the urge to panic, he floated on his back until the initial pain had worn off and he was able to strike out once more for the shore, using a less energetic stroke this time.

He had gone two hundred yards before anyone noticed him. He heard shouts behind him. A moment later the first musket balls whistled towards him, but by then he was beyond effective range for sharpshooting. By the time he waded up the shingle beach out of the surf he walked with insouciant slowness to show his contempt. As a final act of defiance, he dropped his trousers and bent over to let them get a good look at what he thought of their marksmanship. Between his own legs he could see the opium hulk upside down, one of the gun-ports amidships opening as they ran out a thirty-two-pounder long gun . . .

Molineaux swore, hitched up his trousers and broke into a run as the gun boomed. The shot screeched through the air towards him with a sound like canvas tearing. He flung himself flat on the ground as the shot burst over the beach. Pellets of canister showered down on the shingle close by. He quickly picked himself up and ran further uphill before they had a chance to reload.

When he reached the crest of the spine of hills that ran the length of the island he glanced back. On the beach below a long boat had landed and men armed with muskets swarmed ashore. To the east, the sun was just peeping over the horizon. Molineaux turned and ran back to where he had left Mei-rong with the *yolo*.

It was twenty minutes after dawn before he reached the cove where he had left her. She was still waiting for him when he stumbled out of the trees on to the shingle. 'Cast off!' he called to her, breaking into a sprint for the last stretch.

'Where Missee Killigrew?' she demanded.

'He's not coming. Get pushing, Mei-rong, or else we'll have unwelcome guests.'

They put their shoulders to the boat and shoved it back into the water. At last it floated clear and Molineaux collapsed in the bottom while Mei-rong stood on the stern to pole the boat out through the breakers with her sculling oar. 'Missee Killigrew, him spilum?'

'Killigrew dead? Don't be daft. He's got the devil's own luck, that one.' Molineaux hoped it was true.

The *yolo* was a cable's length from the shore by the time the men from the opium hulk appeared behind them. They fired a desultory volley from their muskets but none of the shots even came close.

'You makee someone plenty angry,' said Mei-rong.

Molineaux grinned and glanced ahead. They could see the peaks of Hong Kong island only six miles away.

He pondered what he had overheard. He would have precious little to tell Commander Robertson when he got back to the *Tisiphone*: that Killigrew had been captured and was being taken to Zhai Jing-mu's lair – somewhere between Hong Kong and Swatow from the sound of it – but that only narrowed it down to a hundred and fifty-odd miles of coastline, not counting every creek and inlet. It was hardly calculated to divert Robertson's rage at Killigrew's escape.

Bannatyne and Zhai Jing-mu were planning something, that much was obvious. But what? Molineaux had a feeling it would not be anything good. He hoped Killigrew would find out and then manage to get away and back to Victoria in time to reveal all. But that was too much to hope for, even from a man like Killigrew. Molineaux wished he had knocked Ultzmann out when he had had the chance and rescued the lieutenant. This time Killigrew had bitten off more than he could chew.

They had covered almost half the distance, and Green Island, off the westernmost tip of Hong Kong, was just coming into view, when Molineaux spotted a plume of smoke in the direction of Cap-sing-mun Passage. After a few minutes the base of the plume was revealed as a steamer headed for Victoria Harbour.

'Maybe we catchee tow, catchee Hong Kong,' said Mei-rong.

'Maybe,' Molineaux agreed dubiously.

To his surprise the paddle-wheeler altered direction, a few points to starboard, so that it was coming towards them.

The steamer ploughed through the waves, a bone in her teeth where the foam churned at the foot of her stem. Molineaux expected her to slow or turn when it came within a cable's length, but she did no such thing: she just kept on coming.

'Maybe him no see we,' said Mei-rong, sculling the *yolo* out of the steamer's path.

The steamer changed direction again to follow. It was less than fifty yards away now, and bore down relentlessly on the flimsy boat. The white tiger figurehead seemed to pounce at them.

'She's seen us, all right!' Molineaux jumped up from where he sat and lunged across the stern. He caught Mei-rong around the waist and the two of them hit the water together. He was still towing her clear when the steamer's prow ripped through the boat amidships. There was a great splintering crash which momentarily drowned out the plashing of the paddle-wheels. The bow wave lifted Molineaux up and he was still trying to get his bearings when he saw the steamer's starboard paddle-wheel bearing down on him. He tried to swim out of the way but once again cramp paralysed his limbs. He stared helplessly as the paddles filled his vision, each one slapping down against the water viciously, closer, closer . . .

A strong hand caught him underneath the chin and pulled him clear with only inches to spare. Even so the backwash almost sucked him under, but the same hand grabbed a fistful of his hair and dragged him back to the surface. Mei-rong, God bless her. Like any Tanka girl, she could swim like a fish.

'You oh-kay?' she asked him.

Coughing and spluttering, it was all he could do to nod. As the stern of the *White Tiger* passed them, he saw Shen standing on the rail, glaring down at them malevolently. Molineaux expected the steamer to turn and try to run them down again, but she just altered course slightly and continued on her way. Probably Shen did not think they would be able to swim the last three miles to Hong Kong.

If Molineaux had been alone then the comprador would have been right. But the tireless Mei-rong had enough strength for both of them. She stayed with him the whole way, urging him on when he had the strength to swim, towing him behind her when his limbs finally gave out. At one point he felt his mouth fill with water and he thought he was drowning – he was so far gone he was not sure that he cared – but the next thing he knew she was dragging him on to the beach of Belcher Bay. Then she collapsed on the shingle beside him and they both lay there gasping for breath while the midday sun warmed their bodies.

Molineaux had no idea how long he lay there, but after a while Mei-rong gained strength sufficiently to start complaining in a torrent of Cantonese. He did not understand a word of it, but it did not sound like the kind of language polite young ladies used. Realising her mother tongue was wasted on him, she switched back to pidgin English.

'Bloody bastard barbarian! My bloody takee them to *yamen*! No *yolo*, no home, no cash; no cash, no rice! My starvum! Mei-feng alla time warnee my 'bout bloody bastard barbarian, she tellee me no mixee *fan kwae*. What for my no listenee?'

'You can take them to the *yamen*, all right,' gasped Molineaux. 'They deliberately tried to murder us!'

'You takee murder charge to Hella, you bloody bastard barbarian devil-slave! My sue him for losum plenty cash!'

'Bring him up on deck,' ordered Ultzmann. Two pilongs – dressed in the same black pyjamy suits and crimson turbans as the Triads who had attacked Killigrew on both of his visits to the joss house on Hollywood Road – seized him and hoisted him to his feet. 'Watch him,' warned Ultzmann. 'He may be pretending to be more badly injured than he really is, to lull us into a false sense of security.'

Killigrew feigned nothing. The Triads on the smug boat had amused themselves on the voyage by beating him, and now he could barely stand. Nevertheless, as he was dragged on deck he tried to observe as much as possible. If by some miracle he was able to escape, he would do so carrying vital intelligence which would serve the Royal Navy well when it came here to destroy Zhai Jing-mu's fleet.

For there could be no doubt he had finally tracked the pirate to his lair. He counted about three dozen junks in the harbour, most of them carrying nine guns in each broadside. The largest – Zhai Jing-mu's flagship, to judge from the display of steamers and black and red flags – had forty-two guns in total. All in all it was a formidable force. But there was no sign of the *Golden Dragon*.

Killigrew had been kept below deck during the voyage from Cap-sing-mun, but he guessed they could be no more than twenty or thirty miles east of Hong Kong. So close to the seat of British naval power in the South China Seas, yet perfectly safe thanks to their secluded location in an arm of the bay hidden from the open sea.

The smug boat moored against the jetty and while the crew started to unload the cargo of opium, a boat was sent to the flagship to inform Zhai Jing-mu of the arrival of their special guest.

Ultzmann took Killigrew ashore. Even though the lieutenant had both his hands tied behind his back, Ultzmann did not take his pepperbox off him for a moment. The two Triads threw Killigrew to the ground outside one of the huts in the village.

Killigrew watched as the boat from the jetty reached Zhai Jing-mu's flagship. A moment later he recognised Zhai himself, resplendent in his white clothes and crimson sash, climb down into the boat.

He turned to Ultzmann. 'I thought the Triads wanted to overthrow the Ch'ing Dynasty because they allowed us barbarians to smuggle opium into their country?' he said thickly. 'And yet here they are, helping them to do it!'

'Regrettable but necessary,' said Ultzmann. 'The Brotherhood of Heaven, Earth and Man must have money to buy arms before it can overthrow the Ch'ing Dynasty. Smuggling opium is the quickest way to make that money.'

'Who's going to sell them those arms? Bannatyne, I suppose?'

Ultzmann chuckled. 'Oh, I think you'll find the Triads have a far greater role for us Westerners in the overthrow of the Ch'ing Dynasty than you can ever imagine, Herr Killigrew. And when the Ming Dynasty is restored, this whole country will be made strong enough to resist the bullying tactics of the British. No longer will China be crushed and humiliated by your Royal Navy. With modern shell guns and steam-powered ships, China will be able to defend herself.'

'You think Bannatyne cares about their revolution? He's

only interested in making money. You can't believe his promises. It was men like him who urged the British government to go to war with China in the first place, so he could continue to import opium. The last thing he wants is to see China strong enough to defend herself. Even he's not stupid enough to equip Chinese with Western arms. He wouldn't do it for all the tea in China.'

Scrunching up the shingle beach from where the boat had landed, Zhai Jing-mu grinned. He had a crimson eye patch now to match his sash. 'That is where you are wrong, Killigrew. All the tea in China is *precisely* what he is doing it for.'

Killigrew stared at him, and then nodded. 'A total monopoly of the tea trade?' That would make Bannatyne the richest man in the whole world; and the most powerful.

Zhai lifted up his eye patch and thrust his face close to Killigrew's. The socket was empty, just an ugly mess of scar tissue. 'Take a good look at your handiwork, *fan kwae*. This was your doing!'

'My heart bleeds for you,' sneered Killigrew.

Zhai kicked him savagely. 'Mock now, while you still can, barbarian. Soon you will be begging me for mercy.' He turned to one of the Triads. 'Bring out a table. Get some coals burning in a brazier and heat up some irons until they are red-hot.' He turned back to Killigrew. 'You think that kick I gave you just now hurt? You do not know the meaning of pain. But you will soon, I assure you.'

# *XVI:*

# *The Mæander*

'You think we don't know what it is that you and the *tai-pan* are up to?' Killigrew asked Zhai Jing-mu. 'You're planning to provoke another war between Britain and China.' He was spread-eagled on a table while four pilongs held him down, one at each wrist and ankle. Ultzmann watched while Zhai Jing-mu turned the irons in the brazier. They were already starting to glow red-hot.

'You're insane,' said Killigrew. 'Can't you see? The Chinese can't win, not against steamships and shell guns. You know as well as Bannatyne that if there is a second war, the British won't hold back the way they did in forty-two. British public opinion will demand that this time the Chinese be taught a lesson. What on earth can you hope to achieve by it? Such a war would be utterly ruinous for China . . .'

Zhai Jing-mu took an iron from the fire and held it up to his single eye to examine its glowing tip. He frowned, and returned it to the fire. 'Precisely so, Mr Killigrew.'

'But of course . . .' Killigrew could have cursed himself for not realising it sooner. 'That's exactly what you want, isn't it? Another war with the barbarians will be the downfall of the Ch'ing Dynasty. The Manchu administration in

Peking will topple, and the Triads will be ready to seize government.'

'A fascinating theory, Mr Killigrew,' said Zhai. 'But of little use to you now. Tomorrow, at the hour of the pig, the first shot in our little war will sound out, heralding a new era in Chinese history. But you, my friend, will not even live to hear that opening shot.'

'You're off your head. You think the British will fight a war to put you in power in Peking?'

'Why not? When my fleets, and my contacts with the Triads, will have helped them to defeat the hated Manchus? You know as well as I do that the British government has no interest in controlling China directly. Much better to install an administration friendly to British trade, which will open more ports to the barbarians.'

'On the condition that only Bannatyne's ships are allowed to deal in tea and opium. And what do you think your friends the Triads will have to say, when they discover that all along you've been planning to help the very barbarians you promised to help them drive out?'

'I have nothing to fear from the Triads. I know their methods, their leaders, their hiding places. Once my puppet is installed on the Dragon Throne, the menace of the Triads will be crushed for ever.'

'Hear that, Ultzmann? You've got to hand it to your friend here, the way he's been playing everyone off against each other: Manchus, Triads, the China traders. Does Bannatyne think that Zhai Jing-mu won't go back on his promise to him, the way he's so willing to go back on his promise to help the Triads?'

Ultzmann looked uncertain, but said nothing.

'Perhaps if the Triads were here instead of you, we'd be hearing a very different story,' persisted Killigrew. 'About how he intends to renege on his promises to the barbarians, to put the Triads in an unassailable position of power in

Peking, and to drive all barbarians from the Celestial Kingdom.'

'Herr Bannatyne knows what he's doing,' said Ultzmann. But even he no longer sounded convinced.

'Silence!' snapped Zhai. 'We have heard enough from you, Killigrew.' He took one of the irons from the brazier and approached the table. 'Unless, that is, you wish to scream. That would be music to my ears. An eye first, I think. Do your own Christian scriptures not teach: "An eye for an eye, and a tooth for a tooth"?'

He leaned over Killigrew with the glowing iron and slowly brought it nearer and nearer to his face. The *lao-pan*'s single blue eye glittered as he relished the moment. Killigrew's attention was transfixed by that glowing tip as its searing heat came close enough to warm his cheek and bring tears to his eyes.

'You'd better make up your mind whose side you're on, chop chop, Reverend,' Killigrew called in desperation. 'Help me now, and there's a chance you'll live through this. But don't think neither Bannatyne nor Zhai Jing-mu will betray you.'

'You're not taken in by his foolish chatter, are you, Ultzmann?' asked Zhai.

'Of course not!' stammered the missionary.

'Good. Because you know what will happen if you do not co-operate. You see, Killigrew, there is no one to help you now . . .'

An excited jabber came from the direction of the jetty. Everyone around the table looked up to see seven more junks sailing up the creek, battered and battle-damaged: round shot embedded in their timbers, masts missing, gaping holes ripped through their mat-and-rattan sails, and scorched paintwork. Someone on one of the junks was signalling.

'What is he saying?' demanded Zhai.

'They have been pursued here by two barbarian ships,'

said the man holding down Killigrew's right wrist. While he was concentrating on the signals, he relaxed his hold just enough for Killigrew to raise his arm a couple of inches off the table until the backs of the man's hands touched the red-hot iron held by Zhai. He screamed as his flesh sizzled, and released the lieutenant's wrist.

Killigrew grabbed the iron in Zhai's hand and smashed it against the head of the man who held his left wrist. As the man went down, Killigrew was able to sit up and parry a sword-stroke from the man who had held his right wrist. As the man raised his sword for a second blow, a shot sounded. Surrounded by enemies, Killigrew knew it could only have been aimed at him. He looked down at himself in search of the bullet wound, and then realised he had felt no pain. He glanced up at the swordsman. A bullet-hole had appeared in his forehead. He dropped his sword and sank to the shingle.

'Let him up.'

As the pilong holding Killigrew's left leg backed away from the table, Killigrew twisted. Ultzmann stood with his pepperbox in one hand, smoke curling lazily from one of the muzzles.

Killigrew rolled off the table and snatched up the sword before moving to join Ultzmann. Zhai and the remaining two pilongs – one of them nursing burned hands – backed away, but more pilongs armed with *gingalls* and pistols ran up the beach towards them.

'You betrayed me!' Zhai hissed at Ultzmann. 'It was you who brought the barbarian ships here!'

'No. But since they're here . . . it is obvious the Englander is right, Zhai. It is over. The Royal Navy has found your lair.'

'Over?' Zhai laughed derisively. 'My dear Reverend, it is only just begun! But for *you*, it is over. And before you die, I want you to know that Ai-ling will soon die also. Once my men have used her for their entertainment. And I should warn you, some of them have deliciously depraved tastes . . .'

'You *Arschloch*!' Ultzmann screamed in rage. He pointed the pepperbox straight at Zhai, but the *lao-pan* was faster. Before the missionary could fire, the *lao-pan* drew a dagger from his sash with a movement like lightning and flung it. Ultzmann fell back into Killigrew's arms with the dagger embedded to the hilt in his chest. '*Rettet sie!*' he gasped in desperation. '*Um Himmels willen, passt auf, dass ihr nichts zustößt!*' He coughed, blood spilling from his lips, and lay still.

Killigrew had no idea who Ai-ling was, or what Ultzmann's last words had meant – as luck would have it, German was one of the few languages he did not speak – but there had been no mistaking the anguish in the missionary's final moments.

Killigrew looked up at Zhai.

'Kill him,' the *lao-pan* ordered irritably.

One of the pilongs charged at Killigrew with a sword. The lieutenant snatched the pepperbox from Ultzmann's dead hand in time to shoot the pilong in the stomach. He turned the pepperbox on Zhai Jing-mu, but the *lao-pan* was already running back down the beach gesturing at Killigrew. 'Shoot him! Shoot him!'

Killigrew squeezed off a couple of shots at Zhai Jing-mu's back but missed as the *lao-pan* threw himself flat on the ground. Killigrew fired the last two shots at the pilongs charging towards him, kicked over the table to give himself some cover from the bullets which started to whistle in his direction, and then turned and ran.

He dashed along the side of the creek, leaping awkwardly from boulder to boulder as the bullets spanged amongst the rocks. His only chance was that the pilong who had read the signals from the returning, battle-scarred junk had not been mistaken. If Western ships had pursued a flotilla of junks into this cove, it seemed unlikely they would give up and turn back. If they were close enough for him to swim out to, he was saved. If not . . .

The wide creek meandered around a headland, and as Killigrew clambered over the rocks for higher ground he suddenly found a wide bay spread out before him. There were two ships at the entrance to the bay: a forty-four-gun frigate flying the white ensign, towed by the Peninsular and Oriental Company steamer SS *Shanghae*.

A ball from a *gingall* ricocheted off the rocks close to his feet and a splinter of rock stung him in the leg. He dropped down behind a boulder as more bullets soughed over his head.

A moment later the first pilong leaped over him. Killigrew jumped up and tackled him from behind. He managed to get on top of the pilong, pushing him face down into the shingle, and pulled the *gingall* back against his throat until he had throttled him. Two more pilongs appeared on the rocks above him, armed with a pistol and sword respectively. He shot one with the *gingall*, bracing the stock against the ground, and then used the heavy gun to parry a sword-stroke from the other before smashing the butt into his face.

The rest of the pilongs were not far behind, nearly two dozen of them. Killigrew picked himself up and ran until he was as close to the two ships as he could get on the land. They were nearly half a mile out to sea, but he could see a gig closer in to shore, sounding the depths over the sand bar at the mouth of the bay. He waded into the surf, waving his arms desperately above his head, hoping the sound of the pilongs' guns would reach the ears of the men in the ships and draw their attention to his plight.

Bullets ploughed into the water around him. A moment later a gun boomed from the side of the frigate and a shot roared over his head, to burst over the pilongs on the shore behind him: canister shot.

He dived into the water and swam out to the gig with a

strong crawl stroke, although after his exertions on shore his strength was close to giving out. Seeing he was in difficulties, one of the seamen in the gig jumped overboard and swam to meet him, helping him cover the last few yards. He managed to get his arms over the gig's gunwales and clung there, panting. There were three other seamen in the gig, along with two faces Killigrew recognised: Assistant Superintendent Cargill of the Hong Kong Police, and Captain the Honourable Henry Keppel.

If Killigrew had ever had a surrogate father after his own had died, it was Keppel. It was four years since Killigrew had served on the *Dido* and his old captain was about forty now, but the blue eyes beneath his bushy red eyebrows glinted as mischievously as ever. A younger son of the Earl of Albermarle, he was a small man, less than five feet tall, but he more than compensated for it in terms of personality and strength of will.

'Hullo, my boy!' he remarked with cheerful aplomb, as if he and Killigrew had bumped into one another on Pall Mall instead of at the entrance to a pirate lair in the South China Sea. 'Up to your neck in it as usual, eh?'

'Permission to come aboard, sir.'

'I don't know. What do you think, Haines?' he asked the coxswain, with his customary crooked smile. 'Should we let Mr Killigrew into the boat?'

'He do look kind of bedraggled, sir.'

Aided by the seaman who had jumped into the water to help him, Killigrew scrambled over the gunwales and collapsed in the stern sheets. Grinning, he ran his fingers through his sopping hair to sweep it back out of his eyes. 'I'm certainly glad to see you chaps.'

'That doesn't make what I have to say any easier, Killigrew,' Cargill said apologetically. 'I'm afraid you're under arrest.'

'I take it you didn't come all this way just to arrest me?'

Killigrew asked once he was ensconced in a tub of deliciously warm water in one of HMS *Mæander*'s cabins.

Seated on the bunk, Keppel shook his head. 'We're on routine pirate-hunting duties. Captain Morgan received word that pilongs have been ravaging the coastline in these parts shortly before we arrived in Hong Kong. We set out to give chase at once. Mr Cargill here kindly agreed to come along and act as interpreter.' He gestured to where the assistant superintendent stood in the open doorway, and Cargill inclined his head with a smile.

'When we got to one village, Mr Cargill spoke to the people there and they told us they'd only recently paid money to this fellow Zhai Jing-mu to stop him from torching the place,' continued Keppel. 'We gave chase and a few miles further on found another village; in flames, this time. We crammed on every stitch of sail and sighted a fleet of fourteen junks. When we closed with one of them Mr Cargill hailed them.'

'Naturally they told us they were peaceful trading junks carrying salt to Hong Kong,' said Cargill. 'But we could see them tricing up their stink-pots and boarding nets, and clearing their guns for action.'

'We got in three broadsides first and managed to sink three of the junks, but then the wind dropped and they drew off with their sweeps,' said Keppel. 'We put the boats in the water to tow us, and gave chase. The next morning found them a mile or so ahead of us, then a light easterly air sprang up and we hauled to the wind on the starboard tack. That was when the *Shanghae* put in an appearance.'

'How did they get caught up in this, sir?' asked Killigrew.

'One of the China traders chartered her to search for the *Coquette*,' explained Cargill. 'Another damned clipper gone missing.'

'Not Bannatyne?' Killigrew demanded suspiciously.

'Bannatyne? No,' said Cargill. 'We signalled that all in sight were enemy, and she gallantly steamed to the attack.'

'That was when things started to go wrong, though,' put in Keppel. 'The *Shanghae* took a shot through her boilers, and while we were chasing one of the junks inshore we ran on to an uncharted reef. My first lieutenant gave chase with the pinnace, cutter and gig and managed to catch another junk, but the rest got away. The *Shanghae* got her engines going and towed us off the reef, and we gave chase and . . . well, here we are.'

'What brings *you* here, Killigrew?' asked Cargill. 'When I saw you yesterday, you were supposed to be under arrest on board the *Tisiphone*. Then I learned you'd slipped overboard with one of the hands.'

Killigrew grinned sheepishly. 'Sorry about that. I knew Bannatyne was in with Zhai . . .'

'What?' exclaimed Keppel. 'Are you trying to tell me that Blase Bannatyne is in league with the pilongs? That's preposterous!'

'That's what I keep telling him, sir, but he won't listen to me,' said Cargill.

'Lucky for us all that I didn't,' said Killigrew. 'I went aboard the *Buchan Prayer* to find proof.'

'And did you?' asked Cargill.

Before Killigrew could reply, there was a knock on the door. 'Enter!' said Keppel.

Cargill withdrew from the doorway to allow the *Mæander*'s first lieutenant to enter. 'We've finished charting the bar, sir,' he announced, saluting. 'It's fairly shallow all the way across, but we think we've found a channel where we can slip through.'

'Good work, Mr Bowyear,' said Keppel. 'We'll cross the bar at high tide.' He checked his fob-watch. 'That's two hours from now. Have the decks cleared for action.'

'Aye, aye, sir.' Lieutenant Bowyear turned to leave.

Killigrew's voice arrested him. 'Hold on, sir. You're not planning to sail after them up that creek, are you?' he asked Keppel.

'I don't see why not. There's only seven of them.'

'Correction, sir. There were only seven of them when you chased them into this bay. But they've just met up with another thirty-five of their friends. Including Zhai Jing-mu's flagship.'

'Zhai Jing-mu is here?' Cargill exclaimed in shock.

Killigrew nodded. 'You've stumbled on to his base of operations, sir.'

'How the deuce did you find it?'

'The Reverend Werner Ultzmann had me brought here after Captain Ingersoll caught me on board the *Buchan Prayer* last night. You want proof that Bannatyne's in league with the pilongs, Mr Cargill? The fact I'm here at all speaks for itself.'

'Hardly proof, Killigrew. Perhaps it ties in Ingersoll and Ultzmann, but . . . you understand, I'm only thinking of what a jury will believe after Mr Bannatyne's lawyers have had a chance to work on such testimony.'

Killigrew narrowed his eyes at the assistant superintendent. 'And what do *you* believe, Mr Cargill?'

'I'm a police officer, Mr Killigrew. It's my job to prove, not believe. What I *believe* is neither here nor there.'

'All this will have to be settled later at Mr Killigrew's court martial,' Keppel said firmly. 'If there *is* a court martial, that is, which I'm very much beginning to doubt. When a junior officer finds a pirate nest the navy's spent years searching for, it's damned bad form to court martial him by way of thanks.' Keppel's promotion to post-captain predated Morgan's, so his arrival at Hong Kong made him the senior officer on the station. 'I'd say taking care of Zhai Jing-mu must be our first priority.'

'Killigrew's right, though,' said Cargill. 'You can't take on that many junks with just one frigate and a lightly armed civilian steamer.'

'No,' agreed Keppel. 'But we can try to keep the swine bottled up here until reinforcements arrive from Hong

Kong.' He stepped across the tub and bent over the desk, swiftly scrawling a dispatch. When he had finished he blotted it, put it in an envelope and handed it to Bowyear. 'Take this to the captain of the *Shanghae* to deliver to Captain Morgan in Victoria.'

'Aye, aye, sir.'

'And see if you can find the wardroom steward. Mr Killigrew looks as though he could do with a drink.'

A Chinese steward emerged from his cubbyhole, took one look at Killigrew and then ducked out of sight just behind the door. '*Hai?*' he asked Keppel with a bow.

'Be so good as to fetch Mr Killigrew a brandy, steward.'

'*Hai.*' The steward bowed again and crossed to the drinks cabinet on the far side of the wardroom.

Keppel exchanged bemused glances with Cargill. 'It seems our new steward is shy about the human form, Mr Cargill.'

Killigrew stood up in the bath and tried to get a better look at the steward's face, but the Chinese, as if aware of the scrutiny, kept turning his head away so that all Killigrew could see was the queue which hung down his back. Keppel handed him a towel and he started to dry himself. 'New steward?' asked Killigrew. 'How long's he been aboard?'

'This is his second day. We hired him in Victoria yesterday when our old steward was suddenly taken ill with stomach cramps. Why do you ask?'

'No reason. I just thought perhaps I'd seen him somewhere before. At the Hong Kong races, maybe, or in a joss house in Tai-ping-shan.'

'Entirely possible, I suppose.'

The steward returned with Killigrew's brandy. He had acquired an oilskin hat and wore it ludicrously low on one side of his head so that, as long as he kept his face in profile, it was concealed from the lieutenant. He handed the glass to Killigrew.

'Thank you, Mr Li.'

'Name no Li,' said the steward. 'Name Deng.'

'Of course it is,' Killigrew said with a thin smile.

After his bath, he changed into a spare uniform loaned to him by Bowyear, who was roughly his size, and was given something to eat in the wardroom where he recounted his adventures aboard the *Buchan Prayer* and afterwards to Keppel, Cargill, and the *Mæander*'s officers. After dinner he joined Keppel and the *Mæander's* master on the quarterdeck for a cheroot and the three of them gazed across to the mouth of the creek in the gathering gloom of dusk. The *Shanghae* had long since headed back to Hong Kong, and the *Mæander* was alone off the mouth of the bay, the only thing between Zhai Jing-mu's fleet and the freedom of the open sea.

'What do we do now, sir?' asked Killigrew. 'Wait until re-inforcements arrive?'

Keppel nodded. 'Not much else we can do. I've had Mr Bowyear double the anchor watch in case the pilongs try anything tonight, but I expect they'll be busy turning their anchorage upstream into an ambush in preparation for our attack. Should be quite a brisk fight tomorrow, eh?' he added with obvious relish.

Killigrew thought about it. 'Brisk' was one word for it. But he would have been lying to himself if he had tried to deny that he was looking forward to the chance to pay the *lao-pan* back for Peri's murder.

'Zhai Jing-mu's slipped through my fingers too many times, sir, and at terrible cost. It won't happen again.'

The *Mæander*'s master chuckled. 'A regular fire-eater, sir, just like his father used to be,' he told Keppel.

'You knew my father?' Killigrew asked him.

'Certainly, sir. Back in the twenties your father and I were unemployed on half-pay, so we joined Admiral Cochrane in helping the Greeks win their independence from the Turks. But you must know all about that. I can see you've inherited your looks from your mother, but from what I've heard your spirit is all your father's. Always dashing off impetuously, risking his neck in pursuit of one ideal or another.'

None of this matched with the mental image Killigrew had conjured up of his parents. He was astonished. 'I had always assumed my mother was the fiery one. You know, what with her being Greek and all.'

'Your mother? Good Lord, no. No, your mother was always a lady. Demure, softly spoken and kind, she was. Lovely girl. Except when she was killing Turks, of course. She loathed them with a passion. Still, she couldn't match your father when it came to being a buccaneering, jump-first-and-look-later sort of swashbuckler. Hot Celtic blood, I always supposed – but I was always glad he was on our side, bigod! Captain Spitfire, the men used to call him.'

Keppel checked his watch. 'Well, I don't think we'll see much activity tonight. I'm off to bed to get an early night. I suggest you do likewise, my boy. Tomorrow's likely to be a long day.'

Killigrew lingered on deck alone to finish his cheroot and thought about what the master had just told him about his parents. Everything he had previously assumed had just been turned on its head. All his life he had struggled to emulate his father, a man whom he had always pictured as being a staid and proper gentleman. Yet there had always been part of him which found it difficult to control his passions and act in a gentlemanly way; he had always assumed it had come from his mother; it was like being two people at the same time, constantly at war with his inner nature.

He remembered what the Taoist priest had told him at the joss house in Tai-ping-shan: two conflicting influences in his life – *yin* and *yang* – two people he would never meet again who would always be with him. His father and mother, of course; he had been a fool not to realise it sooner. Perhaps it was time for him to stop trying to suppress his passionate nature, but to make the most of it. Instead of trying to be one thing or the other, he would accept that he was both. Perhaps the two combined would be greater than the sum of their parts: after all, he was neither his mother nor his father, but the product of their union.

He chuckled to himself. 'Captain Spitfire, eh?'

The *Mæander*'s gunner overheard him. 'Sir?'

Killigrew flicked the stub of his cheroot overboard. 'I'll show you tomorrow.'

There was a knock at the door to the first lieutenant's cabin. 'Come in,' called Bowyear.

A marine private entered and brought in a couple of jugs of steaming hot water. 'Seven bells, gentlemen.'

'Thank you, Marine Fawcett. You can go first at the wash-basin, Killigrew.'

'Thanks.' Killigrew climbed down from the hammock which had been slung in Bowyear's cabin for him. 'Mind if I borrow your shaving things?'

'By all means.'

'Much obliged.' Killigrew worked up a lather and applied it to his face before scraping at his bristles.

'I wonder if we'll be finished here in time to get back to Victoria for the dragon boat festival?' said Bowyear.

'Christ!'

'What's the matter?'

Killigrew studied the nick he had carved in himself in the mirror above the basin. 'I'd forgotten it was tonight.'

Bowyear grinned. 'Damned inconsiderate, these pilongs. You should've told Zhai Jing-mu you had other plans.'

Killigrew did not smile. If there was some plot due to be hatched that night, then it was entirely possible that the fact Zhai Jing-mu was holed up in his lair would prevent it from coming to fruition. But if Bannatyne was behind it then Killigrew suspected the *tai-pan* would have taken every eventuality into account.

He dressed while Bowyear shaved and washed himself, and then the two of them joined the rest of the officers for breakfast in the washroom. Afterwards he took his cup of tea on deck and found the Chinese wardroom steward balancing on one leg on the gunwale, performing a sequence of almost balletic movements in slow time.

Killigrew moved to stand in front of him. 'Good morning,' he said in Cantonese.

'Good morning,' the steward replied evenly, neither looking down nor breaking off his sequence.

'Do this every morning, do you?'

'When it is practical. These are my *t'ai chi chu'an* exercises.' Li moved gracefully into a new position: left knee drawn up as far as it would go, right hand raised in a fist above his head and his left hand held level with his stomach, palm upwards. 'This is called "Lion Opening Mouth".'

'I see,' Killigrew said dubiously.

'*T'ai chi chu'an* exercises focus the mind and spirit, and aid meditation, as well as developing muscles, posture, and correct breathing technique.' Li brought his right hand down and his left hand up until they were level in front of his face, at the same time stretching his left leg out before him parallel to the deck. Then he bent his leg at the knee and stretched his arm out on either side.

'And you find balancing on a gunnel helps?'

'In *t'ai chi chu'an*, as in so many things in life, balance is the key.'

Killigrew shrugged. He was not in the habit of criticising other people's beliefs, so long as those beliefs did not harm other people. He made a gesture with his tea cup that was half-toast, half a motion for Li to carry on, before crossing to where Keppel had emerged on to the quarterdeck.

'You do realise he's a Chinese spy, don't you, sir?' he murmured.

'Good Lord, yes,' said Keppel. 'But you know what the Admiralty's unofficial policy is on letting the Chinese see Western technology.'

'Let them see as much as they like and hope they'll be impressed into acknowledging our superiority?'

Keppel nodded. 'Complete waste of time, of course. Benjamin Franklin obviously never travelled in the Orient, otherwise when he said that nothing was certain in this world except death and taxes he would have added John Chinaman's unshakeable conviction in his total superiority to all other races of mankind. Still, if I'm going to have a spy on board my ship, I'd much rather know exactly where he is—'

'Sail ho!' cried the look-out at the masthead.

It was the *Shanghae*, returning with reinforcements following in her wake; or rather, *reinforcement*, for the only vessel she sailed with was the *Tisiphone*. The paddle-sloop hove to alongside the frigate. Ordinarily it would have been Captain Keppel's privilege as the senior officer of the three ships to ask the captains of the other two vessels to meet him on board the *Mæander*; but since Killigrew had to be taken back to his own ship, Keppel decided to hold his council of war on board the paddle-sloop.

Commander Robertson and Lord Hartcliffe awaited them on the quarterdeck. 'Shall we go down to my day room, gentlemen?' suggested Robertson. Keppel might be the senior officer present, but Robertson was the host and it was up to him to take the initiative.

They made their way below. 'Good to have you back, Killigrew,' Hartcliffe murmured in Killigrew's ear.

'Any news of Mrs Bannatyne or the *Golden Dragon*?'

'Seaman Molineaux says he overheard Captain Ingersoll tell the Reverend Mr Ultzmann the *Golden Dragon* would be in the Cap-sing-mun anchorage at midnight tonight.'

'If Bannatyne hasn't changed his plans,' agreed Killigrew. 'Still, that's one rendezvous the good reverend won't be keeping.'

'He's dead?'

Killigrew nodded. 'Another of Zhai Jing-mu's victims. I persuaded him to change sides at the last moment, not that it did the poor devil much good . . .'

Hartcliffe coughed into his fist, a quarterdeck signal that Robertson was approaching.

'I shall want a full written report of your activities since the moment you jumped ship the day before yesterday, Second,' growled Robertson. 'When I've seen that I'll decide what punishment to give you for disobeying my orders. That can wait until after we've dealt with these pilongs, mind,' he added, indicating that he expected Killigrew to redeem himself today.

They entered the day room and Killigrew was mildly surprised to find Admiral Huang waiting for them. The admiral rose to his feet and bowed to the British officers.

'Gentlemen, I believe you all know Admiral Huang of the Imperial Chinese Navy,' said Robertson. 'The admiral's fleet of war-junks is following from Canton and should be here in a few hours. Governor Bonham and Governor-General Xu both agreed it would be politic if this was a joint Anglo-Chinese operation.'

The commander did not have to explain further: everyone in the room understood that there would be no arguments with the Chinese authorities about the legality of the operation if a Chinese admiral were party to it.

Keppel got proceedings underway. 'I suggest we start by considering the position,' he said without preamble. 'Since Lieutenant Killigrew has actually been up the creek where the pilong fleet is anchored, he's kindly volunteered to put us in the picture.'

Killigrew unrolled a rough sketch-plan he had drawn up. It showed the shape of the creek as he could best remember it, with the jetty and the village marked on. 'This shows the positions of the enemy's junks as they were when I last saw them late yesterday afternoon,' he explained. 'I think we can rest assured they'll have changed since then.'

'How many junks?'

'I saw thirty-five with my own eyes, not including the seven that the *Mœander* chased into the bay. They hadn't anchored when I was forced to make my rather hurried departure. Most of them carry about nine guns in each broadside but the largest, Zhai Jing-mu's flagship, carries twenty in each broadside and two stern guns. There may be more junks hidden further up the creek; I'm afraid I didn't get a chance to check. There was also a smug boat tied up at the jetty. That's all I can tell you for now.'

'We've sounded the bar and found a channel through into the bay,' added Keppel. 'It's not deep, but the *Mœander* should be able to scrape through at high tide.' Of the three ships in the flotilla, the *Mœander* had the deepest draught.

'When's the top of high water, sir?' asked Robertson.

'Half-past seven this morning,' said Keppel. He had already checked the almanac and had no need to consult his notes. 'And again at five this evening.'

'It's nearly seven now,' said Robertson. 'Do we go in at once, or wait for the Chinese junks and then go in this evening?'

Keppel turned to Huang. 'Admiral?'

'Every moment we delay gives Zhai Jing-mu more time to prepare his defences,' said Huang. 'And the longer we delay, the more time he has to escape overland.'

'Very well,' said Keppel. 'Unless anyone has any objections, we'll go in this morning. Commander Robertson will lead the attack in the *Shanghae*, if Captain Carfax is agreeable . . .?'

The captain of the *Shanghae* inclined his head. 'What will our strategy be?'

Keppel scratched his head, as if puzzled by the question. 'We go into the creek and shoot up everything in sight.'

Everyone nodded approvingly.

'The *Tisiphone*, under Lieutenant Lord Hartcliffe, will follow the *Shanghae* towing the *Mæander*.' Keppel checked his fob-watch. 'To your ships, gentlemen, and clear for action. We enter the bay in twenty-eight minutes' time.'

They went up on deck. Hartcliffe asked the boatswain to give the order to beat to quarters, while Robertson and Captain Carfax transhipped to the *Shanghae* in one gig and Keppel returned to the *Mæander* in another.

The *Tisiphone* manoeuvred to take the *Mæander* in tow. On all three ships the hands scurried to and fro in the familiar frenetic ballet of clearing the decks for action. Every man knew his post. Netting was strung up over the decks, the anchors raised and the gun crews got into position. Both the *Shanghae* and the *Tisiphone* already had steam up. As soon as the *Tisiphone* and the *Mæander* signalled they were ready, Robertson and Cargill climbed back into the *Shanghae*'s gig and rowed to the prow to lead them in over the bar, sounding out the channel as they went. The flotilla could only sail as fast as the oarsmen in the gig could row, so they moved off slowly at first, the *Mæander*'s sails reefed and the paddle-wheels of the two steamers turning lazily.

Admiral Huang had stayed on board the *Tisiphone* and stood on the quarterdeck with Hartcliffe and Killigrew, who had retrieved his cutlass and pepperbox from his cabin.

With the *Tisiphone* less than half a cable's length astern of the *Shanghae*, Killigrew could clearly hear the voice of the leadsman to the *Shanghae*'s gig as he measured the depth with a lead-line and called out the soundings. 'By the mark, twain . . . and a quarter, twain . . . and a half, twain . . . and a quarter, twain . . .' The gig moved up and down the bar as the leadsman searched for the channel.

The three ships hove to and waited.

'Zhai Jing-mu's flagship must have a draught of at least three fathoms, from the size of her,' said Killigrew. 'If that could get through at high water, then so can the *Mæander*.'

'. . . and a half, twain . . . a quarter less, three . . . a quarter less, three . . .'

'The tide will be turning soon,' said Hartcliffe.

Killigrew gripped the rail tightly. 'Doesn't matter. Zhai's fleet isn't going anywhere, and if we have to wait until this evening then we'll have the added advantage of Huang's junks to help us.'

'And a half, twain,' the leadsman's voice droned monotonously. 'And a quarter, twain . . . and a half, twain . . .'

Hartcliffe directed his telescope across the bay towards the mouth of the creek.

'You won't be able to see them yet,' said Killigrew. 'The main anchorage is a good five miles upstream of that headland.'

'By the mark, four!' the leadsman called out triumphantly, finding the channel where the depth increased to eighteen feet. 'And a quarter, four . . . and a half, four . . . a quarter less, five . . . by the mark, five . . . and a half, five . . . and a quarter, six . . .' On the far side of the bar, the bottom plunged away quickly.

'Looks like they're through!' said Hartcliffe, and a moment later the *Shanghae*'s paddles began to turn as she followed the gig through the narrow channel. He turned to Midshipman Cavan. 'Ask Mr Muir to take us ahead, slow.'

'Aye, aye, sir.' Cavan went below to the engine room and soon the *Tisiphone* was towing the *Mæander* in her wake.

Killigrew glanced aft and saw the current before the bar carry the *Mæander* to the left side of the channel. He signalled desperately for the helmsman on the frigate to steer to starboard before they were grounded. Orders were relayed across the frigate's deck and her head began to come around, but it was too late; a moment later a slight shudder ran through the *Mæander* and she seemed to drop astern.

'She's grounded!' warned Hartcliffe, and turned to Cavan, who had just returned on deck. 'Tell Mr Muir to stop all engines immediately.'

'Aye, aye, sir!'

The cable between the *Tisiphone* and the *Mæander* grew taut. For a moment Killigrew feared it would snap, and the frigate would become grounded. It was touch and go: a moment later the frigate slid forwards once more. 'It's all right, she's free.' Killigrew turned back to where the midshipman was halfway through the after-hatch. 'Belay that last order, Mr Cavan! The *Mæander* is free.'

Then all three ships were across the bar and crossing the deep bay to the mouth of the creek. The *Shanghae* hove to long enough to take the gig back on board and then advanced once more, ahead slow, the leadsman at the channels still calling out the soundings every so often as they groped their way blindly up the uncharted creek.

Killigrew strolled the length of the *Tisiphone*'s deck, inspecting the gun crews and making sure that everything was ready for the coming fight. He paused by the pivot gun in the forecastle, where Molineaux had been appointed to replace O'Connor as captain of the gun. 'I see you made it back all right, Molineaux.'

'Aye, aye, sir. I did understand you right back on the *Buchan Prayer*, didn't I?'

'Perfectly right, Molineaux. I've already commended you in my report to Commander Robertson.'

Molineaux's face fell. 'I'd rather you hadn't done that, sir.'

'Oh?'

'Well, when I got back on board the *Tisiphone* yesterday, Commander Robertson said the only reason he wasn't going to punish me for going adrift with you was because he was certain he'd soon have you yourself to throw the book at.'

'It's nice to know our captain has such confidence in me,' Killigrew said wryly. His inspection finished, he returned to join Hartcliffe and Admiral Huang on the quarterdeck.

'Did you have any success in learning more of the Triads' plot?' asked Huang.

'Some. As far as I can gather, they're trying to start a war between Britain and China. The idea is that the Manchu regime will be so weakened by another war, the Triads will have no difficulty in overthrowing the Ch'ing Dynasty.'

'I suspected as much,' Huang snorted contemptuously. 'The Imperial Grand Council will not initiate such a war, I can assure you.'

'Bannatyne and Zhai know that. My guess is they're planning to commit some atrocity against the Europeans in Hong Kong which will have the people in Britain screaming for Chinese blood.' Killigrew thought hard, trying to remember what little Zhai Jing-mu had told him in the hope it would reveal a clue. 'Zhai said something about the first shot in the war. Perhaps they're planning to assassinate Governor Bonham.'

'The Portuguese didn't declare war when the Governor of Macao was murdered by the Triads,' pointed out Hartcliffe. 'Besides, Governor-General Xu Guang-jin has been invited to sit with Bonham in the gubernatorial stand to watch the dragon boat race. Supposing the assassin missed Bonham and hit Xu by accident?'

'Governor-General Xu has been forced to remain in Canton due to illness—' The admiral broke off and stared at them both in horror.

'You think Xu might be a part of it?' asked Hartcliffe

Huang shook his head. 'Inconceivable. The Governor-General is a close friend of mine. We studied together for the civil service examinations in Peking. He would never be a party to a plot against the Dragon Throne.'

'Perhaps not,' said Killigrew. 'But suppose someone slipped something into his food? Nothing fatal, you understand; just something to give him stomach cramps, like whatever you gave the *Mæander*'s steward to make a place for your man Li.'

Hartcliffe nodded slowly. 'If something happens to Bonham tonight and Governor-General Xu is conveniently absent, no one will believe for a moment that the Chinese authorities were not party to the assassination. The public back home will be howling for Chinese blood. War will become inevitable . . .'

Killigrew was about to reply when a shout carried across from the *Shanghae*'s look-out: 'Sail ho!'

The *Tisiphone*'s own look-out raised his telescope and peered up the creek.

'What can you see?' Hartcliffe called up through the speaking trumpet.

'Four, five . . . no, at least twenty, twenty-five of them! They're anchored in close order across the creek!'

'Trying to bar the passage,' surmised Killigrew. 'The rest must be further upstream.' On an impulse he took the telescope from the binnacle, crossed the deck and ascended the ratlines. He stopped at the maintop and gazed up the creek. The junks were just as the look-out had described them, moored bow to stern across the whole width of the creek. There were twenty-seven of them in all.

He descended to the deck once more and described what he had seen to Hartcliffe. 'Looks like they're ready for us. I recognised Zhai Jing-mu's flagship in the centre of the line.'

'You think Zhai Jing-mu himself is on board? I would have thought he'd be skulking somewhere towards the rear.'

'Not he. He may be a pirate and a murderer, but he's courageous, I'll say that much for him. Besides, his junk has the biggest broadside of them all. They wouldn't want that missing from their ambush.'

'Well, if they're ready for us, that cuts both ways.'

The boatswain's mates piped for silence. It was important for the crew to be quiet when they went into action: soon things would be noisy enough as it was, and they would need to hear orders clearly. But there was more to the silence than that: there was a palpable air of tension on board. Killigrew shared the crew's trepidation. One navy paddle-sloop was more than a match for any junk of war, but three European vessels against forty-two junks? He hoped they were not biting off more than they could chew. And there was always the danger that Zhai Jing-mu had one more trick up his sleeve . . .

# *XVII:*

# *A Dragon Throne in Hell*

---

The PS *Shanghae*, HMS *Tisiphone* and HMS *Mæander* rounded another bend in the creek, and then there was less than a mile of water to where the junks were anchored. Zhai Jing-mu had daringly decided to defend the creek at its widest point, so that he would be able to bring more guns to bear on the flotilla.

'*Mæander* is signalling, sir!' warned Midshipman Cavan.

The frigate in the *Tisiphone*'s tow was so close Captain Keppel could easily have called his instructions across to the sloop with his speaking trumpet; but there was a greater chance that someone in Zhai Jing-mu's fleet would understand English than be able to interpret naval signals.

Neither Hartcliffe nor Killigrew needed to raise their telescopes to understand the signal hoist: '*Shanghae* to take left flank, *Tisiphone* will tow *Mæander* to centre three cables from flagship, cast off tow, and take right flank.'

'So we have to run the gauntlet of half their line before we get in place, eh?' a sailor with a Liverpudlian accent grumbled. 'And get into position while we're about it.'

Killigrew did not recognise him at first, which was strange, because he had taken care to get to know the names of all the hands during the voyage from Portsmouth. Then he saw the sailor take out a comb and tidy his hair, as if he were going on a run ashore as opposed to into battle. The gesture reminded Killigrew of where he had seen this man before. 'It's Endicott, isn't it?'

The Liverpudlian turned with a blush. 'That's right, sir. Ordinary Seaman Seth Endicott.'

'When did you come aboard, Seaman Endicott?'

'Yesterday morning, sir, with the other new lads.' He jerked his head at three companions.

Killigrew realised that these men had been brought on board to fill the gap left by the deaths of Dando, Firebrace, Gadsby and O'Connor. Later he would have to find out the names and ratings of the other three newcomers, but now was not the time. 'You don't approve of Captain Keppel's tactics?' he asked Endicott.

'I didn't mean that, sir.'

'I should hope not. I also take it you didn't mean to speak after the boatswain's mates had piped for silence?'

Endicott hung his head.

'You're allowed one mistake in my watch, Mr Endicott, and you've used yours up already. Watch your step.'

Abashed, the Liverpudlian nodded and went about his work in silence.

Smiling faintly, Killigrew studied the line of junks through the telescope once more. They were less than a mile away now, and he was close enough to see the springs which ran from the junks' sterns to their anchor cables, so that their bows did not turn as the tide flowed into the creek. He checked his watch. 'What time did Keppel say high tide was?'

'Half-past seven,' replied Hartcliffe. 'Must be on the turn by now.'

Killigrew nodded and returned his watch to the fob-pocket in his waistcoat. 'Don't you lads fret,' he told Endicott and his companions. 'Captain Keppel knows what he's doing.'

A sound like thunder rolled across the creek, reverberating off the hills on either side, and twenty-one plumes of smoke billowed from the gun ports of Zhai Jing-mu's flagship to merge into one cloud which hid the junk from sight. Even as the first balls hurled up great fountains of water before the *Shanghae*'s bows, the guns of the other junks boomed in quick but ragged succession. About a cable's length ahead of the *Shanghae*, a wall of water boiled out of the creek, momentarily blotting out all sight of the line of junks. Even as the last echoes of the broadside died away, Killigrew could hear the spray thrown up sheeting back down into the water with a loud hiss.

The pilongs had fired first, and their shots had all fallen short.

'Full steam ahead, Mr Cavan!' snapped Hartcliffe. 'Take her three points to starboard, Ågård.'

'Aye, aye, sir!' As the midshipman descended to the engine room once more, the helmsman and his assistant span the wheel, bringing the *Tisiphone*'s head a couple of points to starboard until the paddle-sloop was making for the flagship at the centre of the line.

The paddle-wheels churned with renewed urgency, slapping the water rhythmically. As the two steamers raced to get into position before the pilongs could reload their guns, the *Shanghae* veered off to her allotted position at the left flank of the line.

'We've got the flagship in our sights, sir!' called the gunner. 'Want us to open fire?'

'Hold your fire!' Hartcliffe called back. 'Captain Keppel would never thank us if we snatched the prize from under his nose,' he added *sotto voce* to Killigrew. 'Stand by to alter course to starboard!'

'Aye, aye, sir!' The gunner directed his team to pivot the bow-chaser on its racers until it was ready to fire through one of the gun ports on the port side of the bow.

The *Tisiphone* was less than three cables' lengths from the line of junks now.

'Stand by to let go the tow rope . . . let go!'

The cable was dropped in the *Tisiphone*'s wake. Behind them, the *Mæander* glided closer to the line of junks under her own momentum, at the same time putting her helm hard over to bring her broadside-on to the enemy,

'Hard a-port, Ågård!' ordered Hartcliffe.

'Aye, aye, sir!' The quartermaster brought the *Tisiphone*'s head around to starboard so that they sailed parallel to the line of junks. They were only three hundred yards away now, close enough for Killigrew to see the pilongs on deck, bare-chested and glistening with sweat as they worked to reload their guns beneath the glare of the morning sun. They had almost finished and any moment now the *Tisiphone* would be caught broadside on to the pilongs' guns.

Except that Keppel had timed it to a nicety. The pilongs had almost finished reloading when the ebbing tide suddenly swung the junks on their springs so that they lay in a bow-and-quarter line with their broadsides bearing across one another's sterns. The pilongs on the deck, who only a few seconds earlier had been preparing to sweep the creek with a maelstrom of shot with quiet confidence, now ran to and fro across their decks jabbering in panic as they tried to rectify their new headings. A great cheer went up from the *Tisiphone*'s deck.

'Pipe down!' roared the boatswain. The men at once fell silent.

'Thank you, bosun,' said Hartcliffe. 'Open fire, Guns.'

'Aye, aye, sir!' The gunner turned to Molineaux and the captain of the thirty-two-pounder abaft of the *Tisiphone*'s port-side paddle-box. 'Fire!'

Both guns boomed at once, hurling round shot at the junks ranged to the *Tisiphone*'s left, and both were bang on target, each blowing a hole through the planks of a junk's hull. Then the two gun crews raced one another to be the first to reload ready for their next shot.

Astern of the *Tisiphone*, the *Shanghae* engaged the two junks at the far end of the line, the only pilong vessels which could bring their guns to bear on the *Mæander*. The *Mæander* herself, meanwhile, had anchored three hundred yards from the centre of the line and her port broadside boomed repeatedly as she exchanged shots with Zhai Jing-mu's flagship and the junks around her.

The pilongs on the junks opposite the *Tisiphone* worked furiously, hauling on their springs to bring their broadsides to bear while the paddle-sloop's gun crews had free reign to hammer their opponents unmolested. Within moments two of the junks had been blown out of the water by well-placed shells from Molineaux's bow-chaser, while two more had taken a battering from the thirty-six-pounder and a fifth was in flames.

Then the junks which were still in a position to put up a fight had hauled round their heads until their broadsides had been brought to bear, dashing any hopes of an easy fight. The pilongs kept up a well-sustained fire, hurling shots at the paddle-sloop as fast as they could reload their old-fashioned guns, but their shooting was wild. Some balls flew across the *Tisiphone*'s bow, others fell astern, but most fell short. Only a couple of dozen went home. One ball passed through the signal locker and the gun room; another struck the port-side paddle-box, smashing the bath and harness casks, before landing on the quarterdeck and rolling between Hartcliffe and Ågård, who stood less than three feet apart. The ball ploughed on until it smashed through the captain's skylight and plunged into the cabin below.

Ågård cursed. 'Would you take the helm from me for a moment, sir?' he asked Killigrew. He had to shout to make himself heard above the din, but his voice was otherwise calm.

The lieutenant glanced at him. The passing ball had doubled-up the quartermaster's cutlass and forced the point into his calf. Blood streamed from the wound.

'Of course.' Killigrew helped Ågård's assistant with the wheel. The quartermaster coolly pulled the cutlass-point from his leg – blood gouted – and then bound up the wound with his neckerchief. 'Better get down to the sick berth and let Mr Westlake take a look at that, Ågård. Holcombe can take your place.'

'I'll be all right, sir,' said Ågård, resuming his place at the helm. 'The sawbones is going to have his hands full with properly wounded men to want to worry about a little scratch like this.'

Ships and junks continued to pound one another. The noise was terrific and a thick pall of smoke hung over the creek. On the decks of all three European vessels the gun crews had stripped to their waists to work their guns, while ship's boys scurried to and fro between the guns with powder, shot and shells. Killigrew did not imagine that the scenes on board the junks could be much different.

With so much sweat and energy expended by the Tisiphones, Killigrew was starting to feel like a spare part. He was ready to help the boatswain direct the hands to clear away wreckage or carry the wounded below, but there was little wreckage and no one was seriously wounded; not on board the *Tisiphone*, at least. He was also ready to take Hartcliffe's place if the worst should come to the worst, but thankfully his friend seemed impervious as he dominated the quarterdeck. There was no sign of his usual diffidence.

Wherever there was a space along the port-side bulwark the marines lined up to shoot at the pilongs on the decks of the junks with their muskets, while the pilongs returned their fire with *gingalls*. Killigrew was tempted to blaze away with his pepperbox, but knew at that range he would be wasting shots.

The contest was still undecided, but while all three British vessels had taken a battering, at least they were all still afloat and in action, which was more than could be said for the junks. Of the fifteen or so that were still afloat – with so much smoke drifting across the scene, it was hard to be certain of anything – at least half were ablaze. But the pilongs showed no sign of surrendering, proving that Killigrew's earlier assessment of Zhai Jing-mu applied equally well to the men who followed him. There was no let-up of shots from the crews who were still capable of operating their guns.

Killigrew ducked as another wild shot snatched a spar off the foremast, and it plunged to the netting immediately above his head in a tangle of rigging. 'Everything all right, Molineaux?'

'Just plummy, sir!' Molineaux replied, beaming, and turned briefly to address his men. 'Come on, you idle bastards! Get your fingers out of your bum-holes and get that gun reloaded, damn you! Where's the next cartridge? Ah, there you are. Well don't just stand there like a black slug in a cunny-warren, boy! Pass it to the loader!'

Killigrew smiled. Clearly Molineaux was enjoying himself immensely. The lieutenant lingered by the bow-chaser long enough to see the gun crew put their next shell into a junk, shredding it into so much driftwood in the wink of an eye, and then made his way back across the ordered chaos of the deck to where Hartcliffe stood on the quarter-deck.

Hartcliffe pointed through a break in the smoke torn by a sudden gust of wind to where they could just see a dozen men climbing over the far side of Zhai Jing-mu's flagship into a fast rowing boat. 'Looks like even Zhai Jing-mu thinks he's beaten.'

It was hardly surprising. The flagship was ablaze now, and even as Killigrew and Hartcliffe watched another shell from the *Mæander* exploded inside the big junk's magazine.

A great flash lit up all the smoke scarlet with a tremendous boom. A moment later the junk had disappeared in a dense volume of smoke mixed with pieces of junk, masts and men. The very sides of the junk seemed to open out. A cheer rose up from all three British vessels, and Admiral Huang clapped his hands together with a delighted cry. 'How-how-ah!'

When the smoke cleared the junk could be seen to be settling down, with only her lofty stern and the mizzen-mast showing above the water, Zhai Jing-mu's red, black and gold ensign now ragged at the tip of the mast. About a hundred yards away the rowing boat could be seen racing up the creek.

'Damn it, the blackguard's getting away!' exclaimed Hartcliffe.

'Has Keppel seen? Perhaps if we signal . . .' Killigrew glanced across to the becalmed frigate and his heart leaped into his mouth. 'Look to the *Mæander*!'

Although stricken, Zhai Jing-mu's flagship had not sunk and its blazing stern now drifted loose of its anchor cable, carried downstream by the ebbing tide towards the helpless frigate.

The crew of the *Mæander* had seen their peril. If the blazing junk ran into the frigate then Keppel and his crew would find it impossible to stop the blaze from spreading through the rigging. What little wind had stirred the air earlier had died altogether and there was no point in the *Mæander* setting her sails, but they had tripped their anchor so they could drift with the tide before the burning junk. But the junk, with most of her hull beneath the water, was moving faster and bore down inexorably on the frigate.

'We'll have to help them!' said Hartcliffe. 'Full ahead, Mr Cavan!'

'Aye, aye, sir!' Cavan set off on another visit to the engine room.

Hartcliffe turned to Ågård. 'Hard-a-starboard!'

While they waited for the engine to start up and give the *Tisiphone* some way, Killigrew realised that the paddle-sloop would never make it. The *Mæander* was almost half a mile away, and with every passing second the ebb tide carried her off further, at the same time bringing the blazing junk closer. Frigate and junk were less than fifty yards apart and the two would be locked together before another minute had passed.

And then a miracle happened. The *Shanghae* suddenly burst forth from the thick bank of smoke on the far side of the *Mæander*. Somehow Commander Robertson had seen the frigate's peril from his own position and steamed to the rescue while the *Tisiphone* had still been getting her engines started. Now the *Shanghae* nosed into the narrow gap between the *Mæander* and the blazing junk. Putting her starboard bow to the frigate's side, she began to push her clear of the fire-raft which the junk had become.

The frigate's weight slowed the *Shanghae* for a moment, and now it was the steamer which was threatened by the blazing junk. The junk came close enough to scorch the paintwork on the *Shanghae*'s sides, and then the steamer's paddles bit at the water once more and won enough momentum to carry both vessels clear of the drifting junk. Killigrew felt relief wash over him.

The *Tisiphone*'s engines started up, once there was no need for them. 'Ah, there you are, Mr Cavan,' Hartcliffe said as the midshipman's head bobbed up through the hatch. 'Ask Mr Muir to stop the engines, there's a good fellow.'

Cavan sighed and went below once more.

Killigrew took stock of the situation. The last of the junks had been silenced. They were all in confusion, the ones that were ablaze drifting into the others and setting those alight as well. Pilongs jumped overboard on all sides, swimming desperately for the shore. Wherever one could see through the thickening smoke, the only sight was that of the heart of Zhai Jing-mu's once-proud pirate fleet sinking in flames.

'*Mæander* is signalling, sir,' said the yeoman of the signals.

Both Hartcliffe and Killigrew could read the signals for themselves: *Go after ZJM.* Mæander *and* Shanghae *will finish off here.* The frigate was too deep-draughted to risk proceeding any further up the creek.

'Mr Cavan!' called Hartcliffe.

The midshipman was just emerging from the hatch once more. 'Sir?'

'Ahead slow, if you please.'

'Aye, aye, sir.' Cavan rolled his eyes insubordinately and disappeared yet again.

'We should rig up some kind of telegraph running from the quarterdeck to the engine room, so that orders can be relayed instantaneously to the engineer,' remarked Killigrew.

'Nonsense,' said Hartcliffe. 'It's good exercise for the snotties.'

The paddle-wheels churning slowly, the *Tisiphone* nosed forwards between the junks that blazed on all sides. They steamed through the thick smoke, fires showing dimly through the acrid fug. Here and there voices could be heard crying out plaintively in Cantonese as a pilong called out for help to comrades who no longer lived. On more than one occasion a pilong swam towards them only to realise too late it was a British vessel he was turning to for help. When they saw their mistake they would swim off in the direction from which they had come, but one of the marines invariably put a musket ball between their shoulder blades and they slipped beneath the waves.

Killigrew wiped his streaming eyes with his handkerchief and peered through the smoke ahead in case an undamaged junk should suddenly loom in front of them. The gun crews stood by their loaded guns, ready to fire. The smoke thinned out and then the *Tisiphone* had burst through on the other side. There was still no sign of any more junks, and the creek stretched open before them. On either side Killigrew could see pilongs wading ashore and scrambling up the banks to disappear into the trees. Several of the marines levelled their muskets.

'Belay that!' said Killigrew. 'Save your powder and shot for men with fight left in them.' Perhaps the fleeing Chinese might one day return to the sea to renew their careers as pilongs, but Killigrew had bigger fish to fry.

Specifically, Zhai Jing-mu. Whatever else happened this day, Killigrew would see the *lao-pan* punished for Peri's murder, or die himself in the attempt. The fast rowing boat, which had slipped away from the side of the flagship only moments before she had been blown apart, was now half a mile ahead of the *Tisiphone*, disappearing around the next bend in the creek. Killigrew ordered the leadsman to the chainwales to call soundings. Zhai Jing-mu appeared to be getting away, but the *Tisiphone* could not go any faster for fear of running into shoal water; perhaps the pilongs were deliberately trying to draw them into the shallows of the uncharted creek.

Around the next bend they came within sight of the village, where the smug boat was still tied up at the jetty and the four unfinished junks stood in the stocks. 'Those'll have to be fired,' said Hartcliffe.

Killigrew nodded. 'We'll take care of that on the way back. We can't afford to waste any powder and shot until we know there are no more sea-worthy junks to be dealt with.'

'Ambush?'

'You can be sure of it. Zhai Jing-mu's got fifteen more junks in this creek somewhere, and they'll be waiting for us.'

'All right, everyone keep a sharp look-out!' ordered

Hartcliffe. 'If anyone spots a junk, I want to be the first to know about it!'

As the *Tisiphone* moved around the next bend, the creek grew narrower. Everyone on deck was silent, and the only sound to be heard was the throb of the engines and the plashing of the paddles.

Killigrew eyed the tree-lined banks of the creek. 'He's out there somewhere . . .' he murmured, to himself as much as to Hartcliffe. He frowned. There seemed to be something wrong with the densely packed foliage on the west bank.

He was about to draw Hartcliffe's attention to it when a cry came from the forecastle, 'Two junks, two points off the starboard bow!'

The junks came into view less than two cables' lengths away as the *Tisiphone* rounded a slight headland which jutted into the creek, and a moment later both opened fire with an ear-shattering broadside which hurled round shot through the air towards them. The *Tisiphone*'s fore top-mast was snapped off with a splintering crash and plunged through the netting over the deck, narrowly missing the bow-chaser's crew. They worked on, and a moment later scored a direct hit on one of the junks with their first shot, a shell which ripped the junk apart.

Even as the echoes of the explosion were drowned by the cheers of the men on deck, a splintering, crackling sound came from behind them and Killigrew twisted to see a huge fence of interwoven leaves and branches come crashing down to reveal a hidden side-channel. Within seconds no less than half a dozen small, fast junks were propelled from the channel by their sweeps, opening fire on the *Tisiphone*'s stern. Killigrew felt the deck tremble beneath him as a shot smashed through the windows of the captain's quarters.

'Hard-a-starboard!' ordered Hartcliffe, manoeuvring to bring the greater part of his firepower to bear on where the greatest threat lay, with the six junks which had emerged to cut off their line of retreat. A moment later the *Tisiphone*'s port-side thirty-two-pounder boomed and set one of the six junks ablaze.

'Man overboard!' yelled a voice from the forecastle.

'Who the devil's fallen overboard at a time like this?' Killigrew wondered.

'He'll have to wait until we've got ourselves out of this pickle,' said Hartcliffe. 'Stop engine!'

Endicott ran across to the quarterdeck.

'Why aren't you at your quarters?' Killigrew demanded angrily.

'It's the Chinese admiral, sir,' said Endicott. 'He's the man overboard. He jumped. Molineaux said you'd want to know.'

Killigrew ran to the side and saw the admiral swimming strongly to where the remaining junk ahead of them was moored. Now that the first junk had sunk, he could see what had been hidden before: the fast boat which slipped away from Zhai Jing-mu's flagship moments before it had exploded was tied up beside the second. Admiral Huang had obviously seen it and decided to grab the big fish for himself.

Killigrew cursed. He could not believe his eyes. It was impossible to imagine any Western admiral behaving in such a foolhardy manner, not even Nelson. But then English translations of Chinese words were notoriously inaccurate and Killigrew reflected that it was not beyond the realms of possibility that Huang's title, translated as 'admiral' by the British, actually meant something along the lines of 'escaped lunatic'.

'It's Huang all right,' he called to Hartcliffe as another round shot screeched between the *Tisiphone*'s foremast and mainmast, parting a backstay.

'That's all I need!' groaned Hartcliffe. 'If a Chinese admiral gets himself killed while in the care of the Royal

Navy, Bannatyne won't need to start a war between Britain and China; we'll have done his job for him!'

'Want me to go after him while you take care of those fellows?' Killigrew indicated the six junks behind them, now off the *Tisiphone*'s port quarter.

Hartcliffe nodded. 'Take the second cutter.'

Killigrew quickly picked out a crew and they lowered the cutter into the water abaft the starboard paddle-box while the *Tisiphone* exchanged shots fast and furiously with the junks to port. Two more junks had been blown out of the water by the time Killigrew slid down the life-line and landed lightly in the stern of the cutter.

'Bear off and give way with a will! Cheerly does it!'

The cutter skimmed so swiftly across the water that it was only a few yards behind when Admiral Huang hauled himself up the side-ladder on to the junk's deck. The admiral certainly had courage. Killigrew directed the marines amongst the cutter's crew to give him covering fire, and one of the marksmen brought down a pilong who appeared at the entry port directly above the admiral.

'Rowed of all! Watch for stink-pots!'

The cutter bumped against the junk's side and Killigrew rushed up the side-ladder without waiting to see if his men followed. He flung himself over the bulwark, kicking a pilong in the chest as he did so, and drew his cutlass to parry a sword-stroke aimed at his neck. Huang was there, enthusiastically hacking and slashing expertly with his own sword like a man half his age. The pilongs were so tightly packed around Killigrew there was no room for any skilful fencing; all he could do was hack, thrust and shove. Savage, screaming faces surrounded him on all sides. He narrowly avoided being skewered on a sword-point and drew his pepperbox in his left hand. Pressing it hard against a pilong's side, he pulled the trigger and the pilong fell away.

Then the rest of the cutter's crew swarmed on to the

junk's deck, and months of cutlass drill paid off as they butchered the pilongs expertly and the deck ran red with blood. The pressure around Killigrew was relieved enough for him to look around and take stock of the situation. A well-aimed blow from Huang's sword saved a British seaman's life: the admiral was clearly perfectly capable of looking after himself.

Then Killigrew spotted Zhai Jing-mu, unmistakable in his white suit and crimson sash, halfway up the companion ladder to the high poop deck. Zhai paused to aim his pistol at Huang. Killigrew raised his pepperbox and fired. The shot narrowly missed, but it was enough to put Zhai off his aim. Scowling, the pilong took his other pistol from his sash and fired at the lieutenant. The bullet splintered the bulwark behind him. Zhai threw the pistol at Killigrew's head and resumed his ascent.

Killigrew ducked and ran across the deck. A pilong moved to block his path, sword raised. The lieutenant brought him down with a shot in the chest. He slid his cutlass back in its scabbard and ascended the companion ladder to the poop. Another pilong appeared above him. He pulled himself close to the ladder to avoid a sword-thrust, and then leaned out to shoot the pilong under the jaw.

'Behind you, sir!' Cavan was busy defending himself with his cutlass against a pilong swordsman, but he was able to draw Killigrew's attention to the man who ran at his back with a spear. Killigrew twisted and shot his would-be assassin, and then shot the man fighting Cavan for good measure. Cavan waved his thanks and then ran to help Molineaux, while Killigrew resumed his ascent of the ladder. He paused just beneath the top rung, and then bobbed up, pepperbox first, sweeping the poop with the muzzle. Zhai Jing-mu was climbing over the taffrail, preparing to jump over the side and swim for the shore.

'Stop right there!' shouted Killigrew.

Zhai Jing-mu twisted and, recognising his nemesis, he jumped overboard. Killigrew climbed on to the poop and ran to the taffrail to see Zhai Jing-mu swimming for the shore, less than thirty yards away.

Huang joined him at the taffrail. 'Shoot him!'

'No bullets.' Killigrew glanced over the deck. The Tisiphones were getting the upper hand wherever he looked and Cavan seemed to have the situation under control. Glancing across the creek, Killigrew saw the *Tisiphone* had sunk all but one of the junks which had appeared astern. He hooked his pepperbox to his belt and scabbarded his cutlass. He was not going to let Zhai Jing-mu get away this time. 'Cover me.' He swung one leg over the taffrail, then the other, and dived into the water.

Zhai reached the shore twenty yards ahead of him and turned with his sword drawn to attack Killigrew as he emerged from the shallows, but a shot sounded behind the lieutenant and he saw an explosion of dust amongst the rocks at Zhai's feet. He twisted in the water and spied Huang at the taffrail with a smoking *gingall* in his hands. Molineaux was also there and he took the empty *gingall* from Huang, exchanging it for a fresh one. As Huang took aim once more, Zhai turned and bounded away from the water's edge, climbing the steep bank like a mountain goat.

Killigrew staggered out of the water and scrambled up the rocks after him. At the top of the bank the ground levelled out and he saw Zhai making for a small farmhouse. He drew his cutlass and charged after him. The *lao-pan* disappeared into the farmhouse and emerged a moment later leading a sturdy pony by a halter. Somehow it did not surprise Killigrew that the pilong admiral had had an escape route planned all along.

The pony was already harnessed and Zhai swung himself into the saddle. He gazed up the track leading inland, glanced at Killigrew, and then at the track again as if trying to make up his mind. Then he tugged on the pony's bridle and charged to meet Killigrew. When he was only a few yards away he drew his sword and aimed a slashing blow at Killigrew's neck.

The lieutenant ran backwards to receive the attack. As Zhai swung, Killigrew tried to duck and parry at the same time. He tripped and fell heavily, narrowly avoiding landing beneath the pony's hoofs. The cutlass skittered from his hand.

He stood up, but Zhai had wheeled the pony for his next charge before he could recover the cutlass. Killigrew instead ran to meet him, dropping on the ground before the pony. The beast instinctively leaped over the prone man. Caught off guard, Zhai had to drop his sword and cling on for dear life to avoid being thrown from the saddle.

Killigrew jumped up and sprinted after him. Zhai looked about, but the lieutenant had positioned himself behind and to the left of the pilong, in his blind spot. Zhai had to wheel the pony before he saw Killigrew, and by then it was too late. The lieutenant seized the *lao-pan*'s left arm in one hand and his sash in the other. He hauled Zhai out of the saddle and hurled him over his head to land on the ground.

Zhai rolled over and over. As Killigrew approached him, the pilong snatched up a stone and threw it at Killigrew's head. The lieutenant staggered back, stunned. Zhai was on his feet in an instant. He drew a dagger from his belt and hurled himself at Killigrew. The lieutenant caught him by the wrist with his left hand, but the pilong hooked one foot behind his leg and tripped him over. Killigrew went over backwards and Zhai landed on top of him. His face a snarling mask of rage, Zhai tried to force the tip of his dagger into Killigrew's left eye, but the lieutenant refused to relinquish his grip on the pilong's wrist.

With his right hand, Killigrew clawed at Zhai's face and dragged his eye patch down until it was around his neck.

Then he reached behind Zhai's head and pushed the thong away, twisting it until the pilong gagged, his one remaining eye bugging from his skull while the empty socket made his face look even more demonic. With his left hand he swept Killigrew's arm away, breaking his grip on the eye patch. He seized the lieutenant's throat in his left hand and squeezed. Killigrew felt himself choking. As his grip weakened on Zhai's wrist, the pilong pulled his arm free and then raised the dagger for a blow to the heart.

Killigrew closed his eyes and braced himself for death. Above him, Zhai's body shuddered violently. When the death blow did not come, he opened his eyes again. Zhai was staring at him with a shocked expression on his face. He glanced down at his chest. Following his gaze, Killigrew saw a bloody hole in the pilong's chest big enough to stick a fist in. He could see daylight on the other side.

Zhai Jing-mu lifted his gaze to stare at Killigrew in bewilderment, and then his one blue eye rolled up in his skull and he slumped sideways.

With a shudder of disgust, Killigrew pushed the grisly corpse off him and twisted to see Huang marching towards him with a *gingall* carried on one shoulder and a beam of satisfaction on his features. Molineaux followed behind him.

'Looks like the goddess T'ien Hou finally won through for you,' Killigrew muttered thickly, rubbing his throat where Zhai had gripped it.

'For both of us, Lieutenant.' As Molineaux helped Killigrew to his feet, the admiral marched across to where the pony stood. The beast shied away skittishly, but Huang calmed it and took the saddle bags from its back.

'You oh-kay, sir?' asked Molineaux.

Killigrew nodded. Zhai was dead, Peri was avenged, but somehow he did not feel satisfied. It was not because he had not had the privilege of killing Zhai himself, but because he could not help feeling that even Zhai Jing-mu had only been a puppet in all of this.

Drawing his sword, Huang marched back to Zhai Jing-mu's corpse and decapitated it with a single blow. He picked up the head by its queue, put it in one of the saddle bags and slung the bags over his shoulder.

'A gift for my emperor,' explained Huang, seeing the expression on Killigrew's face. 'Will you not do the same for your queen when you have killed Bannatyne?'

Killigrew shook his head. 'Somehow I don't think she'd be amused.'

They made their way back to where Huang and Molineaux had left the fast boat they had come ashore in. All of the junks which had tried to outflank the *Tisiphone* were sunk now. Killigrew and Molineaux rowed the admiral back to the junk, where they found Cavan and the others tidying up the mess. There were no prisoners: the pilongs had fought to the last man.

'Everything under control, Mr Cavan?'

Ashen-faced as he wiped blood from his cutlass, the midshipman nodded. His face was streaked with tears. Glancing down, Killigrew saw a large damp patch on the crotch of his pantaloons. 'Don't feel embarrassed, Mr Cavan. No one's going to laugh at you. There isn't a man aboard the *Tisiphone* who didn't do exactly the same thing when he got his first taste of real fighting, and anyone who tells you otherwise is a dammed liar.'

'Even you, sir?'

Killigrew nodded gravely. 'Even me. And even Robertson. Just remember that next time he's weighing you off, and it won't seem so bad.'

Cavan managed a wan smile through the tears. 'What happened to Zhai Jing-mu, sir?'

'If he's planning to seat himself on any more dragon thrones, he'll have to find himself one in Hell.'

'Sir!' yelled Molineaux.

Killigrew turned and what he saw filled him with dismay.

The remaining seven junks of Zhai Jing-mu's fleet were sailing down from the head of the creek. Several of them opened fire with their bow guns, sending up plumes of water all around the paddle-sloop.

He turned to Cavan and the others. 'All right, let's see if we can't turn this junk on her springs and bring her broadside to bear! You there! Get those guns shotted and run out, chop chop!'

Even as the seamen on the deck of the junk cleared for more action, another shot sounded, the unmistakable boom of a sixty-eight-pounder, and a moment later one of the seven new arrivals was blown apart by a direct hit from a shell. In the same moment, the *Shanghae* came into sight around the spur of land astern.

The *Tisiphone* fired her starboard-side thirty-two-pounder and another of the newcomers received a direct hit which set her poop deck ablaze. Within seconds the rest of the junks had raised white flags.

Molineaux mopped his cheeks with a handkerchief. 'Permission to heave a huge sigh of relief, sir.'

'Permission granted, Able Seaman.'

'Is it over?'

'Not quite.'

# XVIII:

# Jobbernowl

The flotilla remained in the creek into the afternoon. Zhai Jing-mu's ammunition store was rifled for powder and shot which could be used on board the *Mæander* and the *Tisiphone*, while Killigrew and a team of men set fire to the four unfinished junks in the stocks. Three of the junks which had been captured intact would be towed back to Hong Kong as transports for the prisoners and then auctioned for prize money; the rest would be destroyed so that they could never be used by pirates again.

Cargill came ashore to interrogate the *lao-pans* of the captured junks. 'Ask them if they know anything about a plot due to take place in Hong Kong tonight at the hour of the pig,' suggested Killigrew.

'Zhai Jing-mu's dead, Killigrew,' said Cargill. 'I'm sure whatever plan he and his friends concocted between them died with him.'

'I wish I could be so sure . . .'

One of the prisoners suddenly broke away from the rest of the group and lunged at Cargill, bawling in Cantonese so rapid Killigrew could not follow a word he said. The others tried to take advantage of the diversion to make a break for it. One of them slipped past Killigrew but he blocked the path of the rest and covered them with his pepperbox. Cargill had dropped his pencil and notebook and was grappling with the *lao-pan*. Molineaux went to help him, but Cargill laid the *lao-pan* low with an uppercut. A moment later more bluejackets had arrived on the scene to surround the pirates.

Killigrew glanced over his shoulder. The pilong who had broken free had almost made it to the corner of a hut when Keppel stepped into view in his path. The pilong tried to side-step him. Keppel quickly assessed the situation, seemed to make way for the pilong, but then tripped him up as he passed. The pilong landed heavily on his face. Keppel picked him up by the scruff of his neck and dragged him across to where the rest of the prisoners were being held. 'Did someone mislay this?'

'Thank you, sir,' said Killigrew.

Molineaux bent over and retrieved Cargill's pencil and notebook from the ground. 'You dropped these, sir.'

'Ah, thank you, Seaman . . .'

'When I was a kinchin, I always wanted to be a "D".'

'A "D"?'

Cargill smiled thinly. 'Thieves' cant, Mr Killigrew. He means a detective. I shan't ask where he learned such an expression.'

'When you were a child, Molineaux, you were a petty thief,' said Killigrew.

Molineaux shrugged. 'Just the other side of the coin, sir.' He was about to hand the notebook to Cargill, but could not resist opening it and pretended to read a page at random. 'One: do shopping. Two: pick up laundry. Three: beat suspect to death in order to extract confession. Four: tell superintendent the suspect sustained his injuries falling down the stairs.'

'It doesn't say that,' Cargill protested wearily.

Molineaux grinned. 'Just my little joke, sir.' He held out the notebook and the pencil. Cargill was about to take them when a frown clouded Molineaux's features and he snatched it back.

'Could I please have my notebook back?' Cargill protested.

'Give it back to him, Molineaux,' Killigrew snapped irritably.

'Wait a moment, sir.' The seaman reached inside his shirt and pulled out a grimy piece of paper with some numbers pencilled on the back. He stared at the paper, then flipped open the notebook in his other hand and stared at that before glancing back to the paper. 'Sir, I think you'd better take a look at this.'

Killigrew smiled sheepishly at Cargill. 'You don't mind if I humour him, do you?'

The annoyance on Cargill's face was plain to see, but he shrugged wearily as if he could not be bothered to protest.

Molineaux held both the notebook and the paper for Killigrew to see. The paper had clearly been soaked in sea water at some point and was all crumpled and torn, but both the printers' ink and the hand-written information had been fast long enough not to have run too much. The ink was faded but still legible.

It was a receipt for an eight-inch shell gun.

'Where did you get this?' Killigrew demanded of Molineaux.

'On board the *Buchan Prayer*, sir, on Ingersoll's desk. Look at the tails of the Gs, sir, and the capital Es.'

A look of panic appeared on Cargill's face. 'Give that to me!' He tried to snatch the receipt from Molineaux, but the seaman held the paper above his head and took a step back.

Killigrew laid an arm across the assistant superintendent's chest to hold him back. 'I'd say you've got some explaining to do, Mr Cargill,' he said.

'All right, so occasionally I do a little paperwork for Ingersoll,' blustered Cargill. 'That's not a crime, is it?'

'Filling out receipts? Weak, Cargill, damned weak. You'll have to do better than that.'

'Can I say it, sir?' pleaded Molineaux. 'Please let me say it. I know all the words and everything.'

'Be my guest.'

Molineaux stood in front of Cargill. 'Assistant Superintendent Cargill, I am arresting you on suspicion of colluding with pirates and conspiracy to murder.' He reached into Cargill's coat pocket and drew out a pair of handcuffs. 'You do not have to say anything at this time, but anything you do say may be taken down and used as evidence in a court of law.' As happy as a clam at high water, Molineaux cuffed Cargill's hands behind his back. 'I always wanted to say that to a peeler.'

Killigrew smiled thinly. 'That's the biter bit.'

'Surely you don't believe . . . ? The whole thing is preposterous, gentlemen, simply preposterous! I'm an assistant superintendent, for God's sake. What could I possibly have to gain by helping Zhai Jing-mu?'

'How much did Bannatyne promise you?' demanded Killigrew. 'You've been spying for him all along, haven't you? You were the one who made sure that the preparations for Zhai Jing-mu's trial dragged on as long as possible, to give the Triads more time to rescue him. And you were the only one to survive the attack on the gaol when Zhai Jing-mu was rescued. Why weren't you invited to Bannatyne's ball? Because you had to help the Triads rescue Zhai Jing-mu?'

'Damn it, man! I was shot!'

'In the leg. Very easy to shoot oneself there without doing too much damage.'

'I hope you know what you're doing, Killigrew,' said Keppel.

'Doing?' Cargill was livid. 'I'll tell you what he's doing. He's making a big mistake, that's what he's doing!'

'I don't think so, sir,' said Killigrew. 'I should have seen it earlier. Cargill here's been blocking every lead to Zhai Jing-mu every step of the way. The prisoner who was poisoned at the gaol: the bakery had nothing to do with it. You were terrified I was going to persuade him to tell me where Zhai Jing-mu's base was, weren't you?' he asked Cargill. 'The morning we interrogated that poor fellow Chan I noticed you kept looking at your watch, as if you were waiting for something to happen. Then news of Lieutenant Dwyer's death arrived. Was that what you were waiting for? The information which you knew would make me lead Peri Dadabhoy into a trap?' Killigrew struggled to keep his voice calm, but inside he was filled with hatred: Cargill had been as responsible for Peri's death as Zhai Jing-mu himself. 'When you heard I'd survived, you murdered the prisoner in case I came back to renew my interrogation of him. Then there was the Triad I captured outside the joss house on Hollywood Road. You were careful to kill him before he could tell me anything.'

'He was going to stab you.'

'I've been thinking about that. I couldn't work out how you could have seen that dagger from where you stood; even I couldn't see it, and *I* was standing right over him. Now I understand: you *couldn't* see it, could you? Not until after he was dead, when it gave you a perfectly good explanation as to why you shot him.'

Cargill was starting to look pale. 'This is insane. You can't prove any of this.'

'Sooner or later we're going to find Verran. One of you two is going to talk. You both know it's Bannatyne I'm after, so why should you swing for it? Whichever one of you turns Queen's evidence first, wins. The loser goes to the scaffold. You've got a head start, Cargill. I suggest you make the most of it.'

The police officer slumped in total dejection. Then a greasy smile slid across his face and he chuckled. 'You'll have to catch Verran first.' It was as close to an admission of guilt as he was likely to get.

'Don't concern yourself on that account,' said Killigrew. 'We shall.'

'I don't think I have anything more to say until my lawyer is present.'

'Very wise,' growled Keppel.

They put the prisoners in irons aboard the three junks which had not been destroyed and Cargill was taken on board the *Tisiphone* and put in irons in the lee waist with a marine to stand guard over him.

All three of the vessels in Keppel's scratch flotilla had sustained damage in the battle. The *Tisiphone* was the worst hit: both the captain's day room and the wardroom behind it smashed up by the round shot which had penetrated her stern, but Commander Robertson was clearly delighted with a day's work well done and surveyed the damage to his quarters and personal possessions with an uncharacteristically sanguine expression.

The *Tisiphone*'s engineer, Muir, made one of his rare forays from below decks. 'We took a shot in the engine room, sir,' he reported to Killigrew as Keppel explained the implication of Cargill's guilt to Robertson. 'One of the connecting rods is bent out of kilter.'

'Lucky it didn't go through one of the boilers. Can you fix it?'

Muir grimaced. 'I've managed to jury-rig it, sir, but it won't hold for long. It'll need to be replaced as soon as possible.'

'Haven't we got spares aboard?'

'That *was* the last spare, sir. I put an indent in at the dockyard two months ago, but you know what they're like.'

Killigrew nodded. 'Will it hold until we get back to Hong Kong?'

'I'd be happier if we went under sail power only.'

'We need wind for that, Mr Muir.' The breeze had died away to leave the three vessels becalmed.

Molineaux appeared at Killigrew's elbow. 'Sir.'

'That was good work, Molineaux, spotting the similarity of the handwriting on the receipt to that in Cargill's notebook.'

'Thank you, sir. But I still can't help wondering why Cargill should make out the receipt instead of Ingersoll. Unless Bannatyne wanted to be sure there was no way it could be traced back to one of his employees.'

Killigrew stared at him for a moment as the implication of Molineaux's words sank in, and then checked his watch. It was almost three thirty: only five and a half hours until the hour of the pig. He crossed to where Keppel and Robertson were talking on the quarterdeck. 'Sir? We can't waste any more time here. We *must* get back to Hong Kong as quickly as possible.' He explained his theory quickly to both officers. 'If Bannatyne's planning what I think he is, we can't afford to take any chances. He won't know that Zhai Jing-mu's dead; no one in Hong Kong will, until we get there, and that will be with only an hour or two to spare.'

'That's all very well, Second, but the *Shanghae* took a shot in her boilers and ours were damaged,' said Robertson. 'Unless you can whistle up a wind for us, I'm afraid we're becalmed.'

'Sir?'

'What is it, Muir?'

'It's only twenty-five miles to Hong Kong. I reckon there's a good chance the jury-rigged connecting rod will hold out till then.'

'What if it doesn't?'

'If it breaks . . . well, it might do some serious damage to the engine. I mean, we could be in dock for weeks.'

'Leaving us stranded, at the mercy of the wind, you mean.'

'We're at the mercy of the wind now,' Keppel pointed out. 'If Killigrew's right – and he usually is – we can't just sit here and do nothing. There are some ponies in the village. I'll send Lieutenant Bowyear and some men overland to Kowloon; they should be able to get a fishing boat there to row across to Victoria.'

Killigrew snapped his fingers. 'That's it, sir! The fishing station at Kowloon! If there's a shell gun lined up at the governor's stand, that's where it'll be.'

'Would it be close enough?' wondered Keppel.

'Extreme range, sir. But firing from a fixed platform, with plenty of time to measure the charge and line up the shot – a good gunner could be bang on target with the first shot.'

'All right. Bowyear will ride for the fishing station at Kowloon to find that gun. Robertson, you take the *Tisiphone* and try to warn the governor. The rest of us will follow under sail with the prisoners, and pray for you. Remember, if Bannatyne can make it look as though the Chinese were behind this atrocity – and with his partner in the House of Commons he shouldn't find that too difficult – then the public will soon be baying for another war with China and anything we say to contradict them won't matter a damn.'

'Do you have any idea how many rumours of plots, assassinations and uprisings cross my desk every week?' Governor Bonham tilted his head back so his valet could tie his cravat. He stood before a cheval-glass in the dressing room of a house he had to rent from one of the China traders; although a site had been chosen and the land had been cleared, building work had not yet begun on an official residence for Her Majesty's governor, plenipotentiary and superintendent of trade. Bonham was obviously used to receiving enquiries from naval officers at all hours of the day and continued to dress for the evening's festivities as he gave them an audience.

'No, sir,' Killigrew said innocently. 'How many?'

Bonham glared at Killigrew. Robertson motioned impatiently for his second lieutenant to be quiet.

'Enough to mean that if I paid any attention to all of them, I wouldn't be able to do my job,' said Bonham. 'In fact, the whole machinery of government would come to a standstill. Did it ever occur to you that that might be exactly what the Triads desire?'

'Sir, I'm not asking you to heed all of them,' said Robertson. 'Just this one. It's more than a rumour. Lieutenant Killigrew has had titbits from known members of Triad-affiliates – to which Able Seaman Molineaux is a second witness to some – and we've also had it independently confirmed by a Chinese informant.'

Bonham smiled tolerantly as his valet helped him into his coat. 'Listen to yourself, Commander. A Chinese informant? A naval lieutenant with a reputation for being excitable, and a common sailor? Hardly what I'd call reliable sources.'

Killigrew could feel his temper welling up within him like bile, but checked himself. It would be wisest to leave the talking to Robertson.

'A naval lieutenant with a proven track record in getting results, sir,' said the commander. 'And I'm not asking you to halt the machinery of government, just to cancel your attendance at the festivities tonight.'

'And lose face in front of the Chinese? I'm sorry, Robertson, but it will take more than some nebulous notion of a conspiracy to make me do that. You don't even know what it is that these conspirators are planning to do.'

'They've got a gun,' said Killigrew. 'Probably an eight-inch shell gun, by the sound of it; Able Seaman Molineaux found a receipt for one on board the *Buchan Prayer*. My guess is they're planning to fire it at the stand overlooking the harbour. That might put a spoke in the machinery of the island's government,' he could not resist adding. In addition to Bonham, General Staveley and all the island's senior officers and officials had places in the stand, along with their wives.

Bonham's valet adjusted his sash until the governor slapped his hand away in irritation. 'An eight-inch shell gun cannot be an easy thing to conceal, Mr Killigrew. You find me your shell gun, and maybe then I'll listen.' He smirked. 'Of course, once you've done that, I trust you'll attend to the matter so that there will be no need to call off the celebrations.'

'If there's nothing more I can say to dissuade you, sir . . .' Robertson saluted and motioned for Killigrew to accompany him out of the room. The butler saw them to the door.

'You wouldn't think it would be so difficult to persuade someone to permit you to save his own life, would you, sir?' sighed Killigrew.

Robertson rubbed his temples wearily. 'I don't know, Second. Bonham's got a point. It does sound rather far-fetched. All we've got to go on is cryptic hints and suppositions. If we're wrong about this, we're both going to look pretty foolish come midnight when the celebrations have passed off without a hitch.'

'Oh, I hope we're wrong, sir,' said Killigrew. 'I *pray* we're wrong. If looking foolish is the price I'd pay for that, I could bear it.'

Hartcliffe was waiting for them outside with a dozen bluejackets from the *Tisiphone*, some of them with black eyes and bruises. 'Well?' Robertson demanded impatiently.

'Bannatyne's not at his house or at the factory, sir. We searched both thoroughly.'

'What happened to your men?'

'Some of Bannatyne's men didn't like us barging into the factory. They tried to stop us.'

'Hope you gave as good as you got.'

'Paid back in full, sir, with interest,' said Hartcliffe. 'The butler at the house said Bannatyne had been called on an urgent trip to Macao for a business meeting. He couldn't tell us any more.'

'I might have known he'd have an . . . what are those things called, when you're somewhere else at the time of the crime?' asked Robertson.

'An alibi, sir?' offered Killigrew.

Robertson nodded. 'He's clever, damn him. We know that something ghastly is going to happen tonight, yet all the evidence we have to support our theory could so easily be construed far more innocently.'

'What did the governor say?' asked Hartcliffe.

'Everything's going ahead as planned.'

'Did you tell him about Bannatyne's involvement?'

'Don't be ridiculous! We wanted him to take us seriously, didn't we? "Excuse me, your excellency, but we believe there's going to be an attempt to blow up the gubernatorial stand at the festival tonight, and we think Blase Bannatyne is behind the conspiracy." ' Robertson snorted. 'I'm not even sure I believe it myself.'

'We've still got just over an hour, sir,' said Killigrew. 'I'll take some men across to Kowloon and turn that fishing station upside down.'

'Sorry, Killigrew,' said Hartcliffe. 'I'm afraid Mr Bowyear beat you to it. I bumped into him on the wharf; he'd just come from Kowloon. His men searched every inch of that fishing station and found nothing. He left them on guard there in case Bannatyne showed up with the shell gun, and came across to find us. He went back to join them as soon as he'd spoken to me.'

Killigrew sighed. 'He's wasting his time. If the shell gun isn't there already, then it was never Bannatyne's intention to use the fishing station in the first place. It must be somewhere else. Somewhere behind the stand, perhaps.'

They all turned to where the hills of Hong Kong showed faintly against the night sky. 'Too exposed,' said Robertson.

'Not at night.'

'They'd have wanted to make sure the gun was in place in plenty of time,' said Hartcliffe. 'It needs to be somewhere hidden, but with a clear shot at the stand.'

'What do we do now, sir?' asked Killigrew.

'I don't know,' Robertson said heavily. 'But I've a feeling you're going to be brimming with ideas.'

'Sorry, sir. I'm as much at a loss as you are.'

'Hmph.'

They climbed into the carriage Robertson had commandeered from the harbour master and rode back to Victoria. The house Bonham rented at Spring Gardens was to the east of the town, almost a mile from the centre. Long before they reached the corner of Queen's Road and Pedder Street, however, the crowds became so thick that the carriage was making almost no progress at all.

'We'd be quicker walking,' snorted Killigrew. 'With your permission, sir?' Robertson nodded and he opened the door and jumped down.

'Killigrew!' Robertson called after him.

The lieutenant turned back. 'Sir?'

'You heard what Her Majesty's plenipotentiary said. Find him your shell gun. You've got one hour.'

Killigrew nodded and turned away.

The crowd engulfed him at once. It seemed as if the entire population of Victoria and Tai-ping-shan were out on the streets for the dragon boat festival: Chinese men and women in red clothes, European men in their finest tail-coats and women in elegant ball gowns fanning themselves against the sultry air of the summer night. Every building was bedecked with paper lanterns. Chinese bands played their exotic, twangly music at a frenetic, joyous tempo while dancers twirled streamers and tumblers performed in every open space, spinning plates on bamboo canes or forming human pyramids. Chinese children ran about screaming and laughing, to the delight of the Western ladies and the annoyance of their husbands and fathers. On Harbour Master's Wharf, the oarsmen of the dragon boats performed their *t'ai chi chu'an* exercises to limber up before they climbed into their vessels for the great race. On the roof of his houseboat, Prince Tan was entertaining what Killigrew guessed would be honoured guests; if he had not been otherwise occupied, he would have liked to spend the evening with the mandarin himself. The delicacies would be exquisite, he knew, and the houseboat would provide a grandstand view of the race.

Firecrackers burst like a ragged volley of musketry in a street nearby, startling him. He whirled and came face to face with a dragon: a carnival dragon, its long body supported on a series of bamboo poles, each pole held separately by a man. The men were acrobats as much as puppeteers, following the lead of the one who controlled the head in perfect synchronisation to make the dragon whirl and swoop above the crowd.

Killigrew turned away and bumped into a wizened vendor who tried to sell him a packet of rice wrapped in silk and tied up with brightly coloured threads. He waved the old man away irritably and forced his way through the crowd, disorientated by the whirl of lights, faces, activities, spectacles and noise.

He came to where the governor's stand had been built in the open space in front of the barracks. None of the big-wigs had taken their places yet, and the empty seats looked like one of the few places where he could get some respite from the chaos.

'Excuse me, sahib!' A noncommissioned officer of the Madras Light Infantry, the evening's guard of honour, tried to stop him. 'But those seats are by invitation only.'

'Oh, shove off!' snapped Killigrew.

The soldier hesitated uncertainly, and then saluted. 'Yes, sahib!' The NCO about-turned and marched away.

Killigrew sat down at the centre of the stand and gazed across the sea of faces on the wharf to the harbour beyond. If his tenuous theory was correct in all its assumptions, then the shell gun had to be located within a direct line from where he sat; it would be hidden behind something, but behind something which could quickly be moved aside when the time came.

But there was no shortage of hiding places. Any one of a hundred *yolos* and sampans which crowded the waterfront could have concealed such a weapon; it would take hours to search them all, and there were only forty minutes or so left. The hour of the pig began at nine o'clock, the time the dragon boat race was due to commence, and Killigrew guessed the attack would be timed to coincide with that.

He became aware of a shuffling noise beneath his feet. Glancing down he could just make out a lantern moving around in the empty space beneath the stand. A sudden cold feeling stirred inside him. He had become so fixated on the idea of a shell gun, it had never occurred to him that Bannatyne's plan might be much simpler than that. Taking Guy Fawkes for his inspiration, all he had to do was pack the space beneath the stand with gunpowder and set it off at the appointed time.

Trying to act as casually as possible, he stood up and sauntered to the end of the stand. Then, ignoring the stairs, he vaulted over the rail and ducked under the stand, drawing his pepperbox as he did so.

A shadowy figure played the beam of a bull's-eye about the floor.

Killigrew levelled the pepperbox. 'Stop right there! Identify yourself!'

'Able Seaman Molineaux, HMS *Tisiphone*,' came the prompt reply. 'That you, Mr Killigrew, sir?'

The lieutenant sighed and hooked his pepperbox to his belt. 'For Christ's sake, Molineaux! What the devil d'you think you're doing?'

‘I thought maybe Bannatyne might have packed this place with gunpowder, but no such luck. I was jawing with a havildar a while back; he said they checked under here even before they heard the rumours of an attack, and their patrols are pretty regular.’

‘Come on, Molineaux.’ Killigrew sat down on the front row and took out his cheroot case. He lit one, and then found himself offering the case to the seaman.

‘Sir?’

‘Go on. Help yourself.’

‘Thank you, sir. But I don’t smoke.’

Killigrew had his hip flask on him. ‘You drink, don’t you?’

Molineaux stared at the proffered flask uncertainly, and then accepted it. He took a deep pull and gasped. ‘Lumme, sir! That’s smooth!’

‘John Jameson’s finest,’ agreed Killigrew. He gestured to the seat beside him. ‘Oh, sit down, man, for God’s sake! You’ve been on your feet as long as I have, if not longer.’

‘Thank you, sir.’ Molineaux sat down beside him, but failed to look comfortable.

‘What do you think, Molineaux? Is there really a plot to start a war between Britain and China, or am I just being paranoid?’ Killigrew laughed bitterly. ‘It’s rather rum, when you consider it. All my life I thought I knew all the answers to everything. What was wrong, what was right . . .’

‘You ain’t done so bad so far, sir, if you don’t mind my saying.’

‘Right now, Molineaux, I’d trade the secrets of the universe for the answer to one simple question: where would I put that shell gun if I was Bannatyne?’

‘But you’re not Bannatyne, sir.’

‘That’s my point. I’m supposed to be the one with piratical blood in his veins; the one who can think like them, anticipate them, beat them.’

'Not thinking like Mr Bannatyne isn't anything to be ashamed of, sir.'

'It's not a question of shame. It's a question of losing. I don't like to lose. But right now, Bannatyne's got me fairly stumped.'

'I'll wager that Assistant Superintendent Cargill knows, sir. Let me alone with him for half an hour and I'll get it out of him.' Killigrew could tell that the idea of beating the living daylights out of a senior police officer appealed to the ex-thief.

'But that's the catch, Molineaux. We're supposed to be on the side of law and order. We're not allowed to do that sort of thing. Which is why bastards like Bannatyne win every time,' he added bitterly.

' "It was from out of the rind of one apple tasted that the knowledge of good and evil as two twins cleaving together leaped forth into the world. And perhaps this is the doom that Adam fell into of knowing good and evil, that is to say, of knowing good by evil." '

Killigrew stared at the seaman. 'Eh?'

'Something I read in a book, sir, that stuck in my memory. John Milton, *Areopagitica*.'

The lieutenant nodded. He had forgotten that Molineaux's choice of reading could be astonishingly highbrow for a common sailor who had grown up on the back streets of Seven Dials. But as Killigrew was starting to discover, Molineaux was a damned uncommon sailor.

Molineaux gestured with the hip flask. 'Mind if I . . .?'

Killigrew shook his head. 'Help yourself.'

The seaman took another pull, gasped with pleasure, and then screwed the top back on. 'You know what my ambition is, sir? I want to make something of my life. I want to get on in the navy. Maybe even get rated bosun one day; then I can do all the shouting while some other poor bugger does all the graft. I've dedicated the past six years of my life to that aim. But I'll let it all go by the board if it means we can scupper Bannatyne's plans. Just half an hour, sir. I'll make him blab. You don't have to know anything about it.'

Killigrew knew how serious Molineaux was about his naval career. 'You'd throw all that away, just to save the life of Bonham and the other stuck-up bigwigs that will be sitting here in half an hour's time?'

'You mean to tell me you wouldn't do the same, sir? It ain't the guv'nor, it's the Celestials I'm worried about. Damn it, sir – pardon my French – but I *like* the Chinese. Not just Mei-rong, but all of them. They're clever, they're funny, they know how to have a good time when they get the chance . . . they're just like us, really.'

'I can't say I'm feeling particularly clever at this precise moment in time.'

'Cheer up, sir. The villains don't always win. Remember the Owodunni Barracoon?'

Killigrew smiled faintly. 'I could hardly forget.'

'We beat 'em then; we'll beat 'em again. You'll see.'

Killigrew stood abruptly. 'Come along, Molineaux. It's time we had a few sharp words with Mr Cargill.'

They made their way to where Mei-rong was living temporarily on board her mother's *yolo* with about a dozen small children. Killigrew could not work out who the children belonged to, but he had the feeling that the mother operated some kind of nursery for working Tanka girls. 'We need you to take us across to the *Tisiphone*, chop chop,' said Killigrew.

'One dollar,' said Mei-rong.

'Here's five.' Killigrew sat down in the stern and Mei-rong quickly cast off and started to scull them out to the paddle-sloop. The children all crowded around Killigrew, demanding that he play with them, until Molineaux came to his rescue by keeping them enraptured with conjuring tricks. They did not understand a word of his monologue, but his funny faces kept them in stitches.

*Yolos* had never seemed slower than they did now, but at last they bumped against the *Tisiphone*'s side, and Killigrew and Molineaux climbed up to the deck. 'Wait here,' Killigrew called down to Mei-rong.

She had sensed his desperation. 'Five dollar!'

'Five dollars!' exclaimed Killigrew. He sighed. 'All right, five dollars. But you'll have to wait for it. You know, that young lady is going to make some lucky man a fine business manager one of these days,' he added in an aside to Molineaux.

Hartcliffe was on duty on the quarterdeck. 'Any luck?'

Killigrew shook his head. 'We're going to try talking to Cargill.'

'I've already tried, Killigrew, believe me. He's not talking.'

'You just haven't been going about it the right way,' said Killigrew. 'You may want to go below decks for the next fifteen minutes. And the anchor watch, too.'

'I hope you're not thinking what I think you're thinking.'

Killigrew checked his watch. 'We've got twenty-one minutes, my lord. If we don't find that shell gun by then . . . I'm going to do whatever it takes.'

Hartcliffe shook his head sorrowfully. 'Fanning! Dismiss the watch.'

'Sir?'

'You heard me. I want everyone below decks. That includes you, Private Barnes,' he added to the marine who was guarding Cargill.

'Don't worry,' Molineaux told the marine. 'He ain't going anywhere. We'll keep an eye on him.'

Killigrew stood over the police officer, who was shackled hand and foot. 'We haven't got much time, Cargill. I think you know I'm right about this shell gun; and I think you know where it is. If you don't tell me where it is, and it goes off . . . if *one person* dies as a result, I'm going to kill you.'

Cargill grinned. 'You wouldn't dare.'

Killigrew shook his head. 'Don't put me to the test, Cargill. Which is it to be?'

Molineaux glanced across to where Bonham was already taking his seat in the stand with the other assembled bigwigs. 'Maybe we should take him to the stand and tie him up next to the governor, sir. I reckon he'd talk fast enough then.'

Killigrew checked his watch again. He was starting to get desperate. 'There isn't time. Look, Cargill: in eighteen minutes dozens of people are going to be killed. If that happens, many more will die over the next few months in the course of a senseless war. Do you really want that on your conscience?'

'Come on, Killigrew. You fought in the last war. What about all those men who died then? What did they die for? The Treaty of Nanking? A treaty that the Celestials are refusing to abide by? Five treaty ports, they said; and now they won't even let us in the walled city of Canton. We should have marched into Peking instead of stopping and making peace when we did. We passed up a great opportunity to teach the yellow-bellies a lesson; if there is another war, it will just put right what was left undone in forty-two.'

Killigrew grabbed Cargill by the lapels, lifted him to his feet and slammed him back against the bulwark. 'My patience is running out, Cargill.'

'You've got no evidence against me, Killigrew. Do you really think I'm going to admit my guilt by telling you where that gun is? What kind of a jobbernowl do you take me for?'

Killigrew stared at him.

Cargill looked uncomfortable. 'What?'

The lieutenant grinned. 'You see? If only you'd said that earlier, you could have saved us all this unpleasantness.'

'Said what? I didn't say anything!' protested Cargill.

'My dear assistant superintendent, you really should

take more care about the sort of presents you give – and to whom you give them.'

'Eh? What?' Cargill was bewildered.

But Killigrew was already turning away. 'Come on, Molineaux. We've got work to do.'

'You know where the gun is, sir? I didn't hear Cargill say anything.'

'A little bird told me.'

Killigrew and Molineaux surfaced beneath the bows of Prince Tan's palatial houseboat. Directly above their heads, only a couple of feet above the waterline, a guard armed with a musket stood on the gallery, oblivious to their presence. The two Britons exchanged glances and Killigrew nodded. Then they grabbed an ankle each and pulled the guard's feet out from under him. He fell down and cracked his head on the deck before he could cry out, his musket landing in the water with a splash.

A doorway covered only with a silk curtain led into the houseboat from the gallery and a voice called out in Cantonese from within. Killigrew hauled himself out of the water and on to the gallery, taking up position with his back pressed against the bulkhead by the door.

The curtain was pulled aside and another guard appeared. He saw Molineaux in the water, supporting the body of the unconscious guard, and opened his mouth to cry out a warning. Killigrew's fist smashed into his jaw.

Molineaux handed the cable up to the lieutenant, who tied it in a timber hitch to one of the posts supporting the deck head above. 'That should hold,' he whispered, picking up the guard's musket.

'You sure you want to do this alone, sir?'

Killigrew nodded. 'Prince Tan is – used to be – a friend of mine. He saved my life once. If I can do this without bloodshed, the happier I'll be.'

'And if you can't? You don't know how many men he has on board.'

'You let me worry about his men. Just make sure this houseboat is turned through ninety degrees so that the starboard side points towards the harbour mouth instead of the waterfront.' As Molineaux turned and swam back alongside the cable to where Robertson and Hartcliffe waited on the *Tisiphone*'s quarterdeck, Killigrew pulled aside the curtain and stepped into the passageway beyond. He made his way along it, peeping through the doors on either side as he passed but found no sign of what he was looking for.

A companion ladder led to the deck above. He started to ascend when he heard footsteps above. He quickly ducked back down and hid beneath the steps. He saw feet coming down, thrust the musket's barrel between the steps and swept it to knock the man's feet out from under him. The man fell forward and hit his head on the bulkhead on his way down. Killigrew scrambled over his unconscious body and crept cat-footed up the steps as he heard a voice above call out in Cantonese.

'Chang? Are you all right?'

Killigrew heard footsteps and waited at the top of the stairs. A moment later another guard approached. As soon as he hove into view, Killigrew knocked him out with a right cross. He dragged the body back down the steps and laid it next to the first. Then he ripped down a silk hanging, tore it into strips and used it to bind and gag them both.

Returning to the upper deck, he started to search each of the chambers. The first two he glanced in were deserted, but in the third he found Ai-ling – the Eurasian beauty he had seen talking to Ultzmann at Tan's picnic which seemed like a lifetime ago – tied to a bed. Her eyes widened when he stepped into the compartment. He lifted a finger to his lips, and unfastened the gag.

‘Who are you?’ she whispered in Cantonese.

‘A friend. You’re Ultzmann’s mistress?’

She looked offended. ‘His daughter!’

Killigrew nodded. He should have guessed as much a long time ago. Bannatyne or Tan had somehow found out that the missionary had an illegitimate half-caste daughter. At first they had probably threatened him with exposure; but as their schemes grew more desperate they had kidnapped her and used her as a hostage for the missionary’s help and co-operation.

He wondered if she knew her father was dead, murdered by Zhai Jing-mu; he knew he could not bring himself to tell her now.

‘Prince Tan and Zhai Jing-mu are planning to assassinate the governor,’ Ai-ling said urgently. ‘You must stop them!’

‘Don’t worry, it’s all in hand. They have a shell gun on board; do you know where it is?’

‘The upper deck, I think; I heard them manhandling it on board a few weeks ago.’

‘I’ll deal with it,’ he told her. ‘Can you swim?’

‘A little,’ she said.

Glancing down, he saw she did not have bound feet. ‘Go down to the stern – you know which way that is?’ She nodded, to his relief: he did not have time for lengthy explanations. ‘Go down to the stern and swim across to the British warship two hundred yards astern. Use the cable to pull yourself along if you must. They’ll look after you there.’

‘What about you?’

‘I have to have a word with Prince Tan.’

He accompanied her back to the deck below and watched from the bottom of the stairs as she hurried along the passage and disappeared through the curtained doorway leading on to the stern gallery. At his feet, the bound and gagged men struggled powerlessly. He ignored them and climbed back up the companionway to the upper deck.

He peered through a bead curtain covering the entrance to one of the compartments on the port side of the houseboat, facing towards the waterfront. The shell gun was there, pointing towards a door which opened out amidships towards the stand on the wharf. Only a silk curtain, tied down to prevent it from flapping in a breeze, hid it from any prying eyes ashore.

A team of ten Chinese were readying the gun and they had obviously been well drilled. The gun itself was an unfamiliar make, although the operation seemed simple enough: the percussion lock hit a priming tube in the breech to fire a shell. A box of fifty-six-pound hollow shells stood close by, and another of flannel-wrapped cartridges.

Killigrew stepped through the bead curtain. 'All right, gentlemen,' he said in Cantonese. 'That's quite enough of that. This festival already has all the fireworks it needs. Step away from the gun, please.' He gestured with the musket and the Triads backed towards the far partition.

Prince Tan stepped through behind them, flanked by two more guards. 'What is going on here?' he demanded. Then he saw Killigrew, and smiled. 'Ah, my barbarian son. I think, in my heart, I was expecting you to come sooner or later.'

'It took me a while, your highness, but I got here in the end. Tell your men to stand down. It's all over. Zhai Jing-mu is dead, Bannatyne's vanished; we know all about your plan to spark off a war between Britain and China. It isn't going to work. I'm afraid—' Killigrew broke off when he felt the cold touch of a gun muzzle against the back of his neck. 'Ah.'

Molineaux swam back along the length of the cable to the *Tisiphone*'s stern. Robertson and Hartcliffe waited for him at the entry port. 'Where's Killigrew, Molineaux?'

'He went aboard, sir. Wanted to confront his excellency in person.'

'Damned young fool. Well, as long as we pull the boat clear.' Robertson checked his watch. 'Three minutes to go. Now that's what I call in the nick of time. Go below and tell Mr Muir to start the engines, Molineaux. Full speed ahead.'

'Aye, aye, sir.' The seaman descended by the main hatch to the engine room where the stokers sweated to keep the furnaces burning and the pressure in the boiler just right. It was dark, hot and smoky in the engine room and the air was thick with coal dust. Molineaux would not have been a stoker for – he grimaced at the thought – all the tea in China. 'Turn ahead, full speed, sir,' he told Muir.

The engineer checked the pressure gauge, nodded, and hauled back a lever. Steam hissed and the pistons started to work: slowly at first, then faster and faster. He could not hear the sound of the paddles plashing above the racket of the engine, but he could tell from the motion of the deck beneath his feet that they were moving.

There came a loud snap followed by a clang, and a ghastly screech of rending metal. Something ricocheted past his head and bounced off the boiler casing. Muir swore and hauled on a lever. The pistons slowed and stopped until the engine room was silent but for the hiss of steam.

'What's wrong, sir?' demanded Molineaux.

'Connecting rod's broke. Damn it!'

'You can fix it, can't you?'

'Oh, aye. I can fix it, all right. It'll take a few weeks, but I can fix it.'

'A few weeks! Sir, we've got about one minute. Then it'll be war.' Molineaux sprinted for the upper deck to tell Robertson what had happened, but he knew he would be too late. There was no time to put a boat in the water and send a squad of marines and bluejackets to the houseboat. Now it was all up to Killigrew.

# *XIX:*

## *Fire and Water*

'You think our plan is foiled?' Prince Tan asked Killigrew, who stood with his hands tied above his head to a beam while one of the Triads kept him covered with a pistol. 'Zhai Jing-mu was expendable. He had played his part; he was no more than a pawn. He kept you chasing about the seas while the real plot was taking place right here in Hong Kong, my barbarian son.'

The Triads finished priming the shell gun. 'Is it lined up?' asked Tan.

One of them cut a slit in the silk curtain before the gun's muzzle and peered through. 'Right on target, excellency.'

'Excellent.'

A single pistol shot sounded, startling Killigrew, and a moment later a terrific din went up from the waterfront as the crowd began to beat their drums, cymbals, pots and pans.

The race had begun.

'In just a few moments, as the winning dragon boats cross the finishing line, we shall fire the first shot in the second phase of the great war between Britain and the Celestial Kingdom, and what was started ten years ago will finally be brought to a satisfactory conclusion,' said Tan.

'Two centuries of Ch'ing tyranny will be brought to an end and in time the rightful Ming emperors will be restored to the Dragon Throne.'

Killigrew knew that all he had to do was to keep Tan talking until the *Tisiphone* pulled the houseboat clear of the wharf. He was sure it could not be long now. 'Let me guess. You just happen to be a direct descendant of the Ming Dynasty?'

'A fact my ancestors have kept concealed from their Manchu overlords for over two hundred years. Oh, there are other men with a better claim on the Dragon Throne than mine, but it should not be too difficult to ensure they die heroically fighting the Manchu tyranny in our glorious war.'

'You think the Manchus are tyrants? You don't know the meaning of the word tyranny, Tan. You start a new dynasty drenched in blood, and that's the way it will be for ever.'

'Barbarian blood, Mr Killigrew. Do not think you can dissuade me from this course of action. My whole destiny had led up to this moment.'

'Excellency!' one of the Triads whispered urgently, and nodded to the doorway leading aft. Killigrew followed their gaze and saw Li Cheng standing there.

'Prince Tan? In the name of the Daoguang Emperor I arrest you for high treason,' said Li. 'Tell your men to put down their weapons and release the barbarian.'

Tan stared at him incredulously. 'You came alone? Unarmed?'

Li bowed.

The Triads stared at him, and then burst out laughing. 'Kill him,' Tan said dismissively.

One of the Triads pulled a pistol from his sash and pointed it at Li's forehead. Li's leg flashed out and kicked the pistol into the air. He punched the man in the throat and then caught the pistol on the way down. He used it to shoot the man who held a pistol on Killigrew.

Two Triads drew swords and charged at Li. He threw the pistol at the head of one, knocking him out, and then caught the other by the wrists to stay the blow. A third Triad came at him. Still holding the second at bay, Li kicked him in the chest and threw him back across the room.

Another Triad drew a sword. Killigrew grabbed hold of the ropes binding his hands above his head and hauled himself up to kick the Triad between the shoulder blades with both feet. The Triad staggered into a man who had been lining up a pistol-shot at Li. The shot went wide, drilling a third man in the head.

'Thank you!' Li wrested the sword from the man he grappled with and knocked him out with a *wu-yi* punch.

'I could be even more helpful if you cut me loose.' As a Triad tried to slash at Killigrew with a sword, the lieutenant kicked him in the crotch and he went down with a howl.

'So sorry . . .' Li jumped into the air and somehow contrived to kick two men in the face simultaneously. 'I am a little busy at the moment.' He parried a sword stroke from another man and kicked him away long enough to throw the sword across the room. It spun through the air, sliced through Killigrew's bonds and embedded itself in the bulkhead behind him. His hands free, he knocked out one Triad with a right cross, another with a left uppercut, and turned to pull the sword from the bulkhead.

'Fire the gun!' screamed Tan.

'But the dragon boat race is not yet ended, excellency!'

'Fire it *now*!'

Killigrew saw two of the Triads light the fuse of a shell and insert it in the muzzle of the gun: they did not seem to realise there was no need to light the fuse, the firing of the gun did that automatically. In their panic they had not cut the fuse to the correct length – not that a few seconds would make much difference either way when the shell landed on the gubernatorial stand. Why the devil hadn't the *Tisiphone* towed them clear yet?

Two swordsmen attacked the unarmed Li from both sides at once. He side-stepped, grabbed one by the wrist and whirled him around to receive the other on the point of his sword.

Tan picked up the lanyard to fire the shell gun and flexed his fingers around the toggle. Parrying a sword-stroke from one Triad, Killigrew kicked another in the groin. The man staggered back, cannoned into Tan and knocked him across the breech of the gun.

While Li exchanged fast and furious *wu-yi* blows with one Triad, another tried to strike him down from behind. Killigrew flung his sword. It spun over and over and took the man in the throat. The lieutenant turned and found himself staring down the length of a quarrel resting in a crossbow. He had a flashback: it was the same man who had almost shot him at the gaol, the one who had later shown up as the captain of one of the pilong junks which had 'attacked' the *Golden Dragon*.

Killigrew caught him by the wrists and forced the crossbow up towards the deck head. The two of them struggled for control of the crossbow. They bounced against the shell gun and then rolled on the deck beside the gun carriage.

Inside the barrel, the fuse still burned.

Tan steadied himself and adjusted his grip on the lanyard.

The pilong tried to point the crossbow at Killigrew's face but the lieutenant was stronger. He forced the pilong's arm away, into the space beneath the hammer of the percussion lock.

Tan pulled the lanyard. The hammer fell and the pilong screamed in agony. The firing pin failed to connect with the priming tube.

There was no time to draw back the hammer for a

second try. Aware of the still-burning fuse in the barrel of the gun, the Triads and the guards fought to climb out of the door and the windows.

Tan was knocked down in the panic. He tried to crawl away but Killigrew grabbed him by an ankle and deftly tied the lanyard in a stout knot around it.

'This way!' Li threw himself feet first against one of the bulkheads. The flimsy partition smashed under his weight. Killigrew followed him through. In the next room he saw Li hurl himself through a window. Killigrew jumped out after him, headfirst. He plummeted twenty feet, hit the water, and a moment later the shell burst in the gun's barrel. Red-hot chunks of metal burrowed through the water all around him. He swam down a fathom, aware of flames lighting up the surface above him, and then struck upwards.

When he surfaced, the houseboat was in two halves and sinking in flames. No one was watching the dragon boat race any longer. A few of the Triads who had managed to escape from the houseboat splashed around, striking out for the shore.

A hand grabbed Killigrew by the scruff of the neck. He twisted and found himself hard against the gunwale of the *Tisiphone*'s thirty-foot steam pinnace. Ågård and Molineaux hauled him on board.

'Are you all right, Killigrew?' Hartcliffe called from the stern.

He nodded. 'Why the devil didn't you just pull the houseboat clear?'

'Engine failure. You seem to have managed well enough without help.'

The marines in the boat were shooting at the Triads who swam for the wharf. A Chinese surfaced on the opposite side of the pinnace. One of the marines whirled, levelling his musket, but Killigrew knocked the barrel up. 'He's on our side!'

Li Cheng was pulled into the pinnace and they rowed back to the *Tisiphone*. When Killigrew had climbed up the side ladder he found Robertson waiting for him on deck. 'Good work, Second.'

'Don't thank me, sir.' He gestured to where Li Cheng was climbing through the entry port after Hartcliffe. 'Chalk this one up to the Celestials. Mr Li just saved my life. And averted a small war. Miss Ai-ling?'

'The Eurasian girl? In the sick berth, being properly cared for by Westlake and Strachan. Where the deuce does she fit into all this?'

'She's Ultzmann's daughter. They were holding her as a hostage for his bad behaviour.'

'I see. What about Prince Tan?'

'Dead, sir. That just leaves Bannatyne, Verran and Ingersoll to take care of.'

'Except we don't know where they are,' pointed out Hartcliffe.

'There's a slim chance they still plan to make that rendezvous at the *Buchan Prayer* at midnight.'

Robertson checked his watch. 'We'll never make it in time. It's quarter past nine already, and Muir tells me it'll take weeks to repair the engines.'

'Might I make a suggestion, sir?'

'It's your choice, madam.' Blase Bannatyne faced his wife across her cabin on board the *Golden Dragon*. The fire damage had been repaired and cosmetic alterations had been made to the steamer to disguise it from prying eyes on the other vessels in the Cap-sing-mun anchorage. 'Even as we speak, a train of events which will change the whole course of history has been set in motion. When the war is over, a new dynasty will rule in Peking. A dynasty which will be in my debt. A new treaty will be signed: one giving me exclusive rights to all the tea produced in China. I shall be the richest man in the world.'

She stared at him for a moment, and then shook her head. 'How much money do you need?'

He stared back, as if there were something strange about her question. 'All of it.'

'You're insane.'

'You never understood me, Epiphany. Can't you see my vision? What I'm trying to achieve for us here? When my plan comes to fruition, kings and queens will bow to you. Isn't that what you want?'

'No! Blase, I never wanted kings and queens paying attention to me. Just you. I just wanted you to place some value on the things that interested me, as well as the things that interested you.'

He sighed and stood up. 'I cannot afford the public disgrace of a divorce. You understand that, don't you?'

'Is that the only way you can see to keep our marriage alive? By making veiled threats?' She shook her head. 'It's over, Blase. I just want you to let me go.'

'That I cannot do—' There was a knock at the door. 'Who is it?' Bannatyne called impatiently.

'Cap'n Ingersoll, sir. The look-outs on Lan-tao have reported back.'

'Splendid. I trust everything went according to plan?'

Ingersoll opened the door. His face was pale. 'Something went wrong.'

'What do you mean?'

'Prince Tan's houseboat blew up before the dragon boat race finished.'

Bannatyne stared at him in disbelief. Then his face hardened. 'Killigrew!'

Mrs Bannatyne laughed. She no longer had any sympathy for her husband. He was deranged, twisted. The only reason she had not realised it before was because he had always kept her at arm's length, emotionally. 'You want to rule the world, and you can't even get the better of a junior naval officer!'

Bannatyne slapped her viciously, knocking her out of her chair. She fell to the deck, but refused to give him the satisfaction of seeing her cry. 'Does that make you feel better, Blase? You can't beat Killigrew, but you can beat me, a defenceless woman . . . your own *wife*, for Heaven's sake!'

He scowled, and turned back to Ingersoll. 'Tell Verran to get steam up at once. We're leaving. Fetch all the papers from the safe on the *Buchan Prayer*. And unless you want to be here when the Royal Navy arrives, I suggest you bring your things on board, too.'

'Aye, aye, sir. Where shall I tell Cap'n Verran we're bound?'

'Anywhere but here.'

Molineaux did not recognise the steamer tied up at the landing stage next to the *Buchan Prayer* when Sir Dadabhoy Framjee's pinnace steamed through the Cap-sing-mun Passage. Molineaux manned the tiller while Killigrew and Hartcliffe stood in the bow. 'That's not the *Golden Dragon*!' he protested.

Killigrew raised a telescope to his eyes. ' "*Vermilion Bird*", it says. And if you believe that, you'll believe anything. It's the *Golden Dragon*, all right. I'd recognise her lines anywhere.'

Hartcliffe cast his eyes over the squad of marines and bluejackets, and his eyes fell on Li. 'What the blazes is he doing here?'

'He wanted to come,' said Killigrew.

'That's beside the point. This is navy business, and he's a Chinese national and a civilian.'

'I felt we could use all the help we could get,' said Killigrew, and smiled faintly. 'He seems to know how to look after himself.'

'This will be cutlasses and musket-work, Killigrew. There'll be no place for his *wu-yi* skills here.'

'Yes, milord. Want me to have Molineaux put the tiller over and take us back to Victoria?'

Hartcliffe sighed. 'If he gets killed, Killigrew, it'll be on your head.'

Killigrew said something else to Li in Cantonese; telling him to keep his head down and stay out of trouble, guessed Molineaux.

As they closed with the *Buchan Prayer* Hartcliffe raised a speaking trumpet to address the men on the decks of the opium hulk and the steamer. 'This is Lieutenant Lord Endymion Fitzmaurice Berkeley Hartcliffe, of Her Britannic Majesty's Royal Navy. I order you to strike your colours and permit us to board you!'

Killigrew stared at Hartcliffe, who shrugged. 'Never does any harm to use one's full tally in a situation like this. You'd be amazed how many people go weak at the knees in the presence of nobility.'

A shot sounded from the deck of the opium hulk, and a musket ball whizzed through the air above their heads to splash into the pinnace's wake.

'Weak at the knees they may be, milord, but it doesn't seem to have put their aim off by much,' said Killigrew.

Molineaux glanced towards the *Golden Dragon* and saw some of the men on her poop swinging the stern-chaser around to point at the pinnace. 'Pivot gun off the starboard bow, sir!' he called.

'Make for the far side of the *Buchan Prayer*!' ordered Killigrew.

The men on the *Golden Dragon* managed to get one shot off before the pinnace slipped behind the hulk. It screeched over the heads of the bluejackets and plunged into the water on the far side, sending up a great gout of water which almost capsized the pinnace and drenched everyone on board. Then they were protected behind the hulk, and too close in for the men above them to be able to draw beads on them with their muskets.

'Grappling irons!'

Molineaux snatched up one of the grappling irons and whirled it expertly, as he might whirl the lead when sounding. He let go and it flew up to the rail far above their heads, the rope snaking out behind it. Another seaman did likewise, and both irons caught firm on the rail. Molineaux went up one rope and Killigrew the other. Molineaux was halfway up the hulk's side when he saw a man at the rail above him, sawing at the rope with a knife.

Next to him, Killigrew gripped the rope tightly in one hand and braced his feet against the side of the hulk. He leaned out, plucked a pepperbox from his belt and took careful aim. The pistol cracked and the man fell back out of sight.

Molineaux signalled his thanks and went on and up over the rail. He took off the hook and started to fasten the half-severed rope more securely to the rail. He had almost finished when a guard came at him out of the gloom and swung a musket-butt at his head. Molineaux ducked and drove his fist into the man's stomach. He doubled up to reveal another guard behind him, levelling a musket.

Killigrew swung himself over the rail and kicked the musket aside a moment before the guard pulled the trigger. The musket-ball ploughed into the side of a deck house. The lieutenant landed on the deck and laid the man out with a right cross.

Molineaux finished fastening the rope and a moment later more bluejackets swarmed over the side with daggers, cutlasses, hatchets and belaying pins gripped between their teeth or thrust under their belts. They were followed by Li.

'See if you can find Mrs Bannatyne!' ordered Hartcliffe. 'There's a chance she may still be alive!'

'And if anyone finds the *tai-pan* himself, he's mine!' added Killigrew.

If the lieutenant intended to exact his own brand of justice on Mr Bannatyne, that was fine with Molineaux.

He ducked between two of the deck-houses and came face to face with Ingersoll. Grinning, Molineaux pulled his Bowie knife from its sheath.

'Oh-kay, you sonuvabitch. Let's hear you call me "nigger" now.'

Ingersoll turned and ran. Molineaux pursued him down the accommodation ladder to the landing stage, and up on to the deck of the *Golden Dragon*. Li was right behind him. No sooner had they stepped through the entry port than the two of them stopped short.

Most of the sailors on the steamer were busy lowering the sails or casting off the mooring ropes, but there were still enough left over to form a semi-circle around Molineaux and Li. Behind the two interlopers, the gangplank was raised as the wind began to carry the *Golden Dragon* away from the landing stage.

On the far side of the deck of the *Buchan Prayer*, Killigrew parried a bayonet thrust from one guard with his cutlass, punched a second in the face with the knucklebow, and then stabbed the first in the throat.

Further along the deck, Ågård glanced at Killigrew and his eyes widened in shock. 'Behind you, sir!'

Killigrew whirled and came face to face with Bully Hayes and Eli Boggs, the two *tindals* from the *Golden Dragon*. Boggs levelled a revolver at Killigrew's head.

'Finish him, Eli!' snarled Hayes.

Endicott stepped out behind them and rammed a musket against the backs of their heads like a quarter-staff. Boggs dropped the revolver and slumped to the deck, while Hayes staggered forward and Killigrew knocked him out with a blow from the hilt of his cutlass. 'Much obliged to you, Endicott.'

The Liverpudlian beamed proudly. 'My pleasure, sir.'

'Killigrew!' Hartcliffe's voice came from the other side of the deck. Killigrew ran across to join him in time to see the

*Golden Dragon* move away from the landing stage under sail. Bannatyne stood next to Verran on the quarterdeck, mockingly waving farewell to the two lieutenants. In the steamer's waist, Molineaux and Li were surrounded by Ingersoll and four sailors.

'They're getting away!' Hartcliffe protested.

'The devil they are!' Killigrew slotted his cutlass back in its scabbard and ran back to where he had left a grappling iron hooked over the far rail. He ran to the hulk's poop deck, stood at the taffrail and whirled the iron above his head. It arced up through the air and dropped over one of the yards of the *Golden Dragon*'s mainmast. There was no time to make the rope fast to the hulk's taffrail. The ship's movement pulled the rope tight almost at once, and Killigrew barely had time to swing one leg over the taffrail, and then the other.

He stepped out into space and prayed he had judged the distances correctly.

He plummeted for a couple of feet and then the rope swung him in towards the *Golden Dragon*'s stern. He hauled on the rope to pull himself up, raising his legs beneath them to avoid cracking them on the rail, and then swung across the quarterdeck. He hit the planks and his graceful swoop came to an abrupt and inelegant end as he rolled against the far bulwark. No bones broken, though, as far as he could tell.

He climbed shakily to his feet and turned to where Bannatyne and Verran stood next to Suleiman, the helmsman at the wheel. Killigrew drew his cutlass. 'Hello, Jago. Time for a return match, I think.'

Verran was grinning. He made no attempt to reach for his own cutlass. Killigrew realised what was wrong and began to turn, but he was too late. What felt like a sledge-hammer smashed into the back of his neck. He dropped his cutlass, staggered a few paces and sank to his knees. He flopped on to his back and, through the lights that danced before his eyes, saw Shen loom over him. Then Verran was there, holding the point of his cutlass at his throat.

'Never mind him,' Bannatyne told Verran. 'Shen will deal with Mr Killigrew. You take care of our slant-eyed friend.' The *tai-pan* pointed, and the lieutenant managed to raise his head in time to see Li ascend the ratlines pursued by two Lascars.

Then Shen grabbed Killigrew by the ankles and started to drag him towards the taffrail.

'Three against one,' said Molineaux. 'That's hardly fair.'

Ingersoll and the two sea-cunnies charged as one. Molineaux danced aside, slashed at one of the sea-cunnies with his Bowie knife, dodged beneath Ingersoll's grasping arms, and tripped the second sea-cunny so that he sprawled on the deck.

'Hardly fair to you, I mean,' said Molineaux, dancing back. He ducked behind the jolly boat stowed on deck as they came at him again. One of the sea-cunnies reached for him across the boat. Molineaux seized him by the jacket with his left hand and dragged him across the boat's tarpaulin cover. He brought the haft of the Bowie knife down against the back of his neck and knocked him unconscious.

He slashed at Ingersoll with the knife, but the captain jumped clear. A moment later the other sea-cunny had dashed the knife from his grip with a *wu-yi* kick. It clattered across the deck. Molineaux tried to go after it, but Ingersoll interposed himself.

Molineaux turned and raced across the deck. Ingersoll and the other sea-cunny pounded after him. He stumbled down the after-hatch and through a door into the captain's day room, illuminated by an oil lantern which hung from a nail in an overhead beam. He waited on the other side of the door, and as it began to open outwards he kicked it with all his might. The door smacked into the first man's face and Molineaux heard his unconscious body hit the deck.

Ingersoll came through the door, dagger in hand. He slashed at Molineaux's chest. Molineaux jumped back and bumped into a table. He rolled over it backwards, accidentally catching the lantern with one of his feet and hurling it into a corner. The glass smashed and a puddle of burning oil spread across the deck. Molineaux managed to get both feet on the deck, and then Ingersoll came around the table at him with the dagger.

Li Cheng paused halfway up the ratlines and turned to stamp on the hand of one of the Lascars who pursued him into the rigging. The man cried out and thrust his knuckles into his mouth. Li stamped on his other hand. The Lascar let go with that hand too and only realised his mistake when the ship, moving out from behind the lee of Lan-tao Island, rolled beneath him. He fell backwards with a cry and plummeted into the sea.

Li continued to climb up to the platform at the foretop where he encountered two Malays who had already been in the rigging. The first tried to kick him in the head as he climbed up through the lubber's hole. Li caught him by the ankle and gave his whole leg a twist. The Malay tried to turn away from the pain, lost his balance and fell to the deck.

Li climbed up on to the platform in time to meet the next Malay, who inched his way in from the foreyard. The man threw a punch at his head. Li ducked, and drove the tips of his fingers into the centre of the man's chest. The Malay doubled up in agony and fell with a scream.

Hassan, the *ghaut serang*, came up through the lubber's hole and slashed at Li's feet with a kris. Li jumped over the arcing blade and backed out on to the yardarm, arms spread wide for balance. Hassan tried to follow him. The more orthodox method for moving out on to the yard was to stand on the foot rope while holding on to the spar, but the *ghaut serang* seemed to sense that would put him at a disadvantage to Li, who balanced effortlessly on the yard itself, in spite of the rolling of the ship.

Holding on to the mast for support, Hassan slashed at Li with the kris. The Chinese skipped back further out on to the yard. The *ghaut serang* swallowed hard and let go of the mast, edging nervously out on to the spar. He faced up to Li and slashed at his throat. His arms folded mockingly, Li leaned back slightly and the wavy blade missed his Adam's apple by a hair's breadth. Hassan overbalanced and fell from the yard without Li having touched him. The Chinese shook his head sadly, amazed that the *tai-pan* should employ sailors with no sense of balance to crew his ship.

Suddenly the yard jerked sharply below him. He almost lost his footing, and his arms flailed wildly as he teetered for a few seconds. He had just regained his poise when the yard gave another jerk, and then another.

He heard laughter as he struggled to maintain his footing. Glancing down to the deck – a mistake: it made him feel even dizzier – he saw Verran directing three seacunnies to tug on a rope. Each time they hauled, the yard on which Li stood gave another jerk. Now he could see when each jerk was about to come and brace himself in readiness, it was easier to maintain his balance. He waved mockingly to Verran.

Scowling, the captain went crazy. He drew his cutlass and slashed at ropes left, right and centre. When the third rope parted, the yard suddenly pivoted at the middle and the end on which Li stood dropped down under his weight. As the yard canted he felt his feet slip and the world span around him. He tumbled and fell headlong towards the deck far below.

★ ★ ★

'What the devil does that idiot think he's doing?' Bannatyne demanded. 'He'll bring down all the sails!' He started to march across the deck.

Shen indicated Killigrew. 'What shall I do with this one?' he asked in Cantonese.

Bannatyne did not even glance over his shoulder. 'Throw him over the side. Suitably weighed down, of course.'

Shen grasped Killigrew by the lapels, hoisted him to his feet and propped him up against the taffrail. He picked up a length of chain and wrapped it about the lieutenant's torso a couple of times to make sure his body would sink. Then he bent down to seize Killigrew's ankles so he could tip him over.

Killigrew had only been pretending to be stunned, and now he seized his chance. He snatched a mahogany belaying pin from a rack and smashed it over the back of Shen's head.

The pin snapped. Shen straightened with an expression of mild annoyance.

Killigrew thrust the splintered end of the pin in Shen's face, but the Chinese caught him by the wrist and stopped the thrust short. He twisted Killigrew's arm, whirled him around and yanked his wrist up into the small of his back.

Killigrew gasped. It felt as if his arm was going to be wrenched from its socket. His hand opened and the broken belaying pin dropped to the deck. Shen pushed him away. Killigrew staggered backwards across the quarterdeck and collided with the helmsman, Suleiman.

The assistant helmsman, a Lascar, seized him in a full nelson and held him fast as Suleiman let go of the wheel long enough to draw a dagger from his belt to finish him off. With no one to hold it, the wheel spun crazily as the waves buffeted the rudder.

Killigrew leaned forward and pulled the Lascar over him so that he lost his balance. Then he whirled round and straightened, putting the Lascar back down in the path of

Suleiman's dagger thrust. The Lascar groaned. Killigrew broke free and whirled round again in time to see the Lascar slump to the deck.

Suleiman stared down at what he had done, and then came at Killigrew with a snarl. He thrust like lightning, and before Killigrew could defend himself the blade slammed against his chest.

The two of them glanced down. The dagger's point had caught in one of the links of the chain Shen had wrapped around Killigrew. Before Suleiman could pull back the dagger, Killigrew caught him by the arm. The two of them grappled for a moment. Killigrew forced Suleiman's hand towards the spinning helm. He let go of the arm as the wrist was caught between the spokes of the wheel and the bone snapped audibly. Sobbing in agony, Suleiman sank to his knees.

Another hammer-blow smashed into Killigrew's neck: Shen again. He staggered across to the rail, trying to put as much distance between himself and the Chinese to buy himself enough time just to turn and face his next attack. He turned and braced himself, but Shen was taking his time, his face the epitome of supreme self-assurance.

Killigrew removed the chain Shen had wrapped around him. As Shen advanced on him, he whirled the chain around his head like a flail. He swung it at the comprador. The links wrapped themselves around Shen's head, but the comprador grabbed the chain and hauled on it. Caught off balance, Killigrew staggered towards him and his face met the comprador's fist coming in the opposite direction. He staggered back against the taffrail, dazed, and shook his head muzzily.

Shen unwrapped the chain from his head and tossed it over the side, advancing once more.

The deck heaved violently. With no one at the helm, the *Golden Dragon* was being blown wherever the wind and current would take it; and it only took one glance of

Killigrew's trained eye to see that the sea was intent on carrying them to where white breakers betrayed the presence of a reef in the gloom.

Killigrew pointed. 'If someone doesn't take the helm, we'll be run aground!' he said urgently in Cantonese.

Shen did not make the mistake of turning to look. 'First I shall finish you, and then take the helm.'

Killigrew lunged suddenly at the Chinese, raining a salvo of blows against his face: right jab, right jab, left uppercut, right cross and then the *coup de grâce* – that old left hook that came out of nowhere when they were too dazed to see it coming.

Shen grinned. 'Is that the best you can do?' He jumped into the air, kicked Killigrew in the chest and drove him back against the rail.

The fire in the cabin spread swiftly. Molineaux found himself caught between the roaring flames and Ingersoll's dagger. He faced the dagger, the greater of the two perils, first. Ingersoll thrust at his stomach. Molineaux caught him by the wrist and the two of them grappled chest to chest. The captain was stronger, but Molineaux had his arm gripped with both hands. Ingersoll gave up trying to thrust the dagger into his stomach and instead used his weight to push him back into the flames.

Molineaux's feet struggled for purchase on the deck. He could feel the heat of the flames scorch the back of his neck. He threw himself sideways in desperation, and Ingersoll stumbled into the flames. He let go of Molineaux to beat out the flames where his clothes had caught fire.

Molineaux ducked out of the cabin. He heard Ingersoll's footsteps right behind him. He ascended a companionway and turned to kick Ingersoll in the face. The white man avoided the blow and caught Molineaux by the leg. The two of them struggled in the confined space. Ingersoll slammed the seaman first against one bulkhead and then against the other. Molineaux still stood above Ingersoll and he used gravity to his advantage, falling on the captain. Locked together, the two of them crashed back down the steps to the deck below.

They rolled apart, rose to their feet and faced one another. A terrific shudder ran through the ship and there came a groaning, splintering sound from somewhere forward. Even as Molineaux was thrown against Ingersoll, he knew instinctively that the ship had crashed into something.

Unbalanced, the two of them fell down the next companion ladder to the lower deck. Molineaux lay there for a moment, dazed. It felt as if every bone in his body was broken.

Then Ingersoll was on him again, smashing at his face with his fists. Molineaux seized him by the throat and squeezed. As Ingersoll's eyes bulged from their sockets, Molineaux managed to push him off and roll on top, but then Ingersoll lifted his knee sharply into Molineaux's crotch. Fire blazed through his loins. The two of them tumbled over and over on the deck until they fell down the hatch to the orlop deck.

The water broke their fall. Cold sea water: it surged along the deck as it rushed in through a breech in the hull. Floundering, Molineaux and Ingersoll broke apart to find their feet. The water was only waist deep, but it was rising fast. Realising the ship was sinking, Molineaux turned and tried to climb back up the companion ladder, but Ingersoll caught him by the belt and dragged him down. Then he got both his hands around Molineaux's neck from behind and forced his head underwater.

# *XX:*

## *The Death of the Golden Dragon*

As Li Cheng fell he braced himself for the bone-breaking impact of the deck, but it never came. Instead something caught his ankle and almost tore out his leg. He found himself dangling upside down thirty feet above the deck, his foot caught in the foot-rope of the crazily canted foreyard.

Below he could see Bannatyne shouting furiously at Verran. The *tai-pan* pointed up to where Li dangled. Verran nodded and began to ascend the ratlines.

Li swung against the limp foresail. He could not get a grip on the canvas to pull himself up. He panicked for a moment, and then his scrabbling fingers found a reef point and gripped it. He pulled himself up with one hand, found another reef point with the other and then disentangled his foot from the foot-rope. His legs swung down and he hung the right way up at last.

As he tried to climb back on to the foreyard the ship juddered and canted suddenly, swinging him out with the dangling yard. Verran, halfway up the ratlines, was almost thrown overboard but managed to hang on. Below, Bannatyne and the sailors were hurled to the deck. On either side of the bows, Li could see the breakers boiling white where they surged over the reef. Her bows impaled on the reef, the *Golden Dragon* began to settle in the water.

Verran resumed his ascent. Li swung himself back on to the foreyard and climbed up to where it was trussed to the mast. Just as he reached the platform at the foretop Verran thrust his cutlass at him up through the lubber's hole. The razor-sharp steel sliced through the flesh of Li's calf. He gasped, jumped clear and caught hold of the shrouds which led up to the cross-trees at the peak of the fore topmast. He began to climb, and Verran climbed up after him.

A series of bangs sounded above the pounding of the waves as they smashed the stricken vessel against the reef. Li glanced aft and saw the panes of glass in one of the skylights below shatter as the flames in the cabin roared against them.

He had reached the cap of the fore topmast. Still gripping his cutlass, Verran continued his ascent. 'No place left to run, my slant-eyed friend!'

Li glanced about desperately. The only other way off the fore topmast was via one of the two ropes that ran from the yard-arm ends of the fore topgallant yard to the main topmast crosstrees. There were only two questions: would one of them be strong enough to bear his weight; and could he make it to the mainmast before Verran sliced through the rope and sent him plunging to the deck far below?

Molineaux was not drowning, but he was not far from it, either. He had managed to get his lungs half-full of air before Ingersoll pushed his head under. Now he floundered about, unable to gain purchase with either hands or feet as Ingersoll kept up the relentless pressure.

His knuckles brushed against something solid: a handrail. He searched for it with his fingertips, found it again, got a good grip, and then pulled himself further under.

It was the last thing Ingersoll could have expected and it caught him completely off guard. His hands locked right around Molineaux's neck, he found himself dragged under the fast-rising water before he had a chance to take any air into his lungs.

Molineaux held on tight to the floor timbers, gambling on there being more air left in his own lungs than there had been in Ingersoll's. The pain in his chest grew tighter and tighter, until he felt he must burst if he did not breathe in now. But Ingersoll's fingers still dug into his neck from behind. Perhaps he had miscalculated. Perhaps Ingersoll still had his head above water.

Molineaux could not hold out much longer. He felt his vision misting, his strength giving out. He allowed himself to go limp, hoping to trick Ingersoll into thinking he was dead.

And then the hands were gone. Molineaux surfaced and banged his skull on the low deck head, but he did not mind that, he was just grateful to whoop that sweet, fetid air into his lungs.

Ingersoll was already wading through the chest-deep water towards the companion ladder. Molineaux went after him, but the water impeded his every step. By the time he reached the ladder Ingersoll had slammed down the hatch cover from above.

Molineaux climbed up the companion ladder and pounded on the underside of the hatch cover, but Ingersoll had made it fast. Molineaux climbed back down to the deck. If he could get forward he knew there would be another way up beyond the hold.

The water was shoulder-high now and he was fighting against the torrent that rushed in. He half-swam, half-pulled himself through the engine room. When he reached the door to the hold he had to duck his head under the water, but there was more headroom on the other side.

Chests of opium were stacked high on either side. He swam down the gangway between them until he reached the ladder to the main hatch on the far side. As he climbed up out of the water Ingersoll appeared above him and reached for the hatch cover.

Molineaux grabbed him by the ankle. Ingersoll lost his balance and fell through the hatch. The two of them plunged into the water which swirled furiously between the opium chests.

They turned to face one another in the chin-deep water. Ingersoll's hand came up out of the water and Molineaux realised that the white man had retrieved his Bowie knife. He tried to step back and tripped over some unseen obstruction on the submerged deck. He backed into a stack of chests. Ingersoll slashed at his face with his own knife.

Molineaux ducked beneath the water to avoid the thrust. He caught Ingersoll around the waist and drove him back. Something – possibly Ingersoll's knee – bumped against his face. The water reduced the force of the blow, but it was still enough to enable him to break free before Molineaux could pull him under.

The seaman surfaced. Ingersoll came at him again, stabbing this time. Molineaux backed into the stack of chests once more and noticed one of the ropes which held the chests in place had been slashed through by one of Ingersoll's thrusts. Then the ship gave a lurch as the next breaker forced it deeper on to the reef. The chests at the top of the stack toppled forward. Molineaux pressed himself back against the chests below.

Ingersoll saw his peril but it was too late. He threw up his arms in a futile gesture and then the uppermost chest smashed down against him and drove him under the water. The chest bobbed up again almost at once. Ingersoll followed a moment later, floating on his back. The Bowie knife had been driven into his heart.

★ ★ ★

'Time for number-two *wu-yi* demonstration.' On the listing quarterdeck, Shen circled Killigrew. 'Leopard punch!' One hand whipped out and slammed into the lieutenant's chest. He staggered back in agony. It felt as though his ribs had been driven through his lungs.'

'Venomous snake strikes vital point!' Shen struck Killigrew beneath the armpit. The lieutenant sank to his knees.

'Crane drinks alongside stream!' A fist slammed into Killigrew's face, and he sprawled on his back. He rolled over and tried to crawl away.

'Yellow oriole drinks water!' A foot struck Killigrew in the ribs and knocked him on his side. Barely able to see through the waves of pain that swamped him, he crawled over to the taffrail and pulled himself to his feet.

'Are you paying attention?' Shen's face looked demonic in the light of the flames that shot up through the shattered skylight. 'Civilised Chinese pay much money for this kind of schooling. Kicking the sky!' He lifted his foot into the underside of the lieutenant's jaw. Killigrew's head snapped back and he almost went over the taffrail. He steadied himself just in time to receive Shen's next attack.

'Phoenix-eye punch!' A fist smashed into Killigrew's temple. He span away dizzily across the tilted deck. He knew he could not take much more of this beating.

'Double tiger claws!' Two more fists slammed into him with bone-jarring force. He staggered back again on legs like water. Every nerve end in his body was screaming at him to give up and lie down and die.

Bracing his feet in an effort to stay upright on the canted deck, he faced Shen and wiped his sleeve across split lips. 'You know we have martial arts in Britain, too?'

Shen threw back his head and laughed. Killigrew summoned up the last reserves of his strength and grabbed him by the lapels.

‘Glaswegian kiss!’ Killigrew brought his forehead down sharply against the bridge of Shen’s nose. Dazed, the Chinese staggered back with blood gushing from his nostrils.

‘Ringsend uppercut!’ The lieutenant flicked a boot into Shen’s crotch. The Chinese doubled up in agony. Killigrew span him around to face the raging inferno which blazed up through the skylight.

‘Naval officer kicks hulking brute in backside!’ He slammed the sole of his boot against Shen’s buttocks. The Chinese staggered forwards, tripped over the skylight coaming and fell through with a scream.

Holding one arm across his brow against the intense heat, Killigrew squinted down into the flames. He saw Shen in the cabin below. The comprador picked himself up and staggered about for a few moments, but his clothes were on fire and the smoke and flames blinded him. He blundered about for a few seconds, then finally slumped to the deck and lay down to die.

Breathing hard, Killigrew stumbled over to the bulwark and clung on to it for support. A moment later a dripping wet Molineaux emerged from the main hatch and staggered over to join him. Everyone else on deck was either dead or unconscious. ‘You oh-kay, sir?’

Killigrew nodded. ‘Did you find Mrs Bannatyne?’ he asked desperately as the deck gave another shudder.

‘No, sir. Where’s Li Cheng?’

They both looked about. The only signs of life were in the rigging. Li clung to the fore topgallant yard at the peak of the foremast. Verran climbed up the rigging towards him, cutlass in hand, but Li seemed more interested in one of the fore topgallant braces.

‘He’s going to climb across to the mainmast!’ gasped Molineaux.

‘He’ll never make it,’ Killigrew said grimly. ‘Verran will cut it before he gets halfway . . .’

Both of them were assuming that Li would haul himself along the brace hand over hand. Both of them were wrong.

Li got his feet on the fore topgallant yard and stood up, spreading his arms for balance. Then he stepped out on to the brace like a tightrope walker. 'Jesus Christ!' exclaimed Molineaux. 'He's crazy!'

Li started to walk along the brace; no, he started to *run* across it.

Muda and MacGillivray ascended the ratlines on either side of the mainmast to meet the Chinese at the other end. 'We'd better go and help him,' said Molineaux.

Killigrew had had more than enough for one night, but he could hardly stand by and allow the young Chinese to be butchered. As Molineaux scrambled up the ratlines to port, Killigrew ascended on the opposite side. The *Golden Dragon* was heeling over to starboard and Killigrew's climb was almost vertical as he pursued MacGillivray, but he forced himself onwards and upwards.

The wind blew Li off balance. He teetered for a moment and Killigrew watched with his heart in his mouth. Somehow the Chinese regained his poise and made it to the cap of the main topmast.

Killigrew caught up with MacGillivray, grabbed him by the belt and plucked him from the ratlines. The engineer fell with a scream and was swallowed up by the breakers which surged across the reef.

Muda was only a few feet below Li in the main topgallant shrouds, climbing up with a kris between his teeth. Both Killigrew and Molineaux were too far below to catch him before he reached Li. Verran, meanwhile, crawled along the fore topgallant brace after the Chinese, his face twisted in a snarl of hatred.

Li waited for Muda at the main topmast crosstrees. The Malay reached him, took his kris from his teeth, and slashed at his legs. Li kicked him in the wrist and the kris spun high into the air. Li slammed the sole of his slipper into Muda's face and the Malay plummeted to the deck.

Verran was almost two-thirds of the way along the brace. Li deftly caught Muda's spinning kris by the haft. He swung himself around the topgallant mast and slashed at the brace. Verran stared at him in horror as the blade sliced through the rope. Still clinging on, he swung downwards, headfirst. He hit the mouth of the funnel and plunged down it with a hollow, echoing cry which was cut short as he plummeted into the furnace below.

In the same instant his cutlass clattered to the deck.

Killigrew and Molineaux shinned down the backstays to the deck. A moment later Li joined them and bowed. 'I am sorry I killed your friend.'

'That's all right. I never liked him much anyway.' Mindful that Bannatyne was still loose on board somewhere, Killigrew picked up Verran's cutlass. 'All right, search the ship. We're not going until we find Mrs Bannatyne . . .'

'Don't bother,' said the *tai-pan*. 'She's here.'

Killigrew, Molineaux and Li whirled. Blase Bannatyne stood behind his wife, the muzzle of a single-shot percussion pistol pressed against the underside of her jaw beneath her right ear. In his other hand he had a second percussion pistol pointed at Killigrew. The two of them were silhouetted by the blaze which now engulfed the whole of the stern. The ship's timbers groaned in her death throes as the waves pounded her against the reef.

'Drop the sword!' snarled Bannatyne. 'Now!'

The *tai-pan* and his wife stood too far away for Killigrew, Molineaux or Li to be able to do anything. Raging with frustration, Killigrew threw down the cutlass so that it buried its point deep in the deck, the hilt quivering.

Bannatyne laughed and took the first pistol away from his wife's jaw to cover both Molineaux and Li. 'You didn't really think I'd shoot my own wife, did you?'

It was Mrs Bannatyne who answered. 'As a matter of fact, I did.' She rammed an elbow into his stomach. He doubled up and dropped one of the pistols. With his free hand he threw her against the jolly boat stowed on deck.

Killigrew lunged for him. Bannatyne fired and a white-hot needle bored through the flesh of the lieutenant's shoulder. A moment later a final shudder threw them all to the deck as the ship was wrenched asunder with a splintering groan. The bows sank almost at once and the stern and midships section canted crazily. Li gave a cry and slipped down the smooth deck to be engulfed by the breakers. Killigrew managed to wrap one arm around the skid beams on which the jolly boat rested, and with the other he caught Molineaux by the wrist as he slid past.

The waves rose slowly up the deck, tilted at an angle of fifty degrees. Above them the blazing stern cast a hellish glow over the scene. As the ship sank deeper the tilt of the deck increased.

Molineaux's weight threatened to pull Killigrew's arm from his socket. 'Hang on!' yelled Killigrew.

Above them, Mrs Bannatyne clung to a grating in the deck while her husband, further up the grating, tried to stamp on her fingers. 'Mr Killigrew!' she screamed. 'Help!'

'Sir!' yelled Molineaux.

Killigrew glanced down. The seaman jerked his head to where Bannatyne's other pistol had wedged in one of the scuppers. 'Swing me over!'

The lieutenant started to swing Molineaux to and fro across the deck. At the furthermost reach of the swing, their grips broke. Molineaux bounced off the bulwark and slithered down the deck. He snatched at the pistol as he went and managed to catch hold of a set of pinrails a few feet above the rising water. One end of the pinrail broke away under his weight. 'You'll have to take the shot, sir! I can't make it from here!'

Killigrew nodded. Molineaux hurled the gun up the

deck with all his might. The motion ripped the pinrail away completely and the seaman plunged down.

The pistol skittered past Killigrew and he caught it even as he saw the water swallow up his friend. 'Molineaux! No!' he screamed in horror.

The seaman did not reappear.

Killigrew turned his attention back to where Bannatyne clung to the grating. He lost his grip and slid down to kick his wife in the face. She cried out and Killigrew braced himself to catch her, but she hung on to her husband's ankles now. He caught hold of the grating further down. She scrabbled against the deck in search of a foothold while he kicked at her face again to free himself.

Killigrew thought of Molineaux, and Peri, Li and Ultzmann, and of all the other people who had died thanks to Bannatyne's machinations. There was no doubt in his mind that the *tai-pan* had lived too long. He drew a bead on him. 'Mrs Bannatyne!' he called. 'Let go!'

'I daren't!' she sobbed.

'Let go!' he repeated. 'I'll catch you, I swear it! Trust me!'

She let go and slid down the deck in a blossoming of petticoats. Killigrew fired and then dropped the pistol in time to catch her. Agony tore at his right arm where it gripped the skids and he distinctly felt the bone pop out of its socket. He cried out in pain.

'Are you all right?' she asked.

He gritted his teeth and nodded. He drew her in closer so she could grasp the skid beams for herself. They both looked up to where Bannatyne lay on his back, still clinging to the grating with one hand. He stared back at them in shock, and with one hand reached inside his coat. Killigrew thought he was reaching for another gun, but when the hand came out it was empty and glistened with blood in the firelight.

Then the *tai-pan* lost his grip, slid down a few feet until his legs struck the first of the skid beams. His body pivoted outwards to roll down the deck to where Verran's cutlass was still embedded. Killigrew buried Mrs Bannatyne's battered face against his chest as the razor-sharp blade sliced her husband's head clean off. Head and body bounced into the foaming breakers.

The water was only a few feet below Killigrew and Mrs Bannatyne now, the deck almost vertical. 'Clasp-knife!' he told her. 'In my pocket. You'll have to cut through the ropes holding the tarpaulin cover in place.'

She nodded, took the knife from his pocket, and clambered up the skid-beams to where the jolly boat was stowed. She sliced through the ropes and wrenched off the tarpaulin cover. Favouring his dislocated arm, Killigrew climbed inside. 'Now cut the mooring ropes,' he told her. 'Leave the ones at the top until last. And make sure you're in the boat when you cut them!'

She did as he told her, climbing into the jolly boat alongside him as she sawed at the last of the ropes. 'Hold tight!' he cautioned her.

The rope parted and the jolly boat shot the last few feet down the deck. The bow bumped sideways off the stump of the mainmast and Mrs Bannatyne was thrown against Killigrew. The prow buried itself in the waves, and then came up again and they drifted away from the ship.

A few inches of water sloshed around the bilges. Killigrew took the bailing scoop in his left hand. 'You'll have to row, get us clear of the reef before the *Golden Dragon* goes down. Think you can manage it?'

'I'll just have to try, won't I?' She fitted the oars in the rowlocks and rowed them until they were clear of both the sinking ship and the reef. Once they were out of danger she stopped rowing and shipped the oars, and the two of them watched as the steamer's blazing stern slipped beneath the waves with a hiss. For a second or two the golden dragon ensign which hung from the jackstaff was still visible, ragged and smouldering at the edges, and then that too was gone for ever.

Epiphany Bannatyne cut off his jacket to avoid twisting his dislocated arm and examined the wound in his shoulder where her husband had shot him. 'You're lucky. It's just a flesh wound.' She did not faint at the sight of blood, but bound up his wound gently but firmly to stop the bleeding.

'One day you'll make some lucky chap a good wife,' he told her.

'He can't be any worse than my last husband,' she agreed. 'In fact, I think I could do a lot better for myself.'

He leaned closer to her. The bruises on her face where Bannatyne had kicked her looked appalling, but Killigrew did not imagine he looked any better. 'Did you have anyone in mind?' he asked her.

'If I think of anyone, you'll be the first to know. Mr Killigrew . . . are you a wealthy man?'

'Me? No. Poor as a church mouse. Why do you ask?'

'Perfect.' Her lips slightly parted, she moved her face towards his.

At that moment a figure bobbed up on one side of the jolly boat, and was followed up by a second on the other side a moment later. Killigrew reached for his clasp knife and Mrs Bannatyne snatched up one of the oars, but they were only Molineaux and Li.

'As pleased as I am to see that you're both back from Davy Jones' locker, I must say your timing could have been a good deal better,' Killigrew said ruefully. 'Well, now you're here you can take up those oars and put them to some good use.'

'Don't tempt me,' muttered Molineaux.

'Oars not necessary,' said Li, and pointed. 'Look!'

They all turned to see Framjee's steam pinnace navigating the reef with Ågård at the tiller. Hartcliffe waved from the bows and presently tossed a line across to them. Molineaux and Li let go of the jolly boat and swam across to the pinnace where Seth Endicott helped them on board.

'What happened to Bannatyne, Molineaux?' asked Hartcliffe.

'He's probably trying to bribe Davy Jones into letting him go even as we speak.'

They took the jolly boat in tow and headed back to Victoria. Killigrew tried to get comfortable next to Mrs Bannatyne but something was sticking in his back. He reached underneath him and found a bottle of laudanum. 'Just the thing!' He pulled the stopper out with his teeth and spat it over the side. Before he could take a sip, however, she snatched the bottle from his hand and threw it overboard.

'You don't need that any more.'

'But I only wanted a sip, to take my mind off the pain.'

She moved closer. 'I'll give you something to take your mind off the pain . . .'

# *Afterword*

Alas, all of Kit Killigrew's efforts to avert a second war between Britain and China were for naught: the two empires were at war within seven years. Once again the British were the aggressors, declaring war on China because of their insistence that British subjects guilty of crimes in China should be tried in British courts. The Second Opium War (1856–1860) is sometimes known as the *Arrow* War, after the name of the ship from which a 'British' seaman (actually a Chinese) was taken by the Chinese authorities. The man was tried for murder and found guilty, prompting another outburst of Lord Palmerston's gunboat diplomacy.

It takes two to polka, and the arrogance of the Chinese in believing that all other races on earth – even those they had never encountered – were subject to the authority of the Emperor in Beijing certainly contributed to this second outbreak of hostilities. But the inescapable fact remains that they were well within their rights both to try people accused of crimes on Chinese soil in Chinese courts, and to forbid the import of opium into China, which of course was the cause of the First Opium War (1839–42) – and also the underlying cause of the second. If the Chinese were beaten thoroughly on both occasions, that is as much a reflection of the pacifist Confucian ethos which had been dominant in China for centuries as of the superiority of British technology. While the cultural and technological superiority that China had once possessed over the rest of the world had by the nineteenth century been long permitted to stagnate, perhaps that was a fair price to pay for centuries of relative peace and harmony. Tragically, that peace was only shattered by the arrival of the barbarians.

While I have no wish to make excuses for the men who smuggled opium into China in the eighteenth and nineteenth centuries – they deserved none – it is only fair to point out that until the mid-nineteenth century it was little understood that opium was addictive; indeed, some tried to argue that opium was beneficial. Uncontrolled before the Pharmacy Act of 1868, it was available over the counter in England, as pills, lozenges, pastilles, liniments, and raw poppy seeds, and as the active ingredient in many medicines. 'Kendal Black Drop' was a particular favourite of Coleridge and Byron, but opium was not exclusively a rich man's vice: it was cheaper even than gin, hence its popularity with industrial workers in Lancashire. The withdrawal symptoms suffered by addicts who tried to quit were supposed by doctors to be unrelated ailments. The cure for these 'unrelated ailments'? More opium-based medicines, of course.

Although Killigrew fought in the First Opium War, I had no wish to write in depth about his experiences at that time: there was no way I could see of salvaging anything noble or heroic out of that shambolic butchery. I was more intrigued by events that took place in 1849, the events which inspired much of this novel. In that year the ravages of the pilongs became so difficult to ignore that the Royal Navy decided to do something about them. The worst of these pirates were Shap-ng-tsai and Chui-apoo – the joint inspiration for Zhai Jing-mu – who divided up the south coast of China between them: Shap-ng-tsai would operate to the west of Hong Kong, while Chui-apoo operated to the east. Shap-ng-tsai was blamed for the murder of *Capitão* d'Amaral, the governor of Macao, early in 1849, and shortly afterwards the murder of Captain d'Acosta of the Royal Engineers and Lieutenant Dwyer of the Ceylon Rifles were ascribed to Chui-apoo, whom they were said to have insulted.

In the autumn of that year Her Majesty's brig *Columbine*, in company with the P&O steamer SS *Canton*, chased a fleet of pilong junks to Bias Bay, to the east of Hong Kong, where Chui-apoo had his lair in Fan-lo-kong creek, an arm of Bias Bay. The *Columbine* kept the pilong junks bottled up in the bay while the *Canton* steamed back to Hong Kong to fetch Her Majesty's paddle-sloop *Fury*. The *Columbine* was unable to enter the bay because her draught was too great, so on that occasion it was left to the *Fury* to go in, and she is said to have destroyed no less than twenty-three pilong junks, although Chui-apoo, despite being desperately wounded, is believed to have escaped.

No sooner had the *Columbine* and the *Fury* returned to Hong Kong than they were dispatched westwards to deal with Shap-ng-tsai's fleet, in company with the SS *Phlegethon*, a steamer of the Honourable East India Company. Over the course of several weeks they tracked Shap-ng-tsai's fleet ever westwards, into the uncharted islands in the Gulf of Tonquin, until they trapped the pirates in the Tonquin River. In a battle lasting two days, the two navy vessels and the civilian steamer put paid to no less than fifty-eight pilong junks and suffered only one fatality amongst their own crews. Once again the pilong admiral escaped, but his fleet was destroyed. The fates of both Shap-ng-tsai and Chui-apoo are shrouded in uncertainty, but according to one account Chui-apoo was captured by the British and committed suicide while awaiting trial, while Shap-ng-tsai surrendered himself to the Chinese authorities and was given a commission in their navy!

These events actually took place several months after this novel is set. I brought the action forward to set the climax at the dragon boat festival, which also allowed me to feature Captain the Honourable Henry Keppel, who was in command of HMS *Mæander* at Hong Kong at this time, although I also had to delay his arrival by a couple of months for dramatic purposes. Keppel was one of the great swashbuckling heroes of his day and went on to become Admiral of the Fleet in 1877.

Many other characters in this novel were likewise inspired by real people who were in China at this time. Rear-Admiral Sir Francis Collier did suffer a paralysing stroke in February 1849 – the month Dwyer and d'Acosta were murdered – and died a few months later. There was an Admiral Huang Hai-kwang who took part in the British expedition against Shap-ng-tsai. He arrived with a fleet of six war junks, but knowing they would not be able to keep up he travelled on one of the British vessels. Determined to keep the Chinese end up, on the second day of the battle in the Tonquin River he jumped overboard and swam out to capture a pilong junk single-handed.

Cargill was inspired by Assistant Superintendent Daniel R. Caldwell of the Hong Kong Police. Caldwell also took part in the expedition against Shap-ng-tsai, as an interpreter. He emerges from the pages of this chapter of history as one of the few men who took the trouble to understand the Chinese – he married a Chinese, almost unheard of for a European in those days – for which he was subsequently accused by one of Hong Kong's attorney-generals, T. Chisholm Anstey, of consorting with pirates and being financially interested in brothels. An inquiry cleared Caldwell of these charges, but it was conducted in such a manner – with certain evidence being burned by Caldwell's friends – that though he was never proven guilty, nor was he proven innocent, and in the end it was decided that he was guilty by association with a man discovered to be a pirate and was therefore unfit to hold the office of justice of the peace (a post which by that time he had already quit).

Hong Kong certainly seems to have been a lively place. Writing of the Hong Kong newspapers in the 1840s, Jan Morris informs us:

> We are told of 'astounding rumours implicating certain Chinese residents . . . in dark deeds of piracy and crime'. We are told of the 'diabolic procedures' employed by the hordes of pirates infesting the Pearl River Estuary. We hear at length of 'the ruffian Ingood', who specialized in robbing drunken sailors, and who, having drowned one over-protesting victim, became in 1845 the first European to be hanged in Hong Kong. We read of a plot to poison twenty-five men of the Royal Artillery, of a battle in the harbour between junks and boats of HMS *Cambrian*, of an attempt to burn down the Central Market, of a reward offered for the Governor's assassination, of protection rackets, robberies with violence and incessant housebreaking.*

Hong Kong was a colony based purely on trade and the *tai-pans* of the trading companies must have set the tone. They were hard, ruthless men who would stop at nothing in the pursuit of wealth. Foremost amongst the China traders was the company of Jardine Matheson. Scottish Presbyterians and the epitome of Victorian hypocrisy, they brought God and opium to China, and by no means in equal quantities. Unlike Bannatyne, both men lived long and died millionaires in comfortable retirement, which was more than they deserved. Such wealthy men were extremely influential – like Sir George Grafton,

* Jan Morris, *Hong Kong*, Viking, 1988, pp. 90–91.

both William Jardine and James Matheson returned to England to become members of parliament – and there can be little doubt that it was partly the influence of such men that drove Britain to attack China in the first Opium War.

Samuel George Bonham became Governor of Hong Kong, Plenipotentiary and Superintendent of Trade in 1848, after his predecessor was forced to resign by the opposition of the China traders. Bonham was knighted in 1851, made a baronet the following year, and remained governor until 1854.

Ultzmann is a fictional character, but inspired by a real one: the Reverend Karl Friedrich Gutzlaff, known to British sailors as 'Happy Bowels'. He worked for Jardine Matheson for a while and ultimately became Chinese Secretary at the office of the Hong Kong Superintendent of Trade. When he left the colony for France to raise funds for his missionary activities, the French consul at Macao wrote to his government to warn them, describing Gutzlaff as 'a man of considerable inventiveness, who has always sought to enrich himself . . . I regret to say that there is not a word of truth in the tales of this Sinologue.'* Sir Dadabhoy Framjee is modeled on Sir Jamsetji Jeejeebhoy, the first Indian baronet, who was active in the China trade at this time. He made a fortune from the opium trade, but he at least seems to have ploughed vast amounts of money into charitable works in his native Gujerat.

*Wu-yi* – which simply translated means 'martial arts' – is of course better known in the West nowadays as kung fu (strictly speaking, *gong-fu*). It was practised by Shaolin monks, whose temples became centres of opposition to the Ch'ing Dynasty in the eighteenth century. Another focus of opposition to the Manchus was the many interlinked

* *Affaires Diverses Consulaires*, Quai d'Orsay, quoted in Frank Welsh, *A History of Hong Kong*, p. 164.

secret societies which formed the Triads, of which the Brotherhood of Heaven, Earth and Man was only one. Today the Triads are predominantly criminal organisations, but in the nineteenth century their purpose was very much political. In 1850, however, their efforts were subsumed into the Taiping Rebellion, which the Manchus ultimately crushed in 1864, but only after a bloody war which is said to have cost more lives than the whole of the Second World War. Secret societies continued to be part of Chinese society until Sun Yat-sen overthrew the Manchu Dynasty in 1911: the 'Boxers United in Righteousness' – also known as the 'Harmonious Fists' – of 1898–1900 were one such organisation. If there are still secret societies intent on overthrowing the current regime in China to this day, the Communists aren't telling.

Despite the efforts of the Royal Navy and the Chinese authorities, piracy continues to be a problem in the South China Sea into the twenty-first century. During the 1850s, Westerners seemed to supplant the natives as the foremost pirates in the region for a time. Two of the most notorious were the Americans William 'Bully' Hayes and Eli Boggs. But that, as they say, is another story . . .

# Killigrew and the North-West Passage

## Jonathan Lunn

1852: The most famous rescue mission ever attempted.

Joining the search for Sir John Franklin's ill-fated voyage has long been a dream for Lieutenant Kit Killigrew, R.N. However, a captain more interested in personal glory than the safety of his own crew soon turns the voyage into a reality more akin with Kit's wildest nightmares. And just when he thinks it can't get any worse, a creature of almost mythical proportions starts to pick the crew off one by one . . .

*Killigrew and the North-West Passage* evokes in terrifying detail the true horror of an Arctic winter – the mind-numbing cold and desolate landscapes – and a darkness which seems almost to permeate men's minds. It's Jonathan Lunn's most chilling and exciting novel yet.

Praise for the Killigrew series

'A hero to rival any Horatio Hornblower. Swashbuckling? You bet' *Belfast Telegraph*

'If you revel in the Hornblower and the Sharpe books, grab a copy of Jonathan Lunn's action-packed saga' *Bolton Evening News*

'On a par with Douglas Reeman or Bernard Cornwell' *South Wales Argus*

'A rollicking tale with plenty of punches' *Lancashire Evening Post*

0 7472 6525 9

headline

# Killigrew and the Incorrigibles

## Jonathan Lunn

1850. Seven of Norfolk Island's most notorious criminals have escaped. Kit Killigrew and the crew of HMS *Tisiphone* give chase, eventually tracking them down in the New Hebrides, where a deadly game of cat and mouse ensues. Also in the islands is an elusive figure who has made his fortune from a barbaric trade and is desperate to avoid discovery. Killigrew is about to face his most ruthless opponents yet. But, he remains dangerously distracted by the recent tragedy that preys on his conscience, and his state of mind threatens to achieve what cannibals, prisoners on the run and a vicious trader cannot, as he places himself in the line of danger once too often . . .

*Killigrew and the Incorrigibles* is the third book in Jonathan Lunn's series featuring the unconventional naval hero Kit Killigrew, R. N. The series has been widely praised:

'Let's hear three huzzas for Killigrew, the Victorian naval hero who knocks most of his rivals into a cocked hat' *Northern Echo*

'If you revel in the Hornblower and the Sharpe books, grab a copy of Jonathan Lunn's action-packed saga' *Bolton Evening News*

'Action-packed and well-researched . . . in the vein of Forester and O'Brian but with its own distinctive flavour. Shows great promise' *Good Book Guide*

'A cracking adventure' *Newton & Golborne Guardian*

'A rollicking tale with plenty of punches' *Lancashire Evening Post*

0 7472 6382 5

headline

# Killigrew's Run

## Jonathan Lunn

The Baltic, 1854. Viscount Bullivant has a peculiar notion of a family holiday – spectating at the Crimean War. But becoming prisoners of the Russian secret police was not in their plans . . .

Commander Kit Killigrew of HMS *Ramillies* has more important things to worry about. But Bullivant is a crony of the prime minister, so Killigrew and his men are ordered to rescue the viscount and his family.

Soon they are being pursued through the treacherous Ekenäs Archipelago by the Russian paddle sloop *Atlanta*; and in her dashing captain, Count Mikhail Yurievich Pechorin, Killigrew may finally have met his match . . .

'The Royal Navy's finest is the hero par excellence with the constitution of Indiana Jones, the ruthlessness of Dirty Harry and the ready wit of James Bond' *Northern Echo*

'There are some things you look forward to throughout the year, like birthdays and Christmas. The publication of the next Killigrew novel is in that sort of league now. Exceptionally good' *South Wales Argus*

0 7553 2068 9

**headline**

madaboutbooks.com

. . . the

Hodder Headline

site

for readers

and book lovers
madaboutbooks.com

Now you can buy any of these other bestselling Headline books from your bookshop or *direct from the publisher*.

FREE P&P AND UK DELIVERY
(Overseas and Ireland £3.50 per book)

| | | |
|---|---|---|
| An Evil Spirit Out of the West | Paul Doherty | £6.99 |
| The Outlaws of Ennor | Michael Jecks | £6.99 |
| The Templar's Penance | Michael Jecks | £6.99 |
| Seven Dials | Anne Perry | £6.99 |
| Death of a Stranger | Anne Perry | £6.99 |
| The Legatus Mystery | Rosemary Rowe | £6.99 |
| The Chariots of Calyx | Rosemary Rowe | £6.99 |
| Badger's Moon | Peter Tremayne | £5.99 |
| The Haunted Moon | Peter Tremayne | £6.99 |

TO ORDER SIMPLY CALL THIS NUMBER

**01235 400 414**

or visit our website: www.madaboutbooks.com

Prices and availability subject to change without notice.